Library of America, a nonprofit organization, champions our nation's cultural heritage by publishing America's greatest writing in authoritative new editions and providing resources for readers to explore this rich, living legacy.

CRIME NOVELS OF THE 1960S
VOLUME I

Crime Novels

FIVE CLASSIC THRILLERS 1961–1964

Volume 1

The Murderers • Fredric Brown
The Name of the Game Is Death • Dan J. Marlowe
Dead Calm • Charles Williams
The Expendable Man • Dorothy B. Hughes
The Score • Richard Stark

Geoffrey O'Brien, *editor*

THE LIBRARY OF AMERICA

CRIME NOVELS: FIVE CLASSIC THRILLERS 1961–1964

Published in the United States by Library of America.
Visit our website at www.loa.org.

This paper exceeds the requirements of
ANSI/NISO Z39.48–1992 (Permanence of Paper).

Distributed to the trade in the United States
by Penguin Random House Inc.
and in Canada by Penguin Random House Canada Ltd.

Library of Congress Control Number: 2022944749
ISBN 978-1-59853-737-6

First Printing
The Library of America—370

Manufactured in the United States of America

Contents

Introduction

BY GEOFFREY O'BRIEN

American crime fiction has always tended to reflect the culture's rougher edges and more unstable elements. In the twentieth century, genteel puzzle mysteries in the Agatha Christie mode had their devotees and imitators, but the native product was more typically characterized by an acute awareness of social fissures and mental borderlines. The pressures and dangers of the Prohibition era, the Depression, World War II and its anxious aftermath are never far away. Likewise, the crime novels of the 1960s are suffused with the outward ills and troubled undercurrents of their time—urban chaos, racist hatreds, proliferating drug use, the suspicions and jangled nerves of suburban enclaves, the nihilistic rejection of established moral codes, the dissolution of personality itself—as perceived by very different writers from multiple angles.

As a genre, crime fiction has always also had a symbiotic relation with emerging media and with evolutionary changes in publishing formats. The pulp magazines of the 1920s and '30s fostered the rise of the hard-boiled style exemplified by Dashiell Hammett and Raymond Chandler. In the 1940s—a decade during which crime stories of all sorts maintained a dominant position in the world of entertainment—the same tropes, and often the same writers, could be found in novels, popular magazines, movies, and radio. It was typical for a successful mystery novel to be serialized in a magazine, adapted for radio and the movies, and eventually reissued as an inexpensive paperback. At this moment of peak popularity, the genre embraced a wide range of approaches, from the tough guy school to the psychological realism of women writers such as Helen Eustis and Elisabeth Sanxay Holding. In the 1950s, the success of paperback reissues ushered in the era of paperback originals, driving the remaining pulps toward extinction, just as the conventions of the half-hour radio play migrated to television. Increasingly in evidence was a grittier, more male-oriented vein exemplified by the novels of Mickey Spillane, movies offering violent ripped-from-the-headlines exposés of gangsterism, or televised celebrations of law enforcement such as *M Squad* or *Highway Patrol.*

By the 1960s, crime fiction, although still a reliably popular genre, no longer occupied such a commanding cultural position. Even Ross Macdonald, the preeminent literary heir of Hammett and Chandler, did not become a best-selling author until late in the decade. (Macdonald's work, central to any consideration of crime fiction in the 1960s, is available in three Library of America volumes.) Conventions that had flourished for decades seemed to have reached a point of diminishing returns. The era of the private eye and the romantic noir melodrama along the lines of *Double Indemnity* or *Laura* tended to inspire parody or evoke nostalgia. Other genres emerged as strong competitors to traditional crime fiction: science fiction and fantasy as developed by Robert Heinlein, Frank Herbert, and others (including the belatedly popularized J.R.R. Tolkien), and extended by *The Twilight Zone* and *The Outer Limits*; the fusion of crime story with horror as in Alfred Hitchcock's *Psycho*, from a novel by Robert Bloch; the political thriller making drama out of global crisis, exemplified by best-selling novels like *Seven Days in May* and *Fail-Safe*; the harsh realism and psychological probing of true crime breaking through to a wider public with Truman Capote's *In Cold Blood*; and above all the phalanx of secret agents led by James Bond and given more substantial credibility by the clandestine bureaucrats of John le Carré.

Facing this stiff competition, writers working in a more traditional vein—some of them, like Fredric Brown, Charles Williams, and Dorothy B. Hughes, long-established veterans; others, like Dan J. Marlowe and Richard Stark, relative newcomers—felt the pressure to go beyond the predictable limits of the standard whodunit or police procedural. By widening the breadth of their subject matter, addressing themes that might once have seemed risky, perhaps availing themselves of the audacity allowed by a new permissiveness in publishing, or experimenting with formal approaches befitting a flashier and speeded-up era, the best crime writers reinvented the genre in strikingly distinctive ways.

A writer with his roots in the pulps, equally successful in the crime and science fiction genres, the prolific Fredric Brown was the name Richard Stark. As Westlake commented: "Stark and Westlake use language very differently. . . . Westlake is allusive, indirect, referential, a bit rococo. Stark strips his sentences down to the necessary information." The Parker novels are constructed with a formalist rigor equivalent to a criminal planning a complex heist. Each book is a variation on a theme, with four movements—conception, preparation, execution, and aftermath—and the effect is indeed musical. Despite their immersion in material details, they have a nearly abstract quality that suggests a wide range of possible readings without ever imposing a particular message. They are among the books most consistently admired by other crime writers. *The Score* (1964) was the fifth in the series, which would eventually encompass twenty-three titles; it is notable for the particular audacity of the attempted crime, and the emergence of the actor-thief Grofield as a lighthearted foil to the implacable Parker.

Each of these works establishes a very personal connection with a transitional and often chaotic cultural era, while continuing to draw on the strengths of a mature tradition. The novels collected in this volume, along with its companion volume, *Crime Novels: Four Classic Thrillers 1964–1969*, reveal not so much a period style as a varied and inventive range of approaches. In going beyond earlier templates for crime fiction, these writers continued to redefine its nature and widen its possibilities.

THE MURDERERS

Fredric Brown

Chapter One

I WOKE to darkness, with the shreds of a ridiculous dream keeping me from knowing what had awakened me or even who I was. Then I remembered; it was the automatic alarm clock in my mind which had awakened me; I'd set it for this time because of an appointment. I even knew who and where I was.

I was Willy Griff, waking from a nap in my basement room, and the room was in Mrs. Whelan's rooming house—better known as the Zoo because of the strange characters that it housed. And the Zoo was in Hollywood, the mecca of actors like myself. Correction: other actors; there is none exactly like unto me. Better, perhaps, but never like.

I thought, let there be light; and turned one on. The clock on the night stand under the lamp told me that it was eight o'clock. I had to get up now because of my appointment to meet Lennie, my agent, at the Wilshire Derby at nine. It could be important. Lennie had told me he thought he could bring a television producer along, one who was starting to shoot a new crime series on the Warner lot. Lennie had told me it ought to be good for at least a bit part; the series characters were set but the show would need a full complement of fresh faces every program for the hoods who would not survive the show.

I threw my feet over the edge of the bed, stretched and yawned.

I, Willy Griff, twenty-seven, born of farmer parents in the Imperial Valley, sufferer under Pasadena Playhouse, crucified most of the time since in my efforts to get a foothold above occasional bit parts, but not yet dead or buried. Move over, Brando, I'm on my way.

I walked across to the sink and put cold water on my face, wiped it and studied myself in the mirror to decide whether or not to shave again. The verdict: negative. Just a touch of shadow on my face, as now, made me look more mature and more plausible as a potential crime-show hood. The face I studied was neither rugged nor handsome but somewhere in between; sometimes I wished it were more definitely one or the other, but one works with what one has. And I can think of it as a versatile face; I smiled at myself boyishly, lowering my eyes and then raising them again in the manner of Jack Lescoulie charming housewives with a soft-sell commercial, then I tightened the corner muscles of my mouth and scowled through flat hard eyes, a torpedo with finger itching on a trigger. Yes, a versatile face. I let it revert to its usual expression of slight arrogance—or partially concealed great arrogance—and looked at it again, and approved. I ran a comb through the black hair above it, making it sleek again.

Yes, a versatile and satisfactory face. And why shouldn't I face the world with arrogance, seeing that it's a lousy world I never made. I could have done a better job.

I lighted a cigarette, put on my robe, and went down the hall to the bathroom, deciding I might as well get that trip over with before I dressed.

The door was locked so I stood leaning against the wall opposite until the toilet flushed and in a minute the door opened and Doll came out. "Hi, Willy," she said. And, with a glance at the robe, "Getting up late or going to bed early?"

Doll was a slightly gorgeous redhead, the most attractive female inmate of the Zoo. But she belonged to Solly and was hands-off stuff for that reason. Solly was an ex-wrestler who now managed other wrestlers. He was fifty if he was a day but he was a giant of a man who could still tie any ordinary man into pretzel knots.

But Solly wasn't in hearing and I let my voice go dulcet—sexy instead of arrogant—when I answered her question. "Hi, Doll. Haven't decided yet. Any suggestions?"

I stood watching while she walked away from me down the hall. I knew that she knew I was watching by the way she rolled her hips a little more than she usually did. Provocative, but she was a commodity that's never in short supply in Hollywood.

Back in my room I dressed carefully, but quickly; if I didn't dawdle I'd have time to walk down to Wilshire and save myself a cab fare. The rooming house is on Rondo just off Sunset, not too far a walk. 1515 Rondo is a fleabag and a poor address, but it has the advantage of being central.

I went out, and paused on the top of the two cement steps that led down to the sidewalk; the air felt damp, as though rain might be coming, and I was wondering whether to go back to my room and get a hat and trench coat. A car door slammed, quite close, and I glanced in the direction of the sound. A gray '57 Fairlane was parked at the curb and a man had just left it. He was coming across the sidewalk toward me and since I hadn't yet made up my mind about the coat-and-hat bit, I stepped a little aside to let him pass and enter. I'd never seen him before.

He was big, almost as big as Solly, and like Solly he looked like something from TV wrestling, but in clothes. He wasn't tall, maybe five-ten to my six feet even, but he had shoulders, and a neck like a rhinoceros.

He came up to me, but didn't pass. He said, "Hi, actor-boy. Let's go back to your room." His voice sounded tired, as though he'd been waiting a long time to say that.

I wasn't afraid, not yet, but my mind made like a detective's on a series show, with deductions. He'd been waiting in that car till I came out, so he didn't know my room number. Rather, which room was mine; they don't have numbers on the doors. But he knew something about me since he knew that I was an actor. My name? Probably, since he knew my profession.

I temporized. "I don't dig you," I said. "I've got an important appointment—"

"Look, Griff," he said. (He did know my name and that made it seem less dangerous; at least it wasn't a heist; if he knew my name and profession he'd know I wasn't worth heisting.) "Don't get scared; I'm not going to hurt you—if you play along. I'm a licensed private investigator and I've got a client who wants to talk to you. Now, as soon as I phone him to come around."

"Oh," I said. And *Oh*, I thought. I saw it now. Doris Seaton. I'd been with her this afternoon. Fun and games at a motel.

And John Seaton, her husband, had suspected fun and games and had put a pee-eye on her and he'd been with us when she'd dropped me here at the Zoo at a little before five o'clock. He'd been waiting since for me to come out, since he didn't know my room. But he must have described me and asked some questions somewhere, since he had my name, rank, and serial number.

Well, it had been a nice thing with Doris, while it lasted. She had money and a swank car and I had what I contributed to the relationship. Two months, we'd been making the scene.

But still—why did Seaton want to *talk* to me? Just the fun of reading a riot act to me and telling me, with a hunk of paid muscle for protection, what would happen to me if I saw his wife again?

But maybe I could stall it, on account of my appointment with Lennie. "Listen," I said, "I'm willing to talk to your client, but does it have to be right *now*? I wasn't just putting you on about the appointment. It could be important."

"So's seeing my client, kid. He wants me around when the confab happens so if it's tomorrow it'll cost him an extra day. I give value for a client's money."

He reached around me and opened the door, gave me a push—a gentle one but it carried me across the sill. He took my arm and headed for the phone half a dozen paces down the hall. He let go to reach in his pocket for a dime. But he said, "You can probably outrun me if you want to try. But if we have to go through this again tomorrow, it'll be tougher."

"Okay," I said. "Might as well get it over with now." Maybe, I thought, I could still keep my date if I took a taxi.

When he dialed EX for the exchange I knew I'd been right. Exbrook is the exchange of the Seaton home, in Santa Monica. And a moment later he was saying, "Seaton? All set here. His name is Griff, with a double-f—1515 Rondo, in Hollywood. That's a few blocks west of Highland, and the number is just north of Sunset . . . Okay, just a minute." He spoke over his shoulder to me. "What's the room number?"

"No number. First door to the left after you've gone down the front steps to the basement floor."

He relayed that and then said we'd be waiting in the room.

I led the way down and we went in the room and I closed the door.

"Okay," I said. "Chair or the bed, your choice. And since it's going to take him at least twenty minutes to get here, we might as well not make faces at each other. Do you dig musky? I got a jug of it. Or don't you drink on the job?"

"It's better than nothing. And I'm not on the job any more, exactly." I got the jug and poured us each a glass to drink. He sat down on the chair with his and I took the edge of the bed. Very chummy. "I'm just to stick around till he's through talking with you."

"And take a poke at me if he gets mad and tells you to?"

He grinned. "My license doesn't cover that. Unless in defense of my client. So don't lose your temper, kid. I'll be right outside the door while he's talking and if a rumpus starts I'll be right in. Dig me?"

"I dig you," I said. "How long have you been following us? Or is that a professional secret?"

He shrugged. "Don't see how it matters. Her, for a week. You were with her three times. Same motel each time."

None of this mattered but I was curious. This was the first private eye I'd ever happened to talk to. I asked, "How come you didn't blow the gaff on us the first time?"

"Client didn't want a bust-in. Just wanted to find out who she was cheating with. And the two times before today she dropped you off up on Hollywood Boulevard at a crowded time. I was in my car behind her, but couldn't park in time to pick you up on foot. That's the hell of a tail job in a car. Just dropping you off, she didn't have to park but I would have."

I nodded. "And today she dropped me off here and you stuck outside until I showed. Neat."

My private eye looked at his wrist watch and then downed the final sip of his wine. He walked over to the sink and rinsed out the glass and put it down. Off duty or not, he didn't want his client to find him drinking. The timing was perfect; there was a knock at the door just as he put down the glass. He was closer so I let him open it.

Through it came—well, the best I can do for a first impression is a pear-shaped object. I'd never seen him before, but he could be no one else but Doris's husband. Seat Cover Seaton, he advertised himself, the Santa Monica seat cover king.

Seat Cover Seaton. Pear-shaped, fortyish, or maybe a little more, balding, getting dewlaps prematurely. Dorrie had told me quite a bit about him, but this was worse than I'd been prepared to see. The only nice thing about him didn't show. He had money; he made money.

"Thank you, Mr. Weston," he said, and now I knew the detective's name. Mr. Weston went out.

I was standing now and I didn't ask Seat Cover to sit down; I wasn't going to until he broke the ice and I knew what line he was going to take. I just stared at him calmly, waiting.

And then I almost did a double take, because the silly bastard was crying. Actual tears. It put me down for a moment; what can you do against anything as square as that?

"I'm sorry, Mr. Griff," he said.

The meaning of that eluded me, for a moment. I'd been screwing his wife, in various hotels and motels on his money (vicariously, of course) and *he* was sorry. And he hadn't used it in the southern sense of the word, that he was a sorry object; he hadn't inflected it that way. Then I dug what he'd meant, that he was sorry he was crying and making an exhibition of himself.

But he went on and I didn't have to answer. "Mr. Griff, I love my wife. Very deeply. Before I say what I'm going to say I want to be sure you understand that."

What in hell was he leading up to? I'd imagined that, whatever he was going to say or threaten to do, it would mean the end of my seeing Doris and I'd reconciled myself to that while I'd been waiting. Now I began to wonder. What was he building?

He struggled to make sense. "What I'm trying to say is, I understand. Dorrie is young and I suppose she—well, I mean I understand. But it can't go on, her seeing you. I love her and I don't want to divorce her. I won't if I don't have to. If she—"

I decided to speed things by helping him untangle himself. I said, "Have you talked to her about this, Mr. Seaton?"

"Yes. And she is willing to give you up and give me another chance. But I wanted to talk to you too, so you'd understand and not try to get in touch with her."

Of course I'd get in touch with her. She was too passionate a bitch to lose without trying. And too much in love with me (whatever she'd told him, she couldn't have meant it; it must have been under duress) and too handy to borrow bread money from when I was between engagements. But I'd be a fool to say so and put him on guard. As it was, we'd have to be a damn sight more careful than we'd been, which hadn't been very.

"I understand," I told him. "And, if Doris agrees, I haven't any choice. Besides, I can't afford to support her—at least not the way you can. So—what can I say except okay?"

He nodded slowly. "The only thing is, do you mean it, Mr. Griff? I don't like to make threats, but I want to make sure you won't see her again—even if—even if she didn't fully mean what she told me and calls or tries to see you again."

He was talking a little more firmly and confidently now.

"Mr. Weston tells me you're an actor," he said. "I suppose you play in television?"

I wondered where this was leading but there wasn't any reason not to answer it straight. "Yes," I said. "Small parts to date, but I'm beginning to be known. What did you mean about not liking to make threats? I don't like to be threatened."

"I thought you might not and that's why I had the detective wait outside the door there. You see, I'm in television too—on the other end. I sponsor two programs and have spot announcements on others. I have a lot of friends and connections in television. I wouldn't want to do this, but I can get you blacklisted, make sure you'd never get another part. Not even a commercial."

I frowned. *That* was something I hadn't thought of. Probably I should have. Things like that are done all the time in the rat race. Not to big name stars, unless to a degree by big name sponsors. But I was vulnerable. He could hurt me plenty.

He went on. "I wouldn't want to do that. But I will if I find that you're keeping on seeing Dorrie. Even if she's the one that calls you first."

I said, and managed to keep my voice calm and my face straight, "You won't have to do that, Mr. Seaton. But I'd like to ask one favor of you."

"What?"

"Since I'm going to break with Doris I'd like to do it pleasantly. I'd like to see her once more, if only to say goodbye."

"No! I won't let—"

I held up a hand, traffic cop like. "Don't misunderstand; I don't mean see her privately. And—" I threw some bait I knew he'd fall for, uncertain of her as he was right now "—maybe, since I'm giving her up anyway, I can talk her into really meaning it about loving you again; that is, unless she does mean it already. I've got nothing to lose, and guess I owe you that much."

"That—sounds fair. But how would I know that's what you were telling her?"

"You wouldn't, I guess. I couldn't sell her on that idea with you listening. But you can be sure I won't lay a finger on her, won't even kiss her goodbye, because you can be watching us. Is she still home now?"

He nodded. I said, "Then here's how we'll work it. Drive home and get Doris, take her to—there's a tavern on Vine called Shorty's; she knows where it is if you don't. I'll walk there meanwhile and we'll get there about the same time. She and I can talk in a booth. You can sit at the bar and keep an eye on us."

"Well—you wait here and I'll phone her. If Dorrie says all right, I'll do it."

He went out and came back in three minutes. I'd left the door ajar and he didn't come in, just stood in the doorway. He said they'd be at the tavern in about an hour.

I gave him and the detective time to get clear and then went up to the phone. It was a little after nine but I could find out if Lennie had his producer at the Derby.

They paged Lennie and he came to the phone. He told me I wasn't missing anything businesswise, that the producer had phoned at the last minute and called things off. But that he had a starlet and she no doubt had a friend somewhere, they all did, and why didn't I come anyway? I told him something else had come up and I couldn't. Not that I would have, in any case. I know Lennie's starlets. Anything female that wants to get into movies or television and that he hasn't slept with yet is a starlet in his language. As a flesh peddler he attracts them by droves and maybe once in a while gets one a bit part. But they're all starlets until he's slept with them. Once each; the same chick more than once doesn't appeal to him.

It would take me only half an hour to walk to Shorty's so I had almost half an hour to kill and I went back to my room to do some heavy thinking. About what kind of a pitch I was going to throw Doris and just how I'd throw it.

It would be based on three things. One, that Seat Cover Seaton had money. He probably wasn't a millionaire but he was probably a quarter of one. Two, that if anything happened to him, as people euphemistically say, Dorrie would have that money. And three, that Dorrie was overboard for me, really overboard. I hadn't been the only man with whom she'd put horns on the Seat Cover, but she'd told me, and I believed her, that with me she hit an emotional peak unique in her experience. She'd marry me like a shot if she was free to do so, and if we could afford it.

It ought to add up to something. One way you can add points—one, two, and three can come out six. It can't come out less than half that.

I decided to finish my thinking while walking, and I did.

When I got to Shorty's the Seatons weren't there yet. There were a few customers but I didn't know any of them. Nor even the bartender, which was one reason why I'd picked the place. I'd been in the place only twice before and both times with Doris; we'd sat in a booth and hadn't got into conversation with anyone.

I sat at the bar and ordered a whisky and soda. Sipped at it. I was finishing it when Seat Cover and Doris came in. I stepped down off the stool to greet them. Seaton had a ridiculously determined look on his face; it wasn't the kind of face made for an expression like that. It made him look even more silly than when he'd been tearful.

Doris was wearing a light tan dress that molded her figure perfectly. She was a symphony in yellow and tan. From the top: beautifully dressed blond hair, Doris's face, bare shoulders tanned almost to the shade of the dress—could hardly tell where Doris left off and the dress began. A yellow belt to match her hair. Below the dress her legs were either bare or stockinged to match their tan. Then tan high-heeled shoes that made her just the height I prefer in women, five feet eight. A mink stole, too dark a brown for the rest of the ensemble, was the only slightly discordant note, but she was carrying it over an arm, not using it to conceal those smooth, soft shoulders. I'd never asked Doris's age, but I'd guessed it to be late twenties. About my own age, probably, although I'd told her I was thirty-two.

I tried to see whether she had been crying, but I couldn't tell; there was no redness around her eyes. There might have been a slight puffiness, but that could have been my imagination. Her face, otherwise, was a deadpan. She must be wondering why

I'd arranged a final talk, in her husband's sight. He'd hardly have told her I'd promised to try to get her to go back with him again and be happy.

I said, "Hello, Mr. Seaton. Doris, there's a matter I'd like to discuss with you privately. Will you sit in a booth with me a little while?" And then, looking back at Seaton. "You won't mind, will you, sir?"

He shook his head stiffly and climbed up on a bar stool. And I led Doris to a booth about twenty feet away, being careful not to take her arm or touch her in any way. I put her in the booth so she'd be facing away from Seaton. If what I was going to suggest was going to shock her I didn't want him to be able to watch her face and make any guesses. My face I could keep controlled; it wouldn't give anything away.

I sat across from her and smiled gently, sadly. The expression Seaton would expect me to have, if he was watching. I said, "Darling, would you like to marry me—or at least live with me—marriage wouldn't matter—if that funny-looking thing sitting at the bar wasn't around to stop us?"

No, she didn't startle at all. She must have been expecting it, hoping for it, or something like it. "I'd—love it, Willy. But—wouldn't it be too dangerous for us, now that he knows about *us*, and a detective knows too?"

Smart girl, practical as hell. And dead right, unless I could figure an angle.

I said, "Not dangerous for us, darling. Just for me. You wouldn't have any part in it, or know anything about it until it was over. But first let me tell you what I'm supposed to be telling you, so you'll know. I'm talking you into forgetting me, saying a permanent goodbye to you, and trying to talk you into loving him again. I think you should—pretend to, I mean —whatever we decided about what I just suggested. Second-honeymoon him for a while."

She shuddered a little, but her shoulders were slightly below the level of the booth partition behind her; he couldn't have seen that.

"How did he persuade you to—?"

"To help him? He didn't. It was my idea, to have this chance to talk to you and make arrangements, if you want. And to lull his suspicions for the future, whether or not he'll have cause for them. No, he neither persuaded nor bribed me. He did threaten me—but my career, not my person."

I told her about that.

"Willy, do you really think—?"

I said, "I really—" But then stopped quickly; the bartender was coming to our booth to take our order. Only as it happened, he wasn't; he had a tray with two drinks on it and put them in front of us. "Gentleman at the bar," he said, "sent these over to you."

A whisky soda for me; the bartender of course knew what I'd been drinking. And a gibson for Doris; of course Seaton knew what his wife's drink was.

I picked mine up and looked toward Seaton to nod thanks to him, but he wasn't watching so I touched glasses with Doris instead, and took a sip of my drink.

I said, "It can be done, and safely. There are ways. But—"

"But what, honey?"

"It will take money to get it done safely. Light-of-my-twisted-soul, how much money have you got, or can you raise easily, without him knowing about it?"

"Why—about six hundred. I've got that in a safe deposit box nobody knows about. It's—well, I sort of saved it for mad money, out of the clothes allowance he gives me. I don't always spend all of it, but he thinks I do. And I've got a few pieces of jewelry that he wouldn't miss if—"

"No," I interrupted. "You'd have to hock or sell them, or I would, and it might be traced back if there's an investigation. I hope six hundred will be enough. How soon can you get the money out of the box?"

"Tomor— No, today's Friday. The bank won't be open again till Monday."

"All right, Monday, or as soon after as you can get free and be absolutely sure you're not being followed. I don't think he'll have you tailed any more, or me, but he just might. Don't take any chances."

"I won't. But when will I see you to—"

I said, "Listen carefully; we shouldn't talk much longer. Starting Monday I'll make a point of dropping into—um, The Doll House, every afternoon from two-thirty to three, for a drink. After you've got the money ready, phone me there the first afternoon you're free at that time. I'll figure something meanwhile, how we can meet safely, I mean, and tell you then. Don't phone from home, even if you're alone. Use a public phone, with no one in hearing. Got me?"

"Willy, honey, I'm *scared*. It's one thing to think about something like that, but to *do* it—"

"We daren't talk any longer, darling. Think it over, over the weekend. And if you decide not, call me at The Doll House to tell me the verdict's no."

I finished the rest of my drink and said, "Stay here. I'll send you a Seat Cover. And treat it nice, honey, because we won't have a ghost of a chance if he has a ghost of a suspicion left. 'Bye—and I love you."

I didn't give her a chance to answer; I slid out of the booth and walked over to Seaton, slid onto the stool beside him. I said, "We've said goodbye, and I've convinced her." Nobly, "You go to her now."

He said, "You mean—?" (People *do* say "You mean—?" He'd said it, just like that.)

I nodded and he climbed down from the stool and walked toward the booth. I didn't watch, except myself in the mirror, until the bartender came over to me. I put a bill on the bar and ordered myself another drink. Then I motioned with my head toward the booth and said, "Send them a round on me. Gibson and whatever the gentleman was drinking here." I grinned at him. "We're playing musical chairs," I told him. He grinned back.

Chapter Two

I WOKE to daylight, hangover, and disorientation. I wasn't in my own pad. I was fully dressed except for my shoes. I was alone. I sat up and looked around and managed to orient myself in space, if not in time. I was in Charlie Hayes's pad, on the second floor of the Zoo. Charlie was the only other actor staying there, and the nearest thing I had to a friend under this roof. Actors don't always get along too well, especially when they're hungry, but he and I weren't competitive. He's ten years older than I, smaller, and plays character parts; he's especially good on foreign accents. There was no chance of both of us ever being considered for the same role. And Lennie peddled both of us; in fact, I'd met Lennie through Charlie, who'd been with him for quite a few years.

I knew it must be a wine hangover from the terrible thirst I had. The inside of my mouth was as dry as the inside of one of those bleached cows' skulls you see lying on the desert.

I got off the bed and staggered over to the sink, turned on the cold water. Then while I was reaching for the glass I happened to glance in the mirror over the sink.

My hair had turned gray overnight. And I was dressed in a torn and ragged suitcoat over a dirty and ragged work shirt. I looked twenty or thirty years older. . . .

Then I remembered and, as soon as I'd had a glass of water, laughed at myself for the sudden scare. Yes, I remembered last night, now. At least most of it.

It had been Sunday night and Charlie Hayes and I had decided to do what he called the mission bit, for fun and games and a little virtuoso exhibition of acting. We'd put on ragged clothes, grayed our hair, and used make-up. Not much make-up, because it would have to stand inspection at close range; mostly around the corners of the eyes, a few touches like that. And a fair amount of dirt, genuine dirt. Then we'd taken Charlie's car—it's a jalopy but it runs—downtown. We'd parked it on Winsett and walked to Fifth Street, skid row. Down among the winos.

We'd made a few of the crummy bars, drinking cheap muscatel to get a little drunk and into the spirit of things, and pretending to be drunker than we were. Mixing with other drunken bums, getting into drunken arguments.

Then, when we were worked up to it, we hit a mission and let ourselves get saved, let them stand us up in front of the other bums—the real ones, the pathetic ones—and we confessed our sins and promised to straighten up and become good Christian teetotalers. Charlie even broke down and cried; I didn't go quite that far, but I did a good job.

We didn't corn it, not deliberately anyway. It was Charlie's game; he'd done it a few times before. The whole idea is to play it straight (it's corny enough that way) and if you do or say anything to make either a bum or a Christer even give you a suspicious look, it's a point against you. If you give yourself away you lose.

Sometimes we'd be together and sometimes we'd go into a bar or a mission separately and not know each other, but with each of us keeping an eye on the other to see how he was doing. Charlie says the first time he tried the mission bit he'd done it alone, but it hadn't been much that way. You need an audience, someone who's in the game with you, who knows who you really are and what you're doing, to make it fun and keep you on your toes.

We let ourselves be saved again, and we were prayed over and fed soup and hard rolls, at another mission, and then decided that the game had begun to pall. We picked up a jug of musky and drove home. We were heading for my pad but ran into Solly and Doll who were leaving but changed their minds and decided to join us for a while. So since my pad's a bit crowded with four people, we went up to Charlie's, which is bigger. Solly and Doll didn't stay long, but we got other recruits. Johnny Kaprelian, who earns his bread as a studio messenger but who's trying to free-lance television scripts, brought his portable phono over, and some records; we dug Charlie Parker and Pres for a while. Smoky Conover, our beatnik poet, cut down the volume of a Pres record and used it for background to read a poem against; I don't remember the poem but I remember its title. He called it "The Warp and the Woof and the Woofer and the Tweeter." He had a beatnik girl with him—straight dark hair and a black leotard, *you* know—and for some reason which I didn't hear got mad at her and left her there. She wasn't bad, at least at that time of the morning, and several of us made passes. But it was her night for being cool and she wasn't having any. All she wanted was bongos to play with the music, and there weren't any around, so she ended up bongoing on the back of a prop guitar Charlie had hanging on his wall. Mrs. Whelan, the landlady, came up to ask us to knock off a few decibels on the noise, and stayed for a glass of wine; she's a nice, tolerant old bat. Somebody went out and got another jug. Somebody broke one of Johnny Kaprelian's records and we almost had a fight, but got him calmed down. A couple of fag friends of Johnny's came looking for him and treed him to Charlie's room by the sound of his records; they were both high on weed, but didn't have any, or said they didn't. Charlie told them if they wanted to join the party they'd have to dig another jug. They said they would and left, but I don't remember whether or not they came back. That's about the point where my memory began to get fuzzy and finally went to black. I didn't know whether I'd passed out on Charlie's bed before or after the party broke up.

But whichever way it was, Charlie must have decided it was easier for him to go down to my pad to sleep than to get *me* down there. Or the whole party might have moved on and he could be sleeping anywhere. Obviously he'd been able to navigate after I hadn't been. Well, there had been times when I'd drunk him under the table, too.

After two glasses of water I searched for a cigarette and found one, went briefly to the second floor bathroom and then down to the basement and my own room. Charlie wasn't there but he'd been there; the bed had been slept in and all his clothes, the old ones he'd worn for our little masquerade the night before, were lying on it. He wouldn't have gone anywhere jaybird naked, so I looked for my robe. It was gone, so I knew he was down the hall taking a shower. I drank some more water and in a minute he came back.

"Hi," he said. He sounded as unenthusiastic as I felt. "Some party, man."

"Anything happen after I folded?" I asked him.

He shook his head. "Nothing worth mentioning. Broke up without a row, around four. You lasted till three. The fags didn't come back with more wine, so we ran out. Gawd."

"How's a pickup drink strike you?"

"Wine? Wow, no. Or you got some medicine stashed?"

I had, a half pint of whisky. I got it out and poured us each a shot. I watered mine but he took his straight and then a chaser.

"God, does that taste lousy!" he said. It did, but after a minute my mouth tasted less like the bottom of a rabbit hutch and I felt a little better in general. I took a shower and a shampoo (someday I'd like to try real poo instead of sham) and got dressed. It was half past twelve by then. I had plenty of time to have some breakfast and get to The Doll House for my two-thirty to three o'clock wait to see if Doris would phone me there.

I checked finances and found only change in the pockets of the old clothes I'd worn to skid row, but I'd stashed a five before I'd left for there, and I got it, from my favorite stash for money. With my other few books in a small bookcase I keep a Gideon Bible that I once swiped from a hotel I'd stayed at. Nobody who ever comes to my room would think of picking it up to read, let alone to carry it off, since it's unsaleable and unhockable.

Not that I had immediate worries about money, even if Doris didn't come through with any. I could husband the five to last me till tomorrow and then I could put the bite on Lennie. I had some money coming from a bit on "The Untouchables" (I'd played a technician in a police laboratory) and Lennie's always good for a bite when you've got money coming that will come through him. He knows he'll get it back just by holding it out.

I walked to the drive-in at Sunset and Highland and had me a big breakfast. That would hold me until a late dinner. Two meals a day cuts the budget and the budget is important while you're scrambling to get somewhere. And clothes are more important than eating, in my racket. You've simply got to keep up a front; you never know when you may run into somebody important to you.

While I ate I found myself wondering about, and wondering at, the pitch I'd given Doris Friday evening when Seaton had let me talk to her. Had I been really serious in telling her I'd free her from Seaton by killing him? Murder? *Me?*

That was crazy and I knew it was crazy; I'd just been acting. It's an occupational disease.

I'd wanted to see Doris once more to set up a safe deal to have one more assignation with her, that's all. And, if possible, to con her out of a final spot of money. I hadn't hoped for six hundred, but I could sure use that much. It would fill in a few holes in my wardrobe and let me live for about two months besides, if I stretched it. Six bills isn't to be sneezed at, when you're almost on your uppers.

But, damn it, she'd *gone* for the idea, that was what surprised me. I'd been ready to brush it off as kidding if she'd been shocked. And then talk her around and set up one final date with her anyway, and maybe get a few bucks as a farewell present. Once we could get away with, but we wouldn't dare keep on seeing each other. She had more to lose than I did. Well, she'd probably get an attack of cold feet or common sense. But she'd keep the date to tell me so, and she'd surely bring some money anyway, if not that much. She knew how badly I needed it.

I strolled up Highland to Hollywood Boulevard and turned east toward Vine. Out here they call Hollywood and Vine the crossroads of the world and in a sense it is, but it gives outsiders and newcomers a false impression because they unconsciously compare it to Forty-second and Broadway, Times Square. They're nothing alike. Hollywood and Vine is just a corner like any other corner in a city. But strolling along Hollywood you pass people and I get a kick out of trying to classify them. You don't pass a fraction as many people as you do on Broadway but they average out screwier.

Faggots and call girls, bus boys and Lesbians, actors and dishwashers, visiting firemen and producers, agents, beatniks in barefoot sandals, madmen or fanatics mumbling or talking to themselves, actresses and taxi dancers, con men, torpedoes, junkies and pushers, poets, gigolos, musicians, lushes, pachucos, mistresses, squares, hipsters. . . .

Wrestlers, gamblers, bookies, college kids on the town, tourists staring at every passing face in hopes that the next will be one they recognize as a movie star, bums and millionaires, nobodies dressed to kill and wearing dark glasses in the hope that they'll be taken for stars, vipers, crackpot evangelists and juvenile delinquents, television cowboys, sadists and saints, prostitutes and panhandlers, schoolteachers and bellboys. . . .

You don't see all of those type on any one stroll of a dozen blocks along the Boulevard, but do it often enough, know people, and you'll see them all. I do it often enough, and I know people.

I checked the time when I crossed Vine and I was still going to be too early. I could make one drink last half an hour, but hardly longer, so I didn't want to get there until two-thirty. I killed some time in one of the second-hand bookstores and paid for my visit by buying a paperback copy of a book of American ballads.

Then it was time so I went on to The Doll House. It's a bar that's a lot better than you'd think it to be, from its name, which comes from the fact that the proprietor has been collecting dolls (real dolls, not the Hollywood kind) from all over the world, for thirty years. He's got them from Timbuctoo, from the France of Louis XIV, and pre-revolutionary America. They're in glass cases around the walls, all labeled, and Doris had gone ape over them the first time I'd taken her there. She'd really flipped. Most women do.

I sat at the bar, ordered a highball, and sat waiting for my doll to phone. I'd decided that I didn't think she would, or that if she did it would be to tell me that she'd changed her mind, and goodbye. Well, if that happened it hadn't cost me anything, unless you count the two drinks I had bought the Seatons. And the drink I was having now; I didn't really want it, with a wine hangover still just wearing off.

I sipped the highball slowly, to make it last. There were only a few people at the bar and none of them looked like someone I'd especially like to yak with, so I took the book of ballads I'd just bought out of my pocket and started to skim it. Then I came to "Sam Hall" and stopped skimming.

> "*Oh, my name it is Sam Hall, it is Sam Hall;*
> *Yes, my name it is Sam Hall, it is Sam Hall;*
> *Yes, my name it is Sam Hall, and I hate you one and all,*
> *Yes, I hate you one and all, God damn your eyes.*"

"Yes. We'll leave it at the airport garage. He'll come in a taxi so we won't have both our cars to worry about when we get back. So you and I have time to see one another, the last time for at least a week."

"Wonderful," I said, thinking hard. Yes, counting the time it would take her to get to Hollywood from where she was and the time she'd have to allow for driving to the airport we'd still have a good three hours.

"Willy, while I'm driving in why don't you save a little time by checking in a hotel for us? The Creighton, maybe; it's only two blocks from where you are, and it's a nice place and we've never been there together."

I said, "It's a wonderful idea, darling, except for one thing. Insufficient bread. I've got only about three bucks on me. I was going to borrow some from Lennie if I didn't hear from you. I can't get a room at the Creighton for that, and I haven't any luggage with me either, so I'd have to pay in advance for the room."

"All right, just stay where you are and I'll pick you up there."

"'Kay, but wait. Don't park and come in. It'll take you at least twenty minutes to get here. In fifteen I'll wander out to the curb and be waiting. Save time that way."

"All right, Willy. Only we should have a farewell drink at the hotel, no? Will your money cover that, or should I stop on the way?"

"I can cover a pint and that ought to do it. Or we can get it from room service at the hotel."

"Not room service, honey. They might take half an hour to bring it up and we'd have to stay decent till it came. With time a-wasting."

I laughed and promised to have it when she picked me up.

I finished my drink quickly, went to a liquor store half a block away, and was at the curb in front of The Doll House within fifteen minutes; Doris's MG stopped double parked a few minutes later and took off again when I got in.

"Shall we go to the Creighton?" she asked. "Or—?"

"As good as anywhere," I said. "But don't drive there and let them park the car. Put it on the parking lot on the side street around the corner from it. We'll walk back."

"All right, Willy. But why?"

"Your right name is on the car registration. We wouldn't want the attendant who parks the car to get nosy and compare that with how we register. Dig?"

She nodded. I said, "The odds are way against anything like that, Dorrie, but from here on in we take no chances."

She nodded again. By then she was turning the corner the Creighton is on and she pulled into the parking lot half a block beyond. Before the attendant came I borrowed the keys from her and took one of the suitcases out of the back of the car. I relocked the trunk and put the key back in the ignition just as the attendant came up and gave us a ticket.

As we walked off the lot she slipped something into the side pocket of my coat. "The money, Willy. It's six hundred even. I had about fifty more, but I thought I'd better keep it in the box."

"Right," I said. "With luggage, we won't have to pay in advance, but I will anyway. That way we can leave when we want to without calling attention to the fact we've been there only a few hours."

Her grip on my arm tightened to show she understood and agreed.

We got a room for ten bucks and another dollar got the bellboy out of it. I locked and bolted the door behind him, and when I turned Doris was already wriggling out of her clothes, with her dress up over head. I laughed and caught her that way and held her helpless for a moment. Not that she minded what I did to her during that moment. Then I helped her get the dress the rest of the way off. And the rest of her clothes.

One of the kicks of life—and one thing that must make monogamy monotonous—is the fact that no two women are alike in the way they prefer to approach being bedded. Finding out, subtly, just what they like and doing things their way is a big factor in making them want return engagements. Doris liked me to undress her completely before I even took off my coat, carry her to the bed and put her on it, on top of the covers, kiss her in strategic places until we were both thoroughly aroused, and then watch her lying there while I undressed myself. She told me it made her feel really naked, nakeder than plain naked, if she was that way and was kissed and fondled while I was still fully dressed. A touch of exhibitionism, perhaps, or a little more than that; but she enjoyed being aroused and then having a brief hiatus of not being touched, but of building up anticipation while I undressed, watching her, watching the rise and fall of her beautifully shaped white breasts, the slight anticipatory movement of her firm, tanned thighs. By the time I joined her on the bed we were both ready, more than ready. If our time was brief, I'd manage to hold out a while, but if there was time and to spare for a second time, as now, I'd whisper, "This will be quick, darling," and she'd let go too and we'd still reach climax together, however quickly.

I whispered, "This will be quick, darling," and it was, but it was almost like an explosion. Afterward, despite the relative brevity of exertion, we both lay spent and breathing hard, apart, and then Doris rolled into my arms with a soft moan that said more than the words that followed it: "Oh, darling, that was the *most* wonderful . . ." And I said, and meant, "Yes, it was."

"Willy, I know we're going to have to talk and to plan, but —we can't *do* anything till John and I are back from Mexico anyway, so can't we wait till then? This afternoon—there's so little time and it's the last time we'll see one another for a week at least."

I said, "Get one thing straight, Lady Loverly. *We're* not going to do anything; *I* am. And I'm going to ask you a million questions about Seaton's habits, the layout of his house and office, where he goes, when he goes out, things like that. But that can wait, yes. And you're not going to be in on even the planning."

"But—"

"But no buts. The only thing you'll know, when I've got things set, is *when*, so you'll be sure to have an alibi, even be out of town if you can arrange it. Beyond that, the less you know the better."

"All right— How's about a drink, huh? I feel wonderful."

"That you do," I agreed. I got the bottle of whisky and opened it, found glasses and, luckily, an ice-water tap in the bathroom. I made us drinks and when I came back with them Doris had braced the pillows against the headboard so we could sit and half lie on the bed, braced up enough to sip our drinks.

After we were comfortable I said, "Dorrie, there are a couple, just a couple of questions, I want to ask you now, since we're having a drink anyway, to give me something to start thinking about while you're gone. Okay? I won't take ten minutes."

"All right, Willy."

It was just an act, of course, but I decided to do some thinking and make it look good. Or was I beginning to start thinking about this thing seriously?

"Do you have any servants at home?" I asked.

"Two. A housekeeper-cook—she doesn't do too much cooking because outside of light breakfast we have most meals out —and a maid."

"Do they both live in?"

"The housekeeper does. The maid comes in at ten and leaves at six—unless we're having company for dinner once in a while and then she stays later and gets paid extra."

"While you're in Mexico, will the housekeeper be living there?"

"No, not after tomorrow or before Sunday. She'll get paid just the same, but she asked John if he minded if she went up to Sacramento to visit her sister, provided she came back late Saturday or early Sunday and had the house ready for us by the time we get back late Sunday night. Of course he said she could."

"Good," I said. "Then will you lend me your key while you're gone? I want to look over the house thoroughly—like case it."

"Sure, Willy. Front or back door? I've got both on the key ring with my car keys, on the lot. You'll have to come back to the car with me."

"I would anyway, to carry the suitcase. All right, that will be one thing I can do this week. Let me think which key I'd rather—"

"Wait, honey, I've got an idea. You might as well take both keys as one of them. Because I couldn't pretend to have lost either, off the key ring with the others. You take both house keys, and while I'm in Mexico I'll lose the whole ring, see? There won't be anything suspicious about that."

"But—how'll you drive back from the airport without your car keys?"

"No trouble. John carries the duplicate keys to my MG and I carry the duplicates to his Chrysler. So either of us can drive either car."

"Good," I said. "I'll take both house keys then. And I promise not to swipe anything if I use them."

"Don't joke, Willy." She pulled a little away from me. "Are you *really*—? No, I don't expect it would do me any good to ask that."

"Ask what, honey?"

"Whether you're really going to go through with this, or whether you came up with an idea to get yourself a chunk of cash as a farewell gift from me. Whichever it is, you'd *say* you were going to follow through, so what good would it do me to ask?"

"Doris, what kind of a heel do you think I am?"

She laughed a little. "I don't know. Which kind are you? The kind that would murder a man to get his wife, or the kind that would cheat the wife out of six hundred dollars and not kill her husband?"

"Damn it, Doris," I said. "I—"

She laughed again. "All right, Willy, I won't bug you. See, I'm picking up some of that beat slang you use. But do me one favor, will you? When we get in touch after I'm back, let me know? If you've decided it's too risky—all right, I'll understand. And not expect any money back—because I wouldn't get it anyway. But if you change your mind, *please* be honest about it and let me know. Fair enough?"

"Sure it's fair enough," I said. "And that goes both ways. While you're gone I won't be able to do anything but planning anyway, so if *you* change *your* mind—"

"I won't, Willy. I made up my mind, the minute John confronted me with what he'd learned from that detective that John—had to go. Maybe you were surprised how quickly I agreed when you brought it up."

"I was," I admitted.

"I'm desperate, Willy. You see, he'll never give *me* a divorce because that would give me a share in the community property, or anyway a settlement. But he as much as said that if

I'm ever caught again in—what's that legal phrase, *flagrante* something?"

"*Flagrante delicto.*"

"Then he'll divorce me for adultery and see that I don't get a penny. I'd—well, I just can't go back to being poor. And I'm a passionate woman, Willy. I can't stand John sexually, not very often anyway—it's just disgusting—and never to be able to love anyone the rest of my life— I just can't take it, Willy. I love you and I want you—but if you let me down, I'm going to find someone else who won't. Or kill John myself if I can find a way that's safe. I just *can't* face living with him another twenty or thirty years—until I'm an old woman. That or being poor again. I was a—a waitress when I met John, and that's something I won't face again either."

I slid closer and put my arm around her. "Don't worry, Lady Loverly," I said. "I won't let you down."

And wondered if I was telling her the truth.

I saw that she'd finished her drink. "Want another?"

"Another drink or—?" She laughed. "No, not another drink, now. Hold me awhile."

I killed the little that was left of my own drink and put my glass and hers down on the floor and rolled over to her.

"I love you, Willy. Won't it be wonderful to be *married*? To be together all the time?"

I thought that it really would, for a while. I said, "Sure, Lady Loverly. All that and money too. How much is old Seat Cover worth? Can you make a guess?"

"He told me about a year ago that 'if anything happened to him' I'd have enough to get by on. He said at least a hundred thousand after taxes and everything. It would be more than that now; he's made quite a bit in the last year. And we haven't been spending any more than we did last year. Kiss me, honey."

I kissed her and—you don't want the play by play description. The second time was as wonderful as the first, but in a different way. Slow and leisurely and with variations and experiments. We were still new enough to each other to allow room for experiments, and we were compatible in that neither of us enjoyed sadism or masochism, but everything else. I managed to last a long time while she had several climaxes, each a bit more quiet but a bit deeper and more satisfying than the one before.

Then we lay quiet for a while. I looked at my wrist watch and told her it was time to leave, if she was to have time to eat something before starting to drive to the airport.

We made one final arrangement: next contact. I told her I'd be at The Doll House—same time, same station—next Monday and every day thereafter until she felt it was safe to phone me there after her return from Mexico City. Not from home, and only if she was positive she wasn't being followed. The main purpose would be to tell me what she'd worked out about her own alibi, so I could match it, as nearly as I could, with the Deed.

Monday and every day thereafter until I heard from her. And I asked her not to fail to phone me; even if she changed her mind or chickened out she should phone me to take me off the hook and not make me go to the Doll House indefinitely, two-thirty to three every day forever.

Whether we'd *see* each other whichever day she phoned would depend on circumstances, hers. If she was absolutely sure she was not being followed and didn't have to report in, as it were, for like a couple of hours, why not? Indeed, why not? It wouldn't be safe for us to see each other for at least a couple of weeks, maybe a month, after she was a widow.

We took quick showers and dressed, went downstairs and ate in the Creighton dining room, and then while she waited in the lobby I went up and brought down the suitcase. I got in the car with her and let her drop me off at the Zoo, since it was on the way to Sepulveda, her best route to the airport.

And, besides my own room key, I jangled two other keys in my pocket as I went in. Keys to the gas chamber? I wondered if I was going to use them.

But in a side pocket of my coat was something I was going to use all right, a roll of bills. I'd peeled off a twenty when I'd paid in advance for the hotel room and the change from it had been enough to cover our dinners, since I hadn't been very hungry so soon after a big late breakfast and had had only a sandwich myself.

I counted what was left and it was all there, five hundred and eighty clams. One hundred-dollar bill, four fifties, and fourteen twenties. I put it down on the bed, sat down myself, and looked at it. What the hell was I going to do with it? It was more than I wanted to carry around with me, and more than I wanted to stash here, even in Gideon. Besides, it was too thick a pile for Gideon to hold in his mouth without showing that something was there.

Tomorrow, *if* I'd decided for sure by then that this was just money I'd conned Doris Seaton out of, I could use five hundred of it to open a checking account at a bank. It had been several years since I'd had a checking account; I'd been living from hand to mouth most of the time, at any rate I'd never built up this kind of a surplus. But if I was, even maybe, going to go through with murder, a bank account was out. Sooner or later, if Seaton got shuffled off this mortal coil, the cops would get around to asking me questions and investigating me; I wouldn't want to have to explain where all of a sudden I got five hundred clams to start a checking account. Even if they didn't guess or deduce its source it would make them give me a long, hard second look. A deposit box might be all right, especially if I used a phony name when I rented it.

For the moment I put four twenty-dollar bills in my wallet and stashed the rest, an even five hundred, in my second best hiding place, the torn lining of the beat-up old suit I'd worn to skid row and kept for just such purposes.

Suddenly I didn't want to think or decide anything, not tonight. I wanted to drink or to do something, or both. I took the pint of whisky out of my pocket and looked to see how much there was left; it was about half full. That meant that there was enough to offer Charlie Hayes a couple of drinks with me, if he was home. I didn't want to drink alone.

Charlie wasn't home, ditto Johnny Kaprelian. I started back from the second floor to the basement but on the first floor landing I heard music, Bach played on guitar, Partita in D Minor, the one on which Segovia does such a wonderful job. I wandered down the hall and treed it as coming from the room of our beatnik poet, Smoky Conover. I reached to knock and then decided the music was live, not a recording, so I waited till he'd finished and then knocked. Smoky called out for me to *entrez-vous* and I did.

There were two of them besides Smoky, the beatnik chick in the leotard Smoky had brought to Charlie's room last night and abandoned there, and a tall lanky guy I didn't know, who had the guitar on his lap. He gave me a nod and started on a Bach sonata without saying anything, so nobody else said anything either and I took a cushion off the sofa and sat on it on the floor as the rest of them were doing. And held my peace till the lanky one finished the sonata. He put down the guitar and Smoky said, "That Bach cat, he's far out. You wouldn't think anybody had it that far back. Tex, this bad actor is Willy Griff. Squaresville most of the time, but not quite hopeless."

Tex grinned and I grinned back and pulled the bottle out of my pocket and held it up. "Wanted someone to share a drink with. About eight ounces in here, one good slug apiece, or two easy ones."

I passed it to the chick but she handed it on to Smoky. "I'm floating, man. Weed in technicolor, don't want to spoil it."

"Like more for the rest of us," Smoky said; he took a slug and passed it on to Tex. Tex gauged the contents, put his finger to mark a place and took a long slug that was a good guess; it had emptied to the exact tip of his finger. "Reckon that was my share," he said. "Rather have one Capistrano type swallow than two-three short ones. Thanks." He handed me the bottle.

I took a drink of maybe an ounce and a half, which left a short one apiece for Smoky and me. But I put the bottle down instead of passing it right away. There wasn't any hurry. Tex had picked up the git-box again but he was just doodling minor chords so it was all right to talk and I said, "Right cool Bach, Tex. Was he a Texan? Bach, I mean."

He gave the slow grin again. "Would of been, a couple centuries later. But we ain't all cowboys. Ever dig a Texan named Van Cliburn? He tickles a cool box."

He swung from a wild arpeggio that I'd have sworn had quarter tones in it into something that sounded as though it had been transcribed from Villa-Lobos, and that didn't give me a chance to answer, which was just as well. I leaned back against the wall and settled for using my ears and my eyes. Tex was good; outside of a few top-famous ones, I'd never heard a better classical guitar. He couldn't have been over twenty-two or -three, and he was dressed in faded levis, scuffed cowboy boots, and a Western shirt. A dirty white Stetson that had probably cost fifty to a hundred bucks when it was new was pushed so far back on his head you couldn't see why it didn't fall the rest of the way off, but it didn't. Smoky wore his usual costume of old chino pants, a sweat shirt with *Vassar* blazed across the front (God knows how he ever got hold of it) and barefoot sandals. No beard; he didn't need a beard to mark himself as a nonconformist. The chick still wore the same black leotard, or another one like it. When the Villa-Lobos—if that's what it was—had ended, she opened the eyes that she'd been keeping closed most of the time. "I hate these bastards," she said, "they won't find me some bongos."

Nobody answered her and I picked up the bottle and handed it to Smoky; he drank half and handed it back for me to kill the rest. Which I did.

"This is a drag," the chick said. "Let's make the scene somewhere."

"Somewhere like where, Essie?" Smoky wanted to know. I remembered now that that was her name. "Too early. The beat joints aren't swinging yet. Cosmo Alley isn't even open. What time is it, Willy?"

I told him it was almost nine. "See what I mean? Unicorn might be open but strictly from Touristville this early. Same with The Black Hole, and Cosmo Alley won't open for an hour."

"So let's go to the beach. Caddy's a'wasting."

I started to ask whose Caddy but Smoky was asking Tex if it was okay by him and when Tex grinned and nodded Smoky said, "Okay. Want to read you a poem first, though."

He went over to the dresser and started shuffling through a pile of papers.

"Got it!" he announced triumphantly. "'The Warp and the Woof and the Woofer and the Tweeter' wasn't a title; it was a poem like in itself. I made my mistake trying to write a poem *about* it. I call my new one "Pattern." Here, friends and country boys, feast your eyes."

He handed it to Essie, who was sitting on the bed, and Tex and I sat one on each side of her and read over her shoulders.

We read:

Pattern

Oh, the warp and the woof
And the woofer and the tweeter
And the warp
warp
warp
woof woof woof WOW woof woof woof
warp
warp
warp
And the woofer tweeter
woofer tweeter
woofer tweeter
WOW
tweeter woofer
tweeter woofer
tweeter woofer
Oh, the tweeter and the woofer and the woof and the warp
And the warp and the woof and the woofer and the tweeter.

"Crazy, man," I said.

"Endsville," Essie said.

Tex grinned.

Smoky looked happy as he took it back and folded it, put it in his pocket. "It's the wows at the intersections that make it. Well, let's off to Goville. Or go to Offville. Say, there's an idea in that too. But I'll save it."

We went out. Tex, carrying his guitar case, led the way to a flashy black Cadillac convertible parked a few doors north. I wondered if he made that kind of money playing guitar or if he had a rich father back in Texas. It turned out to be neither. When we got in the car, Smoky and Essie taking the back seat and me sitting up front with Tex, Tex didn't use an ignition key; he leaned forward and twisted some wires together under the instrument panel just back of the ignition lock.

"Don't tell me this car is hot, Tex?" I asked him.

"Well—it's a little warm maybe. But it's a cool set of wheels, man."

"Warm or cool," I said, "do you got to pick something as flashy as this to swipe? Hell, the fuzz can probably recognize it without reading the license plates."

From the back seat Smoky said, "Don't worry about ol' Tex. Like he knows what he's doing."

Tex gunned the engine, then pulled out from the curb and tooled the Caddy around the corner to head west on Sunset. "Don't worry, man," he said. "I know who belongs to this dreamboat. Goin' out of town, left it on a lot and paid for three days in advance. That was yesterday, so I'll be plenty safe if I put it back late tonight."

"Unless the lot attendant misses it and reports it stolen," I said.

He grinned. "He's already missed it but ain't reported it. I'm the lot attendant." He tooled smoothly from lane to lane, passing car after car with effortless ease. "Got any bread, man? I really ought to put five gals in this thing sometime this here now evening, so he won't see the gas gauge down."

"Guess so," I said. "But first stop at a liquor store. I'll pick up some wine so we'll have something to suck on down at the beach."

The only bills I had were the four twenties in my wallet and I didn't want to have to break one of them at a filling station, in plain sight, so they'd all know I was loaded.

"Crazy," Tex said. We were on the Strip part of Sunset now and he double parked in front of a liquor store.

I got out and went into the liquor store. I broke the twenty buying two fifths of muscatel, got back in the car and put the bag with the bottles on the seat between us. Essie wanted to know if anybody had any weed; hers was wearing off. But nobody had any. She said plaintively that an open convertible in motion was the safest place in the world to blast because the smoke blew away so fast nobody could smell it. I offered her a straight cigarette but she said the hell with it, she didn't smoke, except weed.

Tex took Doheny south to Santa Monica Boulevard and then went west on that. A few blocks after we entered Santa

Monica at Centinella, I saw a street sign that read Prince Drive, and I remembered that was the street the Seatons lived on.

A little farther on, Tex stopped at a gas station. While the attendant was putting in five and cleaning the windshield I stepped into the station, picked up the phone book and looked up Seaton's street number. I'd decided I might as well at least take a look at the outside of the place, maybe after we'd had a few drinks on the beach I'd borrow the Cad and go back for a quick gander. I'd never driven a Cad anyway and wanted a chance to try one.

I came back out and paid for the gas and we got going. Tex took Santa Monica clear to the end and turned north on Ocean, took the downhill cutoff to the Palisades Beach Road, which runs along close to the water. It was a pleasant evening and there were quite a few cars parked off the road on the sand, but Tex drove slowly and finally found a place that wasn't crowded, pulled off and parked. There was a bright moon. We got out and walked across the sand toward the ocean. Smoky bitched about walking in barefoot sandals in sand; finally he took them off and put them in his pocket, walked barefoot.

We picked a place to sit, as close to the water as we could without getting wet when the waves rolled in. We opened one of the bottles and passed it around, sometimes just listening to and watching the waves and sometimes talking about nothing in particular.

I learned a little about Tex and Essie. They weren't together; they'd met for the first time that evening when they'd each separately dropped in on Smoky.

Tex wasn't really a Texan; he was from the Oklahoma Panhandle. I'd guessed him twenty-two or -three but he was a little older, twenty-six. He'd been hung up and in trouble most of his life since he started high school, in and out of juvenile court and then police stations, for just about everything on the books. But he had taught himself classical guitar, and he loved it. He knew every beat joint in San Francisco, Los Angeles, Phoenix and Tucson, and had played at most of them, for pay when he could get it and for kicks when he couldn't get money. Sometimes he held down a job on the side, like his current shift on a parking lot, but he was off the grift, as a means of making money anyway. Sometimes he "borrowed" a car, but just for kicks and not to sell.

He and Smoky had met a couple of years ago at a coffeehouse in Tucson, a small one called Oblivion. They'd both liked it, and had both left Tucson when it closed.

Essie's story was simple. She'd been beat since she'd run away from home at seventeen, five years ago, and had gone to San Francisco. She didn't work often, didn't do anything except sometimes draw or paint a little, and dig progressive jazz. She didn't say so in so many words, but she got by by sleeping around, not professionally, but for the use of a pad and other necessities such as food, drink, and marijuana. Once in a while she'd hold down a job long enough to replenish her wardrobe, such as it was. Getting by was all she wanted or expected out of life. She'd been in L.A. only a week and didn't much like it and wanted to get back to San Francisco, but she was hung up. She tried to talk me into taking her there but gave up when I explained that even if I had the dough I couldn't live there on account of television being here.

When we were about halfway through the second bottle of musky, I asked Tex if he'd walk back to the car with me and show me how to wire a hot short, because knowing how might come in handy sometime in a jam. He did. We found a flashlight in the glove compartment and he showed me exactly how he'd cross-wired the ignition in the Cad and told me about the differences in other makes and years, and told me a few kinds that were so complicated I'd better not try them till I had more experience. I dug him.

Then I asked him if he minded if I tried a little run in the Cad and said I'd have it back in half an hour or so. He didn't care, though at first I was afraid he was going to decide to ride along. But I guess he figured he'd lose out on his share of the rest of the wine if he did, so he stood by till I got the Cad started and then went back to Smoky and Essie.

I put the top up and drove back the way we'd come, toward Prince Drive. I was going to take a look at the Seaton place. Just a look, that's all.

Chapter Four

PRINCE DRIVE turned out to be a pleasant little street only three blocks long. The Seaton house was in the middle of the middle block, on the north side. I guessed it at ten rooms. It was hard to judge age in only moonlight, but I guessed it to be neither old nor new, somewhere in between. With the grounds and a swimming pool and—no doubt—a two-car garage in back, something like fifty thousand clams, maybe a little more. Or maybe a little less; I'm no judge of real estate. Anyway, a bit swankier than my underground penthouse at the Zoo.

But nothing I'd ever want to live in, if things should work out so I had the chance to do so. And I knew enough of Doris's tastes to know she'd agree with me. A slightly smaller but more modern place, somewhere like in North Hollywood or on the beach in Malibu, would suit us better. This was a house for squares; the best thing about it would be the price it could be sold for.

There was light in only one upstairs room, no doubt the housekeeper's room. The rest of the windows, both upstairs and down, were dark and, I thought, shielded by shades or Venetian blinds. The housekeeper, Doris had said, would be here until tomorrow and then gone for the rest of the period of the Seatons' Mexico City trip.

I didn't get all this, such as it was, just driving past. I drove to the next corner and then around a block and back; I parked almost across the street from the Seaton place, turned out my lights and turned on a cigarette, and studied the house a few minutes. There wasn't any hurry. Only a few minutes after I'd parked there the upstairs light went out. I assumed it meant that the housekeeper was going to bed, but it didn't because a minute later a downstairs light came on, and then a porch light. I'd been about ready to drive off—after all you can't case a house much in moonlight from the outside—but I decided to wait another few minutes and did, and then a taxi drove up. I quickly put out my cigarette and moved back away from the window as the cabby got out and went up onto the porch. The door opened and he stepped inside a moment to pick up two suitcases; while he carried them to the taxi, the last light went out inside the house, then the porch light, and a tall middle aged ramrod of a woman came out, locked the door behind her, and then went to the cab. I heard her tell the driver to take her to the Santa Monica Greyhound station.

And the cab drove off and that was that. I was alone there in front of the Seaton house with the keys to it in my pocket and there wasn't a light on anywhere in the block. But it was no good, I decided. If the neighbors happened to notice lights going on and off in the house, and knew the Seatons were away, I'd have the block full of cops within minutes. Even quicker if they thought they saw a flashlight being used. And me with a hot Cad parked across the street. No, Willy boy, I told myself, not tonight. I didn't even have gloves to avoid leaving fingerprints. And, even more to the point, I hadn't yet decided to go through with—what I might decide to go through with. No use taking an extra risk casing the joint until I'd decided to take the big risk, until I'd thought a lot of things out.

I started the Cad again and got the hell out of there.

It drove like a dreamboat. I had to keep an eye on the speedometer to be sure I stayed close enough to the limit to avoid being picked up.

When I got back to the beach and parked the car where it had been before, the others came to join me instead of waiting for me to join them again. Tex drove back the way we'd come and to a Hollywood wine and beer bar.

Tex knew the bartender there and as soon as we'd found out the joint wasn't too crowded and nobody else was doing anything, he went back out to the car and brought in his guitar. After a classical number or two, one of the rock-and-roll set went over and put a quarter in the juke box. Tex uncoiled himself and went over to the box, pulled out the plug. The boy who'd put in the money and another who was with him started over, then saw how big Tex was and stopped. Tex said mildly, "Oughtn't do that, man, when somebody's playin' an instrument." He walked around them without even a glance and joined the rest of us at the bar.

The rock-and-roller came over. "You ain't playing now," he said, "so—"

Tex grinned at him. "No, I ain't," he admitted. "But I'd have to listen. You better wait till we leave."

Sullenly the guy went back to his own place at the bar. But he didn't have to wait long to plug in the juke; we had only one drink and then decided to move on. We had a drink this time at another bar close enough so Tex didn't have to move the Cad, but it turned out to be noisy and we didn't stay long.

Essie kept heckling Smoky to find her some marijuana.

"Chickchick," he insisted, "*I* have none. *We* have none." He got a bright idea for bugging me. "Unless Willy here. He usually keeps weed around. But me, I don't even know any contacts to get some at this time of night."

Essie turned to me but I beat her to the punch. "He's snowing you, Essie. I don't mean I never have, but like I don't ordinarily. And I do *not* have any tonight. Why don't you try meditation? Or something. Anyway I'm about due to cut out. Hard day at the office tomorrow."

They decided to drop in at Cosmo Alley for a while but I said I'd chicken out and head back for my pad. So I rode with them to Cosmo Alley, then walked down to Sunset and fed my face at the first hamburger joint I came to. Leaving it, I saw the sign of a liquor store that was still open, so I bought two fifths of muscatel and, for the next special occasion, one fifth of whisky, and then walked back to the Zoo.

It was only one o'clock when I got there and, if nothing more happened, I'd be in bed relatively early, maybe the earliest I'd been to bed since the last time I'd worked. When you work in Hollywood you go to bed early or else; the studios start work at what seems like dawn and you've got to be there bright-eyed and bushy-tailed or you don't get asked back.

I stashed the bottle of whisky and one of the bottles of wine in my closet and kept out the other bottle of wine for a nightcap to sip while I undressed. But before I opened it I decided I'd rather have my nightcap with someone; I hate to drink alone, even if it's only a bedtime drink.

So I took the bottle with me and went up to Charlie Hayes's pad and tried the knob. We regular inmates of the Zoo seldom knock on one another's doors because if we're home but don't want to be bothered we simply lock the door from the inside. An unlocked door is an invitation to come in; a locked one is either a do-not-disturb sign or means we're out. Charlie's was locked.

But as I turned away he called out, "Who is it?" And when I answered he called out for me to wait a minute. I heard the light switch flick just before the key turned. "Come on in," he said. "I was trying to get to sleep, but I couldn't. Might as well yak a while." He was in shorts; he went back to the rumpled bed and sat on it, still rubbing his eyes against the light.

I held up the bottle. "Maybe a nightcap's what you need."

"Maybe another one," he said. "But save yours; there's one opened over there." He waved toward the table where there was a half-full bottle of tokay wine. "Anyway, let's use that up first."

I put my bottle down and poured two glasses from his.

"Know a guy named Tex?" I asked. "I was out at the beach with him, and Smoky and Essie. Nice out there."

"Guy with a guitar? I've met him. But who's Essie?"

"You met her last night. Chick with the tights and leotard. You made a pass at her."

"So did you. So did everybody. God, I'm down tonight, Willy."

"Something happened?"

"Something almost happened. A fat part. A series part, every damn week, that would have put me in clover. Lennie phoned, wanted me to have dinner with him and a casting director from Crest, said it might lead to something on a new show."

"What's the show?" I asked. Crest is one of the big outfits, up there with Warner Brothers and Desilu. If they were casting a new show maybe Lennie could get me in on something.

"A new top-budget adult Western with situation humor. Crest is shooting the works on it and thinks it will top Gunsmoke, Have Gun, and Wagon Train. And run forever. Role Lennie had in mind to peddle me for is a reformed gunslinger who comes to town and gets taken on by the sheriff as a deputy. I wouldn't have been on till the fourth script, but I'd have been a regular from then on. Christ, I'd have had a small part in every script and a big one in some, next to the lead. And the lead is Rod Desmond; that shows you how big it is."

It showed me, and I made up my mind to see Lennie tomorrow. I asked, "And the casting director thumbed you down?"

"Hell, no. He said I'd be perfect and practically hired me. That's what makes it tough titty. Then he mentioned the name of the producer. Manny Radic."

I saw what he meant. Back when, in the McCarthy days, which were before my time in Hollywood, Manny Radic and Charlie Hayes had both been mild Commies, in borderline organizations the witch hunters had decided were subversive. Both had testified, recanted, and cleared themselves, but it had hurt their careers. The damage to Charlie's was worse because Radic—rightly or wrongly; Charlie says wrongly—got the idea that Charlie was the one who'd thrown him to the lions. Radic was a big shot and Charlie a small-timer, and ever since Radic had been Charlie's implacable enemy. And any choice a casting director makes is subject to the producer's approval, so—

Charlie held out his glass. "Someday I'm going to kill that bastard," he said. "But for now, let's kill the bottle."

I poured, and refilled my own glass. We alternately talked and thought our separate thoughts for a while and then Charlie said, "Maybe I can go to sleep now. Mind splitting?"

I didn't mind, but I asked him if he wanted me to transfuse part of my full bottle into his empty one in case he couldn't sleep after all and wanted another slug.

He shook his head. "Got to be bubbling over at ten tomorrow. Tryout for a commercial. Consolation prize Lennie got me."

"Local or national, Charlie?"

"Just local. But once a week, not one-shot."

"Good," I said. "Hope you make it." But I was wondering why Lennie hadn't tossed it my way. Charlie's got things on the ball that I haven't, but only in the way of playing character parts and older men. With my appearance, I could give him cards and spades on a commercial. And while a local commercial spot doesn't pay much—ten to twenty-five bucks—it adds up to a living if you can get enough of them, and makes your face familiar to casting directors and producers besides. And the best thing is that most of them are filmed, or can be, so if you get anything short of a regular role on a series you can keep the commercial too. And if you can go network for a big sponsor you're in clover.

Back in my own pad I found that the double nightcap upstairs had worked. I was sleepy and was dead to the world the minute I slugged the pillow with my head.

And slept until a knock on the door wakened me. It wasn't a loud knock, but I'm a light sleeper unless I go to bed stoned.

I turned on the light and looked at the clock; it was almost four. I called out, "Who is it?"

I couldn't understand the word or words that came back, but it was a woman's voice, not a man's. And for a dazed moment I had the wild and wonderful idea that it was Doris's voice, that something had happened and she hadn't taken the plane to Mexico City. Once before she'd come here in the middle of the night, after Seat Cover had suddenly decided to take a business trip and had left on a late night plane. It had been one of the only two times she'd ever been to the Zoo; we'd decided after that it was safer to meet elsewhere. But maybe at this hour of the morning she'd figured—

I got out of bed and went to the door and opened it. It wasn't until it was open that I realized I was stark naked, the way I always sleep, but by then it didn't matter.

It was Essie, and she wasn't shocked. She said, "Hi, man," and walked in and past me as casually as though she was walking into a dime store.

Chapter Five

I STILL held the door a few inches ajar while I turned. "You the advance guard? Or alone?"

"Like alone. Close it and lock it, unless you don't want me here."

I answered that by closing the door and locking it. I went to the closet and got my bathrobe, put it on.

Essie sat on the edge of the bed and cocked her head at me. I could see by her eyes that she was slightly stoned. She had a long oval face, not pretty but maybe a little bit beautiful, framed by straight black hair worn in a long bob.

"Liked you better dressed the other way, man," she said. "Are you like modest?"

I laughed. "Like cool. Meaning cool in the archaic sense of slightly cold. It can mean that too, you know. In square talk."

"You a square?"

"Call me a square peg who can always use a round hole," I said, and that got a laugh out of her, the first time I'd ever heard her laugh.

"What happened to Smoky and Tex? Sure they're not coming here?"

"I'm not sure of anything, but don't let them in if they do come. I ditched them a little after you did. At Cosmo, it was a drag. Honey, you got a stick or two? I can't look any more wine in the face, but I could sure blast." She came over and put her arms around me, wriggled against me. "You'll unstash some weed, won't you? I'm worth it when I'm on weed."

I put my arms around her, mostly to keep her from wriggling so much. "Would if I could, chick. But Smoky was just bugging me by telling you I keep the stuff around. And there's nowhere, but nowhere, I could dig any this time of the night."

She broke away from me and sat down on the edge of the bed, looking disconsolate. I said, "Tell you what, though. I got a bottle that isn't wine. Want a shot of whisky to finish off the night?" I was wide awake now, and looking forward to. I didn't want her to decide to go somewhere else to find marijuana.

Not with the rest of the night to go and with those very interesting bumps in the front of the black leotard. Besides, I'd never slept with a real beatchick; it might be interesting.

"Okay," she said. "Whisky then. At least that's better than the damn wine I've been drinking the last couple hours."

She took off her shoes and started rubbing her black-stockinged feet. I got the bottle of whisky and twisted the top off. Glasses.

She sighed. "Say, that Charlie cat with the pad upstairs where we met the other night. Would he be home?"

"He would," I said. "But pounding his ear. I had a nightcap with him two-three hours ago. Why?"

"Would he have any weed around?"

"He doesn't use the stuff. I don't either, often. You'll have to live without, tonight."

"'Kay, honey. Pour me one more slug then. I'll sip this one and let's talk awhile."

"Right," I said. "But don't get too sleepy on me." I refilled our glasses and sat on the bed beside her; I sipped my drink too and we talked.

She wanted to know what I thought of Ginsberg and the other beat poets and did I read the *Evergreen Review*, and I was telling her when she put her glass down and lay back with her head on the pillow.

And was like out cold.

I tried to wake her up to get her to undress, but I might as well have tried to wake a corpse. I lifted her legs up on the bed and managed to get her skirt off. What she had on under it wasn't stockings but black tights up to the waist, overlapping the black leotard. I could have pulled off the tights with a bit of struggle but getting a leotard off an unconscious person is tough going so I decided to hell with it. Some cats, I know, get kicks out of having an unconscious female, but I don't swing that way. With a bit of sweat I managed to get her under the covers and let it go at that. Time enough to get her undressed the rest of the way when we woke up in the morning. Or more likely in the afternoon; it was almost five o'clock now.

The only catch was I was wide awake myself now and didn't think I could go back to sleep for maybe hours. Unless, since I was almost stoned myself, I had a couple more drinks and finished the job. I did, cussing myself for having let Essie pass out on me; she must have had a lot more wine than I'd realized.

When I felt myself getting woozy I finished my second drink quickly, took off the robe, turned out the light and was sound asleep, or passed out, as soon as I got in under the sheet.

Chapter Six

I WOKE to bright daylight and raised my head to look at the clock; it was high noon, almost on the head. Then I remembered Essie and realized that I was looking at the clock across where she had been lying and that she wasn't there any more.

I sat up quickly and threw my feet out of bed. Essie was gone, tights and leotard, skirt and shoes and all. I had a sudden sickening thought and went to my pants which were hanging over the back of a chair. My wallet was in the hip pocket but it was empty of money; there'd been sixty-some dollars in it.

I had an even more sickening thought and went to the closet, pulled out the old suitcoat with the torn lining. There wasn't any five hundred dollars in the lining; there wasn't anything at all there. I looked, like you do, a dozen times, in parts of that lining remote from the corner where I'd stashed the cash. I finally convinced my fingers of what my mind had known all along.

I could see just how it had happened. Essie had wakened—or more literally had come to—early. Her first thought hadn't been to roll me, or, finding sixty-whatever dollars in my wallet she would have scrammed out of there without searching the rest of the pad. No, it hadn't happened that way at all. She'd wakened and remembered that she hadn't completely believed me that I didn't have any marijuana stashed; she'd started to look for some, probably the dresser first, then the closet; pockets and linings of clothes in closets are a common stash for pot. She'd felt the linings of the old coat—and had felt something that didn't feel like pot but like the stuff you could buy it with. A wad. She probably hadn't even stopped to count it before she was whipping into her skirt and—then, just before she took off, getting the sudden thought that if I had that much bread stashed I must have some more in my wallet and she might as well look into that too.

High noon. Hi, noon. Hi, Gary Cooper. I threw on clothes and went upstairs, knocked on Smoky Conover's door. He sang out for me to come in. His voice sounded strange.

I went in and found out why his voice had sounded strange. He was standing on his head on a pillow in a corner of the room, his sandaled feet braced against the wall. "Hi, man," he said, upside-down. "Ever try this, Willy? Best thing on earth for a hangover, man. Brings the blood to your head and—"

"You seen Essie?" I interrupted.

"Sure. About eight o'clock this morning she woke me up."

"Say where she was going?"

"San Fran. She'd left her suitcase here in my room; that's why she woke me up, to get it. Said she was going to take a bus to Santa Monica, get on the Coast Highway and start hitchhiking. She's probably well on her way by now. A good-looking chick gets rides easy."

"Damn you, Smoky," I said. "She rolled me, and it's your fault."

He came down from his head-stand and put his other end on the pillow. "My fault? Oh, you mean because I gave her a snow job on your probably having weed? Man, I'm sorry. Thought I was doing you a favor, so she'd end up in your pad."

"How come you didn't want her yourself?"

"I'm on a yogi kick, man. Haven't had a woman for five weeks. Essie slept here night before last and that was a real test. I didn't touch her. But I didn't want to go through it again last night; that's why I shook her. Lose much?"

"Enough," I said. I sat down on the edge of the bed. "Not only what was in my wallet but a hunk I had stashed. She'd never have found that if she hadn't been looking for weed, while I was asleep. Smoky, but do you think there's any chance I might find her before she blows it all? What do you know about her?"

Smoky looked thoughtful. "Not much. Her real name's Esther, Essie's a nickname. And her last name's either Porter or Potter, damn if I remember which. I met her in San Fran when I was up there four months ago, at one of the joints. She stayed with me a few nights. When we split and I came back here I told her to look me up if she ever hit L.A. She did, just a couple of days ago. Asked around the joints, I guess, till she found someone who knew where my pad was."

"You think she really hitched back to Frisco?"

"Not if she hit you hard. Like say hundred bucks. She hates hitchhiking and if she had the fare and enough over to get there with a stake then she's on a bus."

I said, "It was like a hundred all right. So if she was snowing you about how she was traveling she was probably snowing you about destination too."

"Guess that's right. She's probably heading to make the scene anywhere but Frisco. Damn, I'm sorry, Willy. But, man, you shouldn't keep bread like in three figures kicking around a pad no matter how well you stash it. Banks are square but they're safe."

I nodded and let it go at that; couldn't tell him I'd got the money yesterday—only yesterday?—too late to bank it.

Anyway, there wasn't any use bugging Smoky or setting out in three different directions, and broke at that, looking for Essie Porter or Potter.

It was my own damn fault, at least in part. I should have foreseen that if she woke before I did she might start looking around for weed. And even if I hadn't thought of that possibility I should have had the simple common sense to take my wallet out of my pants after Essie had passed out and put it somewhere like between the springs and the mattress on my side of the bed. Then I'd still have sixty-some bucks at least.

Well, it had come easy and it had gone easy. I wondered what kind of a story I could possibly tell Doris that would make sense to her.

Or I could simply never call her, never see her again.

Or I could kill her husband, without expense money. Hell, if I was going to kill him I didn't know how the money would have come in anyway, except to free me from other worries and responsibilities while I was working things out.

I said so long to Smoky and split; I went down to the phone in the main floor hallway. I checked the change in my pocket and found there was almost two bucks' worth, which was good as far as it went. At least I could call Lennie, and have some breakfast before I saw him to put the bite on him.

I called Lennie, and as I should have guessed he was out for lunch and I got his secretary. She's very efficient, but a prune-faced spinster of sixty. Which makes sense for Lennie since, as I've mentioned, he never likes to sleep with the same woman twice; if he had sleepable-with secretaries he'd have to change them too often. Miss Jocelyn was his answer to that problem; she'd been with him ever since he'd left M.C.A. five years before to start his own agency.

Miss Jocelyn told me that Mr. Berg (that's Lennie) planned to be out on the Warner lot after lunch but that he should be back around four and would probably stay in his office until five. I told her I'd be there at four-thirty, and if he came in sooner not to let him get away without waiting to see me.

Then I went back to my room. I made myself a drink out of the fifth of whisky that was still standing on the dresser almost half full, and then I put it away so I wouldn't be tempted to take a second.

I sat and sipped at it, feeling lousy. Not physically; the seven hours of sleep I'd had had been enough and I didn't feel especially overhung. But I felt soured on everything, and especially on beatchicks. Essie could at least have had the decency to settle for the five hundred when she'd found it and have left me the money in my wallet.

But she probably wanted me broke, immobilized, unable to follow her. Well, I *was* broke, immobilized. And she had a better than four-hour start. I might as well write Essie and the money off.

Easy came, easy went. Thank you, Essie, for the most expensive few minutes of conversation I'd ever had.

And, for better or for worse, for making me a murderer. I had to follow through, now, or I was sunk. I could have stretched that money and made it—with what I could pick up now and then acting—last a long time, around the turning point in my career.

Without it, and without Doris as a continuing if slight source of income, I might as well give up. Go square, take a job. But what kind of job was I fitted for? None that would ever get me anywhere.

And, damn it, *I was going somewhere.* I knew I had what it took, everything it took—except money to put up the front I needed for the rat race, and to ride out the waiting periods.

Money I needed, to get out of this underground penthouse, to be able to move to a place where I could throw parties and get invited to parties in return where I could make contacts, make friends among producers and directors. A good agent I needed, not a two-bit one like Lennie Berg, who got by but who'd never brought a client to stardom. A wife with money I needed.

So easy, if I could commit one simple murder and get away with it. What percentage of murderers are caught and convicted? I'd read the statistics somewhere; I didn't remember the percentage, but it was damn small.

A clever man ought to be able to get away with a simple murder, even if he had a motive for it. And I had to face the fact that the police would find out I had had a motive. When Doris and I married, if not sooner. Probably sooner, through a private eye named Weston. If there's one thing you can count on a pee-eye doing, it's reading the newspapers, the crime news especially. I'd have to be ready to have the police question me, probably not later than twenty-four hours after the crime. They'd investigate anyone and everyone who had a possible motive for seat cover removal. Even if the crime looked to be a simple unpremeditated murder committed in the course of a robbery or burglary, as it would have to look. Anything else, anything fancy, would be too dangerous. The crimes that are gotten away with are the simple ones.

Unless other people turned up with motives—I'd have to remember to ask Doris about that—they'd probably suspect me pretty strongly. But if I was careful enough and left no traces, nothing could be proved. If I was careful enough and planned well enough the only serious danger should be during the crime itself—and I didn't doubt my ability to handle Seaton. Being seen entering or leaving the house by a neighbor who might call copper seemed offhand to be the biggest risk. But not a serious risk. Luckily the houses on that block were spaced well apart. There were trees and shrubbery on both sides of the Seaton house: I could reconnoiter by day to make sure, but I thought that the approach and entrance to the house could not be seen by neighbors on either side but only from houses on the opposite side of the street, and there were only two or three of those within seeing distance. The chance of being observed entering or leaving late at night, especially after the houses across the street were dark, was negligible.

I had over three hours to kill before I could see Lennie and there was no reason why I shouldn't get my daylight reconnaissance of the Seaton house and neighborhood over during that time.

I spent a few minutes thinking things out. I didn't want to make any mistakes, even on something so simple as walking by the house in broad daylight. Someone just might see and notice me, be able to identify me later as having been in that block or neighborhood recently. I didn't want a complex disguise, though, so I settled for a very simple one. I found a pair of sunglasses and put them in my pocket and, on the shelf in my closet, I found an old very soft felt hat that would roll up. I put it in my hip pocket.

I walked south to Santa Monica Boulevard and took the bus, got off at Prince Drive. I put on the sunglasses when I got off the bus, and, half a block farther, I took the rolled-up soft hat out of my hip pocket, shaped it, and put it on. Then, after a glance over my shoulder to make sure no one was directly behind me to notice the transition, I gradually changed my posture and walk. I let my shoulders sag and my spine slump, changed my pace and the length of my steps—and seemed (even felt) shorter and older.

The Seaton house looked bigger and a lot more expensive than it had seemed last night in the dark. And I could see that the grounds were well kept up; Seaton must have at least a part-time gardener. But not one who lived in; Doris would surely have mentioned him in that case.

I kept on going, rounded the corner and walked down the alley for a look at the back. The back yard contained a kidney-shaped swimming pool, a double garage, a patio. Nice lawn, but no trees and only low hedges. An approach from this direction could be seen from several houses across the alley or from the back windows of the houses on either side. Definitely, it would be the front door that I'd use.

I walked back by a different route to the bus line, gradually changing my walk back to normal and, one at a time, pocketing the hat and the sunglasses. I got off the bus at Vine and walked north to Lennie's office.

It was four-fifteen when I got there and Lennie wasn't back

yet. But he came in five minutes later, cheerful as always during working hours. Lennie's cheerfulness is almost psychopathic.

I waved back when he waved at me and, knowing the routine, stayed in my chair while he stopped at Miss Jocelyn's desk and got from her the list of phone calls that had come in while he was gone.

Then he turned to me. "Willy, honey," he said, "lot of people here I've got to call back, take me a while. Some in a hurry. If what you want will take only a minute I'll take you first. If you want to make yak a while, I'll have to make at least some of these calls before I talk to you. So?"

I grinned at him. "I'll settle for twenty-five seconds—at a buck a second. I'm flat, Lennie."

He pulled out his wallet, fished out two tens and a five. "'Kay, sweetie," he said. "But make it last. Your check ought to come in any time now—I'll call the studio and see what's holding it up if it doesn't come soon. But, with this, don't forget you'll have had most of it in advance."

"I know," I said. "Which leads me to one other question. Got anything in mind that might get me another check someday?"

"Sure. Lots of things on the fire." He put a fatherly hand on my shoulder, even though he had to reach up to do it. "You know I'm *for* you, sweetie. Lots of things coming up."

He clapped me heartily on the shoulder and went through the doorway to the inner office, closing the door behind him.

Poor little Lennie.

What did I mean, poor little Lennie? A poor agent, but with lots of poor clients. So if he made a few dollars a week apiece, average, from a hundred clients, that was a few hundred dollars a week. Poor little me, not poor little Lennie.

I waved a jaunty goodbye to Miss Jocelyn, poor little Miss Jocelyn, and took my twenty-five bucks down the stairs and to the nearest cheap restaurant. It had to last, that twenty-five skins.

I ate a breakfast, lunch, or dinner, whatever it was, and then walked back to my room. Nothing had changed there except that it was getting dark and I had to turn on the light. And dear Mrs. Whelan, that good old soul, had been in and had made my bed and emptied my wastebasket. And tomorrow I'd owe her more rent. Why, when I'd been temporarily rich, hadn't I paid her a few weeks ahead? Because I hadn't known how temporary my wealth was going to be, that's why. Simple?

I lay down on the bed to think and my first thought was, why didn't I kill myself? Not the first time I'd thought that, by any means. But now, suddenly and for the first time, I had an answer that really made sense. Why should I, when the sovereign state of California would do the job for me free, if I bungled a murder? And if I didn't bungle it I'd be in clover. It made sense. Even if I had only *even* odds of getting away with killing Seaton, it made killing him make sense.

So. Then, even though it was only Tuesday evening and the Seatons wouldn't be back for five days yet, why not take the first step tonight and case the house, inside, so I could make my plans?

Or would it be better by day? I thought about that for a while. By night would be safer as far as the possibility of my being seen entering it was concerned. But I'd have to use a flashlight and there was always a chance of light being seen by a neighbor or even a cruising squad car. True, shades were pulled or Venetian blinds closed at all the windows I'd noticed, but light can always show through or at the edges of a shade, or through chinks in a Venetian blind. Besides, it would be harder to be sure I'd seen everything worth seeing in the big house, if I worked by flashlight.

Well, I asked myself, why not enter tonight, sleep there? Tomorrow morning when I woke I'd be able to take my time looking around, hours of time if I wished, and then leave. True, I'd stand a chance in a thousand of being seen entering late at night; but if, after leaving, I walked briskly I'd probably be out of the immediate neighborhood by the time a neighbor could phone police and a cop car could get there.

And the best time tonight would be shortly after midnight. By then the neighbors across the street would probably be asleep—Santa Monica is an early-to-bed town—and people wouldn't be likely to be looking out of their windows at the dark house across the street. Later, two or three A.M., would be even safer from that point of view, but after the tavern closing hour, one o'clock, cruising car cops have a habit of asking questions of lone pedestrians, even asking them to show identification if they claim to live in the neighborhood. So, between twelve and one. Tonight.

But what if—

Oh, things could go wrong, somehow. But I couldn't see more than one chance out of a hundred of that happening—if I was careful—and if I wasn't willing to take odds like that, if I chickened out even on casing the house, then I might as well forget the whole thing right now.

Chapter Seven

I CAUGHT a Santa Monica bus at a little before eleven o'clock and rode it well past my destination, into the business section of Santa Monica. I wandered around to kill a little time, had a drink in a tavern and then, remembering it might be a long time before I had a chance to eat again, two hamburgers in a diner.

Then I started strolling leisurely home—to Seaton's home. A few blocks away I put on the hat—but not the sunglasses, which would have been too conspicuous after dark—and gradually changed my posture and walk again. Only a very few houses still had lights on and I hadn't, for the last five or six blocks of my walk, passed a single other pedestrian. Since I'd turned off onto Prince Drive, not even a car had driven past.

One block away I put on a pair of gloves. The gloves were white ones so I walked the last block with my hands in my pockets so they wouldn't show. Not that anybody seemed to be watching me.

Both houses across the street from the Seatons' were fully dark. The crepe-soled shoes I wore made no noise that might cause someone to look from a window to see who was going by.

I walked casually and confidently to the door and let myself in with Doris's key, closed the door behind me.

So far, so good. If someone had seen me enter, and knowing that the Seatons were out of town, was phoning cops then I was in for it. Otherwise I was safe at least until I would leave tomorrow. I'd know about tonight, probably within ten minutes, certainly within half an hour at the outside.

I let my eyes get used to the pitch darkness and then took the slight extra risk of lighting one match, holding it cupped while I looked around to see where the furniture was located and found a big and comfortable-looking sofa. I put out the match and put it in my pocket, then navigated perfectly to the sofa by dead reckoning. I sat down on it, took off my shoes and hat, and then lay down full length. Either the cops were coming or they weren't, and I might as well wait for them comfortably.

After a while I knew they weren't coming, and I went to sleep.

It was bright daylight when I woke up, and from somewhere outside, seemingly quite close, was a sound I couldn't identify. I went quickly to the front window—it seemed to come from that direction—and very cautiously moved two slats of the Venetian blind so I could see out.

The sound was coming from a gasoline-powered lawnmower being pushed by a middle-aged Japanese gardener. I swore mentally at Doris for not having told me about him and which and how many days a week he came, when she was talking about other servants. But then I realized his being there didn't matter. His work was strictly outdoors and he'd have no reason to come into the house, nor a key to let himself in. And he no doubt brought his own tools; most of them do.

I went to another window, from which I could see the driveway leading back toward the garage, and verified that. His truck, with other gardening equipment and tools besides the mower he was using, was parked there, halfway back.

Of course I couldn't leave while he was there, out front, but that was no problem; I wasn't going to leave for a while anyway and sooner or later he'd be working around at the back of the house, out of sight of the front door and the street. Meanwhile, maybe his presence was all to the good. I didn't intend to make any noise anyway, but if I did that power mower would be powerful competition for it. Certainly it would take a powerful noise for him to hear while he was running it.

I went back to the sofa and put my shoes on. And then sat there thinking myself into full awakeness because there wasn't any hurry; I could take my time and if I didn't leave till noon, it wouldn't matter.

I wanted a cup of coffee and a cigarette, and considered them. I vetoed the coffee.

A cigarette, yes. I could put the paper match, the ashes and the butt in my pocket and certainly there'd be no smell of smoke left a few days from now. I started to light one and then had an even better idea. I was going to have to flush the toilet at least once, and fairly soon; I might as well do my smoking in a bathroom and I wouldn't have to use a pocket.

I found a bathroom downstairs off a slightly smaller room that adjoined the big living room. I suppose the room would have been called the library, although it held a stereo record player and more records than it did books.

I sat on the edge of the tub and smoked a cigarette. Then, since I wasn't going to stop to do this again and it might be hours before it would be safe for me to leave, another. Just as I finished the second cigarette the power mower quit—but I knew it would have to start again; he couldn't possibly have finished even the front yard, so I waited. And when it roared again a few minutes later I flushed ashes and butts down the vortex and stood up and stretched.

I started at the top and in the room farthest down the upstairs hallway. A bedroom and, I decided after a few minutes, the housekeeper's bedroom. Yes, this would have been where the light had been last night when I'd first driven by the house. The clothes in the closet—yes, definitely housekeeper. I didn't waste much time there, once I was sure of that.

The door opposite that of the housekeeper's room was used as a storage and linen room. Nothing much interested me except a shotgun and a rifle leaning companionably together in one corner. Apparently Seaton hunted, which meant he wasn't gun-shy. Maybe he kept a pistol near his bed. Well, finding that out had been on my agenda in any case.

The next two rooms, one on each side of the hallway, were bedrooms, but obviously guest rooms, from the lack of personal effects and clothes in the closets.

Then, on one side of the hallway, a pair of bathrooms. Back to back, as it were, as pairs of bathrooms usually are, so that the pipes can run up one wall instead of two.

And, outside of closets, that left two big bedrooms upstairs, one across from the baths and one opposite the head of the staircase. No trouble telling which was which; enough things had been left on top of the dresser in each—and especially the dressing table in Doris's—to show who slept where. There was a connecting door between them but I noticed there was a key in the lock, on Doris's side.

I didn't spend any time looking at her bedroom; I concentrated on Seaton's. This was going to be the scene of the crime, and I wanted to know my way around in it blindfolded—or in the dark. Exact placement of every piece of furniture. Exact number of steps from the door to the bed. Things like that. Everything like that.

And the gun, as I'd expected after finding the rifle and the shotgun in the storage room. It was a .32 revolver with a three-inch barrel, break action. A sweet and deadly little thing, shining in its coat of nickel plate. A weapon for short-range work—but how can you shoot at long range in a bedroom?

It was lying in plain sight in a corner of the top drawer of the dresser. The corner nearest the bed, which was about three paces away. Five to ten seconds away, counting the time it would take to get out of bed, open the drawer, find and pick up the gun. I'd just have to get to him before he could get to it, that's all. No sweat at all if he didn't waken until I was opening the door of his room. Still better, of course, if he didn't waken even then.

And what would waken him? Knowing the house, having a key so I could let myself in silently, having a dimmed flashlight so I wouldn't stumble or knock over a lamp that might waken him before I opened the door of his room. And from there. . . .

There was no particular reason for my having to check all the downstairs rooms, but I had time to kill so I did. The Japanese gardener was through mowing grass in the front yard, but he was still there, using electric hedge clippers.

There weren't as many rooms downstairs as up, but they were bigger. The living room took up a good third of the downstairs area. And the kitchen and the library off which I'd found a bathroom earlier, were sizeable. I found only one other downstairs room, a small one off the library. There was a desk in it and a file cabinet; obviously Seaton worked at home at least once in a while.

The kitchen was the only room I didn't enter, because the shades in it hadn't been pulled and I didn't want to risk being seen from a house across the alley. But I stood in the doorway out of range of the windows to look around. And I saw something that convinced me I hadn't questioned Doris nearly enough and was going to have a really exhaustive talk with her. There was a sliding bolt on the back door and it was locked. If I'd tried to enter that way I'd simply have taken an extra and useless risk of being seen and would have had to come around to the front anyway. Giving me a back door key had been meaningless.

The thought sent me back to the front door to make sure there was no way it could be bolted from the inside—something the housekeeper couldn't have done when she left—so it couldn't be opened from the outside. But there wasn't.

I went once more around the house, upstairs and down, making sure that I'd missed nothing that might be relevant, that I'd moved nothing, left no possible trace of my presence. I checked my pockets to be sure I had everything I'd come with. And then there was nothing for me to do but sit down and wait till the gardener went around and started working at the back.

After a while I heard the mower start again and it seemed a long distance away. I went to the kitchen and crouched down low as I went to one of the unshaded windows and raised my head cautiously. Yes, he was now mowing in the back yard, starting at the far end of it, well over a hundred feet away.

I went to the front door, pushed aside the shade and looked out. Nothing was doing, that I could see, at either of the houses across the street.

I put on my hat, my glasses. I opened the door an inch and checked that the snap lock would work when I closed it again from the outside. Casually, I stepped out, pulled the door shut behind me and made sure that it was locked. Then, still facing away from the street, I stripped off my gloves and turned. Walked, casually, to the sidewalk—casually, but with the special walk that made my height, my age and my general posture seem so different.

No one saw me, as far as I could see. I made the corner and turned it. I wanted to run, but instead let my gait change gradually back to normal. I took off my glasses and put them in my pocket. Then the soft hat that rolled up so easily.

Then another corner, and I felt safe. I walked briskly back to Santa Monica Boulevard and to the nearest bus stop corner.

On the bus I found a seat and took a deep but unobtrusive breath. I had made it. A Santa Monica police car drove past the bus and I watched it condescendingly. It wasn't after me.

I got off at Highland and walked north to Sunset, to my favorite big-breakfast eaterie. It was only eleven o'clock, but I was famished. I had a double order of ham and eggs, extra toast, two cups of coffee. Murder, even in anticipation, is a hungry business.

I checked for mail on my way back into the Zoo. There wasn't any for me; I hadn't expected any. I went to my room. It was warm, so I stripped down to shorts to save what was left, after sleeping in them, of the press in my clothes. Then I propped up the pillow on my bed and lay down. Not to sleep, but to think.

Say that the housekeeper and Seaton were both at least average sleepers, if not especially sound ones. Say that I could count, reasonably at least, on both of them being asleep by midnight.

Say that Doris could rig herself a solid alibi some night next week—preferably for all night, but at least for the first half of it. Visiting friends or relatives, out of town if possible. She must have some friends or relatives whom Seaton knew and trusted well enough that he wouldn't be suspicious if she found some reason to be with them overnight, provided he knew where she was and could reach her there.

Yes, it would almost have to be overnight; if she simply stayed out late, he might decide to wait up for her and that would spoil everything. If I saw a light still on, I wouldn't dare go in and would have to wait for another opportunity.

So, sometime during the evening I'd short the ignition of a car and steal it. Move it to a safe place where it would be waiting for me when I was ready for it. At half past twelve I'd drive past the Seaton house, make sure the lights were all out. If so, I'd drive around the corner and park, walk back, and let myself in the front door. Tiptoe, in my crepe-soled shoes, up the stairs, using a muffled flashlight in such a way that it wouldn't be visible from outside.

Reach the outside of Seaton's door. Turn the knob as quietly as I could, and open it.

From there on in, I'd have to play it by ear.

My dim flashlight probably wouldn't waken him if he was sound asleep, and if he was I could take time to close the door behind me. Cross the room and kill him with one hard blow to the head, while he still slept. With a blackjack, if I could figure a way to get one without any possibility of its purchase, or theft, being traced. Otherwise a piece of pipe, wrapped in newspaper. Yes, definitely wrapped in newspaper because I wouldn't want the blow to draw blood and smear the pillow. Blood on the pillow would indicate to the police that he'd been killed in bed and I didn't want them to figure it that way, because then premeditated murder would be indicated.

He was going to be found on the floor, several paces from the bed, in front of the drawer that held the .32 pistol, and the drawer would be open. Maybe even the gun in, or near, his hand; I could decide that later. In either case the indications would be that he had heard a burglar, had been out of bed going for his gun or getting it when the burglar had entered his room. But struck down before he could get the gun or before he could turn and use it.

Oh, it would be first-degree murder even that way, but it would look unpremeditated, murder committed during a burglary because the householder awoke and resisted, or tried to.

Or—if Seaton woke easily, if he was even already awake when I opened his door, maybe actually tried to get out of bed and to the gun, what then? A little more dangerous but surely—three or four steps, I'd be on my feet and ready and he wouldn't, surely I could get to him before he could get to the gun, and drop him, maybe at the same spot to which I'd otherwise be moving him.

But what if he meanwhile let out a squawk or yell? Well, I was pretty sure that the houses there were spaced widely enough apart that it wouldn't be heard outside the house. And, in any case, one discounts a single sound in the night. A single explosion is, after a few seconds of silence, dismissed as a backfire; a single yell, distant or faint, is dismissed as probably the yowl of a tomcat, the howl of a dog, even a louder than usual noise on a neighbor's television set. People don't call police because of a single distant sound. Someone screaming consistently is something else again, but Seaton wouldn't have time for more than one squawk.

Still, there was the housekeeper. If it was a fairly loud squawk and if she was a normal, average sleeper she'd probably hear it. But would she do anything about it? Not without checking, I felt sure. She'd tap on the door of Seaton's room maybe and ask if he was all right. And I could imitate Seaton's voice—a gravelly one but high in pitch, well enough to call out sleepily that I was all right, I'd just had a nightmare.

But that would spoil the picture of the simple burglary with unpremeditated killing. Maybe it would be better to jerk open the door if she knocked on it and swing again. That would still be consistent with the picture I'd try to leave. Burglar forced to kill householder, housekeeper investigates and gets herself killed too.

But that part I might have to play by ear and anyway it would probably never arise; I felt sure I could kill Seaton quickly enough to make it silent. A man's first reaction on being awakened is seldom to scream instantly, no matter what awakens him, and I'd give him no time for a second reaction. I'd have the advantage of surprise, and all the cards.

Then, in either case, downstairs quickly. I wouldn't steal anything and the police would see nothing odd in that; a burglar panicked by having to commit murder would think only of escape, not of carrying through his original purpose. I'd open a window somewhere—and the police would believe the housekeeper had forgotten to lock it and that that had been the burglar's means of entry. Then leave by the window I'd opened and—no, the front door would be safer and the real burglar I'd be impersonating would be fully as likely to use it, to leave the scene of the crime. Back to the car and back to wherever I was going to leave it back in Hollywood. Probably near wherever I stole it, so the presumption would be that it had been stolen just for a joy ride by some teen-ager. Probably at least half a dozen cars are stolen in Los Angeles every night and most of them found the next day. They'd have no way of tying in that particular car to a burglary and murder in Santa Monica.

Timing? With little traffic at that time of night I'd be able to drive it in twenty minutes either way, without speeding. No reason why I should be inside the house more than ten or fifteen minutes. An hour over all. Say the hour from twelve to one, if that fitted with whatever Doris would tell me about

Seaton's sleeping habits. It probably would. The hour from one to two, or even later, if she told me he sometimes stayed up late.

Suddenly I didn't want to think about it any more, for a while. I was spared the need to by a knock at the door.

It turned out to be Smoky Conover. "Hey, man, sad tidings. Tex got busted Monday night."

"The Caddy?"

"The Caddy. The square that owned it got back sooner than he expected, and the fuzz was waiting for Tex on the lot. I just got the word last night. I came to your pad here then but you'd split."

"Tough titty," I said. "Will they hit him hard?"

"Dunno yet. Maybe a year or so, with his record, if the square presses charges. But maybe he can be offsteered. After all, fact that Tex brought it back to the lot was proof he didn't really steal the wheels, just borrowed them. Man, I know Essie peeled you, but maybe you raised some bread since. Can you kick in five? Or get it up by tomorrow? For a mouthpiece to front for him."

"Man," I said, "You can't get a shyster for—"

"Negative. It's fifty. But I went to see Tex in jail this morning and he named a guy I should go see. He gave me all he had —ten bucks—and told me to hock his guitar and case for whatever I could get for it. I got twenty. So I went to see the shyster with thirty and found I was twenty short. I raised five myself, got five from Johnny Kaprelian and five from Tex's buddy on the parking lot. A fin from you and we got it made; the mouthpiece will swing."

I went for the wallet in my pants and gave him one of the four fives I still had left out of my twenty-five advance from Lennie.

I said, "Have a drink. A few minutes isn't going to matter."

He looked at the wine bottle on the dresser. "Don't feel like wine," he said. "But if you want to come with me to see the lawyer I'll let you buy me a drink on the way."

I didn't want to tangle into it that far. So I said, "Can't make the scene; I'm waiting for a cat to drop in here. But there's a little left in a whisky bottle in the closet there. See if it's enough for two shots."

He did and it was. We made two with tap water and he sat down.

Smoky said, "They'll sweat Tex but they won't get out of him about borrowing other cars or anything else. He's been rubber-hosed before, and for worse things."

I asked, "Do they really do that? Here, I mean?"

"Where you been, man? Hollywood fuzz is tough. But if you ever do swipe a car or something, do it here instead of Santa Monica. Those boys really take you apart, and I know. Not first-hand, but like second-hand, from several cats that swung out there."

A sudden chill went down my back. I wasn't planning to steal a car in Santa Monica, only to commit a murder there. And I too had heard how tough Santa Monica cops were, but when I'd thought of being questioned about the murder—as I almost certainly would be; the detective, Weston, would certainly tell the fuzz about the job he'd done for Seaton when he read that Seaton was murdered—it had never occurred to me that maybe I'd be *really* sweated, third-degreed, and that if they didn't swallow my story whole I was a nobody on whom they wouldn't have to pull a single punch. What if they simply picked me for a patsy, even without evidence, and decided to beat a confession out of me?

Chapter Eight

It was warm and I'd been sweating a little, but suddenly it seemed to be cold in the room. But it wasn't in the room; it was in me, in my mind, realizing what I might be facing if I went through with my original plans. But it was something I'd have to think out after Smoky left.

He was saying, "Like this law-cat's a smooth talker. I don't know how tough the square is, the one who owns the Cad, but if he's human at all I'll give the law-cat an even chance of talking him into dropping charges. If not, it's tough. All he can do is plead Tex guilty and try to get the judge to go as light on him as possible. Well—" he drained the last of his drink and stood up, "guess I'll run along."

He held out his hand, flat, palm up, for the beatnik equivalent of a handshake and I put my palm against it for a moment. He said, "Later," and left.

And it kept getting later and I kept getting more and more scared. Did I once say I'm arrogant? Well, sometimes I am, but I can get scared too, and I got scared. Not by Tex having been picked up for the hot car rap; he'd simply been stupid stealing a car off the parking lot he worked at and then taking it back there so he could get caught red-handed. I was smarter than that, at least.

But the third-degree bit, with the Santa Monica angle on top of it. Somehow I'd never figured on that, never visualized it—at least unless I made some silly mistake that gave me away and in that case I'd be a dead duck anyway.

Oh, I'd counted on being questioned. No later than the next day. Even if Weston should by any chance miss reading the papers, the fuzz would get to me just the same. Somewhere in Seaton's office at home or his office at work would be reports from the private agency. If not, then there'd be a check made out to Weston and that would send the cops to him if he hadn't already come to them.

And my story, I'd figured, would be simple and undisprovable. No alibi—if you try to rig an alibi you're dead—but I'd simply have been on the town. From around, say, nine o'clock to maybe around three or four A.M. Some beat joints are open that late and sometimes even later. During the evening I'd have been in three or four taverns maybe, three or four beat joints. Maybe if I was lucky I'd run into news of a party at somebody's pad that would last all night and not get home till after daylight—and preferably hung over, or giving a good imitation of being hung over. At first, and this would make sense, I wouldn't even remember *all* the places I'd been during the evening and the night. Later I could think of the others one at a time, but I never would be sure of the exact sequence and I'd be still more vague about what time I left one place and went to another. So, of course, would be the various people they'd be able to find—with my help—who'd remember having seen me in one place or another. Those times would all be guesses and they never would be able to prove that I'd taken off an hour to kill. Nor even if a doctor's examination of Seaton and an autopsy revealed the exact and correct time he was killed.

That's what I figured, that since I might (they'd think) have a motive they'd suspect me somewhat but never be able to prove anything. Even if, not too long after the killing, Doris and I started to see each other again and maybe even eventually got married, it wouldn't prove anything. That's something that could happen—and probably would happen—even if Seaton were genuinely killed by a real burglar in the course of a real burglary. Why the hell not? Sure, I'd admit and Doris would admit, that we'd had an affair and had got caught out in it by Seaton. And that she'd gone back to him and the affair was over, with him condoning it by taking her on a second honeymoon trip to Mexico. We'd broken off the affair but if Seaton died and left her free, why shouldn't we start seeing each other again, and openly this time? There's no law against a widow going out with a former lover, no matter how extramarital their relationship had been in the first place. Or even for her to marry him, after a couple of months. And by that time, I'd be safe. If I did leave any loose end—and I wouldn't—that could prove I'd committed the murder they'd get me on it right away, or not at all.

Like easy, I'd thought. All I had to do was keep from making a mistake, and I'd be safe.

But would I be safe? If, even without evidence against me, the cops sold themselves on the idea that I was guilty, what would stop them from trying to beat a confession out of me?

The naked straight chair, the bright light torturing my eyes, the relays of tough, brutal cops hammering the same questions over and over to break my will. The flat-handed slaps in the face, the rubber hoses that could deal such agonizing pain and leave no mark.

"*Why did you kill Seaton?*"

"*Did you plan it with his wife?*"

"*Did you kill Seaton?*"

"DID YOU KILL SEATON?"

In relays, for hours. For many hours. The dry throat, the craving for a drink of water after twelve or eighteen hours of thirst. "Sure, sure, you can have a drink—when you've told the truth." "WHAT DID YOU DO WITH THE LEAD PIPE YOU USED?" "WHERE DID YOU THROW AWAY THE GLOVES?" "HOW LONG HAD YOU AND THE DAME PLANNED TO MURDER HIM?"

"All right, boys, get the son of a bitch out of that chair and work him over, he wants some more. Bend him over that table and use the hose on his kidneys. Make the bastard want us to *let* him talk!"

And then, when I was a palpitating pulp, a blob of ache and misery and thirst and need for sleep, the switcheroo. The soft cop talking like a kind uncle, pleading with me to tell the truth so he could stop the others from torturing me. Giving me a cigarette, telling me if I told the truth I'd get only jail, not the gas chamber and that life was worth living, even at San Quentin, that I wouldn't even get Alcatraz if I quit being recalcitrant and told the truth. . . . And if I held out, he'd be called away and the tough boys would be with me again, the pain in my eyes from the bright light, the blows to keep me awake. . . . "How long you and the dame been planning it?" "Where did you throw away the weapon?" "WHEN DID YOU TELL HER TO GET OUT OF TOWN TO GIVE HERSELF AN ALIBI?" "HOW MUCH WAS SHE GOING TO PAY?" "OR DID SHE PROMISE TO MARRY YOU INSTEAD?" "WHEN DID YOU SCREW HER LAST?" "WHERE DID YOU THROW AWAY THE GLOVES?"

Could I take it without breaking?

I've always hated and feared pain. Dentists are nightmares. I've always suffered more in having to decide to go to one than I actually suffered in the dentist's chair once I was finally there.

As a kid, I hated fights, managed to avoid them whenever I could and still not look too chicken. If I couldn't avoid one and found I was getting beaten I'd manage to let myself get knocked cold, or pretend to be, rather than take more punishment than I had to. I'd dreaded lickings from my father. Not that I got many of them—I'd lie or confess, whichever would be least likely to get me licked. Once when I was thirteen, when I'd stolen some money from my mother and had realized I'd inevitably be found out and get my worst licking to date, I'd run away from home to avoid it. I was away a week before the fuzz found me in El Paso and sent me home. To no licking, incidentally; I'd won out there. Running away had been too serious a matter for corporal punishment and it was assumed that I'd taken the money for the purpose of running away, so it became a lesser part of the greater sin of running away. I'd spent a miserable few months with loss of a lot of privileges and listened to a lot of lecturing from my parents, the minister, two teachers. . . . But no licking, and I'd considered myself ahead. The worst part of the punishment was that I was denied a chance to take a part in the school play that year, a part I'd looked forward to getting. Even then, at thirteen, I was stage-struck and knew that I was going to be an actor. An actor, or nothing. I'd give my life, if necessary, to become one. Funny, I wasn't afraid of dying, even then; I was afraid only of pain.

Even tough guys, hardened criminals, break under the third degree. What chance would I have of holding out?

And why hadn't I thought of that? Possibly because my mind had simply rejected the very thought of it until Smoky's conversation had forced it on my consciousness.

It simply canceled the whole damn plan. I . . .

There was another visitor at my door.

It was Charlie Hayes. He said, "Hi. You feel as lousy as I do?"

"Worse," I told him. "Something special with you? A wheel come off the commercial bit?"

He shook his head. "No, I got it. But one-shot and a lousy twenty-five bucks. God damn it, Willy, I'm not getting anywhere. I'm about ready to give up."

"And do what?" I pulled my feet up so he could sit down on the end of the bed, and he did.

"I don't know. Maybe go to New York and try there for a while. Some television shows originate there. And there's the stage, what's left of it."

"Legit," I said, "is as rough as anything out here. And most of the TV shows that originate there are panel shows, or variety things like Sullivan or— Hell, there aren't many dramatic shows you'd have a chance on."

"At least there wouldn't be Manny Radic."

I started to ask him who Radic was, and then remembered. The producer who hated Charlie for personal reasons and had caused and was still causing him so much trouble.

"Is he really that important, Charlie? Yes, this one series role on the new Western; he's producer on that, so I'll grant he's keeping you out of that, if the casting director likes you for the part. But look at all the shows Radic *doesn't* produce."

"He's got influence, Willy, plenty of it. I know for a sure thing I've lost other roles I'd have had a chance for because he found out I was being considered for them and put me down with whoever he knew on the show. And he'll go out of his way to do it. I feel lousy, Willy. Got a drink? I could use one. In fact, I feel like hanging one on. How about you?"

"Wouldn't mind," I said. "But there's nothing here but a little wine, not much of that. And I'm low on bread. About ten bucks to last me till—God knows when."

"I'll go pick up a fifth and—I got an idea. If we stay here, someone'll be sure to join us and a fifth won't go far. I know a better place. Know Maxine Wells?"

"Met her once at your place, that's all. Dancer, isn't she?"

"Chorus gal for money. Writer for love. She's out of town for a week and lent me a key to her pad, account she's got a marvelous record collection and said I could go up to hear some of them while she's away. When I've been up there with her we never get around to listening much."

"Sounds good. Classical or jazz?"

"Some of both but what I had in mind are plays and poems. She's got *Don Juan in Hell*, *John Brown's Body*, *The Lady's Not for Burning*, readings by Olivier, Dylan Thomas, Rathbone—you name it, she's got it."

"Crazy," I said, and meant it. Just the stuff an actor needs to listen to and that he enjoys listening to even if some of it makes him green with envy. And stuff he can't listen to often unless he's solvent enough to have his own phono and collection.

Her pad, he told me, was on Cosmo, only a few doors from the Alley, a flat over a beauty shop. We could walk there. He bought a fifth at the first liquor store on our way and a block farther on when we were about to pass a delicatessen I suggested that I pop for some grub so we wouldn't have to interrupt our listening to go out and eat when we got hungry.

The pad was about what I'd have expected, if I'd bothered to expect anything, from what Charlie told me about Maxine Wells. Neat but not gaudy, everything in good taste and neither square nor far out.

I put my purchases in the refrigerator in the kitchenette. I told Charlie that he was elected to make the first round of drinks because I wanted to look over the record titles and he'd already seen them.

I picked half a dozen records out of a magnificent selection and when he came in with the drinks we listened to them, talking only between records and occasionally replenishing our drinks.

Then we ate the grub we'd brought and talked shop for a while, and finally Charlie, after a silence between us, led off with a new topic. "Willy, why don't we get solvent enough to get ourselves a decent pad like this and share it, get a phonograph—and a tape recorder so we can do things ourselves—and a TV set so we can keep up with things—"

"And keep it stocked with liquor," I added. "And women—which would mean a place a bit bigger than this so we could have separate bedrooms. And— Crazy, man. But how do we get solvent enough? Go in for robbing filling stations?"

"Don't think I wouldn't. Willy, I'd commit murder, for something like that."

I looked at him to see if he was serious, and I couldn't tell.

Chapter Nine

"WOULD YOU? Commit murder, I mean? I mean, seriously."

Charlie lighted a cigarette, inhaled deeply, and blew the smoke out his nose before he answered. "Of course I would. For enough money to let me live the way I'd like to live—the way we were just talking about. And if I figured that the risk of getting caught was slight."

"How slight is slight?" I asked him.

"A hundred to one against getting busted. Maybe higher if it was for *enough* money. That's what's wrong with the filling station bit. Or any kind of stickup. Hell, man, we could hold up a filling station tonight and, a hundred to one, get away with it. But we wouldn't get more than enough for like a weekend binge. So if we wanted to get solvent we'd have to keep on doing it and the odds would keep going up on us. Like mathematically, you take a hundred-to-one chance fifty times and the odds are even you'll get caught. Don't think I haven't thought about it. Maybe everyone does, when the going's tough. Like it is now for us. But for real money, hell yes, I'd commit murder."

"Or for a real break?" I asked him. "Like a fat role on a TV series you think you'd get if a certain producer—?"

"Like a fat role I *know* I'd get." He laughed harshly. "You think I haven't thought about putting Manny Radic out of his misery? That I wouldn't, if I could figure good odds on getting away with it?" He stubbed out the cigarette he'd taken only a few puffs on. "Willy, there's nothing easier to get away with than murder—if you don't have a personal motive for killing your victim, if you're not going to be suspected or investigated or grilled in connection with the crime. Or if you've got an alibi, a *solid* alibi, like being in New York while the murder happens in Los Angeles. So the fuzz won't even think of you in connection with it. Dig me?"

"I dig you. But would you be specially suspect in case Manny Radic got knocked off?"

"Hell, yes. It wouldn't take the fuzz much asking around to come up with my name. Probably other names too, but I'd definitely be on the list. And the others might all have alibis and leave me sticking out like a sore thumb, if you'll forgive the cliché. And trying to rig a fake alibi would be even more dangerous than having none at all. Gangsters can get away with it, but not ordinary schmoes like us. Who do you know that'd risk his own neck to swear to a fake alibi for you?"

I nodded slowly, wondering.

Charlie was wound up now. "Nothing easier to get away with than killing a stranger. Get him alone, kill him, walk away. Unless you're stupid, try it at the wrong time and get caught, what risk are you taking?"

"How about the passion for confession? The Raskolnikov bit, like in *Crime and Punishment*?"

"Nuts. That's strictly for psychos, Willy. Mugs with a death wish; it isn't confession they want, it's punishment. Strictly from masochism."

That was my own opinion, but I was glad to learn that Charlie felt the same way.

"Any more liquor?" I asked.

"Enough for a short one apiece. Your turn to make them."

I took our glasses into the kitchenette, divided the last of the fifth between them and put a cube and a little water in each. I came back and handed Charlie his.

"I got a story," I told him. "A thought I had for a movie plot—or maybe a TV program. Want to hear it?"

He grimaced. "Probably stinks, but I'll listen."

"It's a crime story, suspense. A man wants to commit a murder but he doesn't dare because the odds are against him—the potential victim is an enemy of his or at least someone he has an obvious motive for killing. He knows he'll be investigated and third-degreed if the man is murdered and he figures the fuzz would beat it out of him even if they can't dig any evidence against him.

"While he's sweating he happens to learn that a friend—a guy he trusts as much as he trusts anybody—would also like to kill someone and has the same reason for figuring that he can't get away with it. So they like pool resources. Each one happens to be out of town or something—a hundred per cent alibi, whatever it is—when his enemy gets knocked off. So neither one is ever questioned seriously, let alone suspected. And there's nothing at all to tie the two crimes together, even remotely. . . . Do you think there's a story in it?"

He was leaning back with his eyes closed.

"Got a good ending for it?" he asked casually.

"Yeah," I said. "They got away with it, and lived happily ever after."

He shook his head slowly. "It'll never sell."

"All right," I said, "forget it."

"Are you serious, or just yakking to hear yourself?"

I said, "I'm serious enough to want to talk about it seriously."

"All right, we'll talk seriously. Just who would you be happier without?"

I hesitated, and then realized that I'd already given up the idea, as far as doing it myself was concerned, so I had nothing to lose. I told him the name and he didn't recognize it until I mentioned the seat cover bit; then he remembered seeing it on television and other ads.

"Good," he said. "I never met him. You ever meet Radic?"

I shook my head.

"Fine. We start even. Except for one thing. You know my motive and I don't know yours. It might make a difference on the method I'd use, so better give it to me in a nutshell."

He was right, of course, if only because he would have to understand about Doris having to be warned so she could arrange herself an alibi for the time of the murder.

He didn't like it, the fact that in Seaton's case, a third person, someone besides us, would know the score. But I pointed out that Doris wouldn't know the real score at all, that if for any reason she did turn state's evidence, she could only finger me, not him. And that if my alibi was really solid and provable they wouldn't believe her even if she talked. Besides, why should she spill when she'd be making herself an accessory to the murder?

We both thought a few minutes without talking. Charlie stood up and started to pace the length of the room like a caged animal, his head down and his hands in his pockets. Seven paces each way. I felt like doing it myself, but there wasn't room for two of us to stake out convenient routes so

I stayed in my chair and sat staring up at the ceiling. A thousand things were running through my mind all at once, the main and recurring one being—did I really have the guts to go through with this and kill a man I'd never seen?

Charlie came and stood in front of me.

"I think it'll work," he said. "We'll have a lot of talking to do, swapping plans and details. But that can wait. Only one thing about it really scares me."

"What's that?"

"How do we know one of us won't funk out and lose his nerve? Have you ever killed anyone?"

I shook my head.

"Neither have I. And some people just can't kill—not cold-bloodedly anyway. It's got nothing to do with mysticism or morals or anything like that. Some people just *can't*, no matter how good their intentions are. How do you know you can? How do I know I can?"

I said, "I guess you don't. I guess I don't. And it would be particularly rough on the first guy if he went through with his killing and the second one funked. How would we decide which of us goes first anyway?"

Charlie shrugged. "No problem there. We flip a coin. But what about what I said was the one thing that scares me? Got any ideas?"

I shook my head again. "Charlie, it's just something we'd have to gamble on—if we decide to go through with it at all."

"Not me. I want to know. Or else we forget the whole idea."

"How can we know?"

"By trying it. Tonight."

"You're crazy," I said. "You mean kill someone just for the hell of it? Take the risk of killing just to find out if you can do it?"

"No risk. Or one chance in a thousand. We do the skid row bit, with a difference. We find the saddest looking wino on Fifth Street, take him down an alley to give him a drink and then do him the biggest favor we can possibly do him—with a blackjack. I've got one in my room. A gun, too, but for tonight a blackjack is the deal."

"It's still nuts," I said, "to take even a chance out of a thousand when there's nothing to gain. Listen, we can work it out this way. If the first guy chickens out, nothing's lost. If the second one does—like if I should if you go first, then I split with you whatever I gain by your act. In cash, I mean—not in Doris's fair white et cetera. Or if you—hell, you see what I mean. What's to lose?"

"Nothing, on an advance chicken-out bit. But what if one of us—first or second, it wouldn't matter—makes the scene and then finds he can't follow through, or panics; he'll get busted sure as hell."

"But—"

"Another thing. If either one of us gets busted on this deal, we might as well figure we both do. If you get caught red-handed trying to kill Radic and they try to beat a motive, the whole story, out of you, I'm assuming you'll be talked into coming clean with them. Maybe you would, maybe you wouldn't. Maybe I would, maybe I wouldn't. But I wouldn't trust either of us not to."

"Guess you got a point there, Charlie. But—"

"So I'm not going to trust either of us not to crack up on a real murder, without a dry run first. Just to test our own reactions under pressure, to make sure we won't crack up or chicken out. If we haven't got the nerve to kill someone together—and the nerves to get away with it—what chance have we got of trusting ourselves or each other on solitary kills?"

I said, "It makes sense, Charlie, but—why tonight? Shouldn't we plan it out?"

He shook his head. "Our real murders, yes. But not this one. All we have to do is find the right bum, get him alone, and slug him. We not only can play it by ear, we'll have to. And why tonight? Because the sooner the better. And we're sober, so let's get the show on the road."

"Don't push, Charlie. Give me a few minutes to think."

"All right. Or would you rather be a beat?"

I think I'd have come to agree with Charlie sooner or later, but that argument—or would I rather be a beat?—triggered its own answer. Charlie and I had discussed beatniks plenty, and both felt the same about them. Some of our friends were beat and we liked them despite it, but far from because of it. We, Charlie and I, used hip language for kicks, but we both completely rejected the philosophy. In a sense, working as hard as we did, being willing to do anything or anybody for success in our chosen profession, we were almost the opposite of beat.

Or would I rather be a beat? Hell, no.

I was quiet for a minute. Then, "Charlie," I said, "before we kill somebody just for the hell of it, let's get some things straight. No point in taking a first step unless we're both damn sure we're going to follow through. Right?"

"Right. So—"

"So let me do the talking a minute, or ask the questions. First, you're not sure you'll get that Western series job, even if Radic's six feet under. You know how many slips there are in this God-damn business. What if you go through with this and it doesn't buy you anything?"

"Don't worry about me, Willy. I'll level with you: I hate that bastard Radic so much I'll go in this for free. Even if I knew I'd never get another TV or movie job, I'd go in for this. Does that answer your question?"

"I guess so," I said. "Now ask me. Or rather, don't; I'll tell you. I don't hate Seaton; I haven't that incentive. And I *can* go through with this and have Doris let me down, and I can gain only through her.

"But I don't think she will. I won't use any square word like love, but she's hooked on me worse than I am on her, and that's plenty. And I can keep it that way long enough to get hitched and after that there's community property even if a wheel comes off. I'm tired of being poor and not getting anywhere because I can't put up a front and get to know the right people. I don't want to be rich, but I want to be an *actor*. I'll gamble. I'll go along if you will. Shall we go kill ourselves a wino?"

"Good boy," he said. "You leave right away. We shouldn't leave here together—should from here on in be *seen* together as little as possible. I'll straighten up this pad and wash the dishes and such. You know where I got the wheels parked. Meet you there in like half an hour."

"Right," I said. And left.

I walked across the night and to my room at the Zoo, changed to old clothes and put on make-up, doing a damned careful job of it tonight, because not getting spotted tonight would be more than playing a game for fun. I left the back way, seeing no one, went through the alley and found Charlie's car and waited in it. He came five minutes later.

We talked on the way down, making flexible plans. We'd not be together, we decided, but we'd stay in sight of each other and if either of us found a suitable derelict in any of the joints we'd explore and con him into going somewhere to split a bottle, the other would follow. Or join, according to circumstances. A whistle would be a signal of danger. Things like that.

We parked the car and stayed together until we got to the corner of Fifth. I stood there a few seconds and let Charlie get ahead and then followed him. He passed up two taverns but turned into the first liquor store. I looked in the window until he came out and then went in and bought a flat pint of sherry to put in my hip pocket.

When I came out I strolled the same direction we'd been walking, east, and soon caught sight of Charlie standing leaning against the window of a wino joint that we'd never happened to hit in our several previous slumming expeditions. As soon as I saw him I slowed down; he turned and caught my eye and, knowing I'd seen him, went into the tavern. I didn't want to follow him in too closely so I stopped to stare a while into the window of a grocery store.

The pint bottle in my hip pocket must have showed, the way I was standing, for someone touched my shoulder and said, "Pal, can you spare a drink outa that there bottle?"

I turned around and looked at him, wondering if I should give him one and then take him into the tavern to give Charlie a gander at him. Bringing in my own prospect would be better, in a way, than picking someone up inside. But I decided against it. He was a bum and a wino all right, but a young one, and fairly husky, a hillbilly kid; a lot of them turn wino when they hit a city. He was red-eyed and had the shakes—a hopeless alcoholic who'd probably be better off dead—but why should we take the chance of picking someone who might fight back and give us trouble when there were so many complete wrecks to pick from, old geezers who couldn't blow the foam off a beer? I told him to get lost and he got lost. At least, I guess he did; I never saw him again and he never knew what he missed.

I went into the Blue Lantern Bar, which had no blue lantern anywhere that I could see, and stood just inside looking around. The joint wasn't crowded, but it wasn't empty, somewhere in between. There were six or seven men—Charlie among them—standing at the bar, which had no stools. There were five booths down the side opposite the bar, and three of them were occupied. One by two middle-aged men who were talking excitedly about something, another by an old man alone, the third by two disheveled bleary-eyed females who were pretty obviously ex-whores with nothing left to peddle.

The old man who was alone had his back to me and I decided to go down to the far end of the bar from which I could get a look at his face. I moved down and while I was waiting for the bartender to notice me, I turned sidewise and looked at the old man. He was a derelict, all right, pretty far gone. Age anything over sixty. He looked eighty, but winos age early. Thinning dirty gray hair, rheumy eyes in a wrinkled, shriveled face between jug ears. His gray stubble of beard was at least three days old. His lips were moving in a silent mumble as he stared down into an almost empty wine tumbler. One sip left, and he was saving it. If he was in good shape enough to walk and would still be in good enough shape after I fed him a drink or two here, we couldn't pick a better bet. This one was gone, real gone, and I don't mean that in beat slang. He was for the birds, or the angels.

The bartender came down the bar and I put down a quarter and asked for a musky. He rang up the whole quarter but it was a sizeable slug of wine.

I turned back sidewise, glass in hand, and took a sip of it. The old man looked up just then and I caught his eye and nodded, strolled across. "Hi, Pops," I said. "Remember me?"

"Sure-sure. Siddown. Sure, 'member you. Yer name's—"

"Benny, Pops."

"Sure-sure-sure, 'member you. D'I ever tell ya bout time I was ridin' th' Katy top a loaded reefer an'—" He looked thirstily at my almost full drink and down at his own. He reached for it and then pulled back his hand. He wasn't going to kill that last swallow until he knew I was good for a refill. "Son, thass last drink I had sence—Ya holdin' 'nough ta buy me one, huh?"

"'Kay, Pops," I said. I got a quarter out of my pocket and put it on the table in front of him. I could have gone to the bar and bought him one, but I wanted to make sure he was able to navigate. If he couldn't I'd wasted two bits. We weren't going to carry him out of here.

He gulped down the rest of his drink and pushed himself up out of the booth and lurched once—forgivable since he'd probably been sitting there for hours—but then caught his balance and flew right. He navigated perfectly the few steps to the bar and when he reached it he leaned his forearms against it but didn't put his weight on them or hang on. He was more nearly sober physically than I'd thought; the slur in his voice and the blur in his thinking processes were the cumulative result of years of hopeless alcoholism. He was probably at the stage where he thought better and was better off drunk than sober—and better off dead than alive. Or was I rationalizing? All right, so I was rationalizing.

So my move was to get out as quickly as I could, with my prospect, before Charlie might take off with someone else. We'd agreed that, if one of us left with another man, the other would follow him, so if Charlie left first I'd have to abandon Pops to his fate, whatever it would be.

Pops came back with his wine. He downed half of it at a gulp; no doubt he'd wanted to take that first gulp at the bar but he'd figured that drinking with me would increase his chances of being bought another.

He looked sadly at his half empty glass, wondering how to pace the rest of the drink to increase his chances. I put him out of that misery. "Drink up, Pops," I told him. "And we'll hang one on. I'm holding. Worked all day pearl diving."

I thought for a moment he was going to cry. Then I could see sudden fear hit him, the fear that maybe I was only kidding him. "You *mean* it, Son? You'd really share with an old coot like me?"

I decided I might as well give him a happy moment so I laid it on him. "Pops," I said solemnly. "I know you don't really remember me, you just pretended to. But I remember you

—and you did me a hell of a favor once. Sure, we're going to get drunk together, and on me."

He leaned forward to peer at me closely from his rheumy eyes, trying to place me, to remember favors he'd done people. "Son," he said, "you ain't the kid ten-fifteen years ago I talked a shack outa redlightin', are you? On th' B. and O. near Cincy?"

"Yeah, Pops, that was me. And you've changed some but I knew you the minute I walked in here. Now let's drink to it. Down the hatch."

We downed the hatch and when I lowered my head I saw that now he was actually crying, tears making streaks in the grime of his cheeks, glistening on the gray stubble. But they were tears of happiness. A miracle had happened. At least once in his life, ten or fifteen years before, he had performed a kind deed, had saved a road kid from being thrown from a moving train by a tough brakeman. And here, tonight, that kid had found and recognized him and was going to get him drunk and get drunk with him. At that moment he was probably thinking that this was the happiest night of his life.

The situation was so grotesque that for a moment I considered talking to Charlie and calling off the plot—or postponing it—and following through by taking Pops on a glorious bender instead of into a dark alley. But I controlled the impulse. Tonight was the night he *should* die, struck down in a moment of happiness, never to know what happened to him. He was due to die soon anyway and in misery instead of in glory. Besides, Charlie wouldn't like the idea and might think I'd chickened out and cancel the whole deal. No, I'd go through with it. Now was the time for all good men.

Chapter Ten

I SAID, "Don't bawl, Pops. Everything's going to be all right. From now on. But let's not waste money drinking by the glass. I got a bottle in my pocket and we can go somewhere and kill it. It's sherry. That okay?"

"Sure-sure. You got a room, kid?"

I shook my head. "Just blew in town this morning. But don't worry about that. We can find a good spot in an alley or a back hallway or somewhere."

"Sure-sure. But we don't got to. I know an empty building, couple blocks. Been sleepin' there most nights."

"But don't any other—" I'd started to say any other bums, but caught myself in time— "anybody else go there?"

"Nup-nup. Locked and boarded up, but I found a secret way in, from a areaway. *Keep* it secret, too. But not from you, kid. You can sleep there too, long as you wanta."

"Good," I said. "Let's go."

Pops walked out more steadily than I did. I let myself lurch once, into Charlie's back, so he wouldn't miss seeing me leave and fail to follow.

Outside, Pops headed east to Wall Street and south to Winsett. I'd looked back once to make sure Charlie was following us; he was and I gave him the signal to keep his distance.

I looked around and nobody was watching us but Charlie, who'd just turned the corner. I gave Charlie a stay-put signal, told Pops the coast was clear, and we turned into the dark areaway. About halfway back Pops groped against a wall and stopped, pulled away two loosely nailed wide boards at one end, and went through. "C'mon," he whispered; "floor level's about three feet down, so don't fall." I went through and down, into pitch darkness. He said, "Jist stay still. I'll pull the boards back and then get us a light. Jist stay where you are." I jist stayed where I was while he fumbled around and then walked away. A moment later he struck a match and lighted a candle, and I could see.

It was a big room, empty except for a few things of Pops's at the far end—a wooden crate on which stood the candle, a spread out blanket, and an unrolled bindle. I looked back over my shoulder while I went to join him; he'd hung another half of a blanket over the boarded window so no light would show through.

I took the pint bottle from my pocket and handed it over as I sat down beside him on the spread blanket. "You first," I said.

He drank and handed it back. "Nice place," I told him. "Listen, I got a buddy I travel with, real nice guy named Larry. I know where he is, right near here. Could he join the party and sleep here tonight too? We'll both be blowing town tomorrow so we won't be moving in on you."

He hesitated a second, looking at the bottle, before he said "Sure-sure," and I reassured him. "He'll bring a bottle too, and I'll get another one or maybe two while I'm out. You can work on this one while I'm gone, kill it if you want." I took a short swallow from it myself and handed it to him.

His "sure-sure" was enthusiastic this time. He put the bottle down. "Git over by the window while there's light, an' I'll put th' candle out. When yuh come back I'll put it out agin till you're both inside."

Charlie was waiting, leaning against a building front. "Perfect set-up," I told him. "But we got to go back to Fifth and get another bottle or two. On the way I'll give you the scoop."

On the way I gave him the scoop. I bought another pint of sherry and when we got back Pops let us in in the dark, put back the blanket and then lighted the candle again. I introduced my friend Larry to Pops and we made ourselves comfortable. There was still a little, not much, left in the first bottle and we passed it around once and killed it, and Charlie opened his.

I was reminded, amusedly, by a poem of Kenneth Patchen's called *The Murder of Two Men by a Young Kid Wearing Lemon Colored Gloves*, which Patchen himself read on a record against jazz background. The poem consisted of only two words, the word "Wait," repeated over and over at irregular intervals and with different inflections, and then the word "Now!" and a blaring final chord from the jazz group.

This was the same, except that it was the murder of one man by two men and neither of us was wearing gloves. But we could wait all right; there was no hurry. I said, "Wait . . .

wait" to Charlie and he grinned, digging the reference. We'd heard the record together once.

The second bottle passed a few times. Pops was taking long ones, but not showing the effect yet. He seemed as drunk as when I'd first talked to him, but no drunker. He had a capacity; if we'd really been trying to get him dead drunk we'd have had to go out for more wine.

About halfway through the second bottle, Charlie looked at me across Pops, who was sitting between us and asked "Now?" I said, "Wait," and handed the bottle to Pops for his final drink. When he handed it back and I had hold of it safely, Pops was looking toward me and I said "Now," to Charlie and he swung the short length of lead pipe he'd meanwhile taken from his pocket, once. It was a lead pipe cinch.

There was a sound like the one you produce by flicking a watermelon with your finger, only louder, and Pops fell forward from the waist and then over sidewise. Out cold, if not dead; and he'd never known what hit him—he'd never known that *anything* had hit him.

I reached my hand toward him to put it inside his shirt to feel for a heartbeat, but Charlie said "Wait!"—and said it sharply, not as in the Patchen bit, but as an order—so I stopped my hand and looked at him. He was holding the piece of lead pipe out to me.

"We don't want to know whether he's dead, yet. I gauged that blow to be borderline. To kayo him and maybe or maybe not kill. You hit again about twice that hard before we know whether he's dead or not. That way we'll never know which of us really killed him and which was just the accomplice. Dig?"

I dug him, I saw his point; it made sense. I took the piece of pipe from Charlie's hand and used it, harder than he had. The *thunk* was louder, anyway, and I thought I heard bone crack.

Charlie said, "Good boy. That did it, if mine didn't. And we'll never know which. All right, now I'll give you a hand."

We straightened Pops up and I made sure there was no trace of a heartbeat.

I nodded to Charlie. "Let's put him down again the way he was. It's a more natural position." We did that.

"How do you feel?" Charlie asked me.

"Cool," I told him. "What do you feel?"

"Nothing. Well . . . maybe I'm exaggerating. It was a kick, but not a big enough one for me to want to take the chance again, except for stakes. But let's not talk about it abstractly until we're out of here. Now, first question: the bottles. Shall we take them all with us, or leave one?"

"Take them," I said. "If we left one we'd have to wipe it for fingerprints. Here's the picture we want to leave for the fuzz —whenever the body gets found. This happened in the middle of a drinking bout with another bum. If they'd been working on a bottle or a jug he'd have taken it with him."

"Right. And he'd have taken the weapon with him too, so we take that. Now—" He looked around. "I've been careful about fingerprints. How about you?"

"Same. There are the boards over the window, of course, but they're not painted and too rough to take prints. Same goes for the rough cement of the ledge. Besides, I doubt if the cops will even try dusting. They find dead winos every day, maybe they won't even autopsy him for the cause of death."

"We can't take a chance on that. We've got to assume they'll decide he was murdered and we've got to keep the picture consistent. Our hypothetical other bum who killed him would have turned out his pockets. Let's do that." We did that and found a dirty handkerchief, some matches and fourteen cents in change. We took the matches—they were book matches and once they'd been touched might retain fingerprints—and the change.

We discussed the candle and decided the hypothetical other bum would have left it burning to light his way to the window and because he'd have no reason to blow it out. The candle had been stuck on a tin lid so it wouldn't set fire to the crate when it guttered out. A fire wouldn't have mattered except that it would cause Pops to be found sooner. He might not be found for days, even weeks, otherwise.

We went once more over every point, then triple-checked. Being picked up for questioning by a cop on the way out seemed to be the only possible remaining danger, and we weren't picked up by a cop. In fact, nobody saw us, cop or citizen. Winsett is a quiet street with no taverns and was completely deserted at that hour. Which, if it matters, was one A.M. Less than three hours ago we'd decided, in Maxine Wells's pad on Cosmo, to commit a trial murder. It had gone like clockwork. Almost *too* smoothly, I found myself thinking, and then told myself that was ridiculous. How safe is too safe? Thinking like that can get you into a padded pad.

An hour later we were back in my unpadded pad, killing what had been left of the second pint. We decided to leave the third one intact for tomorrow. Also our plans for me to commit Charlie's murder and for him to commit mine. But we were really going to do it. We shook hands on it.

We planned ahead only one step, a rendezvous for tomorrow when we could swap notes. I'd tell him everything I'd learned about Seaton's habits and habitat, and he'd tell me the score on Radic. We made the date for two o'clock in the afternoon at Maxine Wells's pad. Charlie would get there early because he had the key. From here on in, the less Charlie and I were seen together in public, or visited one another's rooms, the better.

I was dead tired and slept soundly, as far as I know dreamlessly.

We met at Maxine's and decided we were set to stay as long as it took, into or even through the evening, to talk things out. Charlie had brought food and we'd decided on no drinks. I'd brought along the virgin pint from last night, but we were going to kill that only when we were through talking.

I talked first, telling him everything I knew about Seaton and his house and domestic arrangements. I drew diagrams and floor plans; he memorized them thoroughly and then we tore them into tiny pieces and flushed them down. He gave me equivalent and even more detailed dope on Radic, including diagrams—one of the apartment building Radic lived in and one of the apartment itself. He'd been there several times, back when, while he and Radic had been friends, or at least not enemies.

It didn't take us as long as we'd thought it might; it was not quite six o'clock when we finished and Charlie said, "Well, I guess that's it. Shall we flip a coin to see which of us goes first? Or would you rather deal a hand of showdown poker or play a game of gin rummy, or what?"

"Wait a minute, Charlie," I said. "One thing we haven't discussed, expense money. We'll need *some* at least, if only bus fare to the scene of the crime. And if you're as flat broke as I am, I think we'll have to take the added risk of knocking over a filling station or something before we split for one of us to set up an alibi while the other does his dirty work."

He sighed. "All right, I'll come clean. I've got a little stashed for a rainy day, and I guess this is rainy enough. A couple of hundred. If you draw the short straw I'll lend you some bread, like fifty bucks, before I take off to visit my sister in Frisco. Then, after I'm back, another fifty so you can put some mileage on yourself and have a solid alibi somewhere while I take care of your seat cover boy."

"Solid," I said. I took a deep breath, and the plunge. "In that case, let's not draw. I'll go to bat first. You'd have to wait till Seaton's back from Mexico City and also while I set it up with Doris to have *her* have an alibi for D-night. So it wouldn't be for days or even a week before you could do anything. But your friend Manny can go any time."

He grinned and clapped me on the shoulder. "I was hoping you'd say that, Willy. But I wouldn't have suggested it. Well—in that case, I take off tomorrow morning for Frisco. And, in case, I brought the money with me." He took out his wallet and pulled one-two-three-four-five tens out of it and handed them to me. Then another. "Look," he said, "this may be our last time together for a while. Let's celebrate a little. The hell with the lousy sherry. Get a bottle of whisky, a quart, and a couple of quarts of soda to go with it."

He looked at his wrist watch. "I'm getting hungry. Did you eat lunch?"

I shook my head. "A latish breakfast, around ten."

"Okay. Then while you're gone for the whisky I'll make sandwiches for us. When you get back we'll eat and then allow ourselves, say, till nine to drink and make merry. I want to turn in early, get up early and start driving to Frisco."

We did it that way and, after eating, we sat with our drinks listening to music and not talking except when occasionally one of us would think of a question.

We agreed that I'd not make any move against Radic tomorrow; I'd give Charlie a day to reach San Francisco and establish his alibi there. He wouldn't come back till Tuesday, the day after Seaton's first day back from Mexico; that gave me Saturday or Sunday to do my job and have it happen right in the middle of his San Francisco stay.

He'd stretch his stay if necessary, if I couldn't find Radic home and alone over the weekend. He'd know when Radic was dead all right; if his murder didn't rate space in the Frisco papers, it would certainly make the Los Angeles ones, and he'd pick up one every day while he was away.

He'd phone his sister when he got back to the rooming house tonight and make sure the visit was okay with her. He was reasonably sure it would be. If it wasn't, he'd let me know. Otherwise when we split from here we'd not see each other again till he came back.

I'd told him about the business with Essie, to explain what had happened to the money Doris had given me, and he said he'd spend some time scanning the beat joints in San Francisco, and if he ran into her, he'd try to get back whatever was left of my money by threatening her with the cops.

He gave me the key to Maxine's pad, in case I might have use for it, but warned me that she was coming back Sunday and that I wasn't to use it after Saturday and wasn't ever to let her know that I'd had it.

He also gave me a key to his own pad, so I'd have a choice of three weapons he had there. There was the lead pipe we'd killed Pops with, a blackjack and a little pocket revolver—a five-shot thirty-eight—that Charlie assured me no one knew he had. It wasn't registered and couldn't be traced back to him.

We split at nine. He left to go back to the Zoo and I stayed to have the one more drink that would kill the bottle and then took care of dishes and glasses and records and such, locked up and went to kill a couple of hours at the Unicorn. I sat listening to the music—they had a pretty good singer who did medieval folk songs with a lute—sipping espresso and thinking.

Not about the murder we'd committed less than twenty-four hours ago—that was in the past, and safe as houses—but about the murder I was going to commit. Charlie had told me how he'd planned to do it, as I'd told him how I'd planned to do in Seaton, but each of us was free to follow the other's plans or to roll his own.

Charlie's plan had sounded pretty solid to me, and I was going to use it. It would have been much more risky for Charlie than for me because he would have had to use a disguise and Radic might possibly have recognized him despite it, in which case the plan would have flopped. Radic wouldn't know me, even without a disguise. But I'd wear one just in case anyone who saw me entering or leaving the building, or in the neighborhood, wouldn't be able to recognize me if I ran into him sometime later.

Actually, the problem—and it would be my problem, not Charlie's—of giving myself a solid and logical alibi for the time Charlie would be killing Seaton seemed tougher than any of the problems connected with my killing Radic. The catch was that I had no logical place to visit out of town. My parents were dead and while I had a few relatives still living I hadn't been in touch with them for years. Hell, I didn't even *know* anyone, not well enough to visit, outside L.A.

And whatever my alibi was I wanted it to be a logical one and not look rigged. I didn't want just to take off for somewhere for no reason that I could tell the fuzz.

A local alibi would be much less solid. I could stay till four A.M.—by which time Charlie would be long done with his job —at a coffeehouse and see lots of people I knew but they'd be coming and going and probably no one would be able to swear I'd been there all the time. And, as I'd worked out when I'd been playing with the idea of killing Seaton myself, it would take me only an hour to get from Hollywood to Santa Monica, kill my man, and get back again.

It was going to take some figuring. Getting myself jugged on a drunk and disorderly charge, making myself so obnoxious they'd have to hold me overnight, would be solid enough, but it would be out of character for me; I'd never done it before. It would be too solid an alibi not to look contrived.

I went home around one and right to bed. When I woke up it was ten A.M., Friday morning, and Charlie hadn't come down to tell me otherwise, so I knew he was on his way to San Francisco. Which meant it was my move, but not until tomorrow. Wait . . . wait.

I went to the upstairs front hall and phoned Lennie to see if anything was doing. There wasn't, jobwise, although he was as hopeful as ever. But my check had come. There wouldn't be much left of it, he pointed out, after the usual deductions, his commission, and two advances he'd given me against it. It would be thirty-seven bucks and some odd cents. I told him that that was better than a poke in the eye with a sharp stick and that I'd be in to pick it up, as soon as I'd had some breakfast.

The mailman had left a small stack of mail on the hall table while I'd been talking to Lennie and I leafed through it. One piece of mail was for me; it was an airmail postcard from Mexico City, a picture of the bull ring there, the Plaza de Toros. On the message side was only "Dear Willy: Having wonderful time. Wish you were here. L. L."

A trifle indiscreet of her to have sent it, but not much. The "L. L." for Lady Loverly would have meant nothing to anyone but us. The message was obviously in reverse. She was not having a wonderful time—or why should she have sent the card at all?—and instead of wishing I was there, an impracticable situation, she wished that she was back here. I took it along with me when I went out for breakfast and got rid of it in a trash can.

On the whole, I was glad she'd sent it. It showed she was thinking of me and negated the one possibility that would have made everything I was doing ridiculous. If Doris changed her mind about me—which, however remote a possibility I thought it was, was something that *could* happen—then I would have gone to some risk and a lot of trouble for no purpose.

I had a relatively light breakfast, thinking to save appetite for a really good meal later, and then dropped in at Lennie's office and picked up my check from his Miss Jocelyn, keeping my hand in by indulging in a bit of chitchat with her. I cashed the check at the bank on the corner; it was Lennie's bank and I always cashed his checks there because they cashed them without question.

And then I was almost rich with eighty-some dollars, Lennie's thirty-seven plus most of Charlie's fifty, and there wasn't anything constructive I could do today anyway so I decided I might as well shoot a few bucks and have a pleasant afternoon. I took a bus downtown, caught a double bill of two good movies—in one of which I had had a very small role—and then I caught a bus back to Hollywood, had dinner at the Derby, dropped into a bar and picked up a cute little brownette with a retroussé nose and a Kansas accent who had come to Hollywood three weeks before and who was going to become a starlet, and . . . well, I killed the evening and the night with considerable enjoyment—it had been four and a half days since my last rendezvous with Doris—and at no great expense; I woke up in the morning with Charlie's fifty bucks still intact and a few over. In the morning I left after telling her I could send her to an agent who'd do more for her than the one she'd signed with had been doing (and he would, once) and then telephoning Lennie from her room and introducing them over the phone. I had nothing to lose; I'd probably never call her again. Although the door would still be open if I did, after Lennie had taken his turn.

I had breakfast, and went back to my pad at the Zoo, and started work. Today was my day for murder, my first solo murder, if I could find Manny Radic at home and alone this afternoon. I was really going to do it.

Chapter Eleven

I WAS off to commit a murder.

The first step was going up to Charlie's room to get the gun. It took me two passes because I decided it was best if no one saw me going in there or knew he'd left me a key. The first time Johnny Kaprelian was coming out of his doorway; I said hi to him and went on to knock on Smoky's door. Nobody answered, but by the time I'd decided he wasn't home Johnny was downstairs and I let myself into Charlie's room. The gun was where he'd told me it was, an ugly little short-barreled pocket-size revolver and a box of bullets with it. I wouldn't need more than five, at most, but I took the whole box along. After the murder I'd get rid of the gun and the extra bullets with it; Charlie wouldn't want the bullets around without the gun.

I went back down to my own pad and started packing the few things, besides the gun, that I'd need. A dark blue T-shirt, something I'd worn only a few times and would never wear again, a cap, ditto, and my make-up kit. I put them in a brief case and took off. Step one, before I even went to Maxine's pad for the transformation: I stopped at a drugstore to use their phone booth for a call. No use my going any further with things today if it was definite that Radic wasn't going to be home this afternoon.

I looked up his number and dialed it, got a Japanese voice—subtly Japanese; the accent wasn't strong enough for me to try to imitate it—saying, "Mr. Radic's residence. Good morning."

"Mr. Radic there?" I asked.

"No, sir. Can I take any message?"

"No, thanks. But can you tell me when he'll be home? It's something I have to talk to him about personally."

"I'm not sure, sir. I think he'll be home this afternoon—he said something about having some work to do—but I cannot be sure."

"Okay," I told the Japanese voice. "I'll call again this afternoon. I won't bother leaving my name because he doesn't know me, yet."

So far, so good. There was at least a probability that Radic would be home this afternoon, so I'd go ahead with my disguise. And there was at least a possibility that his Japanese servant would be gone. The Jap had one day a week off—Charlie didn't know which day, currently, but he was also free every afternoon from one to six. He might go out or he might stay in his room; that was something I'd find out later with a second phone call, and then there'd be a third. This was going to be Radic's day for phone calls. If nothing more.

I went on to Maxine's and let myself in, started to work leisurely on making myself look like someone who didn't look like Willy Griff. I'm no Lon Chaney; I've never gone into make-up to that extent, and I can't guarantee a job—not one that wouldn't *look* like a make-up job—that my best friend wouldn't recognize me in. But I knew I could do a job on myself that would keep anyone who saw me this afternoon from being able to identify me later if he saw me *au naturel.* And that was all I expected to accomplish.

I swapped my shirt and undershirt for the dark blue T-shirt first, so I wouldn't have to pull it on over the facial job, and then I went to work first with the putty. I built myself an addition on my nose—not a Cyrano de Bergerac job, not increasing the length at all, in fact; just building up the bridge with a twist. A broken nose and one which, because of the build-up of the bridge, looked shorter than my own. I— Why go into details?

When I was through, and it took me about an hour, I put on the cap and the sunglasses, and that was it.

After that make-up job, call me Mack the Knife. Or Hank the Thirty-Eight. But not Willy Griff.

I took my time and did a good job and it was good timing because it was half past twelve when I finished and Koto—that was Radic's boy—was off duty at one and would either be leaving or not. And it would take me a good half hour to walk to the bus line that would take me to North Hollywood, take the bus there, and see what the score was. I wasn't going to phone again till I got within range because the situation there might change while I was en route.

After I'd studied the make-up job at close range in the mirror and had decided that it would pass, and that it would not be recognized as make-up at all unless someone tried to push my nose around with his finger, I did one more thing. I explored Maxine Wells's desk and found a piece of white paper and an envelope. I block-lettered a message on the former and sealed it in the latter.

I loaded all five chambers of the revolver and put it in one pocket, the envelope in another. I put on the cap and the sunglasses and I was as ready as I'd ever be. The time was a little short of one o'clock.

I walked to Highland, caught a bus north, got off at the last stop before the Hollywood Freeway. I was now (I'd studied a map) seven blocks from the scene of a murder.

I walked those seven blocks and it was half past one. I took a look at the outside of the apartment building in which Radic lived and then went beyond it two blocks to a tavern; I went into it and found it had an enclosed phone booth. I used the phone.

The voice that answered wasn't even faintly Japanese. I asked, "Is this Mr. Manuel Radic?" and the voice said yes it was.

I was using my—let's call it my Number Four voice. Just a bit deeper and richer than my normal one. Baritone instead of tenor. I like it, actually, better than my normal voice, but it's difficult to sustain. I said, "You have a Japanese servant, Mr. Radic?"

He said "Yes" a bit testily.

I said, "My name is Harold Grainger, Mr. Radic. I'm with the Immigration Service. I would like to speak with your servant, but first, how long have you employed him?"

"He's been with me ten years. But you can't speak to him because he isn't here. And why would the Immigration Service be interested in him anyway? Koto is a Nisei; he was born in this country." He was getting testier by the sentence.

"Fine," I said. "Then no doubt the report we received that he was in this country illegally is just a mistake. Nevertheless, we *did* get such a tip, and I'm assigned to follow it up by seeing him, however briefly. No doubt he'll be able to show me his birth certificate and end the matter. Can you tell me when he'll be back? When I could see him for a few minutes?"

He sounded just a little more friendly and relaxed, now that he knew it was a false alarm. He said, "Certainly, Mr.—uh

—Grainger. He has afternoons off, and Tuesday all day. Afternoons, from one to six. You'll be able to reach him here any other time."

I thanked him gravely and hung up.

Koto wasn't there.

There was one other thing to ascertain, but I'd better not make the two calls in quick succession. I left the phone booth and went back to the bar, ordered myself a highball, and took my time, like twenty minutes, to drink it.

Then I called Radic's number again; he answered.

My voice was different. "Are you the Manuel Radic who is a movie and television producer?"

He said that he was. I told him, "My name is Walter Klinger, Mr. Radic. You wouldn't know me; I just came out here from New York. My company is about to launch, and sponsor, a weekly show on network. I'd like to talk to you about it and show you a pilot script that we have. Possibly we can get together on an arrangement for you to produce it for us. I can't mention the figure, but it will be a reasonably large budget deal."

"Ummm—I'm busy, Mr.—uh—"

"Klinger," I said. "Walter Klinger. I understand. I was told by—well, the executive at NBC who suggested that I talk to you about it asked that I didn't mention his name—that you were busy. However, this is a job you could possibly take on in addition to your other commitments. We'd like you to be in over-all charge, and we'd like your name and the Radic touch, but we'd give you anyone you might name for an assistant and you could let him handle the routine details."

"Well—I'd like to talk to you, Mr. Klinger, yes. Are you suggesting that we meet somewhere, or that you come here to my place?"

"I just got into town, Mr. Radic," I told him, "and haven't checked in anywhere yet. I'm at the airport and just about to rent a car; I thought I'd call you first. If you're free, I can drive there and worry about finding accommodations later. Or do you have company?"

"I'm working a bit, but I'm alone. And I can knock off the work for a while if you want to come directly here. Do you know how to get here?"

"Yes," I told him. "Thank you, Mr. Radic, and I'll see you as soon as I can get there."

Thank you, Mr. Radic. In two phone calls—I could hardly have asked both questions on the same call—you told me that your servant is out for the afternoon and that you're home alone, without company. And I was about to get there fast, before that favorable situation might change.

I got there fast, like five minutes for walking the two blocks between the tavern and the apartment building. I pressed the right button in the downstairs hallway and got a testy "Yes?" He wouldn't have been testy if there'd been time for Walter Klinger to arrive, but there hadn't been. Walter was no more, nor was—what name had I used?—yes, Harold Grainger, the immigration inspector. They'd served their respective purposes. Besides, my costume would not have fitted either of those gentlemen; neither sponsors' representatives nor immigration inspectors wear caps and T-shirts, unless possibly on the golf course.

I said, "Studio messenger, Mr. Radic. Have something to deliver to you. May I bring it up?" Nothing suspicious in that; the studios do not work on Saturday afternoons, but sometimes their executives do. And they use studio messengers instead of using the mails when a day will be saved.

"All right," he said shortly. The door buzzed and I had my hand on the handle and turned it, and I was in.

The elevator was self-service and I took it to the right floor and pushed the button outside the proper door, and got chimes. Half a minute later the door opened. I recognized Radic from the description Charlie Hayes had given me. Six-seven, slender, dapper, dark eyes and graying hair, if it matters.

I took the envelope I'd prepared at Maxine's out of my pocket. "They'd like me to wait for an answer, Mr. Radic," I said. "It seems to be something in a hurry."

I'd have had to play it by ear if he hadn't grunted and said "Step in, then," at that point. I wouldn't have let him close the door, not without my foot in it, if he'd tried to as I handed him the envelope. But I hadn't expected him to try that, and he didn't try it.

I was inside the door while he was tearing the envelope open, and I unobtrusively closed it behind me and then took out the snubnose thirty-eight and made it ready. I knew what he was reading because I'd written it myself only an hour or so ago. In block lettering, it read: "THIS IS A STICKUP. DON'T TRY ANYTHING AND YOU WON'T GET HURT."

He looked up into the muzzle of the revolver, and he wasn't going to try anything. His size and age gave me every edge, even if I hadn't had the drop on him. His face paled a little, but he managed to keep his voice reasonably level. It rose only a little. "I'm afraid you're making a mistake," he said. "I don't have enough money here to—"

"We'll see," I said, surprised at how calm my own voice sounded. "You've got a wall safe. Open it."

The wall safe bit was the gimmick. Charlie had known that there was one; he hadn't known whether Radic kept any money in it or not but that didn't really matter. The point was that the wall safe was in the room that Radic used for a home office or workroom, and he'd gone to the trouble of having that room completely soundproofed.

"I have a wall safe, yes," he said. "But there are only papers and contracts— I've got about a hundred or so in my wallet, but that's all—"

"We'll worry about the wallet later," I said. "First, take me to the safe and open it."

"All right, but—"

I raised the gun a little higher, and he quit stalling. He turned and led the way—with me right behind him and the gun aimed at the small of his back—through a doorway, down a short hallway, and into the room he used for an office. I closed the thick door carefully behind me and stayed only a few feet behind him while he crossed in front of the desk to the far wall. He took down a Degas print and there was the wall safe. He twisted the dial a few times and pulled it open. He turned toward me. "See, nothing but contracts and papers. No money or—"

I shot him, dead center in his chest. The explosion made a hell of a loud noise in that room and nearly deafened me. But in a soundproofed room, that was all right.

I'd shot people before—three times, I think—in small parts I'd played in gangster-type TV shows, and this really didn't seem any different, or worry me any more. Except in sound.

One of the three times I'd shot a blank, and on a sound stage a shot, blank or otherwise, is a hell of a lot less loud than in a closed smallish room. The other two times I'd clicked an empty revolver because the shots had been at close range, as this one had been, and even the wad from a blank can hurt if it hits you from only a few feet; in those cases the sound of the shot had been dubbed in later.

The main difference, though, wasn't in the sound. It was in the fact that the man I'd shot not only went down but stayed down for keeps.

I'd check, of course, but I was fairly sure I wouldn't have to use a second shot—and hoped that I wouldn't, because having to fire a second time would make it look more like a premeditated murder and less like a killing in the middle of a holdup.

I didn't have to tell myself to be calm. I *was* calm. I put the revolver back in one pocket and took a pair of gloves out of another, and put them on. I bent over Manny Radic. He was in shirt sleeves, wearing a white shirt, and I could see a small circular red stain the center of which was directly over his heart. And it was spreading a little, but very slowly; if his heart had still been pumping blood it would have been spreading a lot faster than that. Just the same, I made doubly sure. I couldn't feel for a heartbeat without getting blood on a glove, but I'd come prepared with a small mirror out of my make-up kit. I held it for a full minute against his nostrils and when I took it away there wasn't the slightest trace of condensed moisture.

I went over to the opened wall safe. I riffled through its contents and found that Radic had been telling the truth in saying there was no money there. There were contracts, a will, stuff like that. I dropped them on the floor under the open wall safe.

I had to roll Radic's body part-way over to get at the wallet in his hip pocket. I took the money in it but didn't bother counting it.

I straightened up and looked around. He'd kept the holdup note and its envelope in his hand while walking ahead of me into the office here and had put them down on the desk to free his hands for the safe opening bit. I took them back, not so much because I feared the fuzz could identify block lettering but because I'd handled them without gloves and there was the possibility of prints.

I made myself stand and think a long moment. I'd taken care of everything except two sets of prints I'd made before I'd put on the gloves, one on the inside knob of the door of this room, one on the inside knob of the outer door of the apartment. I'd pulled each of those doors shut behind me as I'd gone through it. I took care of both of those knobs by rubbing them with a gloved hand on my way out.

Nobody was in the hallway when I pushed the button for the automatic elevator and got it. I peeled off my gloves on the way down, and that was that.

It had gone like clockwork.

I walked back to the bus line, caught my bus back to Hollywood and walked to Cosmo.

I took off the make-up and changed clothes. I got rid of the blue T-shirt and the cap by putting them in the incinerator chute in the hall across from the pad. I burned the note and envelope and flushed them down.

I straightened up the place to leave no sign that I'd used it in any way, and left. I took the overnight case back to my pad at the Zoo and put it and the make-up kit where I always kept them.

And everything was as it had been a few hours ago except that I'd done my job for Charlie and had done it perfectly, without a hitch or a mistake, and it had been as safe as houses.

The only other difference was that now, instead of having only a little over fifty dollars in my wallet, I had a little over a hundred and sixty. The "hundred or so" Radic had told me he had on him had been just that, a hundred and ten.

And the only remaining loose end was the gun and the extra bullets for it. They'd be no trouble to get rid of. A trash disposal can would serve; the gun and the bullets would probably end up on a dump and never be found or correlated with the murder, but just in case they were found and correlated I'd prefer it to be a downtown trash disposal instead of a Hollywood one. So, reluctantly, I decided to go downtown again. I hate bus rides.

But I might as well get the last loose end tied up.

I polished possible fingerprints off every surface of the gun and the box of bullets which I might have touched, wrapped them in a completely untraceable dime store bandanna handkerchief, one I'd bought several years before—I've forgotten why—and which could have no laundry marks because I'd never used it or had it laundered. I put it in the pocket of the sport coat I was wearing and caught a bus downtown. No one happened to be watching me—not that it would have mattered if someone had been—when I dropped it in a trash disposal can on Pershing Square.

I had a drink and thought things through. It had gone like clockwork and there wasn't a possible chance—not a chance in a million—that the police could possibly come up with anything that could lead them to me.

I had it made. It had been an easy gig, just as easy as killing Pops had been. And just as safe.

All a successful murder takes is careful planning, quick and decisive action at the right moment. You don't even need luck, except in the negative sense of having nothing go unexpectedly wrong.

I caught a bus back to Hollywood and on the way I took one further precaution. I didn't see why the police would ever ask me, however casually, what I'd done this afternoon, but on the chance in a thousand that they might, I worked out a story to cover where I'd been, what I'd done. Not an alibi because I wouldn't be able to prove it. But a story that made sense and that they'd not be able to disprove even if they had any reason for doubting it.

It was six o'clock when I debarked at Hollywood and Vine; by now the body should have been found, or might be being found at this very moment.

I strolled west to Diamond Jim's, had myself two martinis and a good dinner. I figured I'd earned it.

Chapter Twelve

I FELT lonesome. Funny, I hadn't, all afternoon while I'd been preparing for Radic, making the scene there, and doing the few things I'd had to do afterwards. I hadn't been alone, then, really; Charlie had been with me. In San Francisco, sure, but in a sense *with* me as much as he'd been with me when we'd taken care of Pops.

But it was all over now and Charlie wasn't with me any more. I'd have given a third of my capital, fifty bucks, to have been able safely to phone him and gloat over the wild way everything had gone, give him the whole gig. But that was out, of course; he wouldn't want to have to explain why he got a phone call from Hollywood right after the murder.

Even more, I wanted to see Doris, spend tonight with her. But that would have to wait, too. She wouldn't be back from Mexico City until tomorrow night and it wouldn't be safe for us to see each other before Monday at the earliest. And even then maybe only for a drink together at The Doll House, if she could safely get away long enough to make it there.

I thought of calling my starlet of last night to find out if she was free, but she probably wouldn't be—at seven o'clock of a Saturday evening—and anyway I didn't especially want to spend the night with her. Was I getting that hooked on Doris? That would be bad; women are to be used, not loved. Getting hooked on one is almost as bad as getting hooked on horse. Or on the horses.

But on a Saturday evening there'd be *something* doing at the Zoo. There almost always was. Maybe even a hootenanny would be starting, early as it was. I started walking there, passed a newsstand and saw there were no editions out subsequent to the one I'd checked a couple of hours ago, and then got impatient because it was another ten blocks and flagged down a taxi.

I went to my room and undressed, went down the hall to shower and took a thorough one because I wanted to be sure there wouldn't be the slightest trace left of the make-up I'd worn that afternoon, and then dressed again.

I went upstairs to the second floor, and started to knock on Johnny Kaprelian's door and then didn't because I heard guitar music and Tex's voice singing down the hall. That meant he'd been sprung and a celebration was no doubt starting.

I went on down the hall and the music was coming from behind Smoky Conover's door, so I knocked. The door opened and the music swelled, but Smoky was standing there blocking my view and he gave me a pushing back gesture—without touching me, though—and stepped out as I stepped back and closed the door behind him.

"What the hell?" I said. "If I'm not wanted you don't have to—"

"It's okay, Willy," he said. "You're more than welcome, but I want to cue you in on something before you go in there. Essie's back, man, and I want to calm you down before you might make the scene and make *a* scene before you yak with her. She's got some of your money left and wants to give it back to you. She's sorry she glommed it."

"Man, you know I wouldn't make a scene. What the hell. How much has she got left of it?"

"I don't know. She didn't say and I didn't ask. But we got a good party going and I didn't want—"

He reached behind him to open the door but I said, "Wait a minute, Smoky. So I don't have to dampen the party with finances, I'll stay out here. You go back in and tell Essie I won't put her down and get her to come out. We'll go down to my room and straighten ourselves out in private. Then we'll like come back and make the scene."

"Crazy. Listen, are you holding?"

I said, "I will be if Essie comes through with enough to mention. Why? Need a few bucks?"

"No. But the party can use a bit of juice; we started hours ago and we're running low."

"Will do. Say, what's with Tex? Free or on bail?"

"Free. The mouthpiece came through, conned the Cad owner into not pressing charges."

"Crazy. Okay, send out our little Essie."

He went back in and a minute later Essie came out. She wasn't wearing the leotard outfit, but a silk fiesta dress with elaborate embroidery and with Mexican sandals. She looked good in it.

She gave me an uncertain smile. "Willy, Smoky says you're not mad. I hope—"

"Course I'm not. But let's not talk here. Come on down to my pad and we'll straighten out."

I led the way downstairs and she followed. In my room we sat on the edge of the bed and I made hostlike noises by asking if she wanted a drink. She didn't, yet.

"Want to tell you how it happened, Willy. I—"

"Let me tell it," I said. "You woke up around dawn and you thought I'd been putting you on when I said I didn't have any pot around. You started looking for some. And when you found five bills it was too much for you to resist. You emptied my wallet too, not because you were greedy but because you were afraid I'd guess or find out where you were going and follow you if I had traveling money left, right?" I inflected the *left*, *right* to make it a pun and she got it and laughed, at ease.

"That's it. I *am* sorry—if you'd have been a square, that would have been one thing. But Smoky had told me you're a right guy, and—"

"So, what's left of it?"

"Three hundred and something. I don't know exactly." She reached in her tooled leather Mexican handbag—something which, like the fiesta dress, was no doubt on me. "I went to Tijuana. I was stoned, really stoned, two days straight in a hotel there. And I replenished my wardrobe some and then—well, I got thinking and here I am."

She came out with a roll of bills and handed it to me. I counted it. Three hundred and thirty dollars. "Three thirty," I said, "You're not holding out, putting me on? You really spent two hundred and thirty-five or thereabouts?"

"I did, honey. I was really stoned, I tell you. Here, you can look." She handed me the purse. "Four singles and some change. All the rest is there."

I didn't open the purse. "But how about the hundred-dollar bill you put in your brassiere?"

She looked startled for a moment. Then she laughed. "I'll let you look," she said. And peeled off the fiesta dress over her head, and then bra and panties, kicked out of the sandals.

"*There*," she said, "And a chick has only one other hiding place. Want to investigate?"

I wanted to and I did, thoroughly. I had this coming, after her having passed out on me too soon five nights ago. She did the opposite of passing out this time, and she was good. Almost as good as Doris. Later, when we dressed, I was feeling good, and feeling generous. Everything had gone perfectly today and was going perfectly this evening. I'd tossed the bills Essie had given me onto the bedside table and I gave her the three odd tens, put only the three hundred even in my wallet with the hundred and sixty some that was already there.

We wandered out and I picked up a fifth of whisky and a gallon of wine. I glanced at a stack of early edition Sunday newspapers and there wasn't a headline about Radic's being murdered anywhere on the top half of the front page; of course there might be at least a bulletin on the bottom half, or a story inside, but I decided to hell with it. Sufficient unto the day is the evil thereof; a Sunday morning edition of a Sunday morning paper would surely have the story, and I could wait. I knew more about it than the newspapers would know, in any case.

We went back and joined the party at Smoky's, and stayed with it. I congratulated Tex on his freedom and he thanked me for what I'd contributed toward his freedom fund. And I slipped him another ten to help him ride out till he got another job; the parking lot owner hadn't been as forgiving as the owner of the Caddy he'd borrowed. What the hell, I was loaded. People have once in a while, not often, slipped me a saw when it mattered. And it made Tex my friend for life, or at least for the rest of tonight.

People came and went; the party became a wing-ding (but never quite a hootenanny) and still there wasn't a single fight unless you count a bit of hair-pulling between the same pair of faggots who'd been at Charlie Hayes's pad the night I'd met Essie. We separated them without any major hassle. Tex passed out at midnight. The liquor was about gone by then and it was later, for most of them, than one might think because the party had started in early afternoon. The few survivors, including Essie and me, walked to the Unicorn to sober up a bit on espresso. I wasn't feeling any pain and neither was she, but the coffee helped and by the time we got back to my pad—we split from the other survivors before they left—we were in good shape. And Essie wasn't on pot and didn't want any; her two days stoned in Tijuana had put her off it for a while.

We got back home and when, after a session of fun and games, she borrowed my bathrobe to go down the hall to the head, I considered whether to worry about hiding my bread. It would be pretty far out for Essie to swipe it a second time, but then again Essie was a pretty far out chick. I counted the money in my wallet and it was four hundred and fifty-some dollars. I left the fifty-some in it and hid the four hundred in four different places. A hundred in Gideon, a hundred between the mattress and the springs on the side of the bed I'd be sleeping on, and a hundred each in two other good stashes.

Essie came back from her shower and we had a nightcap and talked a while. Essie said she was leaving to go back to San Francisco in the morning; she didn't really like L.A. and had stopped over here only, or at least mostly, to square herself with me. She told me she'd pay me back what she'd spent someday, but I told her to forget it. She never would anyway, so I could afford to be generous. Besides, after tonight I wanted a clean break with her, no hangovers. Tomorrow night, Sunday night, Doris would be back. She'd hardly take kindly to learning, if she should happen to learn, that I was shacking up with another chick. I was glad Essie had decided, on her own, to move on. It saved me the embarrassment of having to hurt her feelings by getting rid of her.

From tonight on, Willy, I told myself, your course is going to be a celibate one for a while. Except for Doris, of course, if it turns out to be safe for you to get together once before the time for the alibi bit comes up. It would be silly to take the risk of committing a murder—and I already had—to get a woman and money with her, and then blow the deal for an extracurricular piece. Women are funny; murder they'll tolerate, but not unfaithfulness. From now on I was going to be a good boy for a while.

We got to sleep somewhere between three and four, and when I awakened at noon, Essie was still there and still asleep. But she awakened when I touched her and I remembered my coming celibacy bit and we had one for the road.

And then we were lying there, reluctant to get up and get dressed, when there was a soft knock on the door. I turned to Essie and put my finger to my lips for silence; my first frantic thought was that it might be Doris, back half a day sooner than I'd expected her. But whoever it was, I'd sooner play possum than answer it.

But the knock was repeated a little louder and a voice called out "Willy?" and it was all right because it was Charlie Hayes's voice. I called out, "Just a minute," and quickly put my bathrobe on so I could open the door and step outside instead of letting him in. I pulled it shut behind me.

"Company?" he asked, and I nodded.

"You're back pretty soon after—"

He held up a hand. "It's all right. But I didn't want to stay to talk here and now anyway. Can you meet me at Maxine's pad at like five o'clock?"

"Sure," I said. "But I thought she was getting back today."

"Negative. Checked my mail when I came in just now and there was a letter from her. She'll be another week—got a week's work in a nightclub there and decided to stay for it. You still got the key?"

"Sure," I said. "Just a minute, I'll—" He stopped me as I started to open the door behind me.

"Makes nix," he said. "I'll get it from you there. But you get there early, since you got it, so you can let me in."

"Shall I bring some grub and drinks?"

He shook his head. "Don't think it'll take us that long, this time. Well—bring a pint if you want; we'll have time to split that much. See you later, then." He dropped his voice. "Good boy. From what I read, it looks perfect."

He looked both ways down the hall to make sure nobody was in sight, and then gave me a quick but firm handshake. And a grin.

When I went back in, Essie was adjusting her bra. She asked me if I'd go up to Smoky's room, where she'd left her suitcase again, and get it. She didn't want to put the fiesta dress back on for traveling and besides she wanted her toothbrush and comb.

I dressed and got the suitcase and she finished dressing, putting on the same leotard and tights outfit, with a skirt over the tights, that she'd been wearing when I'd first met her.

I carried her suitcase to the bus line and waited with her till a bus came. She took the bus that would take her to Santa Monica and put her on the Coast Highway.

When we split, I picked up a Sunday newspaper and read it in a restaurant booth while I had some breakfast.

The Radic killing was on the front page, about a half a column with a half-column picture of the victim. About half the wordage was obit stuff, listing his important screen credits and the various television programs he'd worked on, mostly as producer. It was quite an impressive list.

The rest didn't tell me much I didn't already know. The body had been found at a few minutes before six o'clock when the Japanese servant returned from his afternoon off. Police believed Radic had been dead at least three hours, possibly four. Cause of death was just what I'd have guessed it to be, a thirty-eight-caliber bullet in the heart. A safe was open and papers from it on the floor under it. The dead man's wallet had been emptied of money and was lying on the floor beside him. Police theorized that the killer had forced Radic to open the safe at gun point, and then had shot him at close range as he had turned away from the safe. It was not known how much money had been in either the wallet or the safe.

And that was just about all. It didn't say that the police didn't have a single clue to work on, but then again the police weren't quoted as saying they expected to make an arrest within twenty-four hours.

I went back to my room and gathered my money from the stashes, all except the hundred bucks in Gideon; I thought that might as well stay there as a reserve. And was just wondering how to kill the hour or two before I could take off to meet Charlie, when the answer was solved for me by a knock on my door that turned out to be Johnny Kaprelian. He said they were just renewing the wing-ding up in Smoky's room to celebrate Tex's break in having the charges dropped, and why didn't I come up and join.

We went upstairs and to Smoky's room. There were about eight people, assorted—very assorted. I was surprised to see Charlie among them, but we played it cool. There was yak and there was wine—the standby of a Zoo party where whisky usually evaporates too fast—I took one glass of the wine but sipped it slowly as, I could see from the corner of my eye, Charlie was doing with his. Most of the argument was about Kerouac and whether or not he really represented the beat generation. Most of them thought so but a minority said he couldn't possibly make as much money from his books as he did, and still stay a beat.

At a quarter to five I left, saying that I had a date. I knew Charlie would follow me shortly, but not too shortly, so I took my time walking to Cosmo, and picked up a pint on the way. Good Scotch this time.

At the pad, I stacked a few records on the phono, then went into the kitchenette and made us a couple of Scotch and sodas, put them in the reefer to stay cold.

About twenty minutes later Charlie arrived and we drank a standing toast to Manny Radic's soul, if any.

Then we made ourselves comfortable in chairs and Charlie sighed. "Looks like you did a wonderful job, man. I'll do the same; I promise. Seaton's as good as dead, right now. About Radic—tell me the details."

"You tell me why you came back a full day early. Cuts it close, doesn't it? Wha' hoppen?"

"Wha' hoppen hoppened perfectly, Willy. At eight P.M last night I got a long-distance call. Scared me because I thought something might have gone wrong here. But it was, of all people, Lennie Berg. I'd connected with him by phone after we split here last time and had given him Sis's phone number. So if anything important came up he could reach me."

"But why? What if he'd called you the next day and told you he had something and to come right back?"

"That wasn't likely and besides I'd have stalled him. But I wanted this trip to look perfectly natural, everything about it, and is it natural for an actor looking for a job to put himself out of touch with his agent? You'd better do the same thing when you take off, Willy."

"Okay, and if he calls me too soon I'll tell him I've got housemaid's knee or something."

"Don't kid; this is serious. Your alibi has to hold water all the way, including a good reason for your being where you are, and when. Now here's my suggestion. Go to a doctor tomorrow. You're an actor; you can fake symptoms of being on the verge of a breakdown. You can con him into telling you to take a rest, out of town if possible. Then—when you've got it set when Doris will have *her* alibi set up, take a bus somewhere where people go for their health. With the other fifty I said I'll lend you you can ride out a few days at Palm Springs or Arrowhead or—"

"Wait," I said. "Before I forget." I took out my wallet and gave him fifty. "Here's your first fifty back and I won't need the second." I told him about the hundred ten I'd found in Radic's wallet, and the three hundred I'd got back from Essie.

"I'll be damned," he said. "That chick is a real weirdo. Well, fine. Then you're really solvent. Arrowhead then, or anywhere the doctor recommends. Get him to suggest several places, if you can, so you can pick the farthest one. But where, if anyone asks, did you get the dough?"

"Savings, stashed. Like you had a couple yourself. I've worked enough over the past three years that it's not impossible for me to have saved a few hundred. All right, I'll see a doc tomorrow and con him. Know just the guy. I *was* on the verge of a breakdown about a year ago and his advice was to get away from the rat race for a while if I could afford it. He'll give me the same advice now."

"Fine, and with that advice under your belt you can stall a few days till Doris tells you when she'll be set. Well, Willy, want to tell me all the gruesome details? About Radic, I mean. Did you use the exact plan I'd figured out for myself?"

"With a few embellishments. But you go first, because it'll take less telling. How sound did you make your alibi for yesterday afternoon? Will you have more than your sister's word—and Lennie's that he reached you by phone around eight?"

Charlie chuckled. "Know how many witnesses I have to where I was between two o'clock and five yesterday? Twenty or twenty-five. Sis is interested in amateur theatricals and belongs to a North Beach group up there. They're putting on Saroyan's *The Time of Your Life* and she's playing the Kitty Duval role. They're in rehearsal and the cat who plays one of the key roles—Nick—was out, groggy from just having an impacted tooth pulled. They wanted me to walk through the rehearsal and read his lines and I did. You couldn't have picked a solider time, man."

"Charlie," I said, "I'm almost beginning to get worried because things have been *too* cool. First with Pops and then with Manny. Can our luck hold up for one more?"

"Why not, Willy? Don't go superstitious on me and talk about luck. Luck is what you make it. And don't you think I'm as smart as you are?"

"Sure, but—"

"But nothing. Consider your seat cover removed. All I want is a night when you and Doris both have solid alibis. Different ones, needless to say. You could shack up, but that would be pretty far out. And unless you lined up some voyeurs for witnesses, each of you would have only the other's word."

"Don't be an ass," I told him. "That's the *last* alibi I'd pick. Want the blow-by-blow of my bit with Radic?"

"Why not? But hold it till I fix these drinks."

I waited and then I told him everything I had done yesterday.

He nodded. "Good boy. You didn't leave a loose end. Except one small one—and I took care of it an hour ago."

"What was that?" I asked him.

"Nothing much. Maybe my fault, maybe I didn't make this clear to you, but I meant for you to take from my room not just one of the three weapons there—the gun, the lead pipe, and the blackjack—but all three of them. If I'm questioned about the murder, they just might search my room before they verify my San Francisco alibi and I wouldn't want to have to explain what I was doing with a lead pipe and a blackjack. Not that owning them is illegal, but you see what I mean."

"You got rid of them then?"

"Sure, an hour or so ago."

"But what are you going to use to take care of Seaton? You'll need a weapon for that, Charlie. When I was thinking about doing it, I was figuring a blackjack—if I could have laid my hands on one without its being traced to me. A piece of pipe or something, otherwise. Something silent."

Charlie said, "I thought of that but decided the hell with it. I'm not going to use either a pipe or a blackjack on Seaton. I know where I can get another pistol without its being traceable. And—since Seaton hasn't a soundproof room to get himself shot in—I'll make myself a silencer."

"*Make* a silencer? Can you?"

Chapter Thirteen

"NOTHING TO it. Some copper tubing in two sizes, a drill to put holes in it, some tools, some steel wool. I can buy the ingredients anywhere anytime."

"You're putting me on, Charlie," I said. "Where did you pick up this bit?"

"I'm not kidding you. Hell, man, I've been interested in guns, mostly pistols, since I was a kid. Had a nice collection once when I was working fairly regularly—but I had to sell it when the going got rough."

"The hell!" I said. "You never mentioned it."

"Guess I haven't. Well—anyway I can get what I need, outside of the gun itself, for a couple of bucks, and I can fix it up in a few hours with the right set of tools—and I know a guy who has a real cool home workshop and will let me use them a few hours sometime."

"Crazy, but Charlie—why all that hassle? You can handle Seaton easily with a blackjack, and it's just as silent."

He grinned. "Call it envy. Me, a bug on pistols and I never shot anybody with one. All you know about pistols is how to pull the trigger and look at the fun you had yesterday."

I said, "If you feel that way about it, maybe I should have kept— Hell, no. What am I thinking about? Radic and Seaton can't have been killed by the same gun."

"I won't even use the same caliber. I'll get a thirty-two. But you're going to have to do me one thing, Willy. Keep it for me—gun and silencer both—from the time I get 'em until the time I use 'em. Unless meanwhile I'm questioned and cleared on the Radic bit."

"Or keep it at Maxine's pad."

"Good point, will do. At least for the next six days while I'm sure Maxine won't make the scene there. After that—well, maybe there won't *be* any after that. If you and Doris can set up your alibis, the sooner I get this over with the better. You say she's coming back tonight?"

"As far as I know, and I don't think there'd be any change in plan. Seaton arranged to take the week off, but to be back at work tomorrow, Monday morning."

So, that covered it. We had another couple of drinks and yakked a while, but just happy-talk. Before we split we made an arrangement to meet again without having to go to each other's rooms at the Zoo. A deal like the one I had with Doris at The Doll House. Every evening—for a while, until Maxine came back—Charlie would drop in here for an hour, between eight and nine, which wouldn't interfere with his working hours if he got the job he was shooting for. If I had any emergency information, I'd see him here and then. Only in the unlikely event of an emergency would we make contact with each other at the Zoo.

We split. I left first because I'd given Charlie back the key to Maxine's as well as his extra key to his own pad. I killed the rest of the evening at the Unicorn, enjoying the music and the yak but also planning my coming interview with the doctor who was going to suggest that I cut loose on a few days' or two weeks' vacation so I'd be ready to take off the minute I got the word from Doris.

The four hundred and however many bucks in my pocket felt good, like power, like the ability to decide to go anywhere I wanted to go, within reason. Just far enough that I couldn't possibly have sneaked back to do the job and then returned. Like as far as San Francisco—except not there because Charlie had done that bit. Maybe Phoenix, Arizona—as near as matters the same distance—if the quack thought that a warm, dry climate would help whatever the hell was wrong with me.

Midnight made it a night for me because I wanted to get up early and get the medical bit over in the morning, before I might possibly see or hear from Doris tomorrow afternoon. And if she was set for a quick alibi, I wanted to be able to take off the second I got the word to Charlie.

I woke at eight and made a call to Doc Grainger as soon as I was dressed and before I left the Zoo for breakfast. He was able to give me an appointment for eleven.

Doc Grainger was understanding and sympathetic: "You young fellows," he said, "work too hard and play too hard.

You're jittering pretty bad; think you'd like to go to a sanitarium for a thorough rest?"

"Wouldn't a vacation, a trip to get away from the rat race, be just as good?" I asked him.

"Probably, if you go somewhere where you don't know anybody and can stay quiet. That does *not* include Las Vegas, incidentally. Know anybody in Arizona?"

I shook my head.

"Climate's fine there this time of year, and either Phoenix or Tucson is a good spot. Suggest you don't drive: driving's work and makes you keep alert. Plane's too fast, so go by bus or train and get there rested. Get as many hours of sleep a day as you can. Do you sleep well?"

"Usually not," I told him. "Unless I go to bed stoned."

"I'll give you a prescription for some seconals; take two before you turn in. And some tranquilizers. Read. See movies. Take walks after you're rested up. Have a drink or two occasionally if you feel like it but don't go overboard. And don't make friends, don't get involved. Can you manage a week?"

"I think so."

"Good." He started writing on his prescription pad. "Come and see me when you get back."

I thought I might as well round out my excuse for a trip by getting the prescriptions filled so I left them at the drugstore downstairs in his building. Besides, I could really use the seconals, times when I had to turn in early because I had to be at a studio early the next morning.

I killed time in a movie near The Doll House and left in time to get there at two-thirty, and I nursed a drink till it was time for Doris to have called if she was going to call. Well, I'd hardly expected her to call her first day back.

I went home and started preparations for the trip. I gave Mrs. Whelan two weeks' rent in advance and told her I might go away for a few days to a week. I took out my laundry and a few things to be dry-cleaned.

I stopped in a Hollywood travel agency and checked plane flights to Phoenix. The best flight for me was one that took off a few minutes after seven P.M. and got to Phoenix about nine-thirty. I could wire a hotel reservation ahead of me from the airport, check in the hotel about eleven, set myself up an alibi at a bar until closing time and I'd be all set, in case Doris's alibi was for tomorrow night or the next. On that chance I made myself a reservation on that plane; I could cancel tomorrow if it turned out that was too soon for me to go, if Doris failed to call or make the scene at The Doll House.

I rounded out the afternoon by dropping in on Lennie. He was there but didn't have anything for me except cheerfulness and a few minutes' time, which I took up snowing him about the hypertension I'd been having and about my seeing the doctor, and his advice. I said I'd probably take it but didn't know just how soon I'd take off. I told him that if I left, I'd let him know how to reach me there if anything important came up.

So I went back to the Zoo, all my groundwork laid, and then felt the ground seem to drop from under my feet when I read the note in Mrs. Whelan's handwriting that had been shoved under my door. "Willy: A Mr. Seaton called. Wants you to call him at his office before five today or soon after nine tomorrow." And an Exbrook number.

I stared at it unbelievingly. What the hell did *Mr.* Seaton want with *me*?

Well, it was still a quarter to five, luckily, so I could find out without having to wonder all night. I went upstairs to the phone and found I didn't have a dime. But rather than risk missing him by trying to scrounge one I dropped a quarter.

I got a switchboard operator or secretary and then Seaton's voice came on and I identified myself.

"Glad you called today, Mr. Griff," he said, and his voice sounded friendly. "Tomorrow just might have been too late. First, I want to thank you."

"For what?" I said, blankly.

"For talking to Doris. I don't know what you said to her, but she's a completely changed girl. Our second honeymoon was wonderful. Better, I might say, than our first."

"I'm glad to hear that, sir," I said, and I meant it. Doris had done a first-rate job on him and he was off his guard. But why tell *me* about it?

"I understand you act in television, Mr. Griff. Are you—I believe they call it 'at liberty' now?"

"Just at the moment, yes."

"Have you ever done live television commercials?"

"Of course. Quite often."

"I'd like to do something for you if I can. One of my regular announcers quit while I was away, got a full-time job on a movie, and left, naturally; I don't blame him. I'm afraid the job doesn't pay very much but I'll be glad to try you out if you'd be interested: I'd expect you to stay only until you got a better offer, of course. Would you want to see me in my office at nine tomorrow to talk it over?"

"Why—that's very generous of you, Mr. Seaton. But I'm signed with an agent and I'm afraid I can't deal direct." I gave him Lennie's name and phone number and said Lennie would probably still be there if he phoned right away.

I figured Lennie would be calling back so I smoked a cigarette and waited around near the phone, wondering what the hell this would do to my alibi plans. Well, they'd just have to wait till I learned the score.

The phone rang just before five o'clock. It was Lennie. "Got something for you, sweetie. Not big, but it might turn out to be steady. Shall I dish it now, or do you want to drop over? I'll be here till six."

It was about time for me to eat anyway—I hadn't had anything except a big but comparatively early breakfast—so I told him I'd drop over. And did. Miss Jocelyn sent me right into his office.

Lennie was on the phone and I took the client's chair and waited till he put it down.

"Ever hear of Seat Cover Seaton, sweetie?" he asked me.

"Sure," I said. "I know him slightly. He called me first and I referred him to you. So don't pin any medals on yourself, Lennie. Just tell me the score."

It didn't put him down. Nothing, but nothing, can put Lennie down. He grinned cheerfully. "*Wondered* why he asked for you in particular. Okay, sweetie, here's the score. Seaton sponsors several local daytime programs. Likes a different announcer on each, for variety, doesn't want one to become completely associated with his product. Dig?"

There wasn't any point in answering, so I didn't.

"So, sweetie, you're trying out for a three-spot, three announcements at the beginning, middle and end of a half-hour show from half-past eleven to noon. Two minutes each, opener and closer, two minutes in the middle. Five days a week, Monday through Friday. A one-shot would pay you twenty-five, but if you get it steady, it's a hundred a week. How's it sound, sweetie? Just eating money, of course, till something better comes along. Or till I can pile you up some more commercials at nonconflicting hours till you're making a bundle on them alone."

"Not bad, Lennie," I said. But I wanted a door open in case. "But what about doctor's orders and all that jazz?"

"Jazz-schmazz. Your hypertension's not so bad you can't wait till after the Friday broadcast. Then you'll have three days before the Monday one. You can take your damn trip over the weekend, and again the next weekend if you still want to."

Thank you, Lennie Berg. That's the answer, of course. I can have my cake and eat it too, and Doris will just have to arrange her alibi for a weekend night.

I said, "Let me get this straight. Is it an offer or a tryout?"

"Both, sweetie. It's a job offer for tomorrow. You do the regular eleven-thirty broadcast. If they like you—if Seaton likes you, that is—it's a steady job."

"It's a deal," I said.

He told me which studio and whom to ask for and told me to get there at ten.

I got there at ten. The studio manager gave me the scripts for all three commercials and then showed me the set. There were mock-ups of three sets of car seats. There was a different kind of seat cover on each and the manager told me which was number one, number two, and number three and said my scripts were keyed to show me which I was plugging each time. I told him okay and just to let me alone to study my scripts.

I sat down on one of the seats and studied. I'm a fast study; in half an hour I had all six minutes down solid.

At a quarter after eleven a little man with a goatee showed up and introduced himself as Andrews, Seaton's buyer; he said he also handled details on the broadcasts and wanted to know if there was anything I wanted to know. I told him the only thing that worried me was the timing; I'd like to run through one spiel—they were all the same length—and have him time me so I wouldn't run seriously over or under my two minutes. He told me not to worry about it; they were calculated to come out two minutes each at normal pace; I wouldn't miss if I didn't rush or dawdle and anyway a few seconds over or under wouldn't matter because it was a panel show and therefore flexible. Timing mattered importantly only on the final one, because I couldn't run more than a few seconds into the next sponsor's time without being cut off, but that if I timed myself carefully on the first two, I'd be able to judge the last one pretty accurately.

He told me Seaton wouldn't be there but that he'd catch the broadcast on a set in his office and would phone afterwards; I was to stick around after the broadcast until he'd called, which would probably be within a few minutes.

I restudied the first script with one eye on the studio clock and at a minute before time took my place and watched for the red light to flash on front of the camera and when it did I started. I made it easy and casual, and it was a breeze. I'd timed myself by the sweep second hand of the studio clock and I came out five seconds over. I restudied the second script during the twelve minutes I had between commercials and did it almost perfectly, coming out three seconds short. I hit the final commercial on the head, within one second.

As soon as we were off the air Andrews shook hands with me and told me I'd done a fine job as far as he was concerned but we'd have to wait for a call from the boss. He led me to a desk with a telephone on it in one corner of the studio and said the call would come on that phone; it rang the second he'd finished saying it. Andrews answered it. I heard him say, "Yes, Mr. Seaton . . . fine." Then he handed the phone to me and said, "Mr. Seaton wants to talk to you."

I took the phone and said, "Hello, Mr. Seaton."

His voice was enthusiastic. "You did fine, boy. Especially for the first time. Have you talked to Mr. Berg?"

A silly question. Of course I'd talked to Lennie or I wouldn't have known to be here at ten this morning for the broadcast. But I said, "Yes, Mr. Seaton. Right after you called him last night."

"Good, then you know what the job pays and everything. It's yours if you want it."

I told him I did, if it was on the understanding that I could quit on short notice any time I got an acting job that was worth quitting for. He said that was understood, that he could always switch an announcer from one of his other programs to substitute, so I could even take an acting job that lasted up to a week and come back to his program. That was an even better break than I'd hoped for and I thanked him and meant it. An arrangement like that is what you try for. I was almost sorry Charlie was going to have to kill him. But hell, Andrews liked me too and there was no reason to think I couldn't keep the job for a backstop anyway. The outfit was too big to go out of business just because Seaton died; Doris would appoint a manager to take over and keep things running.

I had myself a fine lunch at Diamond Jim's to celebrate and got to The Doll House in plenty of time.

The call for me came just at the end of the vigil, when I'd almost given up.

"Willy?"

"Yes, Lady Loverly. How was Mexico?"

"Horrible. But I did a good job of it, didn't I? John told me he was going to put you on one of his programs and I caught the one this morning. You were wonderful."

"I'm always wonderful."

"Yes, but—Willy, I don't think we'd better see each other again."

Chapter Fourteen

"OH?" I said blankly, feeling a sudden sense of loss—but congratulating myself that at least I'd got a steady job out of the mess.

"Oh, Willy, I didn't mean that the way it sounded. I haven't —changed my mind, if you haven't. I just mean—until it's over and we can see each other openly, get married after a while. Listen, would this weekend be all right for me to—to be out of town?"

"It would be perfect," I said.

"You know where El Centro is?"

"About a hundred miles east of San Diego, on the American side across from Mexicali. I've been there a few times."

"That's where I'm from. My parents still live there and I've got lots of friends. I go back at least once a year for a weekend, sometimes a whole week. I was there only seven months ago the last time, but while we were in Mexico City I talked John into letting me drive down again the weekend after we got back."

"Wonderful," I said, "and the timing is perfect. Be sure you make it solid, stay with people you know and up as late as you can. Especially Saturday night. But maybe Friday night too, in case. When will you drive down?"

"I'll start no later than Friday noon, and be there by dark. Friday night or Saturday night—but not Sunday night. I promised John I'd be back by Sunday evening, so I'll be taking off Sunday noon or early afternoon."

"It might be sooner," I said, "if you get unexpected bad news that brings you back. Where are you calling from?"

"Downtown Santa Monica. I came to do some shopping and I've got a three o'clock appointment for a shampoo and a set, and I want to be home by five-thirty when John gets home. Six at the latest. So I wouldn't have time to see you today. And I've been thinking it over and—we can wait, can't we, darling? I don't *want* to but I can. We shouldn't take chances."

"Very sensible, but—listen, I've got to see you *once*, for about half an hour, to ask a lot of questions. No monkey business, just a talk. There are things I've got to learn and don't want to go into over the phone. How long will this deal at the beauty shop take you?"

"Oh, an hour and a half maybe, if they take me right away. There wouldn't be time today, darling."

"But you can safely run in to downtown Santa Monica again tomorrow?"

"For an hour or so, yes."

"Good. There's a tavern on Third near Wilshire called Rinky Dink's. Can you meet me there at—uh—four o'clock? I'll have my questions ready."

"All right, Willy. But not more than half an hour. What kind of questions?"

"Like what day or days your Jap gardener comes; you didn't even tell me about him. Like whether you knew the kitchen door is kept bolted so the key you gave me wouldn't have been any use. Like how heavy a sleeper your housekeeper is and what time she turns in. Simple things like that but don't start answering them over the phone because there are too many of them. Dig?"

"Sure, Willy. I'll see you. I love you."

"I love me, too," I said. "'Bye, sweet. See you at four tomorrow."

While I was in the phone booth I called Lennie; I'd have to relay to him the results of my phone conversation with Seaton. He was out until four, as usual, and I told Jocelyn that I'd drop in between then and five.

I strolled around to the travel agency and canceled my plane booking for Phoenix, made a new reservation for the same flight Friday evening. Everything was working out just like clockwork.

I saw Lennie at four-thirty and he was enthusiastic.

"I didn't catch your commercials, Willy," he said. "I was busy on the Warner Brothers lot. But when I got back here half an hour ago there was word for me to call Seaton, and I did. It's in the bag, sweetie. Ninety a week for you and ten for me. And Seaton and I agreed it wasn't worth putting anything on paper about, since you'd have to have an escape clause anyway. That's the crazy thing about it, sweetie, that you can quit any time."

"Crazier than that," I said, and I told him what Seaton had told me about being able to take a few days off once in a while if I got a crack at straight acting that wouldn't take up all my time.

"But better than good, baby. Because I think I've got two-three days lined up for you at W. B. week after next. You'd have had a tough decision if it would have meant dropping your commercial."

He stood up to ease me out and I eased out.

I had something to report to Charlie, so I hit Maxine's a little after eight and brought a bottle with me. He was waiting there and we made drinks and then I brought him up to date.

He said that things were looking up for him too. The role he'd wanted on the new western which Radic would have produced was still open. It was too big a role, though, to go without a tryout and he had one lined up for next week.

He had another item of good news; he didn't think the police were going to bother asking him questions about Radic. His name must have come up in the investigation and they'd gone to Lennie Berg to get his current address. Lennie had given it and then they'd asked Lennie if he knew anything about his whereabouts, on Saturday afternoon. Lennie'd told them he was in San Francisco and had told about reaching him there by phone early in the evening. And he'd given them the sister's address there. Since they hadn't come to him right away, Charlie didn't think they would. They'd probably gone ahead—if they'd doubted Lennie's word about the phone call—and checked the rest of the San Francisco alibi, then dropped his name from the investigation without even talking to him.

We agreed to meet again tomorrow night, same time, same station, so I could pass on to him whatever I learned from Doris tomorrow afternoon.

Charlie had been getting ready, too. He'd got a thirty-two revolver—said it couldn't possibly be traced—and had made himself a silencer at his friend's workshop without anyone knowing about it.

He had the pistol, already fitted with the silencer, here in Maxine's pad, in a locked brief case. He offered to show it to me, but I told him to leave it locked up; all I knew about guns was how to point one and pull the trigger.

We both agreed that Saturday night would be best, better than Friday just after Doris and I had left town. And that was all there was to talk about, so we drank and listened to records for a while. I left first this time and Charlie stayed behind to straighten up the pad.

And that was Wednesday.

The eleven-thirty broadcast went as smoothly as the first time, and I put myself in solid with Andrews by suggesting we have lunch together. And, during lunch, making a suggestion that he thought was excellent. I suggested that we move the permanent-prop front seats out a few feet from the wall and put mock-up back seats behind them so we could display the whole set of seat covers in each case. My spiels stressed that the price quoted was not just for what the customer saw but for a whole set—but wouldn't it be better for the customer to *see* all that he was getting for his money instead of having to tell him? It made sense to Andrews and he said he'd take it up with Seaton that very afternoon.

I pointed out that not having to stress that point in every spiel would let me say more, besides just giving the addresses, about Seaton's two branches, in Van Nuys and Alhambra.

Anyway, it got me a free lunch.

I took a bus out to Santa Monica and got to Rinky Dink's well ahead of time so there wouldn't be any chance of Doris's being embarrassed by getting there first.

I nursed a highball at the bar until she came, as beautiful as ever, at four o'clock on the head. We took a back booth with plenty of privacy since none of the other booths was occupied at that time of day.

I asked her the questions fast and got fast answers. The housekeeper usually retired at nine and was, as far as Doris knew, a sound sleeper. So was her husband, although he sometimes read half an hour or so in bed before putting out the light. But he could be counted on to be snoring within ten minutes after the light went out. Yes, he snored, not loudly but invariably and continuously. That was good, I thought; Charlie would be able to tell by listening outside the bedroom door whether Seaton was asleep or not.

Yes, the back door was kept bolted at night; she was sorry she'd forgotten to tell me that. And she hadn't thought the gardener would matter since he came only by day, Tuesday and Wednesday each week, and never came into the house.

No, John probably wouldn't go out Saturday night. Being alone, he'd be more likely to turn in earlier than usual. She couldn't guarantee this, of course, and thought that he might have tomcatted a time or two when they'd had extended quarrels, but now that she was doing the loving wife bit and keeping him happy, she was almost sure that he wouldn't take advantage of her being away to stray off the reservation.

We made two more Doll House phone dates. She was sure she'd be off, driving to El Centro by one o'clock tomorrow afternoon but she'd phone me at The Doll House—long distance if necessary—from wherever she was at two o'clock, so I'd be *sure* she was safely en route and that no wheel had come off her car or her plans.

And I'd resume my Doll House vigils between two and two-thirty as of next Wednesday, which would be the earliest it would possibly be safe and politic for her to call me; she'd no doubt be called back from El Centro on Sunday after the housekeeper found Seaton's body. And Monday and Tuesday would be busy with police investigations and funeral arrangements and appointing someone, probably Andrews, to carry on the business. Probably even Wednesday would be too soon for us to take a chance of actually seeing each other, but she'd try her best to call me at least, and would do it Thursday if Wednesday turned out to be too difficult.

I told her to stay calm if they threw my name at her—as they would as soon as the private detective, Weston, read of the killing and went to the police with his story. She could admit that we'd had an affair, up to the point where we broke it off—the night I'd talked her into going back to her husband. She hadn't seen or been in touch with me since. And if they asked her whether she was going to see me again, she could say maybe, why not, now that she was a widow?

We left and I walked with her to where she'd parked the MG and saw her off in it, the last time I'd see her as a married woman.

I saw Charlie again at Maxine's pad and passed on to him the additional information I'd got from Doris. He was pleased with it and promised me that he'd have no more trouble with

Seaton than I'd had with Radic. We agreed that this would be our last meeting at Maxine's pad. I'd have to see Charlie again only if anything went wrong with my plans or Doris's. In that case I'd simply look him up at the Zoo late tomorrow afternoon or early evening. He'd make a point of being in his room between four and seven, in case I had to get in touch with him. If he hadn't heard from me by seven he'd know I was boarding the plane for Phoenix and that Doris was safely in El Centro, or at least en route there.

Again we had a few drinks and played a few records. With our final drink we toasted each other solemnly and if either of us had the thought that things had been going *too* smoothly, neither of us said it. Why shouldn't they keep on going as smoothly as they had been?

And that was Thursday and the next day was Friday and things were going like clockwork. I made the scene at the studio at ten on the head and started studying my new scripts.

Andrews showed at eleven and told me Seaton wanted me to phone him, either before the broadcast or right after. I wondered what he wanted, and decided to call before the broadcast instead of after. Andrews told me the number and I dialed it and got Seaton.

"Mr. Griff, you're doing fine," he said. "If you're interested in picking up a little extra money, would you like to have lunch with me today?"

My first thought was that I had to be at The Doll House at two for my call from Doris. I said, "I'd like to, Mr. Seaton, but it would have to be an early lunch. I have an early afternoon appointment."

"Would twelve-thirty at the Wilshire Brown Derby be all right? I can phone a reservation so we'll get served right away."

"That'll be fine," I said. "My appointment isn't till two o'clock and I can make it easy."

I went through the broadcast wondering what it was all about. Was he going to give me two of his programs instead of one? Two hundred bucks a week? If so I was damn near tempted to call Charlie's end of the bargain off. I could still see Doris once in a while, if we were extra careful.

I took a taxi to the Derby and got there ahead of him, and was halfway through a drink at the bar when he came.

I downed the rest of the drink and we took the booth he'd reserved for us.

He got right down to business even before the drinks we ordered came. "Would it upset your plans to go out of town over the weekend?"

I didn't get just what he meant at first. My plans *were* to go out of town over the weekend, on that seven o'clock plane to Phoenix. But I didn't want to say I'd planned a trip anyway; he might get a sudden suspicion that, wherever I told him I was going, it might really be to El Centro for a rendezvous with Doris. I didn't want to put any such thought in his mind.

"Go out of town where?" I asked. "And to do what?"

Our drinks were coming and he waited till they'd been put down. Then he said, "To San Diego, to do a few commercials there. I'm opening up a San Diego branch, starting Monday. And I'll be sponsoring one program there regularly, starting then. I've got an announcer lined up for that show, one who lives in San Diego and handles other programs there. I'm sure you wouldn't have wanted that job; it's too far to commute and it would take you away from Hollywood and your acting career."

"It wouldn't be possible," I said.

"Of course not. But what I have in mind would be, if you're interested. With the branch opening Monday I'm kicking it off by buying six minutes of good time Saturday afternoon and another six Sunday afternoon. Both between four and four-thirty in the afternoon. I consider them especially important and I wonder if you'd care to go down and make them. I want an especially good job and I'll pay thirty-five apiece for them, plus your expenses for the trip. How does it sound?"

"It sounds fine," I said. It did; it gave me a much better reason for being out of town Saturday night than my hypothetical hypertension. It was solid, and he was doing it for me.

But I didn't want to sound too eager so I asked, "But isn't it more expensive for you than having the announcer who'll handle your regular program take care of it?"

"Yes, but I'm paying plenty for that time and don't want to take a chance with it. I've never auditioned the guy—his name is Bill Krebs, by the way—so I don't know how good he is. Besides, there's another reason. I like your style and delivery

—it's just the right shade between being casual and being too sincere, and I want him to catch both broadcasts, either at the studio or on his set at home, and study the way you handle it so he can try to do it the same way. Is it a deal?"

"It's a deal," I said. "I think I'll fly down this afternoon, though, instead of tomorrow morning. Give me a chance to see the town. But that's on me; I'll bill you for only one night at the hotel. I'll fly back Sunday evening."

"An extra night won't break me. Know what hotel you'll be at? So I can reach you if necessary?"

"I haven't been to San Diego since I was a kid," I told him. "I don't remember much about it."

"The Metropolitan's where I stay when I go there. Soon as I get back to the office I'll have my secretary phone and make a reservation for you for tonight and tomorrow night. They'll bill me. Got enough cash for your plane fare and other expenses?"

I told him I had. He wrote down for me the name of the branch manager, Harry J. Wilkins, and the phone number of the new branch. He said Wilkins would probably be working at the store Saturday morning, getting ready to open; if not, his home phone number would be in the book. He'd phone Wilkins meanwhile and have him prepared to meet me and take me to the studio. And Wilkins already had the scripts; I could get them as far ahead of broadcast time as I wanted them.

That seemed to take care of everything except eating, so we ate.

We talked over coffee and suddenly I saw that it was one thirty-five and realized I had to get going fast to make The Doll House by two. I tried to leave money for the bill, which hadn't come yet, but Seaton wouldn't let me, so I excused myself and scrammed.

I could have probably made it in time by walking fast, but I wasted five minutes trying to get a taxi before I started walking. I found one at a stand in front of a hotel a block down Wilshire, but we got hung up in heavy traffic and missed out on every stop light, and it was ten after two when I reached The Doll House.

The bartender knew me by now and came over when I took a stool at the bar. "There was a call for you, Mr. Griff, at two o'clock, just a few minutes ago. A lady, she said you'd know who it was."

"Sure," I said. "Did she say she'd call back?"

"No, it was long distance and she just left a message for you. Said to tell you she'd got off early and was at Indio already, on her way."

I thanked him and ordered a drink. I was sorry I'd missed the call; it would have been nice to yak with Doris a few minutes. But the message was enough; she was safely on her way and at least two-thirds of the way. She'd be in El Centro by four or five o'clock.

I went around to my pet travel agency and made the cat there unhappy by again canceling my reservation for Phoenix. But I made him happy by booking the next available flight for San Diego and this time letting him write up the ticket and paying for it. The flight left the International Airport at ten minutes after four. I had plenty of time to go home and pack and catch a cab to the airport.

I knocked on Charlie's door twice, once before I did my packing and once after, but he wasn't home. It didn't matter except that if I could have reached him it would have saved him from having to wait in his room between four and seven for possible word from me that a wheel had come off my plans or Doris's. I considered leaving a note but decided against it. He'd just have to wait and when seven o'clock came he'd know Doris was safely off and know, or think, that I was boarding the plane to Phoenix. It couldn't matter to him where I really was.

A taxi got me to the airport in plenty of time and while I was waiting for the plane to be called I remembered to phone Lennie and tell him about the deal I'd made with Seaton. I'd done it over his head but he'd still be handling the money and getting his cut and I knew he wouldn't mind.

He was pleased. "Wonderful, sweetie. This Seaton character really goes for you. Or do you know where the body's buried or something?"

I could have made a crack about that, but I didn't.

Chapter Fifteen

IT WAS half past six when I checked in the Metropolitan, which turned out to be a rather small hotel, but a nice one. They must have known that my native habitat was underground because they gave me a basement room. But it was a pleasant enough room and had everything a hotel room should have, except a woman.

But this was my weekend for not picking up any women. They might get entangled in my alibi and the fact that I'd been with one just might come out. And I knew just how Doris would take that and didn't want to take any chances.

It occurred to me that I just might want my alibi solid for this evening in case Charlie should change his mind for some reason and do the job tonight instead of waiting till tomorrow. After all, one can drive from San Diego to Los Angeles in a few hours; the fact that I'd checked in my hotel at six-thirty wouldn't give me a solid alibi if I wasn't seen again till tomorrow morning.

So I stayed in my room only long enough to shave and shower and then went up to the hotel dining room and ate, proving my presence there by signing the tab against my hotel bill instead of paying cash. I decided to find out if I could do the same thing at the hotel bar; it would be helpful. If I had drinks there late in the evening and signed for them, giving the bartender a decent tip besides, he'd remember me and be able to vouch for my presence there.

I figured I might as well phone the branch manager and report in, make a date when and where tomorrow to see him and pick up the commercial scripts. I found his home phone and got him there.

He sounded cordial and said he was having a little party at his place and why didn't I come around and join them for a drink? He'd brought the scripts home with him to do a little editing on them, which he'd done, and I could take them with me so tomorrow we wouldn't have to see each other until he met me at the studio half an hour before the broadcast.

I took a cab around. The party turned out to be a poker party and at reasonable stakes. I watched awhile until someone —a guy who worked a night shift and had to be on duty at ten —left the game and I sat in. We played until a little after midnight and I proved my luck was still running high by coming out almost thirty bucks ahead.

It was running even higher when the heavy loser—he was Bill Krebs, the guy who'd be handling the regular week-day programs starting Monday—announced that he wanted his money back and was going to have a game at his place tomorrow, Saturday evening at nine, and everybody was invited, especially the winners.

So I had my alibi for tomorrow night solid and ready-made, without having to worry about anything as tenuous as a bartender remembering me.

Krebs had a bachelor apartment downtown and drove me back to my hotel. It wasn't quite one o'clock and I talked him into stopping in the hotel bar for a nightcap. He gave me his address and told me how to get to the place, only a three-block walk from the hotel. He'd been briefed to catch my two commercials so he could see how Seaton wanted them handled. He said he wouldn't come to the studio, though; he had the day off otherwise and would catch the program on his set at home.

I was tired and wanted a good night's sleep; it had been a big day. So I left a ten-o'clock call at the desk and went to my room and to bed.

My telephone waked me and told me that it was ten o'clock. It was *the* day, and I felt fine. Morning, when I've had a good night's sleep, is my best time for memorizing, so I memorized my scripts for the afternoon commercials as soon as I dressed and before I went upstairs to the hotel restaurant.

I wandered around downtown and then caught a movie. I killed a little more time and took a taxi to the studio. Wilkins showed up a few minutes later and gave me a last-minute price change on one of the seat-cover sets, which he said Seaton had just phoned to him. He said he was busy as hell getting ready for the Monday opening so he wouldn't wait for the broadcast, but would catch the commercials on a set at the store.

I spent the last half hour restudying the scripts, and the commercials went smoothly, even more so than my Los Angeles ones had gone.

Before I got away there was a call for me; it turned out to be from Bill Krebs. He'd seen the show and congratulated me on the way I'd handled the commercials and said he was pretty sure now just what Seaton wanted and he thought he could do it, starting Monday. He wanted to know if I'd have dinner with him at seven at a restaurant he named and said we could go from there right to his place for the poker game. I decided I could wait that long to eat and told him it sounded like a winner.

I took a cab back to town and saw another movie. It turned out to be a lousy one, but it killed the time.

I found the restaurant and Bill and I ate and then went up to his place, a nice bachelor apartment like the one I was going to have for myself in Hollywood starting pretty damn soon. I was feeling solvent enough to regret that I'd paid Mrs. Whelan two weeks in advance, but I could ride out the Zoo that long.

Whether Seaton survived tonight or not, I was on my way up. One way or another. But it was going to be the other; Charlie wouldn't chicken out now.

We talked shop talk—Bill had never tried acting but had made a stab at doing commercials in Los Angeles for a while and had then decided he could do better on his own home ground—for a while and the others, including Wilkins, started to show up. When there were five of us at nine o'clock we started playing. I thought that just about now Charlie would be making his preparations, maybe driving past the place for a preliminary look to see when the housekeeper's bedroom light went on and off and when Seaton's bedroom light would go on.

Two others showed up in the next hour and we had a full seven players by ten. My luck was still in; I won the first pot and stayed ahead. I'd come to like Bill, though, and was glad to see that he was winning too. He deserved it, for the beautiful alibi setup he was giving me.

I stayed ahead, if not much at times, and I'd have gladly been willing to play all night, but the game started to break up about twelve-thirty. But Bill asked me to stay for a final drink and a little more yak and I managed to stretch my stay till one o'clock by being the last to leave. He was starting to yawn then and I couldn't stretch it any further, but one o'clock should be plenty safe. How solid an alibi did I want?

I walked back to the hotel, again left a ten o'clock call at the desk and went to my room.

I'd just hung up my suit coat when my telephone rang.

I stared at it blankly for a moment and then realized what it must be. Only Seaton, Wilkins, and Krebs knew where I was, and only Wilkins or Krebs, most likely Wilkins, would be calling me at this hour and then only if Charlie had done the job early and he himself had just had a call from Los Angeles.

I picked up the phone and said "Hello" into it.

It wasn't Wilkins's voice that answered, nor Krebs's.

Seaton's voice said, "This is Seaton, Mr. Griff. I'm sorry if I woke you up, but—"

"I just got in," I managed to say. "You didn't wake me. Are you calling from Los Angeles?"

Had something gone wrong?

He chuckled. "No, from upstairs in the same hotel. I got a sudden impulse about nine o'clock to be here for the grand opening and I wasn't sleepy so I drove down. Just got in."

"Fine," I said, and I suddenly realized that I meant it. Charlie had missed and the deal was off. I wasn't going to set up another alibi. I had my start now with a steady job and Seaton was happy with me, and he'd turned out to be a nice guy after all. I didn't need Doris's money. With the start I had and with an acting job coming up for me next week—and Lennie wouldn't have mentioned it unless he was sure of it—I was on my way, on my own. The bad days were over.

"Since you're still awake," Seaton was saying, "would you like to drop up for a nightcap? The bar's closed, but I've got a bottle here. Doris is here, too."

"Doris?" It wasn't a very intelligent remark but things were changing too fast for me.

"Yes, I phoned her from Santa Monica before I left and asked her to join me here. Her drive was shorter so she got here first and took a room. I took the connecting one when I signed in a few minutes ago. Can you drop up a minute? My room number is two-one-six."

"Sure," I said. "I'll be right there."

I put my suit coat back on, checked myself in the mirror to see that I didn't show the ravages of a poker game and decided I was all right.

I climbed two flights of stairs and knocked on the door of 216. Seaton let me in, and he seemed bouncy and more cheerful than I'd ever seen him. "Sit down," he said. "I'll make us drinks. Bourbon with ginger ale? Or with water?" I told him water.

I sat on the sofa and looked around for Doris. He nodded toward a door and, with my attention directed, I could hear water running behind it. "Our rooms connect through a bath," he said. "She's taking a shower. She'll put on a robe after and come out to join us."

"Fine," I said. "Don't make my drink too strong. I've been playing poker with your branch manager and with Bill Krebs, and I've had some already." He was my boss now, in a way, and I didn't want him to think I drank too much.

"I know," he said. "I phoned Wilkins just before I phoned you and he'd just got home from the game. That's why I figured I probably wouldn't wake you when I phoned."

He was making drinks back at a table against one wall and came over with two glasses and handed me one.

Just then there was a knock at the door.

He went to open it and there was a sound like *phutt* and he stood with both hands against his middle and started screaming.

And oh my God, my God, Charlie had seen him leave and followed him down, since tonight was the night I'd be alibied in Phoenix.

And Charlie, panicked because Seaton hadn't gone down but was screaming, came into the room kicking the door shut behind him. I yelled at him—I don't know what or why—but he didn't hear me over Seaton's screaming, and shot again. And since a homemade silencer is good for only one shot unless it's repacked, it was a full-scale bang this time that sounded like a cannon going off. And Seaton screamed louder and still didn't go down and Charlie shot a third time and it sounded like the atom bomb.

This time Seaton went down, with a thud that shook the hotel.

Charlie whirled to run out the door and then saw me and his jaw dropped.

And the door of the connecting bath burst open and Doris, dripping wet and naked except for a towel held in front of her, burst out. She saw me, and then Charlie, and then Seaton dead or dying on the floor, and she dropped the towel and started having hysterics. Loud hysterics. And over them there were voices in the hallway and knocking at the door and somebody yelling to somebody else to call the police for God's sake quickly and . . .

And somebody was suddenly laughing; I think it was a guy named Willy Griff, who one minute ago had been on his way to being an actor.

And because there wasn't anything else to do, that's the way we waited till the fuzz came.

THE NAME OF THE GAME IS DEATH

Dan J. Marlowe

I

FROM THE back seat of the Olds I could see the kid's cotton gloves flash white on the steering wheel as he swung off Van Buren onto Central Avenue. On the right up ahead the strong late September Phoenix sunshine blazed off the bank's white stone front till it hurt the eyes. The damn building looked as big as the purple buttes on the rim of the desert.

Beside me Bunny chewed gum rhythmically, his hands relaxed in his lap. Up front, in three-quarter profile the kid's face was like chalk, but he teamed the car perfectly into a tight-fitting space right in front of the bank.

Nobody said a word. I climbed out on the sidewalk side, and Bunny got out opposite and walked around the rear to join me. His dark glasses and bright yellow hair glinted in the sun. The thick, livid scar across his throat was nearly hidden in his week-old beard. Across the street the big clock said five minutes to three. Under it on another dial a long thermometer needle rested on ninety-four. A shirt-sleeved man stood idly beneath the clock.

We crossed the sidewalk and passed through the bank's outer glass doors. I'm five ten, but Bunny towered over me six inches. I could see the rolled-up canvas sack under his arm. In the vestibule the air conditioning bit hard at the sweat on my face and arms. Bunny led the way through into the main floor lobby. He went left. I went right. Two guards on the main floor.

I found my guard showing an old man how to fill out a deposit slip. I moved in behind the guard, and when I saw Bunny's arm go up across the way I slammed the red-creased neck in front of me with a solid chunk of Smith & Wesson. He went down without a sound. The old man kept right on writing. I heard a choked gurgle from Bunny's guard. That was all.

I took my first good look around while I switched to the Colt Woodsman. If we hadn't gotten those two, we were nowhere. A dozen to fifteen customers, scattered. I fired the Woodsman three times, taking out glass high in the tellers' cages each time. Shattering glass is an impressive sound. In the echoing lobby the glass and the little Woodsman sounded like a turret of sixteen-inchers in a china closet.

"All right, everybody," I said, loud and clear. "Everybody stand still and nobody gets hurt."

Nobody moved. Nobody breathed. Bunny vaulted the low gate up in front. I jammed the Woodsman back in my pants, and balanced the Smith & Wesson again in my palm. If somebody fast-pitched us, I might need the three heavier caliber bullets I'd saved by directing traffic with the Woodsman.

Inside the railing with Bunny, two big-assed women huddled together against the door leading into the cages, empty trays in their hands. Right where they should have been at two minutes to three. Bunny motioned with his gun at the cage door. They stared at him, cow-eyed. Inside the cages there wasn't a sound. Bunny whipped the flat of his automatic up against the jawline of the nearer woman. She fell over sideways, mewling. Someone inside opened the door. Bunny stepped in quickly, herding everyone to the rear. He began yanking out cash drawers. Bundles of hundreds and twenties went into the sack. Everything else went to the floor.

The only thing I could hear was the whimpering of the woman on the floor and the clatter and bang as Bunny emptied and dumped drawers. On my left something moved. I turned, and the movement stopped. Dead ahead on the balcony overhead I caught a rapid blur of gray. I belted the guard over backward with the first shot I banged up there. Bunny never even turned his head.

Two minutes, I'd figured, after we took out the first guards. Two and a half, tops. All over town now bells would be ringing, but in sixty seconds we'd be gone. I did a slow turn, eyes skimming the balcony and the main floor. Nothing.

Bunny burst out the cage door, hugging the sack to his big chest. He jumped the railing, landing on his toes. I fell in six feet behind him, and we went out through the vestibule at a fast walk. Bunny had just reached out to open the right hand outer glass door when there was a sharp crack-crack-crack from behind us. The best part of the door blew right out onto the sidewalk. Heat rolled in through the splintered glass in an arid wave.

Bunny unhunched his neck and started again for the Olds. Out on the sidewalk I whirled and took down the remaining half of the door. One high and one low. It made a hell of a noise. Anyone coming through that vestibule in a hurry should have thought again about his hurry with a square yard of glass in his hair.

When I turned I caught a flash of the shirt-sleeved man under the clock across the street running into a store. I headed for the car. I nearly yelled out loud when I saw the kid had panicked. All the way to St. Louis we'd gone for a driver, and now he'd panicked. Instead of staying under the wheel and drawing no attention to the car, he'd jumped out and run around and opened the doors on our side. His face was like wet cottage cheese.

Bunny went through the front door in a sliding skid. The kid took one look at my face and started to run back around the front of the Olds. Across the street something went ker-blam!! The kid whinnied like a horse with the colic. He ran in a circle for three seconds and then fell down in front of the Olds, his white cotton gloves in the dirty street and his legs still on the sidewalk. The left side of his head was gone.

Bunny dropped the sack and scrambled for the wheel. I was halfway into the back seat when I heard the car stall out as he tried to give it gas too fast. It was quite a feeling. I backed out again and faced the bank, tried to have eyes in the back of my head for the unseen shotgunner across the street, and listened to Bunny mash down on the starter. The motor caught, finally. I breathed again, but a fat guard galloped out the bank's front doors, his gun hand high over his head. He got it down in a hurry.

I swear both his feet were off the ground when he fired at me. The odds must have been sixty thousand to one, but he took me in the left upper arm. It smashed me back against the car. I steadied myself with a hand on the roof and put two a yard behind each other right through his belt buckle. If they had their windows open they could have heard him across town.

I stumbled into the back seat and Bunny took it out of there. The Olds bumped hard twice as it went over the kid. Across the street I could see the shirt-sleeved man pumping frantically at his jammed shotgun. I raised the Smith & Wesson, and lowered it again. I still needed every bullet. I couldn't afford any luxuries. I got the car doors closed within half a block.

"Handkerchiefs!" I yelled at Bunny as we flew up Central and spun east on Roosevelt on the red. "Ditch those glasses. Slow it down. Stay in traffic." Without looking back he tossed two handkerchiefs over his shoulder, snatched off the dark glasses, and grabbed up a blue beret from the seat beside him. He crammed it down on his yellow head. With the glasses off and his hair hidden he looked like a different person.

I wadded up his handkerchiefs with my own and tried to staunch the double-ended leak in my left arm just below the short sleeve of the sport shirt. I accomplished exactly nothing. All that stuff about a bullet's initial impact being shock with no pain; that's horse manure. I felt it going in and I felt it coming out. Like a red-hot saw-tooth file.

I reloaded the Smith & Wesson. I ignored the warm molasses running down my arm, except to keep it from dripping on my pants. I watched the lights. The kid had had the lights timed all the way back to Yavapai Terrace, but we didn't have the kid. I couldn't sit still. I wanted to get back south of Van Buren again so bad I could taste it.

They had to figure us for a main highway. Highway 80 East, to Tucson and Nogales, if they'd seen the right turn on Roosevelt. North to Prescott or Wickenburg, if they hadn't. Even west, to Yuma and the coast. There'd be road blocks up by now on every main artery out of town. We weren't going out of town. Not yet.

We'd passed Seventh Street while I was fooling with the useless handkerchiefs, Twelfth while I was reloading. The first red light caught us at Sixteenth. We sat in tense silence with people in cars all around us. My guts shriveled down to pebble size. I opened my mouth to holler at Bunny to make a run for it, and closed my teeth down hard. So far we hadn't even heard a siren.

In motion again we sailed up to Twentieth and turned south. We were back across Van Buren before I even had time to begin holding my breath. Past Adams and Washington, over the tracks to East Henshaw, and back toward town at the light.

Up to Twelfth in the double-back, a left, and then a right. Shimmering in the sun under a eucalyptus tree, the black Ford sat ahead of us on Yavapai Terrace, close enough to a Chinese grocery to assure that kids wouldn't bother it. Bunny pulled in behind it. We might have been three miles from the bank, but I knew we weren't four.

"Get something out of your bag for this arm," I told Bunny. He was out of the Olds before I had the words all the way out of my mouth, over to the Ford, and back again. He had the jacket to my lightweight suit, and a shirt. "Shred it and fold it and tie it around this thing. Tight." Heat and dust and nausea filled my throat as he complied. I choked it down, whacked some of the dried blood crust from my arm, and slung the jacket loosely over my left shoulder to hide the crude bandage.

After glancing up and down the deserted street, I slid out and followed Bunny back to the Ford. I watched the two-handed carry he made with the sack, and for the first time I wondered how much was in it. In a fifty-pound sack with twenty-five per cent hundreds and the rest twenties, a man can walk away with two hundred thousand dollars. If he walks away.

The Olds we'd leave right here. Bunny pulled ahead to get clear, then backed out onto Twelfth again. He headed south, slowly. The street names were Indian—Papago, Pima, Cocopa, Mohave, Apache—but the area was Mexican. The bushy shade trees were stunted and gnarled. The houses were small, sun-blistered, shacky and close together. The front yards were overgrown tangles. Bunny nosed the Ford into Durango Street, and parked across the street from the dark blue Dodge sedan in the middle of the block.

I drew a long breath as he pulled up the brake. "Okay," I said. "New script. Listen close. I'm grounded. We're not going to the cabin in the canyon." With the kid gone and me with a torn-up arm we had to throw away the book. I rummaged in the sack at my feet. The first three bundles I picked up were hundreds. Fifteen thousand dollars right in my hand. I dropped two of them back, found two packages of twenties, and shoved the three into a jacket pocket.

"We split up here, big man. You take the Dodge. Duck into a cheap motel. Don't forget to wash the yellow dye out of your hair. Day after tomorrow after dark pull out and head east. Stay off Highways 80 and 66. Go back on 70. Roswell, Plainview . . . that way."

I tried to think of it all. "Take the sack. At Memphis head south, for Florida. The gulf coast. Pick a small town. When you make it, once a week mail me a thousand in hundreds, not new bills, registered mail. To Roy Martin, General Delivery, Main Post Office, Phoenix, Arizona. Got it? Take off. I'll join you the minute I can travel."

Bunny got out of the Ford and walked around it and opened the door on my side. His big, hard face was solemn. We shook hands, and he picked up the sack and crossed the drowsy street to the Dodge, his shoes making little puffs in the inch-thick dust. There was a layer of it on the Dodge from passing cars. Bunny opened the back deck, rolled in the sack, and slammed down the lid. With his hand on the door handle he looked over at me and waved before he got in and drove off. Just before he reached the corner I remembered the rest of my clothes were in the Dodge. I reached for the horn, and pulled my hand back. I had more immediate problems than clothes.

I sat there with kind of an all-gone feeling. All the adrenalin-charged-up excitement had drained away. My mind chugged busily, but the rest of me was numb.

Letting the sack go with Bunny hadn't been in the blueprint, but it was the best place for it now. I had some scrambling to do, and the first rule of the game is don't get caught with it on you. If they have to sweet-talk you to try to find out where it is, twenty-to-life has a way of coming out seven-to-ten. If only so they can follow you when you hit the street again. Although on this little frolic, plank-walking the guards could have made everything else academic, if they'd done the big somersault. That one on the sidewalk—

Clean away, except for the hole in my arm. And except for the silly bastard kid. If he'd stayed with the car, I wouldn't be sitting here improvising on an iron-clad plan. Yeah, and if wishes were horses, beggars would ride.

I roused myself, with an effort. I had a lot to do. I had a doctor to find. A doctor would be trouble, but I'd cross that bridge when I came to it. I slid over under the wheel and started up the Ford, and then I had a real bad moment. Bunny's strength pulling up the hand-brake was almost too much for my weakened left arm. Salt perspiration stung my eyes fiercely before I finally succeeded in backing it off. The shirt-bandage was sopping.

Turning the first corner, the sun through the windshield nearly seared my eyeballs. The first two signs I slowed down for in front yards were a realtor and a plumber. The third one drew down the money. Santiago E. Sanfilippo, M.D. I drove by slowly. A garage connected with the house. There was no car in the garage, none in front of the house.

I had no time for anything fancy. I drove up the driveway and into the garage. I draped the jacket over my left shoulder again and walked up the enclosed passageway that led into the house. Through a glass panel in the door I could see an office inside. I had to knock twice before a man in white ducks and a white jacket with a stethoscope sticking out of a pocket opened the door.

Dr. Sanfilippo was a tall, thin, young-looking job, coffee-colored, black-eyed, and good looking. He had a misplaced-eyebrow type of mustache. From the look he gave me I wasn't exactly what he'd been expecting to see. "Yes?" he demanded impatiently when I out-waited him. I couldn't see or hear anyone in the office behind him. "This is a private entrance." He looked over my shoulder at the Ford. "Is that your car? What do you mean by driving it into my garage?"

"I'm a patient, Doc," I told him.

"Then go around to the patients' entrance," he snapped. "And get that automobile out of there before you do."

"Let's arbitrate it, Doc." I showed him the Smith & Wesson about ten inches from his belly. He backed up in a straight line until he ran into a desk behind him. I stepped inside and closed the door. "You alone?"

"I'm alone," he admitted. He looked unhappy about it. "I keep no drugs on the premises," he added. His English was better than mine.

"Inside, Doc." I motioned with the gun and followed him from the cluttered office into a small examination room with whitewashed walls and a wash basin in one corner. Both room and basin looked fairly clean. There was a phone in the office, but none in the examination room. There was only one door, and I was between him and it. A framed diploma hung on the near wall, and I stepped up and read it. It looked legitimate, and I sat down on a white stool beside the elevated examination table. I wanted no self-appointed abortionist whittling on my arm.

Dr. Sanfilippo had been watching me warily. I removed the jacket from my shoulder, and his mustachioed upper lip tightened when he saw the shredded, sodden shirt around my arm. "*Madre de Dios!*" he breathed. His black eyes flicked from a battered radio on a green cabinet back to my arm. "You know I'll have to report this," he said huskily.

"Sure you will," I soothed him. "But you're a doctor. First you'll dress it." I held out the arm. "Like right now."

His smooth, trim features still expressed shock. "Those bank guards—" he began, and stopped. He swallowed, hard. His face was suddenly damp.

"The arm, Doc," I reminded him. So the guards had died. Without ever knowing it, Santiago E. Sanfilippo, M.D., had just passed over an invisible line.

He washed his hands in the basin, and after drying them, unwrapped the arm and examined it, front and back. "Large caliber," he said professionally.

"Large," I agreed.

He turned to the green cabinet. "A half an ampule—"

"No anesthetic," I cut him off.

He shrugged. It was my funeral, and for him it couldn't happen soon enough. He was getting his confidence back. He felt superior to the sweaty, gun-holding type sitting in his office with a ragged bloody hole in his arm. Next he'd be planning my capture. I had a feeling this boy was going to make it easy for me.

He laid out a tray of sharp-looking things on the table, and I spread a towel in my lap. He bathed, swabbed, probed, disinfected, and bandaged. He was rougher than he needed to be. "Don't move until I put a sling on it," he said brusquely when he finished.

"No sling," I said. I picked up the dry end of the towel and mopped off my face. I reached in my jacket pocket where it was slung over my knees, and took out the wrapped package of fifty one-hundred-dollar bills. I broke the seal and put it in my pocket, counted out fifteen bills in three little piles of five each on the examination table, and pushed them toward him. "Nice job, Doc."

That changed his expression *tout de suite*. His tongue ran over his lips, his black eyes never leaving the money. He reached out almost tentatively and picked it up, riffled it nervously, then stuffed it into a wallet and the wallet into his pocket again.

I stood up and kicked the stool I'd been sitting on in his direction. "Sit, Doc. Real still." At the basin where he'd washed up I looked in the small mirror at my short black hair and tanned hard face. I laid the gun on the edge of the basin. I ran the water, and found a clean towel. Stooped over, I could watch his feet. If he could get to me before I got to the gun, he was a better man than I thought. One-handed I washed the oil and lampblack from my hair, and the suntan lotion from my face and neck. When I emerged from behind the towel, Sanfilippo stared in rank disbelief at skin a nationality lighter and iron-gray hair a generation older. "You—you're an old man!" he blurted, incredulously.

"Forty-four, Doc." I patted my crewcut. "The snow on the mountain? Just all the years of taking in washing." His mouth hung open. I looked him over. Thin as he was, I knew I couldn't carry him out of the office. "Walk out to the car ahead of me," I told him. "I'm going to tie you and leave you in the garage."

He didn't like it. He thought it over. I could have predicted the instant he brightened. Would I have paid him if I were going to kill him? Certainly not. The stupid bastard never stopped to realize that if I'd been going to leave him around to do any broadcasting, he'd never have seen me out of the war paint. Following him from the examination room, I picked up something from his surgical tray with a bone handle and six inches of steel. I stuck it in my belt.

In the passageway I got out the Woodsman and put it under my armpit, where I could get to it in a hurry. At the car Sanfilippo turned and looked at me expectantly. I kept a careful ten feet away from him. "Think—something's wrong—" I mumbled, weaving on my feet. I did a long, slow pinwheel to the ground, staying off the bad side. From beneath nearly closed lids I could see Sanfilippo's startled look as he stared down at me. My right hand was close enough to the Woodsman's grip to stop his clock if he came after me, or if he tried to run out of the garage. I didn't expect him to do either. I'd tabbed this guy as a weisenheimer, and I was just egotistical enough to want to make him prove himself out.

He took a final look at me, and spun around to the Ford. He flung open the rear door, and I could hear him pawing through the back seat. He left that in a hurry and tried the front. He ripped out something in Spanish, and darted around to the rear. I'd paid him in hundreds. The swag had to be in the car.

He wasn't bad, the doc. I couldn't see what he used—all I could see were his legs under the Ford—but he popped that back deck lid in no time. I heard the whaaang of broken metal as he snapped the locks on my tool chests in the trunk and went through my stuff like an Indian husking an ear of corn. He sounded off again under his breath, and came around the car on the trot. He dived into the back seat again, only his legs outside.

I eased myself to my feet and got over there. Sanfilippo had a knife out, and was slashing away at the seat cushion. He was right down to the springs in a couple of places. I pulled the surgical tool from my belt. He whacked away at the cushion, cursing like a madman, and then all of a sudden my presence got through to him. He started to turn, and I gave him four and a half inches between the second and third ribs. He was looking over his shoulder at me, and the black eyes didn't believe it. I pulled it out and gave it to him again, then grabbed his belt and steered him down outside the car. He went down like a deflated balloon, slowly at first and then with a rush.

His own knife was still in his hand. I left the steel in him after wiping the handle. I reached down again and yanked his wallet from his hip pocket, stripped it, wiped it, and threw it down beside the body. It would be open and shut to any investigator: killed while pursuing a thief from his office. And, for a bonus, no bullets in him to be matched up with what they took out of the bank guards.

I backed the Ford out of there and drove up to Nineteenth and Van Buren to a big motel, The Tropics. I went in and registered, my jacket again over the bandaged arm. "I'll try your Western hospitality till my office gets me out a new sample line," I told the middle-aged desk clerk. "They busted into my car down in Nogales last night and cleaned me. Clothes, samples, camera—the works. I'll pay you for a week."

The clerk clucked sympathetically as he handed me my change. "Excellent shops within a block or two, sir. Sorry to hear of your misfortune. Hope you enjoy your stay with us."

I took the number 24 key he gave me and ran the car down in front of that unit number. I went inside and locked the door. I washed my face, eased down carefully into an inclined chair with a footrest, and closed my eyes. I had a lot of unwinding to do.

The last conscious thought I had before I drifted off was that those people at the bank were sure going to have one hell of a glass bill.

I lived in that chair for a week, outside of short trips to the on-premises restaurant. Without a sling on the arm I didn't dare get into the big double bed. The first incautious movement would have broken the bullet hole wide open again. With a sling on, I might as well wear a sign "Here I Am." I stayed in the chair.

After the first day I didn't sleep much but I dozed all the time. The next morning I caught a bright-looking busboy in the restaurant, gave him a list of sizes, and sent him out for clothes, specifying long-sleeved sport shirts. He came back with stuff that would have turned a bird of paradise pale with envy. I started to heat up until I happened to think it might be a good switch to have people looking at the clothes instead of at me.

The papers that first morning had a ball. TWO GUARDS SLAIN IN BOLD DAYLIGHT ROBBERY. KILLERS ESCAPE WITH BANK'S $178,000. ONE BANDIT, TWO GUARDS DEAD IN DOWNTOWN SHOOTEMUP.

I looked at that figure of $178,000 a couple of times. Even allowing for the bank's president adding in his personal loan account—which isn't exactly unknown—it was still a nice touch.

The newspapers speculated that one of the escapees might have been wounded. The descriptions were interesting, not to say varied. One eye-witness insisted there'd been five of us. The consensus, though, settled for a husky Swede and a little

Mexican. Like I said, I'm five ten. I go one seventy, but I've noticed before that a really big man doesn't always seem so big himself. He just makes anyone with him look small.

FBI IN CHARGE, the papers blared. The dear old FBI. I hadn't talked to them in sixteen years, and I wasn't planning to in the next sixteen. They'd trace the kid's prints to St. Louis, and between here and there they'd tear everything up, down, and sideways. And a hell of a lot of good it would do them; when he left St. Louis, the kid didn't know where he was going, and either Bunny or I was with him all the time to make sure he didn't talk about who he was going with. It should make for less heat on the west coast of Florida.

Way on an inside page there was a short paragraph. Area Physician Stabbed In Garage, the small-type headline said. The story continued: The body of Santiago E. Sanfilippo, M.D., 31, of—. I read it three times before I put the paper down. The police would be out rounding up all known arm blasters and goofball users. It plugged the last hole the kid had kicked in the blue print by not staying with the car.

I wasn't afraid of Bunny's getting picked up. He had the best natural protective coloration I'd ever seen. It was one of the reasons I'd picked him, that and his nerve and his confidence in me. I've been in this business a while. Two guys with guts and a go-to-hell-with-you-Jack regard for consequences have about three chances in ten of pulling off a big, well-planned smash-and-grab. If one of them can shoot like me and the other one is Bunny, the odds are a damn sight better.

The first week I had a fever nearly all the time. The arm needed treatment, but I couldn't get treatment. I swallowed aspirin by the gross. When the thing wasn't throbbing it was itching. I let it throb and I let it itch. The second week my temperature was gone, but my legs felt like two pieces of spaghetti. I'd wake from a nap dripping with sweat, and have to change from the skin out.

It was lonely in that motel room. Around the country when I hide out I always have a dog and usually a couple of cats with me. Animals I like. People I can do without.

For the first five days the headlines had us as having been sighted in half the towns between Guantánamo, Cuba, and Nome, Alaska. After that we dropped back onto the ninth page, and then right on out of the news. The third week I began to take an interest in a menu again, instead of just shoveling something down. The arm was going to be all right. A couple of times when it had been real bad I'd debated slipping down into Nogales and trying for a doctor. I decided I couldn't risk it. If they didn't watch anyplace else in the world, they'd watch that Mexican border.

About the middle of the third week I drove uptown to the main post office. From its front steps I could have thrown a stone kitty-cornered across the street to the bank we'd taken. I could see they had new glass doors up.

I had a wallet full of crap identifying the non-existent Roy Martin. There were two envelopes at the window, and I signed for them. In the car I slit the first one and unwrapped ten hundred-dollar bills neatly sealed in oil-skinned paper. The second was a duplicate. There was no message in either. The return address said Dick Pierce, General Delivery, Hudson, Florida. Bunny had made it big.

Five days later there was another envelope.

Seven days later there wasn't.

The mail clerk handed me a telegram addressed to Roy Martin. I got away from him fast and opened it. IN TROUBLE STAY PUT DO NOTHING WILL CALL YOU. DICK.

I stared blankly at the recruiting posters on the post office walls. Bunny was in trouble, all right, but not the kind I was supposed to think. The telegram was a clinker. When we'd first teamed up, I'd arranged with Bunny that a message from either of us calling for a change in plans had to be signed "Abie."

But that was nothing compared to the other thing the matter with the telegram. If he lived to be a hundred and four, Bunny would never call me about anything. The knife slash that had left him with the livid throat scar had reached his vocal cords. Bunny was a mute.

Bunny hadn't sent the telegram.

The only person who could have was someone who had intercepted a thousand-dollar envelope for Roy Martin. I looked at the telegram again. It had originated in Hudson, Florida.

I drove back to The Tropics and found Hudson on an atlas. It was a crossroads town south of Perry on U.S. 19 on the way down to Tampa.

I checked out.

The soreness was gone from the shoulder, but it was still stiff. It would have to do. Three-fifty, four hundred miles a day, I figured, without killing myself. Five days.

Knowing Bunny, I was sure of the only way he could have been dealt out of the game.

I had business in Hudson, Florida.

I settled down behind the wheel.

II

THE ONLY time I was ever in the pen, the boss headshrinker gave me up as a bad job. "You're amoral," the prison psychiatrist told me. "You have no respect for authority. Your values are not civilized values." That was after he'd flipped his psychiatric lid at his inability to pierce my defense mechanism, as he called it. I had him tapped from the first sixty seconds. He didn't care what I was; he just wanted to know how I got that way. It was none of his damn business. I gave him nothing but a hard way to go.

Oh, I could have told him things. I could have told him about the kitten. I was maybe eleven or twelve. Fifth or sixth grade. I saw this kitten in the window of a pet shop. A blue Persian, although right then I couldn't have told the difference from a spotted Manx. I ran my finger across the glass and watched her little pink nose and big bronze eyes follow it, and I knew she was for me.

I went back to the house to make my case. I wasn't from any underprivileged home. The kitten's price might have jolted them, but I wasn't in the habit of asking for much. I was the youngest in the family and I had a bushel of sisters and aunts. Getting me the kitten became a family project. The family had also had for some time a project to get me to play more with the neighborhood kids. I'd given up trying to explain to them that the other kids gave me a pain, king-sized.

The sisters and aunts did a lot of yatating before I got the kitten. They always did a lot of yatating. Once—I was fifteen, maybe—eight or nine of them were going it forty to the dozen in the living room. I stuck my head in the door and gave them my very best rebel yell. When they climbed down off the tables and chairs, I told them: "The male of the species gives voice." They didn't think it was funny.

But that was later.

I named the kitten Fatima. First syllable accented, all short vowel sounds. It seemed to suit her coppery eyes and smoky coloring. I played with her by the hour. I taught her tricks.

No one teaches a kitten anything it doesn't want to learn, but Fatima humored me. We had a wonderful time together.

I still got a load of guff frequently from the family about not participating more with my age group. That's probably not the way they put it then; it's not the day before yesterday I'm talking about. I paid no attention to them. I had Fatima, and she was all the company I needed. In some moods she was a natural-born clown, but in others she had an aloof dignity. I'd never have believed that anything so tiny could be so fearless. Fatima would have tackled a lion if one had got in her way.

Some organization in the town gave a pet show. YWCA, Junior League, Woman's Club, American Legion Auxiliary, B.P.O.E. Does—I don't remember which, but I remember women were running it. I bought a little red leash for Fatima out of my paper route money, and entered her in the show. I liked having a paper route. It was something I could do myself, not some group project I was always being pushed to get into with a bunch of moronic kids.

Fatima and her red leash knocked their eyes out at the pet show. She was a real ham. She sat up in the center of the outdoor ring and went through her whole bag of tricks, better than she'd do them for me in private. She went through the kitten and cat classes like a streak of blue lightning, and we were brought back for best-in-show. In the ring for the final judging there was Fatima, a big boxer dog, a black rabbit, a hamster, a goat, and a bowl of tropical fish shaded from the sunlight.

The boxer belonged to a kid who went to the same school I did, a fat tub of lard a grade or so ahead of me. I knew him by sight. If I ever knew his name, I've forgotten it. When I saw the boxer, I steered Fatima around to the other side of the ring. She just plain didn't like dogs. The fat boy saw what I was doing, and he followed me in a smart-alecky way. Fatima swelled her throat ruff and hissed at the boxer in a Persian's surprisingly loud hiss. The fat boy laughed. I asked him to move his dog away. Deliberately he gave him more leash. The boxer leaned down for a closer look, and quicker than I can say it, Fatima raked his nose. The boxer snarled, and snapped. Just once.

Fatima lay in the grass, one tiny little dot of blood on her ruff. Her neck had been broken. The big dog nosed at the inanimate bit of blue-gray fur, then looked up at me as though half-ashamed. I didn't blame the boxer. He'd done the natural thing for any dog. I picked up Fatima's body, and turned blindly away. All I wanted was to get out of there. The fat boy —who first looked scared, and then defiant—grabbed my arm and spun me around. "Look!" he crowed. "Lookit him! Cryin' like a baby!"

I beat the stuffing out of him.

The women got me off him, finally. I was scuffed up and so were they. There was a hell of a lot of gabble-gabble. I walked out on it. I took Fatima home and buried her in the back yard.

That was Saturday. Sunday I hung around the house most of the day. Monday afternoon I waited in the schoolyard for the fat boy to come out, and I beat the stuffing out of him all over again.

That night his father came over to my house. There was a big pow-wow. My family was surprised to learn about Fatima's having been killed. They hadn't even missed her. Finally they settled everything to their satisfaction. The fat boy's father would get me another kitten, and I would apologize to the fat boy.

I told them no. I was nice and polite, but I told them no. When they jumped me for reasons, I told them I didn't want anything from anyone. My father took me upstairs for a talk. I listened, and said nothing. When he saw he was getting nowhere, he went back downstairs. The meeting broke up with them all making baffled noises at each other.

The next afternoon at school I had to chase the fat boy from the schoolyard clear over to within a couple blocks from his house before I caught him. It didn't help him when I did.

There was a lot of telephoning around that night. My father was mad. He took me upstairs again and gave me a licking. He said we were going over to the fat boy's house, and I was going to apologize. I was still crying from the licking, but I told him I wouldn't say it after he got me over there. He made a lot of spluttering sounds and walked out of the bedroom. We didn't go anywhere.

Later that night the minister came to our house. He talked to me for a long time. All about the unexplainable things that happen in life, and the necessity for understanding. I understood, all right. What was all the talk about? I understood. I listened to him, though. I was polite. I wasn't going to give them a chance to call me surly or bad-mannered. When he was tired talking, the minister went away. I don't think even he thought he'd accomplished much.

The fat boy wasn't in school the next day. I was disappointed. When I got home there was something for me. The fat boy's father had left a carrying case with a blue Persian kitten. I didn't say anything to my mother or my sisters. I took the case out in the back yard, and when they stopped watching to see what I was doing I walked crosslots downtown to the pet shop and gave the case and the kitten back to the pet shop man. I told him to give the fat boy's father his money back. The pet shop man looked funny, but he took the kitten. He didn't say a word.

When he got home that night my father blew his stack. I didn't answer him back when he started in on me. All I wanted was to be let alone, and no one would leave me alone. My father said I was damn well going to do what I was told to do, and that if the kitten wasn't back in the house by the next night the consequences would be mine. I knew it just wasn't going to be that way.

So when I got a licking the next night it was partly for having caught the fat boy again on his way home from school, and partly for not having gone back to the pet shop for the kitten.

The next day in school I was called down to the principal's office. He talked a long time, too. The gist of it was that one more go-round with the fat boy and I would be expelled from school. I asked him politely what it had to do with school. I can still see his face tightening up, muscle by muscle. He said sharply that I was persevering in an attitude I would regret to the last day I lived, but he never did answer my question.

The fat boy wasn't in school that day, but I got a licking anyway that night for not having brought the kitten home. I got another the next night, and another the next. By then they were ritualistic, without a word being said on either side. I overheard my mother arguing with my father about his handling of me. I was sorry to hear it. I didn't want sympathy. I didn't want anything. I was stronger than they were, and I knew it. I had undivided purpose. I didn't feel like a martyr. I felt like someone doing what he had to do.

At school I was having trouble finding the fat boy. He was leaving by different doors, at different times. It was three more days before I caught him again. The next morning I was back in the principal's office. He wasn't there, but his secretary told me I was expelled. She looked kind of funny at me all the time she was telling me. I just kind of hung around during the day and went home at the usual time.

My mother and sisters were all waiting for me. At first I thought it was about being expelled, but they hadn't heard. They'd bought me a different Persian kitten. I thanked them. I wasn't mad at them about anything. I wasn't mad at my father about anything. Because the new kitten was a poor dumb animal that needed my help, I fed it. I didn't play with it.

My father came home early, in a tearing rage. The principal had called him. When he saw the new kitten and learned where it had come from, he clouded up and thundered at the women about going behind his back. They turned on him *en masse*. It astonished him. They didn't back him up, exactly, but for the first time in better than a week I got to bed that night without a licking. Even to myself I had to admit I was glad of it. My right shoulder had been hurting worse each of the past three days. I made a bed for the new kitten, and went to bed early myself.

By noon the next day I had caught up on lickings. Before breakfast I slipped out of the house and waited for the fat boy on his way to school. By now he screamed just like a girl at the sight of me. I was in the house at ten thirty when my father came home and marched me upstairs. He really laid it into me. These days they might send a twelve year old to a home, or to reform school. Then they didn't. My father didn't know anything to do but lick me. About an hour afterward I was sick to my stomach.

I didn't go downstairs for lunch. My stomach still felt bad and my shoulder was really giving me a hard time. I tried lying down, but that made the shoulder worse. Around two o'clock my mother came into my room. She looked at my eyes, put her hand on my forehead, and called the doctor. When he came he said I had a broken collarbone. He strapped me up like a mummy. He asked a lot of questions about the marks on me. I didn't answer him. It was none of his business. Afterward I could hear him talking to my mother out in the hall.

I took it easy that afternoon. Mostly I wondered how I was going to keep after the fat boy with an arm strapped down. I knew I'd find a way. As it turned out, I didn't need to. I was sitting downstairs leafing through an encyclopedia when my next oldest sister came flying into the house. She ran past into the kitchen without seeing me, and I could hear her breathlessly telling my mother that there was a big moving van in front of the fat boy's house.

The fat boy's family was moving away.

I don't know why I was so sure they were moving out of town. Maybe because I knew they were sure I'd find him if it was anywhere in the same town. I sat there looking at a picture of a Roman legion in full battle-dress, and I felt a deep sense of peace.

And just like that, it ended.

The shoulder healed in five weeks. In eight they let me back into school. Around the house the subject was never mentioned.

In a year I think everyone had honestly forgotten.

Except me.

I made El Paso the first night.

Highway 70 through Mesa, Safford, and Duncan in Arizona brought me into Lordsburg, New Mexico. Between Safford and Duncan the desert is for real. The stark, multicolored rock and sand of buttes and coulees grimly overshadow the sparse greenery of saguaro, mesquite, and palos verde.

Highways 70 and 80 join up at Lordsburg and run together through Deming to Las Cruces. I turned south there on 80 to El Paso. The temperature when I left Phoenix had been eighty-five. Rolling past the railroad marshaling yards in El Paso there was a flurry of snow in the headlights. Altitude makes a difference. The speedometer on the Ford said 409 miles when I pulled into a motel on the east side of town.

I'd pushed it a bit to make El Paso. I had a reason. I had to get my arm attended to before the bandage became a part of the tissue. Across the International Bridge in Juárez I knew where I could get it attended to, and no questions asked.

The motel office had signs on the desk advertising fabulous guided tours of the fabulous city of Ciudad Juárez in fabulous Old Mexico. I had them call their agency, and in thirty minutes a pot-bellied little Mex in a business suit showed up to guide me. He was about thirty-five, and had the eyes of a well-fed weasel. Four dollars changed hands, and we took off in his car.

He was a cheerful talker. Compulsive, rather. He had been baptized Jaime Carlos Torreon García, he told me, but his friends called him Jimmy. He worked for PanAm in El Paso, but lived in Juárez. He guided nights and weekends. Would I care to see the most excellent Mexican filigreed silver, handworked? I regretted that on Mexican filigreed handworked silver I was loaded. Jimmy was too old a hand at the game even to look disappointed.

It was a twenty minute ride from the motel to the bridge. On the way across Jimmy had a sparkling salute for everyone at the check-in stations, English for the U.S. guards, Spanish for the Mexican soldiers. Unanimously profane in their replies to him, none of them bothered to look at me. The number of trips he made over that bridge, he was better known than the president of the country. Either country.

The fabulous city of Ciudad Juárez was—as always—dirty, dusty, and squalid. Except when it rained, and then it was muddy beyond belief. Mexican authorities show a reluctance to put drains in their streets. God sends the rain and the mud. God will take it away.

My mentor headed unerringly for a bar. “My friend,” he told me, with an encompassing wave of his hand at the swarthy, shock-headed proprietor. “He has the finest *cantina* in the old town.”

I looked around at the empty booths and fly-specked walls. “He’s not a relative?” I asked Jimmy.

“My cousin,” he admitted blandly. Since I so obviously knew the rules of the road, he sat down and ordered Canadian Club for us both without consulting my taste.

“Have a couple,” I told him. “Take your time. I’m going to walk around to the Street of the Girls.”

He slid from his stool immediately. "I must go with you," he protested. "They will cheat you, amigo."

"I'm the bashful type, Jaime Carlos," I said. "I'll go it alone. I'll pay you your commission just as you'd get it from the house." He eyed me doubtfully but returned to his Canadian Club.

Out on the street I side-doored it a couple of times to make sure he wasn't following me. I couldn't see any sign of him, although probably at least half the Mexican male population resembled him in outline. I turned up the third street on the left. I hadn't been in Juárez in years, but I knew where I wanted to go. The side street macadam ended ten yards in from the intersection, and the sidewalk vanished and dropped down eight inches to an earthen footpath.

I found the old woman's place with no trouble at all. I recognized the half-rusted-away iron fence around the scurfy, postage-stamp-sized front yard the minute I saw it. The last time I'd been here Ed Morris had been with me. Ed had been pushing up daisies quite a while now.

The old woman looked me over through a hole in the door panel when I knocked. I don't know what she thought she saw, but she unbolted the door. There was no conversation. She tested the bill I gave her under three different lights while I took off my shirt. Her fat hand made a swooping movement somewhere into her clothes, and emerged without the bill.

She went to work on the arm, humming to herself in a tuneless monotone. I'd been afraid she might have to steam the old bandage free, but she cut it carefully in several places and with little dabs of ether worked it loose. She knew her business. It wasn't a painless operation but considering the length of time it had gone unattended it went a damn sight easier than I'd expected.

I looked at the scar while she prepared a new bandage. A beauty contest queen might have hollered foul, but it was healing. The new bandage was smaller and more compact, easier to hide. The old woman never opened her mouth while she put it on. The last time I'd been there she'd looked three years older than the Archangel Michael, and she sure as hell hadn't found the Fountain of Youth in the meantime.

Outside again I headed back up to the corner. As I stepped back up on the sidewalk, I turned automatically for a look behind me. A street light away I could see a figure of Jimmy's general dimensions. It bothered me. I stepped into a doorway and gave the half-seen figure a chance to catch up. I waited five minutes, but nobody passed my doorway. I wasn't satisfied, but I had to be satisfied. I used my handkerchief to wipe the red dust of the earthen footpath from my shoes, and walked back to the cantina.

Jaime Carlos Torreon García wasn't there.

His cousin, the bushy-haired proprietor, looked surprised to see me. "No sport?" he inquired with a raised eyebrow.

"No sportsman," I said. "Too old."

"It comes to all of us," he philosophized, but crossed himself against the approach of the evil day.

Jimmy bustled in the front door. He, too, seemed surprised to see me. His well-managed expressions of first astonishment and then sympathy would have gone down better with me if it hadn't been for the thick coating of red dust on his shoes.

The second I saw it I was in motion. I tossed a bill down on the bar and hustled him out of there before he could speak. Whatever he knew, it was going to stay with him. Let the cousin think my sudden exit the frustrated petulance of a sexual loser. Cousin Jimmy had acquired some dangerous knowledge.

I sat in Jimmy's car and thought it over. Beside me he kept shooting nervous little glances at me. If he had information, I was sure he didn't know what to do with it. He needed to put his head together with someone and plan a financial coup based on his knowledge of the gringo's movements. Jaime Carlos Torreon García had the proper piratical instincts but a deficiency in a method of operation. And he wasn't going to live long enough to acquire one.

"I think I've had enough sightseeing," I told him, turning toward him. Under cover of the movement I got the Woodsman into my hand. "I think you have, too." I showed him the gun. His eyes popped like a frog's on a hot rock. "Drive up to the checkout zone. Tell them 'no purchases' in Spanish. Just that. Nothing more. Let's hear you say it."

"*No compra*," he said huskily.

"That's *all* you'll say," I warned him. "Let's go."

At the barrier he had trouble getting that much out, let alone anything else. We went through in a breeze. I repeated my warning before we reached the U.S. inspection station. Two minutes later we were back across the bridge. I felt better. Trouble in Mexico I didn't want. Authorities there have a habit of tossing a gringo into a flea-infested calaboose and conveniently losing the key. Sometimes a man can buy his way out. Sometimes he can't.

That left Jimmy.

"Drive up one of these side streets," I told him.

He nearly let go of the wheel. "S-señor, don't do this theeng, I beg of you! Don't do—"

"Left, Jimmy. Now." The car lurched around as he yanked convulsively at the wheel. In three hundred yards the street lights spaced out conveniently. We were about half a mile from the motel, comfortable walking distance. "Pull over. Park between the lights." He did so, babbling unintelligibly in a half-English, half-Spanish high-pitched wail. I rapped him on the arm to snap him out of it. "Dump out your pockets on the seat. Be quick."

It was dark, but I could see. About the third item he showered down on the seat cushion was a pocket knife of the type known as Nacional. Heavy-bladed, in a solid casing, it's a lethal weapon. Jimmy was still turning out his pockets. I picked up the knife and opened it.

I don't know if he saw the movement of my arm or heard the snick of the opening blade. He screamed hoarsely and went for the door handle. I grabbed his collar and jerked him back. He collapsed beside me like a blob of melted butter, his high, keening voice yammering at me. I hit him in the belly to shut him up.

In the sudden silence I took his neck in my hand and found the carotid artery with my thumb. I opened the door on my side. A carotid can be messy. I didn't want to get splashed. I braced my heels against the floorboard and reached for him.

And hesitated.

In the quiet I seemed able to think for the first time since I'd seen clinging red dust on this man's shoes. I'd let myself get so upset at my stupidity in letting the fool follow me that I hadn't thought the thing through.

Alive, he'd talk. Later, if not sooner. That I knew.

But dead, his body would talk, and even more to the point. His cousin expected him back with a tale of where he had followed the *turista*. If he didn't come back, the cousin might get nervous. If he went to the police, they'd have little trouble tracing Jaime Carlos to the motel through the agency. I had had the motel call the agency. The motel would furnish the police with a description of me. And of the Ford.

Dead, this man was an anchor around my neck.

Alive? Not much better, but a little better.

I clicked the knife blade shut. "Sit up and listen to me," I said to him.

He gave a kind of shuddering sigh. "S-señor, I *implore*—"

"Shut up. Drive back to the motel."

It took him a full minute to get the car started. His coordination was gone. He drove like a sleepwalker. In the street lights his face looked like wax. The car bounced high as he turned into the motel driveway going too fast. For a second I thought we were going to take out a cabin before he hit the brake and we skidded in the gravel.

I got out, and motioned at him. "Take off, man."

He stared out at me suspiciously. Was it a trick? It didn't take him long to decide if it was—he still liked it better than where he'd been. He tramped on the accelerator. His car hit the street doing forty-five.

He'd been right up to the gates, and he knew it. He might not know why, but he knew it. As a type he should head straight for his bed and stay there with the covers over his head for three days.

But I couldn't count on it.

Five minutes after his tail-lights winked out of the motel driveway, I was headed east in the Ford.

III

IT WAS odd in a way about the fat boy's family leaving town that time. Six years later it was my family who were going to leave.

The way it happened was like getting struck by lightning. I was eighteen, in my senior year in high school. It was late in the spring, and after a succession of chill, rainy days we'd finally caught a hot one. I had my sweater over my arm when I came out the school's back entrance and cut through the parking lot like I did every day on my way home. I saw these four policemen standing in the middle of the lot, and I wondered what they were doing there.

I knew one of them, Harry Coombs, and I nodded as I passed. He said something to the others, and the biggest one, who had been standing with his back to me, turned around to look. "You," he said to me. "Come over here."

I went over to them. I knew who the big one was without really knowing him. His name was Edwards, and he was a sergeant. He was a beefy man with thinning red hair. I didn't like him. No good reason. His voice was too loud. He took up too much of the sidewalk when he swaggered by. Things like that.

He looked me up and down when I stood in front of them. "What d'you know about hubcaps missing from the faculty cars three times a week?" he demanded. He looked hot and uncomfortable, still in his winter uniform.

"I don't know anything about it," I answered him. I didn't, except what I'd been hearing in school assemblies for a month.

The lower lip in his red face swelled pugnaciously. "Harry here says you spend enough time in this parking lot to be able to tell us what's going on," he continued aggressively.

"I said I see him going through here on his way home!" Coombs cut in.

Edwards paid him no attention. "Well?" he said to me.

"You think whoever's doing it waits for me to come by so I can see them?" I was mad. "Or maybe you think I'm doing it?"

"I'll ask the questions," he snapped, scowling. "What's your name?" I told him. I was liking him less and less by the second.

"Now you know you must've seen what's been going on out here. Who you covering up for?"

I looked at Harry Coombs, to see if Edwards was kidding. Harry looked away. "Look, you can't mean it," I said finally. "I don't—"

"Answer the question!" Edwards roared at me.

I turned and started to walk away. He grabbed me by the arm. I've always hated having people put their hands on me. I jerked my arm out of his hand. He must have outweighed me three to one, but I caught him on the wrong foot. He staggered sideways two or three paces. His red face looked bloated.

My sweater fell off my arm, and I stooped automatically to pick it up. Edwards kicked me, hard. I went over and down, flat, skinning my palms on the parking lot cinders.

I scrambled up and went after him, the hate of the world in my heart. Before I could reach him Harry Coombs had me clamped in a bear hug. He was muttering in my ear but I was struggling so hard I didn't hear him. I had my head twisted around yelling at him to let me go. I never even saw Edwards when he stepped up and slapped me heavily in the face.

"Goddammit, sarge!" Coombs said angrily. His arms relaxed, then tightened as I lunged.

"Shut up, you!" Edwards barked at him. "This is a wise one. We'll take him down to the station and talk to him."

"Then take him down yourself," Coombs said. Deliberately he released me. "I'm on duty right here."

"You're on duty where I tell you you're on duty, Coombs," Edwards warned him. "Get him in the patrol car, and get in yourself." The sergeant clumped heavily back to the other two who had been silently standing by.

It was only by an effort of will I kept a hand away from my smarting face. Don't fight it, I told myself. Not here. I walked toward the cruiser parked in a corner of the lot. Harry Coombs tramped along beside me, muttering under his breath.

The five of us rode downtown. I never said a word. In the police station one of the ones who had taken no part previously took me by the arm and led me to a door beyond which were two steel cells with cement floors. He motioned me inside. I went in and looked around. There was a steel cot without even a blanket on it. Nothing else. The policeman didn't close the cell door, but he closed the outside door. I got a good look at his face before he went out.

I sat down on the cot and tried to get myself organized. I knew they'd be coming in. I didn't feel worried, just mad. I knew I was going to get that Edwards some day if it was the last thing I ever did. And if it could be today, so much the better.

I stood up quickly when the outside door opened. It was only Harry Coombs. He closed it and stood with his back to it. "Listen, kid," he said to me hurriedly. "I got through to him at last that you're no juvenile delinquent. He don't think so much of himself right now, but when he comes in here he'll make a little noise to justify himself. Get smart. Do what he says, y'hear?" I looked at him. "Ahhhh, you're as thick as he is," Coombs growled, and walked out.

I took off my shoes and put them on the steel cot beside me, and stretched out on my back. I stared up at the ceiling covered with misty cracks. Do what Edwards told me? Not a chance. Not a bloody chance. If he was on a hook because of me, he'd stay there till his liver and lungs rotted for all the help he'd get from me.

I sat up when the outer door opened again. Three of them filed in, Edwards in the lead. I didn't know the names of the other two, but by now I knew their faces. Harry Coombs wasn't with them. I sat there and watched them come in.

"Let's hear the answers to a few questions, now," Edwards began. His voice was rough. He looked the same, his red face shiny, but even without what Coombs had said I knew he didn't sound the same. His voice said he didn't like where he was. "I want a statement from you as to what you were doing in that parking lot," he blustered. "A signed, witnessed statement."

I didn't say anything. His face grew dark. He walked toward me, slowly. I sat still. "I said I want a statement from you!" he bellowed.

I sat there. Any statement I gave him he could probably twist around for his own purposes. He'd get no statement from me. When I said nothing, Edwards made a slight movement with his left hand. Just a gesture. Testing my nerve. I sat there. "God, how I love you boy scout tough guys!" he said between his teeth. He loomed up over me as I sat on the cot. He jabbed me in the ribs with a stiffened thumb. "Stand up when I talk to you!"

I sat there. He slapped me. My head hit the wall behind me. One of the men with him made some sort of sound, whether assent or protest I don't know. I couldn't see them. All I could see was Edwards' bulk, his red face and his hot-looking little eyes. My own were squeezed hard trying to keep the tears behind them. "Stand up, damn you!" Edwards barked. He stiffened the thumb and advanced it slowly toward my ribs, waiting for me to flinch. I didn't flinch. He jabbed me in the ribs. He jabbed me again. And again. Each time it felt like a red-hot poker.

When I saw he meant to keep it up, I reached around in back of me and picked up one of my shoes by the toe. When Sergeant Edwards' arm moved again, I came up out of there, fast. I smashed him right across the bridge of the nose with the heel of the shoe. I hit him with every ounce I had in me. He went reeling backward, blood spurting like a gusher. Only the men behind him kept him from going down. He rebounded from them and clubbed at me with both fists. He hit me about three more shots on my way down to the floor. On my way up I hit him in the belly with both hands. He knocked me down again.

There was a lot of noise and confusion. People yelling. People hurting me. I couldn't see very well. I went down and got up twice more. I think it was twice. If I could have seen Edwards, I'd have butted him squarely in the middle of his ugly face with the top of my skull.

But I couldn't see him.

And after a while I couldn't get up any more.

It seemed like a long time later I heard my father's voice. I wondered how he'd got there. "—Someone's going to sweat for this," he was saying angrily. "And I don't care if it's you, John!"

I opened my eyes cautiously. I could see from the left one. I was in an iron bed, and my father and John Mullen, the Chief of Police, were nose to nose at its foot.

"Take it easy, Karl," the chief said. John Mullen lived just up the street from us. I'd taken his youngest daughter, Kathy, to one of the school dances. "I'll get to the bottom of it."

"You're damn right you will!" my father said hotly. "And I want him moved out of here to a hospital right this minute!"

"Doc Everhardt says it isn't necessary, Karl."

"Don't try to tell me what's not necessary! I said right now! Don't think you can keep my boy from the treatment he needs just because you've got a stinking situation you'd like to cover—"

"I said I'd get to the bottom of it!" Flint-edged steel ridged Chief Mullen's tone. His voice had risen, too. "The boy could have been at fault, too, Karl."

"Fault? Fault? Good God, John, have you gone out of your mind? If he burned down the orphans' home, should he look like this? I know this Edwards. A thug in a uniform. A disgrace—"

Chief Mullen had seen my opened eye. He walked quickly around the end of the bed. "What happened, son?" he asked quietly. My father pushed in beside him where he stood looking down at me.

I had to make three starts before I could get out anything. "I—fell down," I said finally. My voice was a breathy rasp.

"Fell!" my father echoed incredulously. "Fell?" He stared at me, then whirled on the chief. "What kind of intimidation is this, John? I'm going—"

"Take it easy, Karl." There was a warning note in the official voice. The chief's shrewd eyes were studying me. "Don't forget we walked in here together. Don't let me hear you say 'intimidation' again." He was still looking down at me thoughtfully. "We'll talk to him later."

"We'll talk to him right now, damn it!"

But the chief finally got my father out of there.

I never told them any more than that, then or later. I never knew what Edwards told them. I didn't care. I think my father thought at first the beating had affected my mind. Right from the beginning, the chief came closer to the truth. Day after day he came to the house with patient questions. After a while I stopped answering him at all. Eventually he stopped coming.

I was out of school three weeks until my face healed up. When I went back, I still had three broken fingers on my left hand, and from shoulders to knees I was spotted like a leopard.

I didn't remember anything about the fingers. They must have got stepped on.

Nobody at school—or anywhere else—knew what happened. The police didn't say anything, and I didn't say anything. I found out without too much trouble that the two men in the cell with Edwards that day had been Glenn Smith and Walt Cummings.

I took to skipping classes at school, even whole days. I spent more time out of the house at night than I ever had. The first three marking periods I'd been on the honor roll, and the school office called me in about my sliding grades. They said I might not even graduate if I didn't straighten up. I didn't give a damn. With such a short way to go I didn't think they could flunk me after the marks I'd carried, but I didn't care if they did. I was busy.

Glenn Smith was easy. He was a heavy drinker. I watched him till I found out he spent a lot of time in the Parokeet Tavern. He had a habit of parking his car on the street in back, and walking up a narrow alley to the Parokeet's back door. Sometimes he was in uniform.

Late one night he came back down the alley, staggering a little. I formed a one-man reception committee. I took him from behind, and I lumped him good. I kicked in a few of his ribs, finally, and left him crawling around on the ground like a wingless beetle. He never even got a look at me. I felt good all the way home.

The next morning Chief Mullen came over to school and took me out of my history class. We went outside and sat in his car. He talked for a long time. He didn't accuse me of anything. I knew he couldn't, because Glenn Smith had never seen me.

The chief went on about the idiocy of people attempting to take the law into their own hands. He talked like a damn fool. I'd taken the law into my own hands, and I liked the feel of it. The chief must have seen the expression on my face. He stopped talking and opened his car door. I went back into school.

Walt Cummings took longer. It was better than a month before I found out he dropped in a couple of nights a week at a married woman's a mile out of town. When I had him clocked so I could depend on him, I caught him at her back door one night. I smothered him in wet-down potato sacking as he came out. I got him down, and when I finished with him they carried him in from there. I went home and went to bed.

Chief Mullen was at our house before breakfast the next morning. He was really warm under the collar. He asked me point blank what I knew about Cummings. My father saved me the trouble of lying. He jumped in and wanted to know if the chief was accusing me of anything. Either make a charge you can support, he told Mullen when the chief hesitated, or get out of my house. The chief left, red in the face. I almost laughed out loud. My father didn't ask me anything afterward. He didn't seem comfortable with me.

Two down and one to go. Every time I passed Sergeant Edwards on the street, I smiled at him. Every time I smiled, he scowled. He knew. I wanted him to know. His scowls said plainly he wasn't letting his nerves get jumped up by any crackpot kid. He watched himself, though. He watched himself so well I couldn't get anywhere near him.

School let out. I graduated, barely. My college entrance credits were all shot. I'd have to pass exams to get in. I didn't take the exams. I hung around all summer, into the fall. Twice my father, exasperated, demanded that I get a job if I had no intention of continuing with my schooling. I paid no attention. I had a job. A job I had to take care of before I could look for a job.

Harry Coombs cornered me late one Saturday night when I was coming out of a diner on his beat. He herded me into a corner. "I suppose I'm lucky they sent me out of there before they went into the cell with you that day?" he inquired, prodding me in the chest with his nightstick. I grinned at him. "They're going to sit you down in a square-looking chair one of these days, kid," he told me. "They'll turn on the juice, and there'll be a sizzling noise while they burn your ass up, but you won't hear it. Think it over." He walked away from me.

By October I knew more about Sergeant Edwards than his wife did, but he never gave me an opening. I began to get restless. I didn't know what I was going to do after I got through with him, but I wanted to get it over with and find out.

Then early in November we had an unexpected sleet-and-ice storm. Edwards came up his porch steps that night with his chin shrunk down into his coat collar, careful of the slippery footing. His head was lowered against the stinging blasts. He never saw the piece of pipe I got him with before he reached his front door. When I finished with the pipe, I rolled him back down his porch steps, and went home. He was lucky. Someone found him before he froze to death.

I didn't find that out until morning. Or at least the clock said it was morning but it was still dark outside. A police cruiser came by for my father and me. They hardly gave us time to dress. My father kept asking them what had happened. They wouldn't say anything. In the cruiser my father kept sneaking looks at me from the corner of his eye.

At the station Chief Mullen really gave me a going-over. He was trying to scare answers out of me. He should have known better by that time. For twenty solid minutes I sat there and smiled at him. I never said a word. My father horned in finally and asked Mullen what basis he had for his unfounded accusations. It really flipped the chief. You've got a wild animal running loose around town, he told my father. You've got a choice. Cage him, or leave town. Leave town, he repeated with emphasis. Better all around.

I felt like laughing until I saw the stricken look on my father's face. I couldn't understand it. The chief couldn't do anything. Nobody could do anything. I didn't give a damn what they thought they knew about me. They couldn't prove a thing.

On the way home my father said tiredly he hoped I'd realize some day it was necessary to live with people. He said a lot of other things. I felt sorry for him. He just couldn't stand up to a situation.

I couldn't believe it when the FOR SALE sign went up on our front lawn. I was disgusted. My father was letting them bluff him right out of the game. They couldn't make him do a thing he didn't agree to do. That's why I couldn't understand it. My father was a weakling.

I couldn't let his spinelessness affect my mother and sisters. I left home that night. I knew I could manage. Obviously my father couldn't.

I left.

I never went back.

*

I had to switch cars.

The minute my pot-bellied Mexican guide's tongue came unlatched, the police would get a description of the Ford—and of me—from the motel. It didn't matter a damn they wouldn't know why they were looking for me. It was up to me to change the appearance of what they'd be looking for.

Highway 80 east out of El Paso is a long, straight, black stretch of road. Not many headlights came at me. Ground fog began to drift in from the fields on either side of the highway. It began to close in over the road. I wanted to make time, and if this kept up I wasn't going to be able to make time.

Most of the gas stations I passed were dark. When I came up on a lighted one, I slowed down, tempted. I hit the gas again and went on by. It wouldn't solve anything. I could grab the attendant's car or anything he happened to be working on, but unless I buried him in his grease pit he'd pass the word on that would tie me to the new car. And even if I buried him, the presence of the Ford when I abandoned it would put the collar around my neck for anyone checking the highway from the motel on up the line.

I needed a setup that would let me run the Ford over a cliff, or the equivalent. Even more I needed to get off Highway 80. The john in a girl's dorm doesn't get any more action than that damn highway.

I went over it in my mind. Van Horn is a hundred twenty odd miles east of El Paso. A dozen miles the other side Highway 80 plows ahead due east, but Highway 90 ducks south. It looked like a better choice. I couldn't count on Jimmy's pulling the covers over his head. They could be out looking for me already.

I made it in an hour and thirty-five minutes, fog and all. I had to fight my eyes closing down all the way, and I hit the shoulder a couple of times, dozing off, but at twenty minutes to midnight I turned onto 90 and headed south. It was a narrower road, much less traveled. I began to watch for a motel. When I saw one with a car parked out close enough to the road, I'd drive a mile beyond, walk back, jump the switch on the car in the motel yard, and take off. There'd be nothing to tie the abandoned Ford to the stolen car, even if the best I could do with the Ford would be to run it off into a field.

I couldn't have been more than twenty miles in on 90 with everything around me as black as the inside of a closet when a pair of headlights came on suddenly in my rear-view mirror. A red flasher started bouncing off the Ford. He must have come up behind me with his lights off, because I hadn't seen a thing. I took a quick look at the speedometer. Sixty-five. Should be no sweat there. I heard no siren, but there was no doubt he intended me to stop. He pulled out alongside, then burst ahead and cut in.

I had to jam on the brakes and cut the wheel hard to avoid scraping fenders as he herded me to the side of the road. As he went past me I could see he was in an unmarked car. I hadn't known the Rangers used unmarked cars. Live and learn.

I was ready when he walked back and leaned in the window I'd rolled down. I handed him my driver's license made out to Roy Martin. Paperclipped to it was a twenty dollar bill. I could see a trooper hat silhouetted against the dark, but I couldn't see the face beneath it at all. I could sense rather than see him looking around the Ford's interior before he walked back to the rear and put a flash on the license.

He returned and handed it in to me. The twenty dollar bill was gone. "Drive up the highway a quarter mile," he said. His voice sounded as if he regularly had steel filings for breakfast. "Turn right the first road. A hundred fifty feet in there's a white fence. Turn left and stop. I'll be right behind you." He walked back to the cruiser. I hadn't got to say a word.

I could feel a slow burn coming up. If this sonofabitch thought he was going to take my twenty and then write me up anyway, he was damn well going to find out differently. When I buy someone, I expect him to stay bought.

He pulled ahead to let me out, and I eased back out on the highway. I rolled down the road slowly, watching for the first turn on the right. Even at that I almost missed it. It was hardly more than a dirt drop-off. Halfway into my turn I thought I'd made a mistake, but the headlights behind me turned in, too. I came up to the white fence, and turned left. In twenty-five yards I faced a dead-end, an impenetrable, jungle-like brush tangle dead ahead in the headlights.

I was getting hotter by the minute. I was losing time. I had missed a turn despite his directions, and wound up in this jackpot. The clearing was too small to swing around in. I started to back out. A red glow filled my rear-view mirror. I turned my head. The cruiser was backing into the clearing, sealing me in. Even as I looked he cut his lights.

All of a sudden I had a feeling.

I cut my lights and motor, fumbled a flashlight out of the glove compartment, and went out the door on the passenger's side. The unmarked car, the absence of a siren, this dead-end deserted spot he'd directed me to—

When I heard him walking I put the flash on him. He stopped dead in the beam of light. He was holding a gun, a blued-steel job. He had on a campaign hat that looked like a Ranger's hat. His clothes didn't look anything like a uniform except for the color. The bastard was no more a cop than I was.

He brought his gun up and snapped off a shot at me just as I let go at him with the Woodsman. He turned and started to run. I put one in his ankle that brought him down with a crash. He landed all sprawled out, the gun flying off in the bushes. I got over to him fast in case he had another.

When I got the flash full on him I saw it didn't make any difference. He'd been running on reflex. The hard core of the light shone down on a round, dark hole just a hair to the right of center between his eyes. The little old Woodsman might not have the stopping power of a .38, but it gets there just the same.

It was quiet in the clearing. I walked over and put the flash on the bandido's car. It was a Ford, too. It looked in better shape than mine. I got his car keys out of his pocket and got under the wheel and started it up. The engine vr-r-roomed with power. Something extra under the hood.

It looked like I had won myself an automobile.

I put on the dimmers on both cars and opened the trunks of both. I loaded his gear in mine and mine in his. I took the license plates off both cars and chopped them up with a hammer and cold chisel. With a screwdriver I worked on the red flasher on the roof until I was able to unscrew it. I knocked down the edges of the socket that held the bulb with the chisel, and slapped a square of tape over it. The black friction tape merged with the color of the car. I rummaged around through saws and climbing irons in my tool chest till I found a set of Florida plates. I put them on the new Ford.

I cleaned out my wallet and started from scratch. When I put it back on my hip again I was Chester Arnold of Hollywood, Fla. I had business cards in the wallet identifying Chet Arnold as a tree surgeon. When it pleases me I'm a tree surgeon. A good one.

When I was all set I went back for my unknown benefactor. I dragged him over and stuffed him into the trunk of the new Ford. With the tool chests already in there it was a tight squeeze, but I finally got the back deck lid closed.

I took off out of there.

Out on the highway every five miles I threw a piece of chopped up license plate out the window. It helped to keep awake. Then it started to rain. It doesn't rain often in West Texas, but when it does it doesn't fool around. I hunched down over the wheel, watched the road in the streaming windshield, and pitched license fragments.

Forty miles up the highway I ran into a torn-up section under repair. In those parts they're so sure it's not going to rain they don't bother with the nicety of preserving one lane of macadam. They tear up the road from shoulder to shoulder, roll it, and drive on the dirt till they get the blacktop back on. If it does rain they have a driving rodeo through four to six inches of Texas gumbo. Never let anyone tell you the Texan is not a sporting animal.

It was raining so damn hard that in less than a mile the whole graveled roadbed was solidly under water. The Ford slipped and slithered along. Even at five miles an hour, a couple of times I wasn't sure I was going to make it. It was like driving across a ten mile lake. I had to watch the highway department right-of-way stakes as they glistened in the headlights alongside the road to be sure I was still in the channel.

I finally got out on hardtop again, and for the next ten miles I listened to Texas mud slurp off the undercarriage at every little jounce. From what I could see of it I could have set up a fairsized sweepstakes selling chances of the Ford's original color. I concentrated on driving and staying awake.

When the speedometer said I was two hundred miles from El Paso, I started looking for a deep culvert. When I saw a likely looking one I pulled over on the shoulder. I got out and walked around to the back. I never saw as black a night. It was raining like someone had turned on the petcock and gone off on vacation. I was soaked in less than a minute.

I got the trunk open, and hauled out my passenger. I hoisted him over to the bank and rolled him down it. He went in with a satisfying splash. I got back in under the wheel and started slogging up the highway again. When they found him, no one would connect my benefactor to me or to much of anything else. Ditto the Ford I'd left behind in the clearing.

I'd passed Marfa and Alpine a long way back, clusters of lights in the dripping night. I was between Marathon and Haymond when I dumped the body. Twice on the long stretch between Sanderson and Del Rio I nearly went to sleep. I was driving myself as hard as I was driving the car.

Outside of Brackettville dawn was breaking in a dirty gray sky when I got a leg cramp so bad it pulled my foot clear off the accelerator. I stopped the car and got out and limped around it a couple of times, but I couldn't shake it off. I drove through town with my left foot on the gas pedal and into a motel on the outskirts. I woke up the owner, shut up his grumbling about the ungodliness of the hour, took the key he gave me and headed for the cabin he pointed out.

I figured I was about 450 miles from El Paso, and it had been a long, long day.

I shed clothes all the way from the door of the cabin to the bed, and I was asleep before I was halfway down to the pillow.

IV

A YEAR after I left home I was up in northern Ohio working the midnight-to-eight shift in a gas station on the edge of town. It was colder than a whore's heart up there in December, but it kept me eating. From two to seven I wouldn't average half a dozen cars. I'd sit inside with my feet cocked up on a gasoline heater, and wait for daylight.

Or listen to Olly Barnes.

He was an odd one. I couldn't figure why a good-looking guy with a college degree should spend his time hanging around the station till all hours in the morning, talking to a kid like me. Naturally I thought he was a queer at first. Then I decided he wasn't, but I couldn't make him out. He was slender, with a pale, narrow face dominated by steel-rimmed spectacles, a high forehead, and straw-colored hair. He was about thirty. His hands were small and usually fluttered nervously while he talked. He had a beautiful speaking voice.

Two or three nights a week he'd be around the station till five in the morning. I never could see how he could keep his eyes open on his bookkeeping job. One thing I noticed about him. He talked a lot about the places he'd been and the things he'd seen, but never about the people. He talked travel, books, paintings, opera, ballet; talked with a passionate intensity. In the beginning I tried to tell him he was way over my head with most of what he had to say. When I saw it didn't matter, I shut up and listened. Olly brought me books I didn't read, and tried to hide his disappointment when I admitted it.

And then one morning the police came and took him away. It was about three thirty, and he'd been talking, as usual, when the cruiser pulled up outside. Olly's good-looking face crumpled like wet cardboard when he saw the big man in plainclothes walking toward the station door. I thought he was going to run, but if he thought of it he didn't have time.

The big man stood in the open doorway, cold air pouring in all around him. "Let's take a ride, Oliver," he said. He had a broad, flat face with high cheekbones and no more expression than an iron skillet.

"No," Olly whispered. "No!" That time it was a scream. He did start to run then, aiming at the garage area, but the man in the doorway took two steps forward and picked him off by the shirt-front like I'd scoop a fly from the wall. He half-carried, half-dragged Olly outside without saying another word. The door slammed behind them.

I went outside to the cruiser. It was none of my business, but I went out, anyhow. A uniformed man was driving. I rapped on the rolled-up front window. I could see Olly and the big man in the back seat. Olly was crying. The uniformed man lowered the window and looked out at me. "What's it all about?" I asked him.

He sat with his head cocked as if he were listening for something from the back seat. When nothing came he rolled up the window and wheeled the cruiser around the pumps and out on the highway.

I stood and watched the tail-lights diminishing up the road. It was a bitter cold night, without a star or a light of any kind, except for the lights of the station. It wasn't any of my business. And I couldn't walk off and leave the place. I went back inside, out of the cold. Olly's overcoat still lay on a chair where he'd dropped it when he came in.

Between then and seven o'clock I called the police four times. No one had ever heard of Oliver Barnes. I described the big man. They knew him, all right. His name was Lieutenant Winick. No one had seen him, either.

A little after four it started to snow. Between calls to the police I was kept busy clearing the station's driveways. By dawn there was six inches on the ground, and it was blowing hard. After seven I was too busy to call any more. When my relief came on at eight I had to stay over an hour to help with the rush of cars.

When I was able to get away there were no buses running. I put Olly's overcoat over my arm and walked the mile and a half into town. Drifts were already a couple of feet in some places, and the storm was spraying line-drive sheets of snow. Cold as it was I was sweating by the time I reached the police station. That kind of weather made heavy going.

I didn't really know what I was doing there. I guess I'd always known Olly wasn't exactly a hundred cents on the dollar. Still, a deal like that—

What if it had been me? Wouldn't I have wanted someone to at least find out the score?

I might as well have talked to a wooden Indian as the sergeant at the desk. He asked a hell of a lot more questions than he answered. Who I was. Where I lived. Where I worked. What my interest was. He finally made a pretense of checking the blotter, and said that no Oliver Barnes had been booked for anything. I knew he was lying, but for him that ended it.

I hung around. Nobody tried to run me out, but they didn't make it easy for me to stay. I tried my questions on two or three newcomers, with the same results. The heat in the waiting room kept putting me to sleep every time I sat down. At eleven o'clock I gave up. I left Olly's overcoat at the desk—in case he came in looking for it, I told the sergeant—and went home to bed.

When I woke at four it was still snowing. I dressed and walked back up to the station after getting a cup of coffee at the corner. When he saw me come in the same sergeant spoke before I could. "Lieutenant Winick wants to see you, kid," he said to me. "Inside. Second door on the left."

Winick looked up from behind his desk when I knocked and entered his office. His high-cheekboned features were just as expressionless as they'd been before. He leaned back steeply in his chair, folded his arms, and looked me over. "Stanton said you wanted to see me," he said at last. As though he'd just got the word, and I hadn't been trying since eight thirty.

"Where's Olly?" I asked him.

"In a cell. Where he belongs."

"Why? What for?"

Winick's slitted eyes were unwinking. "Your friend has a bad habit. He coaxes little girls behind buildings and takes their panties down." His harsh voice deepened as his eyes bored into mine. "*Little* girls. Seven, eight, nine. And you know what he does then?" He told me. "Like day before yesterday," he concluded. "It wasn't hard to know where to look, even without the kid's description when her mother brought her in."

The roof of my mouth felt dry. "How good—what kind of a description?"

"Oliver Barnes' description." Winick's voice blared at me suddenly. "Did you know he'd served a reformatory sentence and a prison term for the same thing?"

"No, I didn't."

"Then you know now. You're not very choosy of your company. How long've you been in town?"

"Six months. When—what time did it happen?"

The big shoulders rose and fell in an elaborate shrug. "Five, six o'clock. The kid wasn't sure."

I felt a sense of excitement. "Five or six o'clock in the evening?"

"Five or six o'clock in the evening," Winick agreed with exaggerated patience.

"Then it couldn't have been Olly," I said triumphantly.

Winick smiled. "He confessed."

"Confessed? Look, you said it happened between five and six day before yesterday?"

He was watching me narrowly. "That's what I said."

"Then it couldn't have been Olly. He brought some books over to my place at four in the afternoon day before yesterday, and he stayed talking until I went out to eat at seven. It couldn't have been Olly, you hear me?"

He stood up behind the desk. "You're mixed up on the days. It happens to you night workers. He confessed."

"The hell I'm mixed up on the days! How could he confess to something he didn't do? You—"

"Careful of the territory you're taking in, kid." Winick's voice could have cut wood. "Where do you fit in this? What kind of friend is Barnes to you?"

"Why don't you ask me what kind of friend I am to Barnes? The way I see it, I'm the one he needs. I want to talk to him."

"He's not seeing anyone. He has fits of remorse."

I could feel myself shaking. "Listen, I'll testify Olly couldn't possibly have—"

"You're going off half-cocked, kid," the hard voice cut me off again. "Did you hear me say Barnes had confessed? In detail?"

"You made him confess! He was afraid the minute he saw you. Because he did it before doesn't mean he did it this time. You must have—"

"Listen to me." Winick's voice was quiet again. "He did it. He confessed it. Can you get that through your thick skull?"

"There must be somebody else for me to talk to around here besides you," I said desperately. "You're not even listening. I tell you Olly couldn't—"

"*You're* not listening to *me*." Gimlet eyes drilled into mine. "Barnes is a menace to society. He's proved it. He should never have been out on the street. This time I'm tucking him away for a good long stretch."

"But he didn't *do* it! Not this time, anyway!"

"He did it." Winick's heavy voice was flat with authority. His eyes appeared almost closed as he looked across the desk at me. "Should I ask Barnes if you were with him?"

My hands clenched. "Is that supposed to make me run out of here? By God, I know what I know. I don't care *what* he did before. This he didn't do, and I'll talk till I get someone to listen."

"You sound to me like someone fixing to get his balls caught in the machinery." Winick leaned down over the desk, resting his weight on his big-knuckled hands. "I know what Barnes is. The people in this town know what he is. When you talk to me, you're talking to all of them."

I got out of there.

I didn't believe Winick, but I found out he was right. Everyone I tried to get to listen to me gave me nothing but a blank stare. Nobody would believe it couldn't have been Olly.

And then I found out the hard way some of them weren't going to believe. The next day I lost both my job and my room. Winick had been to see my boss and my landlady. All of a sudden I was on the street with twenty-three dollars between me and the snow.

I stuck around another day, trying to get someone to listen. I was half out of my mind, crazy-mad at the town and the people in it. And at Winick. Especially at Winick. That night I slept till four A.M. in the railroad station with my head on my bag. Winick's cops found me then and threw me out. I must have ground a quarter inch off my teeth, stumbling around the slippery, frozen streets, lugging my bag. I was half frozen by the time the first one-arm coffee joint opened up.

In the cold gray light of the morning I gave up. I walked out to the edge of town and stopped a highway bus and told the driver to get me eleven dollars worth away from there. I purposely hadn't bought a ticket at the bus station because I figured if Winick wanted to keep a string on me he'd have counted on that.

I wound up across the state, a hundred eighty miles away. I

got a job as stock boy in a chain grocery. Three times a week I bought a northern Ohio newspaper and read every word of it, looking for news of Olly.

It wasn't much of a surprise when I finally saw it, three months later. The black headlines said Olly had been sentenced to fifteen years.

That day I quit the human race. I never went back to my job. I've never done a legitimate day's work since. The work I've done since then has always been with an illegitimate purpose in mind. If that was the way it was, they could damn well have it that way.

I bought a gun in a hockshop. I didn't even own a car. The local paper nipped hard at police heels over the series of gas station holdups by a quick-moving pedestrian who always disappeared into the darkness.

I was surprised at how easy it was. I had only two close calls. Once I was scared off before I'd committed myself, and another time I had to stop an attendant from chasing me by shooting over his head.

The money piled up. I knew what I was going to do with it. I bought a second-hand car and learned how to drive it. About ten weeks after Olly started his sentence I drove the hundred eighty miles back across the state. Back to Winick. I rang his doorbell at ten o'clock at night. He came to the door himself. Not that it made any difference; I was all set to go right into the house after him.

I shot him in the face, four times, as he stood at the door looking out at me. He went backward in a kind of shambling trot. "That's for Olly, you bastard," I told him. I don't think he heard me. I think he was dead before his big shoulders hit the floor.

Winick was the first.

He wasn't the last.

I woke up at sundown in the Brackettville motel, humped myself across the street to a combination grocery-restaurant, and loaded up on bacon and eggs and black coffee. I re-crossed the highway and went right back into the sack. I woke up the next time at five thirty in the morning, feeling better physically than I had in weeks.

I had breakfast at the same restaurant, and was ready to leave. I climbed into the new Ford, listened appreciatively to the engine sound when I started it up, and tried to back out of my parking place. The car rocked back and forth, but wouldn't budge. I sat there blank for a minute before it dawned on me what must have happened. All that Texas gumbo I'd run through—when half-dried it had frozen the brakes down tight.

Back across the road I went again. I rousted out a barefoot kid at the restaurant and brought him back with me. He crawled underneath and clawed out a couple of pecks of rich-looking mud. He had trouble freeing the emergency, but finally managed it. I tied a handkerchief on the emergency to remind myself not to use it. Those brakes wouldn't be fully dry for two or three days. I gave the kid two dollars, and he turned cartwheels all the way back to the restaurant.

It was a beautiful morning when I hit the road. After the storm everything was fresh and clear. The highway was dry and there was no traffic that early in the day. At the first straight stretch I laid down on the accelerator to see what the Ford could do. I chickened out at 105, and it felt like I had an inch left. The thing was a bomb. It held the road well, too.

I drove on through Uvalde, San Antonio, Seguin, and Luling. I had lunch in Weimar. In the afternoon I piled on through Houston, Beaumont, and Orange. I made it into Lake Charles, Louisiana, and spent the night there. The speedometer said 469 miles for the day.

I'd pushed it a little because I wanted to make Mobile the next night. In Mobile I could get guns and other things I needed from Manny Sebastian. I had to ditch the artillery I had. One gun traced back to two bank guards in Phoenix, the other to a body floating in a rain-swollen ditch. If Manny hadn't lost his contacts, I could get a Florida license and registration from him to match what I was driving.

I was out on the highway again by six thirty the next morning. Ten miles east of Lake Charles I turned north on Route 165 at a little place called Iowa. I stayed with the new route for twenty miles to Kinder, then headed east again on 190. This was the New Orleans bypass. I sailed through Eunice, Opelousas, Baton Rouge and Hammond in Louisiana, and crossed into Mississippi at Slidell. A few miles further on

190 hooked back into 90 again, and I rolled along the Old Spanish Trail through Bay St. Louis, Pass Christian, Gulfport, Biloxi, and Pascagoula. Along that sunlit stretch I was seldom out of sight of white sand and blue gulf. When I pulled into a motel in Mobile about five o'clock the speedometer said 343 miles.

I washed up, had dinner, and drove downtown to the Golden Peacock, Manny Sebastian's joint. After midnight the place really swung far out, but at this time of night it was quiet. Manny had a finger in a lot of pies. He hadn't seen me in four or five years, but he recognized me the minute I walked in. He came over and shook hands. He'd put on a lot of weight since I'd seen him last, and his jowls and extra chins transformed the face I remembered as jovially ugly into something sinister-looking.

"The back room?" he asked me with a cocked eyebrow.

I nodded. He walked over behind the bar and engaged in small-talk with two of the half dozen customers. In five minutes I saw him select a key from a huge key ring and let himself out through an unmarked door alongside one marked "Office." The unmarked door was just outside the enclosure of the bar. I gave it another couple of minutes and walked around and tapped. Manny let me in and then closed and barred the door. He had a bottle and glasses already out on the small table that was the room's only furnishing besides an old-fashioned iron safe in one corner.

"Long time, man," Manny said to me. "How's old hit-the-squirrel-in-the-eye-at-a-hundred-yards?" He walked to the table and poured and handed me a drink. "What's your problem?"

"Not the same as yours. You talk too much, Manny." I took a swallow of my drink. "How're you fixed on Florida registrations?"

He nodded. "What're you driving?"

"A Ford all over mud on your parking lot." I handed him one of my Chet Arnold cards. "Have your boy run off a license while he's at it."

Manny went to the door and unbarred it. He called someone over to whom he spoke in a low tone, and closed the door again. "Ready in an hour. Like what else?"

"Hardware. A Smith & Wesson .38 and a Colt Woodsman."

He nodded again. "I'll have to send up to the house for the Woodsman. I've got a .38 right here." He was already whirling the dial on the old safe. "I range-tested it myself. Shoots a fraction high and to the left. The Woodsman's perfect."

"You know where they came from?"

Manny looked hurt. "Right out of the factory." He produced the Smith & Wesson with a flourish, still in the original box. "Never been fired except by me, either of 'em."

"Okay, Manny. What's the damage?"

He squinted up at the ceiling. "Oh, say four hundred for the lot. Paperwork comes high these days."

I paid him. Paperwork wasn't the only thing that came high, but I had to have those guns.

"Grab a seat at the bar. On the house," Manny said, pocketing the cash. "I'll give you the office when I get your stuff together. How're things in general?" The shrewd eyes in the larded-over face studied me.

"Quiet."

He chuckled. "A hundred seventy odd thousand quiet?"

I forced my face into a smile. "I read about that. Nice touch. Sounded like Toby Coates. Or Jim Griglun."

"Toby's in Joliet," Manny said smoothly. "And Jim lost his nerve after that time in Des Moines."

"Sometimes a man gets it back."

Manny shook his head. "Not if he didn't have too much to start with." He grinned at me companionably. "Your pawprints were all over that Phoenix job. You ought to miss a shot once in a while."

Out of the mouths of fools. I made a mental note.

"Sorry to disappoint you," I said as lightly as I could manage. "I've been in hibernation." A growing feeling of irritation mounted within me. This kind of earache I couldn't use.

He seemed to sense my mood. "Who should know better?" he said, cryptically enough, and opened the door. "Order up. It's on the house, remember."

I sat at the bar and ordered a highball I didn't want. Through a window at the right I could see out on the parking lot. A slim redhead with a limp was walking around the Ford. As I watched he raised the hood, leaned in and then out, and wrote something down on a piece of paper. The engine number, I thought.

I nursed the drink for half an hour, and then ordered another. I was two-thirds of the way down to the bottom of it when Manny slid onto the next stool and laid a package down on the bar quite openly. "Eddie says that's a real fireball out on the lot," he said to me softly. "I got a wheelman would give his front teeth for it. You want to trade? I'll give you something to boot."

"Not right now, Manny. I'll keep you in mind, though." I picked up the package and went out to the car. I pulled over to a corner of the lot and unwrapped the package. I put the new license and registration in my wallet, and switched loads from the old guns to the new. I tried them for balance. They felt all right. As soon as I had a chance I'd check out the Smith & Wesson. If Manny said it was throwing a little high and to the left, it was probably more than a little.

I drove out of the lot. More from force of habit than from any real belief that someone might be following me, I doubled and twisted over a circuitous route back to the motel. The conversation with Manny bothered me. Manny was a gossip. Never to the wrong people, so far as I knew, but a gossip is a gossip. This driving around the country so soon after a job bothered me, too. Before I'd always had a nice, quiet place to hole up in between jobs. This time I wasn't calling the tune, though.

I promised myself that as soon as I got straightened out in Hudson, Florida, I'd go to earth in a hurry. Back at the motel I sacked in and slept solidly.

The next morning was the fifth day since I'd left Phoenix. I got another early start and left Highway 90 about thirty miles beyond Seminole, Florida, at Milton. On 90-A I busted along through Galliver, Crestview, DeFuniak Springs, Marianna, Chattahoochee, Tallahassee, and Monticello. I was on the homestretch now. At Capps I turned south on U.S. 19. Out in the country I picked out two swift-running rivers about fifty miles apart, and I threw the old Smith & Wesson into the first one and the old Woodsman into the second.

At four in the afternoon I saw a sign at the side of the highway: Town Limits, Hudson, Florida. I was forty or fifty miles south of Perry. I drove through the main square and found a motel on the south edge of town called the Lazy Susan. I'd covered 362 miles since morning. I registered, showered, ate at the motel, went into the lobby and worked my way through half a month-old *Time*, and went to bed early. After that stretch on the road I wanted to start out fresh in the morning.

I had breakfast in town at a place called the Log Cabin. It looked like stucco but could have been stucco over logs. It was early, but the place was busy. It looked like a factory crowd. Not much conversation, even with the good-looking young waitress who wore an engagement ring but no wedding band.

After breakfast I walked around the square. Driving through yesterday, I'd estimated the town at six or eight thousand. This morning I upped that a little. The store windows were clean, and the displayed merchandise looked fresh. There were no empty stores. The merchants must at least be making the rent money.

I walked past the still unopened bank. It was an old building, bristling in its external impression of maximum security. Like a two-dollar watch of the type that used to be called a bulldog.

I bought a local paper in the drugstore, carried it under my arm to the little park in the square, and sat down on a bench in the morning sunlight. The park faced the town hall and the post office. I looked at the post office a couple of times. To be diverted, registered mail almost had to be tampered with by post office personnel. Although of course the packaged money didn't need to have been registered yet at the time it was intercepted.

The paper turned out to be a weekly. I read every line of it, including the ads. It's a habit of mine. Tips are where you find them. I've had a subscription for years under one of my names to *Banking, the Journal of the American Banking Association*. There's a column in it called "The Country Banker," and two of the best tips I ever had came right out of that column. *Banking* used to publish pictures of newly remodeled bank interiors. Lately they've pretty much cut that out. It must have occurred to someone they were being too helpful.

In the Hudson *Chronicle* I read right down to the Help Wanted and the Positions Wanted ads. There's something to be learned about a community from each. I read all the other ads. If there was a tree surgeon in Hudson, he wasn't using the *Chronicle* to attract customers.

I folded the paper up and walked back to where I'd parked the Ford. Main Street in Hudson ran east-west from the traffic light in the square, not north-south on 19. I drove east on Main. When the stores thinned out, I slowed down. The first houses were small, with tiny yards or none at all. No work for a tree surgeon there.

A mile beyond the built-up section of town the whole area south of Main was a swamp. I remembered seeing it on a map as Thirty Mile Swamp. From what I could see of it, it was no kitchen-garden swamp, either, but a fibrous jungle of cypress and mangrove in brackish-looking water, the whole drearily festooned with Spanish moss. At the side of the road beside a shack a handpainted sign said: AIRBOAT FOR HIRE.

I turned the Ford around and started back. Back at the edge of town again I turned north and began crisscrossing the side streets. Gradually I worked into higher ground and an improved residential area. I turned finally into a block-long street with only three houses on it. Big houses. Estates. I slowed down. This was what I needed. Property that needed to be kept up, and people with the money to pay for it. I drove around, and made notes on the edge of my newspaper.

When I'd accumulated half a dozen I headed back to the square and parked. I found a real estate office above the local five-and-dime and climbed the stairs with my paper under my arm. A young fellow hopped up from behind a desk as I entered. He had on a short-sleeved white shirt with a tie. Below the executive level in this latitude the short-sleeved white shirt is practically a uniform. Nobody wears a jacket, and after lunch the ties come off. Nobody is ever in a hurry.

"Yes, sir?" the boy said briskly. He had a nice smile. "Jed Raymond, sir. May I be of help?"

"Chet Arnold," I said, and handed him one of my business cards. "I just came in to pick your brains." I looked at my newspaper. "There's a big white Georgian house up on Sand Rock Road and Jezebel Drive." I looked at Jed Raymond. "Odd name for a street, that."

"Old Mr. Landscombe named it, Mr. Arnold. They do say he had his reasons." Jed Raymond looked up from his inspection of my card. "You want the tree work?" He shook his head doubtfully. "Mr. Landscombe died six months ago, and there's an unholy dust-up about his will. Three sets of heirs suing each other. The estate'll probably be in probate for years." The boy had a soft drawl and a mournfully humorous smile. He had a bright, heart-shaped face under a ginger-colored crewcut. Any woman over thirty would have taken him to raise and glad of the chance.

"Who's the estate administrator?" I asked him. "He shouldn't want the estate to run down."

Raymond looked impressed. "I b'lieve it's Judge Carberry." He pronounced it "Cah'bry." "If it's not he'll know who it is. You could have somethin' there."

I wrote the name down. "How about a fieldstone rancher up on University Place and Golden Hill Lane?"

"Belongs to Mr. Craig at the bank. His daddy used to be in the lumber business. So'd Roger Craig until he had a heart attack a while back. He came into the bank then. Guess his family owned most of it, anyway."

I looked at the rest of my list and decided to skip them for the time being. A judge, and a banker. Better still, a banker who had been in the lumber business. These two looked like solid leads. If I could crack either one, I was in business in this town. "You know your real estate, son," I told Jed Raymond. "Anything in the regulations says I can't buy your lunch one of these days?"

"If I find anything I'll get it amended," he grinned. He tucked my business card into his shirt pocket. "I'll keep this, if you don't mind. I might hear of something for you."

"Fine. I'm at the Lazy Susan now. If I change, I'll let you know. You happen to have a detailed map of the area?"

He reached in a counter drawer and handed me a thickly folded-over packet. "This one's even got the projected streets in the new development east of town." He waved me off as I put my hand in my pocket. "Hope you do y'self some good locally, Mr. Arnold."

I went back down the stairs to the street. I always carry two tool kits with me, a large one to work out of and a small one for show. I walked back to the Ford and got the small one out of the trunk. I tucked two double-bitted axes into the loops on either side of the chest. When a man formerly in the lumber business saw such a kit, I shouldn't have too much trouble getting into his office.

I walked back up the street toward the bank.

V

I WAS twenty-three when I killed my second man. Funny thing: it was in Ohio, too. Massillon. Five of us had flattened the bank on the northeast corner of the main intersection, but one of the boys got trigger-happy inside. In the getaway Nig Rosen and Duke Naylor were burned down in the street before we made it to the getaway car. A mile out of town I got a deputy in a cruiser trying to cut us off. Two days later the rest of us were flushed out of a farmhouse. Clem Powers was killed. Barney Pope and I were bagged.

Barney was an old lag. He knew he'd have long white whiskers before he made it outside again, if ever. Go for yourself, kid, he said to me as we stood in the farmyard with our hands in the air. I'll back your play.

I'd left my gun inside beside Clem's body. That scored the deputy to Clem. I told the mob scene that surrounded us I was a hitchhiker who'd been sleeping in the barn when the bandidos took over, and I stuck to it. True to his word, Barney backed me up. The police didn't believe it, but the jury came close. The identification putting me inside the bank was fuzzy. The guilty verdict was lukewarm.

Even the judge was leaning. I had no rap sheet. They'd checked my prints from Hell to Hoboken, and they couldn't even find a speeding charge. Two things licked me with the judge, finally. I wasn't using my family name, of course, and the probation officer couldn't get a line on me. The judge refused to believe I'd sprung full-blown from the earth age twenty-three without previous documentation of some kind. Also—and fatally—I could produce no visible means of support.

The judge cleared his throat and said three-to-five. I think he'd been considering probation. Barney Pope drew twenty-to-life. We weren't tried for the deputy. They figured they had us cold on the bank job, and on the other there was a question of jurisdiction and identification. The local D.A. didn't want to give up his own headlines by letting us go up on the other charge.

I hadn't graduated overnight to a five man bank detail. Once I'd found out which end of a gun was which, I'd come up the ladder, from filling stations to theater box-offices to liquor stores—the whole bit. I worked alone until I met Nig Rosen. Nig talked me into the Massillon setup. I guess I was flattered. I was far and away the youngest of the five.

We worked four months on that job. I kept my mouth shut, and listened. Parts of it I didn't like, instinctively, it seemed. Afterward I knew I was right. Complicated action with a bunch of hot sparks was no good. Even before we were hit I'd decided that what I wanted in the future was some kind of deal I could control myself.

In the can I had plenty of time to figure how it was going to be the next time. From the middle of my second year on, Doc Essegian was my cellmate. Everyone called him The Doctor. Maybe because he was such a wise old owl. I know he was no medical doctor.

The first three months he never even said good morning to me. Then I had a little trouble with one of the screws. When I came back from solitary, Doc laughed at me. "Don't let it burn a hole in your gut, kid," he advised me. "You're even a better hater than I am, and that's saying something." After that he kind of took me over. "Life is the big machine, kid," he'd growl at me in his after-lights-out rasp. "It chews you up and it spits you out. Don't you ever forget it."

He had the most completely acid outlook on life I'd ever run across. He really knew the score. He was consumptive to his toenails, but over the years he'd given them so much trouble inside they wouldn't certify him for the prison hospital. Each day he systematically coughed up a little bit more of his lungs, and grinned and thumbed his nose. Don't bother telling me it's impossible for our prison authorities to function in any such cold-blooded manner. I was there.

If it hadn't been for Doc I'd have applied for parole when I was eligible at the end of three years. Go ahead, if you can't tough it out, he told me, but remember this: the minute you do it you're the yo-yo on the end of the string. The least little thing they don't like they twitch the line and back you come. Do the five, he urged me. Go out clean. Spit in their eye. Get a decent job, something you can't do with a parole officer checking on you every time you turn around.

You're young, Doc said to me. Develop something you can work at once in a while and show as a means of support when a prosecutor wants to put you over the jumps. Put in time on the job occasionally. Keep a name clean to work under, because when a judge hears no visible means of support, you're gone.

I'd been there already, so I knew he was right. I had an even better reason for listening to him, though. The swag from the bank job had never been recovered. I knew where it was, and Barney Pope knew where it was. Nobody else. They'd about taken that farmhouse to pieces, but they hadn't found it. At least not publicly. A man working alone could have tapped the till. That you never do know till you get back for a look.

The reason I was sure it hadn't been found officially was that every three months I had a visit from the FBI. They always came in pairs, sharp boys, smooth dressers with faces like polished steel. I used to wonder if they came in pairs to eliminate the chance of my splitting with a single man after making a deal.

Not that I ever knocked down to them. I always insisted I was an innocent hitchhiker caught up in the middle of a police-bankrobber gunfight. They knew better, but they couldn't crack me. Each time they came we'd go over the same tired old question-and-answer game about the whereabouts of the boodle. From me they got a big fat nothing.

I found out Doc was right the first time they came back after I was eligible for parole. They turned me upside down as to why I hadn't applied. I told them I liked it where I was. That was the day I moved up to the top of their list. I knew right then that as the first pigeon out of the coop I was due to get a hell of a lot of their attention the second I hit the street. When I did I wanted it to be with as few strings as possible.

I did the bit. The day I walked out of that stinking hole I didn't have to say mister to any man. And I'd made up my mind: I wasn't going back. I didn't care what it took to stay outside. I wasn't going back.

An FBI tail picked me up at the front gate. I rode with it until he got to thinking it was a breeze. The second day I triple-doored him in a hotel lobby, and lost him.

Give the devil his due. With nothing to go on but persistence, they located me at the first two jobs I found. I wasn't on parole, but I lost the jobs. They saw to that. I'll leave it to you whether they didn't want me working so I'd be driven back to the farmhouse and the swag.

I shook them for good finally by hitchhiking up into the Pacific Northwest and hooking on in a lumber camp. I never saw a town for a year and a half. The work damn near killed me at first, but I got to like it. When I came out of there I could handle a crosscut saw and a double-bitted axe with the best of them, and I could do things with a handgun people pay admission to see.

I drifted into tree work later on. It seemed a natural for part-time work, and for getting a close-up look at a few places I was interested in. Like banks. When I worked, I worked hard. If I couldn't promote something for myself, I had no trouble at all catching on anywhere with a crew.

It was eight years before I went back for the Massillon boodle. I didn't need the money—I'd had two good bank pop-overs almost back to back—but it seemed about time. The farmhouse was gone, the farm cut up into a subdivision. I had to buy a lot to do it, but I got the swag. The deed to that lot is still in a safety deposit box in the Riverman's Trust Company in Cincinnati.

In the can nights I used to read before lights-out. At first it was at Doc's insistence. Learn something, you lazy, illiterate slob, he'd say to me. He had two gods, the dictionary and the encyclopedia. I'd read aloud to him because he had incipient cataracts. He could have had them operated on, but I think he was afraid to let them work on him while he had any light left.

An encyclopedia article would start him talking. He'd been everywhere and seen everything, twice. There were no degrees from the school I attended, but I've had to be a complete jerk not to learn.

Doc had been a bank man himself. A blaster, of the old dynamite school. He had a lot of theories, but he wasn't afraid to admit the world had personally passed him by. Forget the gangs, he'd say to me. Forget the big, involved jobs that hang up on the first weak link, because there's always a weak link. Two good men is all it takes, he insisted. Smash them. Never let up on the pressure. Never take a backward step once you're committed.

I listened, and I developed some theories of my own. I worked it out down to a few decimal points while I was up in the lumber camp getting the smell of the FBI blown off me. I divorced myself for all time from the vault-blowing jobs and the armored-truck jobs and the kidnapping-the-bank-manager-and-his-wife jobs. That was the hard way. A fast, clean operation: that's what I wanted. Hit-and-run. Smash-and-grab. They'd get a look for a hundred fifty seconds, average, with the disadvantage of surprise.

When I left the west coast I drove to Atlantic City and looked up Bosco Sheerin. Bosco liked the sound of what I had to say. I was younger than he was, but I insisted on calling the play. Bosco went along with it. He was a happy-go-lucky type, anyway. We had a two year run that was peaches-and-cream. Then one night in Philadelphia the husband of the blonde Bosco had been seeing came home early. Bosco wound up on a morgue slab with foreign matter in his gizzard. I needed a new partner.

All told in eleven years I ran through four partners, but not one of them punched out on the job. They'd have been better off if I'd kept them working steadier, but how much money can you spend? I'm no big liver. I had a shack in Colorado at timberline on the road up to Pikes Peak. In June it would snow half the mornings, and in July there were still six foot drifts in the back yard. I had another place on the Connecticut River near the Vermont–New Hampshire border. If I was there in August, I'd jump over to Saratoga and make the race meeting. I tried to spend part of every winter in New Orleans, but when the notion took me I'd settle down for a month or two almost anywhere.

When Ed Morris was killed in a drunken argument in a bucket-of-blood in Santa Fe, I went a year without turning a trick. Then one night in a tavern in Newark I met Bunny. I watched him for a month, and I liked what I saw. He could handle himself, and he had the big advantage that he could pass as a *deaf* mute. He even knew the finger-language. He'd been small-time before I picked him up, but he did as he was told. After our first job he had complete confidence in me. He was the best partner I ever had.

Bunny—

I couldn't get away from the feeling that the scorecard was going to read five dead partners in thirteen years.

I entered the latched-back doors of the Suncoast Trust Company and approached a gray-haired woman near the railing enclosing the executive desks. "I'd like to see Mr. Craig," I said to her, handing her my card. "He won't know me. If he's busy, I'll wait."

"Will you have a seat, please, Mr. Arnold?" She rose and walked to the desk of a big man in a dark suit. She placed my card in front of him and said a few words. He looked up at me just as I turned from the railing to sit down. His eyes lingered on the flash I gave him of the double-bitted axe in its straps on the side of the tool kit. I sat down to wait.

The bank exterior might have been old-fashioned, but the interior showed signs of a recent face-lifting. Indirect fluorescent lighting was bright without being harsh. The tellers' cages were behind head-high glass panels. The only bars visible were around the vault that stood in the rear with its huge door gaping open.

A safe prediction nowadays is that a bank resculpting job will result in the appearance of a lot more glass at the expense of a lot less steel. Many tellers are as approachable as librarians. They've made it a little too easy. The pendulum's got to swing the other way. These people shoving notes and paper bags through tellers' windows are beginning to get under the skin of bank personnel. To say nothing of bank architects and the bonding companies.

In the forties, knocking off a bank on a smash-and-grab was tough tissue. It will be again. It goes in cycles. Right now the thinking is positively no violence within the bank. Whatever the bank-robber wants, give it to him. Most likely it will be recovered, and if it isn't, it's insured.

Human nature being what it is, people don't always follow the script. Bank guards suddenly acquire hero complexes. So do bank customers. It's a rare banker who hasn't testified at an inquest or two concerning the last moments of just such a paths-of-glory candidate.

The only edge a pro has is in the way he plans his getaway. The amateur is more likely than not to run into the beat patrolman's arms outside the door. Once outside the load, the pro's three-in-ten chances of getting that far blossom into three-in-four of going the rest of the way.

The amounts of cash carried even by branch banks today make anything over a job or two a year an unnecessary risk. It leaves time to study an operation. Most bankers tend to become rigid in their defensive thinking. A little probing for the soft—

"Mr. Arnold?"

I looked up. The big man in the dark suit was standing at a gate in the low railing, my card in his hand. His eyes were again on the tool chest at my feet. I rose to my feet. "Yes, sir."

"I'll have to ask you to keep it brief," he said, holding the gate open. I picked up the tool chest and followed him to his desk. Up close his color was flat-white, and there were pain-lines at the corners of his mouth. He had a big lion-like head with shaggy gray hair. He was still looking at the axe, so before he could sit down I slipped it from its loops and handed it to him.

He swung it lightly in his left hand, his right unbuttoning his jacket before he remembered where he was. He rebuttoned it. "Nice balance," he said. "Feels a bit light, though."

"You're a big man, Mr. Craig."

His mouth twisted wryly. "I *was* a big man." He sat down, running a fingertip along the helve. I hadn't made any mistake in coming here; this man had seen an axe or two before. "Make your own handles?"

"Yes, sir."

"I used to, too. Except for boning and polishing them." He handed me back the axe. "What's your business with me, Mr. Arnold?"

"I'd like to clean up the trees on your place up on Golden Hill Lane, Mr. Craig. They need it."

He nodded. "References?"

"Nothing local. I've been working up around Bellingham, Washington. Ducked out ahead of the rainy season. At your convenience I'd be glad to meet you at your place and show you I know my business. You were in lumber. I couldn't kid you three minutes."

He nodded again. "Per diem or flat contract?"

"Write your own ticket, Mr. Craig. I'll do a job for you, because with your recommendation there's work in this area I should be able to get. Like the Landscombe estate."

"Be out at my place at eight in the morning," he said. He rose to his feet. "When did you get into town, Arnold?"

"Yesterday afternoon." His calling me Arnold with no Mr. in front of it was the best sign yet. I was three-quarters of the way inside the door.

"I like your style. You've rounded up your information and boarded ship here this morning before the sun's over the yard-arm. We've got a breed around here doesn't move that fast. Eight o'clock," he said again.

"I'll be there, Mr. Craig. And thanks."

"Don't thank me yet." His eyes had already returned to the papers on his desk. "If you can't cut the mustard, you don't get the job. And you're right about one thing: you won't be able to fool me. See you in the morning."

"With bells on," I promised. Walking away from his desk I slipped the axe back into its straps. At the counter I caught a fat lady's eye and opened up a checking account with eighteen hundred dollars in cash.

On the way out I glanced back at Craig's desk. I felt sure he'd know about that deposit by the time I saw him in the morning. I wanted him to know. I wanted to look to him like something more than a fly-by-night county-jumper.

Around Hudson, Florida, Roger Craig's good will could be as sharp a tool as any I had in my kit.

That afternoon I called Jed Raymond's real estate office from the motel. "Chet Arnold, the tree man, Jed," I said when I had his molasses drawl on the line. "Where do you recommend I do my drinking in town?"

"There's a place north of town on 19, Mr. Arnold. Its name is the Dixie Pig, but everyone calls it Hazel's."

"The name is Chet, son. Can I get a meal there?"

"If you're not a vegetarian. Hazel's got a habit of running a side of beef between a candle and a light bulb and calling it well-done steak. You've got to watch it her steaks don't get up off the platter and bite you back."

"That's for me. See you out there?"

"Not tonight." Regret tinged his voice. "Tonight I'm doin' a little missionary work with a gal whose daddy's plannin' a development on the edge of town. Ain't it hell what a man's got to do to make a livin'? Say, how'd you make out with Roger Craig?"

"I take a test flight in the morning."

"Hurray for our side. Tell Hazel I sent you out there, Chet. Don't let her bull you around. She's a character."

"Like what kind of a character?"

He laughed. "You'll see." He laughed again, and hung up.

I took a shower, and shaved and dressed. A drink and a good steak sounded just about right. In the early twilight I drove north from the Lazy Susan. Five hundred yards beyond the business district I took my foot off the gas as a big German shepherd burst out of the underbrush and loped along the shoulder of the road in front of me. I was still trying to decide if he was going to cut across the road when a blue sedan swung around me. It must have been doing sixty-five in a thirty mile zone. The driver crossed over sharply in front of me, out on the shoulder, and hit the dog. Deliberately.

At the last second the dog either heard or sensed the car. He jumped sideways, but not far enough. Either the fender or the wheel rolled him down into the ditch. The blue sedan veered back onto the highway and roared off down the road.

I stuck my foot into the accelerator and held it there for three seconds. Then I took it off. I couldn't afford to catch that sonofabitch. If I left him lying in a ditch I could be in trouble on the project that had brought me to Hudson. I braked the Ford, went into reverse, and backed up. Maybe I could do something for the dog.

I stood on the edge of the ditch and looked down. The dog was trying to get up. He had a long scrape on his head and one leg wasn't supporting him. I reached in the car window and got my jacket off the back rest, wrapped it tightly around my left hand and forearm, and scrambled down into the ditch. The shepherd was still trying to get up. "You gonna let me help, fella?" I asked him, and held out the wrapped arm until it touched him. I had to know if he was hurting so bad he'd bite anything that came in contact with him.

He didn't bite. I moved closer, stooped down, and picked him up. He growled a little, but that's all. An animal's got to be in a real bad way to bite me. They just don't do it. He was a big dog, and it was a steep bank, but I made it up to the car and put him on the front seat. I turned around and started back to town. A guy walking on the road told me where I could find a vet.

"Shoulder sprain," the vet said when he'd gone over him on the table. "A few gashes. Nothing serious. He'll be lame for a week. Leave him with me overnight. Your dog? You ought to get tags for him."

As though on cue the shepherd reached up from the table and took my wrist in his mouth, lightly. "I'll get the tags tomorrow," I told the vet. "Give him whatever he needs."

Outside I had to stop and think where I'd been going.

I headed out north for the second time.

VI

I HAD no trouble finding the Dixie Pig. It was a long, low building, encrusted with neon. No cars were parked in front although there were marked-off parking places. I followed a crushed stone driveway around to the rear and found a half-dozen cars. Evidently Hazel's customers didn't care to advertise their drinking habits to the highway.

Inside it was like a thousand others, low-ceilinged, smoke-musty, and dimly lit. The booths were empty. Six or eight customers lolled on the bar stools with their elbows on the bar. Nobody even looked around at me as I sat down.

A curtain rustled in an opening at the center back-bar, and a woman's head poked through. At the sight of a strange face she stepped in to the business side of the horseshoe-shaped bar. My first impression was that she was standing on elevated duckboards. She seemed enormous. I looked again. The back-bar flooring was on the same level as my side of the mahogany. She *was* enormous. Six feet if she was an inch, and bursting every seam of skin tight levis and a sleeveless fringed buckskin shirt that was no more than a vest. Her upper arms for size looked like John L. Sullivan's, but the skin was like a baby's. She had red hair, and a pleasantly wide mouth. She wasn't young, but she was youthful-looking.

"What'll it be, pardner?" she asked me. Her voice was a ripened contralto, deep and rich.

"You're Hazel?" She nodded. "I'm Chet Arnold. Jed Raymond sent me by. Make it bourbon and branch."

She smiled, displaying two gold teeth evenly spaced in the center of the attractive mouth. "Jed's a good kid." She turned to the bottled array behind her, and I watched the smooth ripple of muscle in her forearm as she poured my drink. I couldn't see an ounce of fat on the woman, but I'd have bet she outweighed me twenty pounds. She was the best looking big woman I'd ever seen.

She examined me frankly as she set the drink down. "Stayin' with us a while?"

"Depends," I said. "I'm prospecting. I make like Tarzan for a living, only with more equipment. I swing through the trees with an axe and a saw in my belt."

Her head was cocked to one side as she took me in feature by feature, the powerful-looking arms folded over her superb big breasts. "I'm not so damn sure you've got the face for that kind of work," she said finally. I've been in front of X-ray machines that didn't get as close to the bone as that woman's eyes.

I moved onto the offensive. "You off a ranch around Kingman, Hazel?"

The deep voice warmed. "Not bad for a guess. Nevada, not Arizona. I was raised in McGill, north of Ely. Raised? Make it roped. I get so homesick for the rimrock country sometimes I could bawl like a week-old calf."

"The planes are still flying," I suggested.

She shook her good-looking head. "I'm married to this goddam place. I just drink another fifth of my five-star shellac and forget about it. Did you want to eat?"

"Jed said you featured steak."

"Jed said right. Take your drink over to the booth there." She pointed to a corner. "I'll put the steak on the fire."

When she brought it to the booth twenty minutes later with a mound of french fries and a couple pounds of sliced tomatoes, I ate for a quarter hour without coming up for air. I mean that was a piece of meat.

I was divot-digging with a toothpick when Hazel came back to the booth. "Apple pie? Coffee?" she wanted to know.

I tested my straining belt. "Better raincheck me."

She glanced over at the bar. Everything was quiet. Standing beside me, I had my first look at her feet. She had on worked leather cowboy boots studded with silver conches. They went for one-fifty if they went for a quarter. She slid into the booth opposite me and sat down with her chin propped in her hands. Her calm inspection raked me fore and aft. "Maybe it's not the face," she decided. "Maybe it's the eyes. What do you really do for a living, Chet?"

I reached for my cigarettes, offered her one, and got two going when she accepted. "Your pa should have hairbrushed you out of asking questions like that," I told her.

"My pa never hairbrushed me out of anything I wanted to do," she answered. "Well?"

"I've been known to make a bet once in a while," I humored her.

"That's more like it," she said briskly. "A workingman you're not. What's your action? Horses?"

"Horses," I agreed.

"Is that right?" She straightened up as though someone had turned on an electric current in the booth bench. "D'you remember old Northern Star? I saw him one time at Delaware Park run five an' a half furlongs in a tick less—"

So we sat and played Remember When.

It's a damn small world sometimes. Hazel's first husband had been Blueshirt Charlie Andrews, the man who bet 'em higher than a duck can fly. I'd never met him, but he'd been a pal of a friend of mine who unfortunately attracted a small piece of lead a few years back. This I did not tell Hazel.

In five minutes we found out we'd both been in Baltimore for the Pimlico Futurity in which Platter had hung it on By Jimminy, one of the last big bets the Bradley camp blew before the old gentleman checked to his last openers. We argued whether it had been '43 or '44. I held out for '44.

"I *know* it was '43," Hazel insisted. "It was my first year at the tracks. I was seventeen."

"Which makes you—"

"Never mind the arithmetic, horseman."

"—younger than I am," I finished.

Her inward look turned back down the years. "Charlie Andrews was about the ugliest man I ever knew, I guess. He stopped off for a cup of coffee in a diner in Ely where I was a waitress. He was on his way to the coast, but three weeks later he was still in the diner tryin' to talk me into sharin' it. He was about as subtle as a blowtorch, an' I was green as grass and scared to death. He'd sit across the counter from me, takin' up most of two stools—he was about five five an' weighed two-forty, an' even his ears had muscles—an' he'd say to me, 'Hazel, honey, you got a croup jus' like a thoroughbred mare. I never hope to see a bigger piece of ass.'" She shook her head reminiscently. "He married it to get it. He was a lot of all right, that

Blueshirt man. Although it sure was chicken today an' feathers tomorrow livin' with him. That man would bet on anything."

Some people came in the back door, and she stood up to go back to the bar to wait on them. "Don't go away, horseman," she said over her shoulder. "I don't get a chance to talk the language much these days."

I knew what she meant. It's a special language. When Jed Raymond walked in at eleven o'clock we were still at it, re-running races of fifteen years ago. "You must have had the password, Chet," he said to me. "Our hostess doesn't usually unbend like this to the hoi-polloi."

Hazel reached up from the booth and hit him a casual back-hander in the chest that nearly collapsed him. "This guy is with it, Jed," she said, leveling a thumb at me. "Where'd you find him?"

"He found me," Jed answered when he could get his breath. "Lay off that strong-arm stuff, woman, or I'll call out the militia on you." He sat down in the booth beside me. "One for the road?"

"One," I agreed. "Then I've got to get out of here. I'm making like a workingman in the morning."

Driving back to the motel twenty minutes later, Hazel's big, handsome face danced in the windshield. With her hearty laugh and golden smile she was the most woman I'd seen in a hell of a while.

For a time I'd nearly forgotten the shape of things.

It wouldn't do.

I pulled into Roger Craig's elliptical gravelled driveway at five minutes to eight. I was wearing my poor-but-honest khakis. Craig was already out in the side yard superintending a young colored boy setting up an eight-foot section of slash pine about a foot and a half in diameter. If this was the test it was going to be a joke. Slash pine is so soft I could have handled it with my teeth. Still, Craig was a native, and this was the wood he knew.

I opened the back deck of the Ford and slid out my big tool chest, and a couple of coils of rope. Craig nodded to me jovially. I could see he knew about the deposit. His manner was a lot easier. Unless I cut a leg off, I had the job. He needed the work done, and I was now a customer of the bank.

I strapped on safety belt and climbers, opened the chest and took out a pair of goggles, and unslung the lighter of the axes. "All set, Mr. Craig?"

"Whenever you're ready, Arnold."

I walked up to the pine log and tested it for balance. It was wedged firmly. I settled myself in front of it, digging in with my heels in the soft turf. With wood like this I had no need for a long, over-the-head axe stroke. Just as well for a still stiff arm. I went at it from shoulder height, placing the cuts more with an eye to accuracy than speed. Still, a deep V narrowed rapidly as the axe rang with the mellow sound of good steel, and the fat white chunk chips flew in a solid shower. Chips were still in the air when I stepped back with the pine log in two sections. The colored boy stood off to one side with wide-rounded eyes.

"I wish I could have tried you a few years back," Craig said. There was a wistful note in his voice.

I almost made the mistake of handing him the axe. That would really have been rubbing it in on a heart attack victim. I pushed back the goggles as I caught myself just in time. "I'd have asked for a handicap," I told him. "You've got a press agent downtown. Bright young fella in the real estate office over Woolworth's. He says you could really go."

Craig smiled with pleasure. "Jed Raymond. Good boy. Knows his way around the woods, too." The smile faded. "I get damn tired of being half a man these days." He turned businesslike. "I didn't want to give you buck fever by telling you beforehand, but you were trying out for two jobs. I ran into Judge Carberry at the club last night. Drop around and see him when you finish up here." He held up a restraining hand when I would have spoken. "What do you propose to do for me?"

"I'll do it all." I waved at the driveway. "I'll shape up that low-bush Ficus and wax myrtle when I finish with the trees." I turned to the side of the house. "Just about all of it needs thinning and trimming, especially the live oaks and that shagbark hickory. See the dead limb on that sycamore? On the other side of the house you've got two bad palmettos. The one nearest the house definitely ought to come down. Maybe the other one can be saved." I ran over it in my mind. "All told, two and a half or three days' work."

He nodded. "You're the doctor." He smiled again. "Literally, by God. Jeff here will give you a hand as you go. Just waggle that axe at him when you want him to move." Jeff showed a mouthful of teeth in an expressive grin. "I'll let the Judge know he can expect to see you when you finish here."

"I appreciate it, Mr. Craig."

"Stop in and see me at the bank any time you're ready." He went into the house, and five minutes later his car eased down the opposite loop of the driveway.

I smoked my before-climbing cigarette while I walked around the yard planning the day. One of Roger Craig's forebears had had an eye for trees. There was something for everyone. In the northwest corner he had the biggest magnolia I'd ever seen. It must have gone seventy feet. He had chinquapin, sassafras, sweet gum, red birch, and mimosa. On the other side I'd seen cottonwood and aspen. He even had a chinaberry tree.

It was a bright, sunny morning, and the air felt crisp. I was established in Hudson, Florida, and my sponsorship was the best. With a start like this if I couldn't ease up on the blind side of whoever had sandbagged Bunny, then there was something the matter with me.

I climbed upstairs and went to work. Most of the morning I thinned out tops, occasionally marking a larger limb that had to go. Jeff dogged me from beneath as I moved from tree to tree, raking and burning the scut. At noon I called down to him to grab himself a sandwich. I never stop myself. In the trees food is just so much extra weight. I go right through from eight to four.

In the afternoon I tied three different weight crosscut saws to my belt, and shouldered up a coil of rope. I went to work on the larger stuff. I'd undercut it first, then rope it to the trunk and lower it carefully to Jeff standing beneath when the overcut snapped it off. I wanted no heavy drops tearing up the side of the house or scarring the lawn.

The last half hour I trimmed up stubs and daubed them with paste. I knocked it off at four sharp. I was tired, but not unpleasantly so. The arm had held up well. It was the first real day's work I'd done since I'd cased the bank in Okmulgee, Oklahoma. I'd finally decided against trying, but I'm never too much out of shape.

I packed the gear back into the Ford, told Jeff I'd see him in the morning, and headed for the Lazy Susan and a shower. In the square the traffic light caught me, and I sat there waiting for it to change so I could swing south on 19. I had to hold up for a second after it changed as a slim, red-headed man limped hurriedly across the street in front of me, against the light.

I turned the corner with a teasing tickle in the back of my mind: had I seen him before, or just someone who looked like him? When you move around the way I do, it's hard to fit faces to locations sometimes.

Then it hit me.

The last time I'd seen that limping redhead he'd been out in Manny Sebastian's parking lot in Mobile with the hood up on my car.

I turned into the first vacant parking space.

I got out of the Ford and walked back up the street.

I sat at the wobbly desk in the motel room and spread out under the light the real-estate map of the area I'd bummed from Jed Raymond. On the floor at my feet the German shepherd lay with his muzzle on his paws, his brown eyes watching me steadily. I'd stopped at the vet's and picked him up after I'd spent a fruitless thirty minutes quartering downtown Hudson in a search for the redhead I'd last seen three hundred fifty miles away. I hadn't been able to find a trace of him.

Seeing him meant the honeymoon was over for me. There was only one reason he could be in Hudson. Manny Sebastian had decided to cut himself in on the Phoenix $178,000. It wasn't very bright of Manny. I had to give it a little thought to work out just how I was going to change his mind. Because I was definitely going to change it. First, though, there was the matter of locating the stuff myself.

The shepherd's shoulder was stiff, but he could walk. The scrape on his head had been nothing serious. "How you doin', Kaiser?" I asked him. His big tail thumped the rug. His head came up, and his new tags glistened on his new spiked collar. A twenty dollar bill had straightened me out with the motel proprietor over the added starter in the unit. It wasn't his busy season, so he could afford not to give me an argument.

I turned to the map. Finding the sack with the money in it had suddenly taken on a priority. Since seeing the redhead, I couldn't take this thing in second gear. Slow and easy was out. I had to get moving. I knew Bunny wouldn't have dug himself in too far out of town, but he wouldn't have set up a tent in front of the city hall, either. He liked to batch it alone where he wouldn't attract attention. It was one of the things I'd liked about him.

Looking at the map, I tentatively ruled out the north-south stretch of U.S. 19 above and below the square as the least likely section for Bunny to hole up in. Too much traffic. Too many people. That left Main Street east from the traffic light. And because of Thirty Mile Swamp to the south, it left Main Street to the north. I took a pencil and marked lightly—beginning at the edge of town—two points five miles apart, as close as I could figure it by the map scale. If I drove up every road leading north off Main in that stretch, I might not find Bunny but I might find a blue Dodge sedan with Arizona plates. An automobile is harder to dismaterialize than you'd think. Even the burned-out skeleton of a car would be a starting place.

I looked at my watch. I still had an hour of daylight. "Come on, boy," I said to the shepherd. He was up at once, hobbling but expectant. Out in the yard he was ready to jump up into the front seat when I opened the car door. I picked him up and put him in. "We'll pamper you for a day or two," I told him. He nuzzled my arm and sat down, dignified as a college president.

I went around to the trunk and hauled out knee-high boots, a machete for underbrush, and a steel-shafted number 3 iron for snakes. I'd seen enough of the side roads around Hudson to know I'd be doing as much walking as riding. I'd cover every cowpath a car or a man could get over in that five-mile stretch, and if that didn't turn up anything, I'd mark off another five-mile stretch and do it again. I'd cover it a yard at a time, if I had to. Whatever it took to do it, I was going to find Bunny.

We drove out Main, out of town, Kaiser sitting up to the window as steady as a sergeant-major on dress parade. He had a big head and a wicked-looking mouthful of teeth. His coat was mostly gray, flecked with brown in front. He looked all business, sitting up there.

The first two roads I turned up weren't bad. The third one I took one look, pulled the Ford in off the road, and changed to the boots. I didn't have enough daylight left to do much that night, but I wanted to get the feel of it. In the first hundred yards I found out I had a bull by the nose. Clouds of gnats and mosquitoes dive-bombed me. I lunged through knee-deep brush, chopping steadily, perspiration streaming, only the signs of recent car passage luring me on to end-of-track. When the ruts petered out by an abandoned tarpaper shack I turned around and slogged my way back.

I came out on the road again to find a two-tone county cruiser pulled in behind the Ford, and Kaiser showing a handsome set of fangs to a uniformed man trying to look into the front seat. My brush-crackling progress announced me, and the man turned to look me up and down.

"Deputy Sheriff Franklin," he said curtly. "You'd better keep that damn wolf on a leash." I said nothing. Franklin was a stocky man with a red face of the type much exposed to weather. His gray uniform trousers had red piping on the sides, and his khaki shirt was open at the throat. "What's your business out here?" he asked me.

"I'm a timber cruiser," I said.

"You're a what?"

"I'm scouting the area looking for a stand of second-growth black maple I hear is in here."

He scowled. "We're two hundred miles too far south for black maple. If you know your business, you know that." He glanced in at the weedy-looking trees shooting up in an area that had been viciously slash-cut years before.

I shook my head firmly. "I had a drink the other night with an old-timer who told me they took a million feet of black maple out of here fifty years ago. Should be a buck in it today for the guy that finds the right spot, if the slash hasn't been burned over." Franklin was studying me. "I'm doing a job of work for Mr. Craig and Judge Carberry back in town," I added.

Whatever he'd been going to say, the names stopped him. He wasn't the type to bow out gracefully, though. He swaggered around to the rear of the Ford and made a production of taking down the license plate number. "We keep an eye on these badlands," he said gruffly, and stalked back to the cruiser. He backed out on the road at fifty miles an hour, punched the shift panel on the dash, and roared down the road, wide open.

I changed back to my cordovans, put boots, machete, and golf club back in the trunk, and patted Kaiser's big head as I got back into the Ford. "Good dog," I told him. He rrrrrrr'd deep in his throat, and nipped at my arm. I had a feeling Kaiser and I understood one another about uniforms.

It was full twilight when I got back to the motel.

I began to make it a habit to eat my evening meal at Hazel's. Jed frequently joined me, and we'd sit over a drink and talk, and when the bar wasn't busy Hazel would join us.

Like a lot of salesmen I've known, Jed was a complete extrovert. In a roomful of people he'd crawl onto Hazel's lap and talk baby-talk to her. He had a high-pitched, infectious laugh that turned every head in a room. With all that he was a sharp-witted kid who looked in both directions before crossing the street.

Between them Jed and Hazel knew every living soul for fifty miles. I sat and listened while they rattled family skeletons past and present twenty to the dozen. Early in the game I introduced the subject of the post office. They shook a few feathers loose from that bird, but I couldn't see anything meant for me.

Lucille Grimes was the postmistress, widow of a former postmaster deceased five years. Jed said the town couldn't understand why she didn't remarry, since she had suitors and to spare. He also said zestfully that she was a tall, leggy, cool-looking blonde.

Hazel had her own ideas as to why the beauteous Lucille hadn't remarried. She hinted darkly that the favored suitor already had a wife. Since Hazel, minus her usual spade-is-a-shovel outspokenness, failed to name him, I deduced that he was a Dixie Pig customer. From Hazel's attitude, Lucille Grimes was not one of her favorite people. Jed kidded her about it.

In all of it there was nothing for me that I could see, but that post office bothered me.

It took me eight working days to clean up the Craig and Landscombe properties. Evenings I got out and plowed up the side roads on the north side of Main, and discovered nothing. When I finished with the Craig and Landscombe places, nobody remarked on the fact that I didn't seem to be knocking down any stone walls looking for more work. The sun coast of Florida is an easy-going neighborhood.

Jed led an active social life, even for a young fellow his age. The nights he didn't show up for dinner, after a couple or three times of my eating alone, it came to be understood that if I'd postpone my own meal to seven thirty, Hazel would serve us both in the corner booth. Over coffee and cigarettes we'd sit and swap lies about horses and horseplayers we'd known.

The big girl was comfortable to be around. Once in a while she'd have to get up and tend bar, but not too often. She did her real business from nine thirty to midnight. At the tracks she'd seen them all from Ak-Sar-Ben to Woodbine. She didn't go back as far as I did by a dozen years, but as the evenings passed it was odd to see how many times we'd been in the same town at the same time. She'd seen Papa Redbird win the Arlington Classic in '48, and Rough'n Tumble the Santa Anita Derby in '51. So had I. She'd seen Turn-To win the first Garden State, and she'd been in New Orleans the winter old Tenacious first took charge. So had I. It wasn't the biggest club in the world.

Jed warned me Hazel could be moody, and her drinking a problem. I saw no sign of either. With me I think she had a chance to let off steam that had been a long time bottled up. Blueshirt Charlie Andrews had died five years before of a heart attack. Hazel had rushed into and out of a no-good second marriage, the only legacy of which was the Dixie Pig.

I liked her. I could tell she had guts. I knew she'd spit in the eye of the devil himself.

I enjoyed it, sitting around batting the breeze about the old days, but way down deep inside I was getting restless.

It wasn't what I had come for.

We were sitting in the corner booth one night, waiting for Jed. Hazel, as usual, was talking horses. Like all horseplayers, she had strong opinions. Arguing, she'd get excited; her eyes would flash, and she'd pound the table.

She held out for Citation as the best she'd ever seen. I was on the coast the summer Citation couldn't get past Noor in the stretch four straight races. I know he'd been away a year, and I know he wasn't what he had been. Regardless, I've never since been able to make him the best.

I go with Count Fleet. He didn't beat horses, he murdered them. I saw him win the Walden at Pimlico by thirty lengths. Look it up. Thirty lengths. And don't ask me who he beat. He beat the best there was around. No horse can do any more. When he came out of the far turn with his mane and tail streaming and the rest of them nowhere, it was enough to stop your heart.

It's been one of my secret sorrows that he never bred anything approximating himself as a runner. Stake winners, yes, but no Count Fleets. I think now the big horse will come from one of his fillies. If I owned a Count Fleet filly, all the gold in Fort Knox couldn't buy her. Some one of these days a broodmare by him is going to throw a jimdandy.

The forum broke up when Jed came in. He sat down, and Hazel went out back to start the steaks. The bar became busy with before-dinner thirst quenchers and she didn't come back. Everyone came in the back door. As far as I could see Hazel could have nailed up the front door and never lost a nickel's worth of business.

Jed was in high good humor. "Made a sale today," he informed me. "Drink up, drink up. I'll buy you one. Got to keep the money of the country circulatin'."

"You can buy me a brandy after dinner," I told him. I could see I'd lost his attention. From his side of the booth he could look out over the back parking lot, and he was leaning forward to look more closely.

"Well, well, well," he said softly. "Here's company for us." He stood up, a bright, artificial smile pasted on his face as a tall blonde walked in the back door. "Here's Miss Lucille now," he said loudly enough to be heard by her. "Maybe she'll have a drink with us." He moved out of the booth.

I could hear his laughing cajolery as he intercepted her in the middle of the floor. In seconds he was leading her to our booth. "—Ol' Chet's been admirin' your post office, especially the fixtures that aren't government issue," he was saying. He winked at me as I rose. "Lucille Grimes, Chet Arnold. Chet's a tree surgeon, Lucille." He grinned at her. "I don't need to introduce you in your official capacity. Chet knew who our beautiful postmistress was fifteen minutes after he'd hit town."

"Won't you sit down, Miss Grimes?" I offered, to cut off the flow of words. She murmured something and slid into the booth opposite me. Her face was cool-looking and composed under the blonde hair. Her face was a bit too long and pointed from brow to chin, but with good features. Her skin was pale, and her eyes surprisingly dark for her low-keyed complexion. Despite the lack of high points, there was nothing washed-out in her appearance.

Jed pushed in beside her and called for drinks. Lucille Grimes folded slim, capable-looking hands on the booth table and looked at me directly. "I hear you're a very capable workman, Mr. Arnold," she said. Her voice was low-keyed, too. No stress or strain.

"Thank you, Miss Gr—"

"Hear, hear," Jed interrupted. "Lucille, meet Chet. Chet, meet Lucille. What's all this Mr. an' Miss business?" He stood up and advanced on the jukebox in the corner. He fed it coins and punched buttons indiscriminately. "Dance?" he offered Lucille, returning to the booth. "Illegal, but the custom of the country," he grinned down at me. He returned his attention to her. "Join us for dinner? Private little celebration of mine."

"Another time, thanks." She sounded genuinely regretful. She danced with Jed. She danced with me. I'm not much of a dancer, but she followed me easily. She wasn't nearly as willowy as I'd thought seeing her come in the back door. She filled a man's arms. I tried to guess her age. Thirty, maybe.

I was on the floor with her when the back door opened again to admit a stocky man in gray uniform trousers with red piping on the side and a khaki shirt open at the throat. My friend from the road the other day, I thought, recognizing the blunt red face. He sat down at the bar and ordered a beer.

After another dance with Jed, Lucille excused herself. "It's been very pleasant," she said to both of us. She smiled at us impartially, gathered up gloves and bag, and exited through the rear door. Three minutes later the stocky man left his half-finished beer and followed.

Jed watched me take this in. "They're not usually that obvious, Chet. That's Bart Franklin, one of our risin' young deputies. Known as Blaze, due to a well-advertised short temper. I'm a jack-leg deputy around here myself in emergencies.

Blaze isn't one of our better-loved members. He's gone for the blonde widow."

"Thanks, son. It always helps to know if another dog's after the same bone."

"You go for her?" he asked in a half-protesting tone. "I brought her over because I remembered you asked about her the other night, but—" He shook his head. "It's all yours, man. Yours and Blaze's. I tell you that gal spooks me. Somethin' about her just—"

"Nothing another ten years wouldn't help you to handle," I told him as he sat there wagging his head. The conversation died as Hazel brought the meal. Jed left at eight thirty to keep a date, and I said so long to Hazel shortly afterward.

I drove back to town, parked in the square, and went into my act. A week ago I'd marked off four taverns as the type most likely to have attracted Bunny's trade. Every night I stopped off in two of them for a glass of beer. I'd sit in each for half an hour, exchanging an occasional word with the bartender. They all knew me now when I came in, and had my beer drawn before I said a word.

Starting with the friendliest, in another few days I'd throw each of them the same bait. "What's become of that big, dark, quiet fella used to be in here around this time of night?" I'd ask them. "Haven't seen him lately."

They'd try to remember. A bartender's customers come and go. "Oh, yeah, the big guy," I hoped one or more of them would say, "That's right, he hasn't been around, has he?"

If they remembered him, I might get a lead. I needed a lead, badly. I was on my second five-mile stretch of side roads, and I'd found nothing. If a bartender even remembered the direction Bunny drove off whenever he left the tavern, it would be more than I had now.

I couldn't racket around this town asking for Dick Pierce. A small town is wired together so tight it would be sure to get back to the interested party. Of course if I crapped out all around the green-covered table trying to find Bunny, a direct inquiry was my ace in the hole.

The day I asked, though, I had to be ready for anything.

I wasn't planning on it.

Not yet.

VII

THE NEXT night I was making the second of my tavern stops when the limping redhead made a mistake. He didn't know it was a mistake, because he didn't know I'd seen him in Mobile. I'd just climbed out of the Ford, ready to go inside for a beer I didn't want, when he cruised by in a black sedan at about eight miles an hour. I got a good look at him. He didn't turn his head to look at me. He just went on by. The sedan turned the corner above the tavern, and pulled into the curb and stopped. I could tell by the reflection from the headlights. I knew the redhead was tailing me as plainly as if he'd written me a letter.

I went on inside and had the beer, talked a little baseball to the bartender, Bobby Herman, and gave some thought to the redhead. The minute I'd seen him on the street the day before I'd decided he was a luxury I couldn't afford. That left two things to be settled: finding out if he'd already reported back to Manny Sebastian where he'd followed me to, and how I was going to get rid of him.

I said goodnight to Bobby Herman and went back outside to the Ford. I pulled ahead and turned the same corner the black sedan had turned. There wasn't a car in sight, parked or moving. I circled the block twice without seeing a thing. I was just beginning to get a good mad on at myself for having lost him again when car headlights picked me up from about thirty yards behind me. I don't know where he came from. The sonofabitch was good. Tailing a man in a car without calling attention to yourself takes ingenuity. This boy had it.

I took him back uptown and east on Main from the traffic light. Out on the edge of town I settled down to a steady fifty miles an hour. I was in no hurry. Somewhere out in the boondocks I'd find a place to leave him, permanently.

In the first five miles I found out how he'd been able to follow me all the way down from Mobile without my getting wise. He was an artist with an automobile. When he had room to maneuver he didn't just lock himself onto my taillight and leave me to wonder eventually about the lights in the rear-view mirror that remained the same distance behind. There was only a sliver of moon, but he rode some straight stretches with his lights out. For short distances he'd be bumper-to-bumper with me, and then I wouldn't see him at all for miles. Twice he passed me, once doing about eighty, only to pick me up again from behind. The first time he went by I wasted a look at his license plate. It was carefully, unreadably mud-spattered.

Twenty five miles up the line I came out of the woodsy darkness enveloping the road into a sleepy-looking, wide-place-in-the-highway town with a blinking yellow light at an intersection surrounded by darkened storefronts. The only other illumination was a lighted telephone booth on the main street, just before the blinker. I turned right at the intersection, right again at the next corner, and right again at the next. I was out of the car and sprinting down an alley between two stores before the redhead's headlights turned the last corner and cruised down past the Ford.

The last time I'd parked he'd turned the next corner and pulled in. I was gambling he'd follow a pattern. If he did, I had him in my pocket. I cut left through a bisecting alley, running for the main street.

I was in time to see his headlights arc around as he swung the corner. Sure enough, his car went past me and stopped not fifteen feet from the phone booth. He'd cut his lights before he even stopped rolling. He'd seen I wasn't in the Ford when he went by. In his own mind he could be getting close to the payoff. He was, but not the kind he expected. He climbed out in a rush, took a quick look around the silent town, and started to head back up the street to the corner he'd just turned. He didn't want to lose me.

He didn't.

I stepped out of the alleyway and intercepted him, the Smith & Wesson in my hand. "Hi, Red," I said to him. "How're things in Mobile?"

It would have stopped the average man's heartbeat. This was a different breed of rooster. Even in the poor light I could see him straightening his face out as he went into a deadpan look. "You got me wrong, Jack," he protested.

"Walk up to the phone booth," I told him. I wanted to see his face in the light when I asked him the question that was bothering me. I followed right behind him, shoving the gun under my armpit. "Get inside it," I said when he reached the booth. "Make out you're dialing." He took down the receiver before he turned to look out at me. "Don't make the mistake of putting your hand in your pocket for change."

"You're makin' a big—"

"You must be the wheelman who wanted the Ford," I cut him off. "Manny tell you you could have it if you kept tabs on me for him?"

It must have rocked him, but he didn't lose his nerve. "I don't know any Manny," he said sullenly. "You off your rocker?" He was eyeing me, wondering where the gun had gone. He had a thin, pale face with a scattering of freckles.

"Have you called Manny since you followed me into Hudson, Red?"

He dropped all pretence. "Manny says you're a tough boy," he sneered. "You don't look so tough to me."

"One more time, Red," I told him softly. "Have you called Manny since—"

"Up, with a meathook, buster!" Red snatched the booth door closed with his left hand while he went for the gun in his shoulder holster with his right. His hand was still on its way under his lapel when I put one in his chest and one in his ear. Both of them took chunks of booth glass before they took chunks of Red. He did a slow corkscrew to the booth floor, the freckles stark in his white face. I emptied the Smith & Wesson into the booth, spraying it from top to bottom. I put the last one into the light. Nobody was going to call this one a sharpshooting job.

I went up the alley at a good clip and right-angled back to the Ford. I reversed it up to the next corner without putting my lights on, then retraced the way I'd driven in there. I put my lights on just before I hit the blinker. Lights were popping on in houses here and there as I swung left and headed for the Lazy Susan.

With the booth light out they'd be a while finding Red. When they did, they'd be another while trying to unscramble the jigsaw. I put the Smith & Wesson on the seat beside me in case I had to pitch it if anything came up behind me. I held it down to fifty all the way back. I only passed three cars on the way, and nothing passed me. Kaiser greeted me at the motel-room door. He stretched out at my feet and watched for twenty minutes with only an occasional blink as I cleaned, oiled, and reloaded the Smith & Wesson.

I didn't know whether Manny knew where to find me or not. I knew that if he didn't, he wasn't going to.

I went to bed.

On my next trip out to the Dixie Pig I took Kaiser along with me. There was the usual sprinkling of a dozen cars parked out in back, including Jed Raymond's sports car. I went in with Kaiser padding sedately along beside me, and Jed waved from a booth. I was two-thirds of the way across the floor before I saw Lucille Grimes with her back to me in the booth opposite him.

Jed, with his fey grin, tried to maneuver me into sitting beside Lucille. I pushed him over and sat down beside him. "Good evening, all," I greeted them.

Lucille smiled but didn't speak. Jed reached under the table to pat Kaiser who sat down beside me. I watched closely but Kaiser didn't take any offense. "Hi, there, big boy," Jed said to him. "Who's your gentleman friend, Chet?"

"Kaiser, meet Jed," I introduced them. I noticed that the blonde's long legs were as far withdrawn beneath the booth as she could manage. Evidently Lucille wasn't an animal lover. "Well, folks, what's the chief topic of conversation?" I inquired.

"The star-spangled, unmitigated dullness of life in a small town," Jed answered promptly. "Right, Lucille?"

Her thin smile was noncommittal. "I don't believe I have too many complaints," she said. "And perhaps Chet hasn't always lived in a small town."

Jed got me off that hook. "They're all small," he asserted. "The biggest of them are small, even New York City. How much town can you live in? Outside of a couple of blocks near where you work and a couple of blocks near where you sleep, the rest is as strange as to a visitor from Beluchistan. I'll take little old Hudson."

"Which side of the argument are you on, anyway?" Lucille wanted to know. "You're complaining about dullness, but you'll take little old Hudson. Page the Chamber of Commerce." I thought she looked tired. There were dark circles under her eyes. She kept watching the parking lot through the booth window. So did I, but not as obviously. We hadn't long to wait. A two-tone county sheriff's department cruiser swung slowly through the lot and down the driveway on the other side. The blonde gathered up her gloves and bag. "You'll have to excuse me, gentlemen," she said, rising. "Good night."

"For a guy slaverin' for blonde meat you don't move very fast," Jed accused me when she'd gone.

"You young sprouts just don't understand the logistics of my generation," I told him. "Our theme song is 'But They Get There Just the Same.' Pay attention; you could learn something. Your technique is all wrong."

"Not since I got out of high school it hasn't been," Jed asserted cheerfully. He turned serious. "Listen, don't let me needle you about the widow. She's—well, there's better fish in the creek. Whyn't you let me slip you a number or two from my little black book?"

"Just because a county cruiser circles the parking lot?" I asked him.

He nodded. "So you saw it, too. Blaze Franklin—" Jed hesitated. "Blaze is a little bit primitive. You know? Rednecked all the time. Who needs it to get involved with a thick turd like that?"

"So he's the jealous type."

"In spades, he's the jealous type." Jed pushed his glass around in the wet circles on the table top without looking at me. "I've heard some stories about Blaze." He turned to grin at me. "Some of them might even be true. Hey, Hazel!" he hollered over to the bar in a quick change of subject. "Bring on the fatted calf!"

We ate diligently, with Jed feeding small cuts of his steak to Kaiser, who accepted them with dignity. "You'll spoil him," I told Jed.

"He can stand spoiling. That's a lot of dog. I like his looks." He glanced at his watch. "Say, I got to get going."

When he left I sat around waiting to see if Hazel was going to be able to get away from the bar long enough to sit down. I got a surprise when she did. The first thing I noticed was that she was wearing a dress. She must have changed since she'd served us. It was the first time I'd seen her in anything but the skin-tight levis. Her hair looked different, too. She'd done something to it.

"What's the occasion?" I asked her as she unloaded the tray she'd brought over. I took another look when she set a drink down on her side of the booth table, too. I'd never seen her take a drink before.

"No occasion." Her voice sounded husky. "Every once in a while I take a notion to give the animals something to think about besides my ass." She plunked herself down across from me.

Now that I was looking at her, her eyes indicated that the drink in front of her wouldn't be her first for the day. I remembered Jed's warnings about her drinking. I wondered if the storm signals were up.

She wouldn't have appreciated it, probably, but I decided I liked her better in the levis. They suited her, somehow. In the western ensemble she was the most female-looking mammal I'd seen in a long time. I wasn't the only one to notice it. Every once in a while a half-splashed customer would get carried away by the levis and acquire a sudden biological urge. Hazel fractured the house every time with her rebuttal. "What's with you, fella?" she'd pounce on him in that deep voice, half purr, half growl. "Your insurance paid up? Nobody told you I got my own cemetery out in back for wise guys snatchin' a feel?" Hazel was no shrinking violet. It took a hardy ego to survive that little speech with the speaker looking down on the red-faced snatcher from an average two to four inches superior height.

Hazel tossed off her drink in a swallow and accepted my light for her cigarette. She still had on her cowboy boots, and the heel of one tapped steadily. Kaiser's ears pricked forward as he lay on the floor beside me.

"I need another drink," Hazel announced. She continued right on without waiting for me to reply, if I'd been going to. "I'm not a blonde, but whatever she's got I'll double and throw away the change. I'll be closing up at twelve fifteen tonight. Come back and pick me up."

I opened my mouth, and closed it again. "Twelve fifteen," I said finally.

She nodded, ground out her cigarette in the ashtray, and got up and went back to the bar. She didn't come back.

I had time to kill. On the way into town I thought about Hazel. I liked her. She was easy to talk to. She had a caustic good humor. Despite the gold teeth, when she took the trouble to fix herself up she was a damn handsome woman.

But—

Ahhh, what the hell, I told myself. Play the hand the way the cards are dealt. What did I have to lose?

I backed off in a hurry from that bit of bravado. I knew what I had to lose.

I stopped in at Bobby Herman's tavern. He was the friendliest of the bartenders on my night beat, and I was just about ready to pull the trigger on a few questions to him. As soon as I walked inside I knew it wasn't going to be tonight, though. Blaze Franklin was sitting up at the bar. Must have been a short date. So much for dark circles under the eyes.

He saw me come in, but it took him five minutes to make up his mind to do anything about it. He got up from his stool finally, two-thirds of the way up the bar from mine, swaggered past the half dozen other customers in the place, and pushed himself in on the stool beside mine, his elbows out wider than they needed to be. "Don't b'lieve I've heard your name," he said in a loud voice.

"Arnold," I said. That's all I said.

"Understand you're quite a dancer," he informed me after waiting to see if I was going to continue. I wondered how much of his tomato face was due to weather and how much to alcohol. Around us the little bar-room conversations had died out. He wasn't satisfied to accept my silence. "I see you peart near ev'y day out thumpin' around that bresh out yonder," he said to me. "You keep it up you're gonna put your number 12 down on a still some day an' git your head blowed off."

"I carry a spare."

He didn't get it for a minute. When he did, he clouded over. "You in town for long, Arnold?"

"Depends," I said.

He took a long breath as though holding himself down. "Depends on what?"

I turned around on my stool until I was facing him. "Depends on me," I told him. I looked him up and down for five seconds, and returned to my beer. He put his hand on my arm. I looked down at the hand, and then at him. He removed the hand, his face flushing darkly. I knew the type. He wanted to lean on me just to show he could. I could feel the short hairs stiffening on the back of my neck. It was crazy. This bastard rubbed me completely the wrong way.

Whatever he'd been thinking of doing, he changed his mind. He got up and stalked out the door. Around me the conversation was not immediately renewed. Bobby Herman came sliding down the bar, his long arm going in concentric circles with a dirty bar rag. He was a thin-faced, pimply specimen with lank hair. "That's Blaze Franklin," he said almost apologetically. "He's a little—quick. What was that about dancin'?"

"Haven't the faintest notion," I said. I wasn't supposed to know the blonde was his playmate. Outside we could hear the roar of the cruiser as Franklin petulantly gunned it away. "Quick, huh? Who's he buried?" And as the words hung in the air, I told myself to cut it out. Trouble you can't use. Where are your brains, man?

Herman's laugh was a cackle. "That's a good one. Who's he buried?" He looked up and down the bar to assure himself of a maximum audience. "Well, no one he's stood trial for," he grinned. It was his turn to listen to the sound of his own words in the musty room. His grin faded. "I mean an escaped convict or two—things like that," he amended it hastily. He sloshed the bar rag about with renewed vigor. "Blaze's one of our best young deppities." Having—as he felt—retrieved the situation, he favored me with another smile.

I finished my beer and got out of there. I killed a couple of hours reading at the Lazy Susan, and left Kaiser in the room when I went out again. When I turned into the driveway of the Dixie Pig the lights were out in front except for the night-light. Around in back there was only one car. Hazel's car. She must have been standing just inside the back door waiting for me, because she came out and turned the key in the lock just as I pulled in.

"Let's use my car," she said. She went directly to it and got in on the driver's side. I climbed out of the Ford and walked over and got in beside her. She spun the wheels in the crushed stone backing up.

On the highway she turned south. Past the traffic light in town she leaned on it. She had a heavy foot, but she was a good driver. I watched alternately a full moon off over the gulf and the road unwinding in the headlights. There was no conversation. Sometimes I know ahead of time, but tonight wasn't one of those times.

Fifteen miles down the road she turned left on a dirt road she had to know was there or she couldn't have seen it. About a mile in on it she turned left again, and we bumped along over deep ruts for three hundred yards until a log cabin showed up in the headlights. Hazel switched off the car lights and we sat there and looked at the cabin in the moonlight. "I built most of it myself," she said. "And I mean I drove the nails. Come on."

She was out of the car and up on the little porch and had the door unlocked and open before I had the car door closed on my side. "Well?" she challenged me softly when I came up beside her. "It's a goddam good thing I'm shameless enough for both of us. You weren't going to ask me out. Why?"

"When I think of a good answer, I'll let you know," I told her. She led the way inside and closed the door behind me. I heard the snick of a bolt. In the moonlight that was the room's only light I couldn't make out many details except that the place was furnished.

Hazel came up behind me and dropped her hands down on my shoulders. "Get into something cooler, horseman," she said. She walked into the next room.

I undressed slowly. When I padded in barefoot she was buck naked on the full-sized bed. She could have been the model for all women for all time. Her eyes were closed.

I knelt on the edge of the bed. "Hazel—" I began.

She opened her eyes. Even in the semi-darkened room I could see the golden smile. "Don't you try to tell me I've gone and emasculated you," she said softly. "Come on here to me. You're a man. You'll do all right."

When it became apparent even to her some time later that I wasn't going to do all right, she sat up on the bed. "Get me a cigarette, Chet, will you?" she asked me. She sounded tired. I went back out to my clothes and found my cigarettes. In the glow of the lighter she studied my face. "Is it me, Chet?"

"It's not you."

"You're not a queer." She said it as a statement but with an implied question.

"I don't think I'm a queer," I said.

"But this happens? Often?"

"About half the time."

She blew out a convulsive lungful of smoke. "You shouldn't have done it to me, Chet." Impulsively her big hand closed on mine. "I'm sorry. It was me who did it to you, wasn't it?" The bed creaked under her weight as she changed position. "What do you think it is?"

"Everybody's got his own opium for that sort of thing, I guess." I stubbed out my own cigarette. "Years ago I saw a cartoon in a magazine. A slick-looking battalion is marching along in perfect cadence except for one raggedy-assed, stumble-footed guy out of step with a rock-faced sergeant alongside him giving him hell. The tag line underneath has the out-of-step character telling the sergeant he hears a different drum. The inference being that he can't help it if the rest of them are out of step. That's me. I march to a different band."

"What's the music?" she asked me directly.

"Excitement," I said after I caught myself. I'd nearly blurted out the truth. I'd nearly said "guns." With the air crackling with tension and a gun in my hand I'm nine feet tall and the best damn man you ever saw, right afterward. There's another time, too, but I'm not so proud of that.

"Well, I've read about bullfighters," Hazel said philosophically. "And I've seen gamblers who were on-again off-again with women, particularly when they were losing." She stood up from the bed and walked to the chair where she'd left her clothes. Her superb big body glistened in the moonlight that filtered into the bedroom. She thought of something else and walked over to me and tapped me on the chest with a solid finger. "Forget it, man. Before we take that fence again I'll have my jukebox man wire you up with 'Yes' and 'No' buttons." The attempt at lightness hung in the air between us. Hazel punched me in the ribs. "Let's just scratch tonight from the results, horseman."

But it was a quiet ride back to pick up my car.

In my time I've had a lot of quiet rides.

VIII

At the Dixie Pig the next night I couldn't see any change in Hazel's attitude. There was no reference to the previous evening. I hadn't gone there expecting to find the details of the disaster soaped in on the back bar mirror, but I'm old enough to know it makes a difference and that the difference usually shows. I couldn't see any change in her at all. Hazel wasn't big only in her physical dimensions.

"I hear you're picking on our poor little deputy sheriffs now," she said to me, sitting down in the booth.

"Your hearing's pretty damn good, except that you've got the story all wrong," I told her.

"Not many secrets in this town," she assured me. "Especially not many that take place in taverns." She studied me as I sat there. "You could be underestimating Blaze Franklin, Chet."

It irritated me. "I'm not over or underestimating him. I don't give a damn about him."

"Don't get narky. I'm telling you for your own good. He's dangerous."

"So how come a dangerous man is a deputy sheriff?"

"I don't think anyone around here had the whole picture on Blaze until he had the uniform. It's the badge that makes him dangerous, the leeway it gives him. A psychiatrist would probably say it gives him an opportunity to safely work out his aggressiveness."

"And I suppose he's most aggressive where the blonde is concerned?" I asked sarcastically.

"If you weren't a stranger in town you'd have already heard some stories about that," Hazel said quietly. "Still, something's happened to that relationship lately." She frowned, a network of fine lines indenting her broad forehead. "I see it in her, not in him. She always had a cocky way of flipping a hip that had the pigeons crossing the street to bask in the sunlight. It used to be that when she snapped her fingers, Blaze rolled over. I don't see that now. She's lost weight. Her eyes look like two burnt holes in a blanket. Something's gnawing on her. I'll tell you the truth, I've been wondering if she isn't dipping into the till down there at the post office."

I had to hold myself down from sitting right up straight in the booth. "Why in the hell would she do that?"

Hazel planted both elbows firmly on the table top. "I'll tell you a tale out of school. When Charlie died, he left me some cash. I invested it. Then I wound up with this place. In a small town, that kind of thing gets magnified out of all proportion to the facts."

Her voice took on a brooding quality, as if she were thinking aloud. "Two months ago Blaze Franklin came to me and tried to borrow three thousand dollars. He had a red-hot business opportunity, he said. I'd learned from Charlie years ago how to keep an approach like that from being a problem. Blaze knew that my investments were managed for me by Nate Pepperman, a business consultant with an office up over the bank. I told Blaze to go and see Nate and explain his proposition, and that if Nate gave it his okay I said it was all right for Nate to milk something and finance the deal." Hazel gave me a little-girl grin. "I've seen Charlie send three a week like that to his 'business consultant,' and he'd light up another cigar and tell me that the day the guy okayed such a proposition was the day Charlie got himself a new business consultant. Most propositions when they couldn't lean on friendship turned out to be swiss cheese in texture."

She sobered again, placing her chin firmly in her cupped palms. "It must have been a couple of weeks later that Nate called me about something else, and I asked him about Blaze. I wasn't too much surprised to hear that Blaze had never been near him. A lot of the big-touch boys choke up in a hurry at the idea of trying to explain an if-and-and deal to a gimlet-eye like Nate."

She nudged a cigarette from the pack on the table and leaned forward to accept my proffered light. She blew out a lungful of smoke and licked at a filament of tobacco on her lip. "About the same time I heard from one of my customers that Lucille Grimes had been into his showroom pricing foreign sports cars. That seemed to be two and two adding up to four."

Hazel leveled the cigarette at me. "Then lo and behold, it seemed the very next time I saw Lucille she was burnin' up the rubber on a bright red, brand new MG roadster. I was curious enough about it to make it my business to find out Blaze had paid for it in cash. That's not the way the title reads, but that's what happened. So either old Blaze found himself a golden goose, after all, or Lucille is into the till and waitin' for her pants to be dropped and the paddle to burn her up. She sure looks it."

"Blaze probably saved up for it out of his green stamps," I said.

"For ten days or so Lucille was around everywhere in that car, champagne-bubbly," Hazel continued, unheeding. "Then the blight set in. I don't know what it was, or how he managed it, but the reins are very definitely in Mr. Franklin's hands these days. She looks like a lamp with the flame blown out. It must be that jealous men are hard on the nerves. She really looks like something was grindin' her down. Maybe a man wouldn't notice it, but it's there for a woman to see."

There was a lot that interested me in the story. A hell of a lot. Had I been knocking my brains out on the west coast of Florida's brush-grown back roads and here the two of them had been practically under my thumb all the time? Franklin's persistent interest in my timber-cruising, and then the connection to the post office—

I thought about it when the bar became busy and Hazel went back to it.

I thought about it some more on the way back to the motel.

I was already in bed when something else occurred to me. I got up and slipped into a robe and went outside to the Ford and opened the back deck lid and my big tool chest. I found what I was looking for, a miniature Italian automatic that fired three .17 cartridges. It had a little holster of its own that strapped on a man's shin.

I went back inside and strapped it on mine. I didn't know yet whether Manny Sebastian knew where to find me. When I found out, it could be on goddam short notice. I might need a little extra something like a hidden shin holster going for me.

But right now there was Blaze Franklin.

And Lucille Grimes.

*

I was in the post office lobby at nine o'clock in the morning. The outer doors were opened earlier to allow boxholders to get their mail, but the windows didn't open until nine. Right on the dot Lucille raised the General Delivery window. I could see two clerks behind her, but they were busy in the back end of the long room. I stepped up to the window, in a hurry to get my piece spoken before we were interrupted by someone walking in off the street. "Morning, Lucille," I said to her.

She looked surprised. "Good morning," she said almost as an afterthought. In the light of what Hazel had said I could see that Lucille was looking something less than her best. The deep, dark circles beneath her eyes were still in evidence, and the blonde hair looked less crisp. A trace of blotchiness marred the velvet pallor of her facial skin.

"May I help you?" she asked me.

"Depends, Lucille," I said with a breeziness I didn't feel. Some things I can do, but exchanging light badinage with a semistrange female isn't one of them. As a rule I leave that to the extroverts like Jed, but circumstances alter cases. "How about having dinner with me some one of these nights?"

Her original surprise was obviously redoubled. "I don't believe I should," she said. Having said it, she stood there testing the sound of it. "I really don't think—"

"You're not wearing his ring," I interrupted her. "Or his collar, I hope."

Her chin lifted. "If you're implying—"

"I'm implying I'd like to have dinner with you. Say Wednesday night?"

"I'll—let me think about it." She appeared confused.

A woman came in the door and walked up to the window. I had to step aside. "Wednesday night?" I pressed her as I did so.

"I'll have to—call me tonight," she said hurriedly, and smiled at the woman. "Yes, Mrs. Newman?"

I backed out tanglefootedly under Mrs. Newman's bright-eyed inspection. On the street I had to give only a very small plus to the operation. At least the blonde hadn't refused out of hand. For the moment I'd have to settle for that.

I walked across the street to where I'd parked the Ford and drove out east on Main. For six hours I beat my way up and back two dozen monstrously tangled dirt roads, logging trails, and footpaths, some of them no more than ten yards apart. I sweat gallons. I lost my temper. And I found nothing.

I went back to the Lazy Susan and showered and lay down on the bed for a couple of hours. The constant frustration was beginning to do things to the hair-trigger of my temper. I knew myself well enough to know that if it continued much longer some little shove from one direction or another would send me careening off on a course not necessarily the right one, just because action itself would be a release.

I was still in a bad mood when I whistled up Kaiser and headed out to the Dixie Pig for dinner. The first three minutes out there compounded it. I walked in to find Jed Raymond in the corner booth in the khaki shirt and red-piped gray trousers I'd come to associate with Blaze Franklin. It jarred me. "Where the hell's the masquerade?" I asked Jed. He looked up at me curiously. I didn't like the sound of my voice myself.

"I told you I was a jack-leg deputy in an emergency," he said cheerfully enough.

"So where's the emergency?"

His grin was sheepish. "Opening of a new supermarket." He ran a hand down the uniform. "I'm on traffic. I get called out a couple of times a month."

I sat down in the booth. "You must be younger than I thought. I don't see you somehow in this cops-and-robbers bit."

"Cut it out, will you?" Jed pleaded. "Around here a realtor is expected to either do this or go into politics. This takes less time and money."

"Suppose you had to arrest a real estate prospect, Jed?"

"Now you know no prospect of mine could ever be involved in anything requirin' me to arrest him," Jed replied with dignity.

"But suppose?"

"Suppose the moon is made of green cheese. Suppose the end of the world." Jed grinned. "If I hadn't got the deposit, though, he might have a little runnin' room."

Kaiser padded over to Jed's side of the booth and rested his muzzle on Jed's thigh. Jed reached down and scratched him between the ears, and Kaiser reached up and took Jed's arm in his mouth. Jed growled down at him, and Kaiser growled back. I could tell the dog wanted to play. Jed reached the same conclusion. "You want a little roughhouse, boy?" he inquired, and slid out of the booth and got down on his knees. In seconds the big gray-and-brown dog and Jed's ginger-colored crewcut were rolling all over the floor in a ferocious-sounding mock battle. It sounded so real the bar customers scattered like quail. One of them climbed up on a table.

Jed got to his feet finally, laughing, brushing the floor dirt from his uniform. Kaiser watched him with ears cocked alertly until Jed sat down in the booth again, then came back and sat down beside me. "That's a lot of dog," Jed said to me, and continued on in the same breath. "I heard you're dating Lucille Grimes."

"For chrissake, did she take an ad in the paper? She hasn't even said yes yet, for that matter."

"You broached your invitation in the hearing of a dear lady who can give a large-mouth bass cards and spades," Jed said drily.

I remembered the woman at the post office General Delivery window. "So, she still hasn't said yes."

"But you asked her." Jed held up a hand when I would have bitten off something short and snappy. "Hold it a minute, fire-eater. I feel a little guilt in the matter. Are you trying to prove something to me because I needled your semi-senior citizen status and threw you smack dab up against the shark-toothed widow?"

"Shark-toothed? What the hell are you talking about?"

"I live in this town, Chet. Do you need a blueprint?"

"For God's sake, I asked the woman to dinner. Does that leave me enlisted among her love-slaves?"

"It leaves you on Blaze Franklin's black list," Jed said soberly.

"How come Blaze Franklin's got this town buffaloed, Jed?"

He spread his hands. "You saw him. You sized him up."

"I sized him up," I agreed. "About twenty-five cents on the dollar."

"Goddammit, you're askin' for it with that attitude!" Jed bristled. "Hazel says Blaze came—"

"So Hazel knows about it, too. You sure *you* haven't taken an ad in the paper?"

Jed stared at me. "Aren't you a little touchy? I don't give a damn if you lay the blonde under the traffic light at high noon.

I'm just concerned my big mouth pushed you into something with a stinger attached."

I pulled up on the reins. The kid meant all right. "All right, forget it, Jed. I asked her. She hasn't said yes or no. If she says yes we'll have dinner. If she says no we won't. It's a big deal?"

He folded his hands together on the table in front of him. "A couple of guys who've gone out with our beautiful postmistress have had—accidents. I don't believe she's had an invitation in a year. Until yours."

"How come no accidents happen to Franklin?"

"Maybe because he's got the town buffaloed. These weren't small accidents, Chet."

"I appreciate the concern, but it's premature, Jed. Can I buy you a drink before you go showing off that boy scout uniform?"

"I'll have to ask you to speak with more respect to this minion of th' law, suh. I'll take a raincheck on the drink." Jed rose to his feet, reached down to pat Kaiser on the head in passing, and went out the back door.

For the first time since I'd known the kid, I was glad to see him go. It's strange what the sight of a uniform does to me. On the other hand I was happy to see Kaiser take to him so quickly. If I had to pull stakes in a hurry, it meant I wouldn't be leaving the big dog high and dry.

I got up and walked over to the phone booth and looked up Lucille Grimes' home phone in the directory. There was no one near the booth when I dialed. "Chet Arnold, Lucille," I said when she answered. "How're we fixed for Wednesday night?"

"Oh, ah—" There was a five second pause. She hadn't repeated my name. I wondered if Franklin could possibly be right there with her. Not that I gave a damn. "Would five o'clock be too early? You could pick me up right at the post office."

"Five o'clock will be fine." So she didn't want me picking her up at her home for some reason. "See you then."

"I'm looking forward to it. Good night."

I replaced the receiver. She'd fairly cooed the last words. I felt a tingle at the base of my spine. Something about the way she'd said it—I don't know, I had a feeling. This attractively long-legged female wasn't saying yes only to dinner. Yet there was nothing soft about her. In Dixie Pig conversations I'd surprised an occasional feral gleam under the long-lashed lids. Unless I missed my guess she was a dandy little cutting tool.

Well, so much the better.

For some reason I've never been able to understand, I'm a much better man when I don't like them.

When I got back to the booth Hazel came over and sat down. "Jed coming back tonight after he gets off this deputy routine?" I asked her.

"Accordin' to him, he's goin' courtin'." She checked the bar with a sweeping glance before continuing. "That boy's goin' to make some girl a good husband time he makes up his mind to settle down."

"I wonder what it feels like," I said before I thought.

"You wonder what *what* feels like?"

"Oh, sitting with a girl on her living-room sofa." I tried to pass it off lightly. "Object: matrimony, if you can't get it any other way."

"You never tried it? No, I s'pose not," she answered her own question. She didn't pursue aloud her chain of thought. A silence settled down between us.

"I've been thinking—" I began, finally.

"Do you suppose—" Hazel started in the same breath.

We both laughed, and she waved a hand. "You've got the floor, horseman."

I couldn't seem to find the right words. "Maybe we ought to try it again some night," I said at last.

She didn't reply for a moment. "There's a point to it?" she asked when I'd begun to think she wasn't going to answer at all.

"There could be. You've made a losing bet or two in your day, haven't you?"

"I wish they'd only been cash." She sounded quite sober. "Why do you want to try it again, Chet?"

"Maybe because the next time I came in here after the other night you didn't have 'Chet Arnold is an impotent slob' up on the front in neon lights."

"What the hell do you think I am?" she began indignantly, and then started to laugh. "Can that corn, man. Why do you?"

"It offends my miserly soul to see such a stack of material going to waste."

"I suppose even a left-handed compliment is more than I rate most days around here," she said good-humoredly. "All right, I'll stop fishing." She reached across the table and covered my hand with hers just for a second before removing it again. "And listen, man: the fact you want to is what counts with me. I've been around gamblers long enough to know that a lot of the time they're wired into different sockets." She rose briskly as a glass bottom rapped on the bar. "I'll be back."

I watched her walk away from me back to the bar, and all of a sudden I knew it was going to be all right. I never know how I know, the times I do. I just know.

I waited for her to come back, but the bar stayed busy. I got up finally and walked over to one end of it, away from the customers. "I'll be back at lock-up time," I told Hazel when she came down the bar toward me.

Her eyes widened. I think she started a wisecrack, but choked it off. "I'll be ready," was all she said.

I drove downtown. I had a couple of hours to kill, and I might as well kill them at Bobby Herman's place. I left Kaiser in the car and went on into the tavern. Herman was friendly with me now, mostly because I let him show off his encyclopedic baseball knowledge by asking him trick questions only a buff could know the answers to. Bobby had never seen a major league game in his life, except in spring training, but he read *The Sporting News* religiously, and he remembered what he read. He had the type of mind that could rattle off the batting order lineups for the Yankees and the Pirates in the '28 World Series. I remembered that series myself. That had been the year I'd been expelled from school for stalking the fat boy whose boxer dog had killed Fatima.

Herman's place drew a workingman crowd. He stayed open till midnight, but on week-nights his customers generally packed it in around ten. The last hour he always had time to talk, and over the last three weeks I'd made it my business to see to it that a lot of his talking was done to me.

I was later than usual tonight. There was only one other customer at the bar when I sat down there, and a boy and a girl in the farthest booth. Bobby whisked his bar rag over the mahogany in front of me and slapped down a tight-collared beer. "Big argument in here tonight," he informed me. "You remember the year Cobb an' Speaker wound up playin' the outfield for the Philadelphia Athletics when they were through in Detroit and Cleveland? Well, the argument was who was the third man in that outfield. I say it was Fothergill. Some of the guys say it was Heilmann. Who do you think it was?"

"If you say Fothergill, I'll settle for Fothergill, Bobby," I told him. He grinned, pleased, and retreated to his wash rack and started rinsing out glasses. The only other customer at the bar finished his beer, grunted goodnight, and went out the door. The only sound in the place was the low murmur of voices from the corner booth and the clink of glasses as Bobby placed them on the drainboard. When he looked up my way again I was ready for him. I nodded down the bar in a way that took in two thirds of the tavern. "Say, whatever happened to the big dark guy used to stand down there when I first started coming in? Big, rugged-looking guy."

Bobby paused with a sparkling glass in his hand. He frowned, trying to think. "Big, rugged—? Oh, yeah. The one with the scar on his throat. That's right, I haven't seen him lately. Must've found greener pastures. He wasn't a regular, anyway."

I felt a tight sensation in the pit of my stomach. "He work around here? He reminded me of someone, and I finally remembered who it was. I thought I'd ask him if he was related."

Herman had returned to his glasses. "I don't know if he works around here. He's not a native, though. Real quiet fella. Drove a blue sedan with out-of-state plates. Probably a tourist."

A real quiet fella. Even after seeing it so many times it always surprised me the way the mute Bunny could walk into a bar, get his first beer by holding up a finger as the bartender drew one for someone else, and all the refills he wanted by snapping a coin down on the bar. He never joined a group but always stood just in the background, smiling and nodding at the general conversation. He had a trick of anticipating a direct question and turning his shoulder so that his attention appeared to be elsewhere and the question flew harmlessly over it. I've seen people lose hard cash betting Bunny could talk after they'd been around him for days.

"Could he be staying up at the Walton House? Seems to me I saw a blue sedan parked up there."

"Don't think so." Bobby dried his hands on his apron front. "Every time I saw him pull out of the lot here he'd swing it around and head out east from the traffic light." He paused as if checking his memory. "I don't think he lived in town."

"Oh, well, it's not that important," I said. I looked at my watch. "Put one more head on this thing, anyway, Bobby. Then maybe your sterling salesmanship can get me to exceed my quota."

I started Herman off on baseball again along with my second beer. He rattled along, happy with the sound of his own voice. I had only to contribute an occasional nod. His confident statistics bounced off me as I sat there thinking about Bunny.

It was a comfort to know I'd been right in my guess that Bunny had hidden out east on Main as I'd originally figured. I'd been beginning to wonder. I might be stubborn, but I had no intention of working my way through to the east coast of Florida a side road at a time. With Herman's memory to strengthen my first guess, though, I'd just have to keep at it. Bunny was out there, somewhere. I had no illusions, of course, that I was going to be able to do him any good.

I was out in the back parking lot when Hazel came out at ten after twelve. She had a dress on again. I walked around the Ford to open the door for her, and she loomed up over me a good four inches. I got a whiff of an exotic perfume as she climbed into the car.

"Relax," I told her as I headed down the driveway. "Everything's going to be all right."

"I just hope you're not building yourself up for a letdown," she said doubtfully.

"It's all right," I repeated.

I drove with my left hand and we held hands, her left in my right. The full moon was past and it was a much darker night. I nearly missed the turn-off road completely. I had to back up for it. We jolted down the final rutted three hundred yards, and sat looking at the cabin that was just a darker blotch in the blackness.

On the porch Hazel gave me her key and I opened the door. It was so quiet it hurt the ears. My pulse must have been doing a hundred and seventy. We didn't bother with any lights.

Hand-in-hand we stumbled through the doorway from the living room into the bedroom beyond.

I undressed her myself. With each layer removed she showed up whiter and whiter, until she gleamed in the dark like the phosphorescence in the gulf. I didn't bother with her cowboy boots. She still had them on when we settled down on the bed. She wasn't making a sound. I could hear the click of the boot heels when her legs came together over my back. I went for broke, and made it. Made it so big it was one lumped-up soul-satisfying taste deep in my throat. I could feel the wild pulse in her neck under my lips. When she got excited herself it was a damn good thing for me there were no spurs on the boots.

I don't know how long it was before she spoke. I could still hear her heavy breathing—or was it mine?—and her voice was a deeply muted, husky sound. "Welcome back, horseman. For an off-again, on-again, Finnegan type you cover a spread of ground."

I didn't say anything. I slid my hands beneath her and took a solid double-handful of her powerful buttocks. I pulled her up against me again, tightly.

"Oh, no!" she chuckled. "Honest to Christmas, Chet—" She started to laugh, a full-throated richness of sound that remained in my mind long after it had died out in my ears.

It was the finest sound I'd heard in longer than I liked to think about.

I was on my back, relaxed, smoking a cigarette when Hazel came back into the bedroom and sat down on the edge of the bed. She reached over to punch me on the arm. "You ride a mean rodeo, horseman," she said to me. "An' here you had me thinkin' there was no fire in the boiler at all." I could feel her bending over me, trying to find my face in the dark.

"There's fire enough baby, when the damn engineer's on the job." I threw away the cigarette, remembered too late the wooden cabin, and got up and found a shoe and ground out the cigarette with the heel. I came back to the bed. "Trouble is every so often he takes these two-week lunch hours."

Her big arms reached up and pulled me down beside her. "The hell with it. At the moment I couldn't care less." She

IX

I PICKED Lucille up on the dot of five in front of the post office. "Since it's early enough for a drive, I made a reservation at the Black Angus," I said. "Okay?"

"It's a very nice place," she said in reply. She smoothed her skirt out beneath her, palms flat against the pliant thighs. Her eyes were bright, and her nostrils flared. There was something between us from the second she stepped into the Ford.

I headed north on the highway and just rolled it along. It was about a thirty mile drive. Without being obvious about it, I watched the rear-view mirror. I saw no indication of a jealous man in pursuit, but Jed's warning was on my mind.

We didn't exchange fifteen words on the way. She sat beside me in seeming lassitude. I was satisfied to leave it that way for the time being. I thought I'd have a chance over dinner to probe a little bit and see what it was that made this woman tick.

It didn't work out that way. In the huge dining room she had three cocktails in quick succession. She apologized for the third, but downed it quicker than the other two. I ordered a good meal, but she just toyed with her food. Conversation remained at a minimum. She closed out my tentative leads with terse replies, her tone brittle. Her responses featured incomplete sentences, dangling phrases, and half-finished expressions, punctuated by an occasional dazzling, loose-lipped smile. An aura of almost febrile excitement emanated from her. I almost expected to see sparks fly from her fingers and toes. She was the epitome of promise.

I suggested brandy afterward. She settled for a highball. She had two, then another. She took on a high gloss. She pronounced her words carefully. Leaving, she stepped a little bit too high over the threshold.

In the car she lapsed into complete silence. Her eyes were fixed dreamily straight ahead down the road. If she felt the car slow down as I studied the motels we came up to, she gave no sign. When she did speak, she surprised me. "This one," she said huskily, and pointed. I turned down a long driveway that wound between individual cabins set back from the edge of the road. I stopped at the one marked "Office" and got out and went inside. Lucille stayed in the car.

I registered under the bored eye of the bald-headed manager. With practiced ease he read my "Mr. and Mrs. Chet Arnold" upside down. "Anything special, Mr. Arnold?"

"A quiet one."

"Certainly, sir." He turned to the key-rack behind him.

When he faced front again, I was filling in another card. "That one's for my brother-in-law and his wife," I said, pointing to the Arnold card. "I'll pay you for both."

The manager dropped the key in his hand on the Arnold card and turned to get another. Again he performed his upside-down reading stunt on the second card. "This one's every bit as good, Mr. Reynolds. They're together, the last two on the right."

"Fine." I paid him, picked up both keys, and went out to the car. The keys were numbers 10 and 11. Number 10 was the Arnolds' cabin. Number 11 was the Reynolds'. I drove to the end of the wooded lot and stopped in front of number 11. I got out and let Lucille out on her side, opened the cabin door, and stepped aside to let her enter. "Back in a second," I told her.

I went back to the Ford and backed it off the driveway and around on the grass behind the cabin. I parked it between two trees. We'd eaten so early the sky was still bright overhead, but under the trees it was nearly dark.

Lucille displayed no curiosity about my short trip. She had every light in the place on when I got back inside. She was humming to herself, and moving slowly about the room in a way that suggested a dance step. Her eyes were the biggest part of her face. Without saying a word she began to undress, leisurely.

I went into the bathroom and closed the door. I took off my jacket and my shoulder holster. I removed the Smith & Wesson from the holster and a towel from the rack, and I wrapped the gun loosely in the towel. I put the holster in a jacket pocket, put the jacket back on, and went out, carrying the towel.

Lucille was sitting on the edge of the bed in her panties. She smiled up at me lazily. The tip of her tongue flicked over her lips. I put the towel down carefully on the small night table, and sat down on the bed beside her. I stood her up, between my feet, and made a production of removing the panties. Her thighs were tanned, her buttocks milky. She looked like a two-toned animal.

She crawled onto the bed and lay there face down while I stood up and undressed. I left my shoes on. I walked to the door and locked and bolted it. When I turned, she had rolled part-way over, watching me. Her eyes looked almost filmed. Her head was up an inch or two from the pillow, slightly turned, as though she were listening.

I was listening, too.

I walked back to her. I was only a stride from the bed when we both heard it with no trouble at all. There was a splintering crash from next door as the door of number 10 went down. I could hear the thump of heavy boots as Blaze Franklin blundered around in the dark in the next cabin, looking for the light.

Lucille's eyes widened as she realized I'd somehow sucked him into the wrong cabin. Her breasts bobbed as she filled her lungs to scream. I reached down and slapped her squarely in her bare belly. She got out a gargle. That's all.

I knew Franklin couldn't stay to hunt for us. The Smith & Wesson and my shoes were just insurance against his being smarter than I thought he was. Right now he was all done on this caper. He had no business there. He had to get away from the empty cabin he'd broken into. Not seeing the Ford, he had to think we'd come and gone already.

I covered Lucille's mouth with my hand till I heard the whine of the cruiser pulling away. Even in the dirt the tires sang. I took my hand off her face. It was no blacker under the trees outside than in the depths of her eyes. "You get a bang out of watching him beat them up?" I asked her.

Her mouth was wet. "He makes them crawl," she said almost in a whisper. She didn't look particularly afraid. "What are you going to do?"

"I'll show you what I'm going to do." I took hold of her. She may not have been the best I'd ever had in my hands, but she was a useful piece of machinery. She submitted passively until she realized my intention. She fought hard, then. She was strong, but not strong enough. She hissed like a cat all the time I abused her.

It was four in the morning before we left there.

Fifty per cent of us had enjoyed it.

I drove back to Hudson and let Lucille out up the street from her house. False dawn was lightening the sky. I didn't want to drive right up to her door in case Franklin was waiting for her on her front porch.

She hadn't said a word all the way back to town. She looked around when I stopped the car. It took her a moment to recognize where she was. She opened the car door and got out, then leaned back in to spit at me. "Blaze will kill you for this," she rasped.

I appreciate a good hater. "You've got it all wrong, sugar," I told her. "You're going to have a hard time explaining this to your jealous lord and master. You set up the place, and then you weren't there. What does Blaze use on *you* when he's a little out of sorts? His belt? A jealous man believes what he wants to believe. Blaze is going to figure you as a partner in the disappearance."

I could have counted to ten while she stared in at me. I'd given her something to think about. Without another word she slammed the door and started up the street. She was unsteady on her high heels. I sat and watched her go.

It wasn't hard to see where Jed Raymond had found the adjective "shark-toothed" in connection with the widow Grimes. I owed the kid something for keeping me from making the play with my eyes shut. Franklin and the blonde must have had a Roman holiday with the suitors she'd set up for the deputy to knock over. And of course none of them would talk.

I couldn't show much of a plus on the real purpose of the evening. There hadn't been much of the conversation I'd counted on. On the other hand, it had done me good to vent some poison on a truly poisonous female.

I started the Ford up, and eased through the deserted square in the direction of the Lazy Susan. I parked a block away and came up on it from the rear. I thought I had Franklin figured, but until I knew for sure I had to be ready to see him on short notice. There was no cruiser in the motel yard. I walked completely around it, my feet silent on the grass. Through the office window I could see the night clerk with his head nodding. There was no sign at all of Franklin. Lucille would be lucky if it was tomorrow instead of right now that she was down on her knees trying to explain.

I went into my unit and showered and shaved. It was full dawn when I stretched out on the bed.

I was beginning to get a feeling about Lucille Grimes and Blaze Franklin.

I had to figure out a way of getting at them.

I interrupted Hazel in her preoccupied feeding of potato chips to Kaiser in our booth at the Dixie Pig. "That's the third time in ten minutes you've given me the double-O inspection as if you were looking for ringworm. What gives?"

"Just looking for battle wounds. I heard you had a date with the blonde last night."

"This *is* a small town. You've got her all wrong, though. She's really quite kittenish."

Hazel snorted. "So's a Rocky Mountain panther. I don't get it. Can it be that the light in your baby blues has reformed her?"

"How did she get into the conversation, anyway?" I evaded Hazel. "Let's get to something important, like what's on your schedule after closing tonight."

"I could run out in back and check my social calendar, but I'll take a chance and say I'm free." She smiled, a warm, golden smile. "Did you have a discussion period in mind, horseman?"

"If you can discuss on your back."

"My, my, what a rejuvenation." She knuckled a big hand and pushed gently at mine on the table. The smile on her lips overflowed to her eyes. "Who was the best sprinter you ever saw at four furlongs?"

"I'd have to make it a deadheat among Decathlon, White Skies, and Moolah Bux, I guess."

"Bet you I could give the field a length start an' beat them to the back door tonight." Hazel rose to her feet. "Let me get out of here before I entirely lose my maidenly reserve," she said briskly. She wagged a finger at me. "You watch out for that woman, y'hear? She's tricky."

"And here I thought I'd changed the subject."

Hazel smiled again, and went back to the bar. I took over her job of feeding potato chips to Kaiser. The big dog was gone for potato chips. I'd tested him with a potato chip versus a piece of steak. He ate the steak, but he ate the potato chip first. He'd crunch a chip, and then circle his muzzle with his tongue to get all the salt.

This town had already given me one surprise in the appearance of the redheaded Eddie from Manny Sebastian's parking lot. When I looked up toward the rear entrance of the Dixie Pig between potato chips, I had a second. Lucille Grimes was halfway across the floor heading toward my booth.

Her hands were empty. Her bag dangled loosely from the strap on her arm. That much I took in in the first split second. Then she was standing beside the booth. "Sit down, if you can," I greeted her. "What color welts are you wearing these days?"

She attempted a smile, but her eyes were murderous. She sat down. I watched carefully until she laid her bag aside. I had no intention of playing clay pigeon for this dolly. From the second she started talking it was plain she had herself under a tight rein. "I came by to ask you to dinner tomorrow night."

Now here was a switch. "Yeah? Where?"

"At my house."

Come into my parlor, said the spider to the fly. "At your house? What's the occasion?"

"I want to talk to you." Even she seemed to realize that was a little weak. "I might have a proposition for you."

"What about?"

She manufactured a smile. "Why don't you come and see? Possibly I can use someone as foresighted as you appear to be."

"In the post office?"

She stood up. "Call me in the morning and let me know." She picked up her bag and walked to the door. Her movements weren't as fluid as I remembered them.

I moved out of the corner of the booth away from the window when she went out the door. This was no campfire girl. The dinner invitation had to mean one of two things. Either Franklin was so crazy mad to get at me he was willing to drop a ton on me right in her house, or Franklin had given her such a hard way to go the blonde was looking for reinforcements to get her out from under Franklin. I couldn't see much nourishment for me in either setup.

Of course if it was Franklin and the blonde who actually had short-circuited Bunny—

I decided I'd have to give the invitation more thought.

Out at the cabin I walked from the bathroom into the bedroom and looked down at Hazel tastefully attired in one thirty-second of a sheet. "Come on and let's take a shower, big stuff," I said.

She yawned, and stretched mightily. The effect was spectacular. "You must have otter blood in you, man," she complained drowsily. "The last two nights with you I been in an' out of that shower till my corns are waterlogged. Why don't you just tumble on down here an' relax your—"

As close as we'd been recently it had remained no secret that Hazel was touchy. I leaned down and goosed her, and she bounded from the bed to the middle of the room with a strangled yelp. I aimed my thumb at her again, and she flew into the bathroom. I herded her into the glassed-in compartment and turned on the fine needle-spray. I adjusted it to warm, and stepped in with her. We each took soap and in silence began to lather each other.

The water hissed softly, the single off-center fluorescent light glistened dimly upon sleek flesh, and warm hands glided gently over slippery body contours. It was a moment out of a lifetime. We stayed in the shower a long time.

The place was just about afloat when I stepped out and grabbed a towel. I picked up another one and handed it to Hazel, still in the shower. She turned the water off and buried her wet red head in the towel. I reached in behind her and flipped the handle over to full cold.

"Ooooooh-h-h!" I never heard such a catamount yowl in my life. Hazel boomed out of that shower like a fullback. She ran right over me. I was laughing so hard that when she turned and came after me, I couldn't defend myself. She got me down and enthusiastically banged my head on the tile. I couldn't get her off till I got into her ribs and tickled. She squealed, and rolled away.

Several wet towels and a couple of cigarettes later we were stretched out on the bed, the firefly glow of cigarettes the bedroom's only light. Beside me I could hear Hazel's deep, even breathing. She reached up over me to stub out her cigarette in the ashtray on the table beside the bed, and trailed her hand lightly along my body as she dropped back with a sigh. "You don't happen to think you're pretty far out sometimes reaching for sensations, horseman?" she asked in her rich voice.

"You can tell your grandchildren someday you did it under water," I told her.

She laughed, then sobered. "That parlay breaks down with the first dog out of the box. Children come before grandchildren, unless they've repealed a law of nature."

I didn't like what I heard in her voice. I changed the subject. "I didn't get a chance to tell you before, but I'm invited out to dinner tomorrow night."

Hazel came up on an elbow. "The blonde?"

"In the solid flesh."

In the increased glow of my cigarette as I took a final drag I could see the outline of her features, but not her expression. "Chet," she began, and hesitated. She seemed to be wondering whether to continue. "I don't want to know your business, Chet, and I'm not jealous of Lucille Grimes, but there's something I think you ought to know." She stopped again. I could have made it easier for her, but I didn't. I didn't because jealous was exactly what I thought she was. She made me sorry right away. "Blaze Franklin is asking questions about you all over town, Chet."

Instinct is a wonderful thing. I didn't have a stitch on, but my hand was up reaching for the butt of the Smith & Wesson in the shoulder holster with my clothes in the next room. "Like what kind of questions is he asking?"

"Where you came from. What you're doing here. Where you lived before. How much talking you do about yourself." Hazel's tone was quiet. "I don't want you to think *I'm* prying, Chet. I just thought you ought to know."

"Don't think I don't appreciate it." I thought about Blaze Franklin. It looked as though I had indeed underestimated the gentleman. He wasn't asking those particular questions because of anything that had happened between Lucille and me. I had no damn business lying here bed-bouncing with the wash out on the line and a storm coming up. "Any reaction from the questioned?" I asked Hazel.

"Even Jed was saying it was odd how little we really knew about you." There was no emphasis in the remark. She was reporting a fact. Her hand came up and settled on my arm. "I'm going to say one more thing, and then I'm going to shut up. If you think of anything I can do to help, let me know." She rolled over and sat up on the edge of the bed. "Let's get dressed," she said briskly. "I'm a workin' gal, and I've got to open up in the morning."

It was a fact the life had gone out of the party. We dressed and locked up and went out to the Ford. On the way back to town I had time to think about Hazel's last remark. "'If you think of anything I can do to help, let me know.'" That was just short of putting it in writing that she was on the team. More than that, she didn't care what the name on the uniform was. In my life I've run into few blanket endorsements. The big woman was all gold and a yard wide.

I appreciated it, as I'd told her, but I was damn well going to put a stop to it. She could get nothing but hurt.

It was two thirty when I turned into the Dixie Pig's crushed stone driveway and let her out beside her car. The routine good nights were an anticlimax.

I drove to the motel. There was only one reason Franklin could be asking those questions about me. He was interested in my interest in the saw-grass swamps and savanna intermingled with pine-land, salt meadows, and mangrove thickets on the east side of town. Franklin had stamped the brand on himself. Franklin was the reason I had come to Hudson.

Granting the fact, it left unanswered questions. How had a mulehead like Franklin outmaneuvered Bunny? Bunny could break him up with his bare hands. And why was Franklin nosing around me when by all rights he should have been lying doggo hoping nobody was looking in his direction?

I didn't know.

I didn't know, but I knew I was going to start finding out at dinner with Lucille Grimes.

There was no question now about my accepting that unwilling invitation.

For two thirds of its length the dinner was an eighteen-karat flop. We sat at opposite ends of a six foot table, and were served by a kid in a maid's uniform. Lucille sat at her end with an expression like an aristocrat among the peasantry. All I could think of was Lady Bountiful among the poor.

It was obvious that with the lady at the head of the table I was a stink in the nostrils. It was interesting that feeling as she did about me, Franklin had been able to force her into issuing this dinner invitation. It made Hazel a hundred per cent right about who was wearing the pants in the corporation.

Franklin was pushing her to set up the deadfall again. He didn't know what had happened to her that night. She wouldn't tell him. Franklin would naturally assume that after this expression of her majesty's gracious favor I would press hard for another date. Lucille knew better, but she had to go along with the idea.

It gave me an idea of my own.

"Glad to see you finally wised up to Franklin," I said to her when the little maid disappeared after serving the dessert.

Lucille's mind had been a long way off. Probably gloating over a mental image of me staked out over an anthill. She came back to earth in a hurry. "Wised up?"

"Sure. What the hell you ever saw in a jerk like that I'll never know. A big bag of wind." It was no trouble to make that sound convincing. "Having me to dinner like this shows you're a smart girl. You should have cut him loose a long time ago. You and I, now—we could really play chopsticks together on the same piano."

She didn't swallow it hook, line and sinker. Not at first. Her eyes were suspicious as I oiled up both sides of my tongue and greased her liberally. She couldn't believe at first I was so stupid as not to know her reaction to me, but the suspicion gradually died. She was used to such a response, for one thing. By the end of the meal she'd come as alive as though someone had just reported my painful demise. She was tossing them back to me as fast as I batted them at her.

Lucille was no fool. I was giving her an out on a problem on which she hadn't been able to see daylight. As far as Franklin was concerned, this was the way it was supposed to go. If she could report progress to him, that was a load off her back. If she could report progress that turned out to be fact, and that put my neck under the knife, why how lovely. She had nothing to lose.

She didn't overplay her hand a bit, either. "I was very angry with you the other evening," she said gravely. "I thought you were a gentleman."

Even the boob that I was supposed to be couldn't let her get away with that one. "You'd just set me up to get cut off at the knees, sweetheart. You're lucky I didn't really get mad at you."

"But you know I wasn't going to do anything—I wasn't—"

"You were just going to sit there and cheer. You got what was coming to you. Just like Franklin's going to one of these days." I threw that in as an afterthought. If she were really getting restless under the Franklin thumb—

She didn't appear to notice the opening. Honest curiosity shone for an instant through the genteel façade. "I admire clever men. Whatever led you to take rooms in two different names?"

"Self-preservation. I was at the head of the line when it was passed around. Look, maybe I was too rough with you, but admit it, you had it coming. I don't see why that means we can't get along. You're a smart girl. You and I make a much better team than you and Franklin. Just don't you try any more cute tricks and we'll be all right. I don't like bossy women. Do as you're told and we'll have no trouble."

I almost expected to hear her grinding her teeth after that little speech, but she smiled sweetly. She was a cinch to bring along a sawed-off baseball bat herself to our next motel room assignation. It oozed out of every ounce of her without her realizing it that she just couldn't wait to drag down into the dust the nose of this loud-mouthed braggart who had abused her. "I'll admit I'm not used to such a—such a forceful man," she said. "Shall we have our coffee on the patio?"

We had our coffee on the patio. I buttered her up some more. She buttered me up some more. Instead of the silver fingerbowls that were placed on our trays twin showerbaths would have been more appropriate.

She finally cut across the radius of the circle to the hub of the wheel. "What are you really doing in this area?" she asked me directly. "I never have believed that black maple story."

"A man can make a quick dollar if he stumbles onto the right patch of second growth out in that timber," I argued.

She wasn't ready now to let me get away with it. "You don't seem to me like the type of man interested in making a few dollars at a time."

I drained off the rest of my coffee and set my cup down with a gesture of finality. I rose to my feet. She rose, too, surprised. "You talk too much, sweetheart," I told her. I walked around the little marble table and took her by the arms, just below the edges of her short-sleeved dress, harder than I needed to. "You're going to have to break that habit." I shook her gently to and fro, not hard, but her face whitened at the pressure on her arms. "I'll give you a chance starting tomorrow night at dinner. Pick you up at five?"

"I'll—all right. Five," she said breathlessly.

"Okay." I let her go. Her hands came up instinctively to caress her arms. My handprints stood out on them lividly. "Thanks for the dinner. See you at five tomorrow. Good night."

"Good night," she echoed numbly.

I went down the outside walk to the street without going back through the house. I would have given a dollar bill to know what she was thinking as she stood there and watched me go. But on second thought I realized it would have been a dollar wasted.

She'd see to it that Franklin took me tomorrow night.

So she thought.

I'd see to it I took the pair of them.

I was positive now. Tomorrow night I'd wind up the whole ball of yarn.

I drove back to the motel and parked in the yard. It was still early, but I didn't feel like going out to the Dixie Pig. I opened the motel unit door carefully because Kaiser had a habit of sleeping against it. He wasn't against it this time. He was sprawled in the lefthand corner with his head at an awkward angle.

"Close the door," a voice said from behind it. Manny Sebastian's fat figure stepped into view. His hands were empty. The hands of the sandy-haired, bucktoothed man who moved out beside him weren't empty. A blued-steel revolver was trained steadily on my chest.

I stepped inside and closed the door.

X

BUCKTOOTH MOVED to my right, the gun steady. "Don't get careless," he said. His eyes were red-rimmed and wild-looking. I could see him only from the corner of my eye as his free hand snaked under my jacket and delicately removed the Smith & Wesson from its holster. He tossed it to Manny.

"He carries a Colt, too," Manny said. His round, swarthy face was shiny with perspiration.

From behind me Bucktooth gave me the shoulders-to-knees handpatting treatment. He discovered the Woodsman in my pants pocket. He didn't make the mistake of trying to take it out himself. "Throw it on the bed," he ordered me. "And be goddam careful how you do it."

I fished the .22 out with thumb and forefinger, and tossed it at the bed. I could see Manny relax. I wondered how the bastards would feel if they knew I still had the little three-shot .17 caliber puff adder on my shin.

"Let's get out of here," Bucktooth said from behind me.

"We're going to take a little ride," Manny informed me. He was mopping at his streaming features with a soggy handkerchief. My Smith & Wesson was in his other hand.

I went over and knelt down beside Kaiser. He was still breathing. There was a ragged, bleeding furrow on his head between his ears, right alongside the still half-healed one from his trip into the ditch. I stood up and turned around. Bucktooth had moved in only six feet away from me, his gun reversed in his hand, the butt exposed. "Did you hit the dog, you sonofabitch?" I asked him.

"Just like I'll belt you if you make one more move like that without being told," he snarled.

I walked into him, swinging.

"Don't shoot! Don't shoot!" Manny bleated from behind me. "He's got to talk first!"

Bucktooth stepped back far enough so I missed him with my first swing. He stepped right back in again and clubbed at me with the gun. I got my head out of the way, but he landed on my left shoulder the same instant I smashed my right hand into his belly. I was staggering sideways when he doubled up. Before I could catch my balance Manny clocked me on the back of the neck with my own gun. I was on my knees all of a sudden without realizing how I'd got there. The room whirled sickeningly.

"Cut it out!" Manny said sharply to Bucktooth, who was lunging at me with upraised gun. Manny stepped in between us. "You can have your fun later." Bucktooth hesitated, his red eyes slitted. Reluctantly he backed away. "Get up," Manny said to me. I got to my feet, wobbly. "Where's the stuff?"

"Fifteen, eighteen miles out in the swamp," I mumbled.

"Didn't I tell you he'd say that?" Bucktooth growled.

"And didn't I tell you it didn't matter what he said?" Manny rebutted. "If it isn't wherever he takes us to, then you exercise that gun butt." He waved the Smith & Wesson at me. "Let's get going."

"Can't find th' tree—at night," I said.

"I don't expect to. We'll go in the morning. Right now we'll go to our place. Less chance of an interruption."

"The dog goes with us," I told him.

"Now here's one practicin' to be a character," Bucktooth said in a wondering tone. He shoved his face into mine. "The dog goes nowhere, jerk!"

"I'll show you where to leave him," I said.

Bucktooth made a sound deep in his throat. Manny caught his arm as he started to swing it. "We can't leave the dog here looking like that in an empty room," he said. He looked at me. "What's your play?"

"I know someone who'll take care of him," I answered. "Open the door. I'll carry him."

"No!" Bucktooth said violently.

"Pick him up," Manny said to me. "The dog will make a good excuse if we run onto anyone," he shut off his angry partner. "Shut up, will you? Rudy Hernandez told me years ago the guy was like this about animals."

I picked up Kaiser. In the shape I was in it was a hell of a lift. Bucktooth was right beside me. "Pretty soon I'm gonna ask you what happened to Red, pal," he said softly. "Right now you make one wrong move or one bit of noise an' you've had it. I won't kill you, but you'll wish I had. I'll break every bone in your stupid face."

"Open the door," I said.

Instead he leveled the gun at me again. "I'll cover you from the doorway till you get him in the car," he told Manny.

Manny opened the door. It was black night outside. I carried Kaiser out. Manny pointed to a big station wagon parked on the rim of the driveway. He opened the front door on the passenger's side. There wasn't a soul around. I climbed into the front seat with Kaiser on my lap. Manny got under the wheel. In seconds I could hear Bucktooth crawling into the seat behind me. I don't know if I could feel or sense his gun three-quarters of an inch from the short hairs at the back of my neck.

Manny took the wagon out of there. I'd intended to take Kaiser to the Dixie Pig, but rolling through town I saw a light on in Jed Raymond's second floor office. "Pull in anywhere here," I said. Bucktooth's gun came up level with my head as the car swung into the curb.

"What's the play?" Manny said to me again.

"See that light up there? I'll carry the dog up one flight of stairs and leave him outside the door of the real estate office."

"And I suppose you'll okay that, too," Bucktooth rasped at Manny.

"I'd just as soon humor him till we get our hands on the stuff," Manny said defensively. "This is one stubborn sonofabitch."

"I'll unstubborn him or anyone else in three an' a half minutes, guaranteed," Bucktooth snapped, but he opened his door and got out. He opened my door. "Come on, you. Sometimes I think the whole damn world's crazy."

I lugged Kaiser up the stairs and laid him down gently outside Jed's door. Bucktooth stayed a yard behind me all the way. I knew that if Kaiser came to before Jed found him, the big dog would smell Jed inside and wouldn't leave.

We were back in the wagon in two minutes. I felt a lot better. Jed would take care of Kaiser. I knew Kaiser liked him. Now I could concentrate on getting rid of these mongolian idiots.

Manny headed north on U.S. 19. About two miles above town he turned into a second-rate motel. "No noise," Bucktooth warned me as we got out of the wagon. By way of emphasis he banged me viciously in the ribs with his gun butt when Manny's back was turned. I nearly went down. Stumbling inside the motel room, I began to make plans for Bucktooth.

With the door closed, Manny turned to me. "How do we get to the stuff?"

"Airboat," I said.

Manny nodded.

"Air what?" Bucktooth wanted to know.

"Airboat," Manny told him. "They use them in swamps. An airplane engine on a plank, practically. No draught. They say they'll float on a heavy dew. I've seen movies of them."

"What's the arrangement when we get there, Manny?" I asked him. I didn't want him thinking I was going too easily. I wanted him unsuspicious.

If I'd ever been in doubt about their plans for me, the glance they exchanged removed it. "A three-way split," Manny said finally. "If it's all there," he amended it. "There's enough for us all." Bucktooth turned his head but not before I saw his ugly grin.

There was only one bed in the room. Bucktooth motioned me to a chair. "Squat, pal," he said to me. He produced a length of manila and efficiently roped me to the chair, my arms to the arms, a leg to each front leg. Manny tested the job, then stretched out on the bed, taking off only his shoes. Bucktooth soon joined him. They left the light on.

The room grew quiet. My head hurt. My ribs hurt. My legs went to sleep. I was uncomfortable, but I wasn't too upset. My time was coming. Daylight would signal the beginning of the end of the line for the two men on the bed.

When I got these two city types out in the swamp, I'd leave them there, permanently.

I must have dozed off eventually, because their stirring around woke me. The light was still on, but at the edges of the curtains I could see early morning sunshine. "Where do we get the airboat?" Manny asked me while Bucktooth was unwinding the rope from around me.

"We rent it. There's a place about seven miles east on Main Street." My arms weren't in bad shape after the night in the chair, but I couldn't stand up. I massaged my legs. It was ten minutes before I could walk. Bucktooth glowered impatiently while I hobbled around.

As soon as we got outside I could tell from the sun and the haze it was going to be a hot, humid day, a real stinger. So much the better. East of the traffic light in town we stopped for breakfast. They took turns going in while one stayed in the station wagon with me. Manny brought me out coffee and a sweet roll.

Out beyond the edge of town I didn't have to say a word. Manny saw the shack with the hand-painted sign "Airboat For Hire" I'd noticed my first day in Hudson. He pulled the wagon in under a tree. "Bring him on down when I signal you," he said to Bucktooth, and walked down to a little dock. We could see him talking to a slatternly looking woman, and in a couple of minutes a boy hand-poled an airboat up to the dock from around behind the shack. Manny raised his arm.

"We won't need any conversation," Bucktooth said, nudging me. We went down the path. I could see Bucktooth looking distrustfully at the wide-planked, battered hull with its high, platform seats, and the big propeller encased in wire mesh. Three or four of the planks were fresh where someone had ripped out the bottom on a snag.

I stepped up onto the boat and started the engine. It was an old type with a hand throttle and a rudimentary tiller. I revved it a few times, listening, then slowed it down and tested the plugs and the battery. I checked the gas gauge and the compass. I had no intention of being left high and wet in the swamp myself.

When the kid who'd brought the boat around saw I knew what I was doing, he wandered off back to the shack. The woman had already disappeared. "Can't you run this thing?" Bucktooth demanded of Manny when the kid left. "I don't like him runnin' it."

"I can run it," Manny said. I knew he couldn't from the way he said it. "He's the one who's got to find the right spot, though. Just keep an eye on him."

He climbed up into one of the front platform seats. Bucktooth settled himself in the dishpan cockpit, facing me, his back braced against a platform strut. He could watch every move I made in the navigator's bucket seat. "You'll get wet down there," I said.

"Just you see to it I don't get wet, pal," he answered me. I would have preferred them in reversed positions. Manny had the keys to the wagon, and my Smith & Wesson. "How long's this going to take us?"

I shrugged. "Hour and a half each way." It wasn't going to take a third of that if I had my way.

I eased away from the dock. Bucktooth stared nervously at the brackish water lapping the boat's low sides. Up on the platform I could see Manny flinch the first few times I rammed the boat over deceptively solid-looking areas of saw-grass.

The sun beat down on us. In no time there were black patches of perspiration on Manny's back and under his arms. Bucktooth was sweating freely, too. Under the gnarled cypress trees with their trailing moss there was shade but no coolness. The swamp was a miasma of sticky heat. I turned right and left through wide channels, enough to get them thoroughly confused. I kept an eye on the compass, and an eye out for mangrove roots that might have tipped us over or stove in a plank. Beneath the thick, green jungle growth overhead the engine didn't sound as noisy. Mosquitoes and gnats hummed around us. Manny and Bucktooth swatted busily. My hide is tougher. Once or twice Manny turned to look back at me. I could see that for the first time he was beginning to have doubts about the expedition.

I gave them enough time to get relaxed, then began watching for a wide-enough space between the trees off the channel accompanied by a low-lying branch of the right height. I passed up a couple that didn't look exactly like what I wanted.

When I saw one that did, I didn't wait any longer.

The tree-opening was on the left, more than wide enough to slip the boat into. "Alligator!" I yelled, and pointed to the right.

"Where?" They bellowed it together. Bucktooth turned in the direction I pointed. Manny stood up to look. I slammed the throttle wide open and aimed hard left. The boat stood up on its port gunwale as it darted between the trees. The low-lying branch caught Manny in the chest. He went off the platform like an ice cube from a spilled cocktail glass. He slingshotted into the tree on the right. Even above the engine roar I could hear the splash he made as he hit the mud below.

With the tiller hard right and two thirds of the way around the first tree I shut the engine off. Bucktooth had grabbed with both hands to save himself from sliding overboard, and I reached down and slipped the little .17 caliber out of its shin holster. As we drifted back out into the main channel, Bucktooth started to turn to check on the shut-off engine. "Don't turn a thing but your head, man," I told him, my voice loud in the sudden quiet. Looking over his shoulder, he turned white when he saw what I had in my hand.

Desperately he looked up at the platform for Manny. His gaze sped then to the space between the trees, and his eyes bugged out at the sight of Manny in the mud, only his legs visible above the greenish water. The legs were kicking feebly.

"Drop your gun in the water," I directed him. I didn't even blink while he did it. I needn't have worried. His nerve was gone. He was ashen, and his hands were shaking. He was a long way removed from the gun-toting bully who'd taken so much pleasure in pushing me around last night. "You don't deserve it, but I'll give you a choice," I said. "I was going to leave you out here, with the heat and the mosquitoes and the bugs and the snakes and the alligators. You'll never make it in. I doubt if I could myself." His whole face was wet as he stared at me. "You won't go easy if you stay, so I'll give you the choice. Stay, or take one dead center from this." I waved the little handgun.

He couldn't speak at all for a second. "You'd—you'd shoot me?"

I laughed. "What the hell were you planning to do to me? Come on, make up your mind. Which is it going to be?" His eyes darted wildly in all directions. "Take the bullet," I said. "You'll go out of your mind out here in twelve hours." His chest was heaving as he tried to pump air through his constricted throat. "Take the bullet."

"No!" It was wrenched from him forcibly.

"Okay." I ruddered the boat over to a little saw-grass island with one half-grown scotch pine slanting up out of it. "Jump."

"Listen, you wouldn't—"

"Jump, you bastard. Or catch the bullet."

I moved my arm. He jumped. He shrieked as he went in up to his knees in the gelid ooze. He grabbed at the tree, and yelled again as something slithered away under his hands. He kept trying to pull his legs up out of the muck.

I started the engine and turned the boat around. The last I saw of him he was halfway up into the tree that was doubling over under his weight. If he was making any noise I couldn't hear him over the engine.

I went back to Manny Sebastian. His legs were under water now, too. I had a hell of a time pulling him far enough up out of the mud to get my Smith & Wesson out of his pants. I didn't bother with the keys to the wagon. I dropped him back in. If it was any consolation to him, I don't think he drowned. His neck was broken.

I rode the compass back to the shack. I poled in the last half mile and beached the airboat three hundred yards beyond the dock, behind a point. As long as the station wagon stayed there for security, the crackers weren't going to worry too much about their boat. By the time they started to I'd be long gone from Hudson.

I walked a mile, then hitched a ride into town. I made and remade plans all the way. I had a date with Lucille for five o'clock. I was through fooling around. Five o'clock was going to be the payoff, but I had a few things to do first.

In town it must have been ninety, but it felt almost chilly compared to the swamp. I went into the truck-stop diner south of the traffic light in the square and had a meal. I could hardly believe it when I looked at my watch and saw it was still only ten thirty in the morning.

I borrowed a sheet of paper, an envelope, and a pencil from the girl cashier. I took a couple of napkins and practiced composing telegraph messages. I finally hit on one I thought would do the trick. ARRIVING SOON MEET ME LAZY SUSAN URGENT YOU NOT FAIL ME. I addressed it to Dick Pierce, General Delivery, Hudson, Florida, and I signed it Roy.

I copied it out on the sheet of paper and sealed it up in the envelope along with two one-dollar bills. On the outside of the envelope I printed "Western Union." I sat there in the diner by the window watching the northbound, over-the-road, diesel-rigged, big vans pull into the yard, and I watched the drivers as they came in and sat down at the counter.

When a likely-looking middle-aged man came in off a furniture rig, I gave him a five-dollar bill and the envelope and asked him to drop it off at the Western Union office wherever he was at noontime. He said he'd be sure to do it. I sat there till he pulled out of the yard and up the road.

When that message hit the deck in the Hudson Western Union office it would be sent around to the post office and delivered to Lucille Grimes. When it was I should get a little action for my seven dollars. The telegram with that signature should give Lucille Grimes and Blaze Franklin something to think about besides Chet Arnold.

I walked from the diner to the motel. Inside I took the phone off the hook. If Jed was trying to call me about Kaiser, better he should think the line was busy than that he couldn't reach me. I took out the Smith & Wesson and I spent thirty minutes cleaning, oiling, and completely refurbishing it. Then I got into the shower and did the same for me.

At noon I was back uptown and parked across the street from the post office. Through the big front window I had a good view of the General Delivery window. The alphabetized slots were right behind the window. I'd specified noon for the sending of the telegram because from twelve to two Lucille was in the post office with just one clerk, and almost always handled the front herself.

I spread a newspaper over the steering wheel, and settled down to wait. I could feel the pressure building up. I don't have nerves, but I get keyed up. Everything around me is magnified a couple of dozen times, including the tick of a watch and the color of the sky.

It was hot in the car, even with the windows down, but not as hot as where I'd just come from. Not as hot as plowing up and down half-grown-over back roads on the east side of Main, either. I was through with that stuff. This little deal was going to pop the weasel right out of the box.

It was one twenty-five when the Western Union kid rode up on his bike. He kicked it up on its stand and went on inside. I saw him lay the telegram down on the counter, and in a minute Lucille appeared at the window and picked it up and looked at it. She looked at it a long time. I could see the kid reminding her she hadn't signed for it.

She scribbled her name, and the kid went out. She never even looked at the General Delivery slots behind her. Telegram in hand, she made a beeline for the back. Telephone call, I told myself. I folded up my newspaper and laid it on the seat beside me. In three minutes Lucille was at the front door. I could see her explaining something over her shoulder to the clerk she'd moved up to the front window.

She came out and walked hurriedly to a red MG parked three doors down the street. A double-parked delivery van had kept me from noticing it before. She climbed in, backed up, and ripped up the street. I was facing the wrong way. I swung in a wide U and took out after her.

She hightailed it through town, straight north on 19. I dogged her at a distance. I didn't need to stay too close. I knew where she was going. No farther than it took to meet Blaze Franklin, Deputy Sheriff, in some kind of privacy.

Actually they didn't bother too much about the privacy. From a quarter-mile behind her I watched her pull off onto the shoulder of the road. She tucked the red MG right in on the tail of a two-tone county cruiser. Blaze Franklin's thick-bodied figure was out of the cruiser and on the way over to the MG before its wheels had stopped rolling.

From a curve away I had no trouble at all in seeing his red face and the yellow flash of the telegram as he snatched it away from her and tore it open. She'd been afraid to open it herself, evidently.

Franklin climbed into the MG beside her. Their heads stayed close together for what seemed like fifteen minutes. I'd have given a quarter to be a fly on the windshield during that conversation. When Franklin jumped out of the MG and headed for the cruiser, I was ready. I swung around and headed back to town. At the first intersection I turned off and parked. In less than a minute the cruiser came flying down the highway, its siren rrr'ing. Franklin was hunched over the wheel, his tomato face like a bulldog's.

Three minutes later the MG came by. Lucille's face was white and strained-looking.

I followed along behind.

Curtain going up.

*

When I walked into the office of the Lazy Susan two hours later, Blaze Franklin was cocked up against the wall in a straightbacked chair, big as life and twice as nasty. If it had been me that's where I'd have been, too, but I still had to grade him A for nerve.

After the first quick look when I came in the door he paid no attention. Mr. Franklin had other things on his mind now than Chet Arnold. They had to figure now they'd had me in the wrong picture. I asked at the desk for mail, not that there ever was any. The young clerk behind the desk tried to engage Blaze in conversation after he'd finished with me. Franklin bit his head off neatly in about eight well-chosen words. The kid turned a dull red, and subsided.

I went out and walked down to my unit. From it I could see the office, and I could see Franklin. Twice in the first few minutes he got up and picked up the phone on the desk without a by-your-leave and made a call. It suited me fine. The longer he sat there the more things he could think of to go wrong. I wanted him shook. I hoped the phone calls were to Lucille. I wanted her shook.

Most of all I wanted Franklin right where he was. His uniform made it hard for me to move openly against him. I could kill them both, but that wouldn't get me the bundle. As long as Franklin was nailed down here, I could be sure of getting to Lucille with no interruptions. And if she gave me a hard time about where the bundle was, I'd shake her till she atomized.

I watched him off and on for another hour. He made a couple of more phone calls. He was a busy boy. At four fifteen I shaved and started to change for my date with Lucille. Buttoning my shirt, I went back to the window. I couldn't see Franklin. I could see the chair he'd been in, but he wasn't in it. I waited a couple of minutes. Wherever he was, he didn't come back.

I finished dressing in a hurry. I shoved the .38 in its holster, slipped into my jacket, and crossed over to the office. In the first quick look around I could see Franklin wasn't anywhere inside. I looked at the clerk. "The bird-dog gone?"

He didn't spit, but he almost did. "Good riddance."

"He say where he could be reached?"

"He said nothin'."

"He get a call from anyone?"

The kid shook his head. "He made enough of 'em, though. The last one he swore an' banged up the receiver an' took off."

I went outside and sat in the Ford. What in the hell had happened? Nothing on earth should have moved Blaze Franklin out of that chair. That telegram from Roy Martin should have made him afraid to move. He should have sat there, getting madder and shakier by the minute. That telegram should have immobilized him.

He must have seen that his only chance of keeping the lid on—once he read the telegram—was to intercept Roy Martin, and dispose of him quietly. Nothing should have been able to move Franklin away from that motel office.

I went back over it step by step. Gradually the only logical answer forced itself on me. I'd underrated the sonofabitch. Suppose he'd been smart enough to call the point of origin of the telegram and ask for a description of the sender? Once he knew the circumstances under which it had been sent he was right back in the saddle. With the telegram exposed as a phony, how much brains did he need to figure out who'd sent it up the road to have it bounce back here off his noggin?

So why hadn't he rushed into my motel unit and shot me up, down, and sideways and triumphantly hauled in the riddled corpse? It was exactly what he should have done. If he had the sense to short-circuit the booby-trap I'd set up for him, how could he have missed the obvious follow-up?

There was something I didn't understand.

Something I didn't know.

It was time I learned it.

I started up the Ford. Nothing was changed, really, except that I had to keep an eye peeled for Franklin.

I drove up to the post office to collect Lucille.

XI

SHE WAS standing out on the sidewalk when I pulled up in front. I opened the door and she got in. "Let's stop for a drink at the Dixie Pig first, shall we?" she said without any preliminary greeting at all.

My first impulse was to refuse. In the first place I didn't want to wave this long-legged blonde under Hazel's nose. I sneaked a glance at Lucille as she sat beside me, eyes straight ahead. She looked and sounded as brittle as glass. She might as well have worn a sign; whatever had pulled Franklin away from the motel, she knew about. The Dixie Pig was now just another gambit in the game.

Okay. We'd go to the Dixie Pig.

But not together. I drew up in front, reached across her and opened the door again. "You go on in. I just remembered I'm supposed to pick up a few dollars a guy owes me. I'll be back in ten minutes."

She didn't like it, but what could she do? She climbed out reluctantly and closed the door. "Hurry back," she said with an attempt at a smile. The shark's teeth were polished to a high gloss.

I circled the Dixie Pig driveway, and saw right away the hunch had paid off. Snuggled in among the six or eight parked cars was Franklin's cruiser. It had to be Franklin's. That's why she'd brought me here, so that he could without difficulty take up the trail for what they both felt would be the final act of the drama.

I pulled out on the highway again and in half a mile found a shiftless-looking country grocery. I stopped in and bought two pounds of brown sugar. Back in the Ford I opened it and set it down carefully on the seat beside me. I drove back to the Dixie Pig and around to the back parking lot. There was a hole two parking spaces away from the cruiser. I nosed into it.

I sat there, watching the two windows that looked out on the back parking lot. I couldn't see anyone in either booth. I picked up the sugar, got out of the Ford, walked around the rear of the car between it and the cruiser, removed the cruiser's gas cap, dumped in the brown sugar, slapped the cap back on, and crushed the bag and stuffed it in my pocket. It might have taken me six seconds. The sugar I spilled was indistinguishable on the crushed stone.

I brushed off my hands and walked in the Dixie Pig's back door. If they'd seen me drive in, I was right on schedule.

Franklin sat at the bar, his back elaborately to the door through which I'd entered. Lucille bounced up from a booth, so quickly she had to have seen me drive in. She met me in the center of the floor. "I don't think I feel like a drink right now, after all, Chet. Couldn't we wait till we eat?"

"Anything you say," I told her. We turned to the door. It was a rush act of superb proportions. I hadn't been in the place thirty seconds, but Franklin was already gone from the bar, ready to take up the pursuit in the cruiser. Behind the bar Hazel all but stood on her head trying to attract my attention. I avoided looking at her as we went out.

The cruiser was gone. Franklin would pick us up on the highway. How would he know whether to go north or south? I found out how he knew. "There's a new restaurant south on the highway, Chet. If you're feeling experimental, I understand it's quite good."

"Anything you say," I repeated. Full twilight wasn't many minutes away when I ran back down the driveway and out onto the highway. "How far is this place?"

"Oh, a dozen to fifteen miles. It's supposed to be quite attractive." Her voice was as cool as a mountain brook. Only the hands clenched in her lap betrayed her inner tension.

Fifteen miles was the superlative of fine. Franklin shouldn't be able to fetch half that before the sugar in his gas line froze his engine down tight. It was a bonus that he'd be decommissioned outside of town.

South of the square I switched on my lights. I watched the shoulder of the road. About a mile beyond we passed a car pulled off on the right, almost indistinguishable in the gathering darkness. If I hadn't been looking for it, I never would have seen it. In the rear-view mirror I watched its parking lights come on as it rolled out on the highway behind us. The wolf was in the sheep-fold. We played follow-the-leader down U.S. 19 in the deepening twilight.

He dogged me from so far back I couldn't be sure where I'd lost him, or if I actually had. He hadn't needed to stay too close because he knew where we were going. After a few miles there were no lights of any kind behind me. I didn't think even Franklin would be running that letter-S stretch without them.

It was a silent ride. Each of us was busy with private thoughts. Lucille roused herself when we'd been on the road about twenty minutes. "You'll have to watch for the turnoff," she said, leaning forward in the seat. "There's a big white sign, and then it's off to the left about a mile."

Naturally they wanted a place not on the main highway. We both saw the sign at the same time. I was already slowing down when Lucille pointed. I turned into a graveled side road at eight miles an hour. No lights of any kind turned in behind us.

A half mile in a wagon-road branched off in the headlights. I turned up it. "Not that way!" Lucille said sharply. I paid no attention. I went up it about fifty yards, pulled up the brake, and cut the motor and lights. Insurance in case a raging Franklin again proved himself shrewder than I'd anticipated and succeeded in commandeering another car.

"Plenty of time for food," I said to Lucille, and slipped an arm around her. My purpose was to keep her from fleeing if she suspected anything. She didn't. She humored me to the extent of lowering her head on my shoulder. She was content to await the arrival of the rear guard. It was full dark under the trees.

I wished I could see her face. It would have interested me to be able to read her expression. As far as I was concerned, Lucille Grimes was already dead. It was just a question of when, and how. In a way it was too bad. This was a really talented bitch.

Right that second she gave me a demonstration of it. She grabbed the horn ring on the steering wheel. The horn blatted twice. She was reaching for the lights when I caught her arm. She sat there tensely with her arm in my grip, waiting for Blaze Franklin to come up out of the darkness and kill me.

I could sense the shriveling of her self-confidence when nothing happened. "You beginning to get the idea he's not coming?" I asked her. "He's not splitting with you, Lucille. He's splitting with me. Your boyfriend's sold you out. I'm supposed to bury you twenty yards off this side road."

It shook her to her heels, but she was too smart to go for it completely. "He'll kill you," she croaked. She tried to look over her shoulder.

"Where is he, then?" I needled her. "Get smart, woman. It's lucky for you I like you. Now get on the ball and steer me to the money. I'll take care of Franklin for you."

There was only one thing she could think. Even if Franklin hadn't sold her out, if he'd flubbed his end of the deal she had to protect herself. She knew who I was, and she knew there was no reason on earth I shouldn't leave her body in the bushes beside the car. Her steel-trap mind should have been telling her she was in perfect position to play it cool right down to the finish line, and then choose up sides with the winner.

I couldn't understand why she hesitated so long.

"We—we never found the money," she said at last. Her voice was husky. "Only the thousand in the envelope and a few thousand on—on him." She drew a quivering breath. "If only I'd never mentioned to Blaze the big, odd-looking man who mailed such queer—" Her voice died away.

So that was why Franklin wanted me alive. He hoped I knew where the bundle was. The funny part of it was, I did. Now.

I tightened the grip on her arm. "Franklin killed him before he found out where the money was?"

"He—yes," she whispered.

So Franklin hadn't been able to crack Bunny. I started up the Ford. "Tell me where he was staying, Lucille." She was silent. I turned my head to look at her. Her face was just an indistinct pale oval. "Tell me," I warned her. "Franklin might not have been able to find it, but I'll find it."

She told me. She had trouble getting it out. The directions would have put Bunny's place north of town. I pulled on the dash light. She was watching me, and she backed off as far as she could go. I crossed my hand over my chest and drew the Smith & Wesson. Her face crumpled with fear. I took hold of her and pulled her toward me, reversed the gun, and slashed her across her soft inner arm with the front gunsight. She cried out in pain and shock as the blood welled. "I'm giving you a chance to change that story," I told her. "Because if we get where you send me and there's nothing there, that's what happens to your face till my arm gets tired."

She changed the story.

The new one put Bunny's place east of town, which sounded a lot better to me.

I got out of there. Lucille sat huddled in the seat beside me. I hadn't expected her to go to pieces so completely. The way I'd sized her up she should have had no trouble at all riding with a foot on each saddle till either Franklin or I got dumped. She must be scared to death of Franklin.

We were on the right side of town but it still took us nearly an hour to get there. I had a funny feeling riding east on Main past the shack with the sign out in front, "Airboat For Hire." The side road Lucille reluctantly directed me up couldn't have been more than a couple of miles beyond the point where I'd been so painfully slogging over brambled trails. No wonder Franklin had been getting itchy.

It was a small cabin way out in the middle of nowhere. I got out of the Ford and ran a flashlight around the building. No telephone wires. Fine. I circled it cautiously. In the rear a mound of cut branches loomed up in the light. I pulled off a couple. There sat the blue Dodge, up on blocks.

So Lucille hadn't lied to me. I returned to the Ford. She still sat in it, motionless. I had to take her by the arm again to get her out. She didn't want to come with me.

I got a chisel and maul out of the trunk of the Ford, herded Lucille up to the door ahead of me, and broke the lock. A wave of dry heat rolled out at me as it opened, a musty, long-closed smell. I wondered if this was the right place, after all. I kept a good hold on Lucille's arm.

Inside I closed the door and stationed her away from it. I walked through the place. A skillet was still on the two-burner stove. Bunny's clothes hung neatly on hangers. There were two more locked doors. A couple of swings of the maul disposed of both. There was nothing at all in the first room. I beamed the flash rapidly around the interior of the second one, and then it hung there, motionless.

I'd found Bunny.

He was face down on the rough pine flooring. His wrists were handcuffed to ringbolts in the floor at right angles to his head. The ringbolts were new. Fresh pine sawdust was still visible where the holes had been drilled for them.

Dry as the air in the place was there was another odor. Bunny had been in the cuffs a long time. With his chest flat on the floor and his arms spreadeagled, not even his great strength could achieve leverage. In a final contortion he had thrown himself onto his right side. The bone of his left knee glistened at me out of raw-looking meat, the trousers and flesh long since abraded away in his ceaseless struggle with the flooring. His upper left arm was mincemeat where he'd gnawed at himself.

He'd lain in the cuffs till he died.

Which kills first, hunger or thirst? I couldn't remember. I couldn't think.

The game had dealt Bunny a tough hand. Looking into Franklin's gun, he must have temporized, thinking he'd find a spot to turn it around. He hadn't counted on the cuffs. He'd gone into them, but he hadn't cracked. How do you break a stubborn man? You starve him. When he's out of his mind with hunger and thirst, he'll lead you to anything he has.

If he's not too far out of his mind. With the hunger, the thirst, and the maddening heat, Franklin had returned to the cabin one day and found a mindless animal that could never lead him to anything.

I stooped and examined the head, cruelly battered from endless, raving contact with the floor. There had been no merciful bullet.

Franklin had left him to die.

Franklin and Lucille Grimes had left him to die.

I knew now why she'd been so afraid to come in here with me. She'd known exactly what I was going to find.

I straightened up and drew the Smith & Wesson. I walked out into the other room.

"Blaze did it!" she screamed when she saw my face. "Blaze did it! I wanted to let him—"

I shot her in the throat, three times.

"Tell your story in hell, if you can get anyone to listen," I told her. She thrashed on the floor, blood pulsing between the fingers of the hands clasped to her neck. "If they can patch up your lying voice."

I stepped over her. I had work to do.

I went outside, into the clean darkness. I looked up at the stars to orient myself. I knew where the sack would be. For a cache out in the country, Bunny and I had always followed a pattern. From the front door of the cabin I stepped out due north as accurately as I could figure it. I knew it wouldn't be more than thirty or forty feet from the cabin.

In the daylight it would have been a cinch, and even in the dark it wasn't hard. My feet told me as soon as I hit softer earth. Bunny had planted something green over it. I ripped it up, pulled the chisel out of my pocket that was the only tool I had, and tore into the loose ground. A foot below the surface I ran into the sack.

I hauled it up and by the light of the flash made certain that the bulk of the swag was still in it. Then I reburied it, stamping down the earth. No sense lugging it around with me. I'd be back for it. I'd be back for it when I brought Blaze Franklin out here and roped him down to Bunny's body and left him to die in the same way he'd left Bunny.

I went back inside for a look around. Lucille was unconscious. Bubbles of blood pulsed gently now instead of jetting with each ragged breath. She wouldn't last long. She was lucky. If I hadn't been so mad that I hadn't stopped to think, I could have figured a different end for her. She was just as guilty as Franklin.

Death I'm used to, but Bunny's infuriated me. Where would Franklin be now? Back at the Lazy Susan, probably, chewing up the rug. He had to hope I came back there. He'd get his wish in a way he never expected.

I went back out to the Ford and got out of there.

I drove straight to the Dixie Pig. I wanted Franklin so bad I could taste it, but I had another errand first. I scouted the back parking lot carefully. No two-tone cruiser. I parked beside Hazel's car and went on in.

Hazel was behind the bar that had a half-dozen customers. Her face lighted up when she saw me. She made a circling motion with her hand that beckoned me behind the bar, and held up the hinged flap at the far end. I walked on in and out through the hanging curtain in the center of the back-bar. I'd never been out there before. It was set up as a lounging room, with a couch and a couple of chairs, a Primus stove and a coffeepot.

"Get a bag packed," I said to her when she came through the curtain behind me. "I'll be back for you in an hour."

Her big hand caught mine and squeezed it, hard. "Listen to me, Chet. Please." Her voice was low and intense. "Franklin has everyone out looking for you. There's half a dozen of them waiting for you down in the motel yard. They never dreamed you'd come back here."

So. End of the line in Hudson, Florida. And I couldn't get Franklin. I couldn't? The hell I couldn't. I held out my hand to Hazel. "Forget what I said about a bag. Give me your car keys."

She turned to her handbag on a chair. "Chet, please let me come—"

"Tell them I took the keys away from you," I cut her off. I couldn't take her with me now. I was something less than even money to make it. "Forget what I said about packing a bag." She handed me the keys. "Tell them I took—" I shut myself off. I was starting to repeat myself. I punched Hazel in the eye. Big as she was she went over backward and landed on the couch. The eye would be her alibi. "So long, baby," I said from the curtained opening. I didn't look back. I didn't want to see the expression on her face.

I drove down to the motel in her car. They should have been looking for my Ford. It turned out they were looking for anything. I'd no more than rolled into the yard and opened the car door when some eager beaver tapped his headlights. Instantly three more sets came on. I was semi-circled by cruisers. The motel yard looked bright as day.

Blaze Franklin came roaring out of the nearest cruiser, waving a gun. He had to be first. He couldn't let me talk. At ten yards I put five in a row into him a playing card could have covered. He went down, bellowing like a wounded bull. He *was* a wounded bull. A dark red stain spread over the front of his uniform trousers. He'd live. He wouldn't enjoy it. I put the last one into his jaw as he flopped on the ground, to keep him quiet if I made the getaway good.

Firecrackers were going off all around me. They couldn't shoot worth a damn. I dived back in under the wheel and aimed the car straight ahead through the largest gap in the encircling headlights. Gravel spurted. Someone shot out the windshield. I ducked flying glass, bumped over the lawn, through the flower bed, around the swimming pool, and over a white picket fence. I jounced down onto the highway and floored the accelerator. For the first five-hundred yards part of the fence kept banging against the front wheels of Hazel's car. Then it fell off.

Behind me were lights and sirens. No shortage of either. I busted right through the square and set sail for the Dixie Pig. In the souped-up Ford I at least had a chance of outrunning them. Right now I could just about smell the overheated engines behind me.

A thousand yards from the Dixie Pig I cut the lights, got over on the shoulder, and drove in darkness. If there had been anything parked out there it would have been Katy-Bar-the-door. I whirled the wheel hard when I saw the lighter outline of the crushed stone driveway. I took a section of hedge with me, but I made the turn. I belted it around to the back. Outside on the highway the cruisers screamed on by.

I yanked up the emergency and lit running. The door on the driver's side of the Ford stood open. I didn't remember leaving it open. I came to a sliding stop beside it, my hand on the butt of my .38 when I saw a dark figure on the other side of the front seat. I came within a tick of blasting it before I recognized Hazel. "Get the hell out of there!" I ordered her, trying to listen for sounds on the highway.

"Take me with you, Chet," she pleaded. "Give me a gun."

"Don't make me do it, baby," I warned her. "Get out of the car."

She got out. I could see she was crying. "Chet—"

"Stop making these losing bets, will you?" I got in under the wheel. "Get back inside and keep your mouth shut." I backed up, swung around, and rammed the Ford down the driveway. The last I saw of Hazel was the glitter of the silver conches on her cowboy boots in the big swing of the headlights.

I doubled back toward town. There were bound to be road blocks north and south on 19. I'd head east, on Main. The added power of the Ford felt good under my foot. I blasted the road. Approaching the traffic light I slowed down. I'd just started to make the left-hand turn when there was the snarl of a siren practically in my ear. Somebody in the posse had had the brains to leave a trailer. He was headed the wrong way, but I saw the shine of his lights as he swung around after me. My forty-five-mile-an-hour turn carried me up onto the sidewalk before I got straightened out on Main.

I really rolled it away from there. I was doing eighty-five on a road built for forty. The Ford was all over the road. I watched the dark ribbon of macadam unroll in the headlights. Behind me the wailing shriek of the siren pierced the night, but I was outrunning him. Then I burst out of a curve into a long straight-away, and far up the road winked the red lights of trouble.

Road block.

Instinctively I lifted my foot off the gas, but I still rolled up on it fast. A spotlight came on when they saw me. A tiny figure stood out in the road, waving me down with flapping arms. I sized it up. Two cruisers across the road, their snouts extending way out onto the shoulders. Three quarters of a car's width between them in the center. Ditch on the right. Open field on the left. And in the rear-view mirror the lights of the trailing cruiser rapidly gaining.

A road block you do or you don't. I mashed down on the gas and headed for the center opening between the end-to-end cruisers. I just might rip my way through. The fool with the flapping arms stood right in the center of the gap. The headlights picked him up solidly. Roaring down on him, I was suddenly looking through the windshield into the white, strained face of Jed Raymond.

I hoped he'd jump. Jed was a nice kid. If he didn't, though, he'd have to take his chances, as I was taking mine. I couldn't have been twenty yards from him—and he hadn't made a move—when Kaiser pranced out in front of him from behind a cruiser, head cocked, tongue lolling, tail waving.

My brain sent me straight on through, over the dog and Jed, to try the odds with the cruisers. But hands spun the wheel, hard left. Somebody else will have to explain it to you. I missed them both, caromed broadside off the left-hand cruiser in a whining, ear-splitting shriek of tortured metal, and hurtled a hundred fifty yards down into the field. The front wheels dropped suddenly into a ditch. There was a loud whump, and the Ford stood up on its nose. The doors flew open. I flew out. I hit hard, and rolled.

I didn't lose consciousness. I still had the gun. The Ford was down on its knees in front, its ass-end up in the air, the wheels still spinning. I started to crawl over to it, and knew in the first second my right leg was broken.

Up on the road the spotlight pivoted and crept down through the field. It caught me, passed on, hesitated, and came back. There was a sharp crack, and a bullet plowed up the ground beside me. Rifle. Sounded like a .30-.30. I crawled over the uneven ground to the Ford, underneath the back wheels where I could see up to the road. I reloaded in a hurry, and got the spotlight with my third shot.

They turned the other cruiser around—the one I hadn't hit—and its spotlight started down through the field. I popped it out before it reached me. Not that it made any difference. More red lights, sirens, and spotlights were whirling up to the roadblock every second now.

I reloaded the Smith & Wesson again. Nothing for it now but the hard sell. Nothing for it but to see to it a few of them shook hands with the devil at the same time I did.

To get me in a hurry they had to come through the field. By now they knew enough not to be in a hurry. The .30-.30 went off again, and a large charge of angry metal whanged through the body of the car over my head. The rifle would keep me pinned down while they circled around behind me.

The spotlights were crisscrossing each other in an eerie pattern in the open field, but one of them had the Ford pinned down steadily. A hump in the ground kept me in shadow. I couldn't see anyone coming through the field.

I heard the rifle's sharp crack again. Above my head there was a loud ping!! Suddenly I was drenched to the waist in gasoline. The .30-.30 slug had ripped out the belly of the gas tank. I swiped at my stinging eyes and shook my dripping head. I looked up just as gas from my hair splashed onto the hot exhaust.

Whoom!!

I saw a bright flare, and then I didn't see anything. The explosion knocked me backward under the car. I rolled out from beneath it. I didn't even feel the broken leg I was dragging. I couldn't see at all. My eyes were gone. I could hear the crackle of flames. Part was the Ford. Part was me. I was afire all over.

I tried to smother the flames on the ground. It didn't help. I still had the gun. I hoped they could see me and were coming at me. I knelt up on my good leg and faced the noise up on the road, bracing the Smith & Wesson in both hands. I squeezed off the whole load, waist-high in a semicircle. I think the last shot exploded in the chamber from the heat of my burning hands. I threw the empty gun as far as I could in the direction of the road.

There was a dull roaring sound in my ears. I tried to put out the fire in my hair. I rolled on the ground. I could smell my own burning flesh.

The last thing I heard was myself, screaming.

XII

I WAS in black darkness for six months. I may have gone a little crazy, too. I gave them a hard time. I went the whole route: baths, wet packs, elbow cuffs, straightjackets, isolation. I stopped fighting them a little while ago. They don't pay much attention to me now.

Even before I could see again, I knew what I looked like. I could feel the reaction, when a new patient was admitted, or a new attendant came on duty. Hazel came to see me four or five times. I refused permission for her to be allowed in.

They don't know that I can see again, that I'm not crazy. They think I'm a robot. A vegetable.

I'll show them.

I have a hermetically sealed quart jar buried in the ground up in Hillsboro, New Hampshire, and another in Grosmont, Colorado, up above timber line. There's nothing but money in both. I don't need it. All I need is a gun. Some one of these days I'll find the right attendant, and I'll start talking to him. It will take a while to convince him, but I've got plenty of time.

If I can get back to the sack buried beside Bunny's cabin, plastic surgery will take care of most of what I look like. With a gun, I'll get back to it.

That's all I need—a gun.

I'm not staying here.

I'll be leaving one of these days, and the day I do they'll never forget it.

DEAD CALM

Charles Williams

I

THOUGH IT had been less than four hours since he'd secured everything on deck and come below, Ingram awoke just at dawn. He turned his head in the faint light inside the cabin and looked at his wife asleep in the opposite bunk. Rae, wearing sleeveless short pajamas of lightweight cotton, was lying on her stomach, her face turned toward him, the mop of tawny hair spread across the pillow encircled by her arms, her legs spread slightly apart and braced, even in sleep, against the motion of the ketch. She never minded, he thought; some people grew irritable and impossible to live with on a sailboat too long becalmed, with its endless rolling and slatting of gear and its annoying and unstoppable noises of objects shifting back and forth in drawers and lockers, but except for an occasional pungent remark when the stove threw something at her she took it uncomplainingly. They weren't in a hurry, she pointed out, they were on their honeymoon, and they had privacy measurable in millions of square miles.

Without even consciously thinking about it, his mind received, filtered, and evaluated each of the individual sounds in the orchestration of creaks and minute collisions going on about him, oblivious to the total melody but capable of becoming instantly alert at the mere suspicion of a note that was out of place. Nothing was rolling or banging on deck; everything was still secure topside. The metallic bumping just beyond his feet in the galley section of the cabin was the teakettle sliding against the rails that kept it on the stove. The click and intermittent rattle above it were dishes shifting minutely inside their stowage on the bulkhead above the sink. The creaking was only a timber working normally as she swung and swung back; if a boat didn't have flexibility it would break up against any kind of sea, like a car smashed against a wall. That sound of something rolling back and forth was a pencil loose in a drawer. The clock struck four bells. He stretched luxuriously. Six A.M. Hot. Dead calm. But at least they'd sailed out of yesterday's grapefruit rinds. They'd had a light southeasterly breeze for six hours last night, which should put them at least another twenty-five miles along their course.

After sliding out of the bunk, he put on water for coffee, moving silently about the galley so as not to disturb Rae. He stripped off his pajamas, picked up a towel, and mounted the companion ladder to the cockpit. Everything on deck was drenched with dew; it stood in great sweaty beads on the brass cover of the binnacle, and the bottoms of the cockpit cushions he'd reversed last night were as wet as if they'd been rained on. It was full daylight now, and the towering escarpments of cloud to the eastward were shot with flame. Not a breath of air stirred; the surface of the Pacific was as unwrinkled as glass except for the heave and surge of the long groundswell running up from the infinite distances of the Southern Hemisphere.

Standing naked in the cockpit, he leaned over and peered into the binnacle from sheer force of habit to check the heading of the ketch as she lay dead in the water except for her rolling. She was lying 290 at the moment, almost abeam to the swell. He turned and looked forward. Everything was secure. Wind or no wind, it was morning, it was beautiful, and it was good to be alive. He was where he wanted to be, at sea with a sound boat and with Rae. They were nineteen days out of the Canal, bound for Tahiti and the islands to the south, tied to no schedule, free of the frustrations and annoyances of life ashore.

He grinned suddenly and made an impatient gesture with his hand. Goofing off. The water for the coffee would be boiling in a few minutes. Reaching inside the companion hatch, he switched off the masthead light, and went forward. Shoved under the lashings of the dinghy atop the deckhouse was a short ladder. He pulled it free, hung it over the port side, stepped over the lifeline, and dived. After coming to the surface, he swam with a powerful crawl stroke up along her side, under the bow, and back down the other side. He turned on his back and floated some fifty feet astern, looking up at her with affection.

Saracen was thirty-two feet on the waterline, forty over-all, ketch-rigged. She was mahogany planked over oak frames and had been built less than ten years ago by a New England yard. She wasn't as fast as some, nor as tall and long-ended and patrician of line, but she was reasonably dry on deck and with her short overhang forward and her deep forefoot she pounded very little in a seaway. Deep-water cruising was what she was built for, he thought, and she was good at it. She'd take you there as fast as you needed to go, and she'd bring you back from anything a sane man would take her into.

He swam back, climbed aboard, and stowed the ladder. In the cockpit he rubbed himself down vigorously with the towel and tied it around his middle. He was a big man, no longer young—he was forty-four—with a flat, windburned face and cool gray eyes. The hair was dark, atrociously cut some five days ago by his wife, graying deeply at the temples, and his shoulders and back were hard and rope-muscled, burned dark by the tropical sun. Along his left hip and in back of his left leg were the slick, hairless whorls of old scar tissue, relic of an explosion and fire aboard a boat when he'd operated a shipyard in Puerto Rico, but the limp was long since gone.

He started below to dress and make the coffee, but paused with one foot on the companion ladder to take a last look around the horizon for squalls. They could make up very fast here in the belt of calms along the Line, even in the early morning. There were no clouds that looked suspicious at the moment— His eyes stopped suddenly and returned to the sector off the starboard bow. He'd seen something. Or had he? Yes, there it was again, a tiny speck almost over the rim of the horizon. It disappeared and came into view again. Without removing his eyes from it, he reached inside the hatch and lifted the big seven-by-fifty binoculars from the rack on the after bulkhead. It was a boat.

At that distance, even with the glasses, he could make out nothing about it except that it appeared to be two-masted and was carrying no sail at the moment. He stepped back to the binnacle and checked the heading. It was bearing about 310 degrees. He looked at it again, but it was impossible to tell whether or not anyone was on deck; it was, in fact, visible at all only when it rose to the crest of a swell. Rae would want to see it, he thought; it was the only sign of life they'd sighted since leaving Panama nearly three weeks ago. Well, it'd still be there after breakfast; nobody was going anywhere until they got some wind.

He went below and pulled on khaki shorts and sneakers. The water was boiling now. He measured out the coffee and poured it. While it was running through he wound the chronometer. He checked the barometer, giving it a little tap with his fingernail. It was steady at 29.91. He entered it in the log, along with the time, and the notation, "Calm. PC to clr. Mod. S'ly swell."

Rae rolled over and sat up, yawning. She brushed the tawny mane of hair back from her face and grinned. "Hi, Skipper."

He perched on the side of the bunk and kissed her. "Hi, beautiful."

She made a deprecating gesture. "Everybody's beautiful when he first wakes up. It's called the blotched, rumpled, and bleary-eyed look; beauty shops can't duplicate it. Mmmmm, I was having a wonderful dream."

"About what?" he asked.

"Fresh water. There was a sunken tub about the size of Rhode Island, with two hundred pounds of bath salts in it—"

"Miss all that too much?"

She rumpled his still-wet hair. "Silly. Who'd want to be a clean widow when she could be a dirty sailor's wife?"

"Watch your language, Mate. I just bathed in the Pacific Ocean."

"God, the English language, at seven o'clock in the morning. I mean the dirty wife of a clean sailor."

"Okay, Moonbeam McSwine. How about a cup of coffee?"

"Love it." She swung long bare legs off the bunk and disappeared into the head, which opened off the narrow passageway between the forward and after compartments. She came out a few minutes later, face washed and hair combed, and sat down on the bunk with her legs braced against the one opposite. He handed her the mug of coffee and a lighted cigarette. "We've got company."

"You mean somebody else is using our ocean?"

He nodded. "I just sighted him."

"Who? Where?"

"Three or four miles away, to the northwest. Looks like a yacht. Yawl or ketch."

"Where do you suppose he's going?"

He grinned. "Nowhere at the moment. He's becalmed too."

"If we could get together and all whistle for wind at the same time, like a grievance committee, or a delegation—"

"This won't last much longer. We whittled off another twenty or thirty miles last night. In a few more days we ought to be picking up the Trades."

"Oh, I'm not complaining. Being becalmed has its points."

"It does?" he asked. "I can only think of one."

"That's the one. Nobody has to be at the wheel."

"I thought you liked to steer."

"I do." She smiled roguishly. "And no further comment, not at this hour of the morning."

"You're a hard woman. Look, I intended to run the engine a few minutes today to dry it out; if you want to, after breakfast we could run over and hail our neighbor. You like to gossip awhile, or borrow a cup of sugar?"

"Sure. But could I have a swim first? Or is he within binocular range?"

"Not unless he's got the Mount Palomar telescope. Anyway, you could wear a suit."

She sniffed. "Swim suit? Fine pagan you are."

After they'd cooked and eaten breakfast and washed the dishes, he returned to the cockpit. The sun was up now, glaring brassily on the polished surface of the sea. *Saracen* had swung around on the swell, but he checked the bearing on the compass and located the other boat without difficulty, using the binoculars. It was off the starboard quarter. Rae came up, wrapped in a terrycloth robe and carrying a towel. "Which way is he?"

He handed her the binoculars and pointed. She searched for a moment. "Mmmmm. There he is. Is he really that small, or just so far away?"

"He's a long way off."

She grinned. "Far enough, I think. I can't even tell if there's anybody on deck."

She went forward, hung the ladder over the side, unbelted the robe, and let it drop. She stepped across the lifeline, poised for a moment, dived cleanly, and came to the surface almost immediately with a flip of her head to clear the hair from her eyes. He walked forward along the port side, watching the water around and below her, faintly uneasy as he always was when she was down there. Motion pictures to the contrary, sharks didn't always travel on the surface with their dorsal fins conveniently showing. "Don't go too far from the ladder," he warned.

"I won't."

She swam back and forth several times and came back to the ladder. When she had her feet on the bottom rung and the lifeline in her hands, he said, "Wait there a minute." He turned and ran below, grabbed a saucepan, and pumped a quart of fresh water into it at the sink. She watched, puzzled, as he came hurrying back. He knelt and poured it slowly over her head, washing the salt water out of her hair. She began to laugh, and when he put down the saucepan she sprang the rest of the way up the ladder and threw her arms about him. "It's because I love you," he said, as wet now as she was.

She kissed him again, and then broke up into laughter once more with her face against his throat. "I was thinking of that woman the Taj Mahal was built for."

"Why?"

"When she was alive, I bet even *her* husband didn't pour a whole quart of fresh water in her hair."

"Probably nothing but emeralds."

"The clod." She pushed back. "But I'd better get some clothes on. They just might have bigger binoculars over there."

He went back to the cockpit. She dried herself with the towel, wrapped it about her head, put on the robe, and went below. The engine controls were in the cockpit. He set the choke, switched on the ignition, and turned it over with the starter. It caught on the third or fourth try, coughed once, and settled down to a steady rumble. He let it idle a few minutes to warm up, and shoved the lever ahead. Taking the wheel, he brought her around and steadied up on the approximate bearing of the other craft. Now that they were under way, the rolling lessened almost miraculously, and the slight breeze of their passage felt cool against his face. He reached for the glasses, picked up the boat again, brought *Saracen* a few degrees to the right to line it up dead ahead, and checked the compass course. Three-fifteen was about right.

"Honey," he called down the hatch, "when you come up, will you bring me a cigar?"

"Right, Skipper. But don't get there too fast. If we're going calling, I've got to dress and put on my face."

"Take your time. It'll take a half-hour or more."

She came on deck in about five minutes, dressed in Bermuda shorts and a white blouse. Her still-damp hair was combed back and tied with a scrap of ribbon, and she'd put on lipstick. He lit the cigar she handed him. She picked up the binoculars and turned forward, searching for the other craft. The sun struck coppery highlights in her hair as she swayed with the motion of the ketch, balancing easily on bare feet.

"Still can't tell whether there's anybody on deck," she said.

"She's a long way off yet," Ingram replied. "And they could be asleep—" He broke off at a muttered exclamation from Rae. "What is it?"

She spoke without lowering the glasses. "I thought I saw something else. Between here and there."

"What?"

"I don't know. It was just a speck, and it's gone now—no. Wait. There it was again."

"Turtle?" he asked.

"No-o. It'd have to be bigger than that; it's too far away. Here, you take a look."

He slid over and stood up in the cockpit. She took the wheel and repeated the compass course. "It's almost dead ahead," she said. "I only had a couple of quick glimpses of it, but I think it was right in line with the other boat and probably three-quarters of the way over to it."

He put a knee on the starboard cockpit cushion and leaned to the right to get out of line with the masts as he adjusted the glasses. He picked up the other craft and studied it for a moment. Ketch-rigged, he thought, and probably a little larger than *Saracen*. There was no one visible on deck. She was almost abeam to the swell and rolling sluggishly. He lowered the glasses a bit and began to search the slickly heaving surface of the sea that lay between.

"See anything?" Rae asked.

"Not yet." Then he did. It was only a speck in the distance, showing for an instant as it rose to the broad crest of a swell. It dropped from view. He marked the location in reference to the other craft and tried to hold the glasses steady to catch it when it came up again. *Saracen* rolled, and he lost it. "Had it," he said. "Wait—here it is again." It was in view for several seconds this time, and he was able to make out what it was. "Dinghy," he announced.

"Adrift?" she asked.

"No. There's somebody in it."

"Odd place to go for a row."

Ingram frowned, still studying the tiny shell. "I think he's coming this way. Must have sighted us and started to row over."

"That's doing it the hard way," she remarked with a puzzled glance at the back of his head. "Why wouldn't he crank up the auxiliary? He must have one."

"I don't know," Ingram said. "Unless it's out of commission."

In another few minutes the dinghy was within easy view without the glasses, continuing to advance across the slick undulations of the sea as its occupant pulled rapidly at the oars, never pausing or even slowing the beat as he turned his head from time to time to check his course. It would have been long since obvious to him that *Saracen* was under way and headed for him, and Ingram wondered why he didn't merely rest on the oars and wait. Judging from the distance remaining to the other yacht, he'd already rowed well over a mile, apparently at that same racing beat. The occupant was a man, bare-headed, wearing a yellow life-jacket.

He was less than a hundred yards away now. Ingram reached down and cut the engine, and in the sudden silence they could hear the creak and rattle of oarlocks as the dinghy came on, its pace unchecked, across the closing gap. *Saracen* slowed and came to rest, slewing around on the swell, port side toward the approaching boat. The man looked around over his shoulder but did not hail. He was going to hit amidships. Ingram stepped quickly up on deck and knelt at the rail. He caught the bow of the dinghy and tried to fend it off, but a last explosive pull at the oars had given it too much momentum, and it bumped anyway. It swung around against *Saracen*'s side. The man let go the oars. One of them started to slide overboard, but Ingram grabbed it with his other hand and dropped it into the dinghy. "Okay," he said soothingly. "Just take it easy."

The other paid no attention. His lips moved, but he uttered no sound, his eyes reflecting some furious intensity of concentration that excluded all else. Ingram took a turn around a lifeline stanchion with the dinghy's painter and held down a hand to help him on deck. The man caught his arm between elbow and wrist with a grip that made him wince. The other hand caught the stanchion, and he came up all in one plunging and desperate leap that kicked the dinghy backward against its painter and almost capsized it, clawing his way over the lifeline and catching the handrail along the edge of the deckhouse. The suddenness of it caught Ingram unawares, and when the man crashed into him he fell backward and sat down abruptly on the deckhouse coaming. For some reason his glance fell on the other's hand, the one holding on to the handrail. It appeared to be infected from a small wound or cut across the knuckles, but it was the grip itself that caught his attention. The fingers were locked around the handrail so tightly they were flattened and white beneath the tan.

Hunger? he wondered. No, a starving man wouldn't have had the strength to lunge aboard that way. More probably thirst. "Water," he said quietly to Rae. "Not too much."

But she had anticipated the request and was already going down the ladder. The man inched his way aft, clinging tightly to both the lifeline and the handrail along the deckhouse, as though suspended over some terrifying abyss. Ingram followed closely behind him to catch him if he stumbled. The man made it to the cockpit and sank down on one of the cushions, looked around him at the sea with a shuddering motion of his shoulders, and slumped forward with his face in his hands.

Rae came hurrying up the ladder from below with an aluminum cup partly filled with water. Ingram took it and touched the man lightly on the shoulder. "Here you go," he said. "Just take it slow, and there'll be more in a minute."

The other looked up, blankly at first, and then with dawning comprehension as though aware of them for the first time, and Ingram was conscious of the thought that the face bore none of the ravages he'd always read of as associated with extreme and prolonged thirst—no cracked and blackened lips or swollen tongue. It was, in spite of the growth of golden beard, a boyish and strikingly handsome face, tanned and slender but not haggard, and unmarked by anything except perhaps exhaustion. The gray eyes were red-rimmed as if the man hadn't slept in a long time. Besides the life-jacket he wore only white sneakers and a pair of faded khaki shorts, and it was obvious he was not only quite young, probably still in his early twenties, but powerfully built and in top physical condition.

"Oh," he said. "Thanks. Thanks a lot." He reached for the water, almost indifferently, drank, and put the cup down beside him on the cockpit seat. Ingram saw with surprise that he hadn't even finished it. He drew a hand across his face and made a shaky attempt at a smile. "Man, am I glad to see you." Then he added abruptly, like a small boy suddenly remembering his manners, "My name's Hughie Warriner."

"John Ingram," Ingram said, holding out his hand. "And my wife, Rae." Warriner started to get up, but Rae shook her head and smiled. "No. Just rest."

"What's the trouble?" Ingram asked.

Warriner gestured wearily toward the other yacht rolling on the groundswell a mile away. "She's going down. She's been sinking for days, and I doubt she'll last through the morning."

"What happened?"

"I don't know," the young man replied. "She just seemed to open up all over. I've been at the pump for a week, and almost continuously for the past two days, but I couldn't keep up with it. And since around midnight it's been gaining faster all the time."

Ingram nodded. It would, as she settled lower in the water and additional seams were submerged. Warriner went on, "I thought I was done for, till I looked over here awhile ago and saw you, and then I was scared to death a breeze would come up and you'd go on without ever seeing me. I fired off a couple of flares, but nothing happened. I guess you couldn't see 'em that far away in sunlight—"

"It was probably while we were below eating breakfast, anyway," Ingram said. "And the water's up in your engine now?"

"Yes. But it hasn't worked for a long time anyway. I tried calling you on the radio, but of course if you hadn't seen me you wouldn't have yours turned on, not out here. So my only chance was to try to get over to you with the dinghy before you caught a breeze." He sighed and brushed a hand across his face again. "And am I glad you saw me."

"Yeah, that's cutting it a little fine." Ingram grinned briefly and reached for the ignition key to start the engine again. "But we'd better get on over there. How many aboard?"

"Nobody," Warriner said. "I'm alone."

"Alone?" Involuntarily, Ingram straightened and looked out across the metallic expanse of sea toward the other yacht. Even at that distance it was obvious she was larger than *Saracen*. "You were trying to take her across the Pacific single-handed?"

"No. There were four of us when we left Santa Barbara. . . ." Warriner's voice trailed off, and he stared down at his hands. Then he went on quietly. "My wife and the other couple died ten days ago."

2

"OH, HOW AWFUL!" Rae cried out and checked herself barely in time to keep from adding, "You poor boy!"—in spite of Warriner's being in the neighborhood of six feet and probably not more than six or eight years younger than she was. Already drawn by the clean-cut, boyish appearance, good looks, and obvious good manners in the face of disaster, she felt a stab of almost motherly compassion and an illogical desire to take him in her arms and comfort him. "How did it happen?" Then she went on hurriedly, "But never mind. You can talk later. Can I get you something to eat? Or some more water?"

"No, thank you, Mrs. Ingram, I'm all right," Warriner replied. "But I could use a cigarette if you have one."

"Of course." She produced them from the pocket of her shorts and held out the lighter. "And why don't you take off that life-jacket? It's hot enough without wearing that thing."

"Oh . . . sure." Warriner looked down at it uncertainly and began unfastening it. He placed it on the seat beside him. "I guess I forgot I had it on."

Ingram's cigar had gone out. He relighted it and tossed the match overboard. "What happened?" he asked.

"It was some kind of food poisoning." Warriner stared somberly at the smoke curling upward from the cigarette forgotten between his fingers. "They all died in one afternoon, within four hours. It was horrible. . . ." He shook his head and then went on in the same flat, mechanical voice. "No, there's no word for what it was like, alone in the middle of the ocean with three people sick and dying, one after the other, all in different stages of the same symptoms, and not being able to do anything about it. And knowing after the first one died there was no hope for the others. My wife was the last one, just at sunset. And the terrible part of it was I wasn't even sick. I just stood there and watched them die, like something that was happening on the other side of a glass wall I couldn't get through."

Rae reached down and put her hand on his shoulder. "I'm sorry," she said. "But don't talk about it now. You've got to get some sleep."

"Thank you," Warriner replied, "but I'm all right. After the first couple of days I managed to snap out of it and get going again. And it was about then I began to notice the bilges were filling up with water and that it took longer every day to pump them out. Before long it was so bad I didn't have time to think about anything but staying afloat. Maybe that was what saved me from cracking up."

"Do you know what the poison was?" Ingram asked.

Warriner nodded. "The only thing it could have been was a can of salmon that must have spoiled. I didn't eat any, because I don't like salmon."

"Had it been opened a long time?"

"No, just a few minutes before they ate it. But it wasn't commercially canned; it was some Russ and Estelle—they were the other couple—some they put up themselves. Every year Russ goes up to the Columbia River for a week's fishing when the Chinook run is on, and when he catches any they have some of it smoked and Estelle cans the rest because Russ claims—I mean, claimed—" Warriner took a deep breath and went on —"claimed it was better than the commercial pack. When we started out on this cruise to Papeete, they had four or five cans left over from last year, so he put them in the stores. About ten days ago—at least, I think it was ten days, I've lost all track of time—it was Estelle's turn to fix dinner. It was hot and muggy and nobody was very hungry. But she happened to remember the salmon and thought she might be able to make some kind of salad out of it by cutting up pickles and onions and putting mayonnaise on it. I didn't eat any; I always figured salmon was for cats, so I made myself a sandwich out of something."

"And nobody noticed anything wrong with it?" Ingram didn't know why he asked. There didn't seem to be much you could do to change the outcome of a tragedy that had happened ten days ago. "The can wasn't bulged or anything?"

"If it was, she didn't notice it. Frankly, she'd had about three rum sours before she went below to fix it. We'd all had, for that matter. And if there was an odor, the onions must have covered it up.

"That was around seven P.M. The next morning between six and six-thirty Russ came up from below—I was at the wheel—and said Estelle was feeling nauseated and upset and wanted to know if I had any idea where those pills were that we'd brought along for the tourist trots. I turned the wheel over to him and went below to look for them.

"I thought they might be in the medicine closet in the head amidships, but when I got down there Estelle was in it, and I could hear her vomiting. When she came out her face was white and sweaty and she looked bad. She didn't have much on, and when she saw it was me instead of Russ she motioned for me to look the other way and ran forward into their cabin. I found the pills and got a glass of water and called out to her. She said it was all right to come in, she was in the bunk. I gave her one. She swallowed it, but she kept rubbing her hand across her face and shaking her head. 'Brother, that rum,' she said. 'It must have had a delayed-action fuse on it.' Her voice sounded funny, as if she had something stuck in her throat.

"I asked her if she was sure it was the rum, and she said, 'I don't know. But you look fuzzy around the edges; I can't get you into focus.' She held out her hand and looked at it and said, 'God, a Picasso hand. It's got seven fingers on it—'"

"What?" Ingram interrupted. He frowned. "Wait a minute —double vision. There's something I've read, or heard—"

"Botulism," Rae said.

"What's that?" Warriner asked. "You mean you don't think it was the salmon?"

"Yes, it probably was the salmon," Rae explained. "Botulism's a very dangerous type of food poisoning that attacks the nervous system. I remember reading an article about it somewhere. I don't remember the other symptoms, but I do recall the double vision and the trouble in speaking or swallowing."

"Do you know what the treatment is?" Warriner asked. "We had a pretty good medicine chest and I tried everything I could think of, but if it turns out that some simple thing we had aboard could have saved them . . ."

Rae shook her head. "You can put your mind at rest about that. I don't think there is any treatment except an antitoxin, which nobody'd have in a first-aid kit. Even if you'd been an M.D. you couldn't have done anything for them."

"Oh. I guess that helps. A little, anyway." Warriner went on. "She looked bad, as I said, but I didn't realize then how sick she was. I guess she didn't either. Anyway, about that time we took two or three heavy rolls and I heard the sails begin to slat, so I went back on deck. I thought the wind had died out again and we'd have to sheet everything in—we'd been becalmed off and on for the past two days, just a capful of breeze now and then from all around the compass. But when I got up in the cockpit, that wasn't it; Russ had left the wheel. He was hanging over the rail, vomiting, and she'd come up into the wind.

"He said he thought he'd got a touch of it too. Even then it'd never occurred to any of us it could be serious; it was just a joke, like the *turista*. I told him where the pills were, and to go on back and turn in and not to relieve me at eight unless he was sure he was all over it. He went below. The breeze held on, fairly steady out of the west; we were making at least four knots, and not too far off the course we wanted, so I didn't want to leave the wheel, even when it was eight o'clock and he didn't come up.

"About eight-thirty I heard somebody moving around in the galley and decided at least one of them was feeling better, but it was Lillian—my wife. She brought me a cup of coffee, and one for herself, and was sitting in the cockpit drinking it when all of a sudden she doubled over with a cramp in her stomach. She ran below to the head. Nobody was able to take the wheel, and *Orpheus* was always a cranky boat; she wouldn't steer herself on any point of sailing. So I doused everything and went below to see how they were. Russ and Estelle were still in their bunks, when they weren't trying to get back and forth to the head. And now *Russ* was complaining that everything looked fuzzy, and he was having trouble talking. Lillian didn't have any symptoms like that yet; she was just nauseated and crampy. But I was beginning to be scared, real scared, thinking of all that empty ocean between us and a doctor. It almost had to be some kind of food poisoning, and everybody decided it must have been the salmon because I hadn't eaten any and I wasn't sick—at least, I wasn't so far. I got the medicine kit out and started through the first-aid handbook that came with it. It was no help; there wasn't anything about food poisoning in it at all, just a lot of jazz about what to do if somebody swallows lye or iodine or something, and how to treat burns and fainting spells and broken bones.

"By ten o'clock Lillian was beginning to have the same symptoms, the fuzzy vision and difficulty in swallowing or talking. The breeze had died out, and it was like an oven below deck with the sun beating down. Russ and Estelle were having trouble breathing. I gave up pawing through the medicines long enough to rig an awning over the cockpit, intending to move them up there, but by now they were too sick to make it up the ladder. I couldn't carry them, not with the boat rolling the way she was, lying becalmed. I rigged wind-chutes, which was stupid, because there wasn't a breath of air moving, but by this time I was so panicky I didn't know what I was doing. I gave them the *turista* pills, and aspirin, and paregoric, and I don't remember what else, but by noon neither Russ nor Estelle could swallow anything any more. They couldn't even talk. All they could do was lie there and fight for breath.

"Russ died a little after three in the afternoon. I hadn't thought there could be anything more horrible in the world than standing there listening to the two of them fighting for breath in that stifling cabin and not being able to do anything to help them, but there was. It was when I realized that only one of them was making that noise now; Russ had stopped. Which meant there was no hope for the others either. Estelle was unconscious by that time, so she didn't know he was dead. Lillian was still conscious and just beginning to fight for breath, but she was in our cabin, aft of the doghouse, so she didn't know either.

"Then Estelle died, less than an hour after Russ. The rest of the day is kind of mixed up and run together; I can only remember crazy pieces of it—Lillian asking me how the others were, and I'd say I'd go see, and I'd go into the forward cabin where they were both dead and then come back and say they were getting much better now and that she'd be over the worst of it in a little while. Then I'd go out of the cabin to pray, so she wouldn't see me. I remember going up on deck once; maybe it would work better up there in the open. I hadn't prayed for anything since I was a kid, and I guess I didn't know how; it struck me once that it seemed like I was trying to negotiate with God, or strike a bargain, or something. I kept saying two of them were gone, couldn't He leave one?

"Lillian died a little after six. When the sound of her breathing stopped, the silence was like something screaming in my ears, and I let go of her and ran up on deck and the sun was just going down. The sky was red in the west, and the sea was like blood, and everywhere there was that terrible silence that went on and on and on as if it was pressing in on me from all around the horizon. . . ." Warriner dropped his face in his hands.

Tears were overflowing Rae's eyes. "I'm sorry," Ingram said, conscious at the same time of something that disturbed him. It was the word *theatrical* intruding on the perimeter of his mind, and he was angry with himself at this apparent callousness. Try it on your own stiff upper lip, he thought, before you throw any rocks; try ten days of it without hearing another voice and you might get a little purple about it too. He wished uncomfortably that he could think of something to add to the simple "I'm sorry," but nothing was going to help the boy except the passage of time. He reached toward the ignition key to start the engine. "But we'd better shag over there and see if we can salvage some of your gear before she goes under."

Warriner shook his head. "There's nothing worth going after. It's all ruined by the water—radio, sextant, chronometer, everything—"

"How about clothes?"

"These will do. Anyway, I don't think I *could* go back aboard. You understand, don't you? It isn't only their dying. Remember, they all died *below deck*. Can you imagine what it was like, what I had to do?"

Ingram nodded.

Warriner's face twisted. "Talk about the dignity of death, and last respects to the dead—pallbearers and bronze caskets and music and flowers. I dragged my wife's body up a companion ladder with a rope—"

"Stop it!" Rae cried out. "You've got to quit thinking about it!"

"I understand," Ingram said. "But you don't have to go aboard; I'll take care of it, if you'll just tell me where to find things—"

"But there's not anything, I tell you!"

"We ought to get your passport," Ingram pointed out. "And whatever money you have aboard. We're bound for Papeete, and you'll need it for your passage home from there. Also, there's the log and ship's papers—"

Warriner gestured impatiently. "The log and ship's papers and passport and money are all pulp and sloshing around in the bilges in three feet of water. If I haven't already pumped them overboard."

"I see," Ingram said, wondering if he did. "But there's another thing. Is she insured?"

"John." Something in Rae's voice made him turn. She went on sweetly, but with a glint in her eyes he'd never seen before. "I don't think we're being very hospitable, or very considerate. Mr. Warriner needs sleep more than anything at the moment, so I'm going to fix a bunk for him. If you'll just come with me and move those sailbags, dear."

She went down the ladder. Ingram followed, conscious of the rigidity of her back as she traversed the rolling cabin and went through the passage at the forward end. The narrow compartment in the eyes of the boat held two bunks, slanted inward toward each other like the sides of a V, but was used only as a locker now. There were cases of food, unopened buckets of paint and varnish, and coils of line, all neatly stowed, and the bunks themselves were piled with bags of sails. There was no hatch above, only a ventilator, and the compartment was dimly lighted by the two small portholes above the bunks.

She pulled the door shut and came close to him. "John Ingram!" It was a whisper, but forceful. "I'm ashamed of you; I never realized you could be this insensitive. Can't you see that boy's on the ragged edge of a nervous breakdown? For heaven's sake, stop asking him questions and let's try to get him to sleep."

"Well, sure, honey," he protested. "I realize what he's been through. But we ought to make *some* attempt to salvage what we can—"

"He doesn't want to go back on there. I'd think you could understand that."

"He doesn't have to. I told him I'd go."

"But why? He said there wasn't anything worth trying to save, didn't he?"

"I know. But obviously water wouldn't ruin everything. Clothes, for instance. Also, he contradicts himself."

"What do you mean?"

"The radio, remember? He said it'd been ruined by the water. But he'd just got through telling us he called us on it."

She sighed. "Why do men always have to be so literal? Do you think he's some kind of machine? John, dear, he lost his wife and his two friends all in one afternoon, and then spent the next ten days utterly alone on a sinking boat, and he probably hasn't closed his eyes for a week. I'd be doing well to remember my own name, unless I had it written down somewhere."

"All right—" Ingram began.

"Shhhhh! Not so loud."

"Okay. But you'd think he'd at least want to bring off some of *her* things, wouldn't you? And there was another thing I was about to explain to him. If that boat's insured, he's going to have a hell of a time trying to collect, with no logbook and just his unsupported word she was in sinking condition when he left her—in a dead calm, with no weather making up. The underwriters are going to ask for a statement from me, and I can't corroborate it. How can I? I'll just have to tell 'em she was afloat when I saw her. And that I hadn't even been aboard and didn't know how much water she was taking."

"He said she probably wouldn't last through the morning, and we're not going anywhere in this calm, so we'll still be in sight when she goes down. But let him get some sleep!"

"Sure. God knows, he probably needs it." Still vaguely dissatisfied, he tossed the sailbags into the other bunk and threw a lashing on them. He went back to the cockpit. Warriner was slumped on the starboard seat with the binoculars beside him, as though he'd been looking at the other yacht. Sunlight struck golden fire in his hair, which had been crew-cut originally but had grown long over his ears. Handsome kid, Ingram thought, and then wondered if that could be the reason for his—well, not distrust, exactly. That was overstating it. Call it reservation.

"You asked me if she was insured," Warriner said. "I'm sorry to say she's not. We thought the premium was too high for the risk involved. And also, that if she was lost, we probably would be too."

"Is she pretty old?"

"Yes. Over twenty years. I guess we got stung when we bought her."

"You didn't have her surveyed?"

"Well—yes. That is, not by a professional, but a friend of mine who's real savvy about boats."

Ingram nodded but refrained from any comment. Under the circumstances, it was too much like kicking a man when he was down to elaborate on the foolishness of buying a twenty-year-old yacht without a professional survey, especially since this was a little on the self-evident side at the moment. "You don't know what caused her to open up that way? Have any bad weather?"

Warriner shook his head. "Not recently. That is, except for a few squalls, which never lasted very long. It was just age and general unsoundness."

Ingram was struck by a sudden thought. "You say you were bound from California to Papeete—aren't you pretty far east? Seems to me you'd have crossed the Line nearly a thousand miles west of here."

"We were taking it by stages. Down the Mexican coast to La Paz, and then by way of Clipperton Island." Warriner made an attempt at a smile. "Look, I'm sorry I got dumped on you this way. But I can pull my weight, and it *will* shorten the watches. And I'll keep out of your hair as much as possible; it's not much fun having a third party around."

"Forget it," Ingram said, feeling uncomfortable for some reason. It was the first time he'd ever heard of a shipwreck victim apologizing for his existence, and he tried again to put his finger on exactly what there was about this boy that he couldn't quite like. There didn't seem to be any answer. "Hell, we're just happy we came along when we did."

Warriner made no reply. Ingram picked up the glasses, braced himself against the mizzen boom, and searched out the other yacht. She was near enough now to make out details on deck, but he couldn't tell whether she was any lower in the water than she had been. She wasn't down by the head or stern, but there was no doubt she had water in her, and plenty of it, from the drunken way she lurched on the swell, taking too long to come back each time she rolled. She had a short, rather high deckhouse with windows rather than portholes located near amidships, and in silhouette was vaguely reminiscent of a motor-sailer rather than a conventional sailing yacht. Dumpy-looking, he decided, and probably cranky as hell and slow. Big auxiliary, no doubt, lots of greenhouse for cocktail parties, and probably built for somebody who never used the sails except when he ran out of gas. Still, Warriner probably had upwards of $30,000 invested in her, and it was a sad way for a boat to end. "She's still on an even keel," he said, without lowering the glasses. "You sure we couldn't gain on it, by pumping and bailing together—at least enough to start locating the leaks and calking 'em?"

Warriner shook his head. "It's hopeless. It's been pouring in since around midnight. Nearly six inches in seven hours."

Ingram glanced down at him and then returned to his scrutiny of the other boat without comment, still aware of that nagging sense of dissatisfaction. Something about the whole thing disturbed him, but he couldn't put a finger on it. Just what was it? Warriner was certainly in a position to know how much water was coming into her. And when you stopped to take a good look at it, saving her was only a pipe dream. Even if they could pump her out enough to plug a few of the leaks, the kid would never make land in her alone. She was too big for one man to handle, even without the necessity of being at the pump twelve to fifteen hours a day.

3

THE SUN was hotter now. He turned, searching the horizon for any darkening of the surface of the sea that would indicate the beginnings of a breeze. Rae came up the ladder. "Your bunk's all ready, Mr. Warriner. Try to sleep until this time tomorrow."

Warriner smiled. "Please call me Hughie. And I don't know how to thank you."

"You don't have to. Just get some rest."

"In a little while. For some reason, I don't feel sleepy at all."

She nodded. "You've been wound too tight for too long. But I know how to fix that." She disappeared down the ladder and came back in a minute with a bottle containing a little over an ounce of whisky. She poured it into the cup that was still beside him. "There's just about enough here to do it." He drained it and accepted the cigarette she held out. "By the time you finish that," she said, "you're going to collapse all over. Just try to make it to the bunk when you feel yourself start to go."

"Thank you," Warriner said. "You're very nice."

She tossed the bottle overboard and perched on the edge of the deckhouse to light a cigarette for herself. The bottle landed with a faint splash just off the port quarter, rolled over as a swell passed under it, and started to fill. It righted itself, its neck out of water. Ingram glanced at it indifferently, and then forward, conscious that Warriner's dinghy was bumping as *Saracen* rose and fell. They'd have to cast it adrift; there was no room to stow it on deck, and of course they couldn't tow it. He looked around and was about to mention this when he stopped, arrested by something in the other's face.

Warriner was staring past him with an almost frozen intensity, apparently at something in the water. Ingram turned, but could see nothing except the bottle, which was about to sink. It had rolled onto its side again as another swell upset it, and water was flowing into its mouth. A few bubbles came up, and it went under. Puzzled, Ingram glanced back at Warriner. The other had risen from his seat and leaned forward, clutching the port lifeline with a white-knuckled grip as he stared down at the bottle falling slowly through sun-lighted water as clear as air. Drops of sweat stood out on his forehead, and his mouth was locked shut as though he were stifling, with an effort of will, some anguished outcry welling up inside him. The bottle was six feet down now, ten, fifteen, but still clearly visible as it continued its unhurried slide into the deepening blue and fading light beyond. Warriner's eyes closed, and Ingram sensed the effort he was making to tear himself away from whatever hell he saw in an innocent and commonplace bottle falling into the depths of the sea, but they came open again almost immediately, still full of the same hypnotic compulsion and horror, like those of a bird impaled on the freezing stare of a snake.

Ingram opened his mouth to ask what the matter was, but caught Rae's eyes on him. She shook her head. They both looked seaward and in a moment heard Warriner sit down again. The whole thing hadn't lasted more than a few seconds. Probably doesn't know we even saw it, Ingram reflected. But what was it? Terror? Terror of what? For some reason he was thinking of the way Warriner had come aboard, the trancelike stare, the convulsive lunge onto the deck, and the way his fingers had flattened themselves around the handrail.

"Breeze coming!" Rae called out suddenly. "Anybody for Papeete?"

Off to the south the surface of the sea was beginning to darken under the riffles of an advancing cat's-paw of wind. Ingram sprang on deck and began casting the gaskets off the mainsail. Rae had run forward and was breaking out the jib. Long months of practice had made them a smoothly functioning team, and by the time they could feel the faint movement of air against their faces a cloud of billowing white Orlon was mounting against the sky. Rae came aft to take the wheel. The mainsail filled. *Saracen* began to move, almost imperceptibly at first, and when she had gathered enough way to come about Ingram looked around and nodded. Rae brought the wheel hard over; she came up into the wind, hung for an instant, and fell off on the port tack, toward the southwest and Tahiti.

For a moment he had forgotten Warriner, but when he turned from setting up the mainsheet to trim the jib, he found the other already hauling on it. Warriner threw it on the cleat and straightened. "How about the mizzen?"

Ingram nodded and began taking off the gaskets. "Might as well get everything on her; the breeze might last for a while. But you go ahead and turn in."

Warriner smiled. "I think I will, as soon as we get this up." He seemed to have recovered completely from the horror of a few minutes ago. They hoisted the mizzen and trimmed the sheet. Ingram leaned over to look in the binnacle. "Can we make 235?" he asked Rae.

"Easy," she replied. "We're to windward of that now." She came right a little. "Here we are—230 . . . 233 . . . 235."

Ingram glanced aloft at the strands of ribbon on the shrouds and started the mainsheet a little. *Saracen* heeled slightly under a puff and began to gather way. He turned to Warriner. "We're going to have to cast your dinghy adrift. No room to stow it."

Warriner nodded. "Yes. Of course."

Ingram loosed the painter from the lifeline stanchion, coiled it, dropped it into the dinghy, and gave the boat a push away from the side. It drifted back and began to fall behind in the wake, riding like a cork over the broad undulations of the swell. Warriner had turned and was staring toward the other yacht, which was off the starboard quarter now that they had come about. The dinghy was a hundred yards astern, growing smaller and looking lost and forlorn in the immensity of the sea.

"Well, if it's all right with you, I guess I'll turn in," he said at last. "If the breeze holds, I can take over tonight."

"Don't worry about it," Rae said. "You'd better rest for a couple of days. There'll be something for you to eat when you wake up."

"It'll be pretty hot down there," Ingram added, "but if you leave the door open you'll get a little circulation of air from the ventilator."

Warriner nodded and went down the ladder. He paused once to turn for a last look at the other boat before his head disappeared below the level of the hatch. When Ingram looked around at Rae, her eyes were misted with tears. He leaned forward and peered down the hatch. Warriner was going through the passage into the forward compartment. He couldn't hear them if they spoke in normal tones.

He slid back close beside her. "What do you make of it?"

"That thing about the bottle?"

"Yes."

She shook her head. "I don't know. But grief does strange things—grief and complete isolation."

"But just a sinking bottle—"

"Obviously it wasn't a bottle he was seeing." She paused, her eyes fixed moodily on the compass card. Then she went on, "What's a sea burial like?"

"I've never seen one, thank God, but from what I've read, you sew the body in canvas and weight it with something. Why?"

"I'm not sure, but . . ." She gestured helplessly.

"I think I know what you mean," Ingram said. "But I'm not sure I agree with you." Wrapped in white Orlon, with the water this clear and the boat lying dead in the water above them, the bodies would still be visible a long way down if you wanted to torture yourself by leaning over the side and watching them disappear into the dark down there. "But that's only morbid. This was worse. Horror—I don't know what you'd call it."

She nodded thoughtfully. "I know. But being utterly alone afterward . . ." Her voice trailed off. The breeze had dropped to a whisper. *Saracen* ghosted through the bald spot for a few yards, the sails beginning to slat; then it picked up again, only to die out once more in less than fifteen minutes. *Saracen* rolled heavily, booms aswing. Ingram sheeted them in. He stood up, still disturbed, and annoyed at himself because he didn't know why, and trained the binoculars on the other yacht. Then, with a gesture of impatience, he made up his mind.

"I'm going aboard her."

Rae looked up. "Why?"

"I don't know. There's something about the whole damned thing I can't quite swallow; no matter how I turn it, it won't go down. Look, Rae, anybody who managed to get this far from land in a boat without killing himself must be a sailor, and that's not the way a sailor abandons one. Just because somebody else comes along going in the same direction—like a hitch-hiker. You'd bring something off, or you'd go back for what you could salvage."

"You don't believe she's sinking?"

"All I know is she's still afloat." He continued to study the other yacht. As far as he could tell, there was no change in her trim or amount of freeboard. Well, it didn't mean anything, actually; it could be hours, or even days, before she went under. He was probably being silly.

"Did he say whether she was insured or not?" she asked.

"He says she's not."

"Then it'd be pretty expensive, wouldn't it, just going off and leaving her in the middle of the ocean?"

He frowned. "Yes, but that's still not what I mean. If she's leaking at all, he'd never make port in her alone; she's too big for singlehanded sailing, to say nothing of being at the pump all the time. He almost has to abandon her, but not the way he did. I keep getting the feeling he doesn't want *anybody* to go aboard."

"But why?"

"I don't know. Admittedly, it doesn't make any sense. But look—you'll notice he didn't turn in until we were under way. And had cast his dinghy adrift."

"That was probably just coincidence."

"Sure. It could be."

"You're going to put our dinghy over?" Rae asked.

"No." He turned, searching for the other one. He could still see it when it crested a swell, several hundred yards astern. "We'll pick his up again. No strain, if we get another breeze."

Saracen had begun to swing around on the swell, to a southerly and then a southeasterly heading. Ingram stood up again with the glasses and could see the water beginning to darken once more to the southward. He looked at his watch. It had been nearly thirty minutes since Warriner had gone below. He slipped down the ladder, crossed to the passage going into the forward compartment, and looked in. Warriner lay on his back, his eyes closed, breathing heavily.

He came back to the cockpit just as the breeze began to stir again. It was out of the south, to starboard on the heading they were on now, and the other yacht lay perhaps a mile and a half away on the port bow, with the dinghy somewhere in between.

Saracen began to move ahead. He motioned for Rae to steady up where she was, and stepped forward to search out the dinghy. In a moment he saw it top a swell almost dead ahead. There was a long boathook lashed atop the deckhouse. He slid it free and looked down to windward, hoping the breeze would continue strong enough to give them steerageway. As far as he could see the surface was riffled and dark. He stepped back to the break of the deckhouse and spoke quietly to Rae. "See it?"

She nodded. "Now and then. When it comes up."

"Good. We'll take it on the starboard side."

Five minutes passed. The breeze faltered but came on again before they lost steerageway. It was less than fifty yards away now. Ingram motioned her a little to port and stood ready with the boathook. The dinghy began to slide past along the starboard side, less than ten feet off. He hooked it neatly at the bow, hauled it inward, and got hold of the painter. He led it aft and made it fast with a grin at Rae. "Nice going."

It was a run almost downwind now to the other yacht. He started the main and mizzen sheets and studied her through the glasses. She was lying on a westerly heading, abeam to the breeze. "Right just a little," he said to Rae. "We'll come up astern and lay to about a hundred yards off."

The gap began to close slowly, and then more slowly as the breeze faltered. It stopped altogether, and the sea became like heaving billows of silk, blinding off to starboard with the glare of the sun. Then, just before *Saracen* began to yaw on the swell, it came on again. The sails filled. The distance was less than a half-mile now.

"I don't like that sluggish way she rolls," Rae said.

"She's got water in her, all right," Ingram agreed.

"Are you sure it's safe to go aboard?"

"Sure. She won't capsize, with all that keel under her. And she won't go under all at once."

"But suppose you're below? You might get trapped."

"I won't go below if she's that close. I can tell when I get on her."

They were still over two hundred yards away when the breeze died again. *Saracen* drifted forward a few yards and began to wallow as she slewed around. Ingram surveyed the remaining distance with exasperation, and searched the horizon on all sides. "Slick as a bald head," he said and sheeted the booms in. "This'll have to do. I'm going aboard."

"Why not start the engine?" she asked.

"He might wake up."

"I doubt it." Then she caught his meaning. "Why? What difference does it make if he does?"

He hesitated; then he shrugged. "I don't like the idea of leaving you on here alone with him. Unless he's asleep, I mean."

"Why, for heaven's sake?"

"I don't know. It's stupid, I realize, but there's just something about him I don't quite buy. Not till I know more about him."

"Well, of all the worriers."

He grunted. "You're probably right. But let him sleep, anyway." He loosed the dinghy's painter and hauled the boat up alongside. Before he stepped down into it he took a careful look around the horizon for squalls. It could be highly dangerous if one made up suddenly while Rae was alone, with all sail on her. There was nothing, however, that looked even remotely suspicious. "If you get another whisper of breeze," he said, "work her on down and come about off the stern. I won't be long."

"Right. You will be careful, won't you?"

"Sure."

"Wait. Don't you want to put on that life-jacket?" It was still lying where Warriner had taken it off.

He grinned. "What for?" Nobody could capsize a dinghy in a sea like this. At the same time, he wondered why Warriner had been wearing it. Timing himself with *Saracen*'s roll, he stepped lightly down into the dinghy and pushed away from the side.

It rode like a chip on the oily groundswell, and reflected sunlight glared in his face as he shipped the oars and began pulling toward the other yacht. As he drew nearer, he could see the sails were sloppily furled and that the deck was littered with an unseamanlike mess of uncoiled and unstowed lines. The main boom rested on its gallows frame, but the mizzen swung forlornly back and forth, banging against its slackened sheets. She was at least six inches below her normal waterline, he thought, and her movements were heavy and sluggish, like those of a dying animal, as she lurched over and back under the punishing rays of the sun. He felt sorry for her, as he always did for a boat in trouble. He changed course slightly to pass under her stern and come up on her starboard side. Her name and home port were spelled out in ornate black letters edged with gilt against the white paint of her transom.

ORPHEUS
SANTA BARBARA

He was still some twenty yards away, rounding her stern, when he heard a crash from somewhere inside the hull, followed in a moment by another. Apparently something had come adrift, a drawer or a locker, and was slamming back and forth on the water inside her. He pulled quickly up along the starboard side and, as she rolled down on the swell, caught one of the lifeline stanchions. After shipping the oars, he gathered up the painter and stepped on deck. He was near amidships, opposite the doghouse. As he made the painter fast he could hear the flow and splash of water inside her hull, sweeping from side to side as she rolled. He didn't like the feel of her under his feet. Better make it short, he thought.

Aft of the doghouse was a slightly raised deck, enclosed by a low railing, which extended back almost to the mizzenmast and the helmsman's cockpit. There was a skylight in the center of this, apparently above the after cabin. It was closed and secured. He stepped aft, feeling her unsteady lurch as she rolled, ducked under the main boom, and looked into the doghouse hatch. There were only four steps leading down, since the top of it was quite high above the deck outside. There was no water here, but the deck was covered with a litter of charts and scratch pads and pencils from a drawer that had slid out of the chart table on the starboard side. He came on down the steps and looked quickly around. The port side and that part of the starboard side forward of the chart table were taken up with settees covered with some white plastic material. On racks above the chart table were a radio-telephone and radio direction-finder.

Aft, beside the steps leading up on deck, was a low doorway, and amidships at the forward end was another. The latter was open. He stepped over to it and peered through. Steps led downward to the main cabin, which was in ruin. At the after end, on the port side, were a sink, stove, refrigerator, and stowage cupboards, while to starboard was a table surrounded on two sides by a leather-covered settee. Everything was drowned, and the cabin was filled with the dank odor of wetness and decay. Water at least two feet deep swirled back and forth, crashing into the stove and refrigerator and settee and dripping from the bulkheads and ceiling, all intermingled with rolling cans from some burst locker, sodden articles of clothing, and books from an emptied bookshelf. It was sickening. At the forward end was a doorway which probably opened into a lavatory, and to the left of it a curtained passage to the forward cabin. He stepped down and splashed through the swirling debris to the passage and peered in. The two bunks were rumpled and dripping, and water rocked back and forth between them. It was just as Warriner had said. He wondered what he was looking for.

He turned and hurried back to the doghouse. Through the windows he caught a quick glimpse of *Saracen* gracefully riding the groundswell two hundred yards away, still becalmed. The mere sight of her was comforting after the ruin below. The door at the aft end of the doghouse was closed and secured with a hasp, through the staple of which a pair of dividers had been dropped. He pulled the dividers out, and as he turned to toss them on the chart table his eye fell on the ship's log, behind a clip on the bulkhead above it. He frowned, puzzled. Warriner had apparently been telling the truth otherwise, so why had he lied about that? He'd said the logbook was pulp, sloshing around in the bilges. And that the radio and chronometer and sextant were all ruined. Nothing up here was wet at all. And as water rose in the cabins below, wouldn't he have brought his passport and money and other valuables up here where they'd stay dry? It would be the natural thing to do. They might be in one of the other drawers of the chart table. Well, he'd look for them in a minute. He pushed open the door and peered down into the after cabin.

A dark-haired woman who appeared at first glance to be completely nude was huddled on the far end of the right-hand bunk, her back against the bulkhead at the foot of it and her legs drawn up under her chin as if to get as far as possible from the door. One hand was up to her mouth and her eyes were wide with fear, which changed to amazement and disbelief as she stared into his face. She cried out, "Stop! Stop, it's not him!" And in the same fraction of a second Ingram saw the other one reflected in the panel mirror mounted on the after bulkhead between the bunks. A man was standing just below him, to the left of the steps leading down, a big man, naked from the waist up, with a broad, beard-stubbled face smeared pink with diluted blood running down from a wound somewhere in the sodden mess of his hair. In his upraised hand was a billet of wood, apparently the end of a drawer he'd pulled from under one of the bunks and smashed. He'd been poised to bring it down on Ingram's head, and when the girl's piercing outcry stopped him he tried to recover. At the same moment *Orpheus* lurched over to starboard, and he fell into the water washing back and forth across the cabin sole. He pushed himself to a sitting position in the water with his back against the other bunk, brushed a hand across his bloody face, and looked up at Ingram with a hard and bitter grin.

"Welcome to Happy Valley," he said. "Where's the All-American psycho?"

"Get on deck!" Ingram snapped. "I'll be back." He whirled and plunged up the steps into the open, ducked under the main boom, and dropped into the dinghy. His hands fumbled as he loosed the painter. Two explosive strokes with the oars brought him into the clear past *Orpheus*'s stern, where he could see across to *Saracen*. Her position was unchanged except that she had swung around and was lying broadside to.

Rae was alone in the cockpit.

He breathed softly and dug in the oars, feeling sweat begin to run down into his eyes. He came up the broad slope of a swell and ran down the other side like some frenzied, two-legged waterbeetle in flight for its life. It's all right, he told himself. It's all right. There's no reason the crazy son of a bitch would wake up. Then, across a hundred and fifty yards of open water, he heard the growl of the starter. Rae was coming to pick him up.

4

He tried to signal to her. At the risk of capsizing, he stood up in the dinghy and frantically sliced the air in horizontal sweeps of his opened hands, but she was bent over the controls now and didn't see. The starter growled again, and this time the engine started with a coughing backfire that spread gooseflesh between his shoulderblades. One of his oars started to slide overboard. He grabbed it and dropped to the seat again. Muscles writhed across his back as he dug them in and lunged, flinging the dinghy up the side of the swell. He was to blame. She'd been watching with the glasses and had seen the way he'd exploded out of the doghouse and run across the deck, and, knowing only that there was something urgent about his getting back, was trying to help. *Saracen* was swinging now, under way and foreshortened as she began to bear down upon him. The gap was only a hundred yards, and closing. Some of the fear began to leave him. It was going to be all right. He heard her cut back the throttle and drop the engine out of gear. Then when he turned his head again he felt himself grow cold all over. There was a spot of golden color just to the left of the lined-up masts. It was Warriner's head. He was standing on the companion ladder, looking aft.

Nothing seemed to move. There was a piercing clarity about every detail of the scene—the foreshortened hull pointed toward him, the little curl of bow wave under her forefoot, the tall spires of Orlon achingly white against the sky, and just this side of Rae's face that spot of gold like a medallion poised on edge above the cambered top of the deckhouse—but the whole thing was frozen like a single frame of motion-picture film with the projector jammed. *Saracen* was seventy-five yards away, with Warriner's head just beginning to turn. A few seconds either way could decide it, but they were something over which he no longer had any control.

Maybe nothing would happen. Maybe he actually *had* forgotten the people he'd locked in there to drown. Or if he'd really been asleep, maybe his reaction time would be off just enough to make the difference— The film jerked then, between the down-thrust oars and the stroke, and the projector began to run. Warriner's head swung on around, and he saw the dinghy and the sinking *Orpheus* beyond. He leaped the rest of the way into the cockpit, and his figure merged with Rae's.

Ingram heard the engine race, still out of gear. It slowed and came back up again almost in the same instant, with the load on it now. Which way would he turn? At the risk of a fraction of a second's raggedness in the beat of the oars, he had to turn his head and look. *Saracen* loomed over him less than four lengths away, the gap closing faster now as she gathered speed, but she was already beginning to swing to starboard. He dug in his left oar and spun the dinghy around almost at right angles to cut across her course.

Saracen, in a hard-over right turn, was on his left now. He could see Rae fighting to reach the ignition switch. Warriner, holding the wheel with one hand, threw her back. She fell to her knees on the short section of deck aft of the cockpit, but sprang up and flung herself on him again. Ingram's eyes stung with sweat, and the oars were bending as he threw the dinghy forward. The engine roared at full throttle; *Saracen*'s bow was swinging off faster now than he was gaining, but the stern was still coming down toward him. Twenty yards . . . fifteen . . . The locked and struggling figures in the cockpit suddenly burst apart. Warriner's fist swung, and Ingram saw her fall. She lay in a crumpled heap on the afterdeck, unmoving, one arm dangling over the stern as if she were calling out for help. Ten yards . . . four . . . three . . . The turn was completed now, and the stern was beginning to draw away from him. He gave one more desperate heave on the oars, stood up, and flung himself at the rail. The dinghy kicked backward under him. His outstretched hands were two feet short, and then he was in the churning white water under the quarter.

He was already behind the propeller, or he might have lost an arm. He felt the solid kick of the water thrown back from it whirl him over, and then his head was above surface and *Saracen*'s stern was ten yards away. It dipped as her bow rose to an oncoming swell, and for an instant he could see Rae's figure face down on the afterdeck, her hair very dark against the bleached and weathered teak. "Jump!" he yelled. "Jump! Get off!" She lay motionless.

For the first time in his life at sea he completely lost his head. It lasted for only a moment, and when he realized what he was doing, that he was threshing madly at the water, trying to swim after *Saracen*'s receding stern, he got control of the panic inside him and brought himself up. Lifting his face above water, he roared out once more with all his remaining breath, "Jump, Rae! Jump!" The limp and dangling arm was his only answer. She was either badly hurt or unconscious.

The dinghy was behind him. Both oars had slipped overboard. He found them, threw them back in, and lifted himself in over the transom. He was more scared than he had ever been in his life, and the whole scene came to him through the winy haze of a desire to get his hands on Warriner and kill him, but there was no time to give way to futile emotion. He whirled the dinghy about and sent it racing across the two hundred yards of open water toward *Orpheus*, trying not even to think except of what he had to do, as if it were an exercise. *Saracen* was going straight away, and he could still see Rae's figure on the stern.

He turned his head. The man and woman had come on deck and were standing just aft of the doghouse, watching him. He shot the dinghy across the few remaining yards, slammed into *Orpheus*'s port side, and pulled in the oars. Neither of them had made a move to take the painter. He grabbed it himself, leaped on deck, and made it fast. "Have you got any glasses?" he asked.

The man grinned bleakly. "You didn't seem to do any better than we did. Maybe you have to be crazy yourself to outguess him."

Ingram caught himself just short of smashing him in the face—not because the man was already hurt or because he was probably in no way to blame, but merely because it would waste time. "Binoculars?" he asked again. "Where are they?"

The man jerked a thumb toward the doghouse. "Rack, just inside the door." But the woman had already taken a step down the ladder and reached for them. Ingram lifted them from her hand without thanks, without even seeing her, and whirled, bringing them to bear on *Saracen*. She was still going straight away on the same course. As he adjusted the knob, she leaped sharply into focus, every detail distinct. Rae still lay huddled on the afterdeck, as far as he could tell in the same position. Warriner was at the wheel, looking forward, apparently into the binnacle. Maybe he had forgotten she was there. Then Ingram realized the futility of any conjecture as to what went on in Warriner's mind. "Have you got a spare compass?" he asked without lowering the binoculars. "Boat compass, or a telltale in one of the cabins—"

"There's a little one in a box in the chartroom," the man said.

"Get it," Ingram ordered, "and set it in the dinghy. Then put your azimuth ring on the steering compass and keep calling out the bearing of that boat."

"And what's all that jazz for?" the man asked. He hadn't moved.

Ingram lowered the glasses then and looked at him for the first time. "You do what I tell you to, you son of a bitch," he said, "and do it now. My wife's still on there. If he throws her overboard, I want to know where. And if I don't get to her in time because I didn't have a course, and a compass in that dinghy, you'll go next."

"Just a minute, friend—" the man began, but Ingram had already turned away and locked the glasses on *Saracen* again. She was at least a half-mile away; he could still see Rae lying on deck, but less clearly now. He heard the woman say, "Oh, stop it; just do as he says. You find the compass, and I'll get the azimuth ring." He paid no attention. He was trying to make a cold appraisal of the several possibilities while at the same time struggling in the back of his mind with the dark animal of fear. This might be the last time he would ever see her, this dwindling spot of color fading away toward the outer limit of binoculars, but that was something he couldn't think about. If he lost his head, there was no chance at all.

She must be still unconscious, because as far as he could tell she hadn't moved. If Warriner threw her over now, while she was still out, she'd drown. The longer he waited, the more chance there was she'd be conscious and able to swim, but on the other hand, the farther out she was, the more it increased the odds against finding her in time, even with a compass course to follow. In a dinghy you were too low in the water, with a groundswell that was running higher than your head. And he *had* to see when it happened.

It was already growing difficult to make out the deck. He was too low. He tore his eyes away from the glasses long enough to leap up on the doghouse and brace his legs against the doomed and melancholy rolling of the boat, and for an instant he was conscious again of the forlorn banging of her gear and the rushing sound of water inside the hull. If he got her back, they'd only drown together when this derelict finally gave up and died. Well, you could only take one thing at a time.

Somebody was calling him from the cockpit. It was the woman. "Bearing 240 degrees."

"Thanks," he said, without looking around. It was difficult to hold the glasses steady enough now to make out the figures on deck; Warriner must be still running the engine at nearly full throttle, to be that far away. Rae was still there, but in another few minutes he wouldn't be able to see her at all. But if Warriner let go the wheel long enough to put her over, *Saracen* would swing around; that he'd be able to see.

"No change. Still 240," the woman said.

"Right."

Minutes dragged by. He lost all track of time. His arms ached, trying to hold the glasses still. The sun beat down on his head, and he could feel sweat run in little rivulets across his face. He could no longer see *Saracen*'s deck at all, but her course continued straight on toward the southwest without a bobble. She must be still there. . . .

"Still 240."

It was hopeless now; he might as well admit it. Even if he knew exactly where it happened, the odds were astronomical against finding her in time at that distance. It would take the dinghy three-quarters of an hour to get there, and even the slightest deviation from the course would increase the area by square miles of rolling ocean, all of it exactly alike.

"That'll do for the moment," he called out to the woman. "Your auxiliary's under water? I mean, it won't run at all?"

"No," she said. "It's completely submerged. There's no fuel, anyway; we used it all."

He swung the glasses, searching for signs of wind. It would take a half-gale, he thought, to move this cistern through the water, even if they could keep it afloat. As far as he could see in every direction, the surface was as slick as oil. *Saracen* was hull down, fading over the rim of the horizon. Swept by fear for Rae and black rage at his own helplessness, he wanted to curse and slam the binoculars through the doghouse roof. Instead, he leaped down on deck and turned to the man, who was in the cockpit beside the woman. "How long have you been pumping?"

"It's been getting a little worse every day for the past two weeks," the other replied.

"And you haven't been able to hold it at all, or locate the leaks?"

"I think all her seams are opening up. We could keep up with it at first by pumping two or three hours a day. After a while it took six. And for the past thirty-six hours there's been somebody on the pump every minute—that is, till around sunup this morning, when he slugged me and locked us in there. No warning at all—the crazy bastard just blew his gasket and tried to kill us—"

Ingram cut him off. "We haven't got time for the story of your life. How bad's that cut on your head?"

The other shrugged. "I'll live. Long enough to drown, anyway."

"Better have it looked after." Ingram addressed the woman. "Take him below and clean it and put Mercurochrome or something on it. If it needs stitches, cut the hair away, and call me—I mean, if you've got sutures and a needle. When you come back, bring up two buckets and a couple of pieces of line eight or ten feet long."

"What for?" the man asked.

Ingram turned toward him. "That's twice you've asked me that when I told you to do something. Don't do it again."

The other's grin hardened. "So don't throw your weight so hard, sport; you might throw it overboard. You may be Captain Bligh on your own boat—"

Ingram walked back to the break of the raised deck and stood looking down at him. "You finished?"

"For the moment. Why?"

"I'm going to tell you, if you're sure you've said all you've got to say. You mentioned my boat." He gestured bleakly toward the southwest. "There it goes. My wife's on it, with a maniac, unless he's already killed her. I don't know what he is to you, and I don't care, but he came off this boat, if you follow me. So let's understand each other, once and for all; we're going after him in this tub if we have to walk and carry it on our backs, and it's going to stay afloat if you have to drink the water out of it with a straw. I haven't got time to kiss you or draw you a diagram every time I tell you to do something, so don't ask me any questions. And I'm pretty close to the edge, so don't bump me. That clear now?"

There was no fear in the other's eyes and no bluster, only that hard-bitten humor. "Sounds fair enough, sport, if you know what you're doing. But be sure you do; I'm allergic to stupid orders."

"Right," Ingram said. "How about the radio?"

"Kaput."

"The receiver too?"

"Yeah. Whole thing was powered by the main batteries."

"Why didn't you bring the batteries up here somewhere before the water covered them? That occur to you?"

"They were already discharged. No more gas for the generator."

No power, no radio, no lights, Ingram thought bitterly. "All right. Go fix your head. And don't be gone all day."

They went below. He turned to the pump, which was located against the after side of the doghouse. It had a stirrup handle which was normally covered by a plate flush with the surface of the deck when stowed, but the plate was off now, the handle extending upward. Warriner was up here alone, pumping, when he sighted us, he thought. But instead of calling the others, he slugged the man and locked them in the cabin. Why? He muttered savagely and grabbed the handle; there was no time to waste wondering about the motivations of a psychopath. It was a good pump that could lift a lot of water, and there was no indication of its being clogged. He could hear the water going overboard in a solid-sounding stream as his back bent and straightened.

He started to think of Rae and then tried furiously to make his mind go blank. He'd go crazy. He stepped up the tempo of his pumping. Where the hell were those two? Were they going to take the rest of the summer? Then he realized they hadn't been gone five minutes. They came back up, carrying two ten-quart buckets, one of them apparently the gurry-bucket from the galley. The man was carrying a length of small line. The blood was washed from his face, and he was wearing a Mexican straw hat with an untrimmed and unbound brim, to protect his head from the sun. "No hemstitching necessary," he said.

"Okay. Take the pump a minute," Ingram directed.

"*Jawohl, mein Führer.*" He grabbed the handle as Ingram let go, and began throwing a hard, steady stream of water over the side. Ingram glanced at him as he stepped back to the cockpit. Clown? Hard case? Idiot? What difference did it make? The azimuth ring was still on the compass. When *Orpheus* rose to a swell he got a snap bearing of the tiny feathertip of white that was all that remained now of *Saracen*'s mainsail. It was 242 degrees. Apparently Warriner was still holding the same course. What did that mean? Anything, or nothing, he thought. Dealing with a deranged mind—what was the use even trying to guess?

The ventilating hatch above the after cabin was closed and secured with a steel pin. He slid the pin out and threw the cover all the way back on deck. The opening was on the centerline, directly above the space between the two bunks below. The other two watched, the man continuing to pump, while he grabbed up the line, cut off a piece about eight feet long, and made one end fast to one of the buckets. He dropped it through the opening, gave a flip of the line to upend it as it landed in the water swirling back and forth across the cabin sole, and hauled it up again hand over hand. He pivoted and threw the water over the side. It was going to work, but it was awkward because of the main boom, which was directly over the opening. He freed the end of it from its notch in the center of the gallows frame, shoved it out to the end, and lashed it. It was all right now. He could stand right over the hatch with his legs on opposite sides. He dropped the bucket again, filled it, and flung the water overboard.

"Okay, let your wife take the pump," he said to the man. "That's a little easier. You bail here."

The man made a burlesque bow to the woman, with a flourish toward the pump. "Pamela, little helpmeet—"

"Shut up," she said. She began pumping. There was something puzzling about the exchange. Ingram didn't know what it was—or care.

He handed the man the bucket. "You know how to dip water at the end of a line?"

"Well, I once poured some out of a boot. Not that I like to brag—"

"Have at it," Ingram said.

The bucket landed on its side, shipped a pint of water, came upright, and floated. After yanking the line back and forth a half-dozen times, the man succeeded finally in sinking it. He hauled the water up.

"I meant without taking all day," Ingram said. "Look." He demonstrated, flipping the bucket so it landed in a dipping position and came up full all in one motion. "I want five or six buckets a minute out of there."

"Think it'll do any good?"

"I don't know," Ingram replied curtly. "But you haven't been able to keep up with it with the pump alone. If we don't gain on it this way, put on your swim trunks. The nearest land's over that way, twelve hundred miles."

"Geez, don't scare me like that. For a minute I thought you said twelve thousand."

Ingram turned away without reply and gathered up the other bucket and the rest of the line. Between the forward side of the doghouse and the foot of the mainmast was another hatch, secured with dogs. He kicked the dogs loose with his feet and opened it. It was over the centerline of the main cabin, and in the dim light below he could see the debris-laden water pouring mournfully back and forth as *Orpheus* rolled. He made the line fast to the bucket and dropped it. He hauled it up, full, and threw the water overboard. This near the mainmast, the boom was in his way, and he had to crouch to avoid it. It was uncomfortable, and after a while it would be back-breaking.

Drop . . . haul . . . turn . . . throw . . . He counted. It was nine seconds. Call it a conservative six buckets a minute

—ten a minute between them. They were ten-quart buckets, twenty pounds of water. Six tons of water an hour, with maybe half that much more from the pump. They'd soon know how fast it was coming in; if they didn't lower it this way, and damned fast, they were done for. They couldn't keep up this pace for very long, all three of them working at once. Somebody had to sleep, and if they ever got a breeze one had to be at the wheel.

There was something else that had to be done, too, within the next few minutes. He straightened, looking down toward the southwest. There was no trace now of *Saracen*; she was gone over the horizon. He reached up and unshackled the halyard from the head of the mainsail and made a sling from what was left of the line they'd brought up, leaving a free end about four feet long. He shackled the sling to the end of the halyard, retrieved the binoculars, and slung them about his neck.

"I'll need both of you for a few minutes," he called out to the man. They came forward. "Think you can hoist me to the top of the mast?"

"Sure." The other looked up at the spar swinging its dizzy arc across the sky. "Better you than me."

"Why not me?" the woman said. "I'm the lightest."

Ingram shook his head. "It's not easy. If you lost the mast it'd beat you to jelly before we could get you down."

He didn't like the prospect himself, with *Orpheus* rolling her rails under and two people he didn't know on the other end of the line, but there was no help for it. He loosed the halyard fall from the pin on the forward side of the mast. "Keep a turn around the pin," he said. "And take it slow. When I get up to the spreaders I'll tell you when to stop and when to heave."

He climbed atop the boom, stepped into the sling, took a turn around the mast with the free end of the line, and made it fast to the shackle. "Okay. Hoist away." The halyard came taut, with his weight suspended in the sling, and he began to move upward in short jerks, two or three feet at a time, with his legs locked around it while he pulled upward with his arms. The first twenty feet were not too bad, but as he continued to mount his arc increased, both in distance and in velocity, with the resultant snap at the end more abrupt and punishing. He reached the spreaders, the horizontal members extending out at right angles to the mast. This was the dangerous part. He had to cast off his safety belt momentarily in order to pass it around the mast above them.

"Hold it a minute," he called out. With both legs and one arm locked around the mast, he worked at the knot with his free hand. It came loose. If he lost his grip now he'd swing out and then back against the mast with enough force to break his skull. The mast swung down to starboard, snapped abruptly at the end, and came back. His arms and legs were slick with sweat, almost frictionless against the varnished surface. He changed arms, caught the dangling piece of line with his right hand, passed it up over the spreader and around the mast. Gripping the mast with his right arm again, he made the end of the line fast once more to the shackle with his left hand, working solely by feel.

"Up easy," he called out. "Slow. About two feet."

He came up, got one leg across the spreader, and then the other. "Okay, hoist away." He went on up. Three feet from the masthead light and the blocks at the top of the mast, he called out, "That'll do. Make it fast." He hoped they knew how.

This was no place for a queasy stomach, he thought. It was like riding a bucking horse making forty feet at a bound. While he was groping for the binoculars he looked down at the deck sixty feet below. Most of the time he was out over the water; he crossed the deck only through the vertical sector of his swing from one side to the other. The centrifugal force at the end of the roll when the mast stopped abruptly and started back felt as if it were going to tear him loose and hurl him outward like a projectile from a catapult.

He brought the binoculars up with both arms wrapped about the mast, and swept them along the line of the horizon off to port. At first he was afraid he'd waited too long. Then his pulse leaped. There she was, a minute sliver of white poised just over the rim of the world.

"If you're made fast down there," he called out, "one of you give me the heading."

"We can't see her from down here," the man yelled back.

"No. I mean our heading. How are we lying?"

The woman went aft and peered into the binnacle. "Two-nine-oh," she shouted up at him.

He looked down at the deck, estimating the angle on the bow. Call it four points, he thought. Forty-five from two-ninety left two-forty-five. *Saracen*'s bearing had remained practically unchanged from the first. Warriner was apparently headed for the Marquesas.

If he had thought to fool them by changing course after he was over the horizon, the chances were he would have already done it. *Orpheus*, with her bare masts, had long since dropped from sight from over there, and he'd probably assume he was equally invisible. Or would he? Just because he was unbalanced or mentally sick didn't mean he had to be stupid. Witness that story he'd made up about the deaths from botulism.

He put the glasses back to his eyes. The little point of white thinned and disappeared, then came up again. Was she still on there? What was happening now, or had happened already? He closed his eyes for an instant and prayed. When he opened them and looked through the glasses again, *Saracen* was gone over the curvature of the earth. He looked around at the slickly heaving, empty miles of the equatorial Pacific shimmering under the sun without even the suspicion of a breeze and felt sick. Automatically he glanced at his watch to note the time. It was 9:50.

5

FAR TO the northward a squall flickered and rumbled along the horizon, but here they appeared to hang suspended in a vacuum while the sun beat down and the oily groundswell rolled endlessly up from the south. The air was like warm damp cotton pressing in on them, muggy, saturated, unmoving. Perspiration didn't evaporate. It collected in a film over the body, a film that became rivulets, now running, now stopping momentarily, now moving again with the irritating feel of insects crawling across the skin. It ran down into his already sodden and clinging shorts and dripped into his sneakers. His back ached from crouching under the boom.

Dip, lift, throw—it went on without stop. The man was working silently above the after cabin, throwing water with a machine-like regularity now that matched his own, and he could hear the steady stream from the pump. It had been an hour and ten minutes since he'd come down from the mast. They'd thrown out nine to ten tons of water, at least, and still the buckets came up full. He'd made no attempt to get a sounding before they started; it was unnecessary. The problem was too elementary to need any measurements—either they got the water out of those cabins this way within a few hours or they were done. If it continued to rise, or even if it remained at the same level, they had no chance, because they obviously couldn't keep this up indefinitely. And whenever they stopped to sleep or collapsed from exhaustion, she'd go down.

He was dehydrated, and the ropy saliva inside his mouth tasted like brass. He wondered if they had fresh water that wasn't contaminated, and then remembered Warriner hadn't been suffering from thirst. Straightening, he looked aft. The woman was tiring; it was evident in the strained and set expression on her face. And the man, though there'd been no word of complaint, was in pain from the blow on his head. It showed in his eyes, below the level of that hard-boiled and half-contemptuous amusement with which he seemed to regard everything that happened.

He walked aft and took the pump handle. "Better take five," he said. "And get a drink. It's not going to help things if you keel over." He turned to the man. "You too."

"I'll bring some water," she said and went below. Ingram bent to the pump. In a moment she came back, carrying a saucepan full of water and a cup and a pack of cigarettes. She set the water on top of the doghouse, lit one of the cigarettes, and sat down on deck with her feet on the steps of the doghouse hatch. There was no protection anywhere on deck from the brutal weight of the sun, and the trapped air below would be stifling. The man took a drink and sat down on deck with his legs dangling in the hatch where he'd been working. After he'd had a cup of the water himself, Ingram went on pumping, driven by the compulsion to hurry, to do something, anything, and by fear of his thoughts if he stopped.

"How about one of your cigarettes, honey?" the man asked.

The woman tossed them toward him silently, without even looking at him. He lit one and asked Ingram, "How much gas you figure you had aboard?"

Ingram continued to pump. "Maybe a hundred and fifty miles at normal cruising speed. Wide open, the way he left here, not much more than half of that—if he doesn't burn the engine up first."

"So call it a round hundred," the man said. "It's been a long time since I diddled around with the pi-r-square jazz, but won't that work out to a good-sized piece of ocean?"

"Yeah," Ingram replied. "With nothing else to go on, about thirty thousand square miles."

"I had a hunch you couldn't carry it around in a cup. And that's not to mention the fact he's not going to stop just because he runs out of gas. We get a breeze, he'll probably get one too. The wind blows on the nutty as well as the beautiful and the pure in heart. Shakespeare. Or was it Salmon P. Chase?"

"I said with nothing else to go on," Ingram pointed out curtly. "We know which way he left here, and it's almost a cinch he's headed for the Marquesas. That's the reason I went up the mast, to see if he'd changed course. He hasn't. And if we ever hope to make land, the Marquesas are the best chance we've got. So why not follow him? And see if we can keep this thing afloat? But don't let me influence you, if you've got a better suggestion."

The other shrugged. "Keep your hair on. I was just trying to estimate the chances. Not good, huh?"

"No," Ingram said. He was about to mention that they had one advantage in that Warriner would have to sleep sometime, but bit it back. It presupposed his being alone on *Saracen*.

The man glanced up as if he'd read his thoughts. "There were just the two of you?"

Ingram nodded.

"Naturally, you never know what a creep'll do, but she might have a chance. He likes a woman around to cry on."

Ingram wanted desperately to reach for this ray of hope, but he'd never been good at self-deception. "And go into port somewhere with a witness?"

"Golden Boy's not so hot at the long-range view. He might not think about that for days, especially with a nice bosom to throw himself on with his Kleenex."

"Will you, for Christ's sake, shut up?" the woman asked wearily.

Ingram glanced at her with curiosity, aware this was the first time he'd actually seen her since that first glance in the cabin, when his only impression had been that she was scared to death and appeared to be naked. Since he'd come back aboard he'd paid no attention to either of them except as to their potential value as tools or pieces of equipment in the matter of keeping this sodden tub afloat and following *Saracen* in it. She was probably in her late thirties, or perhaps even forty, but a strikingly handsome woman in spite of the disarray of her hair and the exhausted and sweat-streaked face. The hair itself was raven black except for a streak of gray, and the eyes were large and brown, but with more imperiousness than gentleness in them. She wore brief white shorts and a white halter which could have been a soiled gray and still appeared like snow against the tan of her body. Under other circumstances he might have noted that she had superb legs, but at the moment he was only wondering if she'd rested long enough to start pumping again. That, and what the hostility was between the two of them. Probably Warriner, he thought, remembering the way Rae had defended him. He seemed to have some fatal fascination for women older than himself. Rae was thirty-five. Then, for the first time, he remembered that presumably there'd been four people on here.

"What happened to Mrs. Warriner?" he asked.

The man grinned. "After marrying Hughie-boy, what *could* happen to anybody? It already has."

The woman exhaled smoke and looked musingly at Ingram. "I'd like to correct the impression you seem to have that I'm married to this specimen of *Pithecanthropus erectus.* I'm Mrs. Warriner."

He said nothing, but his surprise must have showed on his face, for she smiled a trifle wearily and said, "Yes, I am, aren't I?"

"Momma likes 'em young and mixed up," the man said, and Ingram decided today probably wasn't the first time he'd been slugged by somebody. Even people otherwise in full command of their faculties must have found the urge too much to resist.

He introduced himself and added, "We were bound from Florida to Papeete."

"I'm very glad to know you, Mr. Ingram," she said. "But sorry about the circumstances. This fringe-area human being is Mr. Bellew. If you've been wondering why my husband cracked up, perhaps the mystery is clearing. Just multiply your brief acquaintance by twenty-six days."

But there was still the fourth one. "And Mrs. Bellew?"

Bellew turned toward Mrs. Warriner, his eyes bright. "Why don't you tell him, honey? Nobody ever likes my version."

"Estelle drowned," she said. "Or was killed by a shark—"

"Or she was hit by a hockey puck, or some drunk in a sports car." Bellew took a final drag on his cigarette and dropped it between his knees into the water in the cabin. "Hughie-boy killed her."

"That's a lie!" Mrs. Warriner's voice was under control, but Ingram could see the fury in her eyes.

"Oh, not deliberately, perish the thought." Bellew looked at Ingram and made a deprecating gesture with his hands. "Hughie-dear wouldn't even dream of killing anybody—unless she happened to be in the way when he was trying to save his precious neck. Naturally, you can't have that sort of thing. What kind of world would it be without Hughie?"

"You were the one, if anybody was, you blind fool!" Mrs. Warriner started to get up, her self-control beginning to slip. "If you'd watched what you were doing—"

"Break it up!" Ingram's command cut through the scene with a parade-ground bark that halted her. "Both of you! You can fight some other time, if there is one. Get back to work."

With a venomous glance at Bellew, Mrs. Warriner took the pump. The other stood up and reached for the bucket. "And then Hughie hit this nasty old shark right on the nose, and he says you take that, you nasty old shark you. My wife can whip your wife."

Mrs. Warriner started to turn, her face pale. Ingram caught her arm and wheeled her back to the pump. At the same time he barked at Bellew, "Shut up and start throwing water!"

Bellew looked at him with lazy insolence for a moment, as though on the point of refusing out of mere curiosity as to what would happen. Then he shrugged and dropped the bucket through the hatch. "You might have a point there, sport. Drowning makes an awful mess of my hair."

Ingram returned to the hatch forward of the deckhouse, dropped the bucket, and began furiously throwing water overboard, conscious of the wasted minutes. What kind of madhouse was this? With the boat sinking under their feet, you had to tear them from each other's throats and drive them to make them try to save themselves. Well, they'd pump, God damn them; they'd pump till they were standing on their tongues.

What had happened to the fourth one, Estelle Bellew? At the moment he didn't care, but it was a way to keep from thinking of Rae. Didn't they even know? How could one call it an accident and the other say Warriner had killed her? Warriner was fleeing from something, there was no doubt, from some terror that had pushed him over the edge into madness. Or was he only running from Bellew? If you were weak and unstable to begin with, twenty-six days of Bellew's sadistic bullying and amused contempt would drive anybody around the bend. But why in the name of God had they ever started out together in the first place, to sail across the Pacific, four of them in an unsound boat? Well, they must have been friends then, friends and too lacking in experience to know what being cooped up on a small boat for weeks at a time could do to clashing personalities.

But it was futile. His thoughts always came back to the question from which there was no escape. What would Warriner do? But if he were insane, how could you even guess? Where did you start? Would he kill her or throw her overboard because she was a witness to the fact he'd gone off and left three people to drown on a sinking boat? Or worse, did he believe he'd killed Bellew? Presumably, he'd hit him from behind, and Bellew had fallen into the water, probably unconscious. Therefore Warriner might be convinced he was guilty of murder—in addition to whatever had happened to Estelle Bellew—and obviously there could be no turning back and no surviving witnesses. But this was assuming a mind at least partially capable of rational thought, of reasoning from cause to effect, from crime to punishment and how to escape it. Well, hadn't he already shown he was capable of that? He'd made up that very clever and very plausible story about the deaths from botulism just to keep him, Ingram, from going aboard *Orpheus* and discovering what he'd done. The answer probably was that there wasn't any answer, nothing ever clear-cut and definite; even the hopelessly psychotic must have rational intervals. Maybe at times he knew what he was doing, while at others he was completely cut off from reality.

Then what? Rae was no match for him physically; he was a powerfully built man in his early twenties. You could forget that. And there was no weapon— He stopped. The shotgun. It was a twelve-gauge double he'd brought along for hunting in Australia and New Zealand. But it was taken down, the barrels and stock wrapped separately in oiled sheepskin and stowed in a drawer where it could be sealed by customs in ports where it wasn't permitted. She knew nothing about guns; could she ever assemble and load it? No, that wasn't the question. Could she use it? Could she deliberately shoot a man with it? And if she did, what would it do to her afterward? There was nothing pretty about the results of a shotgun blast at close range; she'd have nightmares the rest of her life and wake up screaming— Stop thinking about things you have no control over, he told himself. That's out of your hands; just throw water and keep throwing it. It can't be running in as fast as we're dumping it out now; something's got to give.

It was less than thirty minutes later that two things happened almost at once. The first was a definite indication that they were gaining on the water: as it rushed from side to side with *Orpheus*'s rolling, the bucket would sometimes strike bottom and come up less than full. Maybe less than a foot deep in the cabins now, he thought, if she were on an even keel; they'd thrown out probably that much in an hour and a half of furious pumping and bailing. The other thing was a breeze.

He'd been so intent on bailing, his first awareness of it was the cool feel on his face. He looked up. It was straight out of the west, and as far as he could see the surface of the sea was wrinkled and dark. "Wind," Mrs. Warriner called out at the same moment.

"Right," he said. "Just keep pumping; you can take the wheel in a minute." He dropped the bucket and began casting the gaskets off the mainsail, working feverishly and praying the wind would last. He freed the end of the boom, took a strain on it with the topping lift, and reshackled the halyard to the head of the sail. He hoisted it, tightened it down with the winch, and started on the double for the jib. Then he turned and called back to the other two, "Have you got a genoa aboard?" No doubt he'd regret it by the time he'd manhandled it from one side to the other a dozen times or so in these fluky airs, but every foot of distance was precious. A genoa would add almost the equivalent of another mainsail to her, and it was going to take all the canvas they could get on her to move this hulk in anything short of a gale.

It was Mrs. Warriner who replied, "Yes, there's a genoa, and also a big nylon spinnaker. The sail locker's forward. Do you want me to show you?"

"No. I'll get it." There was a hatchway to the forward cabin. He opened it and hurried down the ladder. The light was dim below deck, the air stifling and saturated with moisture, and water washed back and forth around his legs. In back of the ladder was a doorway opening into the locker in the bows of the boat. The sailbags were stowed in a bin on the port side, some six or eight of them altogether. He began muscling them out and looking at the markings on the sides. There were spare mainsails and mizzens, a couple of jibs, a storm trysail, a spinnaker, and the genoa jib. He looked at this young fortune in sails and wished they'd bought a hull to go with them.

He beefed the genoa back up the ladder, dumped it in the bow, and began unhanking the smaller jib. The breeze was still cool against his sweaty face, and *Orpheus* had begun to come ponderously up into the wind, still rolling heavily. He got the genoa snapped onto the stay, shackled the halyard to its head, and hoisted it. He didn't know where the sheet was, but grabbed up one of the lines littering the deck, made it fast to the clew, led it out around the port shrouds, through the block on the port side of the deck aft of midships, and back to the winch near the cockpit. *Orpheus* swung off to starboard. The mainsail filled, with the genoa aback and blown in against the shrouds. She began to move slowly ahead. When she had steerageway, he brought the wheel hard over; she came slowly up into the wind and fell off on the starboard tack with both the mainsail and genoa full and drawing. He checked the compass. They were heading 220. He came right a little and retrimmed the sheets, but 225 was the best they could do. It wasn't too far from the course they wanted.

He called out to Mrs. Warriner, "You take the wheel now. Bellew can relieve you there at the pump."

She came aft. Bellew moved to the pump, for once without comment. Ingram broke out the mizzen and hoisted it. The breeze had continued to freshen, and now tiny whitecaps were winking on the broad undulations of the swell. During all this burst of furious activity and the excitement of getting under way, the fear had been pushed to the back of his mind, but now as he looked over the side it all came back with a rush, along with a galling and futile anger. Were they moving at all? With the same breeze *Saracen* would have been footing along at four or five knots, but this sodden coffin had little more than steerageway.

"Let me take her again for a minute," he said to Mrs. Warriner. Maybe they were pinching her, trying to point higher into the wind than she would sail. She relinquished the wheel. He came left ten degrees, started the sheets, retrimmed them, tried her farther off the wind, and came back. It was no use. She had no feel of life to her anywhere, no desire to move; she answered the helm with the leaden apathy of a dying animal that no longer wanted anything but rest.

He hadn't expected much, but this was even worse. If you could manufacture your own wind to order, by direction and force, you couldn't make fifty miles a day. He came back to the original course, turned the wheel over to Mrs. Warriner, stepped over to the rail, and looked down. Below the waterline streamers of green hair wove backward with their passage. With ten to twenty tons of water inside her and that pasture on the bottom, he thought, how could you expect anything to move her? "When was the last time she was hauled out?" he asked Mrs. Warriner.

"About eight months ago," she replied. "When we bought her."

Well, that figured; it matched everything else about this expedition. He stepped down into the doghouse and dug a chart of the South Pacific out of the litter on the deck. Even if they weren't going anywhere, they had to have a position, a point of departure. Their last position should be in the logbook, but he didn't trust their navigation. He'd had a good fix from three star sights just at dusk last night; from that, by dead reckoning, they'd made twenty-five miles along a course of 235 degrees. That should be *Saracen*'s position at dawn when he'd sighted *Orpheus*. She was—call it five miles away, on a bearing of 315. That would put her here.

He penciled a cross on the chart: 4.20 South latitude, 123.30 West longitude. The Marquesas were roughly twelve hundred miles to the west southwest, the Galápagos over two thousand miles behind them, and elsewhere nothing but thousands of miles of empty ocean. The chances of their being sighted by a ship were to all practical purposes nonexistent.

And as for ever catching up with *Saracen*, even if they could find her . . . Face it, he thought. She was already far over the horizon, making six knots under power. And when her fuel ran out, she could still outsail this waterlogged hulk with nothing but her mizzen and somebody's shirt.

"The wind's heading us," Mrs. Warriner called out from the cockpit. He went back on deck. The breeze had veered around to the southwest, and she had bare steerageway on a course that was now a little east of south.

"We'll come about," he said. He cast off the genoa sheet, carried the sail forward around the stay and outside the starboard shrouds, and trimmed the sheet on the port tack. They were steering 275 now, which was 35 degrees to the west of the course they wanted. But in a few minutes the wind went further around to the southward and they were able to come down to 245. Then it died out momentarily and sprang up again out of the northwest. He carried the genoa around again. Ten minutes later the wind began to soften once more, and then died with complete finality. *Orpheus* slogged forward a few feet, came to rest, and began to roll heavily in the trough. He looked around the horizon. In every direction the surface of the ocean had the slick, hot glare of polished steel.

They'd made less than a mile. It was 12:10 P.M.

Her face hurt. It was lying on something hard that went up and down and wove back and forth the way the floor had the only time in her life she'd ever been drunk, and there was that same sick feeling in her stomach. Somewhere a long way off there was an engine sort of noise that seemed to have been going on forever, and just audible above it, or through it, a voice was singing. It was an old, very sentimental popular song, one she hadn't heard for years, but it was still familiar. What *was* it? Oh. "Charmaine." That was it. She rolled over. Some powerful light glared beyond her closed eyelids, and she grasped that it was sunlight. She opened them and squinted with pain. Just beyond her was a pair of wide and very suntanned shoulders surmounted by a gold-thatched head. At the same moment the head turned, still singing, and Hughie Warriner regarded her with concern, which gave way to evident relief. He smiled. It was a charming and affectionate smile, and there was something almost chiding about it. She tried to scream, or to move, but could do neither.

The song stopped. "See, you're all right," he said. "Now aren't you sorry you made me do it?"

6

JOHN WASN'T here. The paralysis of shock snapped then, and she screamed. "Where are we? Where are you going? We've got to go back!"

Warriner gave no indication he'd even heard her. She tried to sit up and was assailed by vertigo. The ocean tilted while nausea ballooned inside her, and she collapsed, fighting to keep from being sick. She closed her eyes for an instant to stop the whirling, and when she opened them Warriner had turned forward again to look into the compass. He was sitting in the helmsman's seat in the back of the cockpit, just beyond her legs. He reached a hand around and caught her left ankle, not tightly or roughly, but merely as though to soothe her or to reassure himself that she hadn't disappeared.

She cringed and tried to scuttle backward, but there was nowhere to go; behind her was only the sea. She was cut off; she couldn't reach the wheel or the ignition switch, or even the rest of the boat, without getting past him. There was nothing to hit him with, even if she had the strength.

The hand slid down her ankle and was caressing her bare foot. He turned around again. "You have such beautiful feet," he said. "And women so seldom do. I mean, they do to start with, but they ruin them. Especially European women."

She could only stare in horror.

"In fact, I've often wondered if Gauguin didn't run away to Polynesia simply because he was revolted by the feet of European models." His eyes sought hers in a glance that was amused and intimate, as though they shared some secret joke. "Of course it's silly. It's just something you say to clods at cocktail parties."

Dear God, how did you get through to him? "Listen!" She made it to a sitting position this time, lurched once as *Saracen* rolled, and caught herself with a hand on the lifeline. "Please! We've got to go back! Don't you understand? Turn around. Turn. Like this." She made a lateral motion with her free hand, as though trying to explain the mechanics of wheel-turning to an idiot or to someone who spoke another language. She realized immediately this was wrong, but was too frantic to know how to correct it. She went on, the words tumbling over each other in her haste. "Let me! Let me take it!"

"No." The smile disappeared. He gave a petulant little shrug, as though she had disappointed him, and faced forward to stare into the binnacle again.

She turned and looked wildly astern. How far had they come? At first she couldn't even see the other boat and felt herself begin to give way to panic. Then she made it out, almost hull down on the horizon directly behind them. There was no chance at all of seeing the dinghy at that distance, and she didn't know what had become of John. Except that he wasn't here, and they were already nearly three miles away and going farther with every minute. She was the only chance he had. She turned back and caught Warriner's shoulder. "Go back! We've got to go back!"

He brushed her hand off. "Please, Mrs. Ingram, do you have to shout? You're being unreasonable again."

"Un—un— Oh, God!" She tried to calm herself; if she went to pieces she'd never get through to him. "*Unreasonable?* Can't you understand? My husband's back there. We can't go off and leave him. He'll drown."

Warriner dismissed the whole subject of Ingram with an abstracted wave of the hand. "He won't drown."

"But the boat's sinking—"

"It probably won't. Anyway, he wanted to go aboard there, didn't he? It's his own fault." He turned and looked at her, as though puzzled by her refusal to grasp so obvious a fact. Then he went on, as if talking to himself. "My trouble has always been that I trust people too much. I don't see their real motives until too late. . . ."

It was hopeless, she realized then. Communication was impossible. Then what was left? Try to take the wheel away from him? Even in her desperation she realized the futility of that. And if she provoked him to violence again, this time he might kill her or throw her overboard. It wasn't fear of being hurt or even killed that made her rule that out, or reserve it as a final gamble when everything else had failed, but merely the simple, monolithic fact that her staying on here and staying alive represented the only chance they had. She had to try every other possibility first. But what? Then the answer occurred to her: she couldn't make him turn back, but at least she could stop his going any farther. It was still dead calm, and there was a good chance it would remain that way for hours, or even the rest of the day; if she could disable the engine, John might be able to reach them in the dinghy. But access to it was below; she had to get down into the cabin. Would he let her?

She pushed herself to her knees, grasping the lifeline, and made a tentative move to go past him along the deck on the starboard side of the cockpit. "I—I feel sick at my stomach," she said. "I've got to go to the head."

He gestured toward the rail. "Why not there?"

"I don't like being sick in public."

"No, of course not," he said sympathetically. "I'm sorry. I didn't think of that."

She wasn't conscious of the utter madness of this conversation until she was halfway down the ladder, and wondered if she was losing contact with reality herself. All the landmarks and reference points of rational existence had been so suddenly jolted out of position, she couldn't orient herself. It was as though they were threatened with destruction by the blind and impersonal trajectories of some hitherto placid machine that had run amok through a short circuit in its wiring. Warriner perhaps didn't intend any harm to either of them; they just happened to be in his path. Nor was he threatening her with violence or placing her under any restraint; she was merely powerless to do anything about him.

He couldn't see down into the cabin from where he was, in the aft end of the cockpit; once she was down the ladder she was out of sight. The engine was installed under the cockpit, and access to the compartment was through a removable panel in the after bulkhead of the cabin. She turned and was on the point of lifting the panel out when it occurred to her she had no idea at all what she was actually going to do. Disabling the engine had a fine sound to it—but just *how* did she disable it, and what was she going to do afterward?

The minute it stopped he would come hurrying down the ladder to find out what had happened. And even if she'd succeeded in sabotaging it beyond immediate repair it might be hours before John got here. It would be some time before he was sure *Saracen* had stopped, and it would take at least an hour to row a dinghy this far. She had to have some line of retreat, a place to barricade herself where Warriner couldn't reach her. The companion hatch itself couldn't be fastened from inside. The head? No, the door was too light. Warriner could smash the panel out of it with one kick. The forward cabin, that was the answer. The door was heavier and had a bolt inside. Also there were the cases of stores and the heavy sailbags to barricade it with.

Just hurry, she thought. She lifted the panel out and was assailed by sudden fear as the noise level, already high, increased. Would he notice it? She looked fearfully up at the hatch, expecting to see it darken. Nothing happened. Where he was sitting was almost above it; probably the difference in noise level was too small to be apparent up there. The compartment was dark, but there was a light switch just inside the entrance. She flicked it on and leaned in.

The engine had been running at nearly full throttle for a half-hour, and in addition to its ear-shattering racket the compartment was filled with the fumes of hot paint and burning oil. She felt nausea push up into her throat again. The engine itself was in the center of the small space, with the starting and lighting batteries on her right and a metal locker containing spare parts and tools on her left.

She studied it, searching for a vulnerable spot to attack. Though she had once been a sports-car enthusiast and had for a short period in her life owned an agency for one of the European cars, she knew little more about gasoline engines than does the average woman. She was aware, however, that they could be stopped by shutting off either the gasoline supply or the spark that exploded it. There was a valve in the small copper line coming from the fuel tank to the connection on the engine, but closing that would solve nothing. She could take a hammer from the toolbox and smash the line itself, but that would let the fuel drain into the bilges and convert the boat into a potential bomb. Then how about pulling loose a bunch of wires? That was better, but still not perfect. Warriner could replace them in less than an hour. Then her glance fell on the distributor. There was the answer. Smash that, and the power plant was permanently out of commission.

Then she had a better idea. Why not just remove the cap, where the wires came out? She could take it into the cabin with her; the engine couldn't run without it, and when John got aboard he could replace it and they'd still have the engine intact. She'd watched him take it off to clean the contacts and was certain she knew how to do it. All it required was pulling out those five wires and releasing the two spring clips on the sides, and then it lifted right off. But even that would take longer than the single hammer-blow it would require to smash it, and if he made it down here before she was locked in he would simply replace it after he'd taken it away from her. She paused, undecided, and was about to abandon the idea when another occurred to her.

How many times had John cautioned her never—no matter how short of space she was around the galley—to set anything on the ladder? To the person descending, it was invisible until he'd stepped on it and fallen. She whirled and reached into the stowage racks above the sink and brought out three saucepans. She set them in a row on the next-to-bottom step; under way, *Saracen* wasn't rolling heavily enough to throw them off within the next few minutes, which was all the time she needed.

She bent over and crawled into the compartment. With the metal locker pushing against her back and the bottom of the cockpit crowding her above, it was difficult to balance herself against the corkscrew motion of the boat's stern. Here right up against the engine the racket was deafening, and she could feel herself growing sick again from the fumes. She turned slightly, so as to be headed outward. Now—

She yanked out the wire in the center of the cap. The roar of the engine cut off abruptly. She began furiously snatching out the other four, the ones to the spark plugs. She had three of them loose and was reaching for the fourth when *Saracen* rolled down to port and she lost her balance. She fell over on the engine, her left forearm against the hot exhaust manifold. The sudden pain was too much for her already nauseated stomach. All the strength drained out of her and she collapsed, vomiting onto the floorboards beside the engine. Light footsteps sounded in the cockpit pressing against the top of her head.

Maybe even now there wasn't time to get out. But she had to have the cap; she'd never get another chance. She groped blindly for the last wire and had it in her hand when she was seized by another spasm of sickness. She tore it loose, still vomiting, and clawed at the spring clips on the side. The cap came free. She propelled herself toward the opening, and as her head emerged she saw Warriner's bare legs hurrying down the ladder, above her and to her right. She was cut off; she'd taken a second too long.

Then his right foot came down on the outer rim of one of the saucepans. It flew from under him and he landed amid a metallic crashing at the foot of the ladder. She was out of the engine compartment now, and if she could get by him before he got to his feet she might make it. As she shot past he threw out an arm and caught her ankle. She pulled free but was spun off balance, and she fell over against the port bunk. He had rolled over and was scrambling to his feet. She bounced off the bunk, somehow still clutching the distributor cap, and flung herself toward the entrance to the forward cabin. She was in. She slammed the door, but before she could throw the bolt he hit it from the other side.

It came inward. She had her shoulder against it, but her feet were slipping along the deck as she was forced back. Without something to brace herself against, the outcome was inevitable. She looked behind her and saw the piled sailbags on the port bunk just beyond her legs. Putting her right foot up against them, she managed to straighten the leg enough to lock her knee. It was impossible to force him back, but the door wasn't open enough for him to squeeze through. She could hear his feet sliding on the deck outside as he tried to get enough traction to bring his full strength to bear. A minute went by. She could feel herself growing faint, and her knee was beginning to tremble.

She still had the distributor cap in her hand and tried frantically to think of some way to dispose of it. Maybe she could toss it behind something. No. He knew she had had it when she ran in here; he'd find it, no matter what she did with it. But it was made of plastic; maybe if she slammed it down hard enough it would break. She shifted it to her free right hand

and threw it with the last of her strength against the planking of the deck. It bounced upward at a slight angle, caromed off the sailbags, passed under her straining and almost horizontal body, and came down, spinning, near the bulkhead, less than a foot from the partially opened door, still intact. If he reached in he could pick it up.

He had never uttered a word. She could hear only his labored breathing and the scuffing of his sneakers against the deck on the other side of the door, and the decreasing sounds of water going past the hull as *Saracen* slowed and came to rest. There was a quality of horror somehow in this very absence of speech that made her shiver. She couldn't hold out much longer; her leg was going to buckle any second.

She threw herself suddenly to the left, releasing the door. It flew inward, and he shot past her, losing his balance and falling to the deck between the bunks. She scooped up the distributor cap and ran through the after cabin toward the ladder. If she could only make it into the open before he caught her she could throw it overboard. Her head and shoulders were above the hatch, and she was drawing back her arm to throw it, when she was caught from below. It dribbled out of her hand and into the bottom of the cockpit. She managed to kick free, ran up the last two steps, and leaped into the cockpit after it. She had it in her hand when his weight landed on her from behind and she was slammed down on the port seat of the cockpit with the hand pinned beneath her body.

But he made no effort to reach beneath her and pull it out; his hands were digging at the back and sides of her neck as he tried to close his fingers around her throat. She hunched her shoulders up and pulled her chin down, grinding her face against the cushion. Then his weight was suddenly gone from her shoulders and she was lifted and thrown onto her back. She kicked out with her legs and struck at his face, but his hands were around her throat now and tightening. The contorted face and wild eyes were just above hers, and she closed her own eyes to shut them out.

The struggle was utterly silent except for a faint whining sound he made deep in his throat and the sibilant whisperings of their violence against the plastic cushion. She could no longer breathe, and the sunlight penetrating her closed eyelids began to fade downward through darkening shades of pink toward final blackness. But her hand was free now. Just as consciousness was slipping away she raised it and threw the distributor cap outward. There was no sound of its striking the deck, so it must have gone into the water. Or maybe she was already beyond hearing. . . .

Then, strangely, she was breathing again. The hands were gone from her throat. She opened her eyes. He had stood up and was leaning across her, with his hands on the port lifeline, as though he'd forgotten her. She couldn't see his face. She slid cautiously backward, toward the forward end of the cockpit. He paid no attention. She eased herself upright, poised to leap toward the hatch, and glanced fearfully once more in his direction to see if he had turned. This time she saw his face and understood. She looked outward in the same direction.

It was the distributor cap. It had landed just off the port side, and with *Saracen* now lying at rest on the surface it was sinking almost straight below them through sunlit water as clear as gin. And as he had the other time at the bottle, he was staring down at it with horror and with some sick but inescapable compulsion as it slipped from side to side and then began a gentle spiral that would end in the ooze and the darkness two miles below. The agony of his face was indescribable. He screamed then and collapsed into the bottom of the cockpit with his face pressed into the seat cushion.

She stared, still poised to leap but frozen to the spot. His head rocked from side to side and he clutched the cockpit coaming with a grip that corded the muscles of his forearms. "No, no, no!" he cried out. "I didn't do it! I didn't mean it! It was her fault!" He began to cry then with a ragged sobbing that made his whole body shake.

She was able to move at last. She ran down the ladder on rubbery legs and through the after cabin. After slamming the door between the two, she threw the bolt and began dragging cases of canned stores from under the bunks and piling them in front of it. There were six sailbags. She stacked them against the door also, wedging the last ones against the upright pipes of the bunk frame. She was trembling and drenched with perspiration when she had finished, and collapsed on the bunk, too weak to move. Her face was swollen and painful where he had hit her, and there was an ugly red splotch on the bottom of her left forearm where it had come in contact with the exhaust manifold. She was scared, and she was sick with anxiety for John, but for the moment she was safe. Without an ax to smash the door, Warriner had little chance of breaking in, and there was no ax aboard. And until they got a breeze he couldn't take *Saracen* any farther away. All she could do now was wait it out.

Saracen rolled desolately in the trough of the swell. There was no sound from beyond the door except the normal creakings, slidings, and minute collisions of shifting objects always present on a small boat at sea, and Rae might even have been alone. She tried to make some sense of this thing that had happened to them, but ran immediately into the opaque and impenetrable wall of the fact that Warriner was the only clue to any of it, and Warriner was mad. Where did you go from a starting point like that?

John had suspected there was something wrong with him. If only she'd paid more attention and hadn't waked him up by starting the engine . . . Well, there was no use crying about that now. But what had John found on the other yacht that had made him burst out of the cabin that way and leap down into the dinghy? Somebody hurt or sick? But in that case why was he coming back alone? Wait, she thought, you're close. What he found must have been some proof Warriner was lying, unstable, or dangerous, or all three, and he was rushing back because you were alone here with him. But *what* proof?

Warriner had tried to kill her; maybe he'd already killed somebody else. It was abundantly obvious now he hadn't been chasing her to recover the distributor cap; the chances were he hadn't even known she had it. He'd been intent simply on strangling her because she'd somehow stopped the engine. And his horror at watching it sink had nothing to do with its being a part of the engine; he probably hadn't even recognized what it was. It was the same as with the bottle: he was seeing something else, or somebody.

I didn't do it! . . . I didn't mean it! . . .

Guilt? Terror? Who knew, or could even guess? But the whole story of the deaths from botulism must have been a lie, so it was possible something else and equally terrible had happened. Maybe he was responsible for it— She tensed. He was coming through the after cabin. She sat up and drew back on the bunk, waiting for the impact as he slammed into the door. Would it hold?

Then she grabbed her temples and fought a collapse into hysteria. He'd knocked—a tentative and discreet rap of the knuckles—and said forlornly, "Mrs. Ingram?"

You're not mad, are you, Mama? I didn't know it would hurt the cat. Stop it! she thought. You're beginning to crack up yourself.

He knocked again. "Mrs. Ingram? Please, I didn't mean it! You've got to believe me! I—I just lost my head for a minute because I thought you were against me too. But you're not, are you? You couldn't be. You're like Estelle. The first minute I saw you, I could *feel* you talking to me, the way she did. Mrs. Ingram, what's your first name?"

She could only feel of her throat and go on staring at the door.

"Mrs. Ingram?"

She couldn't be sure, but she thought he was crying. Then in a minute he said petulantly, "Well, you *were* being unreasonable, you know. It was your own fault."

He turned the handle of the door and pushed, and when it failed to open he began to lunge at it in rage, like a child in a tantrum. She watched the bolt in horror, expecting to see it torn off, but it continued to hold. "You want to kill me too, don't you?" he shouted.

Then, as suddenly as it had commenced, the fury subsided. His footsteps went away.

She heard him moving around in the after cabin, and after a while the sound of hammering. It was impossible to guess what he was doing, but at least he wasn't trying to smash down the door. Would John have decided by now that *Saracen* was stopped? Maybe he was already heading for them in the dinghy. She looked at her watch. It was 9:35. He could probably row it in an hour, or maybe even a little less.

But suppose something had happened to him back there when he'd tried to get back aboard? The last she'd seen of him, just before Warriner hit her, he'd been coming toward them as hard as he could row, directly in their path. No, you had to have something to hang onto or you'd go as mad as

Warriner, and faith in John Ingram's ability to cope with anything that could happen at sea was the one solid thing in sight. Even if he'd been run down, he would have got back aboard the other yacht, and he'd have the dinghy with him. And if the other yacht were sinking, he'd keep it afloat somehow—

Her thoughts broke off and she looked around in wonder. It was the growl of the starter she'd heard. Hadn't he even looked at the engine? Didn't he know the distributor head was gone? The engine fired then and settled down to a steady rumble. She heard the clutch engage, and they began to move ahead.

She slumped forward with her face in her hands and wanted to give up and cry. She'd never thought to look in the spare-parts box to see if there was another one. She should have known. John detested engines, but he always said that if you were going to carry the stinking things around they might as well be in working condition when you needed them.

7

HE'D ACQUIRED his first catboat at the age of twelve, and, except for two years at the University of Texas on the GI Bill just after World War II, he'd been around salt water and around boats ever since, most of his adult life as a professional. He'd captained a towboat in Mexico, worked on salvage jobs in half a dozen countries and three oceans, owned and skippered a charter yacht in the Bahamas, and up until eighteen months ago operated a shipyard in Puerto Rico. He'd been in an explosion and fire, and inevitably he'd seen bad weather and some that was worse, but at the moment he didn't believe he'd ever been in a position quite as hopeless as this.

It was 2:45 P.M. Wearing a diving mask, he was some ten feet below the surface on *Orpheus*'s port side, just in under the turn of her bilge, looking at her from below, and the view was a chilling one. She'd never make port. And their pumping and bailing would accomplish nothing except to postpone from one hour to the next the moment she'd finally give up and go to the bottom.

When the breeze had stopped, they'd all three returned to throwing water out of her. Twenty minutes ago, after over an hour's furious and unceasing effort, they had lowered the water level in the main cabin to a depth of around six inches. Their bailing buckets were coming up less than half full each time. He'd knocked the others off for a brief rest and questioned them. Had they hit anything? Driftwood, or a submerged object of any kind? In mid-Pacific, this was admittedly far-fetched, but there had to be some reason for all that water.

It was Mrs. Warriner who supplied most of the answers. "No," she said. "If she did, we didn't feel it."

"When you were running on power, was there any unusual vibration?" If they had a damaged propeller or bent shaft she might have opened up around the stern gland.

Mrs. Warriner shook her head. "No, it was perfectly normal. Anyway, we haven't used the engine in over two weeks."

"We used up all the gas trying to find Clipperton Island,"

Bellew said. "Prince Hughie the Navigator knew where it was, but somebody kept moving it."

She gave him an icy stare but was too exhausted to reply. "How about bad weather?" Ingram asked.

There hadn't been much, at least nothing to bother a sound boat. Two days out of La Paz they'd run into a freak condition of fresh to strong winds which had kept them reefed down for the better part of twenty-four hours. They'd had a couple of days of bad squalls, the worst of which was around two weeks ago when they were trying to beat their way back to Clipperton Island after they'd decided they'd overshot it. The squalls had left a rough, confused sea, and she'd pounded heavily.

"And it was just after that you noticed it was taking more pumping to keep her dry?"

Mrs. Warriner nodded. "I think so. But it wasn't all of a sudden. Just a little more each day. And it must have been about three days ago it began to get really bad and come above the cabin floor when she rolled."

"How was the weather then?"

She thought. "Nothing stronger than light breezes, as I recall. But the day before was squally and rough, and she pitched quite a bit."

Ingram nodded and spoke to Bellew. "When you get your breath, turn to on the pump. I'm going below to see what I can find, and I'll relieve you in half an hour."

He was going through the doghouse when the thought of Rae poured suddenly through the defenses of his mind again, leaving him shaken and limp. No matter how you barricaded yourself against the fear, it lurked always in ambush just beyond conscious thought, ready to catch you off guard for an instant and overwhelm you. What chance did she have? Did she have any at all? Lay off, he told himself savagely; you'll run amok. Do what you can do and quit thinking about what you can't.

Below, in the sodden ruin of the cabins, he'd checked the obvious things first, all the plumbing leading through the hull below the waterline. There were two heads. He couldn't get a good look at the pipes because of the water swirling around them, but he could feel them with his hands. He wasn't looking for a minor leak, but a flood. They were all right; none of them were broken. He crawled through a hatch into the flooded engine compartment under the doghouse. The big two-hundred-horsepower engine was submerged to its rusty cylinder head in oily water surging from side to side. He groped around for the intake to the cooling system and examined the line with his hands. It was intact. Then the leaks had to be in the hull itself—God alone knew where—and there was no way to find them unless you could get her dry inside so you could look.

But you couldn't lower the water with the pump alone, and the buckets were useless after you got it as low as the cabin sole. Maybe there was a fire ax or hatchet aboard; he could chop away the cabin flooring below those two hatches and drop the buckets directly into the bilge. His eyes had grown accustomed to the dim light in the compartment now, and he looked around him, studying as much of the hull as was above the water. She was double-planked; he could see the diagonal seams of the inner skin. He took out his knife and began poking it at random into the wood. On the third plank the knife blade went into it as if it were a piece of bread. He felt a chill along the back of his neck and hurriedly started checking everywhere he could reach, even into the water below him. Large areas of the inner planking and of the frames themselves were spongy with dry rot.

He'd gone back on deck then and asked if there was a diving mask aboard. Mrs. Warriner told him where to find one. After kicking off his sneakers, he'd tossed the end of a line over the port side so he could get back aboard, and dropped in.

How long? he wondered now, peering upward through the mask. It was impossible to guess; too much depended on the weather. In the first hard squall she'd go to the bottom like a dropped brick. In at least three places just above him along the turn of the bilge where the green hair of marine growth waved endlessly as she rolled, he could see the loose butt-ends of planks sticking out where her fastenings had worked loose. Around them the calking was gone, the seams wide open for the full length of the plank. Keeping a respectful distance from the plunging and deadly mass above him, he swam to the surface and forward, around the bow. The starboard side was even worse. He counted six planks where the fastenings were coming out. He swam back and climbed aboard.

Bellew stopped pumping, and they came over to him as he stood dripping on deck under the brazen weight of the sun. "Did you find anything?" Mrs. Warriner asked.

He stripped off the mask and nodded. "Yes. But it's nothing we can do anything about."

"Then she's going down?"

"Yeah. I wouldn't even make a guess as to how long we can keep her afloat, but she'll never make the Marquesas."

"What's causing it?" Bellew asked.

"Dry rot. In the inner planking and some of the frames. It's a disease, generally caused by lack of ventilation, and once it starts it spreads like smallpox. There may have been only a few small patches of it when you bought her, but whoever surveyed her missed 'em apparently, and now it's everywhere. What's happening is that, even if the outer planking is still sound, the fastenings are pulling out; the wood inside is too soft to hold 'em any more. Pounding in those squalls probably started them working loose, and now just the rolling sets up enough play and enough stresses to pull them out. The inner planking's no doubt opening up the same way, and the more she works, the looser it all gets."

"And there's nothing we can do?" Mrs. Warriner asked.

"Nothing except keep pumping."

She sat down at the break of the raised deck and lit a cigarette. She blew out the match and tossed it overboard. "I'm sorry, Mr. Ingram. It's too bad we had to infect you."

Still occupied with the practical problem of survival, and its vanishing possibility of solution, he was caught off guard by this lapse into the figurative. "Infect?"

"With our own particular dry rot. Our contagion of doom. We should have been flying a quarantine flag."

Bellew had glanced involuntarily toward the dinghy still bumping against the side. Ingram saw him but didn't even bother to speak; he merely shook his head. Twelve hundred miles from land, three people in an eight-foot dinghy designed to carry two the hundred yards or so from an anchored yacht to the dock, inside a harbor—a bicycle would be about as practical a lifeboat.

Bellew shrugged. "So it was stupid." Then he went on, his eyes bleak. "But I guess you die hard, with unfinished business."

"Who doesn't?" Ingram asked.

"Sure, sure, you'd like to know what happened to your wife. Me, I'd just like two or three minutes with Hughie-boy." He raised brutal hands and made a twisting motion with them, inches apart. Mrs. Warriner sickened and turned away in a silence that seemed almost palpably to echo with the creak and snap of parted vertebrae. Ingram felt sorry for her. "Never mind," he said harshly to Bellew. "Get back to pumping."

The other fell to without reply. As though conscious of them now only for the first time, Ingram looked at the bull neck and massive shoulders and arms, thinking that Bellew probably could kill a man with his bare hands. It was a good thing he'd got the jump on him to start with. Or had he? It was impossible to tell what Bellew thought, or why he took orders without argument. He had the look of a man it would be very dangerous to push, and the chances were this docility under curt commands was nothing but a realistic acceptance of the facts that Ingram knew the job better than he did and he had more chance of saving himself if he did as he was told.

Ingram sat down in the cockpit to put his sneakers back on. Water still dripped from his hair. Mrs. Warriner sat facing him, on the edge of the raised deck, her knees drawn up, moodily smoking. "What is your wife like?" she asked.

"Why?" He didn't like the question; he saw no reason he should discuss Rae with these people.

"If she knows how to handle him, I don't think he'll hurt her."

"I'd like to believe that," he said bluntly. "But do you mean you *didn't* know how to handle him? When I opened the cabin door down there and you thought it was him, you were scared to death."

The brown eyes met his with perfect frankness. "The circumstances are different. He thinks we're trying to kill him. Also, it wasn't myself I was afraid for."

Ingram nodded, remembering how Bellew had been poised with his club. At the same time, something else disturbed him. Presumably that was her cabin, hers and Warriner's. Then if Warriner was on deck taking his trick at the pump when he'd sighted *Saracen*, why had Bellew been in there? But maybe Warriner had attacked him somewhere else and dragged him in there while he was unconscious. He shrugged. What difference did it make?

"Would she panic easily?" Mrs. Warriner asked.

"No," Ingram said. "I don't think she'd panic at all. Look, she's no high-school girl, or jittery old maid with the vapors. She's thirty-five years old, and she was married twice before she married me. Men are nothing new and startling to her. She's never had to deal with an unbalanced one before, but she *has* been in tight spots, and she's clever and coolheaded and she learns fast. She tried to fight him to get back to the wheel when he took it away from her, but all that happened very fast and it was pure reflex. If she survived—" His voice broke off, and he pulled savagely at the shoelace he was knotting. "If she survived that time, she'd know better than to antagonize him again. She'd play it by ear."

"Is there a weapon of any kind aboard?"

He nodded. "A shotgun."

Their eyes met again. Then she shivered slightly and looked down at the cigarette in her hands. Her voice was very small as she asked, "Could she?"

"I don't know," he said. "Does anybody, till he's faced with it?"

"Is she aware that *Orpheus* is sinking?"

"All she knows is that there was water in her, and that your husband said she was. She won't know what to believe now."

"But the possibility—or probability—will still exist. So they'd be going off and leaving you to drown." She was silent for a moment. "Have you been married long?"

"About four months. We were on our honeymoon."

She nodded. "I can only give you the opinion of another woman who was, in effect, on her honeymoon. Both alternatives are impossible, of course, as long as you continue to weigh them. But inevitably there'll be a point when she has to stop thinking, and it'll become a simple matter of instinct versus conditioning. Instinct is a lot older."

"She may not even remember the gun. Or know how to assemble it if she does—or get the chance, for that matter."

"But she would know better than to try to threaten him with it? You know, the magic wand of television and B pictures?"

"Yes," he said. "She'd know better than to point it unless she was prepared to shoot it." He closed the discussion abruptly and stood up to look down the hatch. There was perceptibly more water in the after cabin than there had been thirty minutes ago. He motioned for Bellew to relinquish the pump.

"I'll take over for a couple of hours. We can't all work all the time, and I want to get some idea how fast it's rising against pumping alone. So the two of you'd better turn in on the settees in there and see if you can get some sleep. You're going to need it."

"Right," Bellew agreed. He started down the steps into the doghouse. Then he turned and asked, "How did he sucker you?"

Ingram explained briefly how Warriner had rowed out and come aboard, and the story he'd told. "It kept bothering me, especially his not wanting to come back aboard here or even wanting me to. But I had no real reason to doubt him, so I couldn't very well force him to, and I didn't like the idea of leaving my wife on there alone with him until I knew more about him. Then he turned in, and I decided to have a look anyway. But apparently he wasn't asleep. You didn't even know he'd left?"

"No," Bellew said. "When we heard you walking around, we thought it was still him. We didn't know he'd sighted a rescue boat when he slugged me and locked us in there. A laugh a minute, that Hughie-boy. Like to run into him again some day."

The contempt in Mrs. Warriner's voice was like a whiplash. "Are you sure that's why he hit you?"

"Why else, baby?" Bellew turned and went on below.

Ingram shrugged and began pumping. Mrs. Warriner remained where she was, turning slightly so she faced him. "I'm not sleepy," she said. "Do you mind if I talk?"

"Go ahead," he said.

She took a drag on her cigarette and stared moodily at the smoke. "I can understand your not wanting to talk about your wife under these circumstances—and least of all to me. But I'm trying to form a picture of her. Not to belabor the obvious any more than we have to, she's the key to this, naturally; we know what's going to happen on here, so if there is to be any other outcome it would have to hinge on what happens on there within the next few hours. You said she was thirty-five, which implies—or should imply—a certain amount of maturity. Is she pretty?"

"Yes," Ingram said. "She's very pretty."

Her smile was fleeting and faintly tinged with sadness. "It *was* a silly question to ask a bridegroom. Is she blond or brunette?"

"Blond," he said, still pumping. "Or in that jurisdiction. Her hair's somewhere between golden blond and light brown—tawny, I think you'd call it—and the eyes are sea-green. High cheekbones, very smooth complexion, beautiful tan. Generally speaking, it's the type of face and coloration that go with high spirit and a very low flashpoint in the temper department, but she grew up faster than the temper did, and somewhere along the line they gave her a sense of humor. Maybe she needed it, to marry me."

"Don't add too much modesty to your other virtues," she said. "It'll sound phony. Does she have any children?"

"No. She had a boy, but he died. Polio."

"I'm sorry. That was the first marriage?"

"The second. The first marriage was one of those kid things, during the war. That is, the Second World War—"

"Thank you, Mr. Ingram. But I know which one you mean. Go on."

"She wasn't quite seventeen, and he was a navigator in the Eighth Air Force. After the war he went back to school on the GI Bill, pre-med student. She worked, and they lived in a Quonset hut—you remember the routine. They were both too young for it, I guess; anyway, he was failing all his subjects and they began to fight and it didn't last. She went back to Texas, and they were divorced. The second marriage was another thing. No divorce; he was killed in an airplane crash."

"How old would the boy be if he'd lived?"

"Around twelve, I think."

"Does she attract children?"

"I don't know," he said. "I've never seen her around any."

"How about the lost, the insecure, the dependent, the scared?"

He saw the shadow of pain in her eyes again and knew what she meant. “She has a great deal of tenderness and sympathy,” he said. “I don’t know how apparent it’ll be after she’s just been slugged—”

“He’ll know, don’t worry. It’s like radar. And he brings it out if it’s been latent for years. With that, plus a reasonable amount of intelligence, I think she can handle him, provided she doesn’t panic.”

“Why does he think you tried to kill him?”

“He thinks Bellew and I are lovers. And that we planned to do away with him and Estelle.” She made no attempt to look away. The brown eyes were completely without expression now, however, and he could only guess at the torment behind them. “Unfortunately, there is some justification for his thinking so. And it’s my fault. I blamed the whole thing on Bellew awhile ago, but that was in anger. I’m probably as much responsible for his crackup as Bellew is, in a different way.”

Ingram was beginning to like her and found that difficult to believe. Maybe she was too accustomed to taking the rap for everything; Warriner had struck him as an alibi artist who’d load it on anybody in sight. “Well, look, your husband’s a grown man, or supposed to be—”

“The type of woman he attracts, or is attracted to, never gave him a chance to be one. And it’s too late now.”

“What happened?” Ingram asked.

For a moment he thought she hadn’t heard. Then she said, “That’s a good question, and I wish I could answer it. Specifically, what happened was a very tragic accident. The accident itself is difficult enough to explain, but to understand why it smashed him you’d have to go back a long way. When was the first time, Mr. Ingram, that you realized it was possible for this environment of ours to be unfriendly, and that it was also possible to find yourself utterly alone in it? I mean, with nobody to take your head in her lap and tell you everything was going to be all right, that the critics were wrong, that the bank must have forgotten to credit your last deposit, that the pathologist must have made a mistake, or the teacher that gave you a D was just being spiteful?”

“I don’t know,” Ingram replied. “Probably a long time ago.”

"Precisely. While you were still quite young, and under relatively harmless circumstances, and over the years you built up—well, not an immunity, nobody's immunized—but call it a progressively higher threshold of susceptibility. It happened to Hughie for the first time at the age of twenty-eight, alone in the middle of the Pacific Ocean without even a lifebelt, and he was there because he'd been betrayed by the one person he'd been conditioned all his life to trust and depend on—his mother, in one of her successive manifestations."

"Aren't you riding yourself pretty hard?" Ingram asked.

"No. I don't think so." She gazed out across the metallic glare of the sea to where the sun had already begun its descent into the west. "If you know the conditions when you accept the appointment, you also accept the responsibility. I let him down."

8

SHE WAS silent for a moment. How did you explain Hughie to a man who'd seen only the wreckage after he'd been shattered by the Pacific Ocean, by Bellew's contemptuous bullying, and by her own misguided attempts to help him? How make him see the wit, the charm, the sensitivity, the genuine talent behind the beach-boy good looks?

Strangely enough, when she'd first met Hughie, a little over a year ago, he'd been living on a yacht. It was on the island of Rhodes, snuggled up under the Turkish coast on almost the opposite side of the world from where she was now, and the yacht, a glittering and obviously expensive yawl registered under the Panamanian flag, appeared to be more or less permanently moored in that harbor astride whose entrance the Colossus had towered two thousand years before. Hughie was living aboard it alone, and he was painting.

Oh, it wasn't his yacht, it belonged to a friend who was only letting him live on it, he'd disclaimed with a refreshing and boyish honesty that couldn't help appealing to a woman who'd known her share of phonies on two continents. It wasn't until somewhat later—too late, in fact—that she learned his frankness had been a little less than complete, that the friend was female, a wealthy American divorcée living in Rome, and that Hughie's relationship to her was one for which "protégé" was as good a euphemism as any. By that time she was—as she would have put it if she'd still been in any condition to view the thing with her old self-honesty and clarity of thought—hooked herself.

She saw him as a talented but too-beautiful boy who was being ruined by a continuously self-renewing matriarchy of lionizing sponsors, benefactresses, patronesses-of-art-at-the-source, surrogate mothers, and rapaciously protective beldames who started out wanting to adopt him and wound up by sandbagging him with the flushed and hectic urgencies of some autumnal reflowering and dragging him off to bed. And by the time she should have begun to suspect the weakness in his character she had made the further discovery that he wasn't a boy at all, that he was twenty-seven instead of the twenty she had thought, and she was hopelessly in love with him.

She was forty years old then and widowed nearly two years, no longer a victim of the grief and numbness of loss but only of its emptiness, the feeling that she must have been left over for something if she could only discover what it was. She'd come to Europe again. Since she belonged to a set to which the jet flight across the Pole was only a commute hop, she had friends in London, Paris, Antibes, Florence, and God knew where else, but she had avoided them, going on instead to Istanbul and then back to Athens and Corfu and a footloose and unscheduled wandering through the Dodecanese, searching for she knew not what. She'd arrived in Rhodes around the middle of July for a four-day stay. She'd met Hughie, and the four days had become a week, and then two, and finally a month.

"He's a painter," she went on. "A good one. And, given a chance, he might have become a great one. It wasn't his fault that women could never leave him alone—"

"If I'm not mistaken," Ingram broke in, "*nothing* is ever Hughie's fault."

She nodded somberly. "To some extent, that's true—if oversimplified. But there are reasons for it."

"I'm not knocking it. Probably a very comforting philosophy, as long as you can keep from having to sign for the mess sometime when there's nobody around to hand it to."

"It's the way he was raised," she said. "He's never had a chance. Even his childhood was against him. He's seen his father only once, and very briefly, in the past seventeen years. Though he's never said so directly, I gather he either hated him or was afraid of him, and probably at least some of it must have been his mother's fault. Certainly the picture that comes through from the few things he has said is one of such utter crudity and brutality it seems a little too one-sided to be quite true.

"His father was—or is, rather—the editor and publisher of a small daily newspaper in Mississippi, an ex-football player at one of the Southern universities, and from all accounts a man whose only passions apparently were drinking, random and indiscriminate affairs with very sordid women, white supremacy, and shooting quail. That plus bullying Hughie because the boy showed more interest in sketching animals than in killing them. It could be that all of this is literally true, in spite of its familiarity, but I wouldn't discount the possibility of a certain amount of editing by the doting mother and embittered ex-wife. At any rate, when Hughie was eleven his parents separated and were later divorced. His mother, who had a little money of her own, took him to Switzerland. He went to a private school in Lausanne but lived with her all the time in the villa she rented there so they wouldn't be separated. She never remarried. You can see the pattern, of course, the possessiveness, the overprotection, the you'd-never-leave-Mumsy-would-you-after-all-she's-done-for-you rubbish. After the school in Switzerland he attended the Sorbonne for two years and then began studying art, also in Paris, and also still living with his mother. She died five or six years ago. There was a little money left, but not enough to keep him going until he could get some kind of recognition as a painter. However—" She smiled with a tinge of bitterness, and went on. "Europe is crawling with middle-aged women eager to help the struggling young artist, especially if he's charming and decorative and well mannered and has no social liabilities like cutting off his ears or wasting too much time painting."

She broke off then with an impatient gesture, as though annoyed at herself. "I'm sorry. You asked me about the accident. As I said, it's difficult to explain how it could have happened. Fortunately you know the interior layout here, which will help. Hughie and I occupied the after cabin, and Mr. and Mrs. Bellew the forward one—"

Ingram interrupted. "But first, who is Bellew, anyway? Somehow, I don't place him in this. Is he a friend, or a neighbor of yours in Santa Barbara?"

"I'm not from Santa Barbara," she replied. "San Francisco. We just bought the boat in Santa Barbara and sailed from there in the beginning." She shook another cigarette out of the pack and held the latter up toward Ingram at the pump.

"No, thanks," he said.

"You don't smoke?"

"Only cigars." He wished he had one, but among the other things he was wishing for at the moment it didn't have a very high priority. "But about Bellew?"

"He's a writer." Then, catching Ingram's look of surprise, she smiled faintly. "No, he *doesn't* remind you a great deal of Proust or Henry James. He's a specialized type of writer; he does articles for outdoor magazines. Hunting and fishing."

"Wait." Ingram frowned. "Bellew? Russell Bellew? I think I've seen some of his stories. Marlin fishing, and hunting sheep in Mexico. With some beautiful photography, as I recall."

"His wife did the photography. She was an artist with a camera."

Ingram stopped pumping for a moment and walked past her to the open hatch to look down into the cabin. In spite of his continuous pumping, the water was still rising. His face was somber as he walked back to the pump.

She lit the cigarette and carefully blew out the match. "Still gaining?" she asked.

"Yes," he said. She was a cool one, he thought; and so, for that matter, was Bellew. That was something, anyway; at least he didn't have a couple of screamers on his hands. Of course there was no telling how they'd take it later on. But then, he added grimly, there was no telling how he'd do, either; it was something you couldn't forecast.

"But we can still hold it by bailing too, can't we?"

"Yes," he replied. "We can now."

"But not for long?"

"Just how long, I don't know. The only thing that's certain is that it's not going to get any better, but it *is* going to get progressively worse, with this rolling. And in a bad squall, as I told you, she could come apart like a bale of shingles. But forgetting the squall, which we can't do anything about anyway, she might last for a week yet. . . ." His voice trailed off.

She glanced up questioningly. "There's something else?"

There was no reason to try to hide it from her, he thought. "Only this—even if we do keep her afloat for another week, after tonight, or tomorrow morning at the latest, it's not going to do any good anyway. There's not a chance in a million we'll be sighted by a ship, not where we are. And even if one happened to pick us up on radar, there's nothing to indicate we're in distress.

"So, as you said, the only thing that could change it is if Rae is still on there and is able to cope with your husband. She might even be able to talk him into coming back. If she does, we'll probably be all right. The second possibility is that she may be able to get control of the boat some way. He'll have to sleep sometime, or . . ." He stopped, floundering.

She nodded, her face devoid of expression. "Or she may kill him. Go on."

If she could manage it, he could too. "Right," he said just as calmly. "But even if she does get control of the boat, it's nowhere near as simple as it sounds. She may never find us again. They're over the horizon now, and unless she knows the course he was steering when he left here, she can't come back because she won't know which way *back* is. Also, at the speed they were going, somewhere around midnight tonight and about a hundred miles from here they're going to run out of gas, and she can't make it back unless she gets some wind. In these conditions, it could take days. Also, at that distance, the accumulated errors of trying to make good a course while she's fighting fluky breezes and calms become so great that after a while she won't know within twenty miles where she is herself.

"She can't call for help, to get a search organized, even if there was anybody out here to look. We've got a radiotelephone, but it won't reach land from here, and you can't call a ship with it because they stand their radio watches on five hundred kilocycles and not the phone bands.

"So if she ever finds us again it'll be within the next twelve hours or so, because if they get any farther away there's practically no chance. Have you got any distress flares aboard?"

"No," she said. "We thought we had a can of them but we've never been able to find them."

"How about oil lamps? We've got to have something she can see if she comes back tonight."

"We have some flashlights. The big long ones."

"Good. They'll do. We'll leave the mainsail hoisted, and lash two of them to the shrouds so they'll shine on it. You can see an arrangement like that for miles."

"That's clever. I wouldn't have thought of it."

"It's an old trick in heavy traffic or poor visibility. Steamship captains trying to figure out what it is may call you things that'd raise blisters on a gun turret, but at least they won't run you down."

"I'm glad—" She stopped.

"What?"

"I was about to commit the incredible *gaucherie* of saying I was glad you'd come along. Let's just say that under other circumstances— May I relieve you at the pump now?"

"Are you sure you're not sleepy?"

"Yes."

"All right. You take over here, and I'll start bailing again."

He moved over to the hatch. Before he dropped the bucket in, he paused to look at an ugly mass of cloud along the horizon to the northeast. It looked like a nasty one, all right, but it was a long way off. He'd just have to keep an eye on it.

Saracen shuddered, protesting the engine vibration, and pitched with a long corkscrew motion as she continued to plow ahead. Here in the tiny compartment the air was stifling. Rae Ingram was conscious of thirst, and of the sour taste of vomit in her mouth. She sat on the bunk and stared unbelievingly at the barricaded door. She must be mad herself; Paradise couldn't have become this nightmare in the few short hours since sunrise, since this morning's dawn when she'd been alone with John on the immensity of the sea, when she'd swum nude beside the boat with that faint but shivery sensation of wickedness—and amusement, because it was a ridiculous way to act at thirty-five—when he'd used a whole quart of priceless fresh water to wash the salt out of her hair because, as he said, he loved her. Could you go from that to this in three hours? Numbly she looked down at her watch. It was 9:50. It had been a quarter of an hour since Warriner had restarted the engine and they'd got under way again.

She tried to force her mind to operate. She was apparently safe enough for the moment from any further assaults upon the door; as long as *Saracen* was under way, he had to be at the wheel. Also, he was apparently dangerous only when opposed. But that was unimportant. She still had to stop him. There was no way she could disable the engine now; she'd already grasped what that hammering was she'd heard in the after end of the main cabin. He'd nailed up the access to the engine compartment so she couldn't get in—at least without making enough noise to warn him. Mad or not, he would have taken some precaution, and that was simpler than trying to lock her in here. The door opened inward, and there was no bolt or hasp on the outside.

Then what? The only other place the engine could be stopped was at the control panel right in front of him in the cockpit. But wait, she thought suddenly. It had already been fifteen minutes since they'd started up again, and the other boat—what was it Warriner had called it, *Orpheus*?—had been almost hull down then. And from the sound of the engine it was still running at nearly full throttle. So merely stopping *Saracen* would do no good now, anyway. By this time they were out of sight over the horizon, and John would never know it. Then the whole problem was changed, and now it was even worse. Somehow she had to get control of the boat so she could take it back— Her thoughts broke off, and she sat up abruptly, feeling a chill along her spine.

Take it back? Back *where*?

She'd forgotten she had no idea at all which direction they'd been traveling since they'd left the other yacht. And with it lost somewhere over the horizon now, where all directions looked the same, trying to go back to it could be just as hopeless at ten miles as at a thousand. First of all and above everything else, she had to find out and keep track of their course. But how?

The answer occurred to her almost immediately. In one of the drawers under the bunks in the main cabin was a spare compass, a small one mounted on gimbals in a wooden box. She sprang up and began furiously hauling the sailbags from in front of the barricaded door. She dragged the cases of stores to one side, slid back the bolt, and peered out. The main cabin was empty.

It took only a minute. She hurried to the sink, softly pumped a cup of water, washed out her mouth, and drank, noting at the same time she'd been right about the access to the engine compartment. The panel was nailed shut. The compass was under the port bunk. Keeping an apprehensive eye on the hatch, she grabbed it out, snatched up a pencil and a pad of scratch paper from in back of the folding chart table, and slipped back inside the forward compartment.

She was about to close the door when another thought occurred to her. While she was able to get out into the other cabin, why not try the radio? If she did it carefully, there was a good chance Warriner wouldn't hear her. Of course! It was worth the risk.

He'd said the radio on the other boat was ruined by water, but he'd also said he'd used it trying to call them. Which was the truth? It would take only a few minutes to find out. If it was still in working order, John would have turned it on, waiting; there was no doubt at all of that. Keyed up with excitement, she set the compass on the bunk with a pillow against it to keep it from rolling off, and slipped back out the door, closing it softly behind her.

The radio was mounted on bulkhead brackets above the after end of the starboard bunk, the transmitter and receiver in one unit. From there she was still invisible to Warriner at the wheel, and by facing toward the hatch she'd be able to see it darken even before his legs appeared if he started down. There was a loudspeaker, but a switch for cutting it out. She threw the switch to the off position, turned on the receiver, and set the bandswitch to 2638 kilocycles, one of the two intership bands.

Still nervously watching the hatch, she lifted the handset off its bracket. This actuated the switch starting the transmitter. The little rotary converter whirred softly; there was no chance Warriner could hear it above the noise of the engine. She put the handset to her ear and adjusted the gain of the receiver. The tubes had warmed up now. Static popped and hissed, but no one was calling. She reached over and turned the bandswitch to 2738 kilocycles. This was dead too, except for the static.

The transmitter was warmed up now. She pressed the handset button and adjusted the antenna tuning control for maximum indication on the meter. It was working beautifully.

"*Saracen* to *Orpheus*," she whispered into the microphone, though there was really no necessity to say anything; as soon as John heard the carrier come on he'd know who it was. There was nobody else out here. "This is the yacht *Saracen* calling *Orpheus*. Come in, please."

She released the transmit button and listened. Static crackled. She waited thirty seconds. Forty. There was no answer. She called again. There was still no response, no sound of a carrier coming on the air. If he was listening, it must be on the other band; maybe it was the only one *Orpheus* had. She threw the bandswitch and retuned the antenna control.

"*Saracen* to *Orpheus*, *Saracen* to *Orpheus*," she whispered. "This is the yacht *Saracen* calling *Orpheus*. Answer on either band. Come in, please."

She cut the transmitter and listened again, turning the bandswitch back and forth between the two channels. The only sound was the eternal crackling and hissing of static from far-off squalls pursuing their violent paths across the wastes of the southern hemisphere. She called twice more on each channel. There was no answer. She replaced the handset, turned off the receiver, and went back inside the forward cabin, wishing now she hadn't thought of the radio.

9

BUT SHE still had the compass. She picked it up from the bunk, removed the lid from the box, and looked about for a place to set it. It had to be oriented as nearly as possible in a plane with the vessel's fore-and-aft centerline, and it had to be secured so it couldn't move. The after bulkhead, she thought, to the right of the door and far enough away from it so it wouldn't be disturbed by moving the sailbags. She set it on the deck with the after side of the box flush with the bulkhead and cast about for something to hold it in place. Not cases of canned goods; cans were steel. One of the sailbags, of course; there was an extra one. She shoved it up against the forward side of the box. That would hold it.

She knelt beside it, studying the movements of the card. It was reading 227 degrees. Then 228 . . . 229 . . . 228 . . . 227 . . . 226 . . . 226 . . . 225 . . . 224 . . . 223 . . . 224, 225, 226 . . . 226 . . . 226 . . . At the end of two or three minutes it had swung no further than from 220 to 231 degrees, and most of the time had remained between 223 and 229. The course he was steering was probably 226 degrees. She glanced at her watch and wrote it down on the scratch pad.

10:14 AM 226 degrees Est. speed 6 knots

That would do it, she thought. All that was necessary now was to keep watch on it to see if he changed. There was no certainty, she knew, that this reading of 226 degrees was anywhere near the actual course, the one he was steering in the cockpit; they might even differ by as much as 20 or 30 degrees. John had already taught her that much about the care and the mysterious natures of magnetic compasses. That one up there had been corrected by a professional compass-adjuster who'd inserted in the binnacle the bar magnets necessary to cancel out the errors induced by the vessel's own magnetism, mostly from the massive iron keel and the engine. This one wasn't adjusted, of course, and was in a different location besides, but it didn't matter as long as it didn't move out of the alignment it was in now. All she had to do, if she ever got control of the boat, was to put it on a general heading of 226 on this compass and then take the correct reading off that one in the cockpit. It wouldn't be easy, and it would take a lot of running back and forth to average out the error of several tries, but it could eventually be done within an accuracy necessary for the job of retracing their route from the other boat. Provided it wasn't too far . . .

For a few minutes she'd forgotten the rest of the problem in her satisfaction at being able to solve this minor part of it, but it all rushed back now and hit her like an icy sea. She sat down, weak-kneed, on one of the other sailbags and regarded end-to-end those two conditions she'd danced across separately and so lightly a moment before.

If she ever got control of the boat . . . Provided it wasn't too far . . .

How was she going to get control of it?

Trying to reason with him, she had already discovered, was futile. Trying to overpower him was so manifestly absurd there was no point wasting time even thinking about it. There was the further fact, already demonstrated, that he regarded any interference with his flight—and probably opposition of any kind—as part of some terrifying conspiracy against his life, and while he was in the grip of this delusion he wouldn't hesitate to kill her. Five minutes later he would be sorry, and he'd probably cry over her body, but that wouldn't do her a great deal of good if she was already dead. Nor, more to the point, would it save John. So anything she tried from now on had to succeed the first time.

In the back of her mind, of course, there'd been the knowledge that in the end he had to go to sleep sometime. Then she would simply tie him up, turn the boat around, and go back to get John. But now, a little fearfully, she brought this comforting backlog out into the light and began to examine it more closely. In the first place, you couldn't tie a man up just because he was asleep; he'd wake up. So she'd have to hit him on the head with something. She knew nothing whatever about knocking people unconscious by hitting them on the head, in spite of the easy and apparently painless way it appeared to be accomplished all the time on television, and unless she was able to overcome her natural revulsion to such an act and did it brutally enough and in the right place he'd only wake up and choke her to death. And in the second place, how about that panel into the engine compartment? If he'd remembered to nail that up so she couldn't tamper with the engine again, he certainly wasn't going to go to sleep and leave himself unprotected. All he had to do was close the companion hatch and fasten it on the outside, and she'd be locked below.

But it was the third objection that finally wrecked it. He wasn't going to sleep—not in time to save John. Whatever horror he was fleeing from was still pursuing him down the dark corridors of the mind, and as long as the engine continued to run, he would. She knew no more about abnormal mental states than the average layman, but she was aware that a man in the grip of obsession or some pathological fear could be immune to fatigue for incredible lengths of time. He'd stay right there at the wheel until the engine died for lack of fuel.

How much gasoline did they have? *Saracen*'s cruising range on power was around two hundred miles. The tank had been full when they left Panama, but John ran the engine for short periods every day or so to charge the batteries and to keep the engine itself from succumbing to the saturated humidity of the tropics. Call it a total of ten hours in the nineteen days. At the moderate speed John drove the engine when he was using it, that would be forty-five or fifty miles. So at cruising speed they should have fuel for a hundred and fifty miles or about thirty hours. But Warriner was running the engine almost wide open, which would increase the fuel consumption tremendously. She wasn't sure how much, but John had said once that beyond a certain point increasing the speed one knot would almost double it. So call it fifteen to eighteen hours, at six knots. And from nine o'clock this morning . . . Sometime between midnight tonight and three o'clock tomorrow morning they would run out of fuel, ninety to a hundred and ten miles from that foundering hulk John was trapped on.

Then what?

The answer was short, inescapable, and merciless. She'd never find it again.

Assume Warriner *was* incautious enough to drop off to sleep in the cockpit without locking her below, and she was able to knock him out and tie him up—she'd have no fuel, of course, to go back with, so she'd have to sail back. In the interminable calms and fickle airs they'd been fighting for the past two weeks, that could take three or four days. But that wasn't the really deadly part of it, not by far. Sailing back, she just wouldn't find the place; she couldn't navigate well enough.

Steering a course under power was one thing; averaging out a course while you were beating all over the ocean on a dozen different headings at varying speeds for different lengths of time, and drifting helplessly at the mercy of uncertain currents for long periods of calm was something else entirely. The only way you could do it over any distance at all was with competent celestial navigation. John was teaching her, and she knew how to use the tables, but she was nowhere near accurate enough yet with the sextant. She could do it if she was trying to make a landfall on some headland visible thirty miles at sea, but if she missed the other yacht by more than four miles she'd never see it at all.

This was besides the fact that at the end of three or four days it wouldn't even be in the same place anyway. Even if it were too full of water to move under sail, currents would still act on it.

And it was sinking. She'd seen herself, from the way it lurched from side to side on the groundswell, there was lots of water in it, and the radio was dead.

Sometime around sunset this evening they would pass the point of no return. After that, they would have used up more than half the gasoline, and every ten minutes would be another mile that nothing would ever buy back—

Sunset. Suddenly, and with such piercing clarity it made her cry out, she saw him struggling in the water, alone on the emptiness of the sea, as the sun went down and the colors began to fade. She could see every line and angle of the face her finger tips had come to know so well, the sun-wrinkles at the corners of the eyes, and that horrible way she had cut his hair; the eyes themselves were open, the clear, cool gray eyes that could be ironic or amused but were far more often gentle, and there seemed to be no fear in them even now but only something she thought was sadness or regret. He made no sound. And there was no lifebelt. If you ever lost a boat, he'd said once, in a place where there was no chance of being picked up, you were better off without it.

She began to shake, all over and uncontrollably, and fell back on the pile of sailbags with the back of her left forearm pressed against her opened mouth while tears welled up in her eyes and overflowed. Why sunset? Why did she have to think of sunset? But she knew, remembering the moments of splendor and that shared enraptured silence when the world was only two people and a boat and a fragment of time poised between night and day. Would he be thinking of them? Would he have to? She was up then, throwing the sailbags behind her to clear the door. She slammed the cases of stores aside as if they were empty, and snatched up a marlinspike she somehow saw in her wildness lying among the coils of rope. Her hand was yanking at the bolt to open the door when some vestige of reason made itself heard at last and she was able to stop herself. She sagged against the bulkhead.

One chance was all she would get. She couldn't throw it away.

He was a young man, with a young man's reflexes. No matter how fast or unexpectedly she leaped into the cockpit she couldn't attack him that way and expect to accomplish anything but her own destruction. And with hers, John's. God, why did she have to be so helpless? There must be some way to stop him. There *had* to be.

It was then she remembered the shotgun.

Her mind slid away from it in revulsion. It edged back, reluctantly but compelled. She could see its dismembered pieces—two, she thought there were—wrapped in their separate strips of oiled fleece in one of the drawers under the starboard bunk. John had never assembled it since he'd brought it aboard, but he did check it from time to time to be sure it hadn't been attacked by rust. He was going to hunt something with it in Australia, or maybe it was New Zealand. In the same drawer were two boxes of its ammunition. . . .

It was sickening. It was impossible. Why was she even thinking about the thing? And there was no use trying to threaten him with it. You couldn't threaten a madman.

She looked down then and saw she still had the marlinspike in her hand. It was over a foot long, of heavy bright steel, gently tapering from one thick end to a point at the other—the classic weapon, she knew from the sea stories she'd read, of the bucko mates of nineteenth-century square-riggers driving their crews around the Horn. She'd never be able to hit him with it from in front, but suppose she could get behind him?

She might. His reactions were unpredictable, of course, but there seemed a chance he wouldn't attack her out of hand if she came on deck, at least as long as she didn't appear to be trying to interfere with him. And he'd turned his back on her before. But that was before she'd tried to sabotage the engine, she thought; he'd be suspicious of her now. Well, she could look out the companion hatch and see how he reacted before she went too far.

There was another thing, too, she thought with growing excitement: once behind him, she could take a quick look into the binnacle and *see* what course he was steering. That would do away with all the trouble and possible inaccuracies of this other way.

The marlinspike would have to be well concealed, but still where it could be withdrawn swiftly and without catching on anything. She experimented. After pulling up the bottom of her blouse, she shoved it into the waistband of the Bermuda shorts and down the outside of her left thigh. But the shorts were a snug fit in this area, and it showed when she walked. She moved it around in front of the hip, where it angled down the hollow of her groin to the inside of the thigh. It had passed inside her nylon briefs, and the steel had a cold and alien feel against her skin. That was better as far as concealment was concerned, but she was aware now of the error of having it inside the shorts at all. When she withdrew it, she had it by the wrong end. The place for it was inside the blouse, which was looser anyway. With the heavy end caught under her arm and only the point inside the waistband, it lifted out easily and quickly and was held just right to swing. Conscious of the extreme shallowness of her breathing, she slid back the bolt and opened the door.

She crossed the after cabin, mounted the first step of the ladder, and peered cautiously out. Her head was still below the level of the deckhouse, but she could see him—or rather, she could see his head and the naked shoulders. He was seated behind the wheel, staring into the binnacle.

He still hadn't looked up, and she had no intention of venturing farther into his territory until he'd seen her and she could assess his reaction. From here she could still make it back to safety before he could get out from behind the wheel and catch her, but going too far would be like misjudging the length of chain by which some dangerous wild animal was secured. She waited, thinking of this and conscious of the incongruity or even the utter madness of the simile. Dangerous? This nice, well-mannered, unbelievably handsome boy who might have stepped right out of a mother's dream? That was the horror of it, she thought. Conscious evil or malicious intent you could at least communicate with, but Warriner was capable of destroying her with the pointlessness and the perfect innocence of a falling safe, and with its same imperviousness to argument.

He glanced up then and saw her. He smiled in evident pleasure and said something she couldn't hear above the noise of the engine. It might be a trick, of course, to entice her within range, but she had to risk it. She went up the ladder, trying to hold her arm as naturally as possible while it clamped the end of the marlinspike inside her blouse. The sea was still like glass, aside from the long undulations of the swell, and after the dimness below she was dazzled for a moment by the shimmering glow of sunlight reflected from it. She stepped out onto the narrow strip of deck along the starboard side of the cockpit, very scared now and pretending to look aft along their wake as though searching for the other boat. Slowly, she thought; stop a minute, and then another step or two, and don't try to smile; that would be too phony—

"No," he said. "Sit down there." He indicated the starboard cockpit seat and then added, "Where I can see you."

It was impossible to tell by his tone or manner whether he suspected her of something, but she hesitated only a second. She didn't have to go all the way back at once, and it would never do to argue with him. "Why?" she asked, but she sat down, some two or three feet forward of the binnacle and the wheel, with her left arm falling naturally at her side.

"Because your face fascinates me," he said, tilting his head slightly to the left and leaning over the wheel to view it better. "You have no idea what a study it would have made the way you were looking up and out at me like some hesitant naiad from a grotto—no. Naiads were Greek. You're Scandinavian."

"Partly," she managed to say. She didn't even know whether he'd meant it as a question or not.

"Oh, definitely Scandinavian. Under your clothes you're probably as blond as snow." He smiled, as though to reassure her that at their level of sophistication there was nothing tendentious in this discussion of her private blondness. "But it was your face we were talking about, the magnificent bone structure. Do you know you'll still be a beautiful woman when you're eighty? I'm speaking as a professional. I'm a painter, and painters always approach a face from the other side, to see what's holding it up. Those high cheekbones and the tilted eyes are racial, of course; people say Slavic, or Tartar, or a half-dozen other things, but to me they're always Scandinavian. If they came out of western or central Asia it must have been along the Arctic Circle. . . ."

He was still too far away to hit, even if he should happen to turn his head. For a moment she saw the whole scene with a sort of wondering horror—a civilized woman of the twentieth century, sitting here with the marlinspike of the Cape Stiff bully-boys secreted against her flesh between her nylon panties and her bra, listening while this handsome boy who was murdering her husband as surely as if he'd used a gun discussed with such charm and evident admiration the structure of her face. How much more of it could she stand? The point of no return was sunset, and if she was still alive then she'd be as mad as he was.

It wasn't that she couldn't do anything, she thought, trying to isolate or identify the ultimate nightmare quality of it; she wasn't tied, or locked up, or even openly threatened, and there was nothing to stop her now from leaping across that narrow space with the marlinspike aswing—nothing except that it might fail, and one chance was all she was going to get. It always came back to that. She had a life expectancy of just one more unsuccessful attempt to stop him, and then John would drown.

Then was she already becoming paralyzed with indecision, like a boy with only one dime in a candy store, unable to make up his mind until the store had already closed and he was out on the sidewalk? She didn't know, but she could see it coming. The stakes were too high, the pressure too brutal. Nobody was equipped to hold entirely in his hands the life of the person he loved above everything else on earth—no, not even in his hands, but poised like an egg on the back of one of them as though for an obstacle race in some macabre party game. Not even professionals, she thought; the surgeon called in another surgeon when the life of his own child was at stake.

10

BUT WHEN he was quiet like this—if not rational, at least for the moment not in the seizure of that torment or terror—why in God's name couldn't she get through to him? It was obvious at a glance what kind of boy he was, and the way he'd been brought up; he'd open doors for you, give you his seat on a bus, or bring you a drink at a cocktail party. And while she suspected there might not be any great strength in him, there was no doubt he was educated, civilized, and probably incapable of deliberate evil or pointless cruelty until this thing, whatever it was, had happened to him. Then why wasn't she able to reach in past the snarled wire-ends of his broken lines of communication and make contact with him, get him to realize what he was doing?

Maybe she hadn't tried hard enough. Or she'd tried in the wrong way; she'd been half hysterical herself, and she'd screamed at him. And then she'd talked down to him, as though it were a recognized fact between them there was something wrong with his mind. Of course, she'd known the error of this the moment it was done, but it was too late to correct.

Anyway, try once more, she thought, and with a better approach; see if you can't establish some kind of contact before even bringing up the subject of going back. Get him to talk about himself? No-o. She hated to throw out the oldest weapon in the arsenal, but there she'd be flirting with the very danger she had to avoid, any reminder of the horror he was fleeing. The past, maybe, but stay away from the voyage; whatever it was happened at sea. Talk about painting, even if you don't know much about it, talk about yourself. That was it, she thought; if she could establish an identity he could recognize, first merely as a woman who was friendly and sympathetic, and then as one he could help in some way, she might penetrate the insularity of breakdown and get through, at least temporarily, to the old behavior patterns. God, if she could only get him to pick up the phone.

". . . it's an overworked word," he was saying, "but definitely valid here. I know I could feel it."

She came back with a start. Was he still talking about her face? "I'm sorry," she said, "but I missed that. What was it?"

"Empathy," he replied. "Sometimes you meet people you're in full conversation with before a word has ever been said. It was that way when I first saw you. Oh, I don't mean the sex thing—though God knows you have plenty of that." Again his smile included her among the mature and the intelligent. He glanced into the compass and then back at her, leaning over the wheel. "I knew we'd like each other. I knew I could talk to you, and neither of us would need an interpreter. But I don't even know your first name yet."

"It's Rae," she said. It was starting out beautifully; he was doing it himself. There were cigarettes and a lighter in the right-hand pocket of the Bermuda shorts. She took them out and tried to light one. In the six-knot breeze of their passage, it didn't take too much acting ability to fail three times in succession.

"Here, let me," he offered.

He lit the cigarette for her and passed it back, and lit one for himself. Good, she thought; one conditioned response might lead to another, and then another. . . . Then it occurred to her she could be oversimplifying just a little the labyrinthine complexities of modern psychiatry; if doctors spent lifetimes trying to find out why a mind went off the rails and how to get it back, there seemed a chance it wasn't quite that easy. But at least she was doing something. *Saracen* heaved up and swayed, quartering the long groundswell. Sunlight shattered into golden points of fire in his hair, and the fine gray eyes were alight with interest as they continued to search her face. She tried not to remember the way they'd looked when he was strangling her.

"Thank you, Hughie," she said simply. Don't overdo it; don't gush.

"*Je vous en prie, madame.*"

"I'm sorry, I don't speak French." She was about to add that John was teaching her Spanish, but didn't. Probably it was best to keep John out of it until she had some kind of bridge across the gap.

"I detect just a trace of Southern accent, I think. From where?"

"Texas," she replied.

"Oil?"

She shook her head. "Every area has its slum dwellers. There are Texans who don't own oil wells."

"See, I knew we'd like each other." Then he added, "I'm from Mississippi. Or was originally." He explained briefly he'd gone to school in Switzerland and spent most of his life in Europe.

"Are your parents still there?" she asked.

"No," he said. "My mother's dead. She died six years ago."

"I'm sorry. But your father is still living?"

The change in him was startling, attuned as she was to every nuance of his expression. "No!" he said loudly. "I mean—I don't know!" Agitation was evident in his eyes, and she could sense his desperate groping through the mists in back of them. Then he appeared to regain control. "I mean, I haven't seen him for years. He still lives in Mississippi, and we never write to each other."

She breathed softly. That had been close. It was obvious she'd made a mistake, but she couldn't understand where or how. Surely his father hadn't been on the boat. Pretend you didn't see it, she told herself, and change the subject, fast.

But he had already fully recovered, as though it had never happened. He smiled at her and said, "Never mind me; you still haven't told me anything about yourself. Except that you're from Texas, which you'll admit yourself is trite. When they get to the moon, they'll find out there's not only a Texan there, but he's already bought it, air-conditioned it, and organized a local chapter of the John Birch Society. *I* could tell you more than that about yourself, just for a start. The chances are you weren't an only child; you had a very good orthodontist when you were young, or ancestors with exceptional teeth; you're warmhearted, and you have a great deal of sympathy and understanding, but you're impulsive; and status probably means little or nothing to you. All surface, of course, and some guesswork. So you take it. Tell me what the leopard was looking for on the slopes of Kilimanjaro." His gesture included all the vast and empty Pacific. "Just a parking place, or did he hear music?"

And the leopard was dead, she thought. But more immediately, that lightning reversal of mood was ominous; even when he was like this, he was further from reality than she'd believed. Well, you still had to try.

"He heard music," she said. "Perhaps not very good music, and maybe even sentimental, or trite. But he also saw something up there."

"What?" he asked. "Samarkand? A trail disappearing into the mist? Not the edge of a map, because maps don't have edges any more. They just say continued on E-12."

"No," she said. "What he saw was simply another leopard listening to the same thing. A rather handsome leopard in a furry and beat-up sort of way, with the same odd taste for Mickey Mouse music and listening to it in strange places. It was like this."

She didn't like doing it; revealing herself this way to a stranger was too much like filling out a Kinsey questionnaire or undressing in public, but, weighed against any possible chance of success, the cost was small. She took a puff on her cigarette and wondered where to begin. Anywhere, she thought, just so you can make him see you.

"One night about a year ago a man came to the hotel where I was registered in Miami, Florida. He was a curt, rather hard-bitten sort of man with too much arrogance and a slight limp, and I didn't think I liked him. And apparently it was mutual; he didn't seem to think too highly of me. I did believe he was honest, though, which was important in the particular circumstances. And the reason I thought he was honest was that anybody that disagreeable and that indifferent to the impression he made on other people almost had to be.

"The reason for our being there—for my being in Miami at all, and for his being in my hotel room—was a yacht, a big two-masted schooner named *Dragoon*. It was mine—or had been. It also had quite a bit to do with the lack of friendliness in the meeting. In the first place, there was probably a sensed difference of attitude as to what a sailing yacht really was. To me it was just a piece of property, like a parcel of land or a stock certificate, that I happened to own, mostly by accident, and which I'd been aboard only once in the two years I had owned it. To him a boat—a good one—represented something else. But besides this, and much more important, was the fact *Dragoon* had just been stolen, and he was suspected by the police of having helped to steal it. They'd picked him up and questioned him, and then released him because they didn't have any actual proof, not enough to hold him. I gathered from the police they'd had a difficult time with him; he wasn't a man who took kindly to being called a thief.

"But first maybe I'd better explain how I happened to own a two-masted sailing yacht in the first place, since I cared nothing at all about boats then. I was a widow, and not even a wealthy one—just a lonely one. I'd been married for a long time and very happily to a quiet and gentle man who was also one of the coldest-nerved and most fantastic gamblers I've ever known. His name was Chris Osborne, and I suppose you'd say he was in the real-estate business, though real-estate speculation would be more like it. By the time he was forty-five he'd already made and lost several fortunes. I'd been his secretary before we were married, but even with that edge I don't think I was ever sure at any given moment whether we were very well off or in debt. Not that it mattered a great deal. Without any children—" She couldn't bring herself to mention the son who'd died. To a boy as young as Warriner it would mean very little anyway, and there had to be a limit somewhere to the coin you were willing to spend to get his attention. "Without any children to leave it to, I could never see any point in piling up money you didn't need. We were happy, which was the thing that counted. Except that of course he was away a lot. I wasn't much good at the social routine, because I'd worked most of my life, and women from better backgrounds and expensive schools could always make me feel awkward and put me on the defensive—I mean the ones who wanted to. So I had a business of my own, just for something to do when he was away, a small sports-car agency. But none of that's important.

"Chris was killed three years ago. He'd gone out to Lubbock to look at a cattle ranch he was interested in, and the plane he was flying went out of control in a thunderstorm and crashed. I won't burden you with what it's like becoming a widow just by picking up the telephone, but it's one of those things you get through some way, then and afterward. It took nearly two years to straighten out his business affairs. He was overextended again and pretty thinly financed on several deals he was working on, and there was a tax case pending with the

Internal Revenue Service. There wasn't a great deal left in the end, but I worked it out as well as I could. And it was something to do.

"But to get on to *Dragoon*. Chris didn't care anything about boats either; he'd simply taken it in as part payment on some deal in Florida real estate, intending to sell it later. Then he was killed, and during the two years it took to get the estate settled and pay off the tax bill it lay at anchor in Key West with a watchman living aboard. Then, just as I started advertising it for sale, it was stolen. Some men got the old watchman drunk ashore and took it out of the harbor one night. The police called me in Houston, and I flew down there. They had only two leads to work on. One was that *Dragoon*'s dinghy had been picked up at sea by a fishing boat southeast of Miami near the Great Bahama Bank. The other was a suspect.

"It seemed a man had been aboard the yacht just a few days before, looking it over, and told the watchman he was interested in it. The watchman remembered his name, and the police picked him up at the hotel where he was staying in Miami and questioned him. They'd found out who he was, and were satisfied with his references—he'd been a charter yacht captain in the Bahamas for a long time, and had operated a shipyard in San Juan, Puerto Rico, until he'd got badly burned in an explosion and fire that destroyed most of it—but they weren't satisfied with his story as to why he'd been interested in *Dragoon*.

"He said he'd been hired to take a look at it by a businessman staying at one of the big Miami Beach hotels, the president of some pharmaceutical firm, who wanted to buy a boat for company entertaining and asked him for a professional opinion of *Dragoon* before making me an offer subject to final survey. But when the police checked, the businessman turned out to be a phony. There was no such company, and the man himself had checked out of the hotel the same night *Dragoon* was stolen. So it was obvious he was one of the thieves. The only thing the police still weren't sure of was whether this man was also one of the thieves or just another victim.

"So that's when he came to see me at the hotel, just after he'd been questioned by the police, this hard-bitten and disagreeable man with the limp. His name was John Ingram, he said, and he was going to help me find my boat. I offered to pay him and was curtly brushed off. There would be no charge, he said. I was glad to have his help, but I still wasn't any fonder of him. I could be stubborn too, and I didn't like having favors tossed at me in that manner.

"But at the same time I began to have a very funny feeling about it. We'd find the boat. We'd find it if he had to sift the Atlantic Ocean with a tea-strainer. Maybe the thieves had made a mistake stealing it in the first place, but their really sad mistake was ever getting this man involved in it.

"He had an idea it was in trouble, probably out there somewhere near where the dinghy had been found, so we chartered a seaplane in Nassau to search the area from the air, and we finally located it aground on a sandbar on the edge of the Great Bahama Bank, about a hundred and fifty miles southeast of Miami. The pilot landed us, with a rubber raft, and we went aboard. Two of the men who'd stolen it were still on it. They'd been trying to run a cargo of guns to one of the Central American countries, when they'd run up onto the Bank from poor navigation.

"John got the boat away from them, refloated it—without a towboat—threaded it through all those shoals and sandbars into deep water again, and sailed it back to Miami. I watched him do it; otherwise I probably wouldn't have believed it. But that isn't what I started out to tell you, not just a story of watching an indomitable man do the impossible against a background I didn't even know existed, nor even the fact that I got my boat back. Long before we reached Florida I didn't care whether we ever did, and *Dragoon* had ceased to be important at all. I was just terrified he was going to sail it into Miami, tie it up, step off onto the dock, and say, 'Now, Mrs. Osborne, there's your goddamned boat,' and turn around and walk away without even looking back. And if he did I knew I couldn't stand it. It was as simple as that.

"I realize you can't even become acquainted with somebody in five days, let alone fall in love with him. But it happened. Maybe it was the slow-motion effect of time and that increased sensitivity to everything you have in an unusual situation. Maybe it was from being with him every minute there in his own element, this world that was so strange and so utterly fascinating to me, as if I were actually seeing him for the first time. As I was. He wasn't an arrogant and disagreeable man at all, but just a very proud one who felt he'd been made a fool of. And a very lonely one. He tried to hide it under all that armor of self-sufficiency, the way he fought the limp from those burns, but it was as clear to me as if he'd been carrying a sign.

"The same thing was happening to him, and he didn't walk away when we got to Miami, but naturally it wasn't as hasty and impulsive as all that, not with either of us. It took some time to clear myself of the suspicion of being some wealthy and socially prominent man-eater who was trying to buy him for a pet, and to convince him that I didn't have any more money than he did. Then he pointed out that I'd seen him only in his own environment, and he'd look entirely different in mine—that is, living and working ashore. That wasn't true, of course, but I knew he would be unhappy. But it was a dead issue anyway; there was nothing in my old life I wanted to go back to. I was as in love with this exciting new world of his just as much as he was, and I had a simpler approach to the subject of environment anyway. Mine was any place that included him. But then I warned you this was sentimental and probably corny.

"We were married six months later, after I'd wound up all the loose ends in Houston and sold everything I didn't want to be burdened with any more. I sold *Dragoon*, which was too big for two people to handle, and we bought *Saracen*. Some day we expect we may go into the charter business in the Bahamas or West Indies, but that's in the future. Now we're on our honeymoon. We're on our way to Tahiti. We realize it has jet runways now, but there are places beyond that don't. We don't know how long the cruise will last nor how far we'll go. Maybe we'll simply go broke. We don't really care. I suppose you could call it a juvenile dream, or flight from responsibility, or refusal to accept the challenge, but everybody doesn't have to listen to the same drum. I like ours. I fell in love with it the first time I heard it, one night on a grounded schooner on the Great Bahama Bank, when I discovered what *he* was listening to and that I was in love with him. I've heard it ever since. I heard it this morning at dawn, becalmed a thousand miles from land, when he woke me winding a chronometer, and in a hundred other places and times and different kinds of weather, and always with him. If it ever stopped, or anything happened to him, I don't think I'd want to go on living." She paused and took a deep breath to steady the shaky feeling inside her. If she hadn't reached him, she never would.

"Now, Hughie," she went on quietly, "don't you think it's time we went back?"

His eyes had been on her face throughout with that same look of interest. Now he appeared to be caught off guard by this abrupt change of subject.

"Back?" he asked politely.

"Yes. To get John."

"You mean back *there*?"

"Yes. We have to, Hughie. You realize that as well as I do—"

He shook his head. "Of course we can't go back."

She held on tightly. Don't scream at him. Don't lose your head. Some of it *must* have got through. "Hughie, please—" But how in God's name could you keep repeating the obvious *without* the appearance of talking down, of explaining something to an idiot? How did you keep it on an intelligent level after you'd said it a dozen times? There simply wasn't any way. "We have to go back now, Hughie. Now, before it's too late."

"No," he said with a little shrug of annoyance. She could see him beginning to go away, as though she had disappointed him again with this revelation of selfishness in her character.

"Hughie, he's my husband. I love him. Do you think I could go off and leave him on a sinking boat, to drown? You can't, either; you know you can't. You're not capable of a thing like that. How could you justify it? You couldn't live with yourself—"

"Do you always have to ruin everything by becoming hysterical? He won't drown."

"But that boat is sinking!"

"Why do you keep saying that?"

"You said it was. You told us yourself."

"I did?" It was obvious he didn't believe it. He glanced into the binnacle, dismissing the whole thing as of no importance. "I don't know why I would have said a thing like that."

"Well, if it's not sinking, why did you abandon it and come on here?"

"*Why?*" He looked up sharply. "Because they're trying to kill me."

She knew she was skirting the precipice now, but there was no way to avoid it. You couldn't plead with him to go back without running into his reasons for not going. "Who's trying to kill you?"

"Both of them." His expression changed then, becoming one of triumphant slyness. "But I fooled them. They'll never get me now, even with your husband helping them."

There it was, she thought. They had come full circle and were back facing each other across the unbridgeable chasm. But at least he hadn't become violent, and if she could stay here and go on talking maybe eventually she could get behind him. The marlinspike was cold and frightening against her flesh.

"Hughie," she said soothingly, "nobody wants to kill you—"

"What?"

"I said nobody wants to hurt you."

The craftiness in his eyes became more pronounced. "You mean I just imagined it?"

She saw the trap and tried to avoid it. "No, I mean it must be a mistake, a misunderstanding of some kind—"

"No! I know what you meant. You think there's something wrong with me, don't you?"

"Of course I don't, Hughie."

"Oh, yes, you do. You're just the same as they were. First your husband, and now you! Poor Hughie's subject to hallucinations!" His voice slipped up into falsetto, apparently in imitation of someone, and was charged with an indescribable bitterness. "You just imagined it, Hughie, dear. Of course you did, darling."

"Hughie! Stop that!" She tried to sound stern and forceful. Maybe she could shock him out of it.

His hands tightened on the wheel, and his eyes were on her with the beginnings of wildness in them. "And I thought I could trust you! I thought you were like Estelle!"

She could only stare in terror then. The name itself seemed to do something to him, to goad him beyond reason. Tendons stood out in his throat, and muscles writhed along his arms and shoulders as he tried to pull the wheel loose, or shake it. He cried out as though something were tearing inside him, and began to shout, leaning toward her across the wheel. She could feel the drops of spittle on her arm.

"*They murdered her!* They tried to kill us both! And you want to take me back there, don't you, so they can finish the job? Oh, I know what you're trying to do!" He half rose from the seat, as if to come out from behind the wheel.

Trying to stop him with the marlinspike would be suicide. She'd only hit him on an upraised arm, and then he'd take it away from her. If she ran, it would almost certainly trigger pursuit, and he could catch her before she could make it to the forward cabin. She did the only thing that was left. She sat still, forcing herself not even to draw back from him. For a second that seemed to go on forever it hung there, and then he dropped back to the seat again.

"*They* did it!" he shrieked. "They did it!" He was staring straight in front of him, and she sensed that he had forgotten her. His lips continued to move, but he made no further sound, and a muscle kicked spasmodically under one eye.

She never knew how afterward, but she forced herself to remain seated for another thirty seconds. Then she stood up slowly and with exaggerated casualness, on legs that trembled and had to be locked at the knees to support her. He paid no attention. She stepped back into the hatchway and started down, still clasping the marlinspike under her arm. At the bottom her legs quit on her at last, but she made it to one of the bunks before she collapsed. She turned then and looked back at the hatch. Sunlight fell into it unobstructed, sweeping back and forth across the ladder treads as *Saracen* rolled. The clatter of the engine went on, and above it she could either hear or feel the pounding of her heart.

It was the starboard bunk she was on—her own, where John came to her when they made love. Above it was the radiotelephone that was powerless to reach him, its very silence a cry for help. And under it in one of the drawers was the shotgun. She had remembered it too easily this time. Her mind slipped away from it with the same revulsion, but she could still see it. She pushed herself off the bunk and ran on into the forward cabin and bolted the door.

It was 11:10 A.M. She raised her eyes from the watch and swept them around the tiny V-shaped compartment that was no longer a sanctuary or a haven but a corner. It even looked like one.

II

THERE WERE two choices, and she had seven hours in which to make up her mind. But both choices were impossible, and nobody could endure this for seven hours.

What happened then?

She could foresee the answer, but she went over it again, just to be sure. Her mind was operating quite coldly at the moment, and she was calm; she was stronger than she'd thought. But then this was only the beginning, and the show hadn't even started yet. She knew what was coming.

She could kill Warriner with the shotgun, or she could go off and leave John to drown. Since neither of these was even conceivable, she had the third, which wasn't an alternative choice but merely a statement of fact or at least of probable truth. Nobody could endure this for seven hours. Her nerves would crack. Sometime between now and sunset her whole nervous system would go up in a puff of smoke like a short-circuited pinball machine; bells would ring, lights would flash, and she'd wind up lying on the bunk staring blankly at nothing while she picked at the fuzz on the blankets. In which case, alternative number two would win by default, and John would drown anyway.

Was that all?

No. There was still one other possibility. At the moment her nerves snapped she might run out and attack Warriner with the marlinspike or with her bare hands. The result of that was foregone.

Then she had to kill Warriner, and she had to do it before just thinking of it drove her out of her mind.

No. She sat down on one of the sailbags with her hands pressed against her temples. Nothing in life could ever be reduced to as simple terms as that. There had to be some other way out of the corner.

Well, where was it? Try them all again.

Hit him with something? He was suspicious of her now, and she couldn't get behind him. And again you ran into the same old limiting factor; you'd get only one blow, and if that didn't work you were dead, and so was John.

Try once more to reason with him? After what had just happened? You could carry on long conversations with him on any subject in the world, except one. At the mere mention of going back, he retreated into his madness and pulled up the bridge.

Well, maybe John wouldn't drown; maybe *Orpheus* wasn't sinking. That there was no way of proving definitely, one way or the other, but she had the evidence of her own eyes that there was water in the boat, lots of water. And why didn't the radio work? Then she thought of something else. The engine didn't work either, or John would have followed them. So everything below was flooded. Even if it weren't in danger of sinking within the next few hours, John would never make port in it. Nobody could pump continuously for twenty days or more. Warriner said there were others aboard, but they hadn't been on deck, and they would have been. So either they didn't exist except in his madness, or they were hurt or already dead.

But at least she could try the radio again. She slid back the bolt and went out, carrying the marlinspike. If he started down the ladder she could throw it at his legs to be sure of getting back in time. She called and listened alternately on both the intership frequencies. There was no answer, no sound except the eternal crackling of the static. At the end of twenty minutes she knew she no longer had any hope of one, that she was only putting off the thing she had to face. She switched it off and went back. Very carefully and precisely she noted the heading on the compass and wrote it down on the scratch pad along with the time.

11:40 AM 226 degrees

It looked neat and businesslike. And there was the illusion she was doing something.

They hit her then from opposite sides, or rather she ran headlong into the second while she was recoiling from the first. The first, of course, was John. He was in the water, drowning, as the sun went down. She leaned forward with her face pressed against the scratch pad on her knees, her eyes tightly closed and then opened again because it was more clearly seen and more terrible with them closed. Then it was gone, as if an automatic projector were changing slides, and she saw the thing that would be there in the cockpit when the shotgun had done its work.

She'd never in her life shot anything with a gun of any kind, but her father and two older brothers had been hunters of quail, and inevitably she had seen a few examples of the mess that resulted when a bird was shot too close under the gun. She had no illusions as to what would be up there. She swallowed, fighting the nausea pushing up into her throat.

Seven hours?

Maybe she could merely frighten him with the gun, point it at him the way they did on television, and say, "All right, Hughie, turn around and go back." This, she knew in her heart, was idiocy comparable to that other cliché of the private eyes and western marshals, the immaculate and neatly packaged death by gunshot wound that never hurt, either the shooter or the shot, but she gathered it to her for a moment in the desperation of her need for some other way out of the corner. Granted there didn't seem to be much likelihood of scaring a man who was already insane from fear, you could at least examine it and try to figure out what would happen.

You had to assume two things, she thought. The first was that Hughie was capable of evaluating two different fears and making a conscious choice of the lesser. Could he? Probably, at least part of the time, but at any specific moment it would be as unpredictable as tossing a coin. The second was that a quaking matron with a gun would be more fearsome than the irrational horror that had already taken possession of his mind. No. Certainly not. The things in the darkness beyond the firelight were always more terrible than the ones that you could see. He'd either pay no attention to the gun at all, or at the mere mention of going back he'd go berserk and charge straight at her.

But it was still worth trying, wasn't it? Even if there was only one chance in a thousand she could bluff him into going back and could control him all the way there without actually having to shoot, at least there would be that one. No. She saw the stupidity of it. Trying to bluff a man she couldn't bluff, with a gun she hoped she wouldn't have to use, was nothing short of suicide. In that second when she was still hysterically voicing threats and praying he would stop before she had to shoot, it would be too late to shoot, even if she could, and he'd have the gun away from her and he'd kill her. If she took it up that ladder at all and committed herself, it had to be with the hundred-per-cent certainty she was prepared to use it. And that she didn't have.

Why not? It was Warriner, wasn't it, who'd backed her into this corner from which there was no other exit?

Legally there was no question of her right to do so. There would be a hearing, somewhere and sometime, at which she would have to testify as to the circumstances, but that was all. She wouldn't be charged with anything, and nobody would attach any blame to her. Then it was simply because of all those nights she'd wake up screaming, and the fact that until the day she died her mind would never emerge completely from the shadow of that unanswered question: could there have been some other way?

So in the end it boiled down to a simple act of purchase, didn't it? If she had no illusions about the price or about the fact she would have to pay it, the terms were clear and understood. For John's life she gave up her peace of mind for the rest of her own. Why not? People gave up their lives themselves for others, didn't they? This was the opposite of heroic, and the act itself was abhorrent, but the same love was involved, the same willingness to pay.

She realized then there was no sense to any of these arguments. You couldn't rationalize killing a man with a shotgun, and you didn't arrive at the deed by any process of thought, of weighing the advantages and disadvantages. If you did it at all, it was after you'd quit thinking, in desperation, when nothing else was left.

And, anyway, she probably couldn't even assemble the gun. John had never done it since it had been aboard, and it had been nearly twenty years since she'd seen her father do it. And it could be a different kind, or a later model. Guns must change over the years, the way cars did, didn't they? Of course they did.

But there were only two pieces.

No, it was just her impression there were only two pieces. There might be more. She'd never counted them, had she?

Well, if she found out she couldn't assemble it, that would settle it, and the torture would stop.

Then, without even knowing how she'd got there, she was kneeling beside the bunk in the after cabin, pulling out the drawer. There were only two rolls of the fleece, one long one and another shorter and bulkier. She ran back into the forward cabin with them and bolted the door. She put them on the bunk and begun untying the cords that bound them.

There were three pieces.

The long roll contained only the barrels, the twin dark tubes fixed side by side, but the other held two pieces. One was the part that went against your shoulder—the stock, she thought it was called—with the lever for breaking it open to put in the shells, and the trigger guard and the triggers. The other piece was a hand-grip sort of thing she seemed to remember went under the barrels just in front of the stock. It was mostly of wood, rounded on the sides and bottom, tapering at one end and fitted with a concave piece of steel at the other. She had no idea how it was supposed to be attached to the barrels.

The barrels themselves had a projection at one end, on the bottom, that must fit into something in the metal part at the front end of the stock. She took them in one hand and the stock in the other and began trying to match them. Yes, there it was. They went together, and formed a hinge. She swung the barrels up, and they locked in place.

But there was still the third part.

And it was obvious it was the wrong piece for this kind of gun, or that something was missing. It was supposed to go under the barrels, right there, and there was nothing to hold it. The concave end must go against the rounded metal end there at the front of the stock. And you could see it didn't even fit; it still stuck out at a slight angle. Well, John must have ordered another one to be shipped to them in Papeete. And since the gun couldn't be assembled without the right piece— There was a little click, and she gasped. The fore end had snapped up into place against the spring tension that held it there.

She stared at it in horror. It was a complete shotgun. It was all there, and it was assembled.

For the third time in ten minutes Lillian Warriner saw Ingram glance off to the northeast where the squall flickered and rumbled along the rim of the world. She could see no appreciable difference in the squall itself. It was still the same swollen mass of purple, shot through with the fitful play of lightning and trailing its skirts of rain, seemingly no larger or nearer than it had been a quarter of an hour ago—but it was Ingram himself she was watching. She judged by the simple fact that he kept looking at it that he was worried about it, though he said nothing. He continued to bail, the gray eyes expressionless.

Well, it wasn't likely he'd be running in circles and wringing his hands. And there was nothing they could do about the squall anyway, except get the sail off, and probably he'd send her to wake Bellew. No doubt there was some quixotic male convention against allowing the porcine bastard to drown in his sleep.

She liked Ingram and was conscious of increasing admiration for him, though this of course only added to the burden of her guilt, while at the same time evoking a mild sort of wonder at her willingness to credit her appraisal of anybody any more after having been so conspicuously wrong about Bellew. No, it wasn't so much that she'd been wrong as that she'd simply had no way of knowing how small even a large yacht could become after a few days at sea. Human beings confined in too small an area were apparently subject to the same laws regarding molecular friction and the generation of heat as gases under compression.

So now not only had they managed to blow themselves up, but the spreading shock wave of disaster had engulfed two other people whose only crime had been the fact they were in the same part of the ocean. The guilt was still hers, and she accepted it, though it seemed a terrible price to pay for the pursuit of an impossible dream, a few minutes of arrant and unforgivable bitchiness, and an accident. There were beckoning avenues of escape: the accident couldn't have been her fault because she'd been asleep at the time, and she'd been goaded into the bitchiness, but these were sleazy evasions and technicalities for which she had nothing but contempt. They were the type of thing that Hughie— She stopped.

Well, it was true, wasn't it? And therein, unfortunately, lay her guilt, the real responsibility from which there would never be any escape—the pursuit of the impossible dream, while she knew it was impossible. She'd known it would never work, that temperamentally she was wrong for him and she'd demand too much of him, but she'd managed to ignore the warnings of her mind.

If only, she thought now in her own contained and private agony, she'd left him alone. She was worse than any of them; she'd utterly destroyed him. Because she did love him. She wondered what crimes the human race could have found to commit without those great ennobling causes like freedom, religion, and love.

She glanced up. Ingram had stopped bailing and was preparing to lower the mainsail. She looked out toward the squall still making up in the northeast. "Is it coming nearer?"

"I can't tell yet what it's going to do," he replied. "But there's no use letting the sails slat any longer."

"Do you want me to help?"

"No. Better keep pumping. Or just rest for a few minutes."

She was conscious of numbness in her arms and shoulders, but she shook her head. "No. I'm all right." She bent to the pump again.

If only she'd left him alone. . . .

The main and mizzen were tightly furled. Ingram finished lashing the genoa rolled up along the lifeline and looked at his watch. It was 3:50 P.M. The sun, though lower in the west, still beat on them with sullen weight in the sticky and unmoving air that felt as if you were trying to breathe in a vacuum. The day was a squall-breeder if he'd ever seen one. There was no sound except water going overboard from the pump and those other and inexorably increasing tons of it sloshing back and forth inside the hull as *Orpheus* lurched over on the swell. The whole northeast sky was black now, but then squalls always looked worse when they were opposite the sun. There was still a chance it would pass to the northward of them, and he didn't want to call Bellew. Not yet. Let him get all the sleep he could. There was a long night ahead of them—if they were still afloat.

He was conscious now of his own tiredness and of the fact he had eaten nothing since breakfast. But he wasn't hungry; it was too hot to eat, even if there was anything aboard not ruined by the water. He picked up the binoculars and climbed atop the deckhouse. Very slowly and carefully he searched the horizon all across the southwest, finding nothing but emptiness. When he lowered the glasses he saw Mrs. Warriner's eyes on him. He shook his head. She nodded, her face as expressionless as his own, and went on pumping.

He stepped back to the ventilating hatch and looked down at the water washing back and forth in the after cabin. It was worse, he thought; even with one of them pumping and one bailing, they were barely keeping up with it. He started to drop the bucket in but turned and glanced back at Mrs. Warriner. She was on the verge of collapse. The hell with it. There was no use letting her kill herself. He tossed the bucket on the deck, then went over and picked up her cigarettes and lighter from the deckhouse.

"Here," he said. He set one of the cigarettes between her lips and flicked the lighter. "Let me take it for a while."

She surrendered the pump reluctantly. "But how about yourself? You haven't had any rest at all. And won't it gain?"

"It'll just have to gain. You're not going to help things by keeling over. And while you're resting, you could finish telling me what happened—that is, if you feel up to it."

She sat down on the deck, facing him. "It's not the pleasantest thing in the world to tell, but since we did this to you, I'd say you had every right to know *how* we did it." She took a puff on the cigarette and went on. "To understand why he thinks we tried to murder him, you need a little background and a thumbnail sketch of the characters involved. Hughie, as I've told you, was an oversheltered boy who never had a chance to grow up; Mrs. Bellew was a rather plain, very gentle woman with an infinite amount of compassion; Bellew, of course, is a pig; and I'm an arrogant and insufferable bitch."

Ingram paused in his pumping. "Do you have to do that?"

She wondered herself. She'd always held a dim view of the therapeutic value of catharsis or confession and regarded all breast-beating and cries of *mea culpa* as being more vulgar exhibitionism than anything else. If you'd bought it, you lived with it as well as you could and with as little fuss as possible. But on the other hand, if you'd wronged another human being, you at least owed him an explanation.

"You wanted to understand, didn't you?" she asked curtly. "I've never been greatly addicted to the use of euphemisms and evasions, and if I thought you were responsible for something I wouldn't hesitate to tell you. To be any good, it has to work both ways."

"I know. But aside from the fact I don't think it's true—"

"Thank you. You *are* nice, Mr. Ingram. But you haven't heard the story."

"No." He resumed pumping. "But there's more to it than his thinking you tried to kill him. Why is he so afraid of water?"

"Because he thinks that's the *way* we tried to kill him, by drowning—"

He shook his head. "No. It's still not that simple." He told her briefly of Rae's throwing the whisky bottle overboard and of Warriner's reaction to watching it sink.

She nodded. "Yes. I know about that part of it." She was silent for a moment, thinking. "I'm not sure I can explain it myself, except that I think it's a fear of drowning carried to the point of phobia. You know what acrophobia is, of course?"

"Yes. A morbid fear of heights. But it has nothing to do with water."

"I know. But in his case I think it does." She nodded toward the sea around them. "When you look out there you see nothing but the surface. So do I; so does everybody. We realize vaguely that two miles down there's a bottom, but we never think of it, even if we're swimming in it—probably even if we're in trouble in it. It makes no difference whether you drown in seven feet of water, or seven miles; you still drown within a few feet of the surface. But you're *in* the water; I think he imagines himself rather precariously suspended on the surface of it, as if it were a film of some kind, ten thousand feet above the bottom. In other words, I get the impression he sees it all the way down. Hence, acrophobia. As I say, I'm only guessing, but how else can you account for that horror when he sees something sinking below him? To him, it's not sinking; it's *falling*. And, like all people with acrophobia, he imagines himself falling with it."

Ingram nodded, though still not convinced she was right. "But he wasn't always like that?"

"Oh, no. He was an excellent swimmer. And skin-diver. It's simply because of what we did to him ten days ago. But you have to understand what happened before, and what the situation was. Explosive is a good one-word description. To begin with, not one of us was competent to take a yacht across the Pacific, and incompetence multiplied by any number up to infinity is still incompetence. Four people who don't know what they're doing—"

"Are simply four times worse than one," Ingram said. "So nobody was in charge?"

"No. Not after things started to fall apart. Hughie, as legal owner of the yacht and the only one with any sailing experience at all, should have been in command, but you can't force a man to command, to fight back, to accept responsibility, if the only responsibility he's ever had in his life was to be acceptable and pleasing to a succession of overprotective women who took care of him. And if you happen to be in love with him and have to stand there helplessly day after day and watch this disintegration under pressure, this thing you can't do anything about, eventually your own frustration may goad you into doing something stupid and cruel and unforgivable. But I didn't intend to make excuses, and I'm getting ahead of the story anyway."

12

"HUGHIE," SHE WENT ON, "has always been obsessed by a feeling for the greatness of Gauguin, and it's been a lifelong ambition of his to go to Polynesia and live among the islands as he did, escape from the rat race the same way, paint the same subjects, experience the same things. So, when we were married in Europe almost a year ago, I let myself be persuaded, in spite of the fact I had some misgivings about it. In the first place, there's no escape from our so-called civilization any more; the twentieth century is something we're locked into and there's no way we can get out; when we got to Papeete we'd probably find the same jukeboxes, the same headlines, the same cocktail parties, the same jet service from here to there, the same Bomb, and the same exhortations to embrace the finer life by buying something. And in the second place, I was more than a little doubtful of our ability to sail a boat down there. But at heart I wanted to be persuaded, and I was. From my point of view there were several things in favor of it. No doubt you can guess what some of them were, but in the interests of clarity they might as well be included in this confession. I'm considerably older than Hughie, and when I met him I was a widow, a fairly wealthy one. You know what he looks like. The picture is trite to the point of banality, except that in this case it's not true at all. He's no glorified beachboy, and we were genuinely in love with each other. And while I bleed very little over the opinions of other people, I didn't want him regarded as something he wasn't—at least, not yet, by the grace of God. I have a small but very good collection of paintings, and I know the work of talent when I see it. I wanted to help him, and in Hughie's case one way of helping him—and me—was to keep him out of the reach of all that gaggle of *soi-disant* benefactresses and panting patrons of the arts who couldn't keep their hands off him."

She broke off with an impatient gesture and then went on. "But enough of that. Hughie bought and studied all the books he could find on yachting and navigation. We chartered a yacht, with a professional crew of two, for a cruise in the western Mediterranean, from Cannes down to the Balearics, to learn as much as we could from practical experience. We came back to the States last winter, bought *Orpheus*, and began getting ready."

She smiled musingly. "Then I think we were betrayed. No doubt you remember the old ploy of crooked gamblers, letting the sheep, the intended victim, win the first few hands in order to increase the stakes. It was as if the Pacific Ocean, or fate, did it deliberately. The passage from Santa Barbara down to La Paz was ridiculously easy. Nothing went wrong at all. The weather was perfect, Hughie's navigation was seemingly accurate enough, the couple with us, who were old friends of mine from San Francisco, were congenial, and we were never at sea long enough for the confinement and too close association to cause any friction, because we made stops at San Diego and Ensenada. If anything had gone wrong in that first leg of the trip we would have been brought face to face with our own inexperience and incompetence, and we'd have had sense enough to give it up. But nothing did, and we were far too overconfident and cocky by the time we reached La Paz.

"Then the other couple had to abandon the trip there and go back to San Francisco because of illness. We lay at anchor in the harbor for nearly three months."

"Were you living aboard all the time?" Ingram asked.

"No. We came back to California, by plane, for several weeks, and part of the time we lived ashore at a hotel. Why?"

"I think that's when the dry rot began to run wild. *Orpheus* may have still been sound enough to make it to Papeete when you left Santa Barbara, but after three months of lying there in La Paz, probably with no ventilation below, she was eaten up with it by the time you sailed."

She nodded. "At any rate, we were stranded. *Orpheus* was too large for two people to handle, even if we'd dared attempt it alone. None of my friends who would have liked to go could get away. We wrote to the yacht broker who'd sold us the boat, and he managed to locate a professional willing to make the trip, a man named Grover or Glover, who turned out to be utterly impossible. He arrived on the plane from Tijuana dead drunk, and somehow managed to stay that way the five days he was in La Paz, without, as far as we could discover, ever taking a drink. And while it might have been interesting from a medical point of view to see if he could stay bagged all the way across the Pacific with no visible intake of alcohol, as a yacht captain he was hopeless. We paid him off and decanted him into the Tijuana plane. So we were on the point of selling *Orpheus* and flying to Papeete to buy another boat there where we could hire an Island crew, when we met the Bellews at the little hotel ashore. Bellew was gathering material for an article on big-game fishing in the Gulf of California, and we became quite friendly in the two weeks they were there. We asked them to make the trip with us."

It was a tragic mistake, but one that had been very easy to make. It was banal to say that Bellew had seemed different ashore, but in the end that was what it amounted to. She supposed they all had, for that matter. Bellew was a man it was easy to get along with sitting around a café table sipping tall iced drinks in a backwater fishing port as limited in other diversions and other friends as La Paz. He'd led an intense and active outdoor life and had a great fund of entertaining stories which he told exceedingly well and with only a little suggestion of boasting. He played the guitar and sang folk songs in the manner of Burl Ives, and he and Hughie, who also sang very well, had two or three times put on highly successful impromptu shows for the other patrons of the hotel. He was big and outgoing and, if a little loud at times, not offensively so, and there was a male competence and assurance about him she'd instinctively trusted because they somehow reminded her of her first husband. It would take more trying circumstances than sitting in cafés or fishing for marlin with him to bring up the other side of the coin, the cruelty and the contempt for any kind of weakness.

Perhaps, on the other hand, Bellew could feel with some justification that he'd been fooled too. He'd claimed no experience with the sea except that highly specialized business of big-game fishing, in power cruisers and usually very near to land, while Hughie, emboldened by the complete success of the trip down the coast from Santa Barbara, had perhaps sounded a little too salty and seagoing, sitting around the drinks.

And she'd liked Estelle Bellew—at least at first. Estelle was a rather shy and only moderately attractive woman of around forty, who was completely wrapped up in her photography and had no apparent designs on Hughie. This turned out to be another mistake, of course. While she didn't have any amatory interest in him—then or later—she did have a great reservoir of unexpended gentleness and compassion she'd never had any occasion to use, living with this hairy and domineering bastard she was married to, and she was possessed of an equally frustrated mother instinct that Hughie brought out in full, especially after it became apparent how badly Hughie needed a mother or somebody to protect him from the Pacific Ocean and from Bellew's abrasive contempt.

"Why did he want to make the trip?" Ingram asked. "Bellew, I mean."

"I don't even know who first suggested it," she replied. "It was just one of those ideas that can burst on the scene fully grown when four people are sitting in a bar with their second or third round of drinks. It was about ten days after we'd met them, and we'd just come in from a day's fishing as his guests on the boat he'd chartered. He already had all the material for the story he was doing on the fishing at La Paz and was sure he could get a story, or perhaps two, out of the trip. I told him we would be glad to pay their air transportation back from Papeete. And, after all, it would only take a month." She smiled bitterly. "We sailed from La Paz twenty-six days ago."

Before they were more than a week out, everything began to go wrong. They blew out a sail in a squall and lost another overboard. Leaks began to show up from opened deck seams so that when they were shipping any water aboard everything below was soaked. They missed Clipperton Island because something had apparently slipped up in Hughie's navigation. They used up most of their fuel trying to beat their way back to it, which was ridiculous, since it was uninhabited anyway, but by now they were no longer acting rationally but only motivated by their endless quarrels. They gave up trying to find the island after it failed a second and third time to appear where Hughie said it was. *Orpheus* began to leak alarmingly, so it took more pumping every day to keep the water out of the cabins.

But beyond all that, it was the old story of clashing personalities jammed into too small a space with nowhere to go to avoid each other. Bellew became caustic, loud-mouthed, and finally insufferable, openly contemptuous of Hughie's mistakes in navigation and seamanship, while Hughie, instead of fighting back, retreated into sullenness and pouting. Estelle Bellew was sympathetic and tried to shield him from her husband. Lillian herself lashed out at Bellew in defense of Hughie—or she did at first, until she decided that wasn't the answer—but at the same time it was lacerating to have to admit to herself that he even needed defending against another man. Some of her hurt and resentment must have showed, for Hughie began turning increasingly to Estelle rather than to her for comfort when he backed down from Bellew. And Estelle tried increasingly to help him, as though he were a boy, and alone.

"That in itself was infuriating," she went on. "The implication was that I was some species of heartless monster who had no sympathy, no feeling for him at all. She had the best intentions in the world, but she simply couldn't seem to understand that that was the trouble in the first place, that he'd never in his life had to accept the responsibility for his own actions or fight for his rights, because there was always some woman panting to shield him from the one and buy him the other. And she was simply doing it again. I was trying to help him in the only way he could be helped—or that I *hoped* he could be helped—by letting him work it out for himself, no matter how I cringed and wanted to go somewhere and cry when he simply retreated into petulance in the face of Bellew's contempt, or no matter how much easier it would have been to set him behind me and then remove Bellew's skin in strips. So I began to treat her—Estelle—with the same insufferable nastiness that Bellew treated Hughie.

"In the end I couldn't stand it any longer—the helplessness of it, I mean—watching Hughie being browbeaten without the spirit to fight back, and not being able to do anything in the world about it except drive him more and more to some other woman for sympathy. I hated both of them, and I hated myself. I blew up. I did the one thing that was guaranteed to hurt everybody. I made an open, deliberate pass at Bellew."

"Well, it's been done before," Ingram said.

"But seldom by people who are assumed to be adult. And seldom with consequences as tragic. It happened one night just at the end of the second week."

It was shortly after dinner and they were all on deck. She was at the wheel, having relieved Hughie just at dusk so he could take a series of star sights while he could still see the horizon. Bellew was sprawled in the cockpit beyond her, while Estelle was sitting alone on the forward end of the deckhouse, looking at the fading afterglow of sunset. Hughie's star sights didn't work out. He'd got three of them, with three lines of position several hundred miles apart, none of which crossed, or were anywhere near the dead-reckoning position based on the equally dubious fix he'd got at noon. Either his figures were wrong or he'd mistaken his stars. A long time went by while he checked and rechecked his work. Then he came out on deck with a star chart, but in the meantime the moon had risen and the stars were fading and hard to distinguish. And Bellew started on him again. Her flesh crawled.

"How's it look, Magellan? We still seem to be in the same ocean?"

Hughie made no reply. He went on futilely trying to match up at least one of the stars with his chart. Her heart ached for him. She wished she could help him. And why, oh why, in the name of God, didn't he turn on the badgering and idiotic *salaud* and tell him to shut up?

"I'll tell you what, Commodore," Bellew went on, "if it turns out we're anywhere near Greeley, Colorado, I got a friend runs a bar there. . . ."

She closed her eyes. Do *something*, Hughie!

He did. Like a sullen child, he threw the star chart on the deck. "Hughie," she called out quickly, trying to save him from utter shame, "let me try. Maybe I could help—" But without even a glance at her he'd already turned and gone forward to Estelle. She could see the two of them sitting close together in the light of the rising moon. She'd bitten her lip to keep from crying, and she could taste blood in her mouth. Then out of some dark and insensate desire to wound them all, herself included, she said to Bellew, "We don't seem to be entirely necessary, do we? But it is a beautiful night, and if you'd like help with some of *your* problems, why don't you bring up a couple of drinks?"

The others had seen, all right—at least the merged silhouette against the moon—and heard the laughter and the singing.

One of them was dead now, and the other was mad, at least partly as the result of it, so she was the only one left—besides Bellew, of course—with any true and rational appreciation of the scene as something to be treasured forever. It had taken perhaps fifteen minutes to sicken herself to the point where she had to go below or jump overboard. She removed the repulsive hand from inside her bra, got up, leaving the wheel untended, and went down to the cabin and locked the door. Hughie never came down at all. Apparently he'd slept on deck.

She went on in a minute. "So there you have the situation. We had everything we needed now for disaster, or for something very messy, but when it came, two days later, it was only an accident.

"I'll try to give it to you in chronological sequence, as we reconstructed it afterward, though it concerned four people in different places, I was asleep through a good part of it, and at the end only two of us were still alive and able to give a coherent account of what had happened. It was two P.M., and we'd been lying becalmed for over an hour, with all sail still set, but the booms sheeted in to keep them from banging. It was Bellew's wheel watch, and he was sitting in the cockpit, keeping an eye out for signs of a breeze. Estelle Bellew was lying in her bunk in the forward cabin, reading, I think, and Hughie and I were in our cabin aft. I was pretending to be asleep; that way we had at least the semblance of an excuse for the fact we weren't speaking to each other. Hughie went out.

"He came on deck. Bellew, of course, was in the cockpit. Neither of them spoke. Hughie went over to the rail and was looking down into the water when he saw the school of dolphin which had been following the boat and playing around under it for the past two days. These are dolphin, the fish, you understand, and not porpoises."

Ingram nodded. "Very beautiful fish, like flame under water. The Mexicans call them *dorado*—golden, or gilded. They like to lie under anything floating on the surface."

"They're the ones. Anyway, while he was looking at them he remembered that Estelle had said she'd like to see if she could photograph them from below the surface if the school was ever around when we were becalmed. So, still without speaking to Bellew, he went back below. Only, when he passed through the deckhouse, he went forward first into the main cabin—that is, the saloon—and called out to Estelle through the curtained passage at the forward end of it, telling her about the fish. She was eager to try to photograph them, so she said she'd put on a swim suit and meet him on deck. Bellew, still aft in the cockpit, heard none of this, of course. Hughie then went back up into the deckhouse and on down into our cabin to put on his swim trunks and get a diving mask and snorkel. But I didn't know it, because by this time I *was* asleep.

"Hughie was below probably only a few minutes, but when he came back up through the deckhouse and stepped on deck Bellew was no longer there. He'd gone below, into the main cabin, to make a sandwich. This, of course, is forward, toward the Bellews' cabin, so—since the two of them hadn't met in the deckhouse—Bellew had no idea Hughie had returned to the deck. Fortunately, you know the layout below, and you can understand why we had to reconstruct this whole thing afterward to try to understand how it could have happened."

Ingram nodded. He could see the tragedy already beginning to take form, like the choreography of some death scene in a ballet, where every movement had to fit.

She went on. "In another minute or two Estelle came on deck from the forward hatch, the one leading up directly from their cabin. She had on her swim suit and was carrying a snorkel and mask and an underwater camera. That is, it wasn't really an underwater camera with a housing, but one of her thirty-five-millimeter cameras that she'd made a watertight bag for with some kind of clear plastic and carried slung around her neck on a cord. Hughie put the ladder over just forward of amidships, and they eased down it into the water—not jumping or diving in because they didn't want to frighten the dolphin.

"It was a rule, of course, since all of us did swim when we had the chance, that nobody should ever go in the water without notifying whoever was on watch. But Hughie apparently thought, since Bellew was gone from the deck, that he was forward in his own cabin and that Estelle had told him before she came up. And Estelle, since Hughie had been the one who'd brought up the whole thing, must have assumed that Hughie had notified him. She hadn't even seen Bellew, because he was in the main cabin. So they put on their masks and snorkels and began trying to get close to the school of fish, which was now moving away from the boat. There was a moderate groundswell running, so even when Bellew came back on deck he probably wouldn't have seen them unless he'd happened to be looking in their direction at the moment they rose to the top or the near side of a swell.

"Hughie has never been completely rational since, and when I saw him again, six hours later he was raving and incoherent, but as well as I could piece it together they'd been in the water about ten minutes and were not over a hundred yards from the boat when it happened. They were fairly close to the dolphin and they'd both dived, Hughie just looking at them while Estelle tried to snap a picture. Hughie came up first, and when his head was above water he was aware that something had changed. It was a second or two before he realized what it was. A breeze was blowing across his face. He turned and looked toward *Orpheus* and screamed. But Bellew didn't hear him.

"As I said, this was at two P.M. I awoke a little after three-thirty and could tell from the angle of heel and the lessened rolling that we'd picked up a breeze while I was asleep and were under way. I noticed Hughie wasn't in his bunk, but paid no attention to it. In a few minutes I got up, dressed, washed my face, and went up through the deckhouse to the main cabin to brew a cup of tea. It was ten minutes of four when I carried it out on deck. Bellew was at the wheel, of course. We were on the starboard tack and probably making around two knots in a breeze that didn't much more than fill the sails.

"Bellew merely grunted when I sat down in the cockpit, but in a minute he said, 'Did you call the great Magellan? Or are you going to take his watch?'

"That was the first second it dawned on me I hadn't seen him anywhere. I jumped up, spilling the tea, and ran below, and I was all the way down in the main cabin before I realized that if he *had* gone to that woman's cabin, if he'd been silly enough to go in there with her husband on deck, I'd already given it away and Bellew would probably beat him to death. I spoke outside the curtain. There was no answer, so I pulled it back. The cabin was empty. I pounded on the door of the washroom and opened it. There was no one in it, nor in the one aft."

She was whimpering and numb with terror by the time she made it back to the deck and saw the ladder hanging over the side. Bellew already had the wheel hard over, and *Orpheus* was coming ponderously about.

She had got her voice back at last and was shrieking at him as she set up the weather runner and trimmed the jib sheet. "*When? How long ago?* You blind, stupid, forgetful fool, you've killed them!"

"Shut up!" Bellew ordered curtly. "They didn't tell me."

"Well, you must have seen them! You were supposed to be on deck!" She broke off then, realizing at last that they were wasting precious seconds on this idiocy when there was so much to be done. They had to figure out the reciprocal of the course he'd been making and estimate the distance they'd come since the breeze sprang up. And none of it was easy. The wind had been erratic, and he'd had to tack twice when it headed him. Their speed had varied from an estimated less than one knot to an estimated three and a half. None of it had been written down because he'd intended to write a rough average of it in the log when he was relieved. She took the wheel, heading back in the approximate direction, while he struggled with the figures. In around ten minutes he had it calculated as closely as they ever would—somewhere to the east-northeast, four to five miles.

She began to hope again. It was only two hours, and they were both good swimmers. Hughie, she knew, could stay afloat four hours easily, and they would have been swimming this way—no, he couldn't even see the masts at this distance, not down in the water. But for at least half the time he would have been able to see them, anyway each time he came to the top of a swell. It was still three hours and more till dark, and she'd get Bellew to hoist her to the top of the mainmast in a bosun's chair. They'd get there in time. Then the breeze began to falter. It came on again for three or four minutes, dropped once more, and then died completely.

They couldn't run the engine. They'd already used up all the fuel. They lay helplessly in the trough and rolled.

They launched the dinghy. Bellew wanted to go because he could row faster, but she insisted. She was two hundred yards away before she realized she didn't have the faintest idea which direction she was going in. She came back and got a compass and set it between her feet, even though she knew it was hopeless looking for them in the dinghy. She was too low in the water to see anything or to be seen. She was far out from *Orpheus* when the sun went down and it began to grow dark. She stood up in the dinghy, calling his name until she could no longer see anything but the distant gleam of the masthead light Bellew had turned on. She rowed back and went aboard. She lay in the cabin in the darkness, trying not to think of what it must have been like to see the boat sailing away from him a thousand miles from land. Bellew came in and tried to speak to her. She didn't even know what he said. He went away, into the forward cabin.

About half an hour later she heard him run through the deckhouse on the way to the deck, shouting, "I heard something." She ran up. The spreader lights were on, as well as the masthead light, but they were glowing only faintly, scarcely brighter than candles, because the batteries were discharged. She ran back into the deckhouse for a flashlight. She began throwing its beam out across the water. Then she heard the sound too, a faint whimpering, but it was coming from aboard rather than from the water. She threw the light forward.

Hughie had come up the ladder and was lying at the foot of the mainmast, his arms locked around it, his face pressed against the wood. His shoulders shook, and he was still making that not quite human sound deep in his throat. She noticed, in that way you sometimes fix your attention on details in moments of overwhelming emotion, that there was a gaping and bluish cut, no longer bleeding, across the knuckles of his right hand. He was alone. Estelle hadn't come back.

"As weak as he was after six hours in the water," she went on, "it took both of us to pry his arms loose from the mast. We half led and half carried him below and put him on his bunk. He opened his eyes; at first they were completely blank, and then he began to recognize us. He cringed back and jumped off the bunk and cowered back in a corner, screaming at us. He was almost incoherent, but we could understand bits of what he was saying. We'd tried to kill him. We'd gone off and left him deliberately. I was only pretending to be asleep and knew he'd gone into the water. And there was something about a shark, over and over.

"In the end, Bellew had to hold him while I injected a sedative dose of morphine in his arm. He fought us, and when he felt the prick of the needle he screamed.

"He never let either of us come near him again. He slept, if he ever slept at all, in the sail locker up forward, with the door barricaded inside. He looked rational, at least most of the time, but he was silent and withdrawn. He would never approach the rail without that look of horror on his face and a death grip on something solid, like a man with acrophobia frozen to a girder a thousand feet above the street. When we'd try to question him about Estelle, he'd go all to pieces and begin shouting again about a shark. I made Bellew stop asking him. It was three days before I got a more or less coherent story of what had happened.

"They'd been attacked by a shark. He still had his mask on, and he swam down and hit it on the snout with his fist, trying to drive it away. That was the way he got that wound on his hand. It had avoided him because he was under the water, but had come up and gone for Estelle, who was threshing on the surface. It cut her in two. There was nothing he could do. He swam out of the bloody water and got away, but the sight of it was too much—that and the fear, and the belief we'd done it deliberately. He cracked up."

So Bellew was right, Ingram thought. He was on the point of asking if she believed the story herself, but realized the futility of it. If she did believe it, it was only because she refused to accept the truth. She, better than any of them, should know what Hughie was really running from, but if she had already made the choice and was determined to accept the blame, argument was useless, and there were more urgent things to think about at the moment. No doubt a psychiatrist could dig it out of her and force her to acknowledge it, but he wasn't a psychiatrist, they were on a sinking boat in mid-ocean, and nine-tenths of his mind was occupied with the cold and relentless struggle to keep the thought of Rae from swamping it. And, in the end, perhaps the specific act for which she blamed herself wasn't significant anyway. The guilt she accepted was the blanket indictment of having been the link at which the lengthening chain of Hughie-protection had finally snapped. She'd been minding the baby when it crawled into the goldfish pond and drowned.

It was possible, of course, that Hughie did think—or had managed to convince himself—that they'd deliberately gone off and left the two of them to die. And naturally he might have an irrational fear of water, after having been in it for six hours in mid-ocean, part of the time in the dark and thinking of the bottom ten thousand feet below him. But neither of these was the horror he was trying to escape, the thing he saw when something was sinking in the water below him. That was Estelle. The only part of it that was difficult to understand was what sick compulsion had kept him there, looking down through the mask at her body falling into the depths after he had killed her.

He'd seen the wound on Hughie's hand. And it wasn't an abrasion such as he'd have received from striking the sandpapery skin of a shark. It was a cut. It had been caused by human teeth, or the broken glass of a diving mask.

So Estelle had panicked and tried to climb up on him to get out of the water, the way the drowning often did. He'd beaten her off with his fists and knocked her out. And the ironic part of it was that, for anybody willing to accept at least a portion of the blame, there'd still have been a way out. Subduing the panicky person who was threatening to drown both himself and his rescuer was an accepted part of lifesaving. Somebody else might have convinced himself he'd hit her only to try to save her, so he could turn her on her back and tow her, and then she'd slipped away from him and drowned before he could get her back to the surface. But not Hughie, who couldn't accept any of the penalty for anything. He'd had to invent his nonexistent shark, which even he couldn't believe. But he *had* to believe it, and go on believing it, or face an unpleasant fact for the first time in his life. And, for a beginner, he'd been handed a rough one to face.

She must have still had the camera slung around her neck. Those 35 mm. jobs were heavy for their size, and with none of the built-in buoyancy from a standard underwater housing it must have been just enough to tip the scales beyond that state of near equilibrium of a woman's body in salt water—any woman except the very thin and muscular and heavy-boned—and keep her falling straight below him after she was unconscious. Even then, the rate of descent was probably very slow, at least until she was down to where the pressure began collapsing her chest cavity. And Hughie had watched her.

No, he thought then, not necessarily. Maybe he'd only imagined watching her; maybe it had already begun in his mind. At any rate, there was the horror, and there was the beginning of that awareness of depth, or of height, upon which he was impaled—seeing the body of this friend, this woman who'd been so good to him and whom he'd killed in panic to save his own life, slide into the ever-deepening abyss below him, still clearly visible at fifty feet, a hundred, maybe a hundred and fifty, and after she had dwindled and disappeared entirely he could go on imagining it—a thousand feet, five thousand, ten thousand, and still falling.

Jesus, he thought, I'm glad I'm carrying it around looking for a place to set it down.

He was aware then that *Orpheus*'s motion was changing. The groundswell was becoming confused as it encountered the mounting seas built up in the squall. He glanced out toward the dark turbulence of the sky in the northeast and the advancing wall of rain that was probably less than two miles away.

"Maybe you'd better call Bellew," he said.

13

WITHOUT ANY remembrance at all of how she'd got there she was standing on the companion ladder, looking out into blazing sunlight and the encircling blue of the sea. Ten feet in front of her the golden impervious head was poised above the binnacle, and she could hear herself shrieking through the clatter of the engine.

"*Go back!* For the love of God, go back before something awful happens! Don't make it happen, don't make it, *please don't make it!*" Her voice skidded up over the rim into hysteria and incoherence.

There was no reply. He glanced at her briefly and then back at the compass with something of the studied avoidance of a diner looking the other way after a waiter has dropped a tray of food, as though he was as disappointed in this uncouth screeching as he had been in her selfishness. Then, with no clear idea how she'd got there either, she was back in the forward cabin, holding onto the upright pipe of the bunk frame with one hand while she ran the fingers of the other across the side of her face and upward into her hair. Something was quivering, either her face or the hand, but she wasn't sure which, any more than she was sure whether she'd actually gone out there and screamed the warning at him or whether she'd just imagined it. No, she must have gone out, because the door was unlatched and open. She could hear it banging behind her as *Saracen* rolled.

The shotgun still lay on the bunk where she'd dropped it, the three separate, improbable pieces suddenly united and frozen into this unmistakable shape of deadliness. She jerked her eyes away from it and looked at her watch, and then a second time in disbelief. It was 12:45 P.M. Time was hurtling past her, and she was beginning to lose whole intervals of it. They were already twenty miles from that sinking boat, and by sunset, when they'd be over fifty, she would have cracked completely. Her chin still quivering, she looked around the tiny compartment again, seeing for the twentieth time only the walls of the trap, this corner she'd been backed into and from which there was no escape except one. She'd tried everything else, and it was hopeless. He was impregnable, unreachable—

Then, with the suddenness of a thrown switch, the wildness and despair were gone, and she was strangely calm. It was as if her mind had come into focus at last, with everything else dropping away until there remained only the two simple, elemental facts she'd been groping for all the time, the only two that mattered at all. John was going to die unless she saved him. And she had the means to do it.

At first she thought the engine had stopped, it had grown so quiet. But when she listened, she could still hear it; it was just farther away, and there was a faint rushing or ringing sound inside her head, as if she had been taking quinine. It was like being enclosed in some huge bubble that protected her from all extraneous sound or thought or interference. It was cold inside the bubble, and there didn't seem to be enough air, because her breathing was rapid and very shallow, but she was invulnerable to everything beyond. She went over and picked up the shotgun.

And this was strange too, with some feeling that she'd done it before and knew exactly what she had to do. It was as if, while her conscious mind was recoiling from it in revulsion, some far level of the unconscious had already accepted the gun with complete fatalism and calmly planned its use. She had to learn how it worked. She pointed it away from her and tried to pull the triggers. Nothing happened. But she'd expected that. Guns had safety mechanisms of some kind so they couldn't be fired accidentally. She began searching for the key to it, and found it immediately, since it was the only part of the weapon not already identified. It had to be this small oblong button just back of the lever that broke it open at the breech so you could put in the shells. She tried to push the button down, but nothing happened. Then it must slide. She pushed it forward, and it did, perhaps a quarter of an inch. She pulled the triggers and heard the clicks, one after the other, as hammers fell on the firing pins.

The shells. Still inviolate within her bubble of cold and unswerving concentration, she went out into the after cabin and knelt before the drawer. There were two boxes of them. Both had been wrapped in plastic and then covered with two or three coats of varnish to protect them from the humidity of the tropics. She'd need a knife. She was making a note of this and reaching over the medicine kit for one of the boxes of shells, when she paused. It was only for a minor part of a second, a fleeting but inexplicable hiatus of movement that was noticeable at all only because ever since she'd accepted this thing and committed herself she'd been going forward with the inevitability of some machine running downhill on rails.

Poised there on the dead center of this almost imperceptible hesitation, with the feeling that somebody was pounding on the wall of the bubble, trying to get in or to attract her attention, she looked down into the drawer, wondering what had caused it. Besides some heavy clothing they wouldn't need until they got down into the higher latitudes, it held only those articles which, in addition to the shotgun, had to be sealed in port by customs—the shells; her cigarettes; John's cigars; the medicine kit, because of the narcotics it contained; and several bottles of whisky and two or three of rum. Then the feeling was gone. The protective concentration closed in around her again, and she was moving ahead. She gathered up the box of shells, picked up a small paring knife from a galley drawer, and hurried back.

It took several minutes to hack her way into the box. She extracted two of the shells and set the box on the deck under the bunk. She broke the gun at the breech with the lever, dropped them in, and closed it. She was fortunate in that her very lack of familiarity with guns spared her the deadly association of those three sounds linked in sequence—the *toinnnk, toinnnk*, of the shells dropping into the ends of the tubular air columns of the barrels, and the metallic click as the breech closed and locked.

But she wasn't so lucky with the blanket. Strangely, the blanket was worse now than the gun, and it might have stopped her except for the furious intensity of her concentration and the momentum she had already gathered. Because she knew what she had to do with it, and do immediately and without hesitation or thought; if she waited, she might never go up there at all, and the act would have been for nothing.

She set the gun down on one of the sailbags, peeled the blanket from the bunk, and held it up before her by the corners with her face averted, like a fireman approaching a blaze behind a shield. The ocean of sickness beyond the bubble surged inward and threatened to collapse it, but she looked down at her feet, her mind shored up against everything but the problem, and decided she could get up the ladder this way and across the cockpit.

She retrieved the gun, took the blanket in her other arm, and went out. The roaring in her head was louder now, so she could scarcely hear the engine. She was cold all over and wasn't sure she was breathing at all; there seemed to be some tremendous weight pressing on her chest. She walked with a stiff-legged artificial gait, like a mechanical toy, fighting the rubbery weakness of her knees, but she was still going forward, still protected and invulnerable. She could see nothing on either side of her. Straight ahead, as if at the end of a long tunnel, the bright oblong patch of sunlight fell through the open hatch, sweeping back and forth across the ladder as *Saracen* rolled. She reached it. She stepped up on the first tread of the ladder and peered out.

She could just see over the hatch coaming, and only his face was visible as he sat in the after end of the cockpit behind the wheel. He was looking down into the compass, and his lips were moving, apparently without sound, though she didn't know for sure because of the engine noise and that roaring in her ears. He glanced up then, straight into her eyes, but there was no recognition, no indication he even saw her. He looked back at the compass, his lips continuing to move. Somewhere inside her a voice was screaming: *Now, now!*

She dropped the blanket beside her on the ladder and brought up the gun, pushing the safety button forward. The barrels reached up and out, resting on the coaming in front of her, and when she put her shoulder against the stock and sighted along them they were pointing just slightly to one side of his face. She moved them over, and when she closed her left eye they were lined up, foreshortened and centered on his forehead ten feet in front of her. She could no longer breathe at all. Her right index finger, like some great unwieldy sausage, came in against the gun, felt the forward edge of the trigger guard, slipped back around it, inside, and lay against the trigger. All she had to do was pull. She tried.

She closed both eyes and let her head fall forward, wanting help from somewhere, but there was no help; she was alone, and if it was to be done she had to do it. When she opened her eyes and looked along the barrels again, the beautiful, hated, mad, impervious head was still there on the ends of them like a permanent decoration installed in a moment of gruesome whimsy by some gunsmith gone mad himself. She tried once more to pull the trigger, and then came down from the ladder with the gun, remembering just in time to push the safety back before she sank down at the foot of it. She couldn't even cry. There were no tears left.

In a few minutes she had strength enough again to gather up the gun and blanket and go back inside the forward cabin with them. She unloaded the gun, dropped it on the bunk, and put the two shells back in the box. That ended it. She knew now. Not even to save John's life could she assassinate in cold blood a boy who didn't know what he was doing.

Or had she actually proved that? she wondered. Maybe all she'd really proved was that she couldn't do it now, at one P.M., still five hours before the deadline, the point of no return. What about then, when she knew she was renouncing all hope of ever seeing him again? But she was too tired, too emptied to think about it now. She had to rest. She sat down on the edge of the bunk, and almost immediately, as the tension uncoiled inside her, she remembered that strange pause or hesitation when she was reaching into the drawer for the shells. Something had been trying to get her attention through the protective armor of concentration. What was it?

It had to be one of the things she'd seen in the drawer. The medicine kit! That was it. But why? Was there some connection with that story Warriner had told about the deaths from botulism and his vain attempts to treat it? No-o. But, wait. She had it then. The narcotics! Hope blossomed, and then just as suddenly it was gone and she sank back into the depths. Of course there was morphine in the kit, and a hypodermic syringe, but what good was it? It was hardly likely Warriner was going to let her stick a needle in his arm and inject him full of opiates. She stopped. Inject? No. There was something else. Then she sat upright. *Codeine!* There was a bottle of codeine tablets in it.

She ran out into the after cabin and yanked open the drawer. The medicine kit was in a wooden box with a hinged cover. She threw the cover up and began searching hurriedly through the bottles, plastic vials, and small cardboard cartons. Aspirin, paregoric, iodine, aureomycin, alcohol, sulfa, sutures—here, this was it. It was a small, square-shouldered bottle with a screw top, its neck stuffed with cotton. She lifted it out and read the typewritten label. "*One tablet for relief of pain. Do not repeat within six hours.*"

There seemed to be fifteen or twenty in it. One, she thought, would make you very drowsy, depending on individual tolerance. She had no idea what a lethal dose would be, but probably anything above four or five might be fatal even to a young man in the prime of life such as Warriner. She didn't want to kill him, even in this painless and unmessy way, but on the other hand too small a dose would be worse than none at all. It would only warn him that he'd been drugged. Three, she thought; that should be safe enough both ways. But how to administer it?

In food, or in something to drink? There'd probably be less chance of his suspecting anything if it were in something to eat. She could pulverize three of them, mix the powder with canned potted ham or something equally spicy to cover the taste, and make a sandwich of it. No, she thought then. The chances were he was going to be suspicious of *anything* she offered him. Irrational he might be, but he was no fool. She thought for a moment. Then she saw the answer, and she smiled for the first time in four hours.

She slammed the drawer shut and strode back to the galley section of the cabin. Having shaken three of the tablets from the bottle, she set them on the tiny drainboard shelf next to the sink and reached up into the stowage racks for a glass. She took two teaspoons from a drawer, set one of the tablets in one spoon and used the heel of the other to crush it, pressing them between her fingers. She dropped the resultant powder in the glass and was reaching for the second tablet when she felt *Saracen* go into a hard left turn and at the same time roll down to starboard. Both the glass and the bottle of codeine tablets started to slide. She caught the glass, but the bottle escaped her and fell on deck. It didn't break, but it rolled and slid all the way across to the starboard side, spilling the tablets as it went. She set the glass in the sink, so it couldn't roll off too, and went lunging after the bottle. She had it and was down on her knees picking up the scattered tablets at the foot of the companion ladder when Warriner screamed just above her. He was already in the hatch, coming down the ladder.

She sprang to her feet and wheeled to run, but it was too late. When she slid through the doorway into the forward cabin he was right behind her and there was no time even to close the door. Trapped now, she turned, seeing the agony of his face and trying to will herself not to fight him. "It was a shark!" he cried out. He caught both her arms in a grip that made them hurt. "It was a shark!" And while she was still struggling with the panic inside her, she began to grasp that he hadn't come down here to attack her. He wanted help, comfort, something he thought she could give him, and if she could soothe him, or at least keep from antagonizing him, she might survive this crisis too. And it would be the last one. Then she remembered she still had the opened bottle of codeine tablets in her hand. She shoved the hand down beside her thigh to keep them out of sight.

"Don't you see, it was the shark!" Then *Saracen*, running at full throttle with no one at the wheel, careened off the side of a swell and went into another hard turn. They lost their balance in the welter of sailbags and cases of stores around the door, and she fell backward onto the bunk. She sat up. Warriner dropped to his knees between the bunks and pressed his face into her lap, encircling her legs with his arms. His shoulders shook. Her left hand was free, but the other, holding the bottle, was trapped by his arms.

She reached down and gently stroked his head. "Of course it was the shark, Hughie."

He raised his head then and looked up at her, and while his eyes were still wild there was nothing dangerous in them. On the contrary, they were almost beseeching, like those of a frightened child. The words began to pour out, tumbling over each other. "It was a big hammerhead, over twelve feet long. I tried to drive it away. I tried to save her. I hit—I hit it on the nose. But she was up on the surface, splashing too much. If she'd come down where I was—they won't bother you under the water, you know that, everybody does—but she wouldn't dive. It was horrible, the shark cut her in two, the water was all bloody. . . ."

She had no idea what he was talking about, but what he wanted was plain enough. He was asking her for exoneration. It was the other boy who'd started the fight or had thrown the football through Mrs. Cramer's window. She stroked his head again. "It wasn't your fault, Hughie. Of course it was terrible, but you did everything you could."

His arms had relaxed their grip around her legs, and she was able to slide her right hand free. While he was still looking up at her face, she brought it up the side of her thigh and shoved the bottle into the pocket of the Bermuda shorts. She sighed. He hadn't seen it.

"You believe me, don't you?" he asked.

"Of course I believe you," she said.

"I knew you would. Somehow I knew it." He hugged her legs again, almost as if in gratitude, and pressed his face against her knees. His voice was almost normal as he went on, "You won't leave me, will you? It's so awful—" He stopped.

She glanced down. He had raised his head again, but this time he was looking at something behind her on the bunk. It was the shotgun. She felt the chill of gooseflesh spread up her back. He went on staring, and then he whispered, "You were going to kill me."

"No. Hughie, no. Listen—please, it's not even loaded."

He still hadn't moved, and his voice was no louder than before. "You want to kill me too."

He reached around behind her and slowly pulled it out by the barrels. There was nowhere she could run, nothing she could do. There wasn't even anything in her mind except the bitterness of the thought that after four hours she'd been within a few minutes of winning, and now she'd lost. Maybe the fear would come in a minute. She was simply too tired to handle more than one thing at a time.

With a wild outcry he lunged to his feet then and swung the gun against the side of the boat. The stock splintered and broke off against an oaken frame above and behind her head. She ducked down between the bunks as he swung again—not even at her, as far as she could tell, but merely in some fury of destruction directed against the gun itself. The barrels rang against the upright pipe of the bunk frame. He beat it twice more against the pipe and threw it behind him, into the after cabin. Above the noise of the engine she heard it slide and bounce along the deck and crash into something, probably the ladder at the after end. At the same moment, while he was turning and off balance, *Saracen* rolled down and the bow swung off on another violent change of course. He fell over against the bulkhead beside the door and slid down atop the sailbag behind which the compass was wedged. He was on his feet almost immediately, facing her. When she'd seen him lose his balance she'd started to scramble up, hoping to get out the door, but there wasn't time. He was right beside it. There was nowhere to go, anyway. She sat down on the bunk again, trying to conceal her fear. *Don't fight him*, she thought; don't try to run. Her only chance to survive was to use her weapons instead of his; there was a lost and frightened boy inside the maniac, and maybe she could reach him. And he could already have killed her with the gun barrels, but he hadn't.

He stared at her wildly for a moment and had taken a step toward her, when he turned, as if he'd remembered something. When he bent over the sailbag she knew what it was. He'd seen the compass when he fell, and the scratch pad with its penciled notations of the course. He lifted the compass out and with another cry of fury he turned and threw it against the starboard side of the cabin. The box splintered, and it fell to the deck in a ruin of broken glass and spilled alcohol.

Then, before he even had a chance to look back at her, she said gently, "Hughie, come here." When the frenzied eyes swung around and fastened on her, she touched her knees, where his head had rested before.

"You wanted to kill me!" he cried out. His hands clenched and opened, and he took a step toward her, coming between her and the door. She saw the hands come up level with her throat, but there was a faint uncertainty or hesitation in his movements now, and she'd detected just a trace of defiance in the outcry. Without that, perhaps she couldn't have found the self-control to do it. She continued to look up at him with perfect serenity.

"Don't be silly, Hughie," she said. "You know I wouldn't hurt you." She wasn't sure herself how she accomplished it, but the tone was squarely on pitch, the voice of all the mothers in the world, firm but still gentle, compassionate, and forgiving. She touched her knees again and said, "Come here, dear."

He came with a rush then. He fell to his knees before her with his face pressed against her legs, and he was crying uncontrollably.

The strength drained out of her, but she managed to remain erect while she gently stroked his head. The clatter of the engine went on. *Saracen* pitched, and the bow swung off onto another tangent in her blind flight across the surface of the sea. Part of it had been luck, she thought, in that the first, compulsive outburst had been directed against the shotgun, but she knew she could control him now. She had nothing more to fear from him. Except that she still couldn't make him go back. But the codeine would take care of that.

Then she remembered the compass and looked across to the opposite side of the cabin, where spilled alcohol still dripped down the planking of the hull. Well, she thought wearily, there must be some answer to that too; she'd think of it in a minute. Apparently after four hours of improvising and feeling your way along the rim of disaster you began to develop a belief there was always another handhold just beyond.

14

Russell Bellew had been dreaming he was packing into the Bitterroot country again for elk when he awoke and he was back on that sinking abortion of a boat and the Duchess of California was poking his shoulder with a pair of rulers. She was looking down at him with that usual expression of hers, as if he were something that had just crawled out of the drain in a bus-station washroom. What the good Duchess needed, besides being knocked on her can a few times, was exactly what she'd have had this morning in about five more minutes if Goldilocks hadn't sighted that other boat and come charging down there with his club just as he got her pinned down on the bunk. Rub it on him for practice, would she?

"Madam called?" he asked.

"Ingram said to wake you."

He loved that bit with the rulers. He slid a hand up the back of her thigh and squeezed. "You should have used a longer stick."

"Obviously." There was no attempt to draw back, or hit him, and she didn't even bother to change expression. "Then you *are* awake?"

He sat up. "What does Hotspur want now?"

"There's a squall coming up."

"So?"

"So the bird of time has but a little way to fly—"

"Shove it."

She tore him off about three-sixteenths of an inch of another supercilious smile, dropped it in his eye, and said, "Yes, of course." She went back on deck.

Cuddly type, the good Duchess. But somebody should have warned her before this that nobody was quite as hard as she thought she was. No doubt she was a better man than that boar's tit she was married to, but she was in for a shock when she found out what it's really like out there when they take the cover off and let you look in. When that ocean started climbing up her leg she'd be screaming her tonsils loose. He didn't like to think about it himself. Well, it couldn't be any worse than jumping into France in the dark with those jugheads down there waiting for you. But that was a long time back. Sport, that was a *long* time back.

But, hell, you had to look on the bright side. Think about Hughie-boy. He wasn't going to drown. It brought the lump right up there in your throat just thinking that Mama's precious made it up the ladder before he chopped it loose. And he only had to kill four people to do it. But we don't mind, do we, fellows?

He went up on deck. . . .

It was 5:10 P.M. when the sun was blotted out and the squall burst around them. Ingram clung to the pump and looked along the deck in the fury of spray and horizontal, wind-hurled rain. Mrs. Warriner and Bellew crouched in the lee of the deckhouse, seeking the little protection they could find. Mrs. Warriner's hair was plastered to her head and face, and Bellew's Mexican hat was long since gone, blown overboard in the first onslaught of the wind. The deckhouse hatch was closed, as well as the two where they'd been bailing, and he and Bellew had lifted the dinghy aboard and lashed it. There was nothing else you could do. Except pray, and keep pumping.

Now that they were inside it, where all directions were the same and visibility was cut to a few yards, perspective was gone and there was no way of telling which way it was moving or how far they were from the edge, but he believed from having watched it as it made up that the worst of it was passing to the northward of them—for what that was worth. It wasn't the wind itself he was afraid of; it was the sea, and that was the same all around them.

It was high, steep-sided, and confused, fighting the groundswell running up from the south. *Orpheus* had too little freeboard now, and she was too heavy-bellied and sluggish to ride with the punch and escape any of the beating she was taking. She pitched, lurched over, and was swept from bow to stern by every breaking sea, wallowing helplessly like some huge but mortally wounded animal. She rolled down too far and hung, pinned there on her beam ends for long moments by the inertia of the water inside her, and Ingram winced, thinking of the stresses as the enormous weight of the keel pulled the other way to bring her back. He could hear the creak and groan of her timbers even above the shrieking of the wind and knew that all the while more of her fastenings were working loose and pulling out of rotten frames and planks below him. Swung around and crouched to protect his face from the stinging of the rain and spray, he continued to pump, wondering about the bed bolts of the engine. And the great keel bolts themselves . . .

But they continued to hold, and in another twenty minutes it began to subside. The sun broke through. The wind dropped and then died completely, and they were still afloat. At six P.M., with the sun low on the horizon, the sea had quit breaking aboard, and they were able to open the hatches to resume bailing. When Ingram looked down at the depth of water in the after cabin he knew there was very little chance she would live through the night.

It was 1:40 P.M., five minutes now since Warriner had suddenly sprung to his feet and run back on deck to take the wheel. *Saracen* was plowing steadily ahead, back on course—whatever it was. Rae Ingram stood beside the sink in the after cabin, crushing the last of the three codeine tablets between the spoons. The bottle containing the others was recapped and stowed in one of the drawers, ready in case she needed more. She dropped the powder into the glass, but it was the other problem she was thinking of. This idea of hers, she felt sure, would still work. Within a few minutes—with any luck at all—she might be in command of *Saracen* again. But what good was it if she couldn't find her way back to the other boat?

The 226 degrees her compass had been reading meant nothing now that he'd smashed it and there was no way to compare it with the steering compass. It could have been as much as twenty or thirty degrees from the actual course. So as far as knowing what their course had been from the other boat, she was little better off than she'd been at the beginning, and now they were at least twenty-five miles away. Somehow she had to find out what he was steering. But how? Try to get a look into the binnacle when she went up? No, that wouldn't work. It was covered, so you could see into it only from the helmsman's seat, and he would be instantly suspicious if she tried to work her way around behind him. He wouldn't let her, and it might even trigger him into another outburst, which would wreck her chances of success with this idea. She couldn't risk it. Getting control of the boat came first. Wait, she thought, beginning to see the solution. The sun. It was shining, and far enough down from the meridian now to cast a good shadow. It wouldn't be exact, but it would be a good approximation, probably near enough to bring her back within sight of the other boat.

Working rapidly now, she dropped sugar into the glass with the powder from the pulverized tablets, put in a few spoonfuls of water to start it dissolving, and squeezed in a whole lemon. Then she opened the door of the tiny electric refrigerator inset in the after bulkhead and took two ice cubes from the tray. She finished filling the glass with water and stirred until there was no trace of the powder left in the bottom and the glass itself was beaded with moisture from the cold. Warriner had been sitting there in the sun since nine this morning with nothing to drink; there wasn't much chance he could resist it—especially if she didn't offer it to him and was drinking from it herself. A little of it wouldn't hurt her.

She carried it up the ladder into the hot glare of sunlight on deck. Warriner looked up from the compass with watchful appraisal but appeared to relax when she sat down on the after edge of the deckhouse beside the mizzenmast, rather than coming down into the cockpit. He said nothing. She ignored him, looking aft as if hoping to see the other boat following them. She took a sip of the lemonade.

The sun was diagonally behind her, falling over her left shoulder, which meant their course was somewhere in the vicinity of southwest. There was a good chance he was steering for the Marquesas or for Tahiti, but she couldn't depend on that because there was no guarantee he even knew the correct course to either of them. She had to narrow it down. Moodily, as if lost in thought, she let her gaze run idly along the scupper on the port quarter, the extreme edge of the deck where it was crossed by the shadow of the mizzenmast.

Of course the shadow was by no means stationary. With *Saracen*'s corkscrew motion as she quartered across the swell, and his deviations on either side of the course he was steering, it moved forward and aft along the edge of the deck as much as two feet or more. But by catching it several times when the boat was on an even keel to cancel out the rolling, she was able to strike an average between the extremes of his steering. The after edge of the shadow would be about three inches forward of that lifeline stanchion, the second one counting from astern. All she had to do, if and when she got the wheel, would be to line the shadow up on that spot, note the heading on the compass, and figure out the reciprocal. But was he going to take the bait? It had already been several minutes.

She looked aft and, without appearing even to notice him, saw that his eyes had been on the glass. She raised it to her mouth, took another sip, and set it beside her on the deckhouse while she reached in her pocket for a cigarette. It was well beaded with moisture, and she knew he could see the ice. How much longer could he stand it?

"What's that you're drinking?" he asked then.

"Lemonade," she said.

"Oh."

She put the cigarette in her mouth, and returned the pack to her pocket. Let him wait. Make him ask for it. Then she saw him look at the glass again and knew she had won. Her only problem had been to make him want it.

There was no way she could lose now, whether he suspected anything or not. If he asked her to bring him a glass, she would merely make another with three of the tablets in it. And whether he did or did not demand to trade after she'd given it to him, it made no difference. But she had an idea he would take the simple way. He did.

"It looks good," he said.

"Would you like me to make you one?" she asked.

There was a trace of slyness in his eyes now. Mother was all right when he was scared and needed her, but she wasn't going to put anything over on him. He was too smart for that. "Why not just give me that one and make another for yourself?"

"But I've already drunk out of it," she protested.

"That doesn't matter." He smiled, as if thinking of some secret joke, and held out his hand.

She shrugged and handed it to him and started down the ladder. Then she turned and asked, "Would you like me to make you another while I'm at it?"

"No, this will do," he replied, still smiling. "And thanks a lot."

Once out of sight at the foot of the ladder, she hurried forward. That should have dispelled the last doubt, she thought, and he'd gulp it right down. How long would it take? Not more than five to ten minutes, probably, but with the first wave of drowsiness he was going to know she'd tricked him and he'd be dangerous until he finally collapsed. She'd better stay here, ready to barricade the door if she saw him start down the ladder, though she didn't believe he'd ever make it this far. Of course there was the chance he might think to close and fasten the hatch to lock her below, but it couldn't be helped. She didn't dare remain on deck. Anyway, noise would never wake him, that thoroughly drugged, and she could tear the hatch cover apart with a hammer and marlinspike and force her way out.

She grabbed a coiled heaving line, which was soft and easy to handle, and the knife she'd used to cut open the box of shotgun shells. With the door just cracked, she peered out, watching the hatch. A minute went by. Three. Ten. *Saracen* continued to plow ahead, apparently still on course. Had he become suspicious of it after all? She was sure there'd been no taste; it was well covered by the lemon and sugar. Then she felt *Saracen* lurch and begin to turn. At the same time a demonic cry shot up above the noise of the engine, like a prolonged scream of rage, and the glass came flying in the open hatch. It narrowly missed the radio and smashed against the bulkhead at the forward end of her bunk. *Saracen* rolled down and turned in the opposite direction. She continued to watch the hatch with apprehension, but sunlight fell through it unobstructed. Almost a full minute went by. Nothing happened except that *Saracen* continued to turn, as if she were going around in a tight circle. She could visualize what had happened. Trying to get up, holding onto the wheel, he'd turned it, and then collapsed across it.

She ran through the after cabin, mounted the first step of the ladder, and peered out. Then she froze. He had fallen forward across the wheel, but now he was moving again, making one last effort to get up. His face was distorted, and he cried out as though in rage against the darkness swimming up around him. One hand reached down to the engine control panel. The noise of the engine cut off abruptly, his arm swung, and she saw the ignition key flash in the sunlight as he threw it overboard.

The brass cover of the binnacle followed it over the side, and then, still screaming, he had hold of the compass itself, swinging in its gimbals. Muscles writhed in his arms and shoulders, and the tendons stood out in his throat. It tore free, and while he was turning with it in his hands to throw it into the sea he fell back onto the seat and collapsed with his head and shoulders on the narrow strip of deck beside him. The compass dropped on deck, burst with an eruption of alcohol, and slid over the side as *Saracen* rolled down to starboard. In the abrupt and almost terrifyingly lonely silence as *Saracen* slowed and came to rest she could only cling to the handrail of the ladder in defeat, and for a moment she wished she had killed him when she'd had the chance. There was no other compass aboard.

Then it was gone, and she was moving ahead. After what she'd been through to get this far, nothing was going to stop her. She had no idea how she was going to find her way back across all those miles of open sea with nothing to guide her, but that would have to wait till she could get to it. The first thing was to tie him. Why, she wasn't quite sure, because he'd probably be unconscious for at least eight or ten hours and if she hadn't found the other boat in five or less she'd never find it at all and after that nothing mattered anyway, but he had to be immobilized once and for all. Maybe it had something to do with having been completely at his mercy for all those years since early this morning, and if there had been any way to embed him in a barrel of hardening concrete up to his neck she would have done it. She stood above him in the cockpit with her heaving line and her knife.

He hadn't moved since he'd fallen. She reached down to touch him, a little fearfully, and then realized nothing was going to rouse him now. He was still behind the wheel, and there was no possibility at all of moving him. He must weigh 180 or 190 pounds, and, inert as he was, it would take a professional weight-lifter to get him out of there. But it didn't matter. She could handle the wheel from the port seat of the cockpit, or standing up. The only thing that did matter was that she had to hurry.

She cut a piece about twelve feet long from the heaving line and bound his wrists together in front of him, going around them and then between them to form an unslippable pair of handcuffs. She stretched his arms out along the strip of deck and made the end of the line fast to a lifeline stanchion. Then she tied his ankles together and anchored them to the base of the binnacle. There was no way he could move at all. His face rested on his outstretched arms.

She stood up, wiped sweat from her face, and looked at her watch. It was 2:20 P.M. Her mind was instantly swamped with all the problems clamoring for attention, calculations of time and distance and the unknown factor of direction and the need to do everything at once, but she brushed them aside. One thing at a time, and the next was to start the engine. She couldn't stand the silence. Normally she disliked the noise as much as John did, but now she needed the comfort of it to be able to think. *Saracen* had come to rest and was rolling forlornly on the groundswell, completely becalmed and helpless on a sea as unruffled as glass and achingly empty in all directions to the far rim of the visible world, where it met the converging bowl of the sky. With John there, it was privacy, but now it was a loneliness that screamed.

She knelt and reached in under the engine-control panel. There were wires coming up to the ammeter as well as to the ignition switch, but she could identify them by location. There were only two to the switch. She twisted and yanked until she had broken them loose. She pulled them down into view and peeled the insulation from them with the knife; then she twisted the ends together, pulled the lever back to neutral, and pressed the starter button. The engine rumbled into life and began to roar. She eased the throttle back to idle.

Now . . .

All she had was the sun, and she'd only have that for another four hours—unless it disappeared before then behind a cloudbank or in a squall. She'd been facing directly aft, and it had come diagonally over her left shoulder, so facing forward she'd want it in the same place. It wasn't much, she thought fearfully. But wait—she could do better than that.

What about the shadow of the mizzenmast, and her mark? If she projected the mark to the opposite side of the boat along the same plane she should be very near the reciprocal of the course he'd been steering. She grabbed up what was left of the heaving line, whirled, and caught the wire lifeline on the port quarter beside the cockpit. Three inches forward of the second stanchion, counting from aft. Right here. She made the end of the line fast, passed it ahead of the mizzen, and went up the starboard side with it. She pulled it taut, and then moved her end aft until it just touched the forward side of the mast. It intersected the starboard lifeline nearly midway between the third and fourth stanchions, again counting from aft. She tied it there, winding the surplus line three or four times around the wire to make it easier to see from the wheel.

At best it was still only a prayer, a stab in the dark. The bearing of the sun was going to change as it moved down toward the horizon, and there was no guarantee at all that Warriner had even gone back to his original course when he'd returned to the deck after smashing her compass. But, she thought, trying to still the fear inside her, all she had to do was come within four miles of *Orpheus* and she'd be able to see her.

She jumped back into the cockpit, pushed the lever into gear, ran the throttle up to about where Warriner had had it, and put the wheel over. Sitting on the port seat of the cockpit beside it, she could see her marker all right. She brought *Saracen* on around until the shadow of the mizzenmast fell on it, swinging back and forth on either side of it as she rolled. As she steadied up, she looked at her watch. It was 2:35 P.M.

How far, how many hours? It was a few minutes past two when Warriner had stopped the engine and thrown the key overboard. From nine this morning, that would be five hours since they'd left *Orpheus*—less the time he'd been below while *Saracen* was running God knew where with no one at the wheel. Call it four and a half hours—twenty-five to twenty-seven miles. At the same speed going back, she should be in the area at seven P.M. That would be a little after sunset, perhaps not quite dark, but by then she would be running blind.

So *Orpheus* had to be in sight by then, because there would be no second chance. If she weren't there, she'd already sunk, or the course had been wrong, and with no compass the latter was as irreversible as the first. Within a half-hour she'd be hopelessly lost herself, with no idea where she was going or where she'd been. She couldn't think about it. She tried to force everything from her mind but the mechanics of steering by the shadow of the mizzenmast and the continuing prayer that the sun would go on shining.

At a little after three she began to see the dark cloud in the north. The squall was still far over the horizon, but she couldn't take a chance of running into it with all sail set; they might be knocked down or dismasted. But she hated to stop, even for a few minutes. It appeared to be moving to the westward at the same time it was coming nearer; maybe it would be gone by the time she got there. But she should take in sail anyway; the main and the jib were going to interfere too much with her view ahead. At a little after four, while the sun was momentarily obscured by a passing cloud, she stopped and took in everything. She was under way again in less than twenty minutes, with the sun visible once more on the thinning edge of the cloud.

Warriner had never moved since he'd fallen. She began to be afraid the three tablets had been too much and she'd killed him. She reached over and touched his throat, and she could feel the pulse. It was slow but steady.

At four-thirty she reached inside the hatch for the binoculars and began to search the horizon to port and then to starboard between corrections to the helm. There was the chance *Orpheus* had got a breeze and John had tried to follow them. Her eyes encountered nothing but the empty miles of water and the far rim of that circle in which they seemed to be forever centered. The noise of the engine went on, they rose and fell in a long pitching motion as the glassy billows of the swell rolled up under her quarter, but they never appeared to move at all.

It was five o'clock. Five-thirty. The squall ahead was moving into the west and breaking up. Scattered clouds began to obscure the sun at intervals, but she went on, looking over her shoulder and trying to judge its position. She continued to search the horizon to port and starboard with the glasses. The sea was empty all around her. By six the tightness in her chest was becoming almost unbearable.

Six-thirty. The sun came out from behind another cloud, and it was far down now, less than a diameter above the horizon and beginning to redden in the haze. The shadow of the mizzenmast was gone. She stood up, holding the wheel with her right hand and steering with the sun just behind her left shoulder while she held the binoculars to her eyes and scanned the sea ahead.

The colors began. Far overhead the fleecy edges of clouds were touched with gold and then pink, darkening to crimson. The sun slid downward into the low cloudbank on the horizon, and in a moment it was gone from sight and there were only the vertical rays of pale lemon extending upward against the sky. Just for an instant the defenses of her mind gave way and she remembered sunsets she had watched with John here in this cockpit in the Bahamas and Caribbean and the Gulf of Panama. She began to tremble. She dropped the engine out of gear, pulled the throttle back to idle, and leaped up on deck. She climbed atop the main boom with an arm about the mast and slowly swung the binoculars all the way around from the already darkening east to the great flame of the afterglow in the west, and there was no sign of *Orpheus* anywhere. It was 7:05 P.M.

15

INGRAM'S EYES were bleak as he looked down into the fading light of the main cabin. If you had any talent for kidding yourself, he thought, now would be a good time to break it out. With the two of them bailing and Mrs. Warriner at the pump, the water had gained several inches in the past half-hour. They must have lost whole planks off her outer skin in that squall.

He turned and searched the emptiness of the sea down to the southwest and then glanced at his watch. It was 6:50. He dropped the bucket on the deck and went back to the others. "Knock off a minute."

Bellew looked at him inquiringly. Mrs. Warriner straightened and pushed damp hair back from a face deeply lined with fatigue. "You mean we're gaining on it?"

He shook his head. "No. We're not even keeping up with it. But a quarter of an hour one way or the other's not going to make any difference, and before it gets too dark to see I want to have one more look around from the masthead."

He slung the glasses around his neck and shackled the sling to the main halyard again. He climbed atop the boom and stepped into the sling with his lifeline around the mast. "Haul away," he ordered. In the confused sea left behind by the squall, *Orpheus* was wallowing even worse than before, but he managed the tricky business of getting past the spreaders without accident. When he was up just short of the masthead light, he called down, "That'll do. Make fast."

They were lying on a southerly heading at the moment. Legs locked against the dizzying swing of the mast, he looked around him. In the east the blue was already beginning to darken with the coming of night, while off to starboard the sun had dropped over the horizon and the western sky was aflame. It was impossible to escape entirely the beauty of it or to seal the mind against all of memory's infiltration, and he was glad he was up here where they couldn't see his face. Then he put the glasses to his eyes and began a cold and methodical search of the horizon to the southwest, fighting the lunging of the mast. He moved on into the south, and around to the east, where the light was beginning to fade. Nothing. Still nothing . . .

Where was she now? Was she still alive? The glasses began to shake. He lowered them and closed his eyes. The feeling passed in a moment, and he had control of himself again. He raised the glasses and came back, very slowly, across the whole area he had searched before, and then on into the dying fire and the wine-red sea of the west. He stopped abruptly. Something came up into his throat, and he swallowed. He tried to swing the glasses back, but for an instant he couldn't. He was afraid to look again.

All right, he thought savagely; maybe you should have sent one of the men. He brought them back.

It was a mast.

Or was it? *Orpheus* rolled, and in the sickening swing out to port and back he lost the spot again. He got the line of the horizon in the glasses once more and inched to the right. There! It was only a tiny pencil stroke seen for an instant against the red glow of sunset. He locked his arms more tightly around the mast in an effort to stop the tremor of the glasses. It came into view, and this time he was certain he saw the other one beside it, the two of them like the tips of two toothpicks held at arm's length before a fire. The shorter one was to the left.

"Lower away!" he shouted.

He knew what they had to do and made up his mind as he came down the mast. Below him, the others looked up silently, their faces almost red in the winy light. He landed on the boom, stepped out of the sling, and jumped down beside them.

"She's over there," he began. When they started to interrupt, he cut them off with a curt gesture. "Wait till I get through. She's going to miss us. She's hull down, even from up there; all I got was a glimpse of the masts against the sunset. She's due west of us, headed north, and she won't get any closer. From where she is, down on deck, we're clear over the horizon, so there's no way in God's world she can see us—"

"There's no way we can signal her?" Mrs. Warriner asked.

"Just one. Set this one afire."

"Oh." She gave him a startled look, and then she was calm again. "Could she see it from over there?"

"I think so."

"You *think* so?" Bellew interrupted. "That's great."

"Shut up." He went on. "There's a good chance. We're to the east of her, so it'll be dark behind us in another fifteen minutes. And there are enough clouds overhead to reflect the glow."

"And if she doesn't see us?" Bellew asked. "But don't bother to tell me, let me guess. We take a taxi to the McAlpin Hotel—"

"We do the same thing we're going to do anyway," Ingram said coldly. "We drown. The water's gained at least three inches on us in the past half-hour, with all three of us working. She won't last till midnight." They were wasting time with this idiotic argument. He swung around to Mrs. Warriner. "It's your yacht, and you're still aboard it—"

"Burn it, of course," she said coolly.

Bellew shrugged. "Okay. What are we waiting for?"

"Will it burn?" she asked. "I mean, this low in the water, and with everything up here wet from the squall?"

"We'll fire it in the chartroom," Ingram replied. "There's no gasoline left at all?"

"No."

"What does your galley stove burn? Bottled gas, or kerosene?"

"Kerosene. There should be several cans of it in the locker forward."

"Right. What about paint stores—turpentine, linseed oil, thinner?"

"There should be some of each."

"Good." He began to issue terse orders. "Get your passports, money, and the logbook; you can't take anything else. Wrap them in something waterproof. Dump the water out of that dinghy and stow 'em in there, along with a couple of flashlights. Put on lifebelts, and then you can give me a hand."

Without even waiting for a reply, he whirled and ran down into the chartroom. He grabbed a flashlight from its bracket and went on down the steps and through the main and forward cabins, where the debris-laden water washed around his thighs. Opposite the sail bin was another locker. He unlatched the doors and yanked them open but could see nothing in the thickening gloom here below. He switched on the flashlight and wedged it between two of the sailbags. In an upper compartment were some tools and paint brushes. He spied a small hand ax and stuck the handle of it in his belt. The bottom of the locker was filled with buckets and rectangular one-gallon cans submerged and bumping together in the water that surged back and forth.

The buckets would be paint. He ignored them and began fishing out the cans. There were a dozen of them, mostly unidentifiable, the labels long since washed off, but it didn't matter. An armful at a time, he carried them up the ladder going on deck from the forward cabin and dumped them beside the hatch. As he made the last trip he saw that Bellew and Mrs. Warriner had returned to the deck, wearing lifebelts, and Bellew had the dinghy up on its side, pouring the water out of it.

The great flame in the west was dying now, and the brief twilight of the tropics had already begun. He grabbed up two of the cans and ran aft.

"What now?" Bellew asked.

"Let's get the dinghy over." With a swing of the hand ax he knocked out one of the windows of the deckhouse and tossed the two cans in on the chartroom table. Mrs. Warriner was holding two flashlights and a package wrapped in oilskins. As she stowed them in the dinghy he noticed the compass had fallen out when Bellew had dumped out the water. It wasn't broken. He put it back in.

"Grab the bow," he said to Bellew. They lifted it over the lifeline and, when *Orpheus* rolled down, set it in the water. It rode lightly on the heavy swell passing beneath them. He handed the painter to Mrs. Warriner. "Take it aft and just wait. Keep it fended off so it doesn't get caught under the counter."

Whirling to Bellew, he said, "Bring up a couple of those spare sails from the locker. It doesn't matter which ones. Dump 'em there alongside the mainmast. And then bring all those cans aft, the ones around the forward hatch."

"Where do you want 'em?" Bellew asked.

"Just forward of the cockpit's all right." He turned and ran down the steps into the chartroom. Quick blows of the hand ax knocked out the rest of the windows. He began yanking drawers out of the chart table and smashing them with the ax after he had dumped out the charts. He tore charts into strips until he had a great armful of paper. He piled this on a corner of the table and threw the splintered drawers on top of it. With another blow of the ax he cut through one of the cans. As the liquid gushed out, he could tell by the smell of it that it was paint-thinner. He poured it over the paper and wood and cut open the other can. This one was kerosene. He swung it, splashing the bulkheads, the deck, and the table. Grabbing up another chart, he flicked his cigar lighter. The lighter was wet and required several attempts before it worked. He held it to the corner of the chart and, when it was burning, tossed it on the pile. With a great sucking sound it all burst into flame at once. He threw the rest of the charts on it and ran out.

Bellew had the two sailbags piled beside the mainmast now and was hurrying back and forth, carrying the cans aft. With his knife open, beginning at the end of the boom, Ingram went forward, slicing through the gaskets of the furled mainsail. When he reached the mast he unshackled the sling and made the halyard fast to the head of the sail again. Two more quick slashes split the sailbags. He hauled the sails out and stretched them along the deck, one atop the other. He grabbed up a line at random, cut off a length, made it fast around the two sails somewhere near the center, and hauled the whole cumbersome bundle over to the base of the mast. He made the line fast to the halyard above the shackle.

Bellew was passing then with the last of the cans. He grabbed two of them from his arms and swung the ax on them. The first was linseed oil. He poured it on the two sails. The other was kerosene. He dumped this on them also, and onto the mainsail, which was dangling in folds along the boom. He could hear the fire beginning to roar below him now, and smoke was pouring through the broken windows. "Give me a hand on this halyard," he called out to Bellew.

They hoisted. The mainsail went up, and with it the great dangling mass of the two spare sails made fast to the head of it. Kerosene and linseed oil began to drip on them.

Bellew grunted. "For that real homey feeling, it ought to be gasoline."

"If it breaks out of the chartroom," Ingram said, "go right over the side."

"Don't give it a thought, sport. I just look stupid."

It was up. Ingram threw the hitches on the pin, and they ran aft. Flame was beginning to lick through the broken windows. "Into the dinghy," he ordered and nodded to Bellew. "You first. Take the oars." Bellew stepped down into it and held it while he helped Mrs. Warriner in.

She protested. "Aren't you going to get in?"

"It won't take three; it'll capsize."

"But you haven't even got a lifebelt—"

He cut her off. "I don't need one. Pull clear and wait for me. I want this thing to go all at once, and go high—the higher the better. Get going." He waved them off. Bellew shipped the oars and they began to draw away in the thickening dusk, heaving up and down on the swell.

There were eight of the rectangular cans on deck at the forward end of the cockpit. He set them up on end one at a time and began swinging the ax. The first was spar varnish. He picked it up and threw it forward. It landed just beyond the mainmast and slid, spilling its contents along the deck. The next was kerosene. It went up the other side of the deck. Turpentine. It followed the varnish. Paint-thinner. That was the trigger, the most volatile of them all. He set it aside, upright on the cockpit seat with his knee braced against it so it wouldn't turn over and spill. Linseed oil. He threw it forward. It bounced and slid, spraying along the deck. The whole interior of the chartroom was a roaring mass of flame now, and he could feel the heat on his face. The varnish on the underside of the main boom was beginning to bubble. He had to hurry. There were only seconds left before it broke out through the roof.

He swung the ax on another can, and another. Some of them had already slid overboard, but their contents had spilled, and the whole deck forward of him was crisscrossed with trails of varnish, linseed oil, turpentine, and kerosene, flowing across the planks and soaking into the seams. The final can was another of paint-thinner. He dropped the ax and picked it up, along with the other can, the one beside his knee.

He ran to the after end of the cockpit and jumped up onto the narrow strip of deck right on the stern. *All right, honey, this is where we are.* Wheeling, he threw the first can straight through a window into the inferno inside the chartroom, and while it was still in the air he threw the other and dived over the side.

Thirty yards away in the gathering night, Lillian Warriner turned and stared in wonder. My God, she thought, they shouldn't match him against just one ocean at a time. Even while his body was still in the air, a great ball of flame burst out of the chartroom, taking the roof of the deckhouse with it and igniting the whole ketch forward of the cockpit in one mighty breath. Fire shot up the oil-soaked mainsail and ballooned in the two sails at the top of it to form—with the force of the explosion and the massive updraft from the heat below—a gigantic torch, a column of flame nearly a hundred feet high. It lit up the sea for a quarter-mile in every direction, and she could feel the heat of it on her skin.

Then he was alongside, with a hand on the gunwale. He dropped his sneakers into the dinghy. They rose as a swell passed under them. "You haven't got much freeboard," he said, "but I think it'll ride if you don't make any sudden moves. If it does swamp, the flashlights are more important than your passports and money. Try to keep at least one of them out of the water. There's no use staying here; keep rowing west."

Bellew turned his head, trying to see the dying band of color along the western horizon. "I'm blind," he said, "with that glare in my face."

"Set the compass between your feet," Ingram said to Mrs. Warriner. "Line it up with the bow, and hold a flashlight on it so he can see it."

She did. Bellew began to pull slowly ahead. Ingram held onto the transom very lightly with one hand and kicked with his feet. When they were a hundred yards away he turned and looked back. It was like a scene from hell, he thought, with the red glare reflected on the black and oily heaving of the sea. The first great pillar of flame had died now that the sails were gone, and they were already in the edge of the surrounding darkness, but she was burning fiercely from bow to stern. The glow in the sky would still be visible for miles.

"Will it last long enough for her to get here?" Mrs. Warriner asked above him.

"No," he said. "It'll burn to the waterline and sink in twenty minutes or so. It'll take her an hour, or an hour and a half. But it doesn't matter; she'll take a bearing on it and have a compass course."

She made no reply. They went on toward the darkness. He thought she might turn for one last look, but she didn't. She remained quite still, her face lowered over the compass between her feet. It was possible she was crying, but if she was, he thought, nobody would ever know it except her.

The same question was in both their minds, he knew, the same dread of what they might find aboard *Saracen*. He thought of the shotgun and shivered.

She'd got under way again because she had to keep moving as long as she could. The silence was out there waiting for her, and once she stopped and killed the engine with the acceptance of final defeat she would be defenseless and she wasn't sure she would survive it.

It was 7:20 P.M. There was still enough faint light and dying color along the rim of the horizon to show her where west was, and there would continue to be, probably, for another ten minutes. Everywhere else it was already night. Across from her, Warriner's naked shoulders and golden head were only a faint gleam in the darkness. She was standing up, holding the wheel with one hand and staring ahead into the north, when something flickered on the extreme edge of her peripheral vision. She turned her head and saw the little tongue of reddish light lick upward over the edge of the world far off to the eastward.

For a second or two she could only stare at it in a sort of stunned disbelief. Then tears came up into her eyes and blinded her for an instant as this gave way to a great surge of joy, but by then she already had the wheel hard over and was coming around. She lined it up alongside the masts and reached for the throttle. The engine noise increased to a roar as it came up the final notch to full wide open.

How far? She'd seen nothing there before, even with the binoculars, which meant it was clear over the horizon—six, eight, or even ten miles away. But John must have seen her against the sunset and then deliberately set *Orpheus* afire because he had no other way to signal her. The only way he could have seen her would have been from the masthead, so there were probably others aboard. But that was unimportant at the moment. She had something to guide her now. That was all that mattered.

In another few minutes the little tip of flame was no longer showing over the horizon, but the glow was clearly visible against the sky. She felt a moment's uneasiness. How long would it burn before it sank? If it were even eight miles away, it would take her nearly an hour and a half to get there. It was almost due east, but that was no help once the last of the light was gone from the west and all directions were the same. She had to have a star or some constellation she could recognize, one still low enough on the horizon to give her the direction. But ahead of her, above the glow, the sky was becoming overcast. Almost instinctively she glanced to the north before she remembered Polaris was below the horizon now. They were south of the equator.

She turned to look astern, and saw the answer, if the sky remained clear enough in the west. Venus had just emerged from behind a cloud. It was perhaps three hours behind the sun, well down toward the horizon directly behind her. She faced forward, less worried now. Twenty minutes passed. The faint reddish glow was still visible ahead, reflected from the underside of the clouds above it. She kept it lined up beside the masts. It began to fade. Then, thirty-five minutes after she had first sighted it, it disappeared with the abruptness of a snuffed-out candle. *Orpheus* had gone down.

Venus was still bright behind her. She went on. It was awkward and not very accurate, trying to steer looking over her shoulder, so she stood up, facing aft directly before the wheel, and tried to keep the planet poised over the end of the mizzen boom. She reached inside the hatch and switched on the running lights. Venus began to disappear in the edge of another cloud. She tried to guess its bearing, but when it reappeared fifteen minutes later it was far around to starboard. She'd been running almost south.

She swung the wheel to bring it astern again and turned herself, to look forward, searching the horizon on both sides and ahead for any tiny pinpoint of light. She must be within two or three miles of them. On all sides the darkness was unbroken. Then Venus faded and disappeared again. The western sky was becoming overcast. Directly overhead stars were visible through holes in the clouds but there was nothing anywhere that was low enough on the horizon to guide her. In two more minutes she was hopelessly lost, with no more knowledge of direction than if she were at the bottom of a well.

She jerked the throttle back and threw the engine out of gear. It was absolutely imperative now that she stay exactly where she was; every turn of the propeller could be taking her away from them instead of nearer. She pulled the twisted wires apart to stop the engine's noise so she could listen as she climbed atop the main boom to search the darkness all around. There was no light, no cry. She came down from the boom and ran below for a can of flares.

There was no fire behind them now; *Orpheus* had gone down nearly fifteen minutes ago. "Still nothing," Mrs. Warriner said above him in the darkness. Each time they crested a swell she searched the sea ahead, while Bellew continued to pull at the oars.

"What time is it now?" he asked.

She held her watch under the beam of the flashlight. "Eight-ten."

It had been fifty minutes. They should have picked up *Saracen*'s masthead light by now. "You've got too much light under you," he said. "Hold the flashlight by the lens so it's completely covered by your hand except one spot right over the compass. Bellew will still be able to see it. Then put that bundle of oilskins across your lap so no light seeps up at all. And when you locate the horizon, don't look directly at it; look a little above. Night vision's better out of the edges of your eyes."

Down in the water and behind the dinghy, he could see

nothing at all. Another fifteen minutes went by. The dark undulations of the swell rolled up under them and slid past in silence except for the creak of oarlocks. "Maybe if I stood up—" she said.

"No. You'll capsize. We're bound to pick her up in a minute. We're still right on course? Bellew, I mean; don't look down at the light yourself."

"Due west all the time," Bellew replied. Then he went on, an undertone of ugliness in his voice. "You know what, sport? Wouldn't it be a real gas if you didn't see any masts over there?"

"I saw masts," Ingram said coldly. It was for Mrs. Warriner's benefit. He had no interest at all in what Bellew thought.

There was a sudden cry from Mrs. Warriner. "I see her! I see her!"

"Where?"

"Way off to the left. My left."

"All right," he said calmly. "Don't take your eyes off it. Bellew, pull your left oar till she tells you to steady up, and then check your compass."

Bellew came around. "Steady. Right there," Mrs. Warriner said.

"Almost due south," Bellew reported. "One-eighty-five to one-ninety."

Ingram swam out from behind the dinghy, and when they rose to the next swell peered into the darkness ahead. He could see nothing at all. He was too low. But why was she so far off course? At a distance of even eight miles she should have passed within a few hundred yards of them. "Can you see the port running light?" he asked.

"No. Only the masthead light," Mrs. Warriner replied. "She must be a mile, or two miles away. Wait. I think I saw the red light then. Yes, there it is. She must have been going away from us, and then turned."

"All right," he said. "Forget the compass for a minute. You can keep Bellew headed straight. Take both your flashlights and hold 'em as far over your head as you can—"

He was interrupted by a sudden cry from Mrs. Warriner, and at the same instant he saw it himself. A rocket arched into the sky ahead of them, hung poised for an instant, and began to float down like some great glowing flower.

"She's lost herself," Bellew said. "Hell, I thought you said she could take a bearing—"

Ingram cut him off savagely. "Save it!" Then he went on to Mrs. Warriner. "As soon as that goes out and she can see again, start waving your lights, pointed straight at her."

She held them ready but made no reply, and he wondered if she were prey to the same chilling thoughts that were running through his own mind. Probably. Anybody but a stupid meathead like Bellew would know something must be wrong aboard *Saracen*. Was she hurt? Or had she killed Warriner and now was beginning to go to pieces? Then the flare went out ahead of them, and Mrs. Warriner was signaling. Several minutes went by while they rose and fell in silence.

Then Mrs. Warriner cried out. "She's turned. I can see both running lights!"

Ingram sighed. She'd sighted them and was coming.

16

THE RANGE was closing. Ahead of her the flashing lights were less than a quarter-mile away. Then it occurred to her he might be in the water instead of the dinghy, and she left the wheel long enough to run forward and hang the ladder over the side. Her knees were suddenly too weak to support her, and she almost fell coming back to the cockpit. It was difficult to breathe, and she was conscious of the pounding of her heart. She stared ahead at the two flashlights as if trying to burn away the darkness surrounding them. Two hundred yards . . .

She brought the throttle back and reached inside the hatch to turn on the spreader lights. The sea was illuminated for twenty or thirty yards on all sides of her, but she could still see the signals dead ahead.

She came hard left, and then right. She pulled the lever into reverse and backed down, racing the engine. *Saracen* came to rest, and the lights were less than fifty yards away, directly abeam. She reached down and yanked the wires apart, and in the sudden silence she could hear the rattle of oarlocks. He was in the dinghy. She leaned across the cockpit seat, staring outward.

Now she could see it. It was coming into the outer limits of the spreader lights. There were two people in it. John was rowing, and there was somebody smaller in the stern. She thought it was a woman— It wasn't John rowing. He was bigger than John. It was somebody she'd never seen before, and the other one was a woman, and there was nobody else. Then she saw the head come out from behind the dinghy, the man swimming, and the upraised arm waving to her. She slid down into the cockpit seat with one hand still feebly clutching the lifeline above her, unable even to raise her head, and her diaphragm began to kick so she couldn't exhale. Every time she would try to breathe out, it would kick and she would inhale again.

Ingram saw her slide down and could see no sign of Warriner. "I'll go aboard first," he said to Mrs. Warriner. She was staring straight ahead, and when *Saracen* rolled down she thought she saw something on the other side of the cockpit, beyond Mrs. Ingram. Something sprawled. "Yes," she said in a controlled but very fragile voice. "Yes. Thank you."

Ingram lunged ahead and went up the ladder while they were coming alongside. Rae was sitting up now, and was apparently unhurt except for that bruise on her face. Beyond her he could see Warriner's body, but in the same glance he saw the bound wrists and the line going forward to the stanchion, and all the breath went out of him at once.

Rae was still looking up at him. "He smash—he smu—he smu—" She tried to point, but he had already seen the uncovered and empty binnacle, like an eyeless socket, and understood. Probably wrecked the other one too, he thought. So she came all the way back and found us with nothing at all. He wanted to say something, but his eyes had begun to sting, and he didn't trust his voice. Without even looking around, he gestured for the others to come aboard and reached down for her arm. She made it to her feet. She went down the ladder, and when she was in the darkness at the bottom of it, she turned.

She still couldn't say anything. She couldn't even cry. She was wrung out, drained, emptied of everything. She could only manage to get her arms up around his neck and cling while his went on crushing her, moving up and down her back as if they couldn't find any place they wanted to stay, while water dripped on her and whiskers ground into her face and the voice was saying, "Oh, Jesus Christ—oh, Jesus Christ—" against her throat.

The last handhold crumbled then, but instead of falling she was floating upward into some welcoming and completely sheltered oblivion, like a child's going to sleep. She felt herself being lifted and placed on the bunk. The arms still bound her, and the voice went on with its profane and ragged whispering, this time into her hair. Then, just before she disappeared entirely into the mist, she heard her own voice say something at last.

"Did you have any lunch?" she asked.

"No," he said. He swallowed and rubbed a hand across his eyes. "I guess I forgot." He kissed her again but knew she was gone. He still knelt beside her, and now he brought a hand up and placed the finger tips very gently against her throat to feel the pulse. And even after he was reassured she was all right, that she had merely reached the limit of endurance and stopped for a moment, he left the hand there, feeling her life run steadily on beneath his fingers. He didn't even know why he did it.

He got up for a cloth to bathe her face, and when he switched on the lights he saw the battered shotgun barrels on the deck beside the ladder. He took a long and shaky breath and shook his head.

She was just beginning to stir again when he heard the voices above him, the one a lashing impassioned whisper, "*Leave him alone!*" followed by the sharp slap of palm on flesh, and hoped she hadn't heard too. After what she'd been through, she deserved at least a few minutes of thinking it was all over. He thought of what was ahead of them and suddenly felt very old and tired. But the only chance they had was to meet it now, and head-on. He ran up the ladder.

Mrs. Warriner was trying to get up from where she was sprawled back on the cockpit seat. Beyond her, Bellew was standing on the narrow strip of deck, trying to turn Warriner's face up with the toe of his shoe. "Wake up, old Hughie-boy, and see who's here."

"All right, Bellew," he ordered, "leave him alone."

The other turned, and in the glow of the spreader lights above and forward of them he could see the insolence in the eyes. "Easy does it, Hotspur. You got your boat back, so just simmer down. This is mine."

"That's right; I got it back. And I give the orders on it. You heard what I said." There was no area for compromise here, not with Bellew. If it meant forcing the issue now, within the first five minutes, force it. But at that moment Mrs. Warriner sat up, the side of her face still red from the slap. Her voice was level and very cold as she spoke to Bellew. "I warn you. Don't touch him."

Bellew sat down on the opposite side of the cockpit. He leaned forward and tapped her on the knee with a forefinger. "Don't crowd me. I've had it. With you *and* your gold-plated fag."

Twelve hundred miles, Ingram thought, in a forty-foot yacht, with the third one crazy. He wondered what Lloyds would quote you on that. "That'll do," he snapped. He felt a little better now that Bellew had sat down. The situation wasn't going to explode as long as Warriner was asleep, or knocked out, or whatever he was. If he could leave the three of them alone for as long as five seconds he might find out.

"It does seem to me," Mrs. Warriner said then, "that one of us might make at least some casual inquiry as to how Mrs. Ingram is." She turned to him. "Is she hurt?"

"No," he said. "Not as far as I could tell. She's had a little too much for one day, and she fainted, but she's coming around now." He turned to go back below. It should be safe enough now, and Mrs. Warriner would sing out if anything happened.

"How'd she get the creep tied up?" Bellew asked.

"How the hell do I know?" he said. "I had some stupid idea that after a whole day of it I might get a chance to talk to her for a minute and a half—" He broke off, realizing he had to keep his temper.

"Sure, sure." Bellew grinned coldly. "I can understand you might have been a little worried. That's where I was one up on you, chum. I didn't have to worry about mine; I knew where she was."

That was the question you always had to ask yourself, Ingram thought, before you jumped all the way down his throat. Suppose it *had* been Rae? But it didn't change anything; it would be as stupid as hating the Pacific Ocean because she'd been swept overboard by a sea. "Bellew, for Christ's sake, don't you think I realize what it's like? But it's just something you can't change; you'll only make it worse—"

"What do you mean?" Mrs. Warriner interrupted.

She knows, he thought; she knows, all right, but she just won't accept it. At that moment Rae's head appeared above the hatch. So he wasn't even going to get a moment to talk to her alone, to fill her in on who these people were and what had to be done. In fact, for at least the next twenty to twenty-five days—assuming they lived that long—he'd never have a minute completely alone with her. He was conscious of a dark and futile anger but choked it off. The situation was still far too dangerous to be crying over lost privacy and interrupted honeymoons.

He sprang to help her and seated her on the after edge of the deckhouse. "Are you all right now, honey?"

She managed a smile. "Yes. Just a little weak from the reaction."

"Aren't we all?" He turned, indicating the others. "This is Mrs. Warriner. And Mr. Bellew."

"Hi," Bellew said. Mrs. Warriner leaned forward and took her hand, and said simply, "Thank you. And I'm sorry."

"It's all right," Rae said. "It's all over now—" She broke off and gasped. "John! The other compass! He smashed that too. We haven't got anything."

Ingram nodded. "I figured he had, or you'd have had it up here. But it's all right. There's one in the dinghy. I can make it do."

He stepped forward and lifted it out. The others had already removed the flashlights and the oilskin package containing their passports. He cast off the painter and pushed the dinghy away from the side. Holding the compass very carefully, he went below and stowed it in a drawer. It was beyond price now, and nothing was going to happen to it until he could get it secured in or on the binnacle. He still didn't know what was going to happen up there. He went back and sat down beside Rae. "All right, honey, if you're up to it now, can you tell us what happened? How did you get him tied up?"

"Codeine," she said. "I gave him three of those codeine tablets from the medicine chest, in a glass of lemonade. I think he's still all right, and it's been over six hours."

The others watched silently while he stepped over and reached down to check Warriner's pulse. He knew Mrs. Warriner would have already, but he wanted to be sure himself. It was steady. "He's okay," he said. He came back.

Rae told them the rest of the story. When she had finished, she looked at Mrs. Warriner. "I still don't know. I mean, if the codeine idea hadn't worked, and he hadn't smashed the shotgun."

Mrs. Warriner touched her on the arm. "I understand, dear. And you'll forget it eventually. We all just thank God it ended the way it did."

"Well, don't break up, girls," Bellew said. "Mama's precious is a-l-l right; he's not hurt. Tomorrow you can draw straws to see who's the lucky girl he'll kill next."

Rae shot a startled and puzzled glance at Ingram. "What happened to him? I couldn't make any sense of what he was saying. Something about a shark."

Before Ingram could reply, Mrs. Warriner and Bellew both spoke at once. Bellew overrode her. "Well, nothing much." He spread his hands in a deprecating gesture. "He killed my wife, and then this morning he slugged me and locked us in the cabin on there to drown when he abandoned ship. But, I mean, hell, nobody minds these little jokes as long as they keep Hughie happy—"

"He didn't kill your wife!" Mrs. Warriner lashed out. "And why don't you go ahead and tell the Ingrams why he locked us in there?"

"Wait a minute! Hold it!" Ingram cut them both off. "Rae's entitled to know what this is all about." As briefly as he could, he told her something of it.

Then he went on, to Mrs. Warriner and Bellew. "I want both of you to listen to me a minute. After your experience on *Orpheus* I shouldn't think you'd have too much trouble understanding what we're up against. We're twelve hundred miles from land, we still don't know when we'll pick up the Trades, and with the very best of luck it could be twenty days or more we're going to be jammed in here. There are five of us on a yacht with cruising accommodations for two, and one's unbalanced and dangerous and is going to have to be tied up and watched every minute to keep him from killing himself or somebody else—"

"Unh-unh," Bellew interrupted. "No sweat at all, pal. All he's going to need is a basket."

"So you're going to kill him? In front of three witnesses. Just what do you do then? Kill us too?"

"I'm not going to kill him. You think I'm stupid, or something? You might say I'm going to immobilize him—"

"Maybe you'd better wait till I get through," Ingram said. "You might change your mind. If you don't, there's a good chance none of us will ever reach land. We've got enough food, and the water will stretch, with rationing. But that's not it. I'm the only one on here that can take this boat down there—the only one who can navigate well enough, in the first place, and the only one who can compensate that compass so we won't be wandering all over hell and halfway back, trying to make a landfall. And I'm not going to stand here and just look on—any more than Mrs. Warriner is—while you make a cripple or a permanent imbecile out of a boy who's not responsible for his actions—"

"Jesus Christ, you too?"

"I said wait till I get through. To beat up a man in his mental condition, you'd have to be sicker than he is. And as I told you, none of us is going to stand here and watch it, so if you lay a hand on him this thing is going to blow wide open. I'd say there's a good chance you can whip me, but if I get beaten up so badly I can't sail this boat or navigate, you're not doing yourself any favor, unless you think you'd like drifting around out here while your tongue swells up and you go crazy.

"And there's another thing I don't think you've thought of. He's scared to death of you, and if you touch him he'll go completely berserk. You may be stupid enough to want to see what'll happen when a man runs amok on a forty-foot yacht with four other people on it, but the rest of us are not. Also, this is no hospital, so what do you do if he dies? So far, everything that's happened has been the result of an accident or bad luck or his crackup, and nobody's committed a deliberately criminal act—"

"You call what he did to my wife an accident?"

"For Christ's sake, Bellew, he panicked! You want to beat him to death because he got scared and lost his head?"

"Captain Ingram!" It was Mrs. Warriner this time. Well, he'd been expecting it.

He turned to her. "Bellew's right," he said wearily, "and you know it. I don't know why you want to saddle yourself with the blame for the whole thing, but your husband didn't crack up because he thought you and Bellew tried to kill him. That's just another place to hide, another way to try to pass the buck. There's no doubt he's afraid of Bellew, and he'll be ten times as afraid of him now, but nobody in his right mind who'd known you for as long as an hour would ever believe anything as stupid as that. He was already irrational when he came up with that gem—"

"Wait a minute!" Mrs. Warriner interrupted. "You still don't know the whole story. Why do you think we were both in that one cabin when you found us? Hughie hit Bellew and locked us in there because when he came below he found this vermin —this incredible, filthy, loathsome pig—already there trying to get into bed with me. What was he supposed to think? If he'd had any doubts before, that would settle them. I hadn't made any noise; being raped was preferable to having Hughie come running down there and probably be beaten to death."

Ingram looked at Bellew, trying to keep the contempt from showing any more than necessary. Don't push him, he thought; he's pretty close to the edge. But the latter was completely at ease. "Rape! Geez! So maybe I was trying to collect what you owed me; it had nothing to do with it, anyway. Hughie-boy already had his club with him when he came down there. He brought it from deck, because he'd already sighted this boat over here."

The son of a bitch, Ingram thought. The dirty, sad—

"If you were that broken up over your wife's death," Rae asked, "how did you ever happen to notice she was missing?"

Ingram gripped her arm and shook his head at her, but neither of the others had heard her anyway.

At least he knew now why Mrs. Warriner insisted on assuming all the guilt, even if she was probably still wrong. "Listen," he said, "that doesn't change anything. He locked you in there because he was already irrational, and he *was* irrational simply because his mind refused to accept the fact he'd been responsible for Mrs. Bellew's death." Then he wondered if he was being very smart. This would only inflame Bellew even more. No, Bellew already knew it anyway, and if he was brutal and stupid enough to want to smash up a boy who was mentally sick, this was merely superfluous and would have no effect on him one way or the other. And somehow he had to reach Mrs. Warriner.

Even while he was conscious of a faint self-disgust for beginning to sound like a cocktail-party psychiatrist, he couldn't escape the feeling that her illogical burden of guilt was probably as dangerous here as Bellew's vindictiveness, and just as likely to trigger an explosion. And certainly it made it a lot more dangerous, and unnecessarily dangerous, for her. Not having any interest at all in what happened to her if anything happened to Warriner, she'd attack Bellew with anything in sight, and the consequences of that wouldn't be anything you'd ever want to remember—if you lived long enough to remember anything. Then, just for a moment, he was tempted to throw up his hands and let the three of them go ahead and kill themselves. Why did he have to defend Warriner, who'd caused the whole thing, when obviously his responsibility was to Rae? Was he going to endanger her life again for that alibi-artist, merely because he was helpless? But he knew he couldn't turn his back on it, even aside from the fact that once it started it couldn't be contained or avoided anyway. And, in the end, there was always Mrs. Warriner. She was worth fifty of the other two, and you couldn't let her throw herself into the meat-grinder from some misguided feeling of guilt.

"For God's sake," he went on wearily, "none of it was your fault, and you're not even doing him any good by trying to take the blame. I'm no head-shrinker, but it seems to me the chances are very good he can be brought out of it, with proper treatment. But he *has* to admit it. I don't think it's a feeling of guilt that made him crack up, but just the refusal to accept the blame. And as long as you go on grabbing all of it in sight, he never will. Jesus, there's no crime in losing your head. Anybody can do it; it's unpredictable. You know that yourself, Bellew—"

"No, I don't, good-buddy. I say nobody but a limp-wristed punk like Hughie-boy could do it, but then I'd never argue with a smart bastard like you. Why don't you write a book?"

He bit down hard on his temper. The whole attempt to appeal to the man had been futile, and any minute it was going to get out of hand. He had to move Warriner, and he'd better do it now, before he waked up. If he could get him shut up in that forward cabin, out of sight, they might make it through the night without an eruption of violence, and by morning Bellew would have had a chance to think twice about it. But getting him out from behind the wheel and down the ladder wasn't going to be easy. He was on the point of telling Bellew to give him a hand when he remembered the old axiom: never give an order you know is going to be ignored.

He turned to Mrs. Warriner. "I think the best place for him is in the forward cabin. The rest of us can use the two bunks in the main cabin in relays, or flake out on deck, subject to the watches we work out. So if you'll take his feet, we'll move him down there now."

"Yes, of course," she said. She stood up.

"No," Bellew said. "As you were."

"What?" she asked.

"Goldilocks stays right where he is." Bellew reached out a foot, put it against her midriff, and pushed. She sat down again.

There was no point in even saying anything, Ingram thought coldly. The act was deliberate and self-explanatory. He was already on his feet, and he hit Bellew as hard as he could just under the ear, as he was getting to his. The only chance he had was to hurt him, and hurt him badly, right at the start. But even as the blow landed, he knew he'd lost. Bellew rolled back with it with the ease and the beautiful reflexes of a pro and counterpunched with almost unbelievable speed for a man his size. Ingram felt the wind go out of him as a fist like a concrete block slammed into his stomach; and then another, which he only partially blocked, hit him over the heart. He started to fall but came back against the mizzen. Bellew hit him twice more in the stomach. Sickness ballooned inside him. He heard Rae shriek behind him, and Mrs. Warriner was trying to get past him to reach Bellew herself.

It was no place to fight; there was no room. He pushed off the mast, blocked Bellew's next punch, and managed to get under his guard with a right. *Saracen* rolled down to starboard. Bellew straightened, off balance, and Ingram hit him again. Bellew went back across the cockpit seat. Ingram swung again, lost his balance, and came down on top of him. They were in the after end of the cockpit, against the binnacle, and Ingram landed with his right forearm across the side of Warriner's face. Warriner stirred and groaned.

Ingram felt an arm lock around his neck and the thumb of the other hand groping for his eyes. He ducked his face down in Bellew's throat and brought his right hand up, grinding the heel of it as he pushed upward, and felt the nose flatten with the tearing of cartilage. Bellew released his neck, pushed him upward, and then kicked out with both feet against his chest. He came up and back, felt his head strike the mizzen boom, and sagged to his knees. Out of the corners of his eyes, he saw Rae emerging from the hatch with the shotgun barrels in her hand, raising them to swing.

Bellew whirled as lightly as a cat, caught her arm, and yanked. She came catapulting up on deck. Bellew plucked the gun barrels from her, threw them outward into the sea, and cuffed her backward across the deckhouse in three smooth and almost simultaneous blurs of motion. Ingram was on his feet again. Bellew turned back to him, grinning and hideous with blood running down his face and onto his chest from the pulpy ruin of his nose. Ingram tried to swing, and then something like the popping of a flash bulb went off inside his head and he was on the bottom of the cockpit.

He wasn't completely out, but dazed and too sick and too weak to get up. He tried. He pushed upward with his arms, felt *Saracen* roll all the way over and spin end-for-end, and collapsed again. He was under the edge of the wheel, and inches in front of his face two feet in white canvas shoes were bound to the bottom of the binnacle with a section of old heaving line. He was absorbing and cataloguing this phenomenon with the bemused wonder of a baby discovering its navel, and only beginning to fit it back into its position in a framework of time and place where everything had blown up and hadn't yet finished settling, when somewhere far off he heard the scream begin. Then the feet moved upward—quite casually, it seemed to him—and the heaving line parted as if it were rotten string.

His mind was clear now, but he still couldn't get up. He fell back on his side and was looking up past the wheel and the binnacle. Bellew, the gory face split in its wolfish grin, was leaning over Warriner. And Warriner was sitting up, cringing backward, still screaming.

"*No, Daddy, Daddy, Daddy, no! No—no!*"

Ingram vomited. He could feel the warmth of it on his hands, and the deck was slick with it as he tried again to push himself up. Mrs. Warriner materialized out of somewhere, flinging herself across his line of vision onto Bellew's shoulders. Bellew shrugged her off. Only half turning, he slapped her backward, and she fell on Ingram's legs.

"Come on, old Hughie-boy, old shark-killer." Bellew grabbed Warriner's shoulders and lifted. He was apparently still talking, for Ingram could see his lips move, but all sound was lost then in another cry from Warriner, a mindless, unceasing, animal screaming that lifted the hair on Ingram's scalp and ran like ice along his back. Warriner lunged upward from behind the wheel, his legs kicking free of the remaining turns of line around them. The line from his wrists to the stanchion gave way. Muscles writhed in his arms. His hands burst apart. Bellew shifted his grip, caught him about the waist, and lifted. He stepped up on the narrow strip of deck between the cockpit and the rail.

Mrs. Warriner was off Ingram's legs then, springing up and toward Bellew. Ingram made it to his knees. Warriner's cry cut off as he saw the water below him, and he spun around in Bellew's grasp, locking his arms and legs around him as if he were clinging to the bole of a tree, and nothing was visible of his eyes except the whites. Ingram got to his feet but fell backward onto the seat. *Saracen* rolled down to starboard. Bellew and Warriner began to topple outward. They were already over the lifeline and almost horizontal when Mrs. Warriner leaped out onto Bellew's back and clamped one arm around his neck while she beat at him with the other hand. All three of them, in one welded and inseparable unit, wheeled slowly over and fell into the sea.

17

"FLASHLIGHT!" he shouted to Rae, who was getting up now. He pushed himself off the cockpit seat and raised it to grope in the locker under it for a diving mask. Leaping to the rail, he looked down. None of them had come up. Bellew, even his tremendous strength powerless in Warriner's cataleptic embrace, couldn't break free, and Mrs. Warriner wouldn't. She'd still be trying to separate them when she lost consciousness. Yanking the mask down over his face, he fell backward into the water.

He turned and peered downward but could see nothing. Farther out, the water was faintly illuminated from the spreader lights, but here directly under the side it was in deep shadow and it was impossible to see under the boat at all. He had only a minute or two at the most. *Saracen* was swinging around on the swell, and by the time he could dive twice there'd be no way of telling where they'd gone under. He kicked downward, swinging his arms in all directions, groping for them. He felt nothing.

Conscious of *Saracen*'s deadly mass plunging up and down on the swell within feet of him, he felt a moment's panic. If he lost his bearings and came up under her he could be knocked unconscious. He swam to his right and started up, and at the same instant he heard them. They were under her, bumping and kicking against the hull in their struggle. Then a beam of light penetrated the water just in front of his face. His head came out of the water. Rae was leaning over the side with a flashlight, shining it downward.

"They're underneath." He gasped. "Shine it in under the counter."

She ran back and threw herself flat on deck aft of the cockpit. Reaching an arm over, she threw the beam of light down and forward, past the rudder. He went under again. He was below the turn of the bilge now and could see the light angling down astern, but everything forward of it was in impenetrable shadow. *Saracen* plunged up and then down, rolling to starboard, toward him. He put a hand up and felt the planking, slick with marine growth, come lunging down against it. He shot downward. It stopped. Pain bit into his palm where it had been cut by a barnacle. As *Saracen* went back to port he swam down and in, raking the area with his arms. Then he saw Warriner and Bellew.

They were almost straight below him, falling away now and dropping into the beam of light. They were still locked together, but no arms or legs moved, and something like a plume of dark smoke was drifting upward and diffusing in the water above them. It was blood, either from Bellew's broken nose or from some wound inflicted on one of them by the keel or hull. He kicked downward but knew at the same time it was impossible. He was already running out of breath, and they were nearly fifteen feet below him, still drifting down. But Mrs. Warriner must be still above them. He *had* to find her. Then his hand brushed something just below him, something soft and fern-like. It was her hair. He entwined his fingers in it and began swimming up and out, away from the hull above him. His chest hurt now, and he wondered if he would make it. He'd been a fool to come under here; his first responsibility was to Rae. Just before he blacked out, his head broke surface and he gulped hungrily at the air.

He was almost under the counter, still too near the rudder and propeller. He swam out, trying to get Mrs. Warriner's head above the surface. Rae had seen him now. "Others—too far down—no use—" He gasped. "Ladder—" It would take too long to tow her around to the other side. Rae disappeared above him, and almost immediately the ladder was dropped over the starboard side, just forward of him. He swam up to it, towing the inert figure behind him. With the beating he had taken from Bellew, he was very weak now, and he wondered if he could get her aboard. Time was precious. She'd been unconscious for minutes.

He ducked under the surface and pulled her across his shoulder. When *Saracen* rolled down to starboard, he got one foot on the bottom rung of the ladder, caught a lifeline stanchion with his free hand, and heaved upward, with Rae helping from above to haul her in under the lifeline until her body was on deck. He came on up himself. They lifted her down onto one of the cockpit seats. Her hair was plastered to her face and she was bleeding from a half-dozen barnacle cuts on her bare legs and shoulders, but she appeared to be uninjured otherwise.

He turned her face downward and began applying artificial respiration. Water ran out of her mouth and drained from her hair, but there was no movement. A minute went by. Two. Three. He was on the point of turning her on her back to try the mouth-to-mouth method he'd read of when he felt her begin trying to breathe again.

She retched and began to gag from the salt water she'd swallowed. He stepped back. She was breathing regularly and without difficulty now. In a few more minutes she opened her eyes. She looked around, blankly at first, and then she screamed. She came off the seat, trying to get to her feet to lunge toward the rail where they'd all gone over. He'd been expecting it. He caught her and forced her back. She fought him, still screaming. Then just as abruptly all the strength went out of her again and she collapsed. She lay face downward while her whole body shook with sobs.

Rae had disappeared. She came running up the ladder now, carrying a glass. Between them they got her upright and forced her to drink. They eased her gently back on the cushion. In a few minutes the crying ceased and she lay still.

"What was it?" he asked.

"Codeine tablet," Rae said. She fumbled a cigarette out of her pocket, but it fell from her fingers into the bottom of the cockpit. She made as if to reach down for it, then merely sighed and collapsed on the other seat. Ingram bent and picked it up for her, but with his wet hand and the water pouring off him and down his arm it was mush by the time he'd straightened. He tossed it overboard. *Saracen* rolled. They looked at each other in silence.

Then Ingram's face twisted. "Maybe if I hadn't hit him . . ."

She looked up. Her voice was thin and very near the edge as she said, "Stop it! And never say that again. He was going to do it, no matter what you did, and you know it. And you saved her, didn't you?"

"I guess you're right."

She rubbed a hand across her face. Then she brought the hand down and looked at its trembling. She clenched it into a fist and opened it. "With luck," she said, "maybe I can keep from thinking about it for ten minutes, and keep from hearing —from hearing—" She swallowed, and went on. "That should be—just about long enough—to get her into that forward bunk and into dry pajamas and wrap a towel around her hair. And then take one of those codeine things myself. Because if I don't make it, you're going to be picking up springs and cog-wheels the rest of the night. Let's go."

Ingram awoke just at dawn. He ached all over, and his stomach muscles felt as if he'd been run over by a truck. He turned his head in the beginnings of light inside the cabin and looked at Rae asleep in the opposite bunk. She was wearing the same sleeveless short pajamas she'd had on yesterday morning, and the mop of tawny hair was spread across the pillow, encircled by her arms. The only thing different was the discolored and swollen area on her face where Warriner had hit her. Just beyond his feet the tea kettle slid and bumped gently against the rails that kept it on the galley stove. Dishes shifted minutely in their stowage above the sink. A timber creaked. It was hot. And it was still dead calm.

He rolled out of the bunk and donned khaki shorts, remembering he could no longer run about the boat naked or clad only in a towel. His eyes softened as he looked down at Rae, and as he put on water for coffee he was careful to make no sound. He went up on deck. It could be yesterday morning all over again, he thought; everything topside was wet with dew, and the surface of the Pacific was as slick as oil except for the heaving of the swell. It was full daylight now, and the few clouds overhead were already edged with pink. Wind or no wind, it was morning, it was beautiful, and it was good to be alive. Then suddenly he was thinking of Warriner and Bellew somewhere in the eternal darkness and the ooze two miles below, and he swore softly as he tried to wrench his mind away. He knew that for years it would keep coming back, leaping out at him in odd moments and without warning to hit him with that unanswerable question: *Would something different, some other way, have worked?*

No. Nothing could have changed it. He'd done everything he could, and in the only way it could have been done. If he'd let Bellew's deliberate provocation go unchallenged, any control he might have had over the situation and any chance he'd have had of saving all of them would have been gone forever. Once authority was lost, you never got it back. And with Bellew doing as he pleased, Warriner would have been doomed anyway. And at some other time, particularly if they were under way, he might not have been lucky enough to save Mrs. Warriner.

He took a look around the horizon for squalls and went back below. He made the weather entries in the log and wound the chronometer. Just as he finished pouring the water through for the coffee, he heard Rae whimper in her sleep. He set the tea kettle down and stepped swiftly over beside her bunk.

Her head was turning from side to side now, and the little cry of pain or of terror was growing in her throat. He dropped to his knees and put his arms about her and began to whisper softly in her ear. She jerked spasmodically, fighting the grip of his arms, and cried out once, but then she was awake. Her eyes were wide with terror, and then confused for a moment before she relaxed and all the tension went out of her. "Just hold me for a minute," she said.

"It won't last forever. You'll quit dreaming about it."

She nodded. "I know. But it may be a long time. The rest of it you could handle, but—oh, God, if only he hadn't said that, *Daddy, Daddy, Daddy*—" Her chin began to quiver and she clenched her teeth to stop it, but tears welled up in her eyes.

"He tried to kill you," Ingram said. "Does that help any?"

"No."

"I guess it wouldn't." He was silent for a moment, and then he went on, "There's not going to be much privacy on here till we get to Papeete, so I want to tell you this now, while I can. I love you."

"That does."

"Does what?"

She managed a smile. "Helps."

He put his mouth down and whispered against her ear. "You're the only one they ever made. Nobody else could have done it—"

"Never mind the junk about what I did. Just tell me again that you love me."

He told her. Then he nodded toward the door into the forward compartment. "While I'm pouring your coffee, take a look in there and see if she's all right."

She rolled off the bunk, opened the door a crack, and peered in. She closed it and nodded. "Still sleeping quietly," she whispered.

She dressed, and they took their coffee on deck to drink it. Ingram lit a cigar, and they watched the sun come up, neither of them saying anything. She started to tremble once as she looked down at the water, but got control of it. He went below to get the compass, to see what it was going to take to secure it in the binnacle, but when he was opening the drawer he heard Mrs. Warriner moving in the forward cabin. He stepped back up the ladder and motioned to Rae. She came down. "Take her something to put on," he said quietly, "and a comb and whatever else she needs to fix herself up. I'll pour her some coffee and take it up on deck."

It was several minutes before they came up. Mrs. Warriner was wrapped in Rae's seersucker robe. Her hair was combed and there was a suggestion of lipstick on her mouth, but her eyes were dead and washed-out, and there were dark circles under them. Her movements were those of a sleepwalker as she sat down in the cockpit and accepted the cup of coffee. She said good morning and thanked him, but it was pure reflex, the ingrained and automatic good manners, and he realized she would have said the same thing if she'd been blind drunk or bleeding to death from a severed artery. But at least she hadn't come running past him to try to jump overboard again. Maybe he was going to get through to her.

She took a sip of the coffee and accepted the cigarette Rae held out to her. "Thank you," she said. She turned to Ingram. "Thank you for saving my life last night." Same tone, he thought. Same inflection. They were of equal value.

He waited till she had finished the coffee, for what strength it could give her. He was sick of making speeches and dreaded it, but it had to be done.

"You heard what he said?" he asked then, abruptly, and apparently with complete callousness. Rae looked at him wonderingly.

"Yes," Mrs. Warriner replied in the same flat tone. The pain showed in her eyes for only an instant and was replaced by that quality of deadness.

"I didn't ask because I enjoy torturing people before breakfast," Ingram went on. "I usually wait till later in the day. But what I'm driving at is that if you did hear him, you know by now it wasn't you he was slamming the door on when he slugged Bellew and left the two of you to drown. It was his father—"

"Yes. Wait," Rae broke in. "I don't know why I didn't remember it before." She told them of Warriner's strange reaction when she'd asked him if his father was still alive.

Ingram nodded. "So there you are," he went on. "He didn't blame you for anything. He didn't think you betrayed him, and he didn't think you deliberately went off and left him to drown. It's just as I told you all along; he was already irrational and didn't know what he was doing; he was confusing Bellew with his father. Probably nobody will ever know what his father did to him, but it was there in his subconscious all the time, and when his mind began to let go—" He gestured wearily. "God, I'm tired of sounding like a discount-house psychiatrist. But don't you see, that was the reason he backed down from Bellew the way he did? When Bellew started bullying him and riding him, the old patterns began to come to the surface again. But I'll get on to what I'm trying to say. You're an adult, and you've probably got more sense than I have, and if you want to go on blaming yourself for something that was never any of your fault from first to last, that's your affair. Aside from the fact that I like you and have a great deal of admiration for you, it's none of my business at all.

"But sailing this boat is my business, and there's a lot of work attached to it. You can help us, if you will, or you can make it tougher by keeping us busy heading you off from the rail because you want to go on torturing yourself like some mixed-up adolescent. Am I making any sense to you at all?"

She nodded, and for a moment there was a trace of life about her eyes, a touch of the old coolness and intelligence. "Yes, you're doing quite well." She turned to Rae. "Mrs. Ingram, I like your husband."

"I'm fond of him at times myself," Rae said.

Mrs. Warriner tossed her cigarette over the side and stood up. "What do we do first? Can I help get breakfast, or shall I be dishwasher?"

Ingram sighed gently. "The first project is that compass. As soon as I can get it installed in the binnacle some way, we'll swing ship and compensate it while we've got the sun low on the horizon. We'll need the azimuth tables, and a watch, and something to use for a new deviation card—" He broke off and stood up himself, looking out to starboard.

"What is it?" Rae asked.

"Wind."

She stood up, and they all turned to look. Off in the northeast the surface of the sea was darkening with the riffles of an advancing breeze. It might die out in ten minutes, or it might never even reach them at all, but it was wind. And today, or tomorrow, or the day after that, they'd pick up the Trades.

THE EXPENDABLE MAN

Dorothy B. Hughes

For my friend, Charlesetta

I

ACROSS THE tracks there was a different world. The long and lonely country was the color of sand. The horizon hills were haze-black; the clumps of mesquite stood in dark pools of their own shadowing. But the pools and the rim of dark horizon were discerned only by conscious seeing, else the world was all sand, brown and tan and copper and pale beige. Even the sky at this moment was sand, reflection of the fading bronze of the sun.

It was good to be out on the road, away from the banging of the town on the other side of the tracks. Driving into Indio after six of an early May evening, the sun-blazing of the earlier hours of the day had become an invisible cloud of heat which lay heavily, suffocatingly, upon the town. Noise had intensified the discomfort, and there was noise—the kind which only a covey of teen-agers in spring could engender. Their cars roared and popped and spluttered, their car radios blared above the din, while their voices screamed and shouted over the combined cacophony.

Hugh's intent, on driving in, had been a stop at an air-cooled drugstore. But once he had seen the size and temper of the invading young people, he settled for a drive-in restaurant. It had been a mistake, this he knew once he had parked. Almost immediately the jalopy which had cut across his way not once but often on his entrance to town, came rocketing back up the street and swung precariously into the drive-in's court. The car was crowded with high school youngsters; he didn't count them, only observed they seemed to be spilling over the sides of the open chassis. He shut his ears to their din and waited for one of the serving girls to bring him a menu. There were three of these girls, dressed in red band-uniform type trousers and wilted white shirts, topped with bolero-length jackets of the same red. Two were no more than teen-agers, the third a little older.

He waited for some time. He would have quit the place but he hadn't eaten since noon. If he were going through to Phoenix tonight, he'd have to eat something now. Between here and

Phoenix, there wouldn't be much opportunity. Therefore he waited, refusing to be driven away by the vulgar young people or the disinclined help.

Eventually, as he knew eventually it would happen, the less pretty of the young waitresses came to his car and thrust a menu at him. He ordered a bacon and tomato sandwich and iced coffee. It was too hot for anything more. There wasn't an undue wait for the order to come and it wasn't bad when it came. The jalopy had roared off with thunderous pipes before then, and he was allowed to eat in peace. Nevertheless he'd been relieved to get out of the town, to cross the tracks into this empty sand world.

He switched radio stations until he found a Los Angeles one with good pop records, lit another cigarette, and settled back into a comfortable driving position. In spite of the heat in Indio, it wasn't too hot on the desert here at sundown, not the way it would have been in summer. Most evenings were still cool, the nights chill, on the desert in May. It should be the same in Phoenix—hot days, cool nights, perfect weather.

He had wound through the small canyon outside of town, and was moving on to the long desert plain, when he noted ahead an extra shadow in the tree shadow marking a culvert. It looked as if there were someone resting under the tree. It couldn't be possible, here, close to fifteen miles out of town. There wasn't a car in sight in either direction, and there was no habitation of any sort in any direction. Yet it looked like a person's shadow.

It was just that. The shadow, raised up from its haunches, waited for his car to approach. He knew better than to pick up a hitchhiker on the road; he'd known it long before the newspapers and script writers had implanted the danger in the public mind. Most assuredly he would not pick up anyone in this strange, deserted land. But he reduced speed when he approached the shadow, the automatic anxiety reaction that a person might step in front of the oncoming car. He passed the hitchhiker before he was actually aware of the shape and form; only after he had passed did he realize that this was a young girl. From the glimpse, a teen-age girl. Even as he slowed his car, he was against doing it. But her possible peril if left here alone forced his hand. He simply could not in conscience go on, leaving her abandoned, with twilight fallen and night quick to come. He had sisters as young as this. It chilled him to think what might happen if one of them were abandoned on the lonesome highway, the type of man with whom, in desperation, she might accept a lift. The car was stopped. He shifted to reverse and began backing up.

As soon as the girl saw that he had stopped, she scooped up her belongings from the ground and started running toward his car. Hugh spoke through the open window. "Do you want a ride?"

She didn't answer at once. She stood there looking through the window at his face. She was a teen-ager, she might have been one of the girls he'd seen at the drive-in. She wasn't pretty; her face was just a young, thin, petulant face, too much lipstick on the mouth, wisps of her self-bleached hair jutting from beneath the gaudy orange and green scarf covering her head. She was wearing tight green slacks. A boy's shirt, too big for her, hung almost to her knees; a dirty white shirt pin-striped in blue. She carried a boy's jacket, a high school club jacket of maroon and gold. She also carried a box handbag of white plastic in one hand, in the other a small canvas traveling bag. She wore white socks and white wedgie sandals, the kind his younger sister said only the cheap girls wore.

He repeated his question, a little impatiently because he didn't like this situation at all, his car stopped here on the road, the girl standing outside looking in at him. At any moment a car from Indio might overtake them, or one appear from the eastern crest of the road. A chill sense of apprehension came on him and he wished to hell he hadn't stopped. This could be the initial step in some kind of shakedown, although how, with nothing or no one in sight for unlimited miles, he couldn't figure.

He spoke up more sharply than was his wont. "Well, do you want a ride or don't you?"

"I guess so." As if in speaking she'd made her decision, she opened the door and piled in.

He set the car in motion again, picking up speed until he hit the sixty-five-mile maximum for this highway. He didn't look at her or say anything more to her. From the periphery of his eye, he saw her set her traveling bag on the floor mat, away from him, close to the door. Her soiled sandal touched it protectively, as if it were filled with gold and precious gems. For no particular reason, he was relieved that his suitcases and his medical bag were locked in the trunk of the car.

Far ahead on the road, he saw the shape of an oncoming car as it lifted itself over a culvert. He switched on his lights. The sky was still pale, the pale lavender of twilight, but the sand world had darkened. It was difficult enough to drive at this hour, the lights would identify the presence of his car to the one approaching. When the other car passed his, headed toward Indio, he saw it was yet another jalopy filled with kids. It was hopped up; it zoomed by, with only scraps of voices shrilling above the sound of the motor.

In his rear-view mirror, he watched until it disappeared in the distance. Just for a moment, he had known fear. It might have been the same group which had hectored him in town. The trap might be sprung by his picking up the girl; they might swing about and come after him. Only when the car had disappeared from sight, did he relax and immediately feel the fool. It was surprising what old experiences remembered could do to a presumedly educated, civilized man.

If the girl had recognized the group, she gave no indication. She was slumped down in the seat, her eyes fixed on the long road ahead.

He held the wheel steady, and lighted another cigarette. He asked then, "How did you get there?"

"Where?" She was defiant.

"On the road. Where I stopped for you."

"I got a ride that far."

"How could you get a ride that far and no further? There are no ranches around."

She considered her answer. "I got a ride that far and then I didn't like—I didn't like it—so I got out."

It could have been true. "Where are you going?"

"Phoenix."

"Hitching?"

"How else could I get there?" The defiance heightened. "I haven't got a big Cadillac and money."

He was going to ignore her remark, but because of his uneasiness, he didn't. He said, "It's a borrowed car." He didn't say borrowed from his mother. He spoke placidly, wanting to diminish her tension. "Does your family know you're hitching to Phoenix?"

"My family doesn't care what I do," she flung at him. She'd have told him it was none of his business but for the fact that, having accepted this ride, she didn't want to take any chances on losing it. "I'm not running away," she said. "I'm going to Phoenix to visit—my aunt."

There had been a perceptible hesitation, his ear was certain. Just as sure as he was that no family, how little they cared for this unappealing girl, would knowingly permit her to hitchhike to another state, so he was sure she'd invented the aunt. Most likely, her family had given her bus fare for the trip and she'd spent it. She wasn't going to tell him whom she would visit and he didn't care.

"What about school?" he asked.

"We got a holiday until Monday. Some teachers' meeting or something."

She didn't hesitate on that, and it explained the number of young people running free in Indio.

"How old are you?" he asked suddenly.

She was angry at the question, but she answered. "I'm—eighteen."

She couldn't have been more than sixteen, possibly no more than fourteen or fifteen. One thing certain, she wasn't any eighteen. She hadn't the maturity which came imperceptibly at that age. His younger sister, Allegra, at fifteen, no matter what she thought, was still a child. Celeste, the older, coming up eighteen, no longer was. This one was a child, telling her whoppers, expecting them to be believed. He knew now he would not drive her all the way to Phoenix. Not across the state line.

He asked, "Where are you from? Indio?"

"No, I'm from Banning." She spoke too fast, lying again. Even she knew she was caught out; she raced on to ask him, "Where you from?"

"Los Angeles."

"What do you do?" The Cadillac was still on her mind.

"I'm a doctor—an intern."

"Really?" She stretched the word, like a credulous child. Yet the answer had somehow taken away her uneasiness, even her resentment. She half turned in the seat to look over at him.

"Really," he said good-naturedly. The response didn't disturb him. "I'm at the Med Center—UCLA."

"Did you go to UCLA?"

"I did my pre-med there and finished at Northwestern. UCLA didn't have a full medical program at the time. Then I did my Army stint and now I'm interning." He was talking with purpose, to keep her relaxed, with a hope of her becoming friendly. If he could get her to that point, possibly he could find out the truth about this trip of hers, perhaps help her. A young girl hitchhiking to Phoenix needed all the help she could find. "Are you in high school?"

"Yeah, I'm a junior." She said it with pride. But if she was a junior, she was older than he thought she was and brighter.

"Do you want to go to college?"

"I don't know. I don't like school much."

Again she was retreating, and he made conversation quickly. "I have a sister, a freshman in college. UCLA. She'll be eighteen this summer. She's a brain, I guess you'd call it. Not that she's always in a book, she's a babe. My other sister, she's fifteen, is a sophomore at L.A. High. She's not so much on books but she's knocking herself out to get college grades so that she can go to UCLA too. She doesn't want to miss the fun."

She said, "If I was going to college, I'd go to UCLA. They have the best teams."

"They usually do," he admitted.

"Did you play football?"

"No. I played some basketball."

"How tall are you?"

He smiled. "Only six and a point. Not tall enough to be a star."

"There's a boy on our team is six seven. All the schools are after him. He's good."

"Where does he want to go?"

"UCLA, of course. If he can get in. You have to have awful good grades to get in there."

"Don't I know it? Doesn't Allegra know it—that's my younger sister."

"Allegra. That's a funny name."

"'Brave Alice and laughing Allegra—'"

She was lost.

"Don't you know 'The Children's Hour'?"

"I never watched that."

He said gently, "It's a poem. By Longfellow."

"I guess we haven't had that in school yet."

He guessed she didn't read anything out of school but comics and lurid romance magazines. He said, "My mother said Allegra was laughing as soon as she was born. My mother learned the poem in school when she was a girl."

The girl asked then, "What's your name?"

"Hugh Densmore. What's yours?"

She hesitated rather too long. "Iris Croom." It might be. The hesitation could mean only that she didn't want him to know her name. Without warning, she asked, "What kind of a doctor are you?"

He didn't quite understand her meaning. He began, "At the moment, I'm not practicing. I'm interning. That means working at a hospital before actual practice."

"I know." She flounced. On television they learned all manner of bits and pieces. "But what are you going to be? A brain surgeon? Or a baby doctor? Or just plain."

"I want to do research," he said. "Cancer research. That's why I'm lucky to get in at Med Center. They're doing exciting things about cancer."

He didn't know if she understood what he was talking about. She was abruptly silent, watching the road ahead. Then again she turned suddenly to him. "I'm hungry."

"I'm sorry," he said. "I don't even have a candy bar. Didn't you eat before you left Indio?"

"I had a malt. But I'm starved now."

She wasn't hinting, there was not so much as a service station in sight. There'd be no place to get food until they reached Blythe. Nor would he stop if there were one, not until he got to Blythe, where he could put her off at the bus depot. "I have some gum." He felt in his pocket and found the package.

"Maybe it'll help." She extracted a stick and handed the package back to him. He unwrapped a piece for himself.

"This'll keep me from smoking so much," he said.

After a moment, she stated, "I guess I'll put up my hair." She rooted in her handbag, found bobby pins and a man's black pocket comb. She pulled off her scarf and ran the comb through her hair. She looked even younger with the lank, badly bleached hair hanging around her face.

"Don't you need a mirror?"

"I have one." She showed him, inset in the lid of her box purse. But she could wind the pin curls without it, there wasn't enough light from the dashboard for her to see in the mirror. By now it was quite dark outside the car. Johnny Mathis was singing from the radio; she hummed with the song.

He wondered again just whom she was meeting in Phoenix in the morning. Or was it simply habit that she put up her hair at night. He asked, "Do you have a boy friend in Phoenix?"

She was immediately suspicious. "Why'd you ask me that?"

"Putting up your hair—"

"I don't want to get to Phoenix looking a mess. It got all wet this afternoon when I was swimming."

He didn't say anything, but it must have been quite a day. From Banning to Indio to the desert highway. Swimming where?

"Are you going to Phoenix?" she asked.

"I am." He was ready for the question, he had been expecting it. "But I'm not going through tonight. I'm stopping over in Blythe."

"Do you have friends in Blythe?"

"No, but I'm too tired to drive through." Actually it was true. "I've been on night duty." Although he'd wanted to walk in on the family tonight, it would be just as well to have some rest and be ready for tomorrow.

"I wish you were driving through." She tied the scarf around her head again, and put on the heavy school jacket. "I'm going to sleep," she announced.

"It's only eight o'clock."

She gave a small but knowing smirk. "I didn't get much sleep last night."

"Do you want to move in back where you can stretch out?"

She considered it, pushing onto her knees and leaning over for a careful investigation. There was nothing on the back seat but his folded jacket. On the floor was a Thermos jug of water. He disliked, from taking family trips as a boy, no doubt, a cluttered car when touring.

She decided, "I guess not. It's warmer up front. I'm used to sleeping in cars." She giggled a little at that, as if it were funny. She turned her back on him, curled herself into the corner, and rested her head against the cushioned seat. She went to sleep almost at once, he could tell by her slightly nasal breathing.

He drove on through the night. The road was good; he hadn't seen half a dozen cars since leaving Indio. He should reach Blythe by around nine o'clock. He began to wonder about the bus schedule to Phoenix. He couldn't simply drop this girl on a street corner. If there was no bus out tonight, he'd probably have to give her the price of a room. In a motel as far as possible from the one where he would stop. He was quite sure she wouldn't have enough money to get one for herself. He didn't have much with him; he never had much money, not on an intern's allowance. Again he wondered if the girl had ever had bus money.

If he had to, he'd lend her what she needed. The aunt could repay him, if there was an aunt in Phoenix. If not, perhaps her family would some day. By now he was in his own mind certain that Iris was a runaway. The sooner he could be shed of her, the safer he'd be. If there was a teletype out for her by now, his position could be more precarious than he wanted to think about.

Worrying about it was pointless. Nothing was going to call attention to them until they reached Blythe. At Blythe he'd see that she was taken care of, and that would end it. And he'd never pick up another hitchhiker, never. Not even a ninety-year-old grandfather or the chief of police.

She wakened when a gargantuan oil truck thundered by, rocking the car. She made a word sound and then for a moment her sleep-dulled eyes looked at him in fear. But she came more fully awake and said, "Oh, it's you. Where are we?"

"About ten miles out of Blythe."

"You're still going to stop there?"

"That's right. But I'll see about your bus first."

"I'm not going on the bus," she said sullenly. "Don't worry about me. I'll get another ride."

He was sharp with her. "What's the matter with you? You can't pick up a ride with strangers in the middle of the night. It isn't safe."

She looked at him for a moment, a level, too-old look. It said she'd let him pick her up and that she was safe with him. Or was she wondering why she'd done it. She said finally, "I can't go on the bus. I don't have any money."

Anger came to his voice. "Now look here, Iris, or whatever your name is, you can't tell me your family let you set off for Phoenix without a bus ticket."

"You don't know my family." Her voice was brittle.

"I don't know your family but I know my family. I know lots of families. There isn't a one that would let a fifteen-year-old kid hitchhike—"

"I told you I was eighteen."

"You've told me plenty of things. You haven't made me believe them. You're not more than sixteen. And unless you're running away from home, you started out with a bus ticket." He calmed down, losing his temper wouldn't help matters. "I'd like to help you. Why don't you level with me? Are you running away?"

"No, I'm not," she flared. "I told my father I was going to Phoenix and he didn't care. He told me to go on and go."

"What did your mother say?"

"My mother ditched us six years ago. She was a tramp."

His hand clenched to keep from striking her. "Don't say that!"

"My father says she was. He ought to know better than you, hadn't he?" she asked insolently.

"Don't you say it," he repeated. "You don't know her side of it. You respect your mother until you know better." It occurred to him, "Is your mother in Phoenix?"

"We don't know where she is. My aunt's in Phoenix."

"Your father's sister? Or your mother's?"

"My mother's."

"And that's where you're going."

"That's where."

"Your father gave you the money to go."

"He didn't give me nothing."

"How did he expect you to get there?"

She said, "I knew he wouldn't give me the money. When he asked me how I was getting there, I told him I'd saved up from baby-sitting."

"You hitchhiked to Indio?"

"I didn't have to. I rode down there with some of the kids."

He was trying to form the truth. "It was the kids who dropped you there on the desert. And drove back again to see if you had a ride. That car we passed—"

"You think you're pretty smart, don't you?"

"No, I don't. I'm trying to find out what happened. That's the way it was, wasn't it?"

She didn't answer him.

"But why? Why didn't you try to get a ride in Indio? You're from Indio, aren't you, not Banning? You were afraid someone might see you trying to hitch a ride there, tell your father."

"That wasn't it," she denied. "It was Guppy's idea. He hitched to Phoenix once. He said they're more apt to stop for you out on the desert than in town. They're sorry for you. In town they think like you do—'take a bus.'"

It disturbed him too much to keep silent, although he didn't want to know, actually was afraid to know. "You were one of the kids in the beat-up car at the drive-in, weren't you?"

She was furtive. "I don't know what you're talking about."

"It was the same car passed us going back to Indio." He demanded fiercely, "Did you have my car staked out from the beginning? Were you waiting for me?"

"I should say not!" she denied with emphasis. "That's not the way it was at all. I wouldn't have—" She broke off. "It wasn't that way," she started again. "I was expecting to get a ride with a family. Not many women would pass up a girl on the highway."

More of Guppy's wisdom, no doubt. With some rancor, he said, "You were willing enough to get in my car."

"It was turning dark and I was getting sort of scared. I didn't want to have to go home and start all over again. My aunt's expecting me. I wrote her I'd be there in the morning."

"And she thinks you're coming by bus."

"That's right. But I didn't tell her which one because I didn't know what time I'd get there."

He studied it. It could be the truth; it could be a pack of lies. It didn't make much difference to him now. He said, "Well, I can't take you on to Phoenix. But I won't just desert you in Blythe. I'll see about a bus and I'll lend you the money for a ticket. You can pay me back tomorrow when I get to Phoenix."

"With what?" she sneered.

He was patient. "I'm sure your aunt will lend you the money. What's her address?"

She made a quick gesture of her head that might have been panic, and again he decided there was no aunt. "Don't you come bothering her," she said. "You give me your address. I'll bring the money to you."

He had no intention of giving her an address. He said, "Never mind that. Just give me your aunt's number. I'll phone before I come, to make sure I'm not bothering her."

His sarcasm was lost on her. She didn't care what he said, she was too involved in putting on fresh lipstick by the dash light. They were coming into Blythe. It was just a small town of the sort you passed through on any highway but for some reason it was, to Hugh, a singularly pleasant one. The wide main street managed to give the impression that it was a main street in spite of being also a state highway. The business section was no more than a few blocks with the usual small-town businesses, the usual wealth of gas stations which cluttered all highway towns, and an abundance of motels, good-looking modern motels. Neon lights were rainbow above the latter, otherwise most of the town was dark.

The bus depot was on the other side of the highway at the western end of town. Hugh pulled around the corner of a side street and stopped the car. "You stay here," he directed Iris. "I'll see what I can find out." He reached for his jacket and put it on.

She was gazing into her purse mirror although there was not even reflected light there. "Hurry up will you? I'm hungry."

He took the keys from the ignition. "I'll hurry." He couldn't make it fast enough to be rid of her, to be solitary and safe again.

He waited on the side of the darkened road for passing cars—it seemed a long time—then cut half on a run across to the depot. A dumpy woman in a yellow cotton dress was behind the ticket counter. She was talking in a desultory fashion with three workmen seated at a table in the lunch section. All of them became silent at Hugh's entrance.

He walked over to the woman. "Are there any buses to Phoenix tonight?"

"They run all night." Unsmiling, she indicated the posted schedule.

He didn't let his expression change as he studied it. But inside, his smile of relief was so broad, he put his hand to his face in fear it might break through. There was an eastbound bus at ten fifty-five. Time for Iris to get something to eat, not too much time to wait after. He had no doubt but that the ticket woman would make certain everyone was aboard when the bus pulled out.

"How much?" he asked her.

"One way or round trip?"

"One way."

"Six thirty-eight."

He took a ten-dollar bill from his wallet. The woman pushed the small bit of cardboard and his change across the counter. He said, "Thanks," and left the place. Again he had to wait to cut across the highway, hoping that those inside the depot weren't watching to see where he was headed. They couldn't see Iris from here, he'd parked the car far enough around the opposite corner to make sure of that.

He wasn't certain she'd be waiting but she was there. As he opened the car door, she greeted him with the complaint, "Didn't you bring nothing to eat?"

He got into the car and closed the door. He said, "There's a bus to Phoenix at ten fifty-five. Here's your ticket."

She took the pasteboard as if it were dirty.

"Put it in your purse so you won't lose it."

"I won't lose it," she said unpleasantly. But she complied, unearthing a red plastic wallet from the handbag, and putting the ticket into the zipper compartment. "Now what am I supposed to do, starve?"

He consulted his watch in the dash light. "It's nine-thirty. You have plenty of time to eat something."

She continued unpleasant. "What do I use for money?"

"How much do you have?"

She emptied the change compartment into her hand. "Seventeen cents."

"That's all?"

She opened all of the wallet compartments. "That's all." She pulled out the pockets of her slacks. "You want to look in my jacket?" She shoved it at him but he didn't touch it. "You can't even buy a hamburger with seventeen lousy cents."

From his pocket, he took the change from the ten. Anything to be rid of her before the local law or a busybody wondered why they were parked here. He said, "Here's three dollars and sixty-two cents. The ticket was six thirty-eight. That's ten dollars you owe me."

Her fingers clutched the three bills and she held her hand palm up for the change. Ungraciously she said, "Thanks."

"There's a café a few doors from the depot. It looks better than their lunch stand."

She was gathering up her belongings.

"Whatever you do, don't miss that bus."

She didn't say anything. She opened the door of the car and backed out, holding the handbag and traveling case against her. She pushed the door shut with her foot. She looked in at him and again said, "Thanks," as if she hated to say it.

He watched until she had darted across the highway and was headed toward the restaurant he'd pointed out to her. He then drove on, and only then did he remember that he'd failed to get the address or phone number of her aunt. He shrugged. Good-bye to ten bucks, ten hard-earned bucks. He couldn't regret too much; he'd have paid out more than twice that to be free of Iris Croom.

He followed the dark country street to its intersection, rounded the block, and returned to the highway. Now that he was rid of her, there was no reason why he shouldn't go on to Phoenix. No reason save that reaction had set in and he knew he was too tired for the long drive. He'd been on night duty for the past month. Last night he'd doubled his job with duty today, a trade to get away early this afternoon. He wouldn't be a safe risk on the road.

He drove the few blocks through the town. There was a large chain motel near the eastern end. He'd stayed there before. He hoped there'd be a vacancy tonight, you never knew. Sometimes even when the sign said there was one, the last unit had been rented just before you arrived.

The vacancy sign was lighted. He turned the car down the circular driveway. Although it was almost three years since he'd been here, he recognized the young woman inside the office. There was nothing distinctive about her. On the street he wouldn't have known her, but in her own setting she was remembered. He was relieved to see her on duty. She'd been a pleasant hostess before, he didn't expect her to be changed.

She wasn't. There was a vacancy and she didn't up the price for him. Five dollars. After he'd taken his kit bag into the room, he was just too tired to drive back downtown and try to find a place where he could eat. It could have been that he was less tired than he was afraid he might come upon Iris again. He settled for an aspirin. Hunger would not keep him awake. He was trained to fall asleep when his head was put to a pillow.

He woke at seven when a loud-mouthed man and woman took off from the next-door unit. He wasn't exactly rested but he couldn't get back to sleep. There was a compulsion to be on his way before any more trouble could develop. And by now he was ravening for food. He shaved, showered, put on fresh linen, replaced his kit in the car trunk, and was ready to leave.

The morning air was cool. Later the sun would be intense but at this hour there was only golden warmth, the color of summer wheat. He drove out to the highway and headed back toward the town to find a restaurant. He changed his mind when he saw the supermarket. Swinging the car into the lot, he went in and bought a quart of milk and a package of six cinnamon rolls. He could have breakfast while he rolled along. It could be better than greasy-spoon food.

He had the car serviced at a nearby station and was on his way. He was as hungry as his passenger had been last night. Before he reached the old bridge that spanned the Colorado, he'd finished a couple of rolls and half the milk. The river was full and lush and green, from green-white winter snow of northern mountains, from spring rains that never fell on this parched earth. Even this early, there were little sunbrowned, near-naked boys splashing along the green banks.

He rolled the car down the other side of the bridge and across the state line to the Arizona inspection station. There were a couple of cars ahead of his under the long sheds. He pulled up. Not until he inched under the roof did he see Iris. She was waiting at the side of the road, just beyond the inspection tables. If possible she looked shabbier than she had last night, unwashed, her hair done up in pin curlers under the dirty scarf, the oversized jacket draped on her shoulders. Her dirty sandal rested against the small traveling bag; the white plastic handbag was clutched to her.

He knew why she was waiting. She thought she could force him to take her along to Phoenix. He wondered if she'd cashed in the ticket and spent the money or if she was saving it to spend in Phoenix. He wondered where she'd spent the night.

He heard the usual questions, "Any fruit? Citrus? Plants?"

"None," he said.

The inspector considered the answer suspiciously. "Let me see in your trunk." He was a fat, sour-looking man, the kind who'd like to make something of Hugh's picking up a dirty blond teen-ager. He'd resented the big white Cadillac the moment that Hugh drove up in it. A second inspector lounged in the doorway of the station.

"Certainly," Hugh said. He got out of the car, not looking toward the girl, and went around to the rear. He opened the trunk. It was as neat as the interior of the car, the way he liked it. His large suitcase, the car case, the kit bag, his doctor's bag, his father's golf clubs. Tools at the side by the spare tire. If he ignored Iris, she might not have the nerve to approach him. Not after pocketing the bus ticket and not using it.

"What's in that one?" the inspector snapped.

"I'm a doctor." Hugh unlatched it. "It's my medical bag."

"Any dope?"

"No, none." Because he'd thought of this inspection when he was packing, he had removed emergency packets for which he had registrations, permits, the works. He was aware that such legalities could make little or no difference to a small-town official bent on trouble.

"Open the other bags." Not please, not even in intonation.

Seething inwardly, Hugh complied. If this big wart-hog threw his clothes around, Hugh decided he would find a way to carry his complaint up to the governor's office.

The man didn't. He snorted at the neatly packed cases and said, "Okay."

Hugh closed the trunk and started around again to the driver's seat. He hadn't quite reached it when he heard the call.

"Dr. Densmore!" Iris was hurrying over to the car. "Dr. Densmore," she shrilled. "I thought I recognized you." On her face was a sickly-sweet innocent smile.

The inspector stopped in his tracks and turned to watch.

"Oh, Dr. Densmore"—she was deliberately speaking too loud—"would you give me a lift to Wickenberg, oh, please? I must have missed my ride and if I don't get there this morning I'll lose my job and I don't know what my mother will say."

Both inspectors were watching, listening; suspicion like hoods over their faces. There was absolutely nothing Hugh could do to escape her. To refuse would have been worse than to accede. He couldn't say he was not going to Wickenberg, there was no way to miss it in this direction.

He spoke politely but aloofly, as if she were the daughter of a man he'd known not well, possibly in a business way. "Why, certainly, Iris. Get in."

Smug triumph flashed in her eyes but the inspectors couldn't see that. She climbed in the car with her belongings and he set it in motion, conscious of the officials following the license plate out of sight. When they were on the road, he asked her, "Why didn't you take the bus?"

"Waste all that money when I could hitch?"

"What did you do with the ticket?"

"Turned it in. I told the lady my plans were changed."

"I suppose you told her I was your chauffeur."

She giggled. "I didn't say nothing about you. I just said I was visiting friends and had decided not to leave yet."

"You're a practiced liar, aren't you?"

"I manage."

"What did you do with the money?"

"Don't worry." She yawned. "You'll get it back. From my aunt, remember?"

"I'll get it back if I have to tell her the whole story. Where did you sleep last night?"

She giggled again. "I didn't. I met up with some kids who knew some of the Indio kids I know. We just kicked around." Her laugh was nasty. "First we spotted your car at that snazzy motel where you stayed. So I knew you hadn't lied to me about staying in Blythe and that I could get a ride to Phoenix with you this morning."

"And if I'd said no?"

"You couldn't. I fixed it so you couldn't." She knew what she'd done, could boast of it. She was an evil little girl. She went on slyly, "I knew why you wouldn't take me on to Phoenix last night. You didn't want to cross the state line with me. So the kids took me out there this morning and I walked across. You got nothing to worry about."

She hadn't known last night. Some of the "kids" must have put her wise.

"What about those inspection officers? What do you think they thought?"

"They thought I was waiting for some friends to give me a ride to work. Then when you came along—you heard me."

"Do you think they believed you?"

"Who cares? Blobs they were. Both of them. Blobs. I'll never see them again."

But I will, Hugh said silently. Every time I visit the Phoenix relatives. And every time I pass this station, I'll be suspect. He didn't say it to her. Whether she spoke it or not, her reaction would be: Who cares? She was interested only in her own affairs. He took another bun from the package and began to eat it.

"Food!" she cried. "Can I have some?"

"Didn't you eat last night?"

"I didn't eat nothing this morning. I'm starved."

She didn't deserve it but he handed the rest of the rolls to her. "You can have these but you can't have my milk. I didn't get any dinner."

"Why not? Didn't you have any more money?"

"By the time I'd taken care of you and found myself a room, I was too tired to do anything but fall in bed."

"At least you got to sleep." She munched on the bun sloppily. "Maybe I ought to sleep now but I'm not a bit sleepy."

"You will be later. Or did you take a pep pill?"

"Of course I didn't," she retorted indignantly. "Where would I get one of those?"

"I thought maybe one of your new friends might have given you one."

She licked one finger. "You're teed off at me, aren't you?"

"Don't I have a right to be?" He drank what was left of the milk.

"I don't know why. I didn't do nothing to you. Unless it's the bus ticket that's bugging you. You'll get your money. Just relax. You'll get it."

"I'll get it," he repeated firmly.

She looked at the carton in his hand. "Is there any of that milk left?"

"None at all." He dropped the container on the seat. "There's some water in the Thermos. It may be a bit stale, I didn't refill it this morning. But if you're thirsty enough, you can drink it."

She scrambled to her knees, leaned over the back seat and lifted the Thermos from the floor. "You want some?"

"No, thank you. You'll find a glass in the glove compartment."

She punched the compartment open, took out the glass and poured it full of water, slopping some of it on her and some on the floor mat. "It's not very good," she said, wiping her mouth with her hand. "I wish you had more milk."

"If I'd known I was having a guest for breakfast, I'd have bought two bottles. When you're through, put the jug back where you found it."

"You're so funny," she said sarcastically. "Ha ha." She finished the water, replaced the glass, banged the compartment shut, and with another scramble swung the Thermos in place. "Maybe we could stop for a Coke in Wickenberg."

"Barring car trouble—God forbid—our first stop will be the bus station at Phoenix."

She said cheekily, "Suppose I have to make a stop."

"I'll pull off the road where there's a bush," he stated. "And no Coke machine."

"I honestly think you would."

"I would," he confirmed.

She believed him and settled back. "Mind if I turn on the radio?"

"No, I don't mind."

She played with the finder until she had a station, there weren't many in this neighborhood. As she had last night, she hummed with the music. When the announcer broke in with an ad spiel, she said, "I wish they'd play that new Johnny Mathis record. Do you like Johnny Mathis?"

"I like him."

"I go ape over Johnny Mathis."

"Personally I prefer Sinatra." He wondered if that dated him, as his mother was dated with Bing Crosby.

At least the music kept her quiet and he could enjoy the morning ride. He'd always had a quickening of the heart when he crossed into Arizona and beheld the cactus country. This was as the desert should be, this was the desert of the picture books, with the land unrolled to the farthest distant horizon hills, with saguaro standing sentinel in their strange chessboard pattern, towering supinely above the fans of ocotillo and the brushy mesquite. Because there had been some winter rain, the desert was in bloom. The saguaro wore creamy crowns on their tall heads, the ocotillo spikes were tipped with vermilion, and the brush bloomed yellow as forsythia.

There was little traffic, never much on this span, and the road was well built. They rolled through Quartzsite and Hope and within an hour were in sight of the weathered curio café and new resort motel of Salome-Where-She-Danced.

Iris sat up brightly. "We could get a Coke here."

"You can get a Coke at Phoenix." He kept his face expressionless, set ahead on the road, driving with care at the reduced town speed. He must attract no attention from country constables or curious tourists while the girl was in his car.

She wailed, "But that's ages!"

They were already out of the town and approaching the shining span of the railway bridge.

"Two hours. One to Wickenberg. Another to the city limits. Maybe another half hour to get across town to the bus station."

"I can't wait. I got to have a Coke, I'm dying."

He made evident his disinterest. "Drink water."

"That stuff! It tastes like you took a bath in it."

"If you're really thirsty, you'll drink it."

"You're revolting." She sulked for a mile, then asked, "You got any more of that gum?"

He put his hand in his pocket, found one stick and handed it to her. She settled down, still sulky but at least near-noiselessly so. She chomped gum. He ignored her. This was his special part of the countryside, the prime of desert and far mountain landscape. The sun was lifting higher and hotter; it was a good thing he'd made an early start.

The hour passed and they were coming into Wickenberg. It meant reduced speed again, and he didn't like it. At this crawl, the people in passing cars, the people on the downtown main street, couldn't help but notice Iris. But at least she didn't open up on her Coke bit. Once free of the outskirts traffic, he pushed up to the sixty Arizona limit. There'd be traffic between here and Phoenix, but the closer he drew to Phoenix, the less he cared. Phoenix was a city. In a city, people were too busy with their own affairs to wonder about a strangely assorted couple.

They wound through the canyon and emerged into the hot flat desert area. There must have been some familiarity with this final stretch which put the excitement in Iris' voice. "I guess I'd better fix my hair." Not for the aunt. There was a boy friend somewhere in the visit. At her age it was strange that she hadn't been babbling about him. She untied the scarf, laid it over her knees and began taking the bobby pins out of her hair.

He was curious. "Did you leave it up all evening?"

"Are you nuts? I took it down in the little girls' room at the café before I met the kids. Then I put it up again before I went to sleep."

"You said you didn't sleep."

She didn't like being called to account. "Not in a bed. I took a little nap in Rocky's car, that's all." She pulled the dirty comb out of her purse and combed out the lank curls. She peered into the inset mirror. "I wish I'd left it up longer. Darn it. Does it look too awful?"

He didn't know how it was supposed to look. He said, "I wouldn't worry about it. Your aunt won't care, will she?" He was holding her to her story.

She tied the scarf under her chin. "No, she won't care. But I want to look nice when I get there just the same."

"A bath and some clean clothes would help."

"I know," she said unhappily. For once she wasn't putting on an act. And he realized what he should have before, she didn't have any clean clothes with her. There wasn't room for them in the small bag.

"Maybe you can borrow from your aunt," he suggested.

"Sure I can. She has lots of clothes, beautiful clothes." She was lying again. "She doesn't care if I wear her clothes. We're the same size. She's real young for an aunt. She'll fix my hair too. She's a beauty operator, she has her own shop."

Poor kid. Poor, poor kid. He was a little ashamed of the ire he'd had toward her. But not enough to forget the lies and the perhaps lies. "You haven't given me her address."

"I don't have a pencil."

"I have a pen." He removed the ball-point from his jacket pocket. By now it was too hot for the jacket but he wouldn't slow the car to take it off.

"I don't have any paper."

He had the letter from his mother which had come yesterday. He slid it out and handed her the envelope. "Write it on the back."

Slowly she inscribed an address.

"Put her name on it. And phone number."

"I don't have her phone number." Reluctantly she wrote a name. He let his eyes touch it when she returned the envelope. Mayble Carney. She couldn't have invented Mayble. No one could.

"My pen?"

She pushed it at him.

"You tell her about the loan right away. Don't make up a big story, just tell her the truth."

She said huffily, "You're sure worried about your money. You'd think it was a hundred dollars."

"Do you know what an intern's pay is?"

"No, I don't."

"It isn't enough to cover bus tickets for strangers," he said.

They reached the city limits of Glendale. Oleanders were a magic wall of rose and white hiding the railroad tracks. Traffic was heavy from now on in; he didn't make conversation. She too was silent, shimmering with anticipation. She kept her head turned to the window, looking out at the buildings and streets. He followed Van Buren into the heart of town.

He said, "Keep your eyes open for the bus station. It's on the left. We'll probably have to go around the block to get to it." Even if a left turn were permitted, the unending line of cars would prohibit it.

They saw the sign at the same time. She cried, "There it is. Just let me off at the corner." Her hand was on the door.

"No, thanks. I'm taking you to the entrance. And you go right inside and telephone your aunt that you've arrived." He'd do that much to get her settled before she looked for more kids to kick around with.

The light changed as he pulled up to the corner and he turned right before she could get out. He circled the block to First Street, drove across Van Buren, and double-parked.

She was out of the car the moment it stopped. She didn't say good-bye or thank you and she didn't look back. But he saw her walk into the station before he rolled away.

The bad dream was over. He was rid of her. He might or might not get in touch with the alleged aunt. She might or might not be told of the loan. He'd rather write off the ten dollars as enforced charity than take a chance on having Iris move into his life again.

2

HIS GRANDPARENTS' home was a large old frame house on Jefferson, freshly painted white each spring. Pink and red roses were climbing the trellises against the porch. The oleanders were a glory of white in the dark glossy green of the tall hedge. He'd spent so many summers here as a child, it was like coming home. He'd never noticed the heat then.

He ran up the steps, across the broad porch, and pushed open the screen door. The air conditioning was welcome. "Anybody home?"

From the dining room he heard the clamor of voices, his grandmother's treble piercing through with excitement. "It's Hughie!"

They were around the big dining-room table, like a scene which never changed no matter how many years he was away from it. His grandmother was smaller and grayer but his grandfather stood tall despite his years. His mother was there; the family had flown to Phoenix earlier in the week. And to his delight, his sister Stacy and her doctor husband, Edward, had dropped in. It seemed impossible that Stacy was old enough to be the mother of a bride. Yet Clytie was twenty, older by two years than Stacy had been when she married.

"The house looks as if it knows there's to be a wedding in it. Where is the bride?"

"The girls had a luncheon at the university," his mother said. "I thought you might be in last night, Hugh."

"I stayed over in Blythe. It was late when I got off." He wouldn't tell her the story, he wouldn't worry her. "Where's Dad?"

"Playing golf. He wanted to escape wedding chitchat for a time."

"Whose clubs? I have his in the car."

Edward said, "Mine. I wish I were with them but I have to get back to the office." With mock woe he added, "Doctors can't take time off, right, Hugh? I'll see you at dinner."

Stacy went to the door with him. By the time she returned, Gram had Hugh plied with more food than he'd seen in years.

Stacy sat down beside him. "We've come up with a housing problem, Hugh. I hope you won't mind too much. We're putting you up at The Palms."

Gram interrupted. "I still say that's foolishness, Stacy. I can make up a nice bed for Hughie on the back porch—"

"And he'd be waked at dawn with the kitchen racket, Gram. You know what Edward said. An intern needs every bit of rest he can get while he's free of the hospital. You don't mind, Hugh?"

Gram tossed her head. "I am not rackety in my kitchen."

"I don't mind at all." Actually he was pleased, though he couldn't say it in front of his grandmother. There wouldn't be much chance to sleep here, not with wedding preparations underfoot. Clytie had chosen to be married in the ancestral home, to walk down the long front stairway as her mother and her mother's mother had before her. With Grandfather to marry her. He was retired now, but once a minister of the Lord, always a minister.

"I am not rackety," Gram said more loudly.

"Of course you're not," Hugh's mother said. "Stacy didn't mean it that way. But Hugh will get more rest at a motel. It's only a few blocks away."

Hugh grinned. "I can be over here before you get that rackety breakfast cooked, Gram."

"You look thin," she accused. "You're working too hard." She said the same thing whenever she saw him. He'd always been her favorite.

"You see," Stacy continued explanation, "with Mother and Dad and the girls with me, and Ellen, Clytie's roommate from Washington—I don't have any more room. John and his parents and brother we put here. That still left a room for you. But at the last minute his grandparents decided to fly out. So there isn't a room."

Gram said, "Putting Hughie out for strangers. I don't hold with that."

"They aren't strangers, Gram," Stacy said with tired patience. She'd obviously been through this a dozen times. "They're almost in-laws. And John's grandfather is a minister just like Gramps. You'll like them."

"Hoity-toity New York people," Gram sniffed.

"Now, Gram, you know John's not hoity-toity. Why would you expect his family to be?" Grandfather asked.

"John's been in Arizona for two years. Time to get over it. They've never been West, John said so."

Gramps said gently, "We'll make them welcome, Stacy. Don't mind Mama. She's just feeling her pepper today."

It was all so homey and safe. Iris was only a small memory far back in Hugh's consciousness. She'd been out of it entirely until this matter of the motel came up, and with it, the strange sense of relief. When he analyzed it, he realized he had had a fear of her finding his car and turning up again. Making trouble. If she turned up at the motel, he could handle her. But she wouldn't. He was quite sure she'd take no chance of being held accountable for that ten dollars. She'd had what she wanted from him, the ride to Phoenix. She wouldn't want to see him again any more than he wanted to see her.

His grandmother had got up from the table and started to carry out the dishes to the kitchen. "I'll pepper you," she told her husband. "Hoity-toity," she muttered as she stomped away. "Hoity-toity."

She'd been born in the Territory of Arizona and was firmly convinced that only Arizonans were to be esteemed. She'd never quite forgiven Hugh's mother for marrying an Angeleno and moving to California. When Stacy married Dr. Edward and moved to Phoenix, Gram had considered it a judgment on her daughter for her own defection. Gram's other children had remained loyal; of the uncles and aunts, none was further away than Tucson.

Hugh said, "I guess I'd better go check in and get my things unpacked. What's the schedule for today, Stacy?"

"Edward has already checked you in, Hugh." She opened her purse. "Here's the key."

"Thanks." It was like Edward; he was always thoughtful about such things.

"The schedule? Tonight's a barbecue at Uncle Dan's. The whole tribe of course and members of the wedding party. Sports clothes."

Gram returned for more dishes. "Barbecue. Cooking outdoors like Indians." She didn't wait for rebuttal but trotted back to her kitchen.

"The Bents are flying in tomorrow morning from New York."

"Want me to meet them?"

"Thanks, but Edward believes we should do the honors. I suppose we should." She sighed. "There's too much to do. Clytie wants Mother and me to drop in on the party this afternoon. You can't imagine the entertainment she's had, Hugh. It seems as if every club on the campus has partied her. There are enough gifts already to furnish a mansion. I don't know where we'll store them until she and John return from Germany. He has European orders, you know."

He knew. It was the European orders which had pushed the wedding up from June to May. John's wing was leaving next week. Clytie would follow after graduation.

"Anything I can do to help—"

"There'll be plenty. Tomorrow is Ellen's bridal luncheon for Clytie. Then there's rehearsal in the afternoon and our bridal dinner at night. We're having it in the private banquet room at The Palms, where you're staying."

"And the main event?"

"Sunday afternoon. Four o'clock. We can't decorate until Sunday, we're using fresh flowers. Oh, we'll keep you busy, Hugh. You'll be run ragged like all of us. If you can get any rest today, make the most of it. You won't have another chance until after the wedding."

"Okay, Stacy. Count me in." He stood up. "When do you want your car, Mother?"

"You'll need it, staying at the motel. I'll ride with Stacy. You can bring the folks out to Daniel's tonight. Six-thirty."

"A pleasure." He stage-whispered to Gram, now folding the tablecloth, "You're going to be my girl at that Indian barbecue and you can so inform your husband."

She snorted, then regained her good humor and laughed.

"Whenever you do want the car, Mother, let me know. Bye, all. See you later."

He drove over to Van Buren and on east to the motor hotel. As he was registered, there was no reason to stop at the desk. He followed the circular drive around to 126, the number on his key. For once he had no rancor at being assigned to a rear unit. His car wouldn't be visible from the street, just in case Iris found some more kids to tour her about the town looking for him. Why on earth should she look for him? He was obsessed and it was nonsense. There was no reason for her to return to haunt him.

The Palms was one of the new luxury motels on the eastern extension of Van Buren. There were no second-rate units. He moved his bags into the bleached-wood elegance, cooled to proper temperature by the wall thermostat. Sliding glass lanai doors opened to a vast expanse of close-cropped green, bisected with bleached white walks. Across the green was a tropical blue pool with clusters of sky-tall palm trees bending over it. Hot-pink umbrellas shaded white tables and deck chairs, hot-pink chaises for sunbathers were grouped at the pool's tiled rim. A faint *plash* came across the lawn as a diver curved from the high board.

The large room with its two oversized beds was meticulously clean, the blue-tiled bath was stocked with good towels, the desk held hotel stationery and guidebooks, the television set worked. There was no reason to expect otherwise. Edward wouldn't select a place without standards of quality. But then you never knew. Remembering stories his mother told of traveling when she was a girl, personally recalling trips he'd taken as a child, he could believe that times had definitely changed.

He hung up his suits and slacks, put away his other clothes in the bureau drawers, laid open his toilet kit on the tiled dressing table. The medical bag he pushed to the back of the shelf. It was two o'clock. Enough of the pre-wedding excitement had entered him to cancel any ideas of sleep. He needed to unwind, but he was so unused to idleness these days, he didn't know how to begin.

Out of simple curiosity, he picked up the telephone directory from the desk and turned to the C's. No Mayble Carney was listed. It could be she lived in a rooming house or had one of those modern apartments with a switchboard. He flipped to the yellow pages, Beauty Parlors. They bore cute names, not those of their owners.

He was just stubborn enough to try to find out if there was a Mayble. He asked the switchboard for Information. When that operator responded, he gave the name and address Iris had written. There was no such person listed at any address.

By now his stubbornness had solidified. There weren't too many beauty shops. He called them, one by one. It took a full hour. Not one had a Mayble Carney working there at present or in memory. He put away the phone and flung himself on the bed. So she'd got by with the lie, the one he hadn't believed could be a lie. He still didn't think she'd invented Mayble. But Mayble wasn't her aunt or didn't live in Phoenix. Possibly Mayble was one of the "kids" in Banning or Indio or Blythe, and Iris had been snickering to herself when she'd put across that whopper.

He'd written off the money, it wasn't that. It was being played for a sucker. He wouldn't suffer because he'd given away ten bucks, not like some of the poor guys who had nothing but their intern's pay. He'd been one of the lucky kids who never knew want, never knew the kind of deprivation which Iris, to look at her, must have lived with all her young years. His family wasn't wealthy but they were comfortable, had always been. He couldn't hold his anger against the girl, she was too miserable a creature. How could she help being what she was?

He got up from the bed. It was still too early to dress for the evening. He decided to go across to the newsstand and buy the Los Angeles papers. Just possibly there might be a report of a missing girl. He didn't have to believe that Iris' father and mother were what she said they were, although that too had had the ring of truth. Like the name of Mayble Carney.

He walked across the green to the motel office. The heat of the afternoon was a shock after the air-conditioned room. It was little wonder that the only guests in view were clustered by the pool. In the lobby the clerks and the bellboys were listless before the evening rush. At the desk he made arrangements for the car to be serviced and washed. With its cross-country dust, it was not fitting for wedding activities. He bought the *Times* and the *Herald-Examiner* at the newsstand. They were mail editions and most of the news would be old, yet the girl had left home yesterday. There could be a mention.

Returned to his room, he searched all the pages with care but there was no story of any missing person. Maybe she wasn't a runaway, maybe that denial had been honest. Leisurely he caught up on the sports and columns, on Gordo and Charlie Brown and Dick Tracy. By then it was time to shower and dress and go gather the grandparents. He wasn't worried any longer. He was actually relieved that there hadn't been an Aunt Mayble to find out who had given Iris a ride to Phoenix.

It was past midnight when he returned to the motel. It had been a singularly happy evening. Lieutenant John Bent was almost good enough for Clytie. As for Ellen Hamilton, Clytie's former roommate—why hadn't any of the family told him what to expect? She was the most beautiful girl he'd ever seen, he who came from a family of beauties.

Ellen carried herself like a model, tall and slender and prideful. Small nose, enormous black eyes slightly tilted, skin like golden sand. Smooth dark hair not worn in one of the silly modern French fashions but with a bang across her forehead, and brushed down to a slight curve just above her shoulders. He could almost believe his mother and Stacy had entered into a conspiracy of silence lest he shy away from her.

He hadn't had half a chance to make headway tonight. John's Air Force friends had surrounded her as if she were a shiny new spaceship. What Hugh had learned about her had been from his mother. Ellen had graduated *cum laude* from Vassar. She was taking special courses at George Washington, preparing for foreign diplomatic service. On that item, he had realized that her father was the Judge, that she was the Washington, D.C., Hamiltons.

It was just as well he hadn't had a chance to be alone with her, he might have fallen. A young doctor, not yet in practice, had nothing to offer an Ellen Hamilton. Moreover, he had no intention of getting involved with any girl until he had paid back the family for their backing him all these years, and was earning enough to support a wife on a decent economic level.

At this hour the cars were parked closely in their lanes at the rear of the units. Not that all the guests were in bed; there were lights behind most of the drawn curtains. The late, late TV show echoed from open lanai doors. He parked as close as possible to 126, locked the car, and walked over to his door. He let himself in, flipped the night latch to keep the maid out in the morning, and put on the lights. He'd left the air conditioning on when he went out; he turned it off now, the motor hum would be disturbing for sleep. It wasn't needed, the night had turned definitely cool. He checked the door screen, it was locked, and he drew the draperies across it, leaving the doors open.

He turned on the TV set, tuning until he found the one with the old movie. He removed his jacket and hung it in the wardrobe, loosened his tie, and stretched out on one of the beds. The soporific picture would relax him for sleeping.

The soft rap on the locked rear door came almost immediately. He didn't comprehend it at first, he took it for an extraneous sound, from the television set or the next-door unit. Only when it was repeated did he know it for what it was, a knocking at his door. His first thought was that it was a mistake, someone at the wrong unit; his second that it was, for some reason, the management. It couldn't be his family. If they'd wanted him for any purpose, they'd have telephoned before coming. He walked slowly back to the soft sound, unfastened the night latch, turned the knob. Only when he saw her standing outside, did he realize that he'd been afraid it might be Iris. She was wearing the same dirty outfit, even to the scarf hiding her hair.

He was furious but he kept his voice quiet. "What are you doing here?"

She spoke almost in a whisper. "I got to talk to you."

"No, you don't." He moved into the doorway, blocking it so that she couldn't push in. "There's nothing whatever you could have to say to me. You go on now. And don't ever come around here again."

"I won't stay but a minute," she protested. "Let me come in just a minute."

"I wouldn't think of it." He spoke with finality. He hoped she would recognize it as such. "Go on home. You could get in a lot of trouble coming here."

And get him into worse trouble. But he wouldn't say that to her, wouldn't put it in her head. She might not know how bad she could make it for him.

"I'm in a lot of trouble." Her head was turned and she spoke under her breath.

"Because you don't have an Aunt Mayble living here and you don't know what to do next?" But she had someone or she wouldn't be able to drive around and discover where he was staying. Or was it possible she had telephoned the motels until she found a Dr. Hugh Densmore registered?

"I do too have an Aunt Mayble. In Denver." She was peering beyond him into the lighted room. She said, "Please, let me in, just for a minute."

He stood firm. "No, you can't come in," he repeated. It was bad enough to have her outside on his doorstep. There was no way of knowing how many persons might be seeing her there. "I tried to help you on the road but I can't help you any more. Go to the Travelers' Aid. They'll see that you get home."

"I can't go home," she said dully. She looked up at him. She said it again with a muted emphasis, "I'm in trouble. Real trouble."

Somehow this had never occurred to him. It was a shock. "Is that why you came to Phoenix?"

She nodded dumbly. She looked sick. "I thought my boy friend would marry me. But he's already married. He didn't tell me that when we were going around together. He's married and got a couple of kids."

He didn't know what to say. Finally he told her, "I think you'd better go to the police and tell them your story. They'll work out something for you." He didn't know what else to advise. Certainly there would be a welfare department in a city the size of Phoenix. Despite everything she was, he was sorry for her. "I can't do anything for you."

"Yes, you can," she said. The old familiar slyness had come into her face. "You're a doctor."

For a moment he couldn't speak. He was frozen with rage. When his voice returned, it didn't sound like his own. "I'm a doctor, yes. A doctor, not a quack. Now you get out of here before I call the police."

He shut the door on her before she could say anything more. He was shaken, he felt physically ill. That she'd had the brazen nerve to come to him for this. And her betrayer, had he been outside in one of those cars watching the scene, waiting to see if she brought it off? He must have driven her here after she had told him it was a doctor who gave her a ride to Phoenix.

If either of them returned, he would call the police. He realized the risk he would be taking, the lies she could tell, her word against his. But the police would check, they would find out that Hugh had never laid eyes on her before yesterday afternoon. He had the strength and the prestige of the University Medical Center behind him, if it came to that. But with that awful sickness of heart, he knew that she could say things which would ruin his hopes of remaining at the university, much less of being granted a research scholarship. There'd always be a residue of suspicion that the girl's inventions weren't all false. How could he prove otherwise? They had traveled together.

While the flickering screen unwound its meaningless story, while the sound track uttered its meaningless words, he waited for another knock on the door. He waited until the picture ended. But there was no more intrusion. She must have believed him when he said he'd call the police.

He undressed, turned out the light, and went to bed. It was a long time before sleep came. He knew how close he was to danger. When he heard the telephone ringing, he came awake at once as he was trained to wake, quietly, completely. He saw that it was morning. He was almost afraid to lift the phone from its cradle. When his mother's voice responded to his hello, he drew a deep breath.

"Did I wake you, Hugh?"

"That's all right. What time is it?" His watch was on the table.

"Ten o'clock. I wouldn't have called but I've an endless list of things Stacy wants done. She and Edward dropped me here at the folks' on their way to the airport."

"Hang on. I'll be there in ten minutes."

He almost made it in ten. Five minutes to shower and shave, five to dress—slacks, sport shirt, loafers. He'd learned in the hospital not to dawdle.

His mother was with his grandmother at the dining-room table, reading the morning paper. He had forgotten about the papers, what might be in them. His mother glanced at her watch. "I wouldn't have believed it possible of you."

Automatically he grinned at her. "Fooled you, eh? Want me to taxi you on the tour?"

"Not until you've had your breakfast," Gram declared. "Sit down, young man." She was off to the kitchen before he could deter her.

His mother said, “Would you? It would be such a help not to battle parking.”

“It would be my pleasure.” Casually, he picked up the section of the paper beside her plate. Sports section. She had the front page.

His grandmother reappeared with a platter of ham slices and three eggs.

“Gram! I’ll be too fat to waddle.”

“Nonsense. They’ve been starving you at that hospital.” She skittered back to the kitchen, to reappear with a plate of hot baking-powder biscuits. “Now eat up. That’s my own strawberry jam in the blue bowl. I’ll pour your coffee.”

He could ask it casually: Any news? He didn’t.

But he wished his mother would comment on what she was reading. Surely she would if there were a missing-girl story. He couldn’t ask for the paper, not with Gram visiting with him. Somewhere along the line of errands, he’d pick up the Los Angeles *Times*. If a California girl were missing, the report would be more complete than in a Phoenix newspaper.

He put aside his napkin. “Sorry to eat and run, ma’am, but that’s the way it is when you’re a doctor.” He kissed his grandmother’s dry cheek. “That’s the best breakfast I’ve had since I was a boy. Remind me to marry you when you get a divorce from Gramps. Where is he this morning?”

“I sent him to the barber shop to get prettied up for the wedding tomorrow.” She gave him a wicked smile. “And to keep him from underfoot while I did my baking. I’m making the wedding cake, did you know that? Clytie didn’t want a boughten cake, she wanted old Gram to make it.”

“Clytie’s a smart kid,” he said. “Come on, Mother. Let’s get with it.”

They left the cool house for the blaze of the street. As they went down the steps, automatically he scanned the neighborhood. There was no one of the size and shape of Iris in sight. He helped his mother into the car and took the wheel. “Where first?”

“The florist’s. To order the corsages for tonight.” She gave him directions. She couldn’t have been more casual when she asked, “How did you like Ellen?”

“So-so.”

"Hugh!"

Her outraged exclamation made him shout with laughter, the first decent laughter he'd had since yesterday afternoon. "You're too transparent, Mother. She's gorgeous, absolutely gorgeous, as you darn well know."

"She's been dying to meet you."

"Sure. And now her dreams are shattered."

"They are not. She likes you."

"Me and the Air Force."

She didn't have an opportunity for rebuttal. They were at the florist's. He let her out and found a place to park further up the block. Ellen Hamilton didn't have to come to Arizona man-hunting. She would have the pick of the lot in Washington and Philadelphia and New York. His family was good, but it wasn't one of the old eastern families whose status went back to Revolutionary days. Except for his grandmother and one branch of the Densmores, none of the lines was more than three generations out of the South. No, he wasn't going to start dreaming any dreams of Ellen. He'd settle for one of Celeste's sorority sisters. By the time he could afford to marry, it would more likely be one of Allegra's.

His mother returned. "Now the stationer's. With John's grandparents coming, we need more place cards for tonight. I hope I can find the same pattern." She touched her temples with her handkerchief. "When I'm in Phoenix, I wish we had air conditioning in the car like the Phoenicians."

"John seems a good guy."

"He is. A real darling. Clytie's a lucky girl."

"What about his luck?"

His mother pretended to sigh. "You're always too quick for me, Hugh. But you might start doing a little shopping around yourself. When your niece gets married, it's high time you started to settle down."

"Don't you think I should wait until I'm earning a living?"

"Hugh, you know your father and I—"

"Okay, okay, lady." He touched her hand. "But you know how I feel about leaning. I've done enough of that. Don't worry, I'll pay you back in rubies some day." The words brought again the uneasiness of what Iris might be saying right now.

"We know you will. But you needn't. Right here, Hugh."

They were in the heart of downtown Phoenix, with no possible place to park. He said, "I'll drive around the block."

"It won't take me long. If they still have the pattern."

He circled several blocks, hoping there would be an opportunity to stop near one of the large newsstands, but there were no spaces anywhere. His mother was waiting on the walk when he returned.

It was the same in the half dozen or so stops. If he could park, there was no newsstand. If he couldn't, the racks were so near yet so far. After a time, he stopped bothering about it. He could buy the paper when he returned to the motel.

At noon his mother said, "I'll have to let the other things go for now if I'm to make the luncheon. Maybe I can get them later this afternoon, I don't have to attend the rehearsal. Do you want to drive me back to Stacy's or shall I drop you?"

"I'm your chauffeur. I shall even wait for you and deliver you to the luncheon party." And with luck, Ellen as well.

"I hate to take your time."

"It's your car and I haven't a blessed thing to do. As a matter of fact, it's fun—like old times."

"You're a charmer, Hugh. Now give me a cigarette and turn right at the next corner."

Stacy and Edward had built in the new section south of town. It was a neighborhood of attractive homes, some large, some not so large, comparable to any city's good suburban development. It took about twenty minutes from town to Stacy's door.

"You're going to have to hump it to make a one-o'clock luncheon, Mother. Where's the event taking place?" He matched her stride up the flagstone walk.

"All the way back to town. The Adams, private dining room. Stacy and the girls have probably gone on. You make yourself comfortable while I rush."

The girls had gone, worse luck. But the Phoenix paper was on the table. And the air of the house was revivifying. He leafed rapidly but thoroughly. There was nothing in the news about Iris. His mother had returned by the time he started to read the front page.

There was never a parking place near the Adams Hotel. He doubled to let her out near the entrance. "I'll be back for you at three and we'll finish off your errands fast. If you don't get some rest before tonight, you'll be on sedatives."

He drove away. He turned on the radio now. He hadn't earlier, preferring conversation with his mother. Since being in residence at the hospital, he hadn't had much time for visiting with her. There was no news coming from any station, nothing but music, not the kind of music he wanted to hear. He turned it off again. He didn't want to go back to the motel but he did want the Los Angeles newspaper. If he were in Los Angeles, there'd be a drugstore on every second corner where he could stop for it and a cold Coke. This was Phoenix. He passed only one drugstore on his drive to The Palms and it didn't look promising.

It was ridiculous to be chary of returning to his comfortable quarters. Iris wouldn't come again. She'd be afraid to. She'd known all right, by his voice and his face, that he meant what he said when he warned her last night. With no more debate, he turned in at the motel, circled to his unit and parked. He walked through the grounds to the lobby. Today's *Times* was on the newsstand. He bought it and the Phoenix paper, then went to his room. The maid had already made it up. He turned the air conditioner to a higher notch, pulled aside the draperies and opened the lanai doors for the view across the green. The swimming pool was decked with sun-tanned lovelies, lobster-red hopefuls, and grub-white newcomers.

He covered both papers with the same thoroughness he had yesterday's and found nothing. Iris had perhaps had a rare moment of truth when she said her mother was gone and her father didn't care what she did. He presumed there could be such parents; he just hadn't ever happened to know any.

He put away the papers. He'd severed his connection with Iris; he didn't have to dwell on it any longer. But he couldn't help wondering what had happened after she'd left last night. The man who'd got her in this trouble would have had to come up with other plans. More likely than not, he'd put her on a bus and shipped her back to Indio. With whatever lies he could invent to fool an expert and make her willing to go. The promise of money. Of sending for her later. If he had a wife and two children, he couldn't have scuttled around trying to find an abortionist for her. Phoenix wasn't a large enough city for a man to be anonymous; he'd hardly risk word of such a search getting back to his wife.

Hugh wished he could have helped her last night. Not in the way which had occurred to her in her desperation, but helped her to get in touch with someone or some organization who would protect her. He had not dared take the risk. In his home town, yes, but not a stranger in a strange city.

At three he was again at the downtown hotel, hopeful for a glimpse of Ellen. She might have been one of the girls just driving off in John's car. His mother came out alone.

"It was a beautiful affair, I wish you could have seen the table, Hugh. Now if we can tick off these errands—"

It took close to another hour. In heat that was pushing the hundred mark. It was four o'clock when he returned her to Stacy's. "As your doctor I insist you lie down for an hour before you start any more activity. Say you will."

"I'll try." She didn't ask him to come in. "Dinner's at eight. Dad and I are picking up the folks tonight. You're escorting Ellen, did I tell you?" She didn't allow him to answer. She went on up the walk.

As he drove away, again he tried the radio, hoping for a news broadcast. Again it was the wrong hour; the same wailing music seemed to be coming over every station. He left it on, turning it down to a subdued murmur, just in case the news cut in.

There was no reason to go back to the lonely motel, to the vulnerable motel. He might as well drop by the grandparents'. Perhaps he could have a preview of the cake. He failed on that; no one, not even Hughie, was to view it until the wedding reception. But he spent a pleasant interlude with the elder Bents, not half as hoity-toity as Gram herself, and John's young mother, who was cooling herself with iced lemonade and his grandmother's palm-leaf fan. Dad and John's father were on the golf course; the heat couldn't deter avid golfers. While Hugh was there, John and his brother Paul, a younger but more serious edition, came in. They'd been swimming at the pool of one of Stacy's neighbors.

"Why didn't someone tell me about that?" Hugh moaned, covering the spurt of anger against Iris which erupted in him. If she hadn't intruded, he'd be having the carefree holiday he'd counted on, not contemplating dark corners of his soul. In his anger, he lost his fear of her. He rose to leave; it was past five. "Have to give myself plenty of time to dude up for the glamour girl."

Without prompting, Paul asked, "Ellen?"

"The line forms on the right," John announced.

"Do you know how many bids for the prom she had the year John graduated?" Paul queried. "Ten! Ten, no kidding."

"Who was the lucky man?"

"I was, who else?" John said. "But then I met Clytie and the other nine had a chance."

His mother said reprovingly, "Ellen's a lovely girl, John. Don't give Hugh the wrong impression of her."

"He's just showing off, Mum," his brother said. "His last blithe bachelor brag. Good luck, Hugh."

"I'll need it with John's winged cronies hovering. Later."

He didn't turn up the power on the radio when he drove away, he didn't think of it. He was almost to The Palms when the murmur came through to him: ". . . girl . . . this morning has not yet been identified . . ." That much, and the announcer launched into a coffee ad.

Hugh drove past the motel, on up Van Buren, flipping the stations but finding no other news. There was a cluster of shops near 36th Street; he remembered a combination variety and drugstore which carried the newspapers. He made a left turn across the road and into the sandy lot. The papers were stacked just inside the door. The black headline thundered at him: GIRL'S BODY FOUND IN CANAL.

The masthead was of the Phoenix afternoon paper. None of the others seemed to have the news. Somehow he managed to fumble a dime from his pocket and carry it to the woman at the cash register in the rear of the store. Somehow he managed to fold the paper under his arm and walk out of the place steadily, unhurried, untouched. Even before reading, he was certain the girl was Iris.

He didn't dare remain here. It was too public a place, he would attract attention. He drove further out on Van Buren toward Tempe, and turned off at a side street, deserted as a country lane. There he stopped the car and fearfully unfolded the paper. The fact that she was unidentified didn't mean that there might not be some mention of her appearance at The

Palms, or of her arrival at the bus station in a white Cadillac with California plates. There was always the innocent bystander who noticed.

She was Iris. Wearing the same green slacks, the same soiled shirt, the same socks and sandals, even the gaudy scarf floating from her hair. There was no mention of the handbag or the traveling case. There was no mention of the high school jacket. The Zanjaros, who patrolled the canal, had discovered the body this morning, floating in the waters on Indian School Road in Scottsdale. The girl was believed to be about fifteen years old. An autopsy would be performed to determine the cause of death. Anyone knowing her identity was asked to come forward.

That was all.

It wasn't suicide. She was too resourceful to commit suicide. Hugh knew the cause of her death. That would be the next story. An illegal operation. A dirty, bungled operation. A murder. A murder committed by two unknowns, the man who had first betrayed her and then taken her to the abattoir, and the man or woman who'd killed her and her unborn child.

Hugh could come forward and identify her. But he dared not. Because he was a doctor, because he had brought her to Phoenix, and because he was so certain that death was the result of abortion, he could not risk telling the police he knew her. They would have to find out some other way. He could only hope they would also find out quickly why she was here and who her boy friend was. If they didn't and if the "kids" in Blythe and in Indio talked, Hugh would become the suspect. And, bitterly, he knew his truth would not be believed.

For long moments he sat there on the road, trying to arrange his thoughts. He couldn't leave town, not without telling the family why, not without spoiling Clytie's wedding. The wedding wasn't important only to Clytie, it encompassed the entire family, four generations of family.

Anyway, to flee in panic was not the answer. It was construed always as the act of a man bloodied with guilt, although in fact the innocent man involved beyond his depth might have more reason to run. Was there any possibility she had been seen at his door last night? He couldn't recall any cars driving up while he talked with her, nor had anyone in that period gone in or out of any of the units in his wing. No one could have been looking out of windows at her, the only windows at the rear were in the bathrooms and were of frosted glass. But he couldn't know how many persons might have seen her cross to his door. Nor could he know whether even now the Blythe inspectors might be hearing the story over the radio, and informing Phoenix of Hugh's license number and their version of yesterday morning's incident. He couldn't deny giving her a ride. Her fingerprints were all over the car.

If only there were someone he could tell his story to, someone who could advise him. There was no one, not here in Phoenix. At Med Center, yes; there were half a dozen colleagues. And there was the Dean, in whom he would have no hesitancy in confiding. But here, no one. Not his father or mother; he would not put this burden on them. At one time his grandfather would have been the perfect one, but he was too old to bear it now. His grandmother was too emotional and she was too old. Not his sister or her husband, not until after the wedding. After the wedding, if there were need, Edward would be the one. He was a respected doctor in town. Enough so to engender respect for his young brother-in-law? Hugh could hope. Perhaps enough so that Hugh's story would be understood and its truth accepted.

Nothing must happen until after the wedding. He would accept whatever ordeal there might be if only nothing were permitted to destroy the pride of the family, gathered together for this joyful moment of its continuance.

The sun was lowering in the sky. He looked at his watch. Six-thirty already, and he started the car. He turned up the radio; there was news coming in. He drove slowly, listening.

There was no new material. Results of the autopsy were not mentioned. Again there was a plea for identification of the girl. He had that much reprieve. His link with her had not been discovered. But fear leaped again. Undiscovered, or suppressed by the police for their own purposes? The police did not give out all their information to the press.

He had to return to the motel; he could postpone it no longer. As it was, he'd be late arriving for his first date with Ellen. He did not know how he could endure the long evening ahead. If only the bridal dinner were being held any place but in The Palms, somewhere private which the police could not know about. If only the police would not arrive until after the last toast had been lifted. If only they would not learn of him until after the benediction tomorrow. If only . . . If only he had never stopped to pick up Iris Croom.

No one was waiting for him at the motel. No one stopped him at the door of his unit; he inserted his key and entered, locking the door behind him. For several seconds he stood there waiting, but no sharp knock sounded. And then he slapped some sense into his head. He was acting like an ass, acting as if he had some guilt in Iris' death. He stripped, started the shower. He had to snap out of it, not become the specter at the wedding feast.

He felt better after showering. He shaved and dressed, for Ellen Hamilton he didn't mind shaving twice in a day. It was seven-thirty when he surveyed himself in the mirror. He didn't look like a man wanted by the police.

What if the police did come to him? His story was straight and true, why should he think it wouldn't come across that way? He transferred wallet and keys, cigarettes and lighter to his pockets, remembered to fold a clean linen handkerchief for his white dinner jacket. He was ready to take off for Stacy's. But just before he opened the door he stopped and bent his head. He prayed silently, prayed as he often had when he was a little boy. *Please, God, don't let anything bad happen to me.*

No one approached him as he got in his car. No one stopped him from driving out of the grounds. His tension diminished and he drove with easy speed to his sister's home. There was no new radio news.

The afternoon heat had softened into balmy evening. The house was lively with light and the sounds of young laughter. He loped up to the door and walked in without knocking. Dr. Edward was adjusting Hale's tie. The youngest cousin was fifteen, this was his first dinner jacket. Ned Jr. at eighteen was an old hand.

Ned asked, "Shall I tell Ellen you're here? She's not half ready."

"I'm glad of that." Hugh sank into a cushioned chair. "I thought I'd be late."

His father emerged from the kitchen with a tray of martinis. "One round only. We don't want any accidents."

"One for me?" Hale quipped.

"When you're twenty-one," Edward said. He gave Hale a push. "Don't touch that tie again."

"But I get champagne at dinner, don't I? You have to let me have champagne," Hale insisted.

The argument must have been going for weeks. Hugh remembered himself at that age, someone's wedding. It couldn't have been Stacy's, he was ringbearer at that one in a velvet suit. It must have been Uncle Wood's, he married late.

"One glass, Edward," he put in his oar.

"One glass then. And sip it."

Hale winked at Hugh. Handsome and perfumed in her gray lace, Hugh's mother came from the bedroom corridor. Stacy followed, slim as a girl in her gold chiffon. And as nervous as if it were her own wedding, not that of her grown-up little girl. "We'd better get on our way. There are always last-minute things to do even with caterers."

"Just wait until I call Exchange, let them know where they can reach me." Edward finished his cocktail.

"Oh, Edward," she groaned. "Not at your daughter's bridal dinner."

He spoke as he dialed. "I'm a little worried about that hospital case. Besides, I have two little mothers waiting, none too patiently, for labor to commence. After nine months with me I don't think they'd settle for a substitute." He spoke briefly into the phone, then cradled it. "Just keep all of your fingers crossed that those babies don't decide to come out at four tomorrow afternoon."

The girls were approaching, the flutter of their voices preceding them. Hugh was surprised at himself; he awaited with the nervous excitement a boy was supposed to have only on his first date. Clytie came first, Celeste followed. Ellen was the last of the three, and Hugh's breath caught. With three sisters, he was usually up on female styles, but the honey-colored sheath which she wore, of some dull clinging material the exact color of her flesh, left him floundering. It could only be a French original, something the girls were always swooning over in the pages of *Vogue*, something you didn't find in L.A., only in Paris. Instead of the inevitable mink stole, Ellen carried a matching scarf, fully twelve feet long, lined in lynx. She told him it was lynx when he asked.

He helped her into the car and took the wheel. But he couldn't find words to entertain her. Once in the car his anxiety recurred. He'd been without news for too long. He wanted to turn up the muted radio but he was afraid of what might have developed in the past hour.

His anxiety heightened as he reached The Palms and turned into the driveway. The private dining room was on the side of the quadrangle furthest from his room. He didn't think the police would be waiting here, and they weren't. But he wondered how long it would take them to trace him to the dinner party. Particularly with the Cadillac parked outside the building.

He helped Ellen from the car. "You're very quiet tonight," she said.

Only then did he realize how withdrawn he'd been during the entire drive. He smiled and quoted lightly, "Problems. Always problems."

"Have I caused them?"

He touched her elbow. "You know, it must be awfully nice never to have to worry about that."

Her eyes slanted at him. "You don't know me very well."

"I don't know you at all." Her arm was satin, her perfume violets in cool rain. Cars were arriving in tiers. He saw no strangers among the wedding guests.

"Are you looking for someone?" Ellen questioned.

He didn't know he'd been that obvious. He must stop dwelling on it. There was no reason to think that the police would be searching for him tonight. Iris hadn't been identified. The last he'd heard she hadn't been identified. Until she was, it was a local story. Nothing to be reported in Blythe or Indio.

He smiled down at Ellen. "The Air Force," he told her. "I'm ready to take them all on tonight."

He doubted that she believed him, but she smiled in return. And they entered the safety of the private dining room. It was filled with guests and music and lifted voices. The long table was festooned with sweet white flowers. Spire white candles pointed their pale flames. Clusters of white camellias were at each setting. All of this for Clytie, secure, happy Clytie. And in a cold and dark place, a girl who'd never had anything lay unwanted, unknown; lay dead.

Hugh found their chairs and seated Ellen. "If I ever have a daughter I'll insist that she elope."

"My sister did. Mother was distraught but I must say Father bore up well."

Hugh didn't sit down until he heard Ellen's disturbed inflection.

"Are you sure you aren't expecting someone? You keep watching the door."

He laughed then and dropped into the chair beside her.

"I could disappear, you know," she said. "The Air Force is most accommodating."

He closed his fingers over her wrist. "Disappear with them at your own risk. I warned you what would happen if they moved in tonight." He could feel the throb of her pulse. "I didn't realize I was watching the door." He must guard himself. "It must be force of habit, expecting someone to rush in with 'Emergency, Dr. Densmore!'"

"It isn't a she?"

He made it definite. "It is not." Not a ghost.

She was laughing. "Or too many shes?"

"Don't believe Celeste. She's inclined to brag about big brother. Gets it from Gram—you know my Gram?"

"I know your Gram. She's in love with you."

"And I with her." And I could be with you. But his eyes jumped from her face to the opening door. It was only a uniformed hotel attendant with a salver of messages for Clytie.

Later he wondered how he ever got through the interminable dinner. He was there, laughing, listening, making the proper responses; eating without tasting, drinking too much champagne, falling in love with the charm of the girl beside him. But he wasn't there, he was in a fearful secret cave, waiting for approaching footsteps to sound, for the shape to emerge, the terrible voice to speak.

It was Ellen who had been speaking. Again he had to ask her what she had said. "I don't even know." She laughed. "Nothing important."

But he saw the puzzlement in her eyes and realized he'd been away once too often. He spoke softly. "I'm sorry. I'm truly sorry." He hesitated but he had to say it, to make her understand. "I do have a problem, a very serious problem."

"Would it help to talk?"

"It would. But not tonight." He recalled his earlier figure of speech. "There must be no specter at a wedding feast." He just touched her hand. "I won't go away again."

There was reassuring strength in her fingers as they clasped his. "Hold tight," she said.

After the dinner there was dancing and it was better then. There was no need for talk with her in his arms. When the Air Force took her away, he danced with Gram, then sat with her, not having to respond to her unending commentary.

At midnight the band played the plaintive bachelor song, "Good-bye, Girls, I'm Through," and the assembled voices were a choir serenading Clytie and John. The evening was over. Nothing had happened. Hugh's relief was so great that he felt light-headed. He found Ellen in her usual encirclement. "Go home, little boys," he said blithely. "The party's over." He caught Ellen's hand, this time his had strength.

Her eyes were bright as jewels. "No more problems?"

"Not tonight. Shall we wait outside?"

She was demurely provocative. "Shall we?"

They skirted the crowd making farewells and slipped out the door into the night. The temperature had dropped to desert cold. They half ran to the parking area.

Before they reached the car, Hugh saw the two men, one large, one slighter, emerge from the shadow of the wall. They weren't in uniform but he knew them at once for what they were. He stopped, stood unmoving, dreading what was to come. Ellen gave him a quick, questioning look. There was no time to explain. The plainclothesmen were on either side of him.

The large one asked, "Hugh Densmore?"

"Yes, I'm Hugh Densmore."

"We've got some questions to ask you."

Hugh spoke courteously, no audible quaver in his voice. "Could they wait until I drive my friends home?"

The guests were spilling out through the doors. They didn't seem to notice what was happening. Perhaps they thought these men were California friends. Again he prayed secretly. *God, don't let the family come out yet. Don't let them know.*

The big man said brusquely, "We been waiting long enough."

If Ellen hadn't been there, Hugh could have questioned them as to their purpose, as an innocent man would. But she was there and he couldn't bear that she should hear their answers. Not until he could tell her the whole story.

He turned to her and handed her the car keys. He said, for her ears alone, "Don't let the family know. Whatever this is, I'm sure it's a mistake and can be cleared up easily."

She didn't say anything; her eyes were enormous with wonder but not with fear.

The big one grunted, "Let's go."

Hugh continued rapidly to her, "Make up something but don't let them know. Please. I don't want them to worry."

"I'll take care of it." She sounded competent. "Call me later."

"Come on," the other detective ordered impatiently.

He left her then, before the two laid hands on him. Their hands were restless. They walked, one on either side of him, rounding the building, moving toward the opposite area.

He asked, "Are you arresting me?"

"What for? You done something?"

"No, I haven't. I don't understand this."

"We just want you to answer us a few questions."

It was worth trying. "I have a room here."

"One twenty-six," the smaller man said. He had the weathered face of a cowboy.

Hugh wondered if they'd searched his room, without benefit of warrant, while they waited for him. Even more he wondered why they'd waited this long. They must have staked out his car. But they wouldn't have known which guest he was if they'd come into the dining room. It might have been the hotel manager who'd kept them from invading the party. Such things were bad for business.

It was worth trying because the night was cold. If they weren't arresting him, it would be more comfortable for them to ask their questions in a warm, lighted room rather than in a cold police car.

He tried to phrase the idea so it would not be rejected. He

wasn't afraid of the men although the big one looked surly and the little one mean. He didn't think they would start something without cause. In the past year there'd been too much national publicity about police brutality and the rights of all citizens.

"We could go to my room," he suggested. "It's over there." But of course they knew where it was, they'd been there.

The big one glowered, as if he'd reject the idea out of hand simply because it was Hugh's idea. But the cowboy said, "Come on, Ringle. We might as well go inside. It's too damn cold out here."

Hugh had been counting on him, the way he hunched his shoulders with his hands dug in his jacket pockets. Their rank was evidently equal, because he led off.

As if it had been his own idea, Ringle said to Hugh, "Come on. You got your key?"

"I have it." They had to walk the long open path, past the swimming pool, to reach his room. The way was out of sight of the cars departing from the dinner. They met no guests. There were the usual lighted draperies in many rooms but no one parted them to look out.

Hugh didn't have to direct the men through the arch to the rear, they knew the way. At the door, he took out his key, turned it, and touched the light switch just inside. He stepped back for them to precede him into the room. The small one scurried in but the big one growled, "Go on," as if he feared that Hugh might cut and run. Or perhaps it was routine.

If they'd been in the room before, they'd left no traces. It was unchanged. He walked ahead and turned on the table lamp. He pushed the switch on the wall heater. "The room heats up fast," he commented. The small man's face was peaked with cold. Hugh was thankful he had turned off the air conditioning before he went out tonight. They might have changed their minds about remaining here; they might have insisted on a warm squad room.

He didn't know the procedure for questioning. He didn't know what were his rights. If you'd never been in trouble, you didn't think of these things. Both detectives were still standing. Hugh indicated the comfortable chairs; he himself took the straight one by the desk, turning it to face the room. Ringle sat down in the big armchair, the other man remained standing close by the heater vent.

Hugh said politely, "I'd like to know what this is all about. You're from the police, I take it."

There was to be no violation of civil rights, at least not yet. Ringle took a folder from his pocket, leaned out of the chair, and held it open for Hugh to glimpse. He didn't let go of it. "Detective Ringle," he said. He pointed to his partner. "Detective Venner."

"And you want to ask me some questions." He was calm. Now that it had happened, his nervousness had diminished. He was also thankful that he'd taken on the champagne early in the evening. Most of it had dissipated while dancing, the last vestiges in the cold walk to this room.

"That's right. You know a girl named Bonnie Lee Crumb?"

He shook his head slowly.

"You sure of that?"

"I've never heard that name before in my life," he said with honesty. Crumb—Croom? And Iris? Something beautiful in her ugly Bonnie Lee life?

"Why'd you come to Phoenix?"

"My niece is being married tomorrow. Dr. Edward Willis' daughter." They'd know Edward. On many cases he was called in by the Phoenix police.

Ringle was suspicious. "You're Doc Willis'—"

"Brother-in-law. He is married to my older sister."

"When'd you get here?"

"Yesterday morning. Around eleven o'clock."

Ringle struck. "You come alone?"

"Yes." He saw the lurking triumph on both of the faces, waiting to spring the trap; the discouragement as Hugh continued, "I gave a lift to a girl outside Blythe. She was coming to Phoenix to visit her aunt. She wasn't with me, simply a passenger."

"Her name wasn't Bonnie Lee Crumb?"

"Her name was Iris Croom." It was too much to hope that the detectives wouldn't detect the Crumb-Croom similarity. "Her aunt's name was"—he pretended to search his memory—"was Carney, Mayble Carney. She owned a beauty parlor in Phoenix, the girl said." Let them look for her too.

"Did you take her to her aunt's house?"

"No, I let her off at the bus station downtown. She asked to be let off there." He explained as if it had all been true. "Her aunt had expected her to come by bus and was meeting her there."

Ringle's lips pursed. "This Iris Croom a white girl?"

"Yes."

"But she let you pick her up?"

He couldn't get angry. And he wouldn't tell the entire story to these two, it was too unbelievable.

Venner piped up. "She was looking at that big white Cadillac, not the driver."

Hugh had long learned to control his voice no matter what burned within him. He said, "I was at the inspection station when she came over to my car and asked for a lift. She said she'd missed her ride." Even as he spoke, he wondered if the inspection officers at Blythe had put the detectives on him. Would they have remembered the name she called out and her shrilled story, or only the white girl asking him for a ride, and the license number of his car? He waited for Ringle to pounce.

But Ringle was addressing his partner. "Ain't you warmed up yet, Ven? Whyn't you sit down?"

"I don't want to sit down." Venner continued to lean against the grill, letting the hot air blow against his thin, shoddy jacket.

Ringle turned back to Hugh. "You read the papers today?"

"I looked them over."

"Read about that girl we found in the canal?"

He couldn't deny it. No one could have missed that headline. "Yes, I read about it."

"Read how we asked folks to come in and identify her?"

He nodded. "Has she been identified?"

Ringle's permanent scowl deepened. "Some kids found her purse tonight. In a ditch about a half mile from where she was found. There was a school-activities card in her wallet with her name, Bonnie Lee Crumb. We put that on the ten-o'clock news."

Venner suggested, "I suppose you didn't hear that news."

"No, I didn't hear any radio reports tonight. I was at a bridal dinner for my niece." As they well knew. He would not suggest an alibi by giving the time of his arrival there.

"Bonnie Lee Crumb, Indio High School, Indio, California." Ringle punched out the syllables as if this information would shake Hugh. Hugh waited for him to continue. "Where was this—uh—Iris Croom from?"

"She said she was from Banning."

Venner insinuated, "How'd you like to look at the one we found in the canal? Maybe you could identify her."

Hugh feigned surprise. "You don't think it's the same girl?"

Ringle said with meaning, "We got a tip."

Venner smirked. "Why do you think we're asking you these questions?"

Hugh was careful. With just the right amount of indifference, he said, "I have wondered."

"Like Ringle says, we got a tip. Right after that report went out on the radio. This guy says a nigger doc driving a big white Cadillac brought Bonnie Lee to Phoenix."

Hugh took a long breath. "Who was your informant?"

Ringle answered diffidently, "The desk sergeant took the call didn't get his name." And Venner continued, "The guy said we'd find the doc at The Palms."

"He gave you my name?"

"Naw, but we didn't have no trouble getting that at the desk here." The implication was in his titter.

Hugh permitted Venner his moment of triumph. Then he spoke, with precision. "It seems to me that this informant is the one you should be looking for. The name Bonnie Lee Crumb was known to him. I never heard it until you mentioned it tonight. The girl to whom I gave a ride was Iris Croom."

"How old was she?" Ringle snapped.

"I don't know. Young. In her teens, I'd say."

"You better come down and have a look at this girl we found." He lumbered to his feet.

Hugh didn't move. "Why?"

Venner took an avid step forward. "You're refusing?"

Hugh said, "If she is Bonnie Lee Crumb, I can't identify her. I have never known anyone of that name."

"Maybe she ain't Bonnie Lee Crumb. Maybe she's Iris Croom. You gonna come or not?"

Ringle stopped his partner's advance. He blinked at Hugh. "You don't have to come. We don't force you. We do everything legal." He turned his scowl on Venner. "You remember the marshal says everything legal."

"I haven't forgot it yet," Venner sneered.

He hadn't forgotten because this was Hugh Densmore and not some poor shabby guy they'd picked off the street or out of a shack.

"I'll come with you," Hugh decided, "if you think it will be of any help." He didn't want to; he didn't trust either of them. No matter what some marshal had said. But he didn't know the legalities, whether he could rightly refuse. Nor did he know if his outright refusal might bring ethical forgetfulness. "Will you wait until I get a warmer coat?" He didn't delay for an answer. He went into the dressing room, turning on the light as he moved. Ringle came casually over to the entrance, where he could watch the change.

Hugh took off his dinner jacket and hung it in the wardrobe. He put on his gabardine topcoat. He looked like a musician at the end of a party, the soft dress shirt and black tie, the tuxedo trousers. It was past one o'clock; he was too tired to go anywhere. He wondered how long it would be before he was permitted to return. If he would be permitted to return.

He switched off the light and returned to the big room. Ringle stepped aside. Hugh remembered, "I don't have a car."

"You can ride with us," Venner said.

He didn't want to ask, "And you'll bring me back here?"

"Sure, we'll bring you back." His mouth was a sneer. "Everything legal."

Hugh continued to be apprehensive but it was too late to change his mind. Ringle was holding open the door. If everything was legal, they'd have to charge him to hold him. And what could they charge him with? Not murder. Not without some evidence.

This wasn't the Deep South. It was Arizona.

3

THEY WALKED through the icy night to where they'd left the car—not a painted police car, a plain dark sedan. They put Hugh in the back seat. Ringle tuned in the police cycle while Venner drove. The radio wasn't like Los Angeles, with never-ending codes coming over. There seemed to be but one item at this hour, a highway accident.

Venner took westbound Washington across town. There were few other cars abroad. Even when they reached the downtown section. When they passed the courthouse without reducing speed, Hugh knew fear. He spoke up. "Where are we going?"

Venner snickered over his shoulder, "To see your girl friend. You didn't think we were keeping her in the office, did you?" After a moment he bared his small teeth. "The icebox isn't big enough." He was the only one who laughed.

They had reached the dead-end circle of the state capitol, and he swerved to the left. Hugh's fear was growing. They were cutting a south-and-west course through a shabby neighborhood he'd never seen before. He'd read of tactics such as this, where a man could be held incommunicado for days.

There were no passing cars to call out to. You couldn't call for help from a police car, anyway; he didn't think you could. When Venner turned down a dark and narrow country lane, panic came up into Hugh's throat. Only his pride kept him from crying out, demanding to know where they were taking him. Pride and the fear. He'd never known fear before, he'd only thought that he had. There were no handles on the rear doors.

Not more than a half mile down the lane, Venner turned a sharp left into an area of low-lying buildings. There was a small sign: COUNTY HOSPITAL. It did nothing to allay the fear.

The place could have been a reclaimed army barracks. The night lights showed faded green brick with darker green trim. There was no sign of life. There was no sound but of insects in the surrounding fields and a sudden scrap of song from a meadow lark awakened by the car's lights.

The car crawled past the buildings, following the driveway to the far rear. It stopped in front of a small blunt building whose night light revealed the legend: COUNTY MORTUARY. Hugh took a breath. Everything legal.

Venner cut the engine. He got out and opened the door for Hugh while Ringle was extracting his bulk from the front seat. "All out for the morgue," Venner chirruped. "Only we don't call it the morgue, the coroner don't like that name. The 'County Mortuary,'" he mimicked.

Hugh walked with the detectives across the recessed outer entrance to the back door. The knob turned under Ringle's heavy paw.

The attendant on duty was an old man. "You again?" he complained. He pushed up arthritically from his office chair. His voice scratched, "You want to see that same girl?"

"Yeah," Ringle said. "Anybody identify her yet?"

"Nary a soul come around. She must of been a floater."

Venner wheezed, "That's what she was all right, a floater!" Again no one else laughed.

The old man shuffled forward ahead of them and opened the door of the storage room. Venner stopped laughing and began to shiver. Hugh was glad he'd thought of the topcoat. The detectives wouldn't get a chance to say that the suspect quaked when he saw the body.

The old man didn't fumble, he knew the slot where she was put away. He rolled out the drawer, folded back the covering. They hadn't done an autopsy yet. That was Hugh's first thought, and with it came a spasm of relief. Surely they wouldn't make an arrest until they knew what caused her death.

He looked the body over carefully, Ringle and Venner and the attendant watching him as if they believed the old fables about Negroes and graveyards. They weren't bright or they'd know that to become a doctor one must study both the quick and the dead.

The girl was Iris—or Bonnie Lee—as he had been sure it would be. No two girls matched the description the police had issued. She hadn't been in the water long enough to be distorted.

Because of his medical familiarity with morgue procedure, Hugh was without emotion. His tension had dissipated in the routine of examination. He looked over at Ringle. "Yes, this is the girl who called herself Iris Croom."

The attendant began covering her again, as he might a sleeping child. Venner left the room rapidly, shaking from the cold. Probably chronic malaria. Hugh followed him, Ringle at his heels. In the office outside, Hugh lighted a cigarette. He had to know if they were calling it murder.

"What was the cause of death?" He doubted that it would enter their heads that as a doctor he knew the autopsy had been delayed. Down the corridor, the metal door banged and the shuffle of the returning attendant could be heard.

Ringle said, "We won't know that until the autopsy."

"It hasn't been done?"

"The M.E. is out of town. Making a speech at the University of Chicago," Ringle said with a blustering pride. Hugh suddenly recalled the national reputation of the Phoenix medical examiner. With a man of his distinction, there'd be no juggling of facts to fit a possible suspect. "He'll be back Monday."

A delay in performing an autopsy wasn't unusual. This one was for Hugh an answered prayer. They wouldn't know until Monday what had killed Iris or if she had killed herself. By then Clytie's wedding would be over. He asked matter-of-factly, "Would you mind taking me back to The Palms now. I'm pretty tired."

Ringle's eyes rested coldly on his face. Hugh met them, unmoved. It was Ringle who shifted. "Will you sign a statement identifying her?"

Hugh gave it consideration. It wouldn't seem to incriminate him further. "I'll sign a statement identifying her as Iris Croom. I didn't know her by any other name."

Venner didn't cover a yawn. "Maybe she was carrying some other kid's school card."

Ringle was preparing a report, leaning on the old man's desk.

Hugh said, "If she was Bonnie Lee Crumb, that man who called you is the one to identify her."

"We told you we don't know who he is." Nor did Ringle care. "He hung up when the sarge tried to get his name." He thrust the paper at Hugh. "Sign this."

First he read it with care. The name of Bonnie Lee wasn't on it. There was a space where Hugh printed the name—Iris

Croom. He signed his name where indicated and returned the form.

No one moved to leave. It would be a mistake to be insistent; they could keep him here all night asking questions if they so wanted. They could make it appear voluntary. Instead of saying anything more, he started moving toward the door. He counted on Venner as before, Venner who looked pinched with weariness. He had it figured right. Venner moved. "Come on, Ringle."

Ringle finished studying the form. He told the old man, "Thanks, Pop. You can go back to sleep now. We won't be bothering you again tonight." Catching up with Venner, he said, "Don't be in such a sweat."

As previously, they put Hugh in the rear of the car. He watched the dark streets out the window as they returned to town. There was no deviation; Venner retraced the route. They passed the courthouse without pause and wheeled over to Van Buren. Ringle said then, "You aren't planning to leave town?"

"Not until Monday. I'm due at the hospital Tuesday."

"Hospital?"

"I'm interning at the UCLA Medical Center."

"You ain't a real doc?" Somehow this was agreeable news to him.

Hugh explained, "I have my degree but I haven't completed my internship. I was given leave to attend the wedding."

Ringle warned, "You better not plan on going back Monday."

"Why not?"

"Might be we'd want to talk to you again. After the autopsy."

Ringle knew, or his suspicions were the same as Hugh's. Only as to her murderer did they differ. Hugh said, "I'll check with you before I leave."

They delivered him to his door, Venner releasing him from the car.

Hugh said, "Thank you" and "Good night."

Venner didn't bother to respond; Ringle made some sound. They had driven away before Hugh had his key in the lock. He went inside, hung the DO NOT DISTURB sign outside on the knob, locked and bolted the door. He'd forgotten about lights and heat when he went out with them; both were still on. The room was too hot but his reaction had set in. Like Venner, Hugh was shaking as if chilled to his bone marrow.

It was far too late to call Ellen, it was almost three-thirty in the morning. A call might disturb the entire household, this he couldn't risk. What was more deterring was the fact that the story was too involved to give over the telephone. He didn't have the strength now to go into it. A realization came suddenly: it might not be safe to talk over this phone. He didn't know how far or how deep the detectives' suspicions extended. They could have a monitor on the switchboard.

Hugh undressed. He couldn't solve his problems tonight. Perhaps in the morning he could figure out what he should do.

When he woke, it was not completely but in a blur. He wondered if he'd missed the bells, wondered at the lazy euphoria which seemed to engulf him. And then he came sharply awake and remembered he wasn't at the Med Center, he was in a Phoenix motel. This was the day of the wedding. And this was the day after the night of nightmare. The girl he'd known as Iris Croom was dead, irrevocably dead, and he was involved.

Innocently involved? No, he couldn't call it innocent. Rather, it was mindless. It was neither; it was a paper chain of circumstance, cut from sympathy and too much imagination. Imagination, yes—why else should he have thought that unless he picked up the girl she would be in danger? Another car would have come along, a family car for which she had said she was waiting, or even another man, a white man. Most travelers, like most men, were intrinsically decent. The end result for Iris would have been the same, cruelly the same. But he needn't have been involved. He was the wrong man to have played Samaritan, and he'd known it, known it there on the road and in every irreversible moment since.

The room was airless. He came out of bed and turned the conditioning to high. He parted the curtains and quickly closed them again, against the searing brightness of the sun. Only then did he look at his watch. He was dismayed at the lateness of the morning. He'd intended to go with the family to Sunday morning services at his grandfather's old church. He wasn't much on churchgoing these days, but when he weekended at home he always accompanied his mother to services on Sunday mornings. It pleased her. Would the eventual headlines read: MINISTER'S GRANDSON ACCUSED OF MURDER?

He shaped up brusquely. That kind of thinking was pure neuroticism. There was no reason to believe that he would become further involved in this death. He had never known Bonnie Lee Crumb. There was someone in Phoenix who had, someone who'd made an anonymous phone call. The police would be searching for him, not harassing an innocent bystander. Yet he was unreasonably relieved that the detectives hadn't returned this morning, that his sleep hadn't been disturbed by a telephone call from headquarters.

Why should they come back to him? He had told them the truth last night, if not all of the truth. For all of his rationalization, he decided he should get out of here and quickly. Before they did return. Before there were reporters and news photographers hammering at the door. It occurred to him to wonder how it was that there were no newsmen last night at the mortuary. The police must be keeping this case well under cover. He didn't know if that was in his favor or not.

They had not put out a teletype with his name last night or as yet this morning. If they had, his sleep wouldn't have been undisturbed. It couldn't be that they would care about protecting Hugh's professional reputation. More likely it was because of the ramifications of the girl's double identity. They could be waiting to move until they made positive identification of Iris as Bonnie Lee Crumb.

He showered and dressed with his mind turning the maybe and if and perhaps and possible until he forced it to quiescence. If he were to emerge from this grim *geste* unharmed, he must walk through it the same man who walked into it. He, Dr. Hugh Densmore, product of his heredity and environment, sufficiently intelligent and well adjusted to his mind and body and color and ambition.

The services would be over, the family should be back at the grandparents', enjoying one of Gram's pioneer meals. He couldn't eat but he'd have a cup of coffee with them. This time he put on his sun glasses before parting the curtains. He slid open the lanai doors. It was another beautiful day, another hot day. There was no policeman on guard outside, no stranger at all. Far across the lawn by the pool, the sunbathers and the swimmers were again gala. He left the doors ajar, with the screen hooked; he liked fresh air with his air conditioning.

As he turned back to the room, he remembered his promise to call Ellen. His hand reached across the desk, then drew away. He wouldn't call her from this phone. He left the apartment, stepping out into the high blaze of noon heat. He'd forgotten he was without a car, he'd have to walk it. He didn't mind the walk, in a way he welcomed it. It would clear his head in a way that driving a car could not. There was no one on guard at this outside door, either.

He cut a rapid crosstown path toward Jefferson Street. Walking in one hundred-degree heat had little resemblance to walking on a Westwood campus. But he didn't diminish his pace even though he knew it to be compulsive. There was need to put as much distance as possible, and as quickly as possible, between himself and the motel. He wouldn't be hidden with the family. He had mentioned Dr. Edward last night. If Ringle and Venner didn't know, they could easily find out where to look for Hugh. His grandfather was as well known as the doctor.

Again the sick feeling overwhelmed him. Surely the police wouldn't interrupt the wedding. But having met Ringle and Venner, he knew that it would make no difference to them. They'd come for Hugh whenever they wanted him. It might even give them a twisted satisfaction to slur their black shadows over the shining white of the bridal ceremony.

When he reached his grandparents' house, he took the porch steps by twos as if Ringle's hand were outstretched to clamp his shoulder. He plunged into the living-room coolness. The voices led him to the dining room. They were at the table, not at one of his grandmother's Sunday chicken dinners, not on the wedding day. But the breakfast they were finishing was equally substantial. None of the young people was present, nor were the out-of-town guests. Only his father and mother and his grandparents.

His mother looked up, appalled. "You didn't walk over here, Hugh! Why didn't you call me?"

They hadn't heard of any trouble. They wouldn't be as normal if they had. He poured himself a glass of water and drank it slowly before answering the concerted hubbub.

"I'm a tenderfoot. Why didn't somebody remind me it would be a hundred and ten in the shade?" His voice sounded normal. He hoped his demeanor didn't belie it. He must remember to be supranormal all this day, not let an inflection or a glance betray the inner nerves.

"Have you had your lunch yet?" It was his grandmother, starting to rise.

Hugh put his hands on her shoulders. "I haven't had my breakfast yet. Don't move. There's enough here for all the starving Chinese." He sat down beside her.

"Those corn cakes are cold. And the bacon."

"You just brought them in, Mama." His father began to serve a plate.

"I'm not hungry," Hugh said quickly. "All I want is a cup of coffee." But he found himself eating; it was easier than arguing. "Where is everybody?"

His father said, "If by everybody you mean the girls, they've gone swimming."

"I thought you planned to go with them," his mother said.

"I planned a full day," Hugh told her. "I overslept." The Sunday papers must be in the front room. He should have thought about them when he first came into the house, before joining the family. Just for a quick look at the headlines. There could be nothing about him in them, not even implied, or his parents would be asking questions.

He heard his mother with his outer ear. "You needn't have sent the car back last night, Hugh. There are enough cars at Stacy's to take care of us."

This then had been Ellen's story. "It's your car."

"Maybe you thought you'd better not drive after the party," his father suggested.

"May be." His grin felt unforced. Ellen might have included such a suggestion. "Those magnums came around pretty often."

They were talking about the dinner and about this afternoon's reception and he tried to listen in case he should be called on for response. They didn't seem to notice his silence; as an excuse for it he kept eating. If he could get away from the table before they did, he could take a moment for the newspaper. The day's plans seemed to involve him; the girls would decorate the house but men were needed for the heavy work.

"Whenever you're ready," he heard his father saying. "You can give me a lift to Stacy's and bring the girls back here with you."

What he saw was his father taking the Sunday paper from the near chair. It had been invisible under the drape of the white tablecloth. Automatically his hand twitched out for it, even as he watched his father hand the folded sections to his mother. "I'm too old for heavy work," his father was continuing heartily. "Besides, after that champagne supper last night, I need a snooze. And once you clear the place of those babbling females, that's what I'm going to have."

Hugh could have asked her: May I have a quick look at the front section? But what answer could he give to her inevitable: Why, is there some particular story . . . ? And she would glance at the front page in passing, would see the headlines about the dead girl. Fear would squeeze her, the fear lying ever-dormant beneath the civilized front, beneath the normal life of a Los Angeles housewife whose husband's income was in near-five figures, whose children had been born and bred and coddled in serenity and security and status.

He did not ask. He rose from the table, made the proper good-bye sounds, and in a flurry of his mother's memoranda for Stacy, followed his father out to the car. He should have emerged with a reassurance granted by the untroubled respite of the dining table. But anxiety smote him as sharply as the sun glare when once he was in the open. He was not able to dismiss it until he was certain that there were no strangers loitering on the street, no unfamiliar cars standing at the curb.

"You drive," his father said. "I don't know whether it's the champagne or the weather, but I'm beat."

As Hugh took the wheel, the anxiety recurred. This was no longer his mother's white Cadillac, this was an item in police reports. He wondered how many eyes would be watching for it as it wheeled in and around the Phoenix streets.

It was important that he make a special effort to match his father's holiday mood. If anyone would sense something wrong in him, it would be Dad. "Anyone with no more sense than to play eighteen holes under an Arizona sun deserves what he feels," he said.

The radio had not come on at the turn of the ignition switch. Ellen must have turned it off manually last night. To protect him, just in case. He didn't turn it on. He couldn't risk it.

The inevitable question was being asked. "When do you have to be back at the hospital?"

"I can take a few days." He had to take at least one more day. If everything worked out right tomorrow, as it surely would, he could fly back in time for duty on Tuesday.

"I was hoping you might have a week, so you could drive Mother home. She's going to stay on with Stacy and help her get rested up. The girls and I are flying out tonight."

How could it be possible to be comforted and fearful at one time? He echoed, "Tonight?"

"I must be in the office in the morning. Your sisters are bellowing to stay longer, but they've missed enough school this week."

Hugh said, "I wish I could stay." And he wished from the bottom of his heart that he could talk to his father about what had happened. But it wouldn't be fair. His father didn't get away often enough from his growing insurance business. Why should he have the vacation spoiled by Hugh's problems? Hugh was a man, not a child. Yet if it hadn't been that they were already in sight of Stacy's, he might not have been able to keep quiet. He'd always confided in his father, from the time he could talk. The dangerous moment passed. He parked in front of the house, and together, he and his father went up the walk.

Approaching the handsome suburban dwelling, for the first time Hugh's anxieties were truly allayed. The Densmores and the Willises weren't the kind of people you pushed around. The flurry of careless voices within the house increased his sense of security.

He called out, "All passengers for the fifty-cent tour to Phoenix, line up at the door. At once. This means now."

He was answered by protests and pleas from the bedroom corridor. The girls were obviously engaged in the multitudinous pre-preparations that were a part of partytime. In the midst of the clamor, Stacy sat on the living-room couch, turning the hem of her dress. "The girls said it was too long," she supplied.

Hugh didn't, couldn't, sit down to wait. He put out his cigarette in an ash tray and automatically lighted another. He was nervous about facing Ellen. He would have to give her an explanation for last night, and the only explanation there could be was the facts of the whole sordid mess. It wasn't something he wanted to tell her. Of all the many girls he'd known and liked and perhaps loved, she was one who might have developed into the real thing. If he hadn't met up with Iris Croom.

When Ellen emerged from the bedroom corridor, he knew he hadn't been wrong in trusting her to handle things the night before. Her competence was implicit in the reassuring way her eyes met his in the moment before she put on her dark sun glasses. There might have been a flicker of relief that he was here, not held by the police. He attempted to move toward her, trying to make it unobtrusive, but his way was blocked by what seemed a roomful of sisters and cousins and nieces and nephews. She too made the attempt. But always before they could converge, the others, as in a ballet, had moved to thrust them apart again. He gave up and raised his voice, "Come on everybody who's going."

The rush through the door began. He watched Ellen approach. There was no chance to speak, for Clytie came pushing after her, calling back to Stacy, "But I have to go, Mother. I've always decorated the wedding arch. Besides, I'd go nuts sitting around here doing nothing until four o'clock."

When Hugh reached the car, the group was somehow mashed inside. With Ellen next to the driver's seat. He wondered if she had arranged it or if it were his sisters' matchmaking tendencies. He was sorry he would have to disappoint them. So sorry, but there was another girl . . . in another country, and the wench was dead.

Through his bitterness, he heard Ellen's voice, almost beneath her breath. "There's nothing about you in the morning paper or on the radio."

He said, as quietly, "It was too late to call you last night."

"I read by the phone until three. Is it—all right?"

He nodded. It wasn't a lie. Everything was all right as far as he knew. He said, "I'll tell you what it's about when there's a chance. Perhaps after the reception we can get away for a while."

"It's a date," she confirmed gravely.

Being able to postpone the recital somehow steadied his nerves. At the house, work, physical work, took over. He and the nephews put up the arch while the girls wrapped the white satin ribbon on the balusters and the handrail of the staircase. There was no time for brooding as they all raced against time to cover the whole with white oleanders and shining green leaves. His mother and Mrs. Bent were doing the dining room, the two grandmothers were stirring in the kitchen. It was near three o'clock before all the groups were satisfied. And he must return to the motel to dress.

He drew Ellen aside, ignoring the wise looks that followed them. "Do you mind taking the crowd back to Stacy's? I'm going to cut out."

"I'll drive you over."

"No," he said, too quickly, too sharply.

She must have known that everything wasn't right, but she said only, "All right. You won't forget we have a date?"

"I won't forget," he told her, wishing that he could forget it, or wishing that it was a date, no more than that. He waited for a moment until attention had been diverted from him, then unhurriedly slipped out to the porch and ran down the steps to the pavement. He struck out slantwise across the wide street, dodging the Sunday afternoon traffic. The heat was no longer ablaze; by now it was heavy, oppressive, as before a storm in the eastern part of the country. In Arizona it didn't presage a storm, merely the late afternoon. He walked as quickly as possible, but it was as if he were walking through shifting sand.

He could have accepted Ellen's offer for a ride, but if Ringle and Venner were waiting for him, he didn't want her exposed to their scrutiny. Last night they had given her no attention, they'd been too busy concentrating on him. Unless they saw her again, they wouldn't remember her. They must not see her again. He couldn't bear the thought of their ugliness touching her.

He was on the side street which led to the motel when he first noticed the car. Noticed yet didn't notice the first time it went by. It wasn't until it passed a second time, more slowly, that he realized it was the same car which had been with him since he'd crossed Washington. By then it was out of sight. He found he could remember nothing, neither color nor shape nor make. Just an old sedan with a man at the wheel. It could have been a plainclothes police car; it wasn't so different from the one he'd ridden in last night. But it hadn't been Ringle or Venner driving, and there'd been only one man in it. The police usually worked in pairs. For the first time it came to him that there would be others besides the police interested in him. The unknown man Iris had come to meet. The man who refused his name to the police. The man because of whom the girl had met death. Three men or one.

The thought slowed his steps and the taste of fear was again in his mouth. Somehow he knew, knew with dreadful clarity, that this man had full intent to make Hugh the killer. He had begun last night with the anonymous call. No, before that he had shown his intent. The first shape had been when he brought Iris to Hugh's door on Friday night. It must have been he who brought her there.

Hugh half ran to the door of his unit. But he hesitated before turning the key and slipping inside. No messages, no persons waited for him. Having no radio, he turned on the television set, not expecting news but just in case. There wasn't any. He blanked out thought while he did what had to be done —another shower, a clean dress shirt, a cotton of lighter fluid to erase a spot of cigarette ashes from his white coat. When he was dressed in his wedding garments, he tried all the television channels but there was still no news. He said aloud, "No news is good news," but he knew he was lying as he said it. If only there were some way, some safe way, to make inquiries of the police. There wasn't. Not for him.

It was time to return to the grandparents' house, but he delayed. He was afraid, he admitted it, afraid to go outside. The fear was not now of the police but of a man without a face or name, a man who knew his face and name and where to find him.

He looked long at the phone. He didn't have to go back alone through the quiet, late afternoon side streets. He could call his sister's house; any one of a dozen cars would stop by for him. He had a good excuse, the wish to arrive for the wedding without passing through six or eight blocks of steam heat. He wouldn't let himself make the move toward the phone. He wouldn't give in to irrational fear. He turned off the air conditioner; the night's chill would have set in before he returned and he couldn't know but what he'd later need a warm room as he had last night. He could delay no longer. He took a last look at the television screen; it was advertising some children's remedy. He cut it off and was on his way.

It didn't seem so hot out now although the sun was still high above the horizon. In his white jacket, he was too visible. He wanted to cut and run but he made himself walk in normal fashion, paying no more attention to passing cars than he would have yesterday or the day before. If that one passed him again, he didn't recognize it. There were so many old dark sedans.

His spirits lifted when he reached the wide thoroughfare of Washington. Certainly nothing would happen here. It was a well-traveled street although there wasn't much traffic on a Sunday afternoon. He followed it to the side street which led over to the Jefferson house. On Jefferson he no longer had to fear. He joined the wedding guests making their way toward the house. He would be anonymous to strangers in the protection of the group.

Within the house, he took a place near the front door. He could step outside to meet them, if the detectives should come. Or if any uninvited guest intruded. But no strangers appeared.

The wedding was quiet perfection. His grandfather pronounced the beautiful old words. The women wept and the men swallowed hard when Clytie's luminous face was turned to meet John's unaccountably solemn one. The bridesmaids were a frieze of summer-leaf chiffon; among them Hugh saw Ellen's flower face only. He wondered how much she had figured out. There was only one big story in the papers and she was not a stupid girl.

Because the wedding was in the home, the guest list was small —the family and a few old friends. But the reception which followed seemed to include the entire community. There was no segregation with Clytie's university friends and John's Air

Force crowd on hand. In a way Hugh wished that Ringle and Venner could have been looking in. They might realize that poor shoddy little Iris couldn't have been the outworn cliché of sexual interest to Hugh.

During the reception, he couldn't remain on guard. He had to mingle with family and friends. With his fingers crossed against intrusion, he had to pretend the joy the others were feeling. Grandmother's towering white cake was cut, the toasts lifted. Hugh limited himself to one champagne cup. He would take no chance on a muddled head tonight.

At six o'clock Clytie tossed the bride's bouquet from high on the flowered staircase. Whatever arrangements John had made for their departure worked. The guests began to drift away. And at last he was free to go, to lift his dangerous shadow from the family's happiness.

If it had been possible, he would have gone alone, silently as shadow. But when he glanced across the room, Ellen's questioning eyes were on him, waiting for his signal. He had committed himself when he asked her help last night; there was no way to eliminate her now. He had to fill in the background for her, despite his reluctance. It was as if he knew that once the story was told, nothing could be withdrawn. From that moment, there must be a relentless march to an inevitable end.

He circled to her side. "Whenever you're ready." It was the first time he'd spoken to her since the beginning of the festivities.

"I'm ready."

"We can skip the good-byes. We'll be seeing the family at the airport later. I'm driving them."

She wasn't a girl who fussed. She retrieved an embroidered purse from somewhere and they left unnoticed among other departing guests.

In the car, he said, "We could go to my room at The Palms but I'd rather not."

She understood. "Whatever you say."

The only place where they could talk without danger of interruption would be a country lane. If the white car wasn't spotted—if he weren't being sought even now on a police call. He drove away, checking the mirror for a following car but there didn't seem to be any. At 24th Street he turned north as far as McDowell, then pointed east toward Scottsdale. The day's heat had softened, enough so in this before-twilight period, that the opened windows of the moving car gave an illusion of evening's cool. Raw green tract houses seemed to have taken over the countryside until they reached the cut. Here the troglodyte rocks and spire cactus were relics of what once had been.

The southern acres of Papago Park were unspoiled, although across the road the government area was newly scarred with a shiny wire fence. Had it been after dark, Hugh would have turned in at one of the sandy bypaths of Papago. But to park on the mesa was to induce attention; passing motorists couldn't fail to notice the big white car. He drove on to Scottsdale Road and turned north toward the village.

Until that moment it hadn't occurred to him that Scottsdale might be dangerous. Iris had been found in Scottsdale, not Phoenix. It was here the police might be watching for him. Or the anonymous man who had known the Scottsdale area well enough to choose a secluded section of the canal road to get rid of Iris. Having come this far, Hugh went on. He couldn't hope to hide, wherever he went. Phoenix and its environs hadn't grown that much.

He had remembered Scottsdale as surrounded by open country. He wasn't prepared for the startling growth the village had suffered, the gash of highway and the intricate, busy traffic pattern where little more than three years ago had been the quiet four corners. He turned off at Main Street and went north again at Miller Road, hoping that way might lead to what once had been. He was discouraged as he passed row after row of paint-clean doll houses.

"This was open fields the last time I was here," he said ruefully, but as he went on he was all at once off the pavement and onto a country lane. He might have been miles from the village, there were fields and an old tree somnolent against the water of a tiny stream.

He did not stop the car, it was too close to the little houses he'd passed. He continued north to the end of the lane and blundered upon the canal road. For a moment he was blunted with shock. It was as if he had entered a maze from which there was no escape whichever way he chose to move. But reason returned. At least he had found a place where it would be safe to talk. Iris had not been murdered here but on the other side of Scottsdale. He drove on, turning to the right away from town, and following the narrow, dusty contours of the road, where the unperturbed water was banked high on the left and on the right were the empty saffron fields. There was scarcely width enough for two cars to pass but there were no other cars, and any approaching from the east could be seen from far off with the whirl of dust to give warning. He pulled up against the side of the road and cut the engine. If any cars came from behind, the rear-view mirror would warn.

He offered Ellen a cigarette, took one himself, and lighted them. He didn't know how to begin, he didn't want to begin.

She spoke before he could. "It's that girl, isn't it?"

He turned and looked into her face. There was no distaste in it, no pity. "I thought you might know."

"What else would have brought the police last night? What else is there?"

He nodded slowly. What else? What else had happened here which could so affect him, a stranger in a strange town? It wasn't like Los Angeles or New York, where there were so many evil happenings.

She said, as if she'd made certain, "You had nothing to do with it but somehow you're involved."

"That's right," he said. "I'm afraid I'm involved."

Almost disinterestedly she asked, "How did it happen?"

He had intended to tell it only in part, but to his surprise he found himself starting on the road to Indio when the jalopy had cut in front of him.

She listened without interruptions. The only thing he didn't tell was the old insults the kids in the jalopy had shrilled at him. Insulated as her life may have been, she still would have heard them too many times. Nor did he mention the car which might have been pacing him this afternoon. By now he was ashamed of having let his imagination trick him into shying at what must have had some everyday meaning, someone looking for a house number or someone early for a rendezvous with a friend. Everything else he told her.

Twilight came down and turned into early evening before he had finished. Together they'd smoked almost a pack of cigarettes. When his ran out, she'd brought hers from her handbag. He concluded unhappily, "And that's it."

For a long moment she didn't speak and he wondered if he had quenched whatever spark of interest she might have had in him. By getting himself so stupidly involved in this affair.

And then she said, it wasn't a question, "You believe the girl was murdered."

"Yes." He was sure of it, as sure as if he'd done the autopsy himself and had proof. "She wouldn't have killed herself. She was too—tough." He explained, "I'm not using the word in the slang sense."

"I know." She nodded. She looked across at him. "Murdered by an abortion."

"Yes." He was reluctant to admit it, as if the admission were further self-involvement.

"And because of the chain of circumstance, you have been picked as the sacrificial goat?" She smiled, but only to soften the implication.

Without hesitation he admitted this as well. "Yes." He went on, "Of course I know I'm building it up. There's no reason why—"

She interrupted him. "There are many reasons why. You know them. I know them. I think you're in for real trouble, Hugh."

He didn't say anything, he couldn't. His hand holding the cigarette was as if a chill wind moved it.

"You need a lawyer."

"No." He rejected it utterly, violently. "What could a lawyer do? I haven't been accused of anything. I haven't done anything." He tried to make her see it. "Having a lawyer would make me look guilty. And I'm not."

She smiled wryly. "Most lawyers prefer an innocent client."

He tried to laugh. "The Judge's daughter."

"Perhaps. I've grown up under the law. And perhaps it's that I've seen too many cases involving innocent people, our people."

He said, "When I need one—if I need one—time enough then."

Without agreeing with him, she accepted his refusal. She asked, "You haven't told your father anything about this?"

"I couldn't. Don't you see? The wedding—"

"You should tell them." She was troubled. "You mustn't let them find out"—she hesitated, then concluded, but not what she'd been about to say—"another way."

He said, "Nothing's going to happen until after the autopsy." He'd convinced himself of this. "If the police had wanted a quick arrest, they could have held me last night when I identified her." He wanted her to see it as he did. "If the autopsy proves she committed suicide, why put my family through all the agony of expecting the worst?"

"You know it isn't suicide, you've said that."

"I know, but only the autopsy can prove it. By then they may have the right man—"

"Don't dream," she said shortly. "You've also said they weren't interested in the unknown informant."

He pleaded his case. "By now they must have talked to her father. He can tell them I never saw the girl until I gave her a ride." Or could he, would he? Did the father know anything about Iris' private life?

Ellen said, almost impatiently, "They won't care who got her into trouble. All they'll want is the man, or woman, who committed an aborticide."

She was right, but he argued, "The boy friend will know who that was. He'll know I had nothing to do with it." And the fear was a knife in him. Because if the police looked for and found Iris' betrayer, that anonymous voice on the phone who must be the same, why would he be expected to tell the truth? He had given them Hugh.

Ellen didn't express her doubts. She only urged, "Tell your family, Hugh."

But he knew he couldn't. Not until it became essential. He couldn't bear it that they too should be in a vise of fear. Suddenly he remembered the time. He switched on the dash lights and looked at his watch. "It's almost eight. We'd better go if I'm to get Dad and the girls to the airport for Flight 305."

She knew he had rejected the idea. She protested no more, only said, "If I can help, Hugh, let me know."

"You've already helped." Like a child he touched her hand in gratefulness.

She smiled back at him but only with her lips. Her eyes remained somber.

The only turnaround was down a dusty bank into a field with a vertical pull up to the road again. The wheels made it. He drove back through Scottsdale and south toward his sister's home. They didn't talk on the drive. Only when they were nearing the house did he have a sudden, disastrous thought. "When are you leaving?"

She said, "I don't know. I think I'll stay on a few days and rest."

"Aren't you in school?"

"I'm taking some courses, without credit. I can catch up. I wasn't returning for another week, anyway. I'm going first to visit some friends in Los Angeles."

He couldn't have the arrogance to believe she was staying on here because of his troubles. But he said, trying to make it light, "I'm glad you'll be around for a few days. As long as I have to stay."

"Of course I'll move from your sister's tomorrow. The Palms looks pleasant."

"It is. But Stacy won't let you move out."

She smiled. "I can be very determined. She certainly needs to be free from company."

"My unit will be available. I'm checking in at my grandmother's tomorrow. She is also a very determined woman."

He didn't want to make the move. But it would hurt his grandparents if he refused without explanation. And he'd have to invent more explanations for borrowing the money from his mother to stay on at the motel.

There was little time to spare at Stacy's, he'd cut it fine. Somehow, while the girls' suitcases were being closed, Ellen managed to change from her bridesmaid's dress to a dark silk with jacket. It took Celeste longer than that to change the contents of her purse.

They made it to the airport close to eight-thirty, the check-in time. Hugh left the group and the luggage at the entrance and circled back to the parking lots. When he returned and entered the lobby, he saw Ringle. It was a large lobby and the big man was far across by the doors which led to the field. Yet he saw Hugh even as Hugh saw him. He didn't move. He stood there, a monolith, as if he were a passenger waiting for a flight announcement. Not a yard away from where Hugh's family was standing.

Ellen was waiting by the magazine racks. Perhaps she too had recognized the detective. Hugh joined her.

"Don't look now but that's Ringle over by the field exit. I'll go to the news counter and buy some cigarettes. Do you think you can get the family outside?"

"I can try."

"I don't believe he'll do anything if I explain. But in case—" He put the car keys in her hand.

She didn't waste time discussing it. She started out. He diverged to the counter and asked for two packs of Ellen's brand of cigarettes. The woman at the cash register passed them across to him and he put down the coins. He stayed there, taking time to open one of the packages while he watched Ellen move to the family. If anyone could manage, she could. The girls would be no problem but his parents might want to remain in the waiting room. She must have been persuasive, for in a moment they were all heading out the door.

He shoved the cigarette pack in his pocket and walked with quick steps across the room. He walked directly up to Ringle. "I'm not going anywhere," he said. "I'm seeing my father and sisters off for Los Angeles."

Ringle grunted. But when Hugh went outside, he followed, obtrusive in his unobtrusiveness. He watched Hugh join the group by the gate.

Dad said, "We decided to wait out here. There'll be a better chance for seats."

The sisters were both talking at once, giving and getting directions for the week ahead when their mother would be away. Hugh handed Ellen the unopened pack of cigarettes.

She smiled "Thanks" while her eyes questioned.

He said, "Thank you for the loan," and hoped his expression conveyed reassurance concerning the situation.

He circled to a position where he could keep an eye on the detective. He didn't think that Ringle would move in now, not unless Hugh started through the gate. But he couldn't be sure, and if it should happen, he was determined to be in a position where he could step up to meet it, not have it touch the family. It seemed an endless time before the plane was called and the passenger gate was opened. The family went on board, waving through the porthole windows to the three left behind. The motors roared, spitting flame, before the big ship taxied away for the take-off. And he had to stand there, still in Ringle's shadow, until his mother saw the flight airborne. After that, he didn't delay. He escorted her and Ellen into the lobby, across it to the outer door, and toward the parking area.

Ringle followed them. Not too close but not far enough for conversation to be unheard. He was by the parking meter when Hugh helped the women into the car. When Hugh drove away, he was still standing there. Perhaps by then it had percolated through his thick head that Hugh had meant what he said, that he wasn't leaving town.

Yet Hugh could not be certain that the car wasn't followed. There were lights at a reliable distance behind him on the road leaving the airport, lights behind him as he left-turned and continued over the country road south to his sister's. It wasn't unusual to be followed by headlights. Now that evening had come, there were plenty of cars on the road, returning from Sunday outings.

It was not until he reached Stacy's house that he was taken with a fear of returning alone to the motel, of being alone through the long evening. He said to his mother, "We won't come in with you. Ellen and I are going to get something to eat."

His mother scarcely covered her pleasure in having Hugh show an interest in Ellen. She opened her purse. "You'd better take my key, Ellen," she said. "I'm sure everyone here will be in bed before you get back." Ellen gave no indication that she hadn't been consulted on Hugh's plans.

Not until they had driven away did Ellen speak. "I'm not really hungry."

"I'm not either," he said. "But it won't hurt us to eat." He admitted frankly, "I didn't think you'd mind. And I didn't feel I could stand an evening of thinking about it."

"We won't talk about it at all," she decided. "At least not until after dinner."

He had turned east when they reached Van Buren. "You

won't mind stopping at the motel while I change, will you? Maybe I won't feel so vulnerable if I can get out of this white jacket."

"Why do you think I changed?" But she seemed relaxed, as if she had put the problem out of mind.

He pulled up at the door of the unit. "Will you come in?" She must come in, not wait in the car, not with the memory of that old sedan driving around and around the block. Not with Ringle hovering.

Before he ushered her through the door, he flicked on the overhead lights. Again he had that overwhelming sense of relief on viewing the room's pristine emptiness.

"Make yourself comfortable," he said. "I won't be long. I'm used to making a quick change."

He went into the dressing room. It wasn't until he reached for his sports jacket that he realized someone had been in the room while he was out. It was an occupational necessity that his personal things were kept in filing-cabinet order. The jacket was neat on the hanger but not where he had hung it. He turned to the dressing table and unzipped his shaving kit. Imperceptibly there was change. He pulled open the two drawers he had been using. His belongings had been searched.

Quickly he pulled his doctor's kit from the wardrobe shelf. This too had been opened and searched. His reaction was hot anger. If they'd wanted to search his things, couldn't they have asked, not sneaked in here while he was away?

They hadn't sneaked in. They didn't have to do it that way. They'd gone to the manager and been furnished a pass key. When the realization came, his rage turned to sickness of heart. Not for himself, but for those who would come after him asking for lodging at The Palms. They'd be measured against Hugh's status, against trouble with the police. *He looked all right but . . . That's what happens when you let them . . .* He could hear the reasonable, deprecating decisions. Or their anger. *I don't care what the law says, from now on . . .* And the tedious inching forward had become a long step back.

He returned slowly to the living room. Ellen was standing there by the coffee table, where he had left her. She said, "There's a message," and extended a slip of paper.

It was a memo from the motel office, a number, and the notation: *Please call.* He twisted the paper in his fingers. He said, "My room's been searched."

She lifted her eyebrows. "You'd better return the call," was all she said. She sat down then in the big chair, the one Ringle had chosen last night.

He went to the telephone, and only after he had lifted it and heard the operator's metallic voice, did he remember that a call from this phone had to go through the switchboard. He was quite certain the message had not been from family or friend. He should have waited for an outside line, not compounded the damage done. But he went ahead, reading the number from the memo slip. The operator's voice repeated it to him, and he heard the sound of her dialing.

If the police had been private, the operator and The Palms' staff would not necessarily know of their visit to Hugh's rooms. Yet in any organization, there was a grapevine of communication which functioned without need of authoritative source or even a spoken word. He could be sure the management would curry discretion, having the police around wasn't good for a hotel's reputation. People were funny about the police. They gave lip praise to law and order, but its myrmidons brought an uneasy feeling even to the most innocent. You could taste it in the atmosphere of the receiving room even when the cops were on errands of mercy. Working in Night Emergency at the hospital had taken most of the unease away from Hugh.

On the other end of the wire a male voice stated, "Scottsdale Police Department."

The words somehow came as a shock. He swallowed and was able to respond. "This is Dr. Densmore."

The voice at the other end also seemed to have been surprised. There was a perceptible silence before it said, "Oh—hold on a minute."

Waiting, Hugh muffled the handset against his jacket sleeve. He said to Ellen, "It's Scottsdale. The police."

She put down the magazine she'd been holding and sat up tall, folding her hands into her lap like a schoolgirl. Her eyes were enormous.

Another voice came on. "Densmore? This is Marshal Hackaberry, Scottsdale. I'd like to talk to you." There was nothing menacing in the voice, it was as normal and hearty as if the man were suggesting a lunch date.

"Certainly," Hugh said. "When would it be convenient?"

"Can you come out here now?"

Hugh's hand tightened on the phone. This wasn't a friendly interview being set up. Did he dare say: *Not now, later. I have a dinner date.* He said, and the hesitancy was in his throat despite his efforts to eradicate it, "Well, yes, I can."

"You know how to get here?"

"Yes, I do." Surely a knowledge of Scottsdale didn't equate with guilt. Every visitor to Phoenix toured Scottsdale.

"I'll be expecting you."

Slowly Hugh replaced the phone. He didn't look at Ellen. "He wants to talk to me." She said nothing. "Now," and he looked into her eyes.

She rose from the chair. "We'd better go."

"Not you." His refusal was explosive.

She smiled as if at a child. "I didn't mean I was going to hold your hand at the interview. I mean I'll drive to Scottsdale with you and wait for you."

"No."

"I want to," she said flatly.

He shook his head and walked back to the dressing room. He didn't care how casually they dressed in Arizona, he needed all possible security. Such a small thing as the campus dress uniform of a white shirt and narrow dark tie was a part of it. He called out to Ellen, hoping she would be more amenable by now, "There'd be nothing for you to do while you waited."

"I'll find something. Or just stay in the car."

"No!" Again he was explosive. He strode back to the room, tying his necktie as he tried to explain. "They know the car. It's part of their—dossier, should I say? You can't stay in it, alone, at night, a girl—"

"So I won't stay in it," she said gravely, and continued, "I'm going with you, Hugh. And I'll find a place to wait, a safe place, where I'll cause you neither worry nor embarrassment."

They were standing too close together, their eyes meeting, measuring their separate thoughts. He was the one who turned away. "All right. I should say thank you. I do need support—I expect you know that from the way I've been behaving."

Her smile was small but reassuring. "I'm not thinking of myself as a pillar. It's just—I couldn't stand the waiting anywhere else."

He understood and he appreciated but he didn't tell her so. Because he couldn't accept the intimacy which was rising between them. He couldn't endure the knowing it must lead to nothing, no more than the finality of a good-bye, it's been fun knowing you.

"I guess I'm as ready as I'm going to be," he said.

They left the room; he checked the door to be sure it was fast. Not that it made any difference. Locked doors didn't thwart the police. But at least he wouldn't be surprised by anyone else.

He couldn't make conversation on the drive to Scottsdale. He was afraid, he admitted to himself that he was afraid, while insisting there was no reason to be. If this were an arrest, the marshal wouldn't invite Hugh to come out for an interview, would he? He'd send the detectives with a warrant. This meeting would be less dangerous than the ordeal with Ringle and Venner last night. Yet Hugh's hands were icy and his heart leaden.

He turned off Scottsdale Road on East Main Street and found a parking place in front of the darkened windows of an Indian arts shop. He did not want to park by the police station; he didn't want Ellen to be seen there. Although this was one of the principal streets, Scottsdale was a village, and by night it was shadowed and quiet. It would have been safe enough for Ellen to remain in the car if it had not been this particular car.

He said again, "I don't know what you're going to do."

"Don't worry about me, please. We'll meet here when you're through. I'll check regularly."

"And if I don't come back?" He had to say it.

"Don't be absurd."

Before he could get out to open the door, she was out of the car. She walked away without turning her head for good-bye. If she hadn't been Ellen Hamilton, she might have been heading for the luxury restaurant near the corner. But she wouldn't try that, not alone, at night; not with him in trouble. She was doubtless going to Luke's, the large lighted drugstore across Scottsdale Road. There'd be no lifted eyebrows much less outright rejection there, no better place at this hour to while away the time.

He removed the keys from the ignition, pushed them in his pocket. As he left the car, the swinging doors of the restaurant emitted a mottled blonde and her beefy tourist cowboy. She shrilled drunkenly into the quiet night. Hugh moved off in the opposite direction.

The pavement ended with this block of specialized shopping area. Beyond was a dusty country lane where the Town Hall, housing the police department, stood. He'd seen it many times, the small brick building which might once have been the village schoolhouse. Steps led up to its porch and it seemed there was always an Indian woman sitting there, a child's head pushing against her long draggled skirt. The reservation lay not far beyond the town. The woman was here even at this hour of night, a toddler asleep in her arms, another child, scarcely older, sleeping against her knee. Waiting for her man who had been invited in for a little talk? No, it wouldn't be that. She'd go home if her man was in jail. The porch was no more than a place where she could wait undisturbed and in safety until her husband finished work or pleasure somewhere in town. It was better to wait for a ride than to trudge the miles with the tired children. She paid no attention to Hugh, she might not have seen him.

He moved to the steps on the right. They led down to the basement door with its sign designating this as the quarters of the Scottsdale police. The light over the door was a white glare. He had to will his feet to descend. If he could have run away, he would have. Facing the essential operation, the patient couldn't run. No matter his fright, he must submit, holding his tenuous courage to wavering hope.

Without further thought, Hugh walked inside. He was in a low-ceilinged basement room. It was not a dank, gloomy dungeon. It was somehow bright and informal, it didn't have the look or smell of a police station. A young officer whose uniform was little different from that of a Scottsdale businessman —tan frontier pants, matching shirt, and black string tie—was in a railed-off sector at the left attending the stuttering police radio. A similar officer was at the water cooler. Beyond a casual glance, neither paid any attention to Hugh. They knew who he was; they must have known. He stood waiting, wishing he knew the protocol. Whether to speak or be spoken to.

Across the room was an open door leading to a private office. The entrance to it was blocked by a large desk of some light wood, the top cluttered with papers and office equipment like any businessman's desk. A third officer materialized in the doorway behind the desk.

"You Hugh Densmore?" he called out, not unfriendly. He was dressed like the others but his belt had handsome silver mountings, Indian silver work.

"Yes," Hugh said.

"Come on in."

He waited for Hugh to cross the room, edge past the desk, and follow into the inner office. Here there was another desk, more cluttered, and a couple of plain chairs which might have been borrowed from a school storehouse. There were two small windows, basement type, high on the far wall. The station was air-conditioned, as was every building in the Phoenix area, but it evidently didn't filter through to this smaller office. A revolving electric fan hummed on a shelf above the desk. The papers on the desk were weighted with desert rocks, a cigarette lighter, a pipe, and like makeshifts.

"I'm Marshal Hackaberry," the officer said. He might have been thirty years or fifty; he had the deceptive weathered face of Western outdoor men. His eyes were horizon-blue, his hair sandy. There was an Arizona twang in his voice. He wore low-heeled cowboy boots with his uniform, the embossed leather worn to a fine finish. He went around behind the littered desk and lowered himself into the revolving chair. He gestured to Hugh. "Sit down."

Hugh took the chair by the desk. All at once he was somehow at ease. He knew why, but only someone who knew the other side of the coin would understand. Hackaberry had looked at Hugh, spoken to him, as to any man he might summon to his office.

"You know why I wanted to see you." It wasn't exactly a question.

"I think so," Hugh replied. "I think it's about the girl who was found in the canal."

Hackaberry nodded briefly. He lifted a thin sheaf of papers from beneath a piece of volcanic rock. "You identified the body."

"I identified Iris Croom."

His eyes shot up to Hugh's face as if expecting to find defiance there. There was none to find. Hugh had merely stated the fact. The marshal looked down again at the papers, tapping them with his forefinger. "I have here the reports of Ringle and Venner." He pushed back in his chair for comfort, and continued, "This is Scottsdale's case. At least for now it is. The girl was found over our line. Do you know anything about the way we work, Mr. Densmore—Doctor?"

"No, I don't."

"We're a marshal's department. Not county, although I'm also a county deputy as are most of my men. Two hats. If it turns out she was killed in the county, not Scottsdale, I'll still be in charge. If, however, the death occurred in Phoenix, the case will go to them."

The marshal had to wait for the autopsy before he could speak more plainly. But this was plain enough to Hugh. If aborticide had been committed in the neighborhood of the motel, the case belonged to Phoenix. If the murder was done by the canal where she'd been found, to Scottsdale. Hugh started to take his cigarettes from his pocket but thought better of it. The need to smoke might give an impression of nervousness.

"The autopsy may give us a lead. But maybe it won't. We may have to do some intensive investigation before we find out. Right now I'm bossman. That doesn't mean Phoenix isn't cooperating with me. We're a small department. When I took over the job a few years ago we had exactly three men on the force. We have fourteen now, but the way the town's growing, that's not enough for plain routine work. When we get a big one like this, we ask Phoenix to help us out. They've got the men and the labs and all the equipment. I'm telling you this so you won't get any ideas you're getting the treatment from both sides. Ringle and Venner are Phoenix Homicide but their chief has assigned them to me for this case. They're working for me."

"I understand," Hugh said.

"And another thing." He worried the papers, not looking at Hugh. "I don't want you getting any ideas that you're going to get a bad beef because you're a—because you're not a white man." He jutted his chin and met Hugh's eyes full with his own. His were like blue flint. "This isn't going to be any race affair. Get that straight. We're after a killer and we're going to get him. And when we get him, we're not going to have things messed up for us by a lot of bleeding hearts or snotty sociologists or NAACP legal eagles. I don't care what color you are, if you killed that girl you'll pay for it. If you didn't, I don't want you."

"I didn't," Hugh said flatly. Again he reached for cigarettes.

This time Marshal Hackaberry noted the move. "Go on, smoke if you like," he said. He himself fished one from a crumpled pack. "Now we understand each other, we can commence. I've got the reports but I want to hear this story myself. Personally. How you picked up this girl in Blythe and brought her into Phoenix."

Hugh took a deep pull at his cigarette. He had given Ringle and Venner no details last night. By now the border inspectors had probably communicated with Phoenix. But it was not this that caused Hugh to make his decision that he would tell the whole story to Hackaberry; it was something in the man himself. He could be wrong. Perhaps the marshal wasn't a straight shooter; it might be an act, so well practiced that it fit him like his old boots. Nevertheless it couldn't be wrong to tell the truth, the whole truth. Right or wrong, the decision was Hugh's. Only by the truth could his innocence be proved. Lies, evasions, suppression could only indicate a measure of guilt. And he was innocent. This was his shield, this his protection.

Hugh put ashes neatly in the glass tray at the side of the desk. "I'd like to start at the beginning," he said.

"That's the place to start." The marshal settled himself more comfortably. He must have been attuned to extraneous sound in the outer office, for he added at once, "Hold on a minute." He was around the desk and over to the doorway, calling out, "Those detectives here yet?" He leaned through the aperture. "Ringle! Venner! Come in here. Better bring another chair, we're short."

Hugh stiffened at the names. It had been too much to hope that he could talk alone to the marshal. Hackaberry had made it clear that the two were his men, their job to find the killer of Iris. They were not here by coincidence; he had sent for them. He must have known there was much more to learn from Hugh than what was in the report. And all the good-fellowship explanatory material was only to pass the time until their arrival?

Ringle came first, grunting what might have been a recognition of Hugh, and lowered his bulk onto the straight chair on the other side of the desk. Venner followed, carrying the extra chair. He placed it in the vicinity of Ringle's, sat down, and jockeyed its placement until he could tilt back against the partition separating this room from the main office. He acknowledged Hugh's presence by drawing back his lips in what might have been a sardonic smile.

Hackaberry was still in the doorway, talking to one of his deputies outside. His words did not carry. Hugh stubbed out his cigarette in the ash tray. He'd like another, but even if the detectives had sworn affidavits that Hugh chain-smoked on his breaks to make up for long work hours without tobacco, they would believe only that he smoked now because of anxiety. As if he could read Hugh's mind, Venner lit a fresh one from his own stub and sighed a deep satisfaction.

The marshal turned into the room again. "Where is your car, Mr.—Dr. Densmore?"

They'd checked. They knew it wasn't out front.

He said, "I parked in the next block. By that Indian shop."

"You wouldn't mind if my men go over it while we're talking? It'll save time for you and for us too."

He did mind. Ellen might have gone back to it in spite of his warning. Or she might look for it before the police had time to replace it. Ellen could cope, that had been made clear to him long before now. And a police request was only the initial polite form of a demand. He knew his hesitancy, although fleeting, had given the wrong impression. He could not help how they misconstrued, he would not mention Ellen. He drew his keys from his pocket and carried them over to the marshal. "She rode to Phoenix with me. You know you'll find her fingerprints all over the car."

"The back seat?" Venner smirked.

"She was never in the back seat!" Only Venner had the power to send him into these quick rages. Perhaps that was the runt detective's function. He controlled the anger before repeating to Hackaberry, "She was never in the back seat. She reached across from the front to get the water jug off the floor. That's the only contact she had with it."

The marshal said, "Let me get this going and you can fill in the whole picture." His boots clacked as he crossed to the door and the keys jangled a counter rhythm.

As he disappeared, the eyes of Venner and Ringle, as if they were iron bars, moved to contain Hugh. He couldn't take it; he looked away, focusing on the blank wall as he returned to his chair.

Venner said to Ringle conversationally, "Maybe I was wrong. Maybe he didn't wait to get in the back."

Ringle's noncommittal grunt could have been a warning. At least he changed the topic. "Did you see Crumb?"

"Yeah. I just come from that."

"How's he taking it?"

"How would you expect him to take a nigger messing with his daughter?"

Hugh forced his eyes to stay on the wall.

But Ringle exploded, "You didn't tell him—"

Venner was laughing so hard that for a moment he couldn't reply. Then he cackled, "Naw, I never mentioned black boy here." Disgustedly he spat. "I told him just what Hackaberry said to tell him—nothing. But when he finds out—" He made an uncouth clicking sound in his throat. "He's not going to like it."

The last words were near-whispered as the marshal burst in, calling over his shoulder, "Don't interrupt me for anything." This time he closed the door soundly before returning to his comfortable chair. Briefly he fingered the papers in front of him, anchoring them with a larger-size rock. He took his pipe from another stack, shifting his ash tray to hold it down. He used his elbow on another segment while he removed the tobacco tin from them to pack his pipe. There was no sound in the room but the measured drone of the fan and the sibilant riff of the flimsies. In the next room, the spluttering police radio could be heard distinctly.

Venner watched the checkerboard maneuvers with his customary sardonic smirk. Ringle appeared lost in his own glum thoughts. Hugh also watched, wondering how much of the business was for effect, how much a habit of makeshift convenience.

Hackaberry puffed the pipe into a waft of smoke and spoke through the stem. "With your permission, Doctor, I think I'll tape this meeting." He yanked open a drawer of his desk, indicated the recording machine which was fitted into it. "That way none of us will have to worry about misremembering."

Again Hugh had no choice. He inclined his head as permission.

Hackaberry set the machine into operation. He stated time, place, those present, and continued, "All present understand this is an informal session. Dr. Densmore volunteered to come here to tell us what he knows of Bonnie Lee Crumb, known to him as Iris Croom. Dr. Densmore is not represented by an attorney, nor is he charged with anything. This is clearly understood?"

There it was, for later introduction in court, if permitted. Ringle growled his response, "Yeah." You could tell he didn't believe in informal questioning. Venner slurred, "Oh, sure." His methods wouldn't be influenced by legalities, not if he could help it.

The marshal repeated to Hugh, "You have no objections to taping?" He needed audible response for the record.

"I have none," Hugh said. Not that tapes couldn't be edited.

"Thank you." Hackaberry stopped the machine, played back what had just been recorded. He was satisfied. The voices were distinct. "Okay." He set the machine again. "You can start in, Doctor. Right at the beginning, when she asked you for a ride at the check station."

Hugh said, "I'd like to start before that. When I first saw the girl."

He had expected, even welcomed, the sensation his words would arouse. In a small way, it would expend some of his hostility to the detectives. But when the response came, the quick ugly anger in Ringle's face, the pitiless narrowing of Venner's lips, it would have been frightening had not Marshal Hackaberry been present. Hackaberry took the statement without any noticeable reaction. He puffed his pipe and asked matter-of-factly, "So you had met up with her before?"

At that moment all three of them were convinced that their suspicions of Hugh were well grounded. Would the full story uproot them? He didn't know, he could only tell them the truth. The truth must be self-evident. He had nothing else to offer, no corroborating witnesses.

He answered the marshal, "Yes. I first saw her the previous afternoon, on the road out of Indio." He kept his attention on the marshal while he told of that initial meeting, his reason for giving her a lift, his growing distrust of her story as they traveled toward Blythe, his decision to put her on a bus there.

When he stopped at the end of that day's story, taking time to light a cigarette, Ringle accused at once, "You didn't tell us none of this."

Hugh took a draught of the cigarette before answering, "I thought that what you wanted from me was simply an identification." He hoped he sounded as innocent as he tried to sound.

Ringle glowered but he said no more.

Hugh took another pull of the cigarette before beginning the events of the next morning. He had left her at the Phoenix bus station, where, allegedly, she would telephone her aunt.

Hackaberry had put down his cold pipe. He was doodling on a pad of paper. "You have that envelope where she wrote down the name and address of her aunt?"

"I have it somewhere at the motel. But there's no such address and no such person here. I called every beauty shop in town. Iris told me later that she did have an aunt of that name who lived in Denver."

"You saw her later." Venner's drawl was pornographic.

Hugh clipped the monosyllables. "Yes. Once."

This was the hard part, this was the part they must believe or his position was hopeless. If they rejected its truth, they would look no further for the abortionist. The marshal, for all his seeming open mind, would have Hugh, as Ringle and Venner already had, fit the role.

Hugh's cigarette had burned to a tip as he talked. He took his time pressing it out in the ash tray, arranging words and scene in his mind. The forthcoming passage must be given in exactly the right way. And he mustn't let a hint of fear or despair or reaction to their cynical disbelief filter through.

The brief pause was too long. The forelegs of Venner's chair came down on the floorboards with a jarring clatter. "While he's figuring out what to say, I'm going to get me a drink of water." He didn't ask, he told Hackaberry. "This is dry work." He hitched up his rumpled plaid trousers as he headed to the door.

"Tell one of the boys to bring in some water," the marshal called after him. "I'm sure Densmore could use some."

Hugh responded to the marshal's seemingly friendly smile. "I could."

Hackaberry pushed up from his chair. "Take a stretch if you want." He himself took a real one, arms upthrust, back arched.

Hugh stood, relaxing while moving away from the desk to the small windows, then returning to his chair.

Ringle didn't get up. "I'd like a can of beer."

"Make it two," Hackaberry said, and smiling again at Hugh, Three."

A deputy came through the door, not with the water but with several sheets of paper which he carried to the marshal. As he started away, Hackaberry said, "What about that water?"

"We're looking for something to put it in, Hack," the deputy explained on his way out.

"Use a milk bottle," Hackaberry shouted after him. To Hugh, he laughed, "We're not as fancy here as you are in Los Angeles, are we?"

Bemused, Hugh said, "I wouldn't know. This is the first time I've been in a police station." He'd never thought of it before; stations were so familiar from movies and television.

Ringle snorted, "You never got a traffic ticket?"

He mustn't antagonize the buffalo further. He tried a smile at him. "Oh yes. I've had my share of those. But I always pay through the Auto Club." And realized at once that he'd done it again. Not for using the service but by taking for granted the use. Ringle's reaction was visible on his face. Such conveniences were for white people; Negroes shuffled in line before a judge.

Venner returned before the moment developed. He carried the milk bottle of water, handed it, snickering, to the marshal, as if remembering a dirty joke. His eyes touched Hugh with malice, but he spoke to Ringle. "Did I miss anything?"

Ringle didn't bother to answer. Hugh accepted the glass of water from the marshal and drank it gratefully. All three were waiting for him to continue the story. Again he addressed himself to Hackaberry, as if the detectives were not in the room. Hackaberry alone might recognize the truth when it was spoken. He told the story of that night, told also his reaction to Iris' suggestion; it was part of the whole truth. He concluded, "I never saw her again, not until these detectives—as a result of an anonymous tip—took me to the County Mortuary last night to identify her body." He stressed the anonymous tip. Perhaps the marshal would realize that the important thing was not to question Hugh but to find that man.

Venner slurred, "All strictly legal, Marshal. He came voluntary."

Ringle slashed in, "And when you identified her, you didn't think none of this stuff was pertinent?" He quoted the word savagely.

"I didn't know the cause of her death," Hugh said. "I only knew I wasn't involved in it."

The marshal was deceptively mild. "Didn't it occur to you when you read the story in the paper Saturday, that the girl in the canal might be the girl you knew?"

Hugh had known this question must come. He also knew that he could not lie, he could only dissemble. He didn't answer too quickly, nor did he hesitate over it. "I don't believe it did. It may have come into my mind fleetingly but there was nothing to support it. I was convinced the girl who drowned herself was a local girl."

"Why?"

"Because of the canal. A visitor wouldn't know about your canal system."

"How'd you know about it?" Ringle asked quickly.

"As a boy I visited my grandfather here every summer."

The marshal's voice expressed doubt. "You mean when you read the story you thought the girl was a suicide?"

"In the story I read, there was no reason to think anything else."

Ringle pounded, "But you didn't come forward to see if you could identify her."

Hugh made himself speak evenly. "That never occurred to me. I thought the girl's family would have identified her as soon as the story was published."

The marshal nodded, as if Hugh's story was credible whether he believed it or not.

And Venner insinuated, "You didn't want it to be your girl, did you?"

Anger rushed into Hugh. At the implication in the question which he could not deny without feeding it. "Did I want it to be the girl I gave a ride to? Certainly not!" He managed to control himself and again direct his words to the marshal. "I hoped she had taken my advice and asked help from an organization which could help her."

"She sure didn't come to the police," Ringle said.

Venner snapped his gum, happy at Hugh's outburst.

The marshal sucked his cold pipe, then suddenly pointed it at Hugh. "We don't know this is murder. The medical examiner won't be back until tomorrow. She could have been bunged up in the water. But one thing we do know—unofficially. She was aborted before her death." He stood up. "We may want to talk to you again after the autopsy. I'll have to ask you not to leave town without checking with me."

The interview was over. Hugh rose. He said, "I'll be moving from The Palms tomorrow to my grandparents' home." Unasked, he gave the address. He wanted to plead: *Don't disturb them, they're old*, but he was afraid it would stimulate the detectives to do just that. Rather, he added the telephone number, suggesting, "You can call me there, if you want to see me again." And hoped he could explain the call if his grandmother or grandfather should receive it. Ringle was stubbing the information into his notebook.

"You'll find your car where you left it," the marshal said. "Thanks for coming in." As Hugh started to leave, he added, "We've borrowed the tools temporarily."

Hugh spun about. Could they believe, could it be possible, that car tools were used on Iris? He was sickened at the thought. The three of them were watching him; to them his shock would be more indication of his guilt.

"You don't mind?" the marshal asked.

He managed to say, "Not at all," and turning again, walked away, aware of the silent eyes following him. He walked on through the main office; the two deputies merely glanced at him, uncuriously, not interrupting their conversation. He opened the door and stepped into the cool night air. Now that it was over, he was trembling.

The Indian woman and her children were no longer on the porch. He looked at his watch. It was close to midnight. And where had Ellen spent the hours? Anxiety for her safety quieted his personal tremors; he hurried away.

The moon was cold and white and high, giving a desert-night brightness to the deserted streets. His car was in the exact place where he had left it. You would not know it had been moved. Ellen was nowhere in sight. The street slept, the village slept. There was no sound, not even the murmur of a car passing on Scottsdale Road. And then as he stood there, the door of the elegant restaurant beyond was opened and a gash of sound cleaved the night. Almost at once it was shut again, closing away the intrusive piano and drunken singing and clamorous laughter. The men who had come out moved raggedly in the opposite direction; nevertheless Hugh quickly got into his car.

He saw then the twist of paper protruding from the ash tray. He turned on the dash light and read the note: "Am at Victor's." Although unsigned, it could only have been written by Ellen. The distinctive script did not belong to the world of Iris. He hoped it had not been in the car when the police were in possession.

He backed away from the curb and drove the block and a half to the large, bright ranch café at the intersection, whose neon beacon spelled Victor's. It wasn't one of the fancy restaurants of the area, it was a hamburger place. Not a dump, it was new, built like a great ranch house of redwood and stone. Despite the late hour, there was a goodly crowd inside. He found Ellen in a booth not far from the door. She gave him a quick, questing glance as he slid into the seat across from her.

He said, "I'm sorry it was so long."

"I haven't been here for long." There was hot coffee and the remnants of a sandwich plate in front of her.

A young waitress came to the table with a menu.

"It's not too late to order?" All at once he was hungry.

"We're open till one." She was neither friendly nor unfriendly.

He ordered; the waitress took Ellen's empty plate and went away.

Ellen said, "Your car was missing."

"They took it. To go over. Your note—"

"After they'd returned it." She studied his face. "Was it bad?"

"No. Not actually. Of course, they don't believe my story. Or rather, they believe it only up to the point where I say I never saw her again."

"What do they say?"

"They don't say anything. They look. Ringle and Venner—"

"They were there?"

"They're assigned to the case. From Phoenix. The marshal—" He broke off, said, "To be honest, the marshal seems to be trying to be as objective as he wants to be." He paraphrased, "He doesn't intend to have the case messed up with 'bleeding hearts.' So he looks objective. But he doesn't believe me any more than the others do." Might as well admit it, to himself as well as to Ellen.

The waitress brought his order. She didn't say anything. She put down the giant hamburger and the coffee without a word. She didn't care whether he was black, white, or mottled; she only wanted to be through with work.

Ellen took up her coffee cup. "Tell me the whole thing. All of it."

Hugh had started eating. "I will," he said, his mouth full. "I will in a minute. I didn't know I was this hungry." But he did know that an ordeal of mind and spirit could lower resistance as much as a physical workout. He finished the hamburger and lit a cigarette before he began to talk. He had enough energy now.

It didn't take as long to tell as it had to endure. Ellen already knew the story. She listened with her eyes on his face, more objective than Marshal Hackaberry. "Tonight wasn't bad," he repeated at the finish, "because they couldn't accuse me of killing her. Because they don't know officially how she died."

"It might not be abortion?" She was too hopeful.

"There was an abortion," he said flatly. "And they know it. They just can't say so until they get a medical report. Not for the record." He shook his head sadly. "It must have been a botched job for them to know." They had probably seen many botched jobs in their duty. The years of Ringle, the ugly years. No wonder he was devoid of sympathy. He continued, "They know there was an abortion but they won't know if that was the cause of her death until after the autopsy. She might have drowned herself, or have been drowned." And what possible reason could the killer have given her, in her pain, to climb with him the high bank of the canal to be put to death? "When they find out, they'll come for me."

"But, Hugh." She was still reaching out for the bent twig of hope. "If it wasn't an aborticide—"

Hugh said distinctly, "They'll come for me because there was an abortion whether it killed her or not." Savagely he asked, "Why should they look for the real abortionist? They've got me. A doctor—"

"A Negro doctor," she emended. "Go on, say it."

"No," he refused with violence. "I won't say it." But after a moment's thought, he admitted, "Perhaps I was beginning to sag into self-pity. I won't even think that way." He crossed his fingers, smiled a small smile. "I hope." Immediately he was grave. "I haven't time for that."

The clock on the wall pointed to one. There were yet a few booths occupied and no one seemed in a hurry, but Hugh picked up the bill. "We'd better get out of here." He hoped he had enough money with him to pay the tab; it would be the final ignominy if he had to borrow from Ellen on their first date. He made it; the cashier's weary mouth managed a "Thank you" as she returned the change.

The night was sharp with cold at this hour, the stars were broken glass patched against the dark sky. He helped Ellen into the car, unobtrusively noting that there was no police car about, nor a strange sedan. Instead of turning south through the sleeping village, out of some compulsion he followed Indian School Road. The shape of the canal rose on the right. Here, but one night ago—could it have been only then?—a living creature of hopes and dreams, joys and troubles, had mercilessly been given over to death.

It must have been appallingly easy to put her to death. Her cries, if she had warning to cry out, would have been heard only by the sleeping. She would not have been afraid until it was too late to be. She trusted the man, by whose act, if not deed, she had been delivered to death. Hugh remembered her childlike anticipatory delight as they drove into the city. She had known no qualms then, she had been sure of welcome. The man—boy—must have panicked to have killed her here on the Indian School Road. Or had she died here because the abortionist had done delayed murder? Or was it that she died on the table and was dumped by the man or woman who had killed her and what would have been a living child? In Los Angeles the victims were dumped more often than not. In an alley with the refuse cans, among the weeds of vacant lots; one had even been flung too late for care from a moving car onto a hospital lawn.

Ellen said, "It was back there she was killed."

"Or died."

She recognized the sadness in him, because she said with emphasis, "You're not to blame yourself. You had nothing to do with it."

"But I did," he told her. "I had too much to do with it." Or not enough. "And everything I did was wrong." He drove on, turning south toward Edward's home. As if it were a sinuous snake, the Indian School Road seemed to follow him.

When they reached the safe suburbs, he and Ellen sat silently for a moment in the darkness of the car. She asked finally, "You don't think the police are through with you?"

She knew the answer, he'd already told her that. "I know they aren't." He broke out in savage frustration, "If I were a detective I wouldn't believe my story. Circumstantially, I fit." He put thoughts into words with crystal clarity. "I'll have to find the abortionist. No one else believes in his existence. I'll also have to find the man or boy she came to meet." There must be the two, to accuse each other, to prove the fact. Was it a plum tree or a peach?

"A good lawyer could help." She'd said it twice; the first time he hadn't heard, only her voice speaking from afar.

"Yes," he agreed. He could admit it now, it was essential to have a lawyer, to ward off arrest until he could find the two guilty ones. A lawyer meant confiding at least in Edward. Edward would know to whom he should go. He sighed his indecision; even after tonight the need didn't overbalance the more important need to keep the family out of this. He didn't know what he should do.

Ellen was waiting for him to continue. When he didn't, she said, "While you were with the police, I telephoned my father in Washington." She didn't apologize. She didn't seem to care whether he would or would not have consented to it. "He'll ring me in the morning with what he can find out." She smiled at his blank face. "You needn't worry. He knows everyone in law worth knowing. He'll find us the right man."

He couldn't help protesting, "Wouldn't it be a lot simpler if I asked Edward about it? He knows everyone worth knowing in Phoenix."

Her "No," was imperative, but she explained, "The police would expect our lawyers to believe your story. Or whether or not they believed it, to defend you as if they did. I told my father what you need." She had thought it out with care; she must have been thinking of little else all day. "A young man, not over forty, but top drawer in his profession; liberal, but not too liberal, no Civil Liberties lawyer, they're suspect from the beginning because they show up in any case involving minorities. As my father says, they're more interested in minorities than in the right or wrong of a case. I may be asking the impossible but I don't want this lawyer to be of any of the minority groups. I want a hundred-percent white American Protestant male. With wife and children, so we'll have them on our side too."

He found himself half laughing. "Is that all?"

She shook her head but she smiled too. "I know just the man in Washington but we're not in Washington."

"You don't think you'll find that kind of man here?"

"We just might. My father is quite a miracle man." She said, "I'll call you in the morning after I hear from him. It will be early—time difference, you know."

He helped her out of the car and together they went up the walk. At the door she said, "I wouldn't put off telling your family, Hugh. Maybe your luck will hold, yet—"

He said what she wouldn't. "I can't expect it to hold forever." The police couldn't keep the newspapers off him indefinitely. Reluctantly he said, "Perhaps I'll talk to Edward tomorrow."

And, saying it, realized he must go to Edward. He was the only person who could give Hugh a lead to the abortionists in the vicinity. Doctors knew. He did not tell Ellen his decision. She might go legalistic on him, think it was the lawyer's business. But the lawyer's future life wasn't threatened. Hugh alone was in the realm of danger where the impossible could—must—be achieved. The two men he must find had had the time to cover themselves beyond finding.

Edward's car was gone from the port. For tonight he could continue to bear his own burden. Perhaps by morning there'd be no need for the fuss of a lawyer and the grief to his kinsman. Perhaps the marshal would ring up to acknowledge his mistake. Why not dream? Without dreaming there was no hope.

Ellen was saying, "Don't worry, Hugh. Go home and go to sleep. It will all look better in the morning. I'm sure the lawyer will clear things up for you without any difficulty."

He said, "Yes, ma'am," and left her there, not even touching her hand in good-bye.

4

HE DROVE without incident to the motel; no news over the radio. There were lights beyond the drawn curtains, the voices of night-blooming young couples poolside lilted with the special heightening of sounds across water. He drove to the rear of his wing and parked. As he opened the door of his rooms, remembering to touch the light switch before entering, the small envelope was livid at his feet.

He took for granted it was a hotel note until he bent to pick it up and saw that it was pale pink, of cheap stationery. It was sealed; there was no name on it, only the room number. With foreboding, he opened it. The message was block-printed in pencil on ruled paper torn from a tablet. It said simply: NIGGER GET OUT OF TOWN.

If it had been meant to frighten or anger him, it failed. For he felt a wild surge of exultation as he read the words. His case was proven, if indeed he had needed this proof. He was the one threat which existed for the murderer or murderers, the only factor which stood between their anonymity and their apprehension.

Someone had had to come here, to his very threshold, to slide the envelope under the door. Someone guilty. How long a watchful waiting there would need to be to accomplish it unseen. The comings and goings of a large motor hotel were constant. Or had the man dared make the move openly, fully aware that no one seeing him would ask questions or particularly notice his form and face. It must have been Iris' lover who wrote and delivered this; the abortionist would not creep that far out of concealment. He need not. He was too accustomed to being outside the law to worry, if he were found out, over one accusation with unsupported evidence. It must have been the man, or someone hired by him to deliver the envelope. Even better if he had hired a messenger; that would create a distinct link, after Iris' death, between him and Hugh.

His eyes were framing the five words, and in a quick decision, Hugh switched off the light and returned to his car. It was only half past one o'clock. Inactivity had suddenly become unbearable. The need to take the offensive at once was compulsive. He knew where Edward practiced—St. Hilary's, a large hospital across town near Thomas Road. He headed toward it. If Edward had finished with the birthing and returned home, there was no loss but a half hour's sleep. He was too keyed up at present for sleep.

Hospitals never slept. There was a middle-aged woman handling reception and switchboard. Behind her a nursing nun in white robe and headdress sat at a table, annotating the day's records. Hugh said to the woman, "Is Dr. Willis still here?"

She said, "I'll see," and checked a paper posted on the partition to her right. "He is," she told him.

"I'm Dr. Densmore from California." That had the sound of professional interest, not a family matter which could wait. "Could you tell him I'm here?"

"I'll see if I can locate him." She moved herself unhurriedly to the switchboard.

The sister came forward. Her smile was as fresh as if it were sun-up, not the weary hours. "Are you the brother interning at UCLA Medical Center?"

He was surprised she would know. "Yes, I am."

"Dr. Willis speaks often of you. That's a magnificent hospital, isn't it? I visited it last summer. I wish we had some of their equipment. Yes, Miss Deane?"

The receptionist was waiting. "Dr. Willis says he is to come upstairs, Sister Rose."

"You know the way?" The sister gave directions. "I hope that young woman delivers easily for Doctor. I'm sure he's tired after all the wedding excitement. It must have been beautiful."

"It was," Hugh told her. He moved off to the elevator. People were nice if you found the right ones. The trouble was there were so many of the wrong ones.

He pushed the button and the elevator rose slowly. Edward was waiting on the delivery floor as the automatic door opened. "I was just having a cup of coffee, Hugh. Join me?" He didn't ask questions, he didn't even seem surprised to have Hugh appear in the middle of the night. He could have heard rumors. Among doctors and nurses an abortion death would be the epicenter of conversation. "I've a room down this way for napping. It'll be a long night. Both of my mothers are in."

He opened the door for Hugh, said, “I’ll get another cup,” and proceeded down the corridor.

Hugh waited on his feet. Now that he was here, it again seemed wrong to inflict this thing on Edward. Yet now it was essential.

Edward returned almost at once. He poured coffee for Hugh, refilled his own cup, and directed, “You take the easy chair. I’ll be selfish and take the bed.” He propped the pillows against the headboard and stretched out, his cup on the hospital table beside him. “Now what’s happened to bring you here at this hour?” His face was cheerful; perhaps after all there had been no rumors yet.

Hugh stirred sugar into his coffee. “I’d rather take a beating than bother you with this. Especially tonight. I know you’re too tired to take it. But I’m afraid to wait any longer.”

From the intonation of Hugh’s voice, Edward was already wary of what was to come. The fear of trouble was so close to the surface in even the most secure of them.

“You read in the paper yesterday about the girl found in the canal?” Hugh forced out the husky words, “I drove her to Phoenix.”

“My God,” Edward breathed. It might have been a prayer.

Hugh tried to speak without feeling, as if it had happened to someone else. “Last night when Ellen and I left the dinner party, two detectives were waiting for me. They’d had an anonymous tip that I could identify the girl. They took me to the County Mortuary and I identified her. Not under the name they had, under the name she’d given me.”

He went back to the beginning, to the discovery of the girl on the road. He stripped the story to its bones; Edward might be called away any moment. But he told it all; it didn’t come easy in repetition, it became more sickening. He concluded, “They’ll do an autopsy on her tomorrow. I am certain they’ll find she was murdered. By abortion or after abortion. And they’ll come straight back to me.”

Edward’s voice was heavy. “There’s no way to prove you didn’t leave the motel that night?”

“No way. And I wouldn’t have had to leave to be the abortionist.”

Edward sighed. "We'd better get you a lawyer first thing in the morning. Before the autopsy results. Roger Hand is our most capable. And prominent. He's served in the legislature. You remember meeting him at the reception today?"

Hugh hated to say it. "Ellen wants a white lawyer."

Edward didn't believe the words.

"She called the Judge, her father, tonight to arrange it. She didn't tell me until after it was done."

Edward shook his head, not understanding. "What's wrong with our own?"

Hugh explained it. "Our own would believe me. She wants someone who would doubt."

Edward thought about it. "She could be right, she could be mistaken. Either way you're bound to come out all right. You've done nothing wrong."

"I wonder." Hugh walked to the window and looked out at the black green of the lawn. "I did something foolish. And that was wrong. I let my sympathy rule my judgment when I picked her up." He changed the subject abruptly, asking what he had to ask. "Have you ever been approached to do an abortion, Edward?"

"Of course I have." Anxiety had gone from Edward's voice; he was on familiar ground.

It hadn't been something in Hugh then, something a girl like Iris could discern.

"I suppose most doctors are asked at some time or other," Edward went on. "Certainly ours are. I doubt if any of them can escape that." His face was thoughtful. "One thing I'll say, Hugh, and it's God's truth. I've never been approached by any of our people. Only by the ofays."

The ugly word was incongruous on Edward's lips.

"Somehow they seem to think that a Negro doctor lacks morality. They become so surprised, almost affronted, when they're turned down. More coffee?"

Hugh said, "I'll get it," returning for his cup.

Edward poured for both of them, continuing, "You'd think they would realize that only a family of better than average economic status, Negro or white, can afford to educate a son medically. Which would rule out bribery."

Hugh lifted his shoulders. "You can't expect the kind of person who comes to you for that reason to be overly intelligent."

"Strangely enough some of them are. Some I've met up with. In their own world, that is. It's only when they come to the dark side that their ignorance shows up."

"They've been taught," Hugh quoted without rancor.

"Yes." Edward smiled reassuringly at Hugh. "Don't let it linger with you. I'm surprised you haven't been asked it before now; interns and students are always considered fair game." He put his head back on the pillows, remembering. "One of the fellows I knew at medical school, a white, although he could have been a Negro, no race has any lien on morality—anyhow, this fellow made enough for all his office equipment before he started practice. He's an important Chicago doctor today."

"I don't see how anyone educated in the meaning and purpose of medicine could."

"There are amoralists in any profession." Edward put down his cup and lit a cigarette. "I wish you'd told me about this when it happened. I would have reported it to our medical association."

"I couldn't. You see that, don't you? I couldn't spoil Clytie's wedding. Even now—" Hugh said desperately, "Only because I must have your help."

Edward's head lifted sharply.

"I must have the names of the abortionists in and around the city. I've got to find the man or woman who did it. The police won't. They have me."

For too long Edward didn't speak. Then he said, "I don't know that I've heard of any cases for some time now. I suppose Mahm Gitty is still at it. She's never been caught yet. She's an old crone who's been a registered midwife for some fifty years. She has a made-to-order alibi whenever she's brought in."

"How do I find her?"

"She's always lived in the Three Oaks district south of town. She hasn't any regular base, she moves from one cousin's shack to another. They're all *primos* in that neighborhood. I've heard the police say that the only way to find her is to poke around the district asking questions. But be careful. They don't like strangers asking questions in Three Oaks."

Hugh said, "There must be others."

"I'll try to get some other names tomorrow. It isn't an easy subject to approach, yet with this girl's death, there will doubtless be plenty of talk going around. I'll do what I can, Hugh."

Hugh moved to the door. All at once he was leaden-tired. Edward must be beyond exhaustion. "One more thing. Don't let the family know anything about this. Please."

Edward spoke quietly. "You may not be able to keep it much longer, Hugh."

"There's no need to worry them yet." Wishing he could hope, he insisted, "It might be they will never have to know."

"I hope so, Hugh. But if they do"—he smiled gently—"they can take it."

There was no opportunity for further words. A nurse rapped and flung open the door; in muted excitement she said, "Can you come now, Dr. Willis? Number One seems to be ready."

Hugh took himself down in the elevator. The nun was no longer at the desk. The receptionist didn't speak to him.

When he was nearing the motel, he passed a police cruiser headed in the opposite direction. For a moment he thought it was Ringle at the wheel. But the car continued east; in his rear-view mirror he watched it disappear.

No further messages had been insinuated under his door. He was asleep when his head touched the pillow.

Ellen's voice on the telephone was as bright as the slant of the sun dividing the drapes on the lanai windows. "I let you sleep as long as I could." His watch hands read quarter to ten. She was speaking with an eager carelessness, girl to boy, in case anyone was listening. "Do you want to come out and get me? I'm moving to The Palms."

"I'll be there as soon as I check out." He tried to shunt his voice out of sleep. "Do we have an appointment in town?"

"Noon. So don't be too long."

"I won't." He groaned out of bed, showered and dressed before packing his suitcases. After the shower, he was awake. When he was ready to leave, he called the desk. "This is Dr. Densmore in 126. Will you have my bill ready? I'm checking out."

He loaded the car and drove over to the office. He hoped there would be no difficulty about a check, he didn't have fifty cents in his pocket.

The clerk on duty was an attractive woman with prematurely gray hair. "I caused you an unnecessary trip, Dr. Densmore. When I looked up your bill, I realized that you were Dr. Willis' guest. I'm sorry."

He'd settle with Edward later—Edward, who thought of everything, even the possible financial status of an intern. Edward, who must by some miracle come up with the right name. He thanked the woman and went out to the car. He didn't leave a forwarding address. Temporarily, the unknown man would be balked in his harassment.

As he waited for traffic to subside in order to wheel into Van Buren, he wondered if the woman had spoken the truth or had purposely created a delay to give her time to report his departure to the police. Well, they already knew. He decided he believed her words. It wasn't a good habit to be suspicious of all motives.

Time was passing too quickly. He could move in on the grandparents later, right now he'd better get Ellen. He anticipated conversation with his mother and Stacy but Ellen was alone, her two small cases in the hallway. She was wearing the same dark silk she'd changed to last night.

"Where is everybody?"

"They went to town to see the Bents off." She pulled on a frost-white glove. "I left the big suitcase for you. It's in Clytie's bedroom."

He fetched it and locked all the luggage in the trunk. With her beside him, he started back to The Palms. "What excuse did you give for staying on in Phoenix?"

She shrugged slightly. "Only that I'd decided to rest up for a few days." She was a direct girl. "They think it's because you're staying over."

"It is," he said bluntly. But not what they thought. His anger, at her being held here by his trouble, was near the surface.

She sensed it and diverted the subject. "I had a battle to move to the motel. But I'm firm."

He managed a smile. "You're an army with banners flying." He didn't want to talk about the trouble, but after all that was the only reason they were together this morning. "I take it we have an appointment with a lawyer at noon."

"Yes, he's giving up his lunch hour to see us. My father had spoken to him before he called me. He seems to think it's a good sign that Mr. Houston would make that concession. Everyone Father questioned gave the same name as first choice, so it would seem he's the lawyer we're looking for. Skye Houston. Incidentally he pronounces it the proper old way, 'Howston.' His office is in that ancient bank building across from the courthouse."

Hugh acknowledged the information with an inclination of his head.

"Now if we can only convince him he should take your case."

"It's not settled?" In his alarm, Hugh almost missed the turn into The Palms.

Ellen explained, "A lawyer doesn't take a case until he has first heard the facts, Hugh."

"I've plenty to learn," he acknowledged. "Do you want to go inside or register from the car?"

"I'll go in. And I think you should go with me. To make it quite normal and free from any indication of hanky-panky." She didn't have to explain that in a courtroom a prosecutor would utilize the meanest fact.

The same agreeable woman was at the registration desk. "Back again the same day?"

Hugh gave her what he hoped was a carefree smile. "Giving a lift to Miss Hamilton. She's been staying at my sister's."

The woman turned the registry card toward Ellen. "I know. Mrs. Willis called me about it."

Ellen's immaculately gloved hand filled in the card.

The woman glanced at it and handed over the key. "I'm afraid the room isn't made up yet, Miss Hamilton." She smiled her eyes at Hugh. "The previous guest just checked out. But we haven't any other space unreserved right now."

It was a lie and they all knew it was a lie, but there was no rancor among them. This clerk couldn't cancel the system; her genuine friendliness was her contribution toward eroding it. Five years ago she wouldn't have had a vacant unit; ten years ago she would have said, "We don't take Negroes," if any had had the courage or spunk to inquire.

She said, "I'll send a maid around right away."

Ellen told her, "There's no hurry. I have a luncheon date in town."

He drove Ellen around to the now familiar door. He carried in her bags and they continued on toward town.

There were no meter parkings open near the courthouse; he hadn't expected otherwise, not at high noon downtown. He drove on First Avenue until he found a parking lot. Until they started walking back, he hadn't actually felt the day's heat. It could have been more than the heat affecting him. His uneasiness over meeting the lawyer throbbed in his temples. He wondered if the Judge had mentioned that Hugh was a Negro, or if when you reached Judge Hamilton's position such subtleties wouldn't occur to you. And he wondered if Ellen had this latent fear when meeting someone new. With her background, it wouldn't seem to be something she had to face, yet how could she escape it entirely? The quickening in the eyes, the certain intonation of the voice, the unspoken awareness: you are black. Even if you were brown or beige or lightly sun-tanned.

The building they approached must surely have been a relic of territorial days. The red brick was weathered to rose, the stone facings were gray not white. There was a secure feeling about its age; it had endured. They entered through the First Avenue door. There was no elevator, only an old uncarpeted stairway leading up and up. Silently they climbed it to the fourth, the top, floor. It was three minutes to twelve when they reached the top, winded, and followed the worn boards of the corridor to the door whose frosted pane was lettered: SKYE HOUSTON, ATTY-AT-LAW. Beneath the legend was another in smaller letters: *Aqui, Se Habla Español.*

Ellen murmured, "*¿Inglés, también?*" as she opened the door. Somehow the absurdity relaxed him and he followed her inside as if he were sure of welcome.

The outer office was minuscule. It resembled a territorial government office, the kind you could see in old engravings. Against the wall was a battered black oak bench with spool back and narrow arms. Behind a low railing with swinging gate were two enormous golden-oak desks, staggered in placement to leave a narrow aisle leading to the interoffice door.

There was no switchboard, only a phone on each desk. The surface of one was cluttered, the other neat, which must indicate the dispositions of the two secretaries. Neither of them was in the room. The sun blazed through two long, narrow windows, looking out on the courthouse across. There was an air-conditioning box on one window ledge, otherwise the cubicle would have been stifling. Even with the box, the room was too warm.

Hugh indicated the telephones. "Should we ring him?"

While he spoke, the twelve-o'clock whistle could be heard faintly through the windows. And the inner door was opened. The tall man in the doorway said, "Hamilton and Densmore?"

Ellen smiled, Hugh inclined his head.

"Come in." He'd known what they were, there'd been no flicker in his eyes. His face was without expression as he stood aside for them to pass through the doorway into his private office.

It was a corner room, looking out on both Washington and First Avenue. It was of old-fashioned dimensions, spacious, particularly in contrast to the anteroom. It gave a comfortable impression, deep leather chairs and couch in dark brown leather, worn in places to chestnut. Old documents rather than the ubiquitous western paintings of this country were framed on the dark paneled walls. The recessed bookshelves were crammed haphazardly, not alone with law books. A large Navajo rug of browns and grays and whites lay on the modern cork-tile flooring. The massive desk, which might have been of walnut, was too old for one to be sure. It must have been hand-hewn in the room, it would never have gone through the narrow doorways. The chair behind the desk was oversize, cushioned in flaking leather. There was no cooling system; overhead two old-fashioned ceiling fans revolved slowly. Yet the room seemed cool.

Houston was a lean, broad-shouldered man, topping Hugh by inches. He wore a dark summer suit, cut like a flannel, a white shirt, and a neat dark tie. His close-cropped hair was sunbleached to pale lemon; he was tanned far darker than Ellen, almost as dark as Hugh. Against this brown skin his eyes were a startling bright blue. He wore heavy horn-rimmed glasses;

when he removed them to gesture, a deliberately induced habit, he looked older. He was probably in his late thirties. There was no indication of what the inner man was like, if indeed there was an inner man. He was as dispassionate as a photograph of himself.

He motioned to chairs. His voice was courteous but devoid of any personal intonation. "Will you sit down? I'm sorry but I must eat while we talk. I have to be in court at one o'clock." He circled behind his desk, which was covered not only with papers but with a white luncheon cloth. He was not a sandwich-and-cup man. There was a steak, a decent green salad, a pot of coffee. He resumed eating. "Your father spoke to me from Washington this morning, Miss Hamilton. He seemed to think that Dr. Densmore might need help and that I might be interested. That is all I know. Do you care to tell me about it?"

He had addressed himself directly to Ellen, as if she were an interpreter between him and Hugh. He was civilized; he accepted Ellen as of his own stature; he had no reason yet to accept Hugh. Hugh didn't resent it, he himself was no different in meeting strangers. Yet it left him unprepared when Ellen said, "It's Hugh's story. I'm merely *amicus curiae*."

Her gesture indicated to Hugh that he should take over. He wondered where to start. And because without the beginning it couldn't be fully explained, he began on the Indio Road. Because of time, he omitted unessential detail as he had for Edward, his own reactions, his thoughts. By now he could sum up the facts economically.

Skye Houston listened without evident reaction. He didn't miss a word, an inflection, although he completed his lunch during the recitation. He'd lighted a cigarette before Hugh was done. At the end he had one comment, "Interesting." As if it had been a piece of fiction. But he lifted his telephone, dialed a number. "Skye Houston here, put me through to the chief, if you please." While waiting he lit one cigarette from the glowing stub of another. "Bruce? Skye Houston. What are the results of the autopsy in that canal case?" He listened, his pencil touching a pad with repetitive marks. When the chief —of police?—had finished, he said casually, "I'm representing him. You may pass the word."

Ellen flashed silent triumph at Hugh. It helped the sick feeling which came over him at the certainty of his further involvement. His name must have been mentioned by the chief.

Skye was dialing another number. "Skye Houston. Have someone give me a buzz when His Honor gets there, will you? Thanks. See you." He rang off and dialed another number before he said to Hugh, "You're right. It's murder." He broke off when his party responded. He identified himself and asked, "Hack in?" While waiting, he broke a long ash carefully into a silver bowl. "Hack? I just talked to Bruce about the canal murder. Are you planning to question Dr. Densmore again?" He gesticulated with his cigarette impatiently. "Why do I want to know? I'm representing him." After a short moment, he asked, "Can you make it tomorrow at three? I'm in court this afternoon." Briefly he listened again, cutting in sharply, "Certainly you can talk to him whenever you like, with or without me. Just remember, I'm representing him." He was more agreeable when he cut in again, "I'll ring you in the morning, Hack. Thanks a lot."

He hung up and set the phone aside. "All right. This is it. There was an abortion. She didn't die of it, although it might have caused death later. It was badly bungled. But she died of a knock on the head. With a wrench or some such tool." He took off his horn-rims and made of them a pendulum. "I'm taking your case. I haven't any business taking it, I've twice as much as I can handle now. But it interests me. I don't get a chance at interesting cases too often, not in Phoenix."

To be uneasy because to the lawyer it was no more than a technical problem, wasn't justified. Why should he have a personal interest in a stranger?

There was a tap on his door, the office had no intercom system. Houston lifted his voice slightly. "Come in."

A head came in, a young, pretty, blond, curly head. A glance touched Ellen and Hugh but with no curiosity.

"What is it, Meg?" Impatience was on the surface.

"You told me to let you know when it was time to go to court, Mr. Houston."

"Let me know when we get a buzz from the clerk. That billy-goat judge has kept me waiting often enough."

The head disappeared quickly.

"Where was I? Oh yes. I'll slough off some of my routine stuff on the needy." He recapitulated, "Yes, I'll take your case. I'm expensive. You may as well know that right now."

Before Hugh could speak, Ellen said something like, "It doesn't matter." He agreed.

"I intend to be governor of this state. My target is four years from now." He spoke coolly, agreeably, but there was an underlying hint of power in him that hadn't surfaced before. It was somehow exciting and strangely reassuring. "I'm going there on your shoulders. This I tell to all my clients. They have a right to know they're building my war chest. Moreover, they have a right to know that without the cases they bring me to win, I wouldn't be tall enough to reach the chair." He began to gather his papers. "I don't say this to worry you. Your credit is good, Dr. Densmore. When I've cleared you, we'll figure out what's fair. Expensive, but fair."

Again the girl tapped and poked in her head. "He's coming."

"Thank you, I'll time it."

She had disappeared before he finished the sentence. Still talking, Houston fastened his briefcase and pushed back his chair. Hugh and Ellen came to their feet. "We must discuss this more thoroughly and make a plan of action. We can't afford delay. What about dinner? Do you mind coming out to my place? It's in the book, Mockingbird Lane. You know, Scottsdale." He came around the desk and shook hands with Ellen. "You, too." It was a directive, not courtesy. "About six-thirty?" He gripped Hugh's hand. "Bring your suits if you want a swim. I find it relaxing after the heat of the day." Briefly he seemed human as he realized, "You must be feeling the heat. You aren't used to it. You won't mind letting yourselves out?" His private door closed behind him; they could hear his tread striking down the corridor.

Hugh looked, bewildered, at Ellen. "You approve?"

"We couldn't have done better. Not even in Washington."

He was surprised at her enthusiasm, he'd never seen her excited before. He was ashamed of his fleeting thought that it was because there had been chemistry between her and Houston; it had been there, he'd sensed it. She was too knowledgeable to let that count. But he didn't express his own doubts as to this lawyer being the right one for him. Perhaps a cold, emotionless legalist who took a case as a hieroglyphic rather than out of conviction was what he needed.

They returned to the outer office. The curly Meg was at the first desk, the cluttered one; a slant-eyed brunette was speed-typing at the other. Meg looked up and said, "Good-bye. Let me know if I can be of any help. Call in any time." She wasn't curious, nor was the brunette who smiled at them as she changed carbons.

Hugh thanked them and opened the door for Ellen. They walked in silence the length of corridor and began their descent of the narrow staircase. What could Hack, who must be Marshal Hackaberry, have said that so annoyed Houston? Why hadn't Houston told them?

Over her shoulder, Ellen said, "He gives you confidence."

"Yes, he has it," Hugh responded. He didn't tell her that he was more afraid than ever.

He had to get away from her; he was unable to contain his impatience to go to Three Oaks and look for Mahm Gitty. He'd forgotten he had had nothing to eat until Ellen said, "Where will we go for your breakfast and my lunch?"

There was no excuse he could give for postponing food; it was past one o'clock and she knew he'd had nothing this morning. He remembered, "There's a bakery cafeteria a couple of blocks from here. Not elegant but friendly and the food used to be good. Will that do?"

"It sounds just right." She was a different girl since Houston, as light of heart as Allegra or Celeste. "Air-conditioned, I hope?" The sun burned down, the sidewalks pushed the descending heat up again into your face.

"Everything's air-conditioned in Phoenix." Deliberately he matched her mood. "Except Skye Houston's office."

They had come upon a newspaper stand; he bought both the Phoenix papers. And realized he couldn't take her to lunch, he couldn't even buy his own breakfast. Somehow he wasn't embarrassed; he could tell the new Ellen with amusement, "I hope you have enough money to feed us. There went my last dime. I haven't had a chance to get to the bank."

She said, "It will be a pleasure."

"A loan," he warned. "Positively a loan."

She laughed at him. "I wouldn't spoil a friendship for a dollar or two."

The cold of the cafeteria enveloped them like a snowfall. They loaded their trays and managed to find a separate table. Without apology, each took up a newspaper, reading as they ate, occasionally reciting a sentence or two aloud. They exchanged papers as they finished the only story.

The morning paper had a rehash of the original news but the early edition of the afternoon paper had headlines of the identification of Bonnie Lou Crumb by her father, Albert Crumb, a mechanic of Indio. There was a front-page news photo of Mr. Crumb's arrival at the airport. The picture showed an unimpressive average man, perhaps in his forties, wearing an open sports shirt and wrinkled slacks. There was no sob story. Mr. Crumb, "tight-lipped and obviously restraining his emotion," had identified his daughter and expressed the hope that "they'd get the punk who did this." If he could get his hands on the killer, "he'll never hurt any girl again." The only mention of the mother was the brief statement that she and Mr. Crumb were divorced when Bonnie Lou was a child. She had not come forward. Iris doubtless had spoken the truth when she had said they did not know where her mother was.

There was also front-paged a blown-up snapshot of Bonnie Lou, taken perhaps a year before, and a cabinet photograph at least two years old, all flaws removed, making her look quite pretty and very young. The paper had been printed before the autopsy results; there was announcement only that it was being conducted. There was no mention of Hugh.

He commented on it, and Ellen admitted, "I don't understand, either. I wonder—it could be they don't want to risk the loss of any sympathy for her. If they're building their case on a sweet, innocent little girl, that false-name business would wreck the impression."

"Or hitchhiking to Phoenix."

She repeated, "I don't understand. Where I come from the newspapers wouldn't defer that much to the police."

Nor would they in Los Angeles. The reporters must know more than they had written. It couldn't be possible that the case wasn't being tongued over in minute detail in both the Phoenix and the Scottsdale stations.

They had finished lunch. On leaving the cafeteria, the blast of the street temperature was unbearable. By the time they had walked back to the parking lot, Hugh felt as if he'd been in a steam bath. He wondered how Ellen managed to appear fresh; perhaps Washington weather was a conditioner. In Los Angeles the thermometer rarely reached these heights.

Not until they were at the car did he ask, "Do you mind driving yourself back to The Palms?"

She was instantly apprehensive. "No. But why?"

He put the keys in her gloved hand. "There's someone I want to talk to."

"Oh no!"

Did she think it was Mr. Crumb or that he'd found out where to find Iris' friend? He couldn't and wouldn't say more. She would try to dissuade him, at least to wait until after tonight's conference. He knew it couldn't wait. Even now Ringle and Venner might be looking for him. That half-heard conversation between Houston and Hackaberry could only mean that the marshal wanted to have another interview with Hugh.

"Nothing to worry about. But I don't want the car." The most foolish thing he could do would be to drive into the Three Oaks district in the white Cadillac.

"In this heat?"

"There's the bus if I need it."

She had to accept his decision, she didn't know enough to countermand it. She opened her purse. "You can't ride the bus for free." She extended a handful of dollar bills. "Don't argue. I'll keep books if you insist."

He took the money. He'd forgotten that a few pennies were his only monetary supply. "Thanks, Ellen. And don't worry. I may ring you up for a lift later."

Her eyes studied him, curiously, thoughtfully. Then she gave her head a slight shake and got into the car. He watched her drive away. He hoped her faith in his innocence wouldn't falter under his refusal to explain. If it did, he could not blame her. She didn't know him well enough for blind faith.

When the car was out of sight, he left the lot. He removed his tie as he walked, folding it into his pocket. He slipped out of his jacket, folding it under his arm. With the collar open, the short-sleeved white sports shirt, wrinkled with dampness, lent an appearance of the kind of young man who might go seeking Mahm Gitty. He didn't remove his dark glasses; everyone wore dark glasses these days. They were no status symbol.

He walked to the nearest service station with Negro attendants. The younger was manning the pump, the older was in the small air-cooled office. Hugh went into the office. A radio was broadcasting a baseball game.

He lent his voice the cheerful informality of Phoenicians. "How's the best way to get to the Three Oaks district from here?"

The man cocked a wary eye. "The best way's to stay out of that district." When Hugh did not respond, he got up from his chair and moved over to the wall where a large map of the city was posted. "But if you got business there, let's see."

Hugh moved beside him.

"How well do you know Phoenix?"

As if he came to town now and again, Hugh said unconvincingly, "I know it pretty well."

The man accepted it as said. His finger pushed along the map. "I guess the easiest way's to go down here. Veer left here and keep going south until you get there."

Hugh asked, "Is there a bus goes that way?"

Again the man gave him a curious eye. "I wouldn't know. Only time I ever go down that way is when I get a call somebody's car is stuck." He must have decided that Hugh was what he appeared, a wayfaring stranger, for he explained, "It's not rightly a district. Just a collection of sharecroppers' shacks, mostly Mexicans. Folks call it Three Oaks because it's built around three old oak trees. When you see them, you're there."

Hugh looked out dishearteningly into the glare of sun. "Is it very far?"

"It's not too far," the man said cheerfully. He wasn't going to walk it. "Not more'n a mile maybe after you veer." As Hugh moved to the door, he added, "It's safe enough daytimes but I wouldn't be caught there alone at night."

"Thanks." Hugh matched the cheerfulness. It wasn't hard to do. He was on his way to something which had purpose.

It could have been no more than a mile, but it seemed ten times that as he moved, sweat-stained, through the heat. He was in the country once he'd veered left, but there was no difference between the heat of country and town save for the lack of shading buildings here. Eventually he saw ahead the three oak trees, tall, heavy-leafed oasis for the crazy-quilt of ramshackle flat-roofed shacks which angled about them. He made for the trees. There were several old wooden benches beneath them. On one, two wrinkled men in farmers' woven straw hats nodded over their knobby canes. On another, a young woman sprawled, surrounded by a bevy of dusty-footed children. The third bench was peopled only by two little boys, dripping ice cream sandwiches down their chins. Hugh sat down on the unoccupied end. The little boys gave him a solemn gaze, then ran off, giggling and gibbering in Spanish.

Hugh could have asked his question of the young woman, she appeared too tired to run away, but he saw then the lean-to grocery store fronting on the makeshift plaza. Surely there would be someone English-speaking there. He rested a little before crossing over to it.

It was insufferably hot inside the dusky store. Flies droned disinterestedly about a ragged bunch of overripe bananas. Behind the counter a stout woman in a housedress splashed with orange butterflies fanned herself with a newspaper.

Hugh removed his dark glasses and assumed the hangdog demeanor and accent the woman might expect from one of his color. "Scuse me," he singsonged, "would you happen to know where I could find Mahm Gitty?"

For a moment she stared at him, suspicious, then broke into furious gesticulating Spanish. He understood some Spanish, but she was speaking too rapidly for him to catch more than a few isolated words. It was probable she knew no English; however, she had recognized the name because it recurred in her torrent.

He didn't give up. When she had abruptly ceased talking and resumed her slow fan, he asked again, "Maybe somebody around here could tell me where Mahm Gitty lives?" This time he stressed the name, looking directly into her eyes and perceiving there the recognition of it.

Again she broke into galloping words, punctuated with Mahm Gittys, ending by raising her voice, "Pepita! *Pepita!*" with an epilogue which seemed to wash her hands of the whole subject.

Pepita appeared, an undersized girl of perhaps twelve years, her black hair, long and dank, hanging about her face. She might have been asleep; she was barefoot and wore only a crumpled wraparound dress. The woman spoke and the girl spoke. They shrugged shoulders at each other and they swiveled their eyes over and again at Hugh. Finally the girl said in heavily accented English, "She don' live here."

But they knew, they hadn't been discussing a grocery order. "I just want to know where she lives," Hugh said. "Where her house is."

The girl stared at him for long moments, not speaking, as if she hadn't understood his words. Then she turned to her mother and again the two were voluble. Hugh waited. Not knowing whether it was better to break into the conversation with demands, pleas, insistence, or hold his peace.

The girl gave a final shrug, shoulders, hands, head, and scuffed to the open doorway. "She live there." His eyes followed her thin brown forefinger to the row of windows and doors, each set in its own small frame box, to the rooftops beyond, any of which could be "there."

He wondered if he might ask her to guide him but knew at once that would but confirm their latent suspicion of him. Instead he asked, "Where the yellow dog is sleeping?"

"No, no. This one." The finger hadn't varied.

"Where the geraniums are on the window sill?"

"This one!" The finger stretched.

"The blue door." Next to the geraniums.

The girl smiled at his success. "The big one," she said. It was perhaps a yard taller than its neighbors.

He said, "Thank you very much," and to the mother, also smiling now, "Thank you, ma'am." Again he stepped into the plaza. He wanted like hell to buy a Coke but he was afraid to force his luck. It might be that only Spanish-speaking were served; it might be they learned North American prejudice after crossing the border. He sauntered past the three oaks and across to the house with the blue door. As he knocked, he glanced back at the grocery store. The girl in the doorway was watching him, the mother's head was shadowed over one shoulder.

He knocked again; there were women inside, he could hear

their voices. Nor did the voices cease as the door was without warning opened by a little boy; it could have been one of the two who'd run away laughing at him. The boy was startled by the appearance of Hugh; he backed away, and without waiting for an invitation, Hugh went inside. He stepped directly into the front room. It seemed filled with women, ancient ones in black, rocking and fanning themselves; a young one, with child, sewing; a painted young one in a tall hairdress reading a movie magazine; a fat matron in a wilting pink sack, her puffy feet bare, who advanced on him. The room was suddenly silent. Her face like stone, she asked, "What you wan'?"

He retreated a step. "I'm looking for Mahm Gitty, ma'am."

"She ain' here."

She could have been one of the crones.

The woman's eyes were hostile. "What you wan' with her?"

There could only be one thing he'd want with her and the woman knew it. He said, "I just wanted to talk to her about something." He made his whine more servile. "You know where I could find her, ma'am?"

"I don' know no Mahm Gitty." Suddenly she padded toward him menacingly. "Get out of here, *gringo*."

He would have laughed but it was no place for laughter. He stayed in character. "Yes'm. I'm going." His departure was rapid. They knew where she was. The harridan knew and the girls and the old Mahm Gitty women. But he'd been afraid to persist. There was evil in the fat woman. He couldn't risk being involved in more trouble.

He walked back to the bench under the tree and sank on it. And now what? It didn't look as if he could go further on his own. He'd have to ask Houston for help. They'd be afraid not to answer Houston's questions. It rankled that he could not bring the same force to bear, that he had to forgo his own social position and become a caricature to ask a simple question. And receive no answer. Until the boy was at his knee, Hugh didn't see him.

"Ice cream?" the boy grimaced.

He sensed it was a trade. "Where is she?"

The round face grew solemn. "She is very sick. They take her to the hospital."

"Mahm Gitty?" He was incredulous.

The boy nodded solemnly. "She is in the hospital for a long time."

"How long?"

"It is two weeks. Two weeks on this Sunday."

Hugh wondered how a child could be sure. "How do you know it is two weeks? Not one week, or three weeks, or yesterday?"

"It is two weeks." The boy was firm. "It is the First Communion Sunday. She is in church and she feels sick. She tries to get up from her knees and she cannot." His eyes widened like dark flowers unfolding. "She falls down. There in the church. They carry her out and they take her to the hospital. She is very sick. Maybe she will die."

Hugh could no longer doubt. And Mahm Gitty was absolved of any present evil.

The boy was standing there. "Ice cream?"

"All you can eat."

The boy, grinning again, ran ahead to the grocery doorway. Hugh followed. The girl and the woman were both waiting inside. Hugh didn't play the old part. He ordered, "A Coke for me and ice cream for my friend."

There was no trouble. The girl uncapped the Coke bottle and handed it to him. The boy was removing from the ice chest a precarious pile of assorted ice cream sandwiches. He shouted, "Thank you, mister," and scuttled away.

The Coke was icy. Hugh drank it in grateful gulps. He tendered one of Ellen's dollars and received the change. Only when he was leaving, did he ask of the girl, "Why didn't you tell me Mahm Gitty was in the hospital?"

"You did not ask me that. You ask me where her house is."

It was factual and he accepted it. The way back to town didn't seem so far as when he'd traversed it looking for the three oaks. When he reached Jefferson, he used a public telephone booth on the lot of another service station. He called Edward's office. Edward was in, but engaged with patients. "If you'd leave your number," the nurse suggested.

"This is his brother-in-law," Hugh told her. "I'll see him later."

It was close to five o'clock. If he were to make Houston's by six-thirty there was no time to waste. He walked over to Van

Buren and caught an eastbound bus to The Palms. He didn't enter the grounds until he was near the unit. The car was there. He knocked at the door.

Ellen hadn't yet dressed; she was in tennis shorts and a white blouse. "You didn't phone."

"I took a bus up from town. Anyone asking for me?"

"No, it's been quiet." She led him to the table by the window. "I made daiquiris." She'd even frosted the glasses.

He sank into the blessedly cool chair and accepted the drink. "I may revive." He knew she was waiting for him to tell her where he'd been but she didn't ask.

"We've only time for one," she said. "I don't want to miss the swim. I didn't go in this afternoon because I was afraid I might miss your call."

He was casual. "You were going in the pool here?"

"Didn't you?"

"I didn't have the guts," he admitted frankly. "I'm no crusader."

"Nor I. But I like to swim. I don't think many of the guests will leave in high indignation if I do. Most of them are darker than I." She smiled slightly. "And somehow I don't believe the management will drain the pool afterwards. It's too expensive a job." Her smile widened. "They may add a bit more chlorine."

He sipped the good drink comfortably. "If you were Lilymay Johnson in for the night you wouldn't dare it."

"I'm not Lilymay Johnson, I'm Ellen Hamilton," she stated coolly. "And if I swim here, that much sooner Lilymay will swim here."

"Of course you're right," he agreed. "It's legal, now it must become custom." He finished the drink too quickly but there wasn't time to dally. "I'll run over to Gram's and change. I'll try to make it back by quarter after. I wonder if Houston is as much a stickler for time with his dinner guests as with his office clients."

"We may find out," she commented.

She followed him to the door, her eyes still asking the question he could not yet answer. He said, "If anything goes wrong, I'll call you."

5

THE FAMILY was gathered in the living room. Waiting for him. For a moment, he felt sick, certain the police had been here. Then Gram spoke spicily, "It's about time." They hadn't.

He had somehow managed his load of luggage, the big suitcase and the small, the plastic car case for his suits, his doctor's kit. His grandfather came to help. "Why didn't you holler?"

He said, "It's all right," but the large suitcase was taken from him.

In the upstairs room which he always occupied here, his grandfather set down the suitcase and fumbled in his pocket. "You had a telephone call."

Hugh was afraid to speak.

"I wrote down the number." He found the fold of paper. "I didn't tell the ladies. They're too curious."

He chuckled a little while Hugh was reading blindly the Scottsdale number.

"You're not in any trouble, Hughie?" Either he had recognized the numerals or Hugh's face had given his turmoil away. "You can always come to me."

Hugh looked across at him, into the compassion and generations of understanding. And he lied. He laughed and lied. "Not at all, sir. It's about the dinner tonight, a lawyer friend of Ellen's." He crumpled the paper and dropped it on the table. "She had the message earlier and passed it on to me."

At least for the moment, his grandfather accepted the statement. Hugh watched the anxiety fade out of the old eyes, the weight lift from the shoulders. And the question came softly, "White friends?"

Hugh said, "Yes. Her father is Judge Hamilton, you know," as if this were enough to explain.

His grandfather said, "You'd better get a move on or you'll be late," and went away.

He'd have to be late. He closed the door to the corridor. He wasn't going to get back to the hospital tomorrow. Not with the police again calling him. He could no longer delay writing to the Dean. The Dean had encouraged him since undergraduate days. He'd sponsored Hugh in Med School, been his mentor in good times and bad. If he could not be trusted with this trouble, whatever happened in the critical days ahead, there was no hope for Hugh's future. Hugh had to trust him.

There was paper in the desk, and envelopes; his grandfather used the room as a library when there were no guests in the house. The letter didn't take too long, he'd been over the story so often. The only personal note he permitted was his hope for an extension of leave. Although he knew the Dean would not betray his confidence, he felt impelled to add the warning: "My family knows nothing at all about this. I hope they will never have to know."

He sealed the letter and addressed it. If he got it off special delivery, it would be delivered to the university in the morning. He put it into his jacket pocket and, unbuttoning his shirt as he moved, went to the head of the stairs. He called down, "Hey, Mother. Please call Ellen I'll be a little late." He didn't wait for her response. He stopped at the bathroom on his way back and started the shower. While he stripped, bathed, and dressed, he refused thought. He transferred the necessary billfold, empty of all but identification, his car keys and addenda. At the last moment, he remembered the crumpled memo and shoved it into his pocket. It was possible that his grandmother or his mother might come upon it and identify the number.

He ran down the stairs to where they waited for him. His mother said, "Ellen said it was all right."

"Thanks. I'll see you tomorrow, Mother. With my dirty laundry." It was a weekend joke. He was half out the door when he called, "Bye, Gram, Gramps. Forgive the dash."

His grandmother snipped, "Ah, love!"

If it were only that. Not this suspended sword over his head. He drove the short distance to the airport, where there were stamp machines. After he'd posted the letter, he returned over 24th Street to Van Buren. It wasn't far to the motel. Ellen was ready, in white, a bright pink cashmere about her shoulders.

Hugh apologized, "I couldn't make it any faster. Should we call Houston that we'll be late?"

She was unperturbed. "I've already called."

She thought of everything, a well-ordered girl.

"Skye had just come in himself. He said not to hurry." This soon it was Skye. And doubtless Ellen. "Shall we go?"

Not until she'd lifted a small waterproof bag, flowered in matching pink and white, did he realize he'd forgotten his bathing trunks. And wondered if it had been a subconscious rejection of swimming in Houston's pool. Counter-bigotry. It wasn't fair to Houston. The lawyer was civilized, that had been apparent in the meeting today. He hadn't asked them to swim as a special treat to the deprived. He had accepted them as his own class and had issued the same invitation he would to such. It was too late for Hugh to change his mind now.

The heat of the day was still heavy over the town. Because of the crumpled slip of paper, a nettle in his pocket, he didn't turn off to cut through the Papago Pass, where the first breeze of evening might be stirring. He would skirt the town of Scottsdale as far as was possible; by now there could be a pickup order out for him, with the big white car for identification. Skirting meant the death road; he wasn't certain of locating Houston's home by way of Camelback. But having forced himself to take the road last night, he was no longer fearful of it. As he turned there, Ellen marked the signpost and became silent.

Last night it had been too dark to see how little the Indian School Road had been changed by time. He drove quite slowly; it wasn't a road for speed, it was no more than a winding, country lane. The canal wasn't visible behind the high banks. Opposite was the old canopy of leafy trees.

They came to the gates of the once serene acres of Brownmoor. Hugh remembered, from years ago, a Sunday afternoon drive with the family; remembered with a pang the dappled walks, the deep shade of the tall trees, the voices of the schoolgirls. Now the grounds stood sad and overgrown and shabby, waiting the final destruction of subdivision. The stables were already gone. At one time, his grandfather had told him on that long-ago day, every variety of native tree and plant had been perpetuated here. It hurt to think that the poison of uncontrolled development, the money greed, if unchecked, would soon reduce not only this oasis but the whole of the beautiful desert valley to the sterility of the tract.

As they followed the road, past a remembered row of neat bungalows with their grass aprons, there was no way to know at what spot Iris' body had been found. All traces of police and sheriff and laboratory activity had been removed. She wouldn't have been visible from the road. Whoever had flung her away had not known how thoroughly the canals were patrolled by the Zanjaros.

In a matter of minutes they were in the town, at the intersection of Scottsdale Road. If it hadn't been for the heavy pattern of traffic lights, and the widened pavement, it might still be yesterday when there was no evil in his stars. He turned north with the lights and drove as far as Lincoln, then cut back to Tatum. It led to the other side of the mountain where the country was molded of golden sand in the setting sun. The homes lay apart from each other, chameleon blurs against the desert earth and sky. Mockingbird Lane wandered north and south and east and west. He followed its contours to the mailbox where HOUSTON was painted in tall letters.

The house was perhaps a quarter mile from the road, long and low, and from the front landscaped only with what was native to the barren land. Saguaro and ocotillo and yucca, and rose-black volcanic rocks. A cedar rail fence surrounded the property. Hugh got out, opened the gate, and after Ellen had driven through, relatched it. He took the wheel again, following the sandy burro path to the house. Ellen lifted the bronze knocker, but before it fell, the door was opened by Houston himself. His smile at Ellen was a welcome untouched by the rigidity of the noon meeting. He was in a terry robe and zoris; he carried a highball glass.

"You'll excuse me for not waiting for you." He divided the smile with Hugh. "I was too damned hot." He closed the door after them and called, "Marcia?" giving the name the Spanish pronunciation.

From what must have been a kitchen wing, a middle-aged Mexican woman emerged. She was wiping her hands on her white apron.

"Marcia, this is Miss Hamilton. And Dr. Densmore. Marcia will show you where to change, Ellen." He explained, "My wife and daughter are on the Continent. I'm hoping to join them in June if I can ever clear my calendar." As Ellen followed Marcia into yet another wing, Houston said, "Hugh, you come with me." He didn't comment on using first names, he made it natural.

"I decided not to swim," Hugh told him.

Houston made no comment which might have induced an explanation, he merely said, "You'll have a drink then while we do?" and led across the huge Western living room to a lanai, and through it onto a patio. There was an outdoor fireplace where mammoth logs were already smoldering. A brazier hung from a spit over glowing coals, ready for the steaks. The long wrought-iron table was set only for the three, all at one end, a hurricane lamp at each place.

The patio was large but not too large to be uncomfortable. It was walled with whitewashed brick, against which the pink and red and snow of oleanders with their glistening dark leaves made a brilliant pattern. The tiled pool, lighted underwater to increase its cerulean blue, lay beyond the dining area.

Skye asked, "What will you drink?" There was no fancy bar, merely a white brick ledge where materials for mixing were set.

Hugh glanced over the bottles. "A light Scotch. I may need a clear head." He took the piece of paper from his pocket. "This call came for me this afternoon. My grandfather took it. I haven't yet called back. It was too late when I received it, if I was to get here in time."

Skye read the number and dismissed it. "Hack will be at home now. I'll ring him later. Don't worry about it." He stuffed the memo in his pocket and took off his robe. In his black wool swimming trunks with his brown skin, he was an even finer figure of a man.

He had seen Ellen coming through the lanai before Hugh did. Hugh said quickly, "I didn't mention it to Ellen." Skye's brief nod was acknowledgment.

She must have known from long experience the impact of her face and figure, for she wore both unselfconsciously. The enormous bright flowers of her suit seemed painted on her. She carried her towel over one shoulder and swung a plain white bathing cap from her forefinger.

Skye walked to meet her. There was an indefinable something which matched them as if they were meant to be a pair. Both were slim, long-limbed, sleek, expensive. Both were tanned, he darkly, she golden. Hugh watched them come together; he didn't hear what Skye said to her.

The first impact of seeing them thus together smote Hugh with the awful aloneness of a stranger in a strange place. He didn't belong where they were. He thrust away such megrims. He'd known from the beginning that Ellen wasn't for him. Nor was she for Skye Houston. This wasn't a social gathering.

He watched them go across to the pool, watched her cleave the air and water in one swift motion. At the splash, Skye seemed to emerge from his dream. He too ran to the tiled edge and shallow-dived into the water.

Hugh drank his Scotch slowly, admitting to himself his envy of them. They swam in long lazy strokes the length of the pool. They were arrows feathered from the high board. They floated with their laughter under the darkling sky and early yellow stars. And he could have held his own in the water with both of them. Being landlocked was his penance for envy.

The fireplace logs were blazing by now; they warmed away the first chill of the desert night. Marcia came and went, lighting the candles, bringing silver and china.

Ellen and Skye finally came out, glistening from the water. She wrapped herself in her towel and let her hair free of the cap before she sat down beside Hugh. "It was wonderful. You should have come in."

Skye said, "Yes." He put on his robe and poured drinks. "You'll have a fresh one, Hugh? Light."

He agreed. There was dinner to come. If he had to see the police later, the alcohol would be dissipated. He couldn't make an obsession of remaining apart from the two.

Skye said, "I'll put on the steaks. They'll be ready to turn when we've had the drinks." It seemed somehow out of character for him to preside over a cook-out but it made him more human. No one mentioned the case as they enjoyed the slow highballs. The talk was cabbages and kings. When the steaks were turned, Skye said, "They'll be ready by the time we're dressed. You'll excuse us for a few minutes, Hugh?"

Hugh said, "Of course," and watched the two vanish into the house. As if it were their home and he the guest. He wondered what it would be like to have a house like this one. With Ellen. Perhaps by the time he could afford it, if ever such time came, it would be possible to build it wherever he wished. Even on Mockingbird Lane. But he wouldn't have Ellen to preside over it. An Ellen couldn't be kept waiting that long. He laughed silently at himself. By the time he had the house, she'd be marrying off her granddaughters.

Skye was the first to return; Marcia behind him brought the coffee container. She and Skye conferred at the brazier until Ellen appeared. This time Skye's smile for her was as if they'd known each other for years. "Your timing is perfect," he complimented. "Now if you'll both come to the table, we can eat."

He served the oversized plates. Marcia brought them to the table and she went away. There was little conversation while they dined. It was close to nine o'clock; the others were as hungry as Hugh was, it was a long time since noon. After eating they rolled chaises into the perimeter of the fireplace. In the flickering light, all of their faces were golden dark. The desert stars were brilliant in the black-blue sky overhead. It was too peaceful to prod with the sharp stick of Hugh's danger. But Skye hadn't forgotten the reason they were here.

He said, "Before I came home tonight, I talked to the marshal."

Hugh spoke without rancor. "He doesn't believe my story."

"Let's say he has a reasonable doubt of it. That's fair. On one side are the things in your favor, on the other the things against you. And some of them work both ways. It's in your favor that you're a doctor at UCLA. It's also against you that you're a doctor, a doctor knows how to abort."

"A doctor knows how to abort. He doesn't bungle it." He spoke with passion.

"He might. If he were in a hurry, without proper facilities. Or if he were doing it under pressure."

"Or if he were a Negro doctor." The words came out more harshly than Hugh intended.

Skye said, "It's in your favor that you're a Negro."

The absurdity of the idea curled Hugh's lips.

"It happens to be true," Skye stated. "In today's climate, no thinking man wants to turn a simple case into an international *cause célèbre*. Furthermore, if he's in politics, he can't risk being branded a bigot. Hackaberry's no different from any of the others. One of these days he's going to have to stand for re-election. So he's leaning over backwards."

"I don't doubt what you say. It's true in a good many cities these days," Hugh admitted. "But my color is also against me.

If as a Negro I'm no longer the expendable scapegoat, I am a complication. You know the marshal would rather I was a white man."

"He would," Skye admitted freely. "He wouldn't have to walk on eggs. Possibly he'd be holding you right now as a material witness."

Ellen said, "You must also admit, Skye, that if a reputable white doctor had given Iris a lift, there wouldn't be this undercurrent to it."

"Maybe so, maybe not."

"At least a white doctor would be given the benefit of the doubt." Hugh tried to keep his voice empty of emotion. "It wouldn't be taken for granted that a quixotic act had a sexual base."

"I'm sure Hackaberry gives you that benefit. As sure as I can be about any man whom I know fairly well."

"That's not the way Ringle and Venner see it."

"Fortunately, it's Hack we have to convince. He knows that your story could be the way you've told it. But it's your unsupported story and it could be another way." He looked directly at Hugh. "How do we go about proving the truth?"

He knew how. He didn't want to divulge it lest somehow the sound of his words would filter through the night and give warning to the hidden men. But this was his lawyer, the man he'd retained to help him. This afternoon had proven he would need all the help he could find. He said, "We must find two men. The one she came to meet and the one who committed the abortion."

Skye thought about it before saying, "It won't be easy."

"I know that. But if we can find the first man, he can give us the second." The police would have ways of getting that information.

"We have no name, no description, no faint clue." Skye was thinking aloud. "How do we find him?"

Ellen spoke. "Her father might have an idea."

"From what he told the marshal, and the marshal believes him beyond doubt, this whole thing is entirely without comprehension to him. He had no idea that his daughter knew a man in Phoenix, much less that she'd been meeting him, shall we say, intimately?"

Hugh said morosely, "The way she lied about everything, as if lies were truth, it wouldn't have been difficult for her to keep it from him."

Ellen suggested, "She may have known her father would disapprove of this man. Perhaps he does know but isn't aware of it."

"That could be," Skye accepted. "But he was most certain that she didn't know anyone in Phoenix. According to him, she hadn't been in Phoenix since she was six years old."

"And that needn't be true," Hugh added. "She could have told her father she was spending the weekend with a girl friend in Banning or Beaumont, and come to Phoenix plenty of times."

Skye said, "If this man killed her to keep his wife from finding out, I don't believe he'd be seeing her in Phoenix."

"If that is the case"—Hugh was figuring out loud—"he met her in Indio. Their affair was carried on in Indio. And he must have had some legitimate excuse to be in Indio. Either business or relatives."

"And some of her girl friends must know who he is." Ellen was suddenly touched with excitement. "I think we start there. With her friends. Girls confide in each other."

Hugh's heart quickened. If they could get a name, they could start moving. All three were silent, examining the idea.

At last Skye said, "I think you're right. We start there. I'll arrange to fly Meg to Indio in the morning. She's young enough to talk to teen-agers on their own level, she won't scare them off as I might." He interjected with some regret, "I wish we could have got to them before their mothers told them to say nothing, not get involved."

"Even so they'll talk," Ellen said, with certainty.

"As to the abortionist, don't think the police have settled on you, Hugh. That's the first action Hackaberry took, in concert with the Phoenix chief. The police have been out covering that ground since the autopsy results were announced."

"They won't find out anything," Hugh said.

Skye lifted his shoulders. "Perhaps not. The muck who are in that filthy business don't come out from under their rocks under average circumstances. With a murder, I doubt if anyone can lift enough rocks to find them. But it could be some informant will come up with something."

"That's why we have to find the boy friend," Hugh said. "He's the only one who can tell us who did it."

"Suppose he won't." Ellen spoke sharply. "How does one go about finding an abortionist? Let's say I wanted to find one. Where would I start?"

"It's an underground," Skye began. "All word of mouth. It isn't something the police have much documentation on, it's even too secret for that. But they figure it starts, and my apologies to Hugh, in the medical profession. A girl is in trouble. She goes to a legitimate doctor. He turns her down. She tries another one, and so on until she finds a medico who's on the ethical borderline, let us say. He's straight but he knows someone who isn't. Perhaps a surgeon barred for malpractice, or a nurse or student who prefers money to ethics. Or it may be a doctor with criminal inclinations; there are such, as in any profession. Perhaps he's gone over the line into illegal operations for quick money. At any rate, she gets a name, and that's the beginning. The word is then passed around. In the office, on the campus, in the bars—God help us, wherever frail man and woman meet together. When the next fellow gets a girl in trouble, he or she doesn't have to go through the initial routine. They ask around and find a friend who knows a friend who has the word." Skye took an angry breath. "The police problem is that neither side will talk. Unless the case becomes a murder, they don't ever hear of it."

"What I was wondering," Ellen said thoughtfully, "is how this man found an abortionist so quickly, after Hugh refused."

"The police are wondering the same thing," Skye stated. "It's not something you can discover in a hurry. It is most likely that he was a previous customer or that he had it set up before the girl came here. Certainly he knew where to go."

Hugh thought aloud. "Iris had told him she was coming to Phoenix and when. She must have. She had none of the hesitancy of a girl who doesn't know whether or not she'll find someone waiting at the end of the journey."

"But you believed she was holding a secret joke," Ellen argued. "It could have been she meant to surprise him."

"No," Hugh denied. "She must have known he would be waiting for her. She couldn't take a chance on not finding him. She had no money."

"How could she write to him? He couldn't have let her know where he lived."

"They had some way to communicate." Hugh was certain.

"By telephone," Skye suggested.

"I doubt that. She couldn't have made a long-distance call from her father's without its showing up on the bill."

"Reverse the charges."

"Not to the man's home. The wife might have answered. And not at his job, unless he has his own business."

It wasn't important now. Skye proceeded, "Somehow she sent word she was coming. And why. And he got ready for her."

There was gall in Hugh's mouth. "He was ready, but when she told him how she hitchhiked to Phoenix with a doctor, he saw a way to save money."

"But why did he kill her?" Ellen cried out. "Why go to the expense of an abortion if he meant to kill her?"

"Did he kill her?" Skye asked rhetorically. "Or did the abortionist kill her when he saw the operation was bungled? Right now that's the most important question for the police. Not the abortion, that problem is always at hand. When they catch one operator, there's a peculiar leniency in the laws that lets him free in no time. But murder's a different matter. It's the murderer they've got to find. They'll admit there may be a man she came to meet, as Hugh claims, but they aren't convinced that man killed her. The operation was a bad one, she was going to die—the logical killer is the abortionist."

Before she could name him. Yes, it was logical. But he wouldn't need a wrench or some other car tool to complete what he had begun. He could make sure she was dead more easily than that.

Hugh flared, "How can they not admit this man? Surely they don't think I made her pregnant?"

"No, they don't think that. But they do think her pregnancy may have come from one of the many boys she knew in her high school. She was a free and easy girl, that's implied in all the information on her. She couldn't do anything about her trouble in Indio, the town is too small. But someone knew where to go in Phoenix. And in Phoenix no one knew her."

"Or she had it arranged with me to take care of her between wedding parties?" The bitterness deepened.

"They don't go that far," Skye said. "They figure it was coincidence she met up with a doctor on the way."

"And the anonymous tip? What about the anonymous tip?"

"The marshal takes that seriously. Ringle and Venner think someone not connected at all with the murder could have recognized the description. Either an Indio boy visiting over here or a Phoenix boy who had met her over there. He wouldn't give his name because he didn't want to be involved in the mess. He was scared. Just like you were scared to identify her after you read that story in the paper. It's a normal reaction."

It could be that way, although Hugh could not admit it. For the identification hinged on what she was wearing. The one who called the police must have seen her in Phoenix.

"How much time do I have?" Hugh asked hopelessly.

"The police don't rush into a murder arrest, Hugh. They want enough solid evidence for the D.A. to go into court and get an indictment. It's true they're in a hurry on this case because they're on a spot. Whenever a young girl is violated and murdered, the citizenry and the newspapers are prone to get hysterical."

"They have enough facts right now for a case against me."

"Not for murder, Hugh. For abortion, yes, perhaps. But that's something the law moves on with exceeding caution. Particularly with a doctor involved. They know that once that accusation is made, the man will never be quite free of suspicion of guilt."

There was nothing more to be gained in worrying the perhaps and the ifs. It was past time to go. If he were to be keen tomorrow, to further his own investigations. The police might be looking into the local abortionists, but because they were police they'd get no answers. And didn't need them, they had enough material to fit the crime to Hugh.

Skye smiled, it was meant to be comfort. "I'm not worried, Hugh. I'm sure Meg will dig up what we need in Indio. We have an advantage just because we're not official."

"I hope so." He looked at Ellen. "We'd better go."

"Yes." She rose. "Just a moment while I get my things."

While she was out of the room, Skye said, "I called your number while I was dressing. Hackaberry wanted to see you but I got him to put it off until morning. Ten o'clock. At his headquarters."

"I'll be there."

"I'll try to make it too," Skye said. "But I may not be able to. My case was continued until tomorrow morning."

Ellen's steps were returning and Skye lowered his voice. "Don't be afraid of them, Hugh. If you're innocent you don't have to be afraid of questioning. But anything you don't want to answer, keep quiet on advice of counsel."

Hugh said again, "I am innocent." Even his lawyer had doubts. By now probably Ellen too.

She joined them at the door. Skye said confidently, "We have a right to believe that when Meg gets back from Indio tomorrow, your troubles will all be over."

"Let me go with her." It wasn't a sudden thought, Ellen must have been brooding about it all evening.

She and Skye looked long at each other. And he shook his head. "You'd better not." His voice was gentle. "You're too civilized."

And what he said was true. Ellen could no more meet in rapport with the inhabitants of a small western town than with the desert lizards. She was too far removed even for intuitive knowledge.

And yet had she been white, Skye could have risked it. All three of them knew it; it was in the trio of silence which held them for that long moment. There was no reproach in Hugh, nor would there be in Ellen, for Skye's rejection. As there was no personal rejection from the lawyer. The silence was recognition of an unalterable fact.

There was little to say as Hugh and Ellen drove back to The Palms. It had all been said. He walked with her to her door.

She opened it and asked, "Will you come in for a stirrup cup, Hugh?" She didn't care much, her thoughts were miles away.

"Not tonight. I'm worn down."

"You are sleepy?"

"It's funny, but I am. Without a prescription." The want to take her in his arms was unbearable. He turned abruptly away. "Good night."

She misinterpreted the reason for his sudden mood, for her thoughts spilled from her. "There must be something I can do! Some way to help!"

He turned back. "You've helped unbelievably."

"There's so much to be done. I can't just stand aside—"

"How do you think I feel?" he cried. "But until we find—"

The ringing of the telephone in her living room was startling. For a moment equal alarm met in their eyes, then she whirled and rushed inside. He was on her heels, stopping only to close the door behind them. There was no logic in his following, undoubtedly it would be her family or friends calling. But it could be his family, with something so dire they would intrude on him here. Had Ringle and Venner come for him?

She had answered before he reached her side. He saw the expression on her face and snatched the instrument from her. A male slimy voice was speaking ". . . another babe shacked up with him . . ."

Hugh broke in harshly, "Who is this?"

"That you, Doc? Don't want to spoil your fun—"

Again Hugh interrupted, demanding, "Who is this? What do you want?"

The jeer went out of the voice. It became tough. Evil. "I'll tell you what I want. You better get out of town before something happens to you. Something real bad. You get the message? We don't like niggers mucking our—"

Hugh banged down the handset and started to the door. Before he was half across the room, Ellen caught him.

"No, Hugh, no!"

He tried to put away the hands clutching his arm, but her arms closed around him, holding him entangled.

"You mustn't go out there. You mustn't!"

He tried to force her away but she clung. Short of hurting her, he couldn't break loose.

"He isn't out there! He's on the telephone!"

The words came through and the fight went out of him. Not the rage which made fear nonexistent, but the will to action.

His arms closed around her and for the moment he stood there holding her, as he'd wanted to hold her. He didn't kiss her, didn't caress her, he simply held her in his arms. After that moment, he released her.

"You shouldn't have stopped me." He pushed open the lanai doors to recover his breath, parting the draperies, gazing out on the peaceful moon-gilt greensward. No one at all was in sight. He closed the curtains before he turned. She had dropped into a chair. The flame of the lighter she held to her cigarette was shaking as in wind. He completed the operation for her, then took the other chair and lit a cigarette for himself. "It was the man we're looking for."

She too had no doubt. "Yes."

"He saw my car come in. He didn't know I'd moved out. He called the room, not my name. He was on a phone somewhere nearby." He was sure of it. Anger returned. "I might have caught him."

"You might have been killed." Her voice was pale. "You might have been lynched."

He said, "He's safe only as long as he's the invisible man. I'm going to have to come against him to find out who he is."

"You may be right." She was breathing more easily. "But rushing out at midnight to lay hands on a white man isn't going to help you. If he killed you, he could and would call it self-defense. He'd need only say you tried to kill him because he knew you'd murdered Iris."

"He'd have to involve himself to say that."

"I can think of a dozen ways he wouldn't have to. So can you. The simplest would be that she came to him, an old friend, with her trouble. That at her request he brought her to you, and that he never saw her again."

"He's not going to kill me," Hugh said. "He needs me to bear his crime."

She couldn't argue with that. She asked, "Would you like that drink now?"

"I don't need it. I'd rather not. He may try again."

"I doubt that. I think he's long gone. He may not have been around here, anyway."

"He had to be. To know I was here. He might have been calling from the lobby."

"That can be checked." She walked to the phone, lifted it, and when the office responded, she said, "This is Miss Hamilton in 126. That call you put through to me a few moments ago, can you tell me if it was from outside the hotel?" After listening to the response, she said, "I wondered. It wasn't for me. It was a mistake." She thanked the night operator and hung up. "It was from outside."

He said, "I think we should try to change your room. I'm afraid to have you stay in this one."

She considered it, then shook her head. "We couldn't ask it without letting too many people know you are concerned in this case. If he should call again, I'll simply say that you've checked out, that I'm the new occupant."

He wasn't thinking of a telephone call but of personal violence. However, if it were the white car that the man watched for, he wouldn't appear at Ellen's door unless it was parked outside. In which case Hugh would be there.

She said, "He must wonder why your name hasn't been in the papers. That must bother him."

He hadn't thought about that. "Yes. He may believe I've been cleared by the police. That would account for his warning me to get out of town, to make me look guilty." Excitement mounted. "He may be afraid I caught a glimpse of him that night, that I can identify him!" He said, "Ellen, he's got to call again! And when he does you'll have to keep him on the phone until I can find him."

She insisted, "He may be calling from Scottsdale. Or Tempe."

"It's the car," he reiterated. "He waited for the car. The timing isn't coincidental. From the time we drove in here tonight until your phone rang was just what it would take to put a call through at this hour, when the lines aren't busy."

She agreed with him but she didn't want to.

"There's that hamburger stand in the next block that stays open until midnight. There's an all-night dispensary right across from the hotel office. He could watch from either of them."

"And there are residential developments all around."

"He can't call from home. He has to have a phone booth or be somewhere with no one around to listen. Tomorrow I'll have a look at those late places."

"You'll be careful what questions you ask."

"I won't open my mouth unless the atmosphere is right. I'm not looking for trouble, I'm trying to get out of it. For all we know, he may work in one of those spots."

"You'd better let the police take care of the questioning."

"The police." As if they cared. But he suddenly said, "Do you think we should let them know about the call?"

"It's too late now. Let Skye do it tomorrow, he's your lawyer."

"Should we call Skye?" He didn't want to. Not at this hour.

She decided, "Tomorrow's soon enough. There's nothing he could do tonight."

"I'd better go." He didn't like leaving her alone, but fatigue had caught up again.

She said, "Let me look outside before you leave. I hate to have you drive alone at this time of night."

He said then what he had been thinking. "I don't like leaving you here alone."

"I won't open the door to anyone. Not without first checking with the office."

Before he could stop her, she had stepped outside onto the walk. He came close behind her and moved past to survey the silent rows of cars. There was no person stirring.

He said, "It's all right. You go back in now." He wanted to have her in his arms, not by accident this time, by design. He was falling in love with her as he'd never known love before, even with full realization of the hopelessness of the situation. Because of a moment of charity on a desert road, he would have to live with the taint of this case forever. That was cold truth. He could never sully an Ellen Hamilton with its ugliness.

"I'll wait until you get the car started." She managed a smile. "We'll synchronize. When the engine's running, I'll dash in and bolt the door."

He couldn't match her smile. It wasn't funny. She stood there framed in the doorway not only until he was under way but until he'd backed out and was turned toward the exit drive. He stopped then until she lifted her hand and shut herself behind the door.

As he drove away, he felt certain he was not followed, but nevertheless he circled several blocks. He wouldn't chance leading the man to his grandparents' home. When he was again on Van Buren, he covered it slowly in the area on either side of the motel. The hamburger stand was closed by now; in the dispensary a tired man stood behind the counter. But Hugh saw what he'd missed before, or seen without seeing, a lighted service station a block beyond the motel. A car parked in front of it could watch The Palms driveway. And there was at hand, on the corner of the lot, the total privacy of a public phone booth.

He was late, six minutes late, the next morning, as he descended the steps of the Scottsdale station; seven minutes late as he stood in the doorway of the marshal's office.

They were waiting for him, the marshal moving the rocks on his paper reports, Ringle sucking a Coke bottle which looked like a toy in his heavy hand. Venner, wearing a damp plaid shirt of pink and yellow-green, was skitting about the small room as if he knew there was to be a pickup order soon.

An innocent man could apologize. Hugh said to Hackaberry, "I'm sorry. Traffic seemed slow-moving this morning." Nothing of how difficult it was to get away from the family without revealing his destination.

"Doesn't matter." Hackaberry waved the apology aside. "I'm running late myself. Have a chair."

Today there were extra chairs, empty ones aligned with Ringle's, two under the windows. Venner, his mouth snaked with disappointment at Hugh's entrance, blocked the latter.

Hugh said, "I'm sorry," and lifted one from Ringle's line, placing it near the marshal's desk. He sat down.

"We couldn't seem to find you yesterday." Hackaberry spoke genially, just as if it weren't important.

Hugh reacted the same way. "So I understand. I was out most of the day." If they wanted to know where he'd been, they would have to ask.

"You know the results of the autopsy?"

"I've read the reports in the newspapers. And I know what Mr. Houston was told."

Ringle rumbled, "Were you surprised?"

Hugh glanced at him briefly, then back to the marshal. "I don't believe I understand."

Venner said maliciously, "We been wondering how surprised you were to find out she'd had an abortion."

Hugh didn't let the insinuation disturb him. He continued to address himself to the marshal. "I hoped the autopsy would not show that she'd been aborted." It might not be wise to say more but he did. "Both as a doctor and as the person I am, I hoped she had been spared that."

Point-blank Ringle demanded, "Did you commit that abortion?"

"No, I did not!" His denial rang out, strong, true. There was no change in the attitude of the three men. They'd been conditioned to the guilty as well as the innocent forthright denials. He might just as well have saved his breath. He continued passionately, "I'm a doctor. I've sworn the Hippocratic oath. Under no circumstances that I can think of, would I violate that oath."

"But you weren't surprised," Ringle said flatly.

"No, I wasn't surprised. What did surprise me in the report was that her death was caused by concussion, not the operation."

The marshal asked, "Why did that surprise you?" He seemed interested.

He might be sticking his neck out, far out, to venture his opinions. But Houston wasn't here to advise him. He knew the interview was being taped and tape could be mutilated. Yet an innocent man would answer, frankly and freely. Hugh said, "Because if he was going to kill her, why would the man take her to an abortionist?"

"You don't think the abortionist killed her?"

"No, I don't," he returned. "I think she was killed by the man who got her in trouble and who found an abortionist for her after I turned her down."

"The mystery man." Venner sounded amused.

Hugh snapped the sentences, "The man she came to meet. The man who drove her to my motel Friday night. The man who telephoned an anonymous tip to the police." He brought out his wallet, removed the ugly scrap of paper and put it in front of the marshal. "The man who pushed that under the door of my room Sunday night. The man who telephoned the motel last night and warned me again to get out of town."

The marshal read the message and held it out to Ringle. The sedentary detective reached across for it, read it without expression, and waited for Venner to cross the room for his reading. Venner read it and tittered.

The marshal said, "You don't know who he is." He held out his hand to Venner for the return of the slip.

"I wish I did."

"He seems to know you."

"He knows my car. He knows my name. He knows the motel where I was staying." He might also know Hugh's appearance but he wasn't going to give Venner a chance for another titter.

Ringle said, "I thought you'd moved out of the motel."

"He doesn't know that; he asked for the room number, not for me by name." He had to go on with the explanation. "I happened to be there when the call came. A friend of my niece's has the room now, I had just brought her home from dinner at Skye Houston's." Deliberately he brought the lawyer's name in, a reminder that he was no longer without support. "Doubtless the man saw my car drive in and thought I was still staying at the motel."

While he was explaining, the marshal's phone had sounded and he had spoken unheard words into it. Now he said, "You can give us the full run-down on that telephone call later. Right now I've got another matter to take up."

One of his deputies was already at the door. With him was an undersized man, his face weathered from outdoor work, his thinning hair plastered with water, his eyes dull. He wore trousers needing a press, unshined shoes. For one wild moment of hope, Hugh believed they'd found the unknown man. And then he knew, from the deference in the deputy's manner, from the demeanor of Hackaberry, who this man must be.

The marshal spoke to the man, "I'm sorry to have to bother you at a time like this but I won't keep you long. Do you mind standing up, Hugh?"

Hugh came to his feet, without haste and without delay. As if he didn't mind. He looked down the room without expression, as if he were to identify the man, not the reverse. And he wondered what thoughts lay beneath the skull with the pasted hair, wondered what regrets would gnaw on a man whose daughter had died as Iris died.

The marshal was asking, "Do you know this man?"

He barely glanced at Hugh. "No."

"Have you ever seen him before?"

This time the man did peer at Hugh, as if to him all dark men looked alike and he was being asked to discover a birthmark to distinguish this one from the others.

"No, I never." The answer came flatly.

"You're sure of that?"

"If I'd seen him before I'd tell you."

The marshal didn't quite know how to phrase it. He asked hesitantly, "You never saw him with your daughter?"

"What you driving at?" Crumb's voice was no longer lackluster; it scraped. "What you trying to make out of her? My daughter wouldn't go with no niggers."

The marshal's voice clamored, "She rode to Phoenix with this man."

No one had told Crumb before. His face turned mottled with the shock. And then he lunged like a terrier toward Hugh. "You murdering bastard! You killed my little girl!"

The deputy caught his arm, held him.

"I didn't kill her," Hugh said. His sympathy for this shell of a man, distraught, bewildered, out of his depth, was stronger than any rancor. "I only tried to help her. She needed help."

Crumb wasn't heeding, he was struggling in the deputy's grasp, shouting obscenities.

The marshal passed Hugh, murmured, "You can sit down," and went to take the man's other arm. Together he and the deputy eased Crumb from the room. Venner began to cock about, his eyes little pointed rocks. Ringle gnawed his thumbnail phlegmatically. Hugh sat down and lit a cigarette. His hands were shaking.

The marshal returned, his boots clattering as he crossed to his desk. He took a last cigarette from a pack, wadded the paper and shot it toward a corner basket. It landed on the floor. "That was Albert Crumb," he said. "Her father." He needn't have said it, possibly it was for the tape.

Venner sauntered back to his chair. "He sure didn't like the idea of a nigger transporting his daughter to Phoenix." The word "transporting" had an ugly sound. If he were smarter than he seemed, he might have chosen it deliberately.

The marshal turned on him. "I don't want to tell you again, there's not going to be any color business in this case. I'm not going to have it messed up with Kluxers or with bleeding hearts."

"I keep forgetting," Venner drawled. But the ugly look he gave Hugh made it clear it hadn't been wise of the marshal to tongue-lash him in Hugh's presence.

Hackaberry went on as if he couldn't stop until he'd said it all. "You're going to handle this the way you'd handle it if Densmore weren't a Negro. That way we'll have a case which will stand up in court, not be sidetracked by a lot of loud-mouths who don't care whether we got the guilty party or not, so long as they're in the headlines. You got that straight now?" He mashed out his limp cigarette. "Let's get back to that telephone call."

Hugh gave a full account of it, even to the final words. He said, "I hung up on him then."

Venner tilted his chair against the wall. "Didn't you want to hear what else he had to say?"

"I did not," Hugh said. To the marshal he continued, "I thought possibly I could catch him at it. There aren't many places near the motel where he could watch for me to arrive and get immediately to a telephone." He confessed, trying not to remember the moments with Ellen, "I was too late. Of course he'd be gone as soon as I hung up."

"Why?" Hackaberry didn't get it. None of them seemed to understand.

"He can't take a chance on being seen. Don't you see, once he's seen, once there's a description, you can find him? And once you find him, there'll be those who can identify him as being with Iris that night."

Ringle took out a notebook. Without interest, he asked, "Where could he be calling from?"

Hugh named the places.

Ringle wrote them down and put away the book. "Why didn't you report the call last night?"

"I didn't think of it until it was too late. He didn't wait around, I'm sure."

"We got things called prowl cars," Ringle said. "Just like you got in L.A. They get around pretty fast."

"I didn't think of that," Hugh said with honesty.

The marshal said, "Well, if you have any more trouble, let us know right away. Next day doesn't do much good."

"I will."

"We'll put a prowl car around the neighborhood tonight."

Hugh wanted to protest. A prowl car would scare off the man. The only chance to find him was to let him go on believing he was safe. He didn't speak up; it would do no good, only cast doubt on there having been a call.

The marshal turned to his detectives. "Do you have any more questions?"

"I got one," Venner said. His mouth was moist. "Did you beat that girl's head in because she wouldn't pay you for what you done?"

Hugh looked to the marshal. His voice was rigid. "I've said it and said it. I am absolutely innocent of any connection with her death."

Venner's chair clicked to the floor. "If you're so all-fired innocent, seems funny you'd hire that big-shot lawyer, Skye Houston, to defense you."

Hugh couldn't contain his anger. "I hired him to try to get a fair deal, not to be railroaded for a murder I know nothing about. Just because I'm convenient."

Venner snapped, "Don't get huffy with me, black boy. It don't pay." He said insolently to Hackaberry, "Black boy's got a temper, hasn't he?"

The marshal choked, "I warn you, Venner."

"Excuse me," Venner sneered. "I must of lost my temper too. I don't like black boys insulting my integrity." He walked out of the room without asking leave.

Ringle said, "Don't worry about him, Hack. I'll keep him in line. I need him on the investigation."

The marshal turned to Hugh. "Nobody's going to be railroaded. But nobody's going to go free who had anything to do with killing that girl." His voice was hard, and his jaw. Like the others, the so many others, he'd have a hard time believing that a Negro doctor had the ideals and ethics of a white doctor. "You are to remain in Phoenix for the time being."

"I've already written the hospital," Hugh said without inflection.

"Very well. You'll be hearing from me." It wasn't a warning, merely a temporary dismissal.

Hugh rose and left the room. He could feel the hostility follow him. Because of Venner, deliberately through Venner, the atmosphere had been changed.

In the outer office, Venner was leaning against the water fountain with the young deputy who had conducted Albert Crumb earlier. He looked at Hugh with spite and said something under his breath to the deputy. The young man laughed, and Venner, delighted with his success, began cackling with him. By then Hugh had reached the outer door, and he went out into the heavy noon. He was shaking with rage, for once the sun felt good. He got in his car and drove away, but only as far as the next block. He pulled in by the small white church. He was in no condition to drive a car until his nerves had calmed. He took off his jacket, laid it on the back seat to dry. He lit a cigarette; it was without taste.

If he were fighting only the routine means of inquiry, it would be hard enough to endure, but to be pitted against personal venom became in time intolerable. The possibility that it might be a deliberate plan, for every man must have a sensitive spot by which he could be broken, made it no less endurable.

The five minutes, ten minutes, he sat there in a square which the growing village had not yet eaten, gave him the tranquillity he needed to set out again. He must discover what Edward had found out, he should report the gravity of the morning's interview to Houston, he wanted to be with Ellen. On his way to Ellen's, he stopped at the Scottsdale branch of Edward's bank. He presented his credentials, gave local references, and had no difficulty in cashing a check. Because it was the closer way, he drove again over the Indian School Road. And for the first time it came to him that the abortionist must be in or near this area. It was highly improbable that the killer, whichever of the two he was, would have risked driving the suffering girl over a long route through town to reach that particular section where he struck. There would be too much danger of interference along the route. Phoenix was well patrolled by city and county police, there was scarcely a stretch of road where you didn't see one of the light blue or light tan official cars.

The murder hadn't been planned. It came out of the botched abortion. This seemed self-evident. There was no reason for the abortion if the man meant to kill. Why had he killed? And, remembering the girl, he knew. Because she had become a worse threat after the operation, because she threatened to tell. The abortionist hadn't killed her, he would have no need of the happenstance tool. It was the man she had come to meet, the man who had driven her to the motel, the man who had driven her to the abortionist's, the man who had driven her away after the operation and had listened to her threats. And that meant there was another car with more evidence in it than in Hugh's. It could mean that the abortionist could identify the man. Hugh was afraid to be hopeful. But it could mean the two would accuse each other.

He had reached the motel. There was no response to his knock at Ellen's door. He walked around to the front of the unit and saw her across the green, just lifting herself out of the pool. She raised an arm in greeting, she must have been watching for him. He remained there by her lanai door while she wrapped the bright beach towel about her and gathered her oddments into the flowered beach bag. Her swimming seemed to have caused no commotion. The sunbathers were somnolent under oiled brown skins, the pool was lively with young people. Under the umbrella tables, older men read newspapers and their women wrote postcards. For most of them Ellen was doubtless only a girl with an enviable tan. Those who may have wondered or known evidently accepted the changing face of society. He'd met with all the varying degrees of civility, of progression and regression as an intern. Unyielding bigots were a minority save in pockets of the Deep South. In today's climate, it was they who could do nothing but retreat behind their warped, sagging fences. No longer could they demand that the fences enclose the rest of the country.

Ellen pulled off her cap as she came across the lawn, shaking down her long, dark hair. When she reached his side, he said, "You needn't have come in. All I want is a private place to phone."

"That you may while I dress."

The sliding door opened at her touch. She hadn't left it

locked. Common sense told him that she'd kept an eye on the room from the pool, that the maids were active all morning in every wing, that the anonymous man must hold a job by day, for his activities, save on Sunday, were all by night. Yet for the moment he was chilled at the thought of Ellen's entering the room to find evil waiting for her.

He said nothing now, unwilling to throw a shadow over the brightness of the morning. "And to invite you to lunch." He displayed his wallet, extracting a bill.

She said, "You don't owe me that much," and "I'd love to lunch but let's have it here. It's much more comfortable than a restaurant." She disappeared into the dressing room and bath. Before he was connected with Edward's office, he could hear the shower running.

Edward was out to lunch. Hugh left his name but no number, saying he would call back. Edward had enough to do without returning calls. Before he could look up Houston's number, Ellen returned, daisy-bright in a full-skirted summer dress. He couldn't tell her she was so beautiful it hurt; he substituted a dry question, "Just how much excess weight did you carry out here?"

She said, "I'm pleased you notice, sir."

"I have a mother and three sisters. I probably know more about femme finery than any male outside Don Loper."

"Then you must know that summer dresses don't weigh much. I didn't have any excess but I may going back. I miscalculated the heat of Phoenix in May. Most of the summer wardrobe I've acquired here." She suggested, "Why don't I call Room Service and order before you finish your phoning? There's a menu in the desk."

"I'd like something cool. Whatever you recommend. My grandmother keeps plying me with hearty meals. She thinks I need fattening." The morning paper was on the table. While she gave the order, he read more completely the front-page story. The turnover brought him to the editorial page. The editor didn't call the police system inefficient, he merely insinuated it as he rang the bells of alarm concerning the safety of young girls in Phoenix. Hugh set the paper away. How long before he'd be thrown from the sleigh to appease the wolves of discontent?

Ellen had finished her call and settled in the wing chair, opening a portfolio and continuing a half-written letter. Hugh called Houston's office. The secretary who wasn't Meg answered, identifying herself. Houston was out, but she said, "I've been trying to reach you, Dr. Densmore. Mr. Houston would like you and Miss Hamilton to come to his house at eight-thirty tonight. Will that be convenient?"

He queried Ellen, and reported, "Yes, we'll be there."

At eight-thirty. That would be after Meg's return from Indio. Hugh's nerves began to quiver. The knock on the door made him start. He wondered if he would ever feel safe again, as safe as he had before Iris.

Ellen was admitting Room Service with the lunch trays. No delaying tactics here. The management was doubtless only too pleased that Ellen chose to eat in her room. The waiter, a gawky young fellow who looked as if he were outgrowing his uniform, arranged the silver and linen and iced food on the low coffee table. He said, "Give me a buzz if you want anything else, Miss Hamilton." He favored Hugh with a nod as he whistled away.

It was pleasant to be lunching here with Ellen, as if they were in their own elegant mansion, looking out over their close-cropped lawn and blue pool. The reason they were together spoiled it. "I hate to have you hanging around here, missing your vacation." He took a French roll from the basket.

"Am I that dull?"

"Ellen!"

"I'm not accustomed to such frankness from young men."

"You know what I mean." He wondered, "Will you still go on to Los Angeles?"

"Certainly. I'm considering driving there with you."

"Delighted." But the bleak prospects made him add, "I wonder if I'll remember how to drive when they let me go."

Her light mood had been surface, an attempt to take his mind from his trouble. "You mustn't get depressed. We're on our way. Maybe you can't see daylight but it's just around the bend."

"I wish I could believe that." Deliberately he returned to unimportant conversation. "Do you know many people in L.A.?"

"Very few. Will you show me the town?"

He exaggerated a groan. "I'll introduce you to some great guys who'll show the town while I'm on duty. The only thing I'll have a chance to show you is the UCLA campus—an hour here, an hour there."

"I think I'll like the UCLA campus."

Without warning their eyes met and held, and in that moment, the game they were playing became real. He immediately turned back to his Russian salad, as if food were more important than furthering their relationship. He would not take advantage of whatever emotions propinquity and absorption in his troubles might have engendered in her. He said lightly, "I hear we have some fine courses in foreign diplomacy. Maybe you'll decide to transfer."

"I might at that." The dangerous moment was gone.

"What made you take up that field? It isn't a woman's."

"No, it isn't. But it could be. There's always need for office help and one needn't stay in that category."

"Okay, Madam Ambassador."

She smiled at him. "I didn't choose the field because I'm a feminist." Thoughtfully, she continued, "We've traveled abroad quite a bit. Because of my father's various assignments. I believe there's a definite need for what I call dark diplomats. A great part of the world is colored, you know."

"You'd rather live outside the United States?"

"Oh no!" She was quite honestly surprised at the suggestion.

"Isn't it easier?"

"To me, no," she said. "In our country, more often than not, we are what Ellison so well describes as invisible. It's just the opposite in Europe. Even in the Orient and northern Africa. As Americans, we are so conspicuous it makes me feel like a cockatoo in a cage. I've never been deep into Africa, I don't know what it would be like for me there, but I don't think I'd be at home. I've been an American for too many generations. Somehow I don't mind invisibility. I'd rather no one saw me as I walk down the street, or pretended they couldn't see me, than to have people nudging and pointing as if I were a freak. Even within its limitations, I like to live my life without comment."

"Then why are you training for foreign service?"

She laughed. "At heart I suppose I'm a crusader, like my father. I don't intend to spend my life in the foreign service, Hugh. I can spare a few years. After that I shall get married, raise a family, and point out proudly to them how much better their lot is than mine when I was a girl. Now tell me your story."

"I'd like to stay in research." He might have been talking about someone else. He couldn't speak of his own future when there was to be none. "However, as I have to earn a living, and want to make a damn good one, I'll doubtless end up in practice."

"You'll specialize?"

"You have to nowadays. Or so the doctors tell me. I'd be content to be a really good old-style family doctor like Edward. Not that I'd ever be the surgeon he is."

"Have you ever thought of a turn at Medico?"

The telephone rang. Neither one of them had actually been free of fear, despite their efforts. Both started at the sound. But she pretended as she went to answer. "We might find ourselves in the same neighborhood overseas," she said. After speaking, she turned, "It's for you," and before he could react, "I think it's your grandfather." She didn't know that increased the decibels of his fear.

The deep, soft voice said, "I'm sorry to bother you there, Hugh, but you've just received a telegram. I thought it might be too important to wait."

The Dean? Hugh said, "Thank you, Gramps. I'll be over in a little."

"We're going out but you know where the key is." Everyone knew where the key was kept. Under the rambler roses on the trellis. He wondered how he could suggest a change of hiding place for the present.

They said good-bye and he replaced the phone.

"Bad news?"

"I don't think it will be. A wire. It must be from the university. I mailed a special to the Dean last night." He sat down at the table. "Bad or good, I'm going to finish my lunch."

She poured more tea into his glass and her own. She'd led him to talk of this and that while they lunched as if there were no doom overshadowing him. Now that he would be leaving, she went directly to what must have been weighting her thoughts throughout the hour. "You were with the police this morning."

"How could you know that?" There was only one way. Skye must have told her.

She said, "You only have that particular face when you've been up against Ringle and Venner."

He admitted, "Yes, they were there. And the marshal. And Iris' father."

"And . . . ?"

"It wasn't good. When he didn't identify me, they told him I'd brought her to Phoenix. Then he called me the murderer."

"Are you afraid?"

"I'm almost past fear. Unless Houston's Meg gets the identity of that man, there's no hope. I'll be charged. Or unless I can find him."

"Did you tell the police about the call?"

"Yes. They're putting a prowl car in the neighborhood."

"That's good."

"It's not good," he denied. "It all but ruins my chance of finding him. He's not going to be active while they're in the neighborhood."

"It may keep you from being hurt." Her words went beyond the simple statement.

He hadn't thought before in terms of actual physical violence, only of facing up to the man, demanding the truth. He wasn't a fighter; he'd never had to be and never wanted to be. As a student doctor he had seen the results of the cruelty of man when reduced to animal viciousness. In particular the cruelty unleashed in today's juveniles, in the gang warfares of the city.

Although he and the police had used "man" as terminology for the killer, Hugh realized at this moment that his mental picture had always been of someone of Iris' generation, of the raucous, acned boys of the Indio experience. Teen marriages weren't unusual. Somehow he had believed that out of the experience of his maturity, he could handle this boy. He had not remembered that boys tended to run in packs. He might not be facing a single adversary.

And there was ever present the fact of color. If the man/

boy attacked Hugh physically, after initial impact, he would be attacking the fact. The hatred of the fact, for him, would justify violence.

Hugh shook the thoughts out of his head. He would not be afraid. If he could find a way to confront the man, he would not hesitate, whatever might come. He didn't want the police there; he wanted it where he could force the truth. Alone, fact to fact. It was the only way he could hope to escape the net being woven by both the police and the killer.

He put out his cigarette. He said, "That wouldn't be very important if it saved my facing trial for abortion and murder." He moved to the door, not wanting to leave this oasis, not wanting to leave Ellen. But there were other things which must be done while he was yet free to do them.

He said, "I'll call you later."

Hugh drove to the Jefferson Street house and climbed the porch steps. Venner was in the swing. Hugh turned to stone. "What do you want?"

The detective's lips were mocking. "I been waiting to see you, *Doctor* Densmore."

He couldn't have arrived while the grandparents were at home, he'd have been inside the house.

"Yes?" When you were arrested you were allowed to make one telephone call. To your lawyer? Houston couldn't be reached; he was in court. To a friend? Edward couldn't be reached. Again the burden would be Ellen's.

Venner gave the old wooden swing a backward push as he got out of it. "You going to ask me inside? I've always been curious as to how you folks live."

It was meant to be insulting but Hugh ignored it. He repeated, "What do you want?"

Venner ceased baiting. "I want your medicine bag." Before Hugh's outrage could become vocal, Venner fumbled a fold of paper from his back pocket. "I got the order here. Signed by the marshal. All perfectly legal."

Hugh accepted the paper. Perfectly legal. He returned it to the detective. The sharp little eyes watched as he took the key from under the roses. The place must be changed. Hugh opened the door. He must be rid of the man before his grandparents returned to face the malice.

Venner gawked around the living room. "Looks right nice." It looked exactly like the living room of anyone's grandparents.

Hugh said curtly, "I'll get the bag."

"Mind if I follow along? I wouldn't want you deciding to remove maybe a knife or a forceps."

Hugh said, "If I'd had any reason to remove anything from my kit, I'd scarcely have waited two days to do it." He started up the stairs, resenting the footfalls behind him.

The yellow envelope of Western Union was propped on the bureau in his room. He didn't touch it; it didn't matter if Venner did see it there. Venner was in the room as Hugh opened the closet door and reached down for the black bag. He could not bring himself to pass it over to the detective. A doctor's bag was sacred to medicine, it didn't belong in lay hands.

He said, "My instruments are sterilized after every use. If I had used them, there'd be nothing to prove it."

"I don't know about that," Venner said. "We got a laboratory that can find a lot of things that aren't there." He held out his hand. "Might be you wouldn't have much of a chance to sterilize stuff, just being a visitor in Phoenix."

He sensed Hugh's resistance, he was enjoying it. He reached further and took hold of the handle. Hugh didn't relinquish it. For a moment they stood there, both clutching the small black kit. Hugh could have jerked it away from him, he was taller and younger and perhaps stronger than the detective. But he didn't dare worsen his position by force. Even if the idea of commandeering the bag had been initiated by Venner, the order was plain. It might be an extra-legal move, but it was legal.

Hugh released his hold, hating the smirk of triumph on Venner's mouth. "Now you got to sign the receipt." He pushed the bag under his arm, deliberately careless, while he pulled the paper from his pocket again. "Sign on the dotted line." He thrust it at Hugh. As Hugh took his pen from the desk, Venner continued, "We wouldn't want that high-toned lawyer of yours to say we done anything illegal."

Silently Hugh returned the signed paper. He started to lead out of his room but Venner didn't follow.

"You're forgetting your telegram," he said. He stood between Hugh and the bureau. He was greedy for the overt act, for one movement from Hugh which he could repulse out of pious legal violence. It had been a near thing when both clutched the black bag. If there had been more space, if they had not been penned in the small aperture between the bed table and the closet door, Venner might have created the excuse.

This was his last chance. When he saw Hugh would not advance, he dangled the kit carelessly from his fingers and with his other hand lifted the envelope. If he dared to open it, Hugh knew he would lose control. He waited, hoping his trembling rage was hidden.

"You haven't even opened it. Don't you want to know who's it from?" His eyes peered as if he could read through the protective cover. "You must be a mighty important boy to be getting telegrams you don't even open."

Hugh refused to speak.

"Catch," Venner said suddenly. He tossed it short toward Hugh. It fell on the rug between them.

Cautiously Hugh bent to pick it up. At once Venner thumped across the room, his heel coming dangerously close to Hugh's hand. But Hugh was quicker. He straightened with the envelope in his hand as Venner passed. He waited for the detective to precede him down the staircase.

Venner wasn't afraid of his rage. He moved lightly, not looking back. It could be he himself recognized how near he had come to his aim, and how damaging it could be to him as well as to Hugh. He had a last word as he went out the front door. "Fresh air sure smells good."

Hugh stood at the door until the car was driven away. Then he moved quickly. He didn't even stop to read the wire. If his grandparents should see him now, they would know something was terribly wrong. He locked the house, replaced the key, and drove away. He didn't know where he was going, he only needed to get out of the neighborhood, to find a place where Venner could not reappear.

He was on North Central when he saw the big drive-in and remembered its objectiveness from previous visits. At this hour it was not crowded. He pulled in, and as soon as his order was taken, he opened the envelope.

It was from the Dean. A day letter in clipped telegram shorthand, but the expanded meaning was plain. There was disbelief that Hugh could be subjected to this misunderstanding, an offer to help in any way possible, and the Dean's assurance that he would arrange things at the hospital for Hugh to be absent as long as was necessary.

Hugh was moved. It was good to know that there was a friend who trusted him. When his Coke came, he drank it slowly and afterwards finished the ice. He was cooled in mind and body when he paid the tab and drove the few blocks to Edward's office. It was about three-thirty. The doctor would be in, and it might be possible to see him for a moment. With every new police move, Hugh knew how necessary it was for him to get on with the search. When he was arrested, there was no one he could ask to continue it. The abortionist would then be safe, not caring that an innocent man was in his stead.

Edward's office was off McDowell, a one-story yellow stucco building housing two doctors, a dentist, an architect, and a pharmacy. All Negro. The white tenants had moved out when the pioneer, the architect, moved in. He hadn't been a crusader; it wasn't easy then or now for a Negro to find good office space.

Hugh drove into the parking lot at the rear and entered the building by the back door. Edward's office was in the front. There were several patients waiting, idling over the magazines. Hugh had met the young secretary-nurse at the wedding reception, but he identified himself and said, "If it's possible to see the doctor for a half minute, I'll wait."

"I'll find out, Dr. Densmore." The patients wouldn't resent a brief conference between doctors. The girl returned almost immediately. "If you'll go into his office, Dr. Densmore, he'll see you when he can. The far door."

He walked into the inner corridor, passed two closed doors, and entered the private office. He sat down across from the desk and waited. The air conditioning made waiting a pleasure. He was tense with hope. It wasn't long before Edward joined him.

"I'm sorry to barge in during office hours," Hugh told him. "But I haven't been able to reach you. Were you able to get any more names?"

Edward lighted a cigarette before taking a key ring from his pocket. "Only two and I must have talked to a dozen people." He fitted the key into the lock of a narrow desk drawer and opened it. He took out a folded prescription blank from his wallet and relocked the drawer. As secretly as if there were other persons in the room, he passed the paper to Hugh.

"The first is a number to call. No name. I had word of it from a nurse, a doctor, and an intern. All professed ignorance of the number; they'd heard of its existence, that was all. I won't tell you which one of them tucked a slip of paper into my hand just as I was leaving the hospital." He gave a muffled sigh. "Somehow I feel that no one I spoke to believed my cover story. They thought I personally wanted to know how to get in touch with an abortionist. My only solace is that I will be able to tell them the truth later. Or so I hope."

"I'm sorry." It didn't help to say it. It didn't relieve Edward's shame or Hugh's own disgust at involving his brother-in-law.

Edward's voice was more muted. "The second is old Doc. Jopher. He lost his medical license years ago, criminal negligence. Operated once too often when drunk. He was a natural to turn to illegal operation. He's served time twice for abortion, but as soon as he got out, he went back to work. No one seems to know if he's in the business currently, there have been no rumors that he is. He's getting pretty old. But somewhere he's finding the money to buy booze. He's usually drunk." Almost apologetically, Edward said, "I don't think he's your man. The police know all about him. He's always questioned if an abortion case is made public."

"And swears he's innocent," Hugh said. "A man like that won't tell the police anything."

"Do you think he'd tell you?"

Hugh shook his head. "But if he's the one, I'll have to find some way to get him to talk. Where does he live?"

"In a little farmhouse north of Scottsdale."

"Scottsdale?" Hugh reacted.

"Yes." Edward was aware of the pertinence. "The directions are on that paper. There's no telephone. But they say he's easy to find, he seldom leaves the place." He put out the cigarette, ready to resume practice. "What about Mahm Gitty?"

"She's out of it. She's been in the hospital for two weeks. I won't keep you longer. I want to get at these."

"Don't be disappointed if they lead nowhere. There may be others no one has mentioned. I may get more information."

"In Phoenix would there be more?"

"There might be dozens." Edward wasn't optimistic. "Destroy that paper when you've done with it. I wouldn't want it to be seen. Did you get a lawyer?"

He realized he hadn't seen Edward since. "Skye Houston."

Edward opened the door. "He's the top man here."

"Ellen's father arranged it."

Edward stopped in the doorway. "Understand one thing, Hugh. We'll all help on the fee. Your father won't have to shoulder all of it."

Hugh faced him firmly. "I'm going to pay every penny of that fee. I'll have to borrow the money but not you or my father or anyone else is going to be out one dime. I'm no longer little Hughie, Edward, this is my responsibility."

Together they walked the corridor, Edward leaving him at the first closed door. Hugh went out through the office, followed by the curiosity of the waiting patients. He'd kept Edward too long from his appointments; it would mean overtime again for an already overworked doctor. Some day he'd make it up to Edward, he didn't know how, but he would.

Again in the car, weighted by the immediate afternoon heat, he took time to reread the information on the prescription blank. Doc Jopher should be the one, but if the police had already questioned him, why should Hugh even dream that he could bring the man to confess? He'd start with the number. If it was so well known in town that three persons had mentioned it to Edward, it would seem the sort of information that Iris' friend could be expected to pick up.

It was not until he'd driven away that it occurred to him to wonder where it might be safe to make this telephone call. Not at his grandmother's or his sister's, they'd be sure to overhear. Not at Ellen's, for she must not know of his activity until it was successfully concluded. He'd have to find a public phone booth, and one where there was no chance of his being observed by either family or friends or police or the unknown man. It eliminated the neighborhoods he knew, and in others he might be intrusive.

He decided to cruise until he spotted a likely booth. He found what he needed at one of the new shopping centers northeast of town. The development was large enough to give him anonymity, but not so large that the phone booth might be in constant demand. Actually there was little reason why the women, darting from one air-conditioned store to another, would need the telephone. They were within a few blocks of their neighborhood homes.

He left the car sandwiched between other cars near the variety store, and went in it, buying a pack of gum to add to the small change in his pocket. Under the arcade he sauntered on to the drugstore, buying a roll of mints, to add more change. Keeping under the arcade, he window-shopped his way to where it ended, and then, as if it were something that had only then entered his head, he walked out into the sun, crossing the sandy expanse to the booth.

There was no one near it. The few cars parked at this end of the area must belong to employers or employees who left the more convenient places for the customers. He closed himself in the booth. It was stifling. He palmed the paper from his pocket, put in his coin, and dialed the number. There was no delay in reaching it.

A metallic recording began without preamble, "If you will leave your telephone number, Mr. Ess will call you. This is a recording. If you will leave your telephone number, Mr. Ess will—"

He hung up. The recording didn't specify how soon the return call might be expected. Minutes? Hours? The sun pouring on the metal roof, the narrow confine devoid of air, made of the booth a dangerous sweat box. Could he remain there safely to await a return call? Did he dare tie up the booth for that long?

He opened the door and stepped outside. There was another possibility. By night Edward's office would be safe from interruption. And Edward knew what he was about. But it would mean giving the doctor's number to the criminal outfit, involving Edward definitely in the dirty business. He had no doubt at all that Mr. Ess would check on a number before he returned the call.

In his frustration and need, it came to Hugh that there could not be a measurable delay in returning the call. Neither party could risk having a third person answer the phone. The area of the booth continued to be avoided. The lady shoppers knew better than to use it when the temperature neared one hundred. Again Hugh entered the box, this time leaving a small aperture for air. Again he dialed the number and reached the metallic voice, but after the repetition of the statement, the recorder stated, "At the beat of five, recite slowly the number to be called," repeated this instruction. The beats were distinguishable and were followed by silence save for the faint movement of the tape. Hugh covered the mouthpiece with his handkerchief, and after the repetition of the five, read off the number printed on the dial. The silent interval was right for a precise reading. He waited and the record went back to its initial statement, "If you will—"

He hung up. He did not dare step out of the booth, someone just might approach to use it. He did open the door wider, not that the hot heavy air brought any illusion of refreshment but it made it easier to breathe.

And he waited. And waited. The perspiration ran down his cheeks like rain, his shirt was like wet paper against his body. He eyed his watch incessantly, then forced himself not to look at it, trying to measure the passage of time in his mind. When he glanced again, three minutes had evaporated. He sucked a mint and his thirst became acute. Why hadn't he bought a newspaper instead of candy and gum? If he had something to read, the time would pass and the phone would ring. He wiped the sweat from his face with the handkerchief, then hung it again over the mouthpiece. And he waited, stepping into the fastness of the booth whenever an occasional car ran to this end of the lot to make its turn. He was tempted to give up, to believe that the organization would not return a booth call for fear of entrapment. But he waited, just a little longer.

And the phone rang. He caught it on the first jangle, pushing the door shut with his foot. "Hello."

A male voice which might have been speaking through a hospital mask said, "Mr. Ess is returning a call to—" and gave the telephone number.

"Mr. Ess . . ." Hugh began.

"Mr. Ess speaking."

It wasn't hard to make the words come haltingly. As they must be spoken by most of those who were forced to deal with this man. "A friend give me your number," Hugh said.

"Speak up," the man commanded. "I can't hear you."

He might be aware that the caller was protecting his voice from identification. But Hugh did not remove the handkerchief. He said louder, “I am speaking up,” and repeated, “A friend give me your number.”

There was silence at the other end of the wire.

“A friend give me your number,” Hugh said again. “You see, I’m kind of in trouble . . . I need some help . . . I got a hundred dollars . . .”

He was interrupted. “The price is five hundred.”

Neither Iris nor any friend of hers would have that amount. Hugh invented quickly. “I got a job. I could pay you a hundred dollars now and—”

Again he was interrupted. Dispassionately. “The price is five hundred. Call again.” The connection was broken.

Thoughtfully Hugh replaced the receiver. He grabbed the soaking handkerchief and in relief stepped outside. Iris had not been put into the merciless hands of Mr. Ess. If by any chance her friend could have raised that kind of money, he would never have wasted it on a girl he wanted only to be rid of.

Hugh walked back to his car and drove away. The stirring breeze cooled him. There was left Doc Jopher. He wouldn’t go there by daylight, it was too close to Scottsdale. He might not be watched as closely as he feared, but he wouldn’t mock fate by taking his car to the house of a twice-convicted abortionist until he had cover of darkness.

contents of a report. Venner wasn't present; it was too much to be hoped that this respite would continue.

When Hugh entered, the two men were immediately silent. They glanced down the room at him, not speaking; Ringle with a ponderous satisfaction, Hackaberry rather as if he'd never seen Hugh before. Hugh waited just inside the door, unsure, unable to understand the changed attitude of the marshal. They could not have found anything damaging in the medical kit or on his car tools. There was nothing to find.

The marshal pushed back his chair. "Did you drive out here this evening?"

"Why, yes." He didn't comprehend.

"Will you show us where you left your car?" The marshal strode down to Hugh, nodded at him to follow. Ringle ambled in the rear.

Hugh said, bewildered, "It's outside, right in front of the Town Hall." He didn't glance toward Ellen as he accompanied the men through the outer office, out the door and up the steps to where the car was parked. One of the deputies, the one who had been in charge of Mr. Crumb, joined Ringle as he passed. For one awful moment Hugh wondered if something had happened to Iris' father, if somehow his car could be involved. But this was impossible. The car had not been left by the motel long enough last night or today to be borrowed and returned. It could not have happened at his grandparents' home; if the killer knew that Hugh had moved there, the harassment would also have moved.

He asked, "Do you want the keys?"

He was ignored. Ringle was half stooping, examining the fenders. Marshal Hackaberry was close by his side. The deputy was there to guard Hugh. Not overtly; he stood apart, but when Hugh moved, he too moved. And his thumb absently rubbed over the leather gun case at his hip.

Ringle was surprisingly agile as he suddenly squatted beside the left front fender. His hand disappeared under it and he looked up at the marshal. "Something's there."

Hugh swept forward, his shadow with him. "That's crazy," he said. "There couldn't be."

The marshal had bent down and pushed his own hand under the curve. He stood up again. He said to Ringle, "Let's see it." Then he looked at Hugh and he sighed. He said nothing, turning his back to watch Ringle. The heavy man was on his knees, his hands working to free something affixed beneath the fender.

Hugh watched, hypnotized, unable to believe. When had this frame been stealthily fitted to him? Last night at Ellen's? The night before? Or as early as Sunday night; while he slept, did the murderer prearrange proof of guilt, to be divulged at the right moment?

Ringle puffed to his feet. What he held was wrapped in a grease-stained piece of flannel, one that might have been discarded at any garage. It was wound with copper wire and heavy black masking tape. The ends dangled unevenly. Ringle loosed the wire and unwound the tape without destroying the pattern made by the cloth. He shook out the contents on his open palm. It was a small, common wrench, indistinguishable from any other of its size and years of use.

Hugh became aware that all three men were studying his face. He said, and he knew he sounded hysterical, "It isn't mine. Someone's trying to frame me. I never saw it before. You know it isn't mine. You took my tools to the lab."

Hackaberry broke through. "We'll go back inside."

Ellen would know from his face as they passed. She would get to Skye in time, before he could be formally arrested, printed, locked up with no hope of proving the truth. He didn't dare look at her lest he start babbling again.

The marshal marched over to his desk. "Sit down," he ordered. They sat as they had on other occasions, Ringle to one side of the desk, Hugh opposite the marshal. The difference was the deputy guarding the door. Ellen wouldn't know, she couldn't hear through that closed door.

Hackaberry bumped down into his chair and picked up his pipe. Ringle carefully deposited the weapon on top of the marshal's papers, as if it were another paperweight. The silence was unendurable, but Hugh kept it during the interminable time it took the marshal to pack his pipe and set it to smoldering. He then said to Hugh, "You're entitled to call your lawyer." There was no more hope, he was to be charged with the murder. "I'll get him if you like."

There was no trickery to the offer, the phone was at the marshal's hand. "Thank you. I would like him here." At least the hysteria was out of his throat, he could speak as factually as the others.

Hackaberry spoke into the mouthpiece. "Get Skye Houston for me."

Would Skye be at home yet? Or was he at the airport meeting Meg? Or with some other clients at dinner? He must be found in time to prevent this arrest.

Hackaberry said, "You deny knowledge of this?"

"You know it isn't mine." Hugh tried to make the words reasonable. "You went all over my car the other night."

"Not under it," Ringle stated.

Hugh continued, separating his thoughts with care, "If it had been mine, if I had used it to murder, you can't believe I'd have kept it in such a precarious hiding place. I'd have had plenty of time and opportunity to get rid of it."

"I don't know about that." Ringle's absent smile held all the knowledge and vagaries of uncounted criminals met in years of service. "Might have been you'd be afraid somebody'd see you throwing it away. Might have worried you that somebody would stumble across it, somebody always does, and it would be traced back to you. Might be you'd figure it was safer to hide it until we let you go home, where you'd know how to get rid of it so it would never turn up."

Hugh said, "You can't trace it to me because it isn't mine."

"We won't find your fingerprints on it." Ringle poked at it with a pencil. "You can tell it's had a good run. But may be we'll find out where it was bought and who bought it."

"I hope so," Hugh declared.

"May be we won't. May be it was bought a long while ago at the five-and-ten or some big hardware store where they won't remember. Could be it was sold in L.A."

It would confirm his guilt to them. It was too much to believe that the murderer had once gone to Los Angeles and bought a simple tool.

The telephone jangled and the marshal grabbed it. "Yeah," he said. "We've got your boy here. The probable murder weapon was hidden under his car." He scowled at the crackling of the earpiece. "That's your opinion. Do you want to get over here before I charge him?" Briefly he listened, then said, "I'll wait just that long." He broke the connection with an angry hand. He said to Hugh, "The lab will find out if this is the weapon. You know that. We'll wait for your lawyer to get here before we continue."

Ringle took out a cigar and lit it. It was a good cigar. He spoke almost affably. "Why don't you make it easy on yourself and tell us what happened?"

Hugh repeated hopelessly, "I've told you and told you. I never saw Iris alive again after I sent her away Friday night. I had nothing to do with the operation or with her death." His words fell into a vacuum of unbelief. And there came to him what should have come before, if he hadn't been disturbed beyond reasonable thought. "Who told you to look under the fender of my car? Did you have another anonymous tip?"

The marshal had the decency to look abashed, but Ringle said, "I don't mind where a tip comes from. As long as it proves out."

Hugh cried to the marshal, "And you don't believe I'm being framed?"

The marshal studied his face, then his eyes went beyond to the door. Skye Houston was entering. He greeted Hugh with a quiet "Hello there" in passing. He stood before Hackaberry, tall, arrogantly disgusted. "Just what is this all about?"

Hackaberry said, "A call came in late this afternoon from a man who identified himself as staying at The Palms. Two nights ago he saw a man—the description fitted Densmore—hiding something under the fender of a white Cadillac with California license plates. This is what we found there." He indicated the wrench.

"Did your informant have a name?"

Hackaberry flushed angrily. "He'd been reading about the murder and worrying about what he'd seen and decided to call us before he left town. No, we didn't get his name. He wouldn't give it. He's a businessman and doesn't want the publicity of being involved in a murder case."

Ringle said without interest, "Venner's looking into it but he won't find out anything. They come and go at the motels. This guy was checking out right then."

Houston was icy. "On this you intend to arrest my client?"

The marshal snapped, "On this and other evidence, I intend to hold him on suspicion of abortion and murder." The scorn on Houston's face made him break out in an appeal to the lawyer, "For God's sake, Skye. With all I have, how long do you expect me to sit on my hands?"

"Until you have one shred of proof."

"Proof? How much proof do I need? He brought the girl here, he admits she came to him to ask—"

Houston interrupted, "You might like to learn the name of the man the girl was involved with."

Ringle's sleepy face quivered to alertness. Hackaberry stared up at the lawyer. He asked finally, "What kind of a gag is this?"

"It's no gag. I can't give you his full name yet but I do have a description and dates of some of his visits to Indio."

"Sit down," Hackaberry ordered.

Skye pulled up a chair, on the far side of the desk.

"Where did you get this dope? How good is it?"

Skye waited, as if considering whether or not he would answer. Eventually he said, "You know I don't have to tell you my source. You could have had these facts before I did if you'd half believed my client's story." With a touch of acid he added, "My information isn't anonymous, it's good. I have a witness."

"Damn you, Skye," Hackaberry began.

"Do you want what I have or don't you?"

Ringle's smoldering anger became a roar. There would no longer be hope of any favor from him, if ever there had been.

The scowling marshal drew paper under his pen. "Shoot."

"His first name is Fred. His surname begins with an O. He lives in Phoenix."

"How many Fred O.'s are there in Phoenix?" the marshal disparaged.

"I haven't checked them out yet. But not too many, I daresay. Not that will fit the other facts. He is young, probably in his twenties. Medium tall."

The description was too vague. The marshal continued making notes but Ringle made no pretense of his loss of interest.

"He wears his hair long, it's bleached blond. When my witness saw him, he was wearing a dark leather jacket and dark trousers."

"And where did this witness see him?"

Skye said with pleasure, "With Bonnie Lee Crumb. When he brought her home after a date."

Ringle was awake again. The marshal put down his pen. "You going to put a name on your witness?"

"Are you going to hold my client on this piece of junk?" Skye's forefinger jeered.

Hugh waited in the awful silence. He could be held; there was more than sufficient circumstantial evidence to hold him on suspicion, the marshal was right when he'd said that. That Houston by legal process might have his client released by morning was of little value. Once Hugh was arrested, once his name became public property, his family was shamed, his medical future without hope.

"You going to give me a name?"

In the silence, Ringle grunted, "Who needs it?" but the two men facing each other didn't hear him. The two were friends. But at this moment there was nothing between them but the contest of their wills shaped by their legal knowledge.

Skye barked a laugh. "All right, I'll give you a name." Hugh felt suddenly weak. It was that close, his being under arrest. Otherwise Skye would never have capitulated. "Lora Mattinor."

"Where does she live?" Ringle was stubbing the name in his book.

"You want me to do all your leg work?" Skye stood up. "Indio, of course. I don't know the address. My client is free to leave, Marshal?"

Hackaberry gave a grudging inclination of his head. "You'll be responsible for his appearance when I want him again?"

As if the suggestion of Hugh's running out was too absurd for comment, Houston gave a short "Yes." He gestured to Hugh. "Let's go, Doctor."

Without a backward glance, Hugh walked out with him. Ellen rose from the chair in the office outside, her eyes deep with anxiety. Hugh had forgotten she was there waiting. Skye put a strong hand under her arm. "It's all right," he assured her. He moved her to the door and up the steps, Hugh behind them.

Night had come down; there was a cold freshness to the white of the stars. Hugh breathed deeply of it.

Skye suggested, "You follow to my house."

Without seeming to move, Ellen was at Hugh's side. "Yes, we'll follow."

Skye waited until they were in Hugh's car, then roared away.

His rear lights were pinpoints far up Scottsdale Road when the stop lights held the white car.

Ellen spoke for the first time. "They didn't arrest you." She lit a cigarette and passed it to Hugh.

"It was close. Until Skye came in like the Marines." Why couldn't his appreciation for the rescue be unalloyed? Because Skye had touched Ellen and Ellen had accepted it as if accustomed? Because he wasn't used to dependency on a white man, on a lord of the manor? The light changed, and as he drove on he briefed Ellen factually on what had happened. In silent apology, making Skye the strong man, the hero.

Ellen was excited. "So Meg did find someone who'd talk."

"Evidently. And got the information to Skye in time. Two Marines."

The pinpoints were ahead, cutting a left turn at the sound of Hugh's approach.

Ellen was confident. "They'll have this Fred O. by tomorrow." Her intonation was that it was all over, just this small detail to be attended.

They'd find the man. This he did not doubt. But it was then that Hugh's acute danger would commence. The steps Fred O. had taken might be crude but they had already proved effective in smearing Hugh with guilt. The man had had plenty of time to concoct the story he'd tell; its culmination would be that Hugh was the abortionist and the murderer. He wouldn't have to prove it, only to accuse and let circumstantial evidence convict.

The foolish days when Hugh had thought the finding of Iris' friend would exonerate him seemed as distant as another life. The car was approaching Skye's place, Skye's car had already turned through the gate.

Hugh tried to speak with enthusiasm. "I'm sure they will." Perhaps Ellen accepted it as such. Perhaps not. She wasn't easy to deceive.

Skye waited at the door for them. "Meg's here." That would be the third car parked by the house. "A good thing she had sense enough to phone me when she landed. Without her information I don't know how I could have talked Hack out of it tonight. What about that wrench under the fender?"

"It was put there. Plenty of chances."

They had entered the living room as they spoke. Meg uncurled from a large chair. "I thought you'd never get here," but her voice fell away as their faces revealed they hadn't been idling. Hesitantly she asked, "Is everything all right?"

"Temporarily," Skye said and stopped. By then they all had seen the little girl on the couch.

Meg said, "This is Lora."

The girl bobbed her head. She was looking from Skye to Ellen and Hugh, then toward Meg for direction.

Meg said, "Lora, this is Mr. Skye Houston, the lawyer. Miss Hamilton and Dr. Densmore."

Again the head nodded but didn't understand. She hadn't expected Negroes. She'd doubtless never before been in a living room with them. She was a homely little thing. She didn't look more than ten, but she must be in her early teens, to be a confidante of Iris—Bonnie Lee. Her hair was in a long unfashionable braid down her back; she had a gopher mouth and eyes set too close together.

Houston said, "You didn't tell me you brought her with you!"

Meg said, "It was a surprise. I thought you'd prefer to hear her story first-hand. It's quite interesting."

"Wait till Hack finds out about this!" But some communication passed from Meg to him and he turned to the bewildered child with his most charming smile. "I'm delighted you could come, Lora. What do you say we have something to eat and then you can tell us all about it." He swerved to Ellen and Hugh. "You haven't had dinner!"

"It isn't important," Hugh said.

"Nonsense. Of course it's important. You can't think when your energy's depleted. As a doctor you should be telling me. Go along. We've got a lot of thinking to do tonight." He herded them toward the kitchen. "See what's in the icebox, Ellen. I'll take the orders here."

Ellen opened the icebox as if she were at home. "What kind of sandwich would you like? There's everything."

Hugh said, "I'd like to take you to dinner—" breaking off as Skye joined them.

"Ice cream and chocolate sauce for the girl and a Coke. God. They've had dinner. Meg just wants coffee." Skye wasn't helpless in the kitchen, like some men; like Hugh's own father, for one. He turned the coffee making over to Hugh and set himself to helping Ellen with the sandwiches.

The intuitive knowledge of each other which had been evident in the first meeting of Ellen and Skye seemed heightened as they worked together. It didn't come from the words they spoke, the meaningless light phrases, it simply was there. It set Hugh silent, apart. If they noticed they would believe it was the weight of tonight's near thing. Not the jealousy which he grudgingly admitted. Not the self-pity he was fighting with every atom of his pride. These two could be gay as tropical fish; they weren't truly in this. Whatever happened wouldn't happen to the personal them. And why shouldn't Skye be conscious of Ellen's charm? He wouldn't be a man if he didn't respond. Being married didn't make him a eunuch.

There was no touch of impropriety in his attention. He could admire without touching. He knew Ellen wasn't a slave wench; she was Judge Hamilton's daughter, of impeccable background. There was no sanity in Hugh's jealousy. Ellen wasn't his. He too dared not touch.

He carried the coffee tray to the living room. Lora imperceptibly shrank back into the cushions as he placed it on the coffee table before the couch. He knew he hadn't been explained to her; she was puzzled, unsure of his presence. She could accept him servicing the tray, but not sinking into the cushioned chair after Meg said, "I'll do that," and took the cord to plug in the urn. The little girl was more disoriented when Ellen and Skye returned, when they all ate together.

Meg eased into the story they waited for. "I didn't have any luck today until I met Lora." The girl preened and smoothed the garnet and pink flowers of her skirt. "I'd talked to all the high school crowd at the malt shop but none of them knew anything about Bonnie Lee having a secret boy friend."

"She only told me," Lora boasted.

"I was about to give up—most of the crowd had gone home—when Lora came up and whispered to me that she could tell me about Fred."

"I didn't want them to know about it," Lora explained as she must have over and again to Meg. "I promised Bonnie Lee I'd never tell. And I wouldn't have only—"

"Only she wants to help us catch the man who killed her friend," Meg said for her.

Lora nodded vigorously. "I certainly do. It's simply awful what happened to her. You don't know who'll be next." It might have been her mother speaking. "It might be me!"

"That's why Lora was willing to fly to Phoenix with me. To tell you the story in person, Mr. Houston."

"I'm grateful, Lora." Houston lived up to Meg's shaping of the scene.

"At first my mother wasn't going to let me come," Lora prattled. "She was afraid it might be a ruse to get me killed too. But after Meg called the Judge—"

Meg's eyebrows were expressive. "I remembered Judge Long was from Indio. Fortunately he was at home and we drove down there, Lora and her mother and I. And fortunately he remembered me from when he was working on that extradition case with you, Skye."

"I just had to come," Lora sighed. "I'd never ridden in a plane before."

Hugh remembered from service days, how many of the boys had never been in a plane before the call-up. In the winged century, if they traveled it was as far as their cars would take them, no more. Most had never been on a railroad train. It was as true for the city dwellers as for the country cousins. He understood Skye's amazement, he'd felt the same reaction.

Houston was growing impatient but he covered it with the practiced smile at Lora. "Bonnie Lee actually told you about this man, this Fred?"

"Oh yes. She told me about all her boy friends. She was terribly popular. Probably she was the most popular girl at school."

Bonnie Lee had to have someone she could talk to; girls were like that in their teens. Hugh's sisters were always rhapsodizing to friends over the phone. Lora was the safe confidante because obviously she wasn't one of the popular crowd. And just as obviously she'd never betray the secrets entrusted to her. Bonnie Lee was her ideal; it was in her voice and shining face as she remembered the girl.

"But Fred wasn't in your school?"

"Oh no. He was older." To Lora twenty years would be old.

"He was from Phoenix. But he used to come to Indio two or three times a week."

"On business?"

"I don't know." Young people never thought of such matters. To Lora, Fred came to Indio to see Bonnie Lee.

"Where did she first meet him?" Hugh asked.

By now she'd accepted Hugh as part of the room and she answered with recollected excitement. "It was terribly romantic. It was during the Christmas holidays when she was working at the ten-cent store, you know, to make extra money, and this gorgeous blond guy came in to buy some candy and she waited on him. It happened just like that! They took one look at each other and fell madly in love." For the moment she'd forgotten the murder. "He was waiting for her when she finished work." She came back to them. "That's how it started."

A married man, picking up an easy girl. To pass the time. Not thinking then of murder.

"Did she know he was married?"

"Of course not!" Lora was indignant. "She wouldn't go with a married man."

Houston said, "You saw him."

"Yes, I did."

"With Bonnie Lee?"

"Of course."

"Did you meet him?"

"How could I? I'm not allowed to go out on dates. My family's so old-fashioned," she interjected. "Besides, they never went where anyone might see them."

To his motel room? The back of a car?

"It was a secret romance," Lora dreamed.

"Why?" Ellen asked. "Did she tell you why?"

"She didn't want her father to find out she was running around with an older man. Besides, he had been cracking down on her going out school nights and Fred only came over during the week. So she had to tell Mr. Crumb she was babysitting, and if she and Fred had been seen around town, her father might have found out she wasn't."

It might have been part of it, Bonnie Lee herself might have believed that the secrecy was her idea. But it wasn't hard to believe that it had been initiated by Fred.

"She lied to her father," Houston stated.

"Yes, but she had to or she couldn't ever have seen Fred."

"How did you get to see him?"

Lora smiled. "I knew she had a date with him that night. It was last February, the night before Washington's Birthday, just before he stopped coming to Indio. There wasn't any school next day so I stayed up reading in my room until I heard them come home. They were laughing it up, not loud enough to wake anybody who wasn't awake, but I heard them. And I looked out my window, I live just across the street, and there he was." She sighed. "Just like she'd described him. Tall, pretty tall, and blond hair with a ducktail, and the leather jacket—"

"You'd recognize him if you saw him again?" Houston put in abruptly.

Lora's mouth drooped. "Well, I didn't see his face, only his back. On the porch." It wasn't good enough. She knew she'd disappointed them. Hopefully she offered, "I'd know him from the back. There's a street lamp at the corner. I had a real good look at him."

Houston helped her regain status. She might be all they'd have to link the unknown man to Bonnie Lee. "You're sure his name is Fred?"

"Oh yes. Bonnie Lee wrote his initials all over her schoolbooks. F.O. Sometimes O.F. Of, you know, in case anyone got nosey."

"But she never mentioned his last name?"

"No, never. But it starts with an O for sure. She was always swooning Fred O, Fred, O Fred, O Fred! She never said the last name though."

And was this too something the man had thought up?

Lora was wound up now, pouring it out, not knowing how much of Bonnie Lee she gave away. A wild girl, the envy of the other girls at high school, the wisecracks of the dirty boys. A girl of whom Lora's parents disapproved yet pitied, remembering a half-neglected child keeping her father's house when she wasn't more than eight years, when the mother left them. A girl who got away with murder—wrong word—when her father was downtown working the night shift at the railroad. A girl who could lie her way out of anything.

"She must have been caught out sometimes," Houston said.

"She was. She was always in trouble at home and at school. But she didn't care as long as it worked out first the way she wanted it."

Lora was right on that. Bonnie Lee, who called herself Iris romantically, wasn't a psychopathic liar; she lied for convenience. After she'd attained what she wanted, she didn't care that the lies were discovered. It wasn't her fault she was what she was; she'd never had a chance to grow up straight. Maybe she would have been a wild kid, anyway. But maybe she wouldn't have been if a mother had been there to help her through adolescence. Men didn't have the gift of mothering. Her father must have tried but he wouldn't know how, and there'd be the job to hold, and all the problems of the household that ordinarily could be shared with a wife. If there'd been someone at home to give the child love and guidance and security. As Hugh's mother gave his sisters. If there'd been someone to talk to other than this unformed worshipping neighborhood child, someone to tell Bonnie Lee that there was a right and a wrong. Someone to say, "Wait" and "Be careful" and "Darling, don't go away yet. Be a little girl just a while longer." Someone to care what happened to her.

Hugh broke through his thoughts. "Did Fred bring her home in a car?"

Lora stopped talking and thought about it. "I don't think so. I didn't see any car. Of course they might have parked it down at the corner but I didn't hear any car. The first thing I heard was them laughing." She explained, "They didn't have to have a car. We don't live far from town. Indio isn't big like Phoenix."

Fred O. didn't have a car; he went over there with someone else, someone else who'd know about his trips.

Now Houston was asking, "Did Bonnie Lee tell you she was planning a trip to Phoenix?"

Lora confessed reluctantly, "No. But we hadn't had a chance to talk lately. She'd been running around with Inky Miller and that crowd." Her nose expressed her distaste. "Inky says she wanted him to drive her to Phoenix to visit her aunt."

The boy with the jalopy. And the aunt wasn't a lie of the moment, she'd been planned.

Lora recalled with pride, "She wouldn't have told me that. I knew she didn't know anyone in Phoenix. Except Fred." Her voice became small, childlike. "Do you think it was Fred murdered her?" She didn't want it to be true. She didn't want her first touch with real romance to be spoiled.

"We think so," Houston said gravely. "We don't know, but we think so."

Her eyes darted to Hugh. Houston caught the implication. He asked, "Have you ever seen Dr. Densmore before tonight?"

"Oh no!" She was outraged at the question. "I never have."

Houston nodded acceptance, then smiled. "I don't think we should keep Lora up any longer, Meg. She's staying at your house?"

Meg nodded.

"I'm sure it's been a long day for her. You'll bring her by the office tomorrow?"

He'd get a signed statement before he turned her loose.

"I'd planned it," Meg said.

He turned the big smile again on Lora. "Maybe we could have lunch together?"

"I don't have to go back to school tomorrow?"

"I don't think we could get you there in time."

The little girl grinned. "That's too bad, isn't it?"

Meg spoke good nights, Lora nodded. Skye went out with them to their car.

Ellen said, "If only she'd met him just once. Face to face."

"If only she knew his full name," Hugh echoed Houston's remark. "But there can't be many Fred O.'s who went to Indio two or three times a week, spent the night, and returned to Phoenix next day." And he thought aloud, "He might not be in the Phoenix directory. Most truckers don't live in the city. If he's a trucker."

"A bus driver," Ellen offered.

"Or a railroad man." Iris would have enjoyed that, the joke on her father. It had to be someone who didn't have a car in Indio. Or whose car or small truck would give away his identity.

Houston returned. "We'll start eliminating the Fred O.'s in the morning. The police may be doing it tonight. But we might get there first. We know more. Someone who had an Indio run at Christmas but no longer has it. She wouldn't have had to come to Phoenix if he was still available in Indio."

Hugh said, "It might be he just stopped seeing her."

"Not in Indio. Too small a town. She'd have found him there if he was still around."

"He could have told her to meet him in Phoenix."

"Not a chance. He wouldn't have had her come here to learn he was married. Too chancey. He wouldn't have wanted her on his hands here." He figured it as he spoke. "She knew where to find him. Not his home, he'd never let her know that."

Ellen said, "The bus station." She repeated it. "A bus driver. She asked to be let off at the bus station."

For a moment there was silence as they looked at each other, hoping. "It could be," Houston said slowly. "It seems too easy but it would fit with his Indio schedule." He took a deep breath. "Sometimes things do fall in line after you get a break."

"Lora is a break?" Hugh asked. She seemed a tenuous one.

"She certainly is. After I get her signed statement in the morning, I don't care how much the police question her." He was thinking of the trial, of his witness, the brilliant defense, the victory of good over evil. He wasn't afraid of the outcome. There might be minor setbacks but the triumph was already in his hand. Academically he might be aware that this triumph would be dust and ashes to Hugh. But he wasn't able to understand that public proclamation of Hugh's innocence would not be able to take away the stain of guilt. "You'll have a drink before you go?" He didn't wait for the answer but began pouring. After handing out the glasses, he sat down beside Ellen. "It's shaping nicely. I didn't expect things to move so fast. Once Fred O. is brought in—"

Hugh could no longer remain silent. "That's when it begins. When Fred O. talks."

Ellen denied him fiercely. "No, Hugh. The marshal won't believe his lies."

"Why not? It's all so logical. He brings her to my doorstep. I say I turned her away and never saw her again. He'll say he left her there and never saw her again. Who is speaking the truth?"

Houston frowned. "There'll be evidence—"

"The evidence is against me. A witness? Not to murder."

"There'll be evidence in his car, or the car he drove that night."

There was a possibility that the scientists by some infinitesimal grain of matter could prove Fred guilty of murder. "But not of abortion," Hugh said. "He will accuse me of the abortion. That will be his revenge because we led the police to him." He said distinctly, "That's all the police are waiting for. Someone to confirm their suspicion."

Skye attempted to speak with the assurance he had earlier but it was a failure. "Let's not borrow trouble. By the time Fred O. gets through lying to the police about everything else, they're not going to be so ready to accept his lies about you as you seem to think. If you didn't abort that girl—"

And still it was the if, even now Skye could have that doubt.

"—no one's going to prove you did."

But who was going to prove he didn't? From a cell he couldn't prove it.

"There's one thing you should know." Houston no longer attempted to hide his troubled frown. "That kid said it at the door. Around school they're saying that Bonnie Lee went to Phoenix with a Negro."

Behind a set face, Hugh's reaction was held.

"She asked me if you were the one."

His voice sounded strange. "What did you answer?"

"The truth. What else could I?" Houston tossed down the rest of his drink. "If only you could remember the license number of that jalopy. I could get those little bastards to tell the truth about your meeting with Bonnie Lee."

"What good would it do?" Hugh asked wearily. "It wouldn't prove I'm not the abortionist."

Not Inky or Guppy or Lora or the ones she spent the night with in Blythe could prove that.

Hugh and Ellen drove away in silence, over the winding deserted roads that led to town. The moon was high and white; each fence post, each clump of cactus was as distinctly outlined as by the sun. The mountains were moon-gray against the deep night sky. A dog barked from a distant house, the only reminder that they were not on another planet.

Hugh said, "Tomorrow I will be arrested."

"This is morbid," she began conversationally, but he cut her off.

"As soon as they talk to Fred O. Skye expects it. He knows he can't prevent it any longer. He's planning my defense."

"He has to plan. What's a lawyer for if he doesn't? Isn't the best offense a strong defense?"

"He'll prove me innocent. When Skye gets through with Fred O., no jury will believe a word he says. But before that the headlines will scream: Dr. Densmore Accused of Abortion. That's what will be remembered, not that I was proved innocent. That's what will stick, my name and that vicious word." He tried to keep the bile from his tongue. "It's all over once I'm arrested. No one wants a doctor with a dubious reputation."

"Why don't you really wallow, Hugh?" she asked quietly. "Make that headline: Negro Doctor Accused." There was anger in her now. "Skye is just as aware as you are of what an accusation can do to your professional life. That's why he's using his prestige, even going outside channels into his personal relationship with the marshal and the police chief and the press to keep you from being officially charged—"

"The press?"

"You don't believe they haven't been around because they don't know about you," she scorned. "They agreed to keep your name out of it because of the circumstances. But they don't like it. If both the marshal and Skye weren't exerting pressure—"

"I'm sorry. I didn't know." And Hugh wondered how often Ellen and Skye had been together, at lunch, cocktails, a swim, for her to know so much more than he did of what was going on. It was none of his business what she did with her spare time. He mocked himself, "No one ever tells me anything."

"You're in good hands, Hugh," she said firmly. "Skye can't make miracles but he can conjure wonders."

They had reached the motel but neither made a move to get out of the car.

She continued, gently now, "If it should happen, don't worry about your family. They'll hear the whole story from me before they can get a garbled account."

"From you and from Edward."

"Dr. Edward knows?"

He had spoken without thinking. "Yes. I've talked to him. I had to."

She didn't seem to wonder why. She only murmured, "Good," as if it were a relief to her that someone in the family shared the knowledge of events. In the interval of silence, each with his own thoughts, the insistence of sound was audible. She said, "I believe that's my phone."

He too had recognized the faint bell. "Answer it!" He was out of the car as he spoke and running lightly from the drive onto the sidewalk and toward Van Buren. When he reached the corner he could see without pausing that in the dispensary across the street there was no one but the clerk, seated behind the counter, a magazine in hand. He chose to turn right toward the service station with the convenient telephone kiosk. But he was halted as a car turned into the main driveway leading to the motel office. For that moment his view ahead was blocked. When the car had passed, he remained rooted where he was. The police prowl car had materialized in that interval. It was stopped near a car at the station curb, a dark unrecognizable sedan. One of the officers was bending to the driver's window, another stood on the corner, not far from the phone booth, talking to two youths. Hugh was too far from the corner to distinguish faces or the make of the car.

He turned and retreated into the motel drive, taking the nearest crosswalk through the green to Ellen's room.

She responded to his knock. "There was no one on the line."

"No." He couldn't contain his disappointment. "The prowl car was there first."

"You think it was Fred O.?"

"Who else?"

"You don't need to go looking for him any longer," she said. "You don't have to take that chance. The police will have him by tomorrow."

She was right. But he had an uncontrollable urge to confront the man in the act of telephoning. With all his theorizing about non-violence, what he wanted was to smash Fred O.'s dirty words down his dirty throat. He said wryly, "The Lord helps those who help themselves."

She countered, "They also serve who only stand and wait." She stepped back from the doorway. "Come in for a cigarette. Until you cool off."

"Not tonight." He made the refusal less blunt. "I'll be underfoot as usual tomorrow. Until our friends arrive—"

What had been banter, by some transubstantiation suddenly was not. If either had spoken in that moment, if either had moved so much as a finger . . . He remembered her laughter, counterpart to Skye Houston's. He kept his hands rigid against his thighs. He managed to make the good-bye casual. "I'll see you in the morning," and she echoed, "Good night."

The palms of his hands were wet. When he was in the car, he rubbed them dry on his coat sleeves, and he was all right again. It was too late to try to find Jopher's home tonight. Particularly with the prowl car active.

He couldn't sleep in the morning. By seven he was dressed, by seven-thirty he heard his grandmother rackety in the kitchen below. He went downstairs. His grandfather was bringing in the newspaper from the front porch.

"You're up bright and early." He smiled. "Would you like to see the paper?"

Hugh's fingers itched but he said, "Thanks, I'll read it later." He might betray his uncommon interest. "Any particular news?" he asked as the old man unfolded it.

His grandfather sat down in the easy chair and looked over the headlines. "Nothing startling. They haven't found that girl's killer yet." No suspicion. Merely the comment of any other man or woman in Phoenix. "Terrible thing that."

"Yes," Hugh agreed. Fred O. hadn't been identified by the prowl officers. You couldn't arrest a man for making a phone call late at night. Hugh went on to the kitchen and visited with his grandmother.

"You going to bring your girl to dinner tonight?" she queried.

"She can't make it tonight." He dared not until he found out what was going to happen to him.

She fussed a bit because she liked to sputter but she didn't insist. It was only out of her hospitality that she was urging the invitation, she was too old to enjoy cooking all day in this heat.

After breakfast it was still too early to go to Ellen's. His mother would be up, she'd be turning to worry if she didn't see more of him. He excused himself. "If Ellen calls, tell her I'm on my way over, will you? I'm going to Stacy's first." That should take care of any calls today.

He found his mother lingering with Stacy and Edward over breakfast. There was no possible way for either the doctor or himself to create a moment alone. Edward left on his calls with the unanswered questions in his eyes.

By ten, Hugh could no longer endure the strain of leisurely conversation and he left for Ellen's. On the way, he decided to stop at the corner station for gas; he was running low. There were two attendants; neither had any special knowledge of him. They were casually efficient.

He went on to the motel, parked outside Ellen's door, but he didn't knock there. Instead he went around to the lanai entrance. If the curtains were opened, he'd know she was up. They were wide, the sliding doors as well. He called from outside the screen, "Anybody home?"

Her voice came from the dressing room. "Come in. It isn't locked."

She reached the living room as he entered. She was buttoning a beach coat over her swim suit. As always she gave him the quick searching glance, to read in his face if things were good or ill. Reassured, she said, "Skye called. He wants you to come down to his office."

"When?"

"As soon as you can. I'm not invited."

"You don't know what he wants?"

"He didn't say." She made it clear. "He deliberately didn't say, so I didn't ask. Come back afterwards?"

"If there is an afterwards."

"Oh, Hugh, don't be silly," she said. Her spirits were high today. Did a morning talk with Houston so elate her? "If this were serious, don't you think he'd have warned me?"

He couldn't deny that. He smiled. "Very well. I'll be back."

The morning's cool was burning away with the mounting sun. The downtown streets were always more intense than where there was grass and sprinkling water. The First Avenue parking lot was full but he eventually found one on First Street. By the time he'd walked from there to the old bank building, his optimism had been depleted by the temperature. He took the narrow stairs slowly; their darkness was relief from the outdoor glare.

Meg was at her desk in the outer office. She said, "It'll be a few minutes. A client just came in."

He should have telephoned before coming. "Where's Lora?" he asked.

"My mother's taken her shopping. I'm meeting them for lunch. Mr. Houston can't make it. Then she'll fly home."

"The police must be wondering where she is."

"They can wait," she said cheerfully, returning to her work.

The morning paper was strewn on the oak bench. Hugh gathered it together. The canal murder was retold to make it seem new. The marshal had given an interview about the search in Indio for clues to the murderer. The autopsy results were repeated in detail. There was no mention of Lora or a man named Fred or of a Negro doctor.

The brown-haired secretary came from the private office with her stenographic notebook. She greeted Hugh, "All clear." Meg spoke through the door to Houston and held it for Hugh to enter.

Skye was involved with papers at his desk. He said, "Find a chair, Hugh. I'll be with you in just a minute," and returned to his work. The owl horn-rims were on his nose; he was as impeccably dressed in a tailored suit as if he practiced in a temperate clime. He looked as if nothing important was on his mind. He completed his notes, clipped them together, and set them in a wire basket. "We've located Fred O.," he stated.

Hugh waited, half in excitement, half in dread.

"The O. is for Othy." He drew a paper in front of him and read from it. "Age twenty-five. Blond, blue-eyed, five ten, weight 164. Drives a 1950 blue Ford sedan." Skye glanced up. "This is from his employment record at the bus company office. He worked for this company from last September until the first of March. He asked then for another run. When he didn't get it, he quit. The manager was pleased rather than otherwise at the solution. Othy was hired as temporary help originally; older men are preferred by the company." Houston set the paper aside. "He is not married."

Hugh pulled up sharply.

"He lives with his mother. She owns a beauty parlor. Out in the 24th Street district."

"No!"

"Her name isn't Mayble. It's Dorcas. That information is from the City Directory."

"Do the police know?"

"We came up with the information about the same time. In reverse order. I did the bus company first. They did municipal records."

Hugh was only half hearing. He was driving into Phoenix, seeing again the excitement mounting in the little girl as she neared the city, neared her meeting with the man she loved, the man she'd come to marry. He could not bear to remember the next night, her despair. He broke in grimly, "He lied to her. To get out of marrying her."

"Yes," Houston said. "He lied to her. He'll lie to us."

"To us?"

"We're going out to talk to him. He works in a garage not far from his mother's shop."

"You want me to go with you?" Now that the moment of facing the man was at hand, he didn't know if he could.

"Definitely. If anyone can start him talking, you can. Because if you're right in thinking he drove the girl to your motel and waited for her, he can't be absolutely sure that you didn't catch a look at him. You know it was impossible. But if he was in sight of your door, he can't know. At least that's how I see it."

Hugh made himself speak calmly. "Have the police talked to him yet?"

"Venner has."

"Venner." His intonation said it all.

"I made the same comment to Hack. Ringle's on the Indio end today. According to Venner's report, Othy never heard of the girl except in the newspaper."

"But his Indio run—"

"There are dozens of men who make that run," Houston said flatly. "It'll take more than that to make him a murderer." He pushed papers into his briefcase and lifted it. "Shall we go?"

Of course Venner would believe Othy. Houston's car was in a private lot nearby, assigned to the building. Its air-conditioned interior made the trip northward a brief one. But the density of the heat was deeper when they left the car and crossed to the open shed with its corrugated iron roof. A porcine man was pounding on an old car in its shade. There were other old cars, all dark sedans, standing in haphazard pattern on the surrounding sandy yard.

The man lifted his red face as Houston queried, "Fred Othy?"

"Round back." He wasn't curious, but then the police had been here earlier. He didn't seem to see Hugh.

They skirted the shed to the rear. Here were dismantled cars, engines and chassis and fenders like crazy players arranged for some monstrous game. At the far end of the premises, a man was dumping debris into one of the empty oil drums standing there.

Skye called out, "Mr. Othy?"

He pushed in his load of rags and metal before turning. "Yeah?" he took his time sauntering toward them.

When he saw the face, Hugh's pulses quickened. He knew this was the right man. It wasn't a good face, it was bony, the complexion bad, pasty despite Arizona sun. The mouth was mean with small unclean teeth. Othy was blond, as Bonnie Lee had told Lora; his hair was lank and yellow; it looked dyed, whether or not it was. It could be that his mother touched it up to keep it from turning dark. He wore it too long into his neck and below his temples.

He was young but not boyish, he could never have been boyish. He wore no shirt, only old, grease-covered khakis. His shoulders were round and freckled but his arms bulged with the muscles of heavy work. He came almost to them, then leaned against an old chassis and lit a cigarette. "What can I do for you?" His feet were long and narrow; he was wearing limp maroon socks and broken brown and white latticed summer oxfords.

"You're Fred Othy?" Skye asked.

"I'm Fred Othy." He paid more attention to the cigarette than to Skye. He might have known Skye Houston by sight. Phoenix hadn't yet grown to the size city where a prominent figure would be lost in the populace. But he was neither suspicious nor frightened at Skye's interest. There was an underlying cocksureness in him; he could afford it, he'd passed the police test this morning.

He was conscious of Hugh's presence and he knew who Hugh was. But after one quick flip of his pale blue eyes to Hugh's color, he ignored him, as if Hugh were chauffeur or handyman to the lawyer.

After his affirmation, both he and Skye waited, testing each other. It was Skye who continued the identification. "I'm Skye Houston."

"Yeah?" Othy's eyes flicked Hugh again but Skye made no introduction. He was so sure of himself, he could ask, "What you want to see me about?"

"You don't know?"

"How'm I supposed to know unless you tell me? I'm no mind reader."

Skye spoke as diffidently as he. "I understand you were a friend of Bonnie Lee Crumb."

Othy was unperturbed. "You're wrong."

"You know who Bonnie Lee Crumb was?"

"Sure. I read the papers. She's the girl got drowned in the canal."

"You didn't know her?"

"I never heard of her until she got drowned." He pitched his cigarette stub at Hugh. It didn't connect.

Skye let his eyes rest on the young man's face for the moment, not too long, just enough for Othy to be forced to wonder what would come next. And it came. "You drove a bus between Phoenix and Indio this past year."

He didn't like the reference but it couldn't shake him; he'd been through this before. "So what. It was a living."

"You didn't meet Bonnie Lee Crumb in Indio?"

"I didn't meet no girls there. I drove the bus over, I drove the bus back. I didn't have no time to screw around with girls."

"You didn't lay over there?"

He was ready to deny it but changed his mind. Instead he shrugged it off. "Once or twice maybe." He was as sure of himself as if he were telling the truth. "I don't remember. You'd have to ask the checker."

Skye paused, then asked, "Why did you quit your job with the bus company, Mr. Othy?"

Maybe Venner hadn't bothered with that. Othy snarled, "I got sick of it. I wouldn't of quit if they'd give me a shorter run but they wouldn't. So I quit."

Without change of expression or inflection, Skye continued, "It wasn't because Bonnie Lee had told you she was pregnant?"

Just briefly, the real Fred Othy was visible, vicious in hatred.

Then his face closed as if he'd pulled down a curtain. Although he tried to recover his previous assurance, he achieved no more than an imitation. "What's the matter, don't you believe me? I told you I didn't know no Bonnie Lee." He hoisted himself off the chassis. "Look, if this is all you got to say to me, you might as well cut out. You're wasting my time."

"Suppose I were to tell you I have a witness who saw you in Indio with Bonnie Lee?"

"I'd say she was a liar." He shot back the words but he was shaken.

"She?"

"She or he." He beetled, "Look, what business is this of yours, anyhow? What right you got to be asking me these questions?"

Ignoring the question, Skye indicated Hugh's presence. "Mr. Othy, have you ever seen this man before?"

Fred O. looked long at Hugh. Framing his answer. If there was, initially, contempt, it changed to actual hate. His lip curled. "No, I never."

"You're quite sure of that?"

He gave Hugh a quick, contemptuous stare. "I'm sure."

Skye then addressed Hugh. "Is that the voice you heard on the telephone, Dr. Densmore?"

"Yes, it's the same voice." Of this, Hugh was certain.

Othy took a step toward Skye. "What is this? A frame? I never talked to no spook on the phone."

"And you didn't inform the police by telephone that Bonnie Lee Crumb had come to Phoenix in Dr. Densmore's car?"

Othy shouted, "I don't know what you're talking about."

Evenly, Skye stated, "I wonder if the sergeant who took that call will also be able to identify your voice."

Othy's grease-stained fists balled. "I don't like this. I don't like it at all."

"You'll like it less when the police go over your car and find Bonnie Lee's fingerprints in it," Skye said sharply. "You may think you've got rid of them all but you can't, not the latent ones."

The boy's fury was diminished by the beginning of fear.

"It's only a question of time," Skye continued. "The police have the same leads I have and better ways of obtaining

"Absolutely, totally clean."

Without speaking, the secretary brought the requested papers to the chief's desk and quit the room. The chief held them out to Houston.

"I don't believe it!" Skye put on his horn-rims before taking the report.

The chief continued amiably, "There isn't one smidgeon of evidence that the girl was ever in Othy's car."

Then why had Fred O. been disturbed when Skye spoke of latent fingerprints? There had to be proof in the car. And it came to Hugh. Othy hadn't used his car, for some reason or other. He'd borrowed—from his mother! Of course, from his mother. He wouldn't have been so upset if it had been the car of a friend, a car which couldn't be traced right back to him. Hugh wanted to blurt out the idea but it was best for him to be silent in this office.

Skye returned the paper. He swung his glasses for emphasis. "This is the boy's car? He didn't make a trade for a new one this week?"

The chief's manicured thumbnail tapped the report. "It's all here. He's had that piece of junk for three years."

It came to Skye then. "He used another car."

"Or he's as clean as his car," the chief said. "And you've got the wrong man. If there is a man."

"My witness—"

"We're looking for your witness. Have you returned her to Indio yet?"

"She's on her way home now," Skye snapped the half-truth. "For the record I didn't know she was in Phoenix when I talked to Hack last night. Yes, I know she came over in my plane with my secretary, but I didn't know it then. Also for the record, we've got the right man. I know when I'm being lied to and Othy just lied in his teeth to me." His voice was flint. "What we haven't got is the right car." He turned on his heel with a short "Thanks," and nodded Hugh toward the door.

The chief's calm voice followed them. "Wouldn't you like the report on your client's fender wrench?"

Hugh froze. Skye half turned. "Yes, I would."

"It was clean too. Or at least, it was rubbed down so thoroughly that not a print can be lifted." He smiled professionally, "Nice seeing you, Houston."

"The same."

Hugh waited until they were outside the building before saying, "It was his mother's car."

"How do you know?" Houston's temper was short.

"I don't know. But if his is ruled out, he must have borrowed a car. There's no other safe way he could take her to an abortionist."

"Why the hell would he borrow a car when he has one?"

"Maybe he was out of gas." Hugh's own temper was raveling. "Maybe he didn't want to waste his gas driving her around town. All I say is that it's logical he'd borrow from his mother. Kids do. Everybody does. Whose car do you think I'm driving here?"

"All right, all right." Houston ended the discussion at the corner. "I'll see if the police are on that angle." His eyes were as distant as if he'd lost the case. And then he saw Hugh and frowned. "Keep yourself scarce today. If there's more news, I'll call you."

Hugh said mechanically, "At Ellen's." He could call in to Ellen. He wouldn't go there; he wouldn't go home. But where to spend the rest of the day? Not driving the white car; it would be a lodestone for the police. He left the lawyer and moved in the direction of the shopping streets of the town. He sauntered with the pavement crowds, feigning interest in display windows. It didn't seem that he had been followed from the chief's office, but because he had no experience in such things, he couldn't be sure. He'd just have to hope he was right. He couldn't spend the entire afternoon walking the hot streets. He crossed and headed in the opposite direction to the nearest motion picture theatre. He was alone, as visible as a rocket, as he approached the cashier's window and bought a ticket.

He didn't know what the current rules were for seating but, remembering childhood, he took a seat in the balcony. There were only three other customers up there, refugees from the truant officer. He hadn't noticed what the picture was before entering; it turned out not too bad the first time around. And the air was cool. The second time was a screaming bore and his summer jacket too light for the continued chill. But he remained in his seat into the third showing, until it would be dark outside.

Emerging at seven-thirty, the warmth of the day past was pleasant on his face. He was inordinately hungry. He'd had no lunch and had been afraid to leave his safety of the balcony for the lighted refreshment counter. If he weren't too late, Ellen might meet him somewhere private for dinner. He passed a news vendor, swung back to buy the evening paper. There was no scare headline, no news of an arrest in the canal murder. They were still seeking clues in Indio.

He began walking toward the parking lot where he'd left his car but he didn't go all the way. Before he returned, before he quit the comparative safety of being just another man on a city street, he had better find out if there were new developments. There were phone booths in the big garish drugstore he'd passed. He returned to it and drank a milk shake while waiting for an empty booth.

In due time, the young girl with dirty blond hair arranged in a grotesque haystack left the booth. She and her duplicate girl friend continued to block the entrance with a detailed retake of her call. He waited in outward patience until they flopped away. He rang the motel and Ellen answered at the first ring from the switchboard.

"Where have you been?" she protested.

"Round and about. Any calls for me?"

His unworried response allayed her anxiety. "Yes, Skye called hours ago, before dinner. He wanted you to get in touch as soon as possible."

"Have you had dinner?"

"I'm just finishing it."

"I'll be out as soon as I get a bite. If I may."

"Don't stop to eat. You can order something here."

He agreed. "I'll be there as soon as I can."

She asked in alarm, "You're not at the police station?"

"No." He could laugh. "I'm downtown. I'll be there soon." He rang off and called Skye's home. There was no answer. Although certain it was futile, he tried the office. No response. He vacated the booth, meeting the glare of the frizz-headed fat woman waiting.

He wove through the crowded store without hindrance and again started to the parking lot. Once out of the main district, the streets were empty and poorly lit. He walked rapidly, close to the buildings. All, with the exception of a small café, were closed. The courthouse loomed across the street, a darkened mass decorated with a few golden globules of light. No longer were old men seated on the benches under the shady trees. After passing the building he cut over to the parking lot. It too was closed and dark, his car was one of few remaining. But it was a park-and-lock, the keys were in his pocket. No one deterred him from driving away. He went out Jefferson, passing the family home, its lighted windows gentle in the night. He'd call the family from Ellen's, let them know he was all right. His absence since early morning might worry them.

At 24th, he went across to Van Buren and drove on to the hotel. But he passed Ellen's unit; he wouldn't leave the car there tonight as identification of his presence. He followed the outside drive and pulled into the circular parking area which serviced the cocktail lounge and restaurant. It was always crowded, his car would be just another one here.

He walked through the grounds to Ellen's. The draperies were luminous across the picture window. A knock at the lanai might alarm her. He went on to the rear door and rapped.

It was opened only a few inches. Then seeing him, Ellen pulled the door wide, locked it after he entered. She looked at him and said, "You're all right."

"I told you I was."

The television set was on in the living room; she turned down the volume, saying, "I couldn't help being worried. Not hearing all day. And Skye sounded disturbed—he wouldn't tell me anything."

"I tried to reach him."

"He's gone out to dinner. He'll call back." She was still examining his face, as if he wore a mask to deceive her.

He said, "I've been to the movies."

"You've what?"

"It was the safest place I could think of. The cliché." He sat on the arm of the chair. "Skye told me I should be scarce today. After we saw Othy this morning."

Her alarm heightened but she controlled it. "You haven't eaten all day?" Her dinner dishes were on the table. She unearthed the menu card from beneath the coffee pot. "Order

He paced, stopped by her chair. "Would you trust me out of your sight long enough for me to go to the office for the L.A. papers?"

Her eyes probed. "Just there?"

"My word I won't leave the motel grounds."

She was reluctant but she said, "Very well." She opened the lanai door. "Go this way. It's safer from outsiders. I'll latch the screen after you."

Outside he took a deep breath of the cooling air. He couldn't have endured the confinement much longer. He had to have a look around. If Fred O. was in the vicinity of the motel, he had to know it. Before he set out for Doc Jopher's. If Fred should sense that Hugh was heading for Jopher's, he'd stop it, whatever he had to do. He couldn't allow Hugh to talk to Jopher. Because it had to be Jopher, there was no one else.

He followed the white walk bisecting the green lawn. At regular intervals there were low-standing amber lamps, like jungle flowers growing along the path. They gave little-enough light, yet if Fred were nearabout, he could recognize Hugh. A middle-aged couple was ahead of him; they turned off at a cross angle. Two high-flying Texas types came out of the cocktail lounge with two nasal, talkative middle-young women. Hugh let them get a good start toward their quarters before he continued on his way. He didn't want to run into minor trouble.

The lobby was enclosed by glass and chrome on three sides. Within it, he would be spotlighted. He entered. Two elderly men were on a couch, boring each other with reminiscences. They gave the inevitable flicker at Hugh and put their heads closer together. One clerk, a woman, was at the desk. The newsstand counters were covered for the night but the dailies were stacked outside, by the magazine and pocketbook racks. He hadn't seen an L.A. paper for some days, he took one of each lying there, the *Times* and the *Herald*. He paid at the desk and went out again.

He walked along the boundary fronting on Van Buren. He didn't step off the grounds. He didn't have to for a look into the dispensary. The lonely clerk was as usual alone and there were no cars parked at the curb. From here he could see only a part of the service station lot. It was peaceful.

When he started back to Ellen's rooms, no other guests were in sight. It would have been a good time for Othy to face him. But there was no incident. Hugh tapped on the frame of the screen and immediately Ellen pulled aside the draperies. She must have been standing there. She said, "You were gone so long."

"I walked a bit. Fresh air. But not off the premises." He asked, "Any calls?"

"No calls. There aren't going to be, Hugh. If there were, it would have been before now. There were three in the hour before you came."

He agreed but not aloud. He'd wait until midnight. In Los Angeles, the case of the girl in the canal had been relegated to unimportant inner pages of the papers. There were fresher murders to report. At midnight the picture ended and he turned off the set. Neither of them had watched much of it. Ellen read a book—it was *Sartoris*—while he dallied with the papers.

She raised her eyes. "Do you give up?"

"I'm afraid I'll have to. Although I don't like to leave you alone." He'd said it so often.

"I don't like to have you go out there."

"I always check a bit before I head for Jefferson." He outlined his circuitous movements of the preceding nights. He walked to the front doors. "I'll go this way. I didn't park outside tonight."

For a moment they stood there looking at each other, then as if she sensed he held private plans, she lifted herself taller and touched his cheek with her lips. "Don't be brave," she said. "You're in enough trouble."

She waited in the lighted doorway until he lifted his hand and moved away. He heard the door close but the light still swathed his path and he knew she was watching. He didn't look back.

7

THE AREA where he'd parked wasn't crowded now, only the cars of late celebrators remained. A young couple backed their convertible out as he approached. The man wasn't Othy.

Hugh got in his car, waited until they'd gone before turning on the engine. Instead of circling out onto Van Buren, he took a side exit. For safety he would have a better look around the neighborhood before traveling to Scottsdale. The prowl car could only be on one street at a time.

The cross street he had inadvertently chosen wasn't a good one. It was too dark, too narrow, too lonely. A small frame house stood on the northwest corner. It was either vacant or everyone in it was long asleep. On the west, for the length of the block, there were only vacant lots. On the northeast corner was a machine shop of some sort, long since shuttered for the night, its back lot littered with rusty shadows. The only indication of life was at the far end of the block where there was a night club of sorts with a painted sign on its roof, lettered black on red: THE CANCAN. The building was an ugly frame shack of a depressing dark red color. The windows were painted black. Here and again on them were vivid scratches, as if the inmates had, in a sudden attack of claustrophobia, clawed a glimpse of a cleaner world outside. In driving to and from The Palms, Hugh had noticed the shack, with an idle wonder at the kind of need for companionship, or hope for pleasure, which would lure a person to it. The dim light over the door, the reflector for the roof sign were the only illumination on this entire block. The street lights from Van Buren on the north and Washington on the south did not carry to the long stretch of the midblock.

He did not know where the car came from. At one moment, he was solitary, driving toward Washington; within a breath, a car without lights darted like a snake into his rear-view mirror. In another breath, he was forced to swerve to a sudden stop, half on the dirt sidewalk; there was no curb. It had happened so rapidly, Hugh was yet without comprehension of its meaning when he pushed open his door and started to get out, demanding, "What the—"

Not until that instant did he understand. Fred O. was getting out of the other car. An ugly smirk was on his face, his muscles and fists were tensing. At the wheel of the marauder car was some friend, hidden by the night, no more than a silhouette with a high-pitched jeering laugh.

In the split second of comprehension, Hugh had the choice of getting back into his car or of continuing his outward movement. He couldn't drive away; he was penned. He got out. It wouldn't be a fair fight but he too was ready. He had inches on Fred, that alone could help him. He did not have the experience or the cruelty. Nor did he have reserves in his car.

Fred waited for him to push shut the door of the Cadillac. The youth's eyes in the night light were hot with satisfaction. Hugh backed away a few steps, hoping to reach open space before he was attacked. If he was maneuvered into the narrow end of the funnel created by the cars, he would be at Fred's mercy. It could be a common strategy of young hoodlum gangs.

He spoke as he inched backwards. "What's the idea? You might have wrecked both cars."

In response, Fred spit directly at the Cadillac. From within the other car, the titter sounded again.

Hugh continued his cautious backing but he didn't make it to clearance. Fred moved up with cold menace. Hugh would not turn and run; he wouldn't have that humiliation forced on him by this scum.

As of yet, Hugh had not openly given recognition. He did now, as a delaying tactic. He said, "You'd better get going. The cops are looking for you."

The smirk twisted to hate. Fred's voice was a monotone. "You goddamn dirty nigger, you won't tell the cops no more about me when I get through with you. You won't tell nobody nothing. Never."

"Aren't you in enough trouble?" Hugh was taut, controlled, waiting for the initial lunge.

"Not the trouble you're going to be in, nigger."

The weight of Fred's whole body followed his fist, a low blow that knocked Hugh against the rear fender of his car.

By making a fast half-turn, he had avoided taking it in the groin. But it put him off balance. He struck back and heard his fist land somewhere on Fred's face, but it was no deterrent. Fred moved in, chopping at Hugh, spinning him, and backing him into the narrows. Irrelevantly, the thought kept jangling through Hugh's mind: he's neglected to turn off the car lights; would they run down the battery?

He was being beaten cruelly. But he kept fighting back. Only his height, offering some protection to his eyes and point of chin, and his reach, which kept forcing Fred to protect his own features, kept Hugh on his feet. He knew he was losing ground, he hadn't the training. And it was possible a rib had been cracked in that first powerful blow.

From the car, the laughter screamed, close to hysteria now. "Give it to him, Fred! Give it to him good!" It was a girl's voice, breathy, shrill. It had never occurred to Hugh that Fred's companion might be a girl. It could have been his reaction of disgust which for that fleet moment took him off guard. A shoulder blow staggered him and, before he could recover footing, Fred's knee thudded into his groin. Hugh doubled over, crumpled to his knees, and automatically covered his face and head with his arms.

"Now you got him!" the girl whimpered ecstatically.

A boot crunched into his side but he held his position, crouching in sheer agony, trying to recover breath. Trying, before he was beaten unconscious, to get to his feet and kill Fred.

"Go on, give it to him," the girl was squealing, and then she broke into a sudden scream. "Jesus, Fred. The cops!"

The boot caught Hugh again but not full strength. There wasn't time for completion. He heard the swoop of Fred getting into the car, the metallic slamming of the door. The girl must have had the motor running but he didn't hear the wheels churn the gravel, the pipes roar. He passed out.

He must have returned to consciousness shortly after. At least no one had delivered any first aid, he was where he had fallen. In the muscle relaxation of unconsciousness, he must have rolled over on his back, but his arms were still rigid, covering his face.

He heard voices, male and female, as from an echo chamber. "He's coming to . . . he moved . . . he isn't dead . . ."

And he heard a disgruntled girl who might have been sister to the girl who drove Fred's car. The words were distinct. "It's only a nigger."

He managed to slit his eyes and he saw the boots. Without volition, his knees jerked up to his chest for a shield. He remembered at once what he must do, get to his feet and kill. And then he realized that these weren't cycle boots, they belonged to a police uniform.

In the background the staccato of a police radio was audible. With effort, he forced his eyes open and glimmered up at the circle of faces illuminated in the spotlight of the police cruiser. He distinguished first the young and anxious uniformed officer, behind him a blur of curious bystander faces, western-looking men, farm-looking women. One of the women had her hair up in leather curlers.

And then he saw Venner. Venner with sly amusement on his lips. Venner who must have identified him before now from the white Cadillac with the California license plate. Someone had turned off the lights of the car.

He kept trying to push up to his feet. The young officer came to his assistance. "Take it easy now," he said. "We've radioed for the ambulance."

Hugh shook his head and blackness spun about him. Someone's strong arm kept him from falling. He slurred, "I don't need an ambulance. I'm all right."

"Now you just take it easy," the policeman repeated. "We'll see."

He heard Venner on the periphery telling the onlookers, "It's all right, folks. Go on home. Go on now."

And he heard a woman twanging, "Well, if they want a witness, I'll testify. It's dreadful." It wasn't the voice which had dismissed Hugh on seeing the color of his face.

The policeman opened the rear door of the Cadillac. "You'd better sit down." He directed Hugh, helped him to sink down to the floor of the car. Hugh's head was thudding, there was blood in his mouth. But he remained almost upright, his feet pressed to the dust of the road, his shoulders held by the door hinges. He managed to say, "Thanks." With his elbows on his knees, his head propped in his hands, he could possibly keep from passing out again.

When the mist cleared, he saw that Venner was standing in front of him. There was a satisfied stench about him. "If you were looking for trouble, you found it."

Hugh managed to extract his handkerchief from his pocket. He dabbed at his mouth. The teeth seemed intact, the blood was coming from a cut or tear of his lip. He couldn't talk too well but he said, "It was Fred Othy."

"That figures." Venner didn't seem too interested.

The officer came into the shadows. "Do you feel up to talking? Do you want to tell me what happened?" His pencil and notebook were visible.

"They ambushed me." Hugh might as well tell it now, he wouldn't be feeling any better later.

"They?" The officer was one of the new type, educated, courteous.

"Fred Othy and the girl. She was driving the car."

Venner snickered, "She must have been a wildcat."

"She didn't get out of the car." To the other man, Hugh said, "I didn't get to see her."

"How'd you know she was a girl if you didn't see her?" Venner jeered.

"I heard her voice. A girl's voice. She was laughing. She kept laughing."

The officer was writing it down in his little book.

Venner said, "You sure do have trouble with Othy and his girls."

Out of sick anger, Hugh asked, "Why aren't you chasing Othy instead of standing here cracking lousy jokes?" He was past caring about Venner's reaction.

There was reaction, immediately. Venner made an abortive forward movement but the officer was there, Hugh's protection. At the same time a siren screamed around the Van Buren corner.

Venner snarled, "Mind your tongue, nigger. I could give you some real trouble."

The police ambulance came to a short stop. The attendants were out of the cab advancing to Hugh. He would not, must not, go with them.

Venner turned his ill-temper in their direction. "It took you bums long enough to get here."

As they converged on Hugh, one said, "We had a three-car crack-up on the Mesa highway."

He was afraid to come to his feet, he might spin out again. He managed to lift a painful grin. "I may not look it but I'm okay."

"That's what they all say," the stocky one said. "Let's ride in to the hospital and find out."

"I've heard all the excuses, I've ridden the wagon myself." With difficulty, Hugh fumbled his wallet from his hip pocket. "I'm a doctor." He passed over his credentials. "If I find I need help, I'll call Dr. Willis. He's my brother-in-law."

Dubiously, the attendant returned the wallet. "You're sure we can't do anything for you?"

"Not a thing. Thanks just the same."

His companion said to the policeman, "You'll put it in your report? Refused medical assistance."

"It'll be there."

Hugh expected possible trouble from Venner but the detective merely bared his teeth. It might be a laugh. Hugh was beginning to breathe more normally. He'd be able to drive home, it wasn't far.

The ambulance wheeled away. The policeman said, "Now if I can finish the report—"

The ambulance diversion had given time for Hugh's head to stop spinning. He gave his name, the reason he had been out at this hour—returning home from a visit to a friend, even the fear of trouble which had caused him to take a circuitous route.

"You mean you're still getting phone calls?" Venner smirked.

"Yes," Hugh said, still not caring. "My lawyer telephoned me that the police couldn't find Fred Othy. He was afraid Othy might be hunting for me."

Venner said to the officer, "How do you like that Skye Houston, running us down after all the errands we do for him?" He jerked his head toward Hugh. "His lawyer." As the officer continued to look puzzled, Venner snorted, "Don't you know who this guy is? He's the nigger brought the canal kid to Phoenix."

Somehow the officer hadn't connected it. He was surprised, then thoughtful. Hugh tasted fear. Possibly the police could take him in on some charge. Disturbing the peace? Or for his own protection? Any excuse would suit Venner. A second beating couldn't be distinguished from the first. Particularly after Hugh refused attention from the ambulance crew; there'd be no report on his injuries.

Hugh appealed, "I've given Marshal Hackaberry all the information I have. It's my lawyer who located Fred Othy."

The officer wrote something, then directed, "Go on with tonight."

Hugh continued his recital, omitting the racial slurs only. Before Venner, he would not speak them. He concluded with a ghost of a smile, "It's a good thing you came when you did. I would have killed Othy."

Venner snorted but the young officer understood. And he asked again, "You didn't get a look at the girl?"

"No. I didn't know it was a girl in the car until I heard her voice. Then it was too late."

"Could you describe the car?"

Hugh shook his head and hammers thudded. "A dark sedan. That's all I know."

"That's the best we could do. He wasn't using lights." The officer put the notebook away. "We were cruising the neighborhood looking for Othy when we spotted the fight. As soon as we turned into the block, this dark sedan took off. It was souped up." He said, "I put it on the radio at once but I couldn't go after the car. I didn't know but what you were dying—or dead."

Hugh was grateful for the kindness but he wished they'd taken after Othy and let him wait.

"He won't get away, don't worry about that." The officer straightened his cap. "Do you want to come down and file a charge against him?" He knew that Hugh wouldn't but he had to ask.

"No," Hugh told him. "He's wanted for something more serious than assault and battery."

Venner shrugged. "Maybe he is. Maybe he ain't."

Hugh said flatly, "He is." He hoped to hell he'd be around when Venner ate dead crow. Slowly he started to push himself to his feet. He wavered and caught onto the door frame.

The young officer was quickly at his side. "Don't you think you'd better let me get you to a hospital?" he appealed.

"It won't be necessary." His entire body agonized with the pain; he didn't know if he could make it but he must. To remain under police jurisdiction meant under Venner. "My head's clear. It's just that I took a thumping." He pushed shut the rear door of the car. The slam of it was like a nail sledged into his brain. But he kept smiling. "If there's any damage I can't repair myself, I won't hesitate to call a doctor."

Every step was agony as he shuffled to the front of the car. He hoped it wasn't showing too much. They stood watching him, the officer anxious, Venner with malicious satisfaction. Hugh managed to open the front door and to slide under the wheel.

He remembered to turn his head to the window to say, "Thanks for turning out my car lights." He didn't know if the officer was responsible but there was no one else to thank.

The motor caught. The wheels came out of the soft dust onto the road. He hoped the police car wasn't going to follow him. He had realized by now that he couldn't go home, not near two in the morning in this condition. There was only one place he could go, back to Ellen. She might be frightened at his appearance but she wouldn't panic, she would cope.

The policeman and Venner had returned to the cruiser. Their engine sounded, their headlights went on, their blinker off. Hugh held his car, lighting a cigarette as excuse for the delay. It looked as if they were waiting for him to make the first move, but something must have come on their radio, for they made a sudden U turn and sped to McDowell. Hugh drove on slowly, cautiously, to Washington, at the next corner taking the cross street to The Palms. From one inch to the next he didn't know if he would be able to make it.

He had to make it. If he fainted at the wheel, he would be picked up by the next cruiser. He would be at Venner's mercy. And Ringle's. He took particular care in making the turn into the motel grounds. He knew the twisting pain it would bring. There was a black Jaguar in front of Ellen's unit, he had to park four spaces away. He inched his car into the curbing, cut the engine and the lights.

He couldn't move, but he must before the blackness closed in again. A few more moments and he could rest. He slid out of the car, cautiously closed the door. He mustn't disturb the guests, if one should see him they would call the police in panic. Not until he reached Ellen's door did he realize that through sleep she would never hear his knock on it. Not unless he hammered loud enough to wake others.

Painfully, pushing one foot in front of the other, he felt his way through the arch and around to the front of the apartments. One more slow step, one more, just one more and he was there. To his relief, the drawn draperies were yet alight. She must still be reading. With one hand pressed against the door screen to keep himself from falling, he tapped with the other.

Almost at once the curtain was pulled aside to reveal her startled face. He swayed away from the screen while she unlatched it and held it open for him. He tried to say something but words wouldn't come. He shook his head and that was wrong. His eyes were swollen almost shut but he saw ahead of him a chair. Blindly, he stumbled toward it. Just before he fainted, he thought with incredible surprise that he saw Skye Houston's outraged face bending over him.

When he half opened his eyes, he was in a strange bed in a strange room. It wasn't a hospital room, you couldn't fool him on a hospital room. He went under again at once but not completely. Far, far away he could distinguish voices. He couldn't hear what they were saying.

He was drugged. At least he was conscious enough to recognize that. He fought against drifting away, fought to force his eyes to reopen. He couldn't see faces, only shapes, but the voices were coming through. In particular Skye's voice, cold, decisive. "You can't question an unconscious man."

"How long's he going to stay unconscious?" That was Ringle.

"Do you think he's feigning?" The anger was more intense. "You've had your own doctor check Dr. Willis' hospital report. What do you want, a miracle?"

"Take it easy." That was Hackaberry. "We know he's in bad shape. Othy lost his temper and—"

"Lost his temper!" Skye exploded viciously. "He tried to kill Densmore."

"All right. So he defended himself brutally when Densmore ran him into the curb—"

Hugh struggled to speak and felt a quick hand on his pulse. He opened his eyes full wide upon Edward's grave face. Edward gave the slightest shake of his head.

Ringle shouted, "He's coming out of it." He must have been at the foot of the bed.

Before his words were completed, Hugh's eyes were reclosed and he had already started to drift into oblivion.

Distantly he heard the marshal's quick "Is he conscious?" and the beginning of Edward's explanation.

As easily as he'd faded out, he returned to the room. Edward's thumb and fingers were still holding his wrist.

The marshal was still declaiming, "—he turned himself in as soon as he found out we were looking for him. Does that sound like he's lying?"

Only moments had passed.

Skye said, "He knew he'd been spotted when he tried to kill Hugh."

"That's just it, he hadn't been. No one but Hugh had seen him. Othy didn't have to tell us about it."

This time Hugh didn't open his eyes; Ringle might and probably was still hawk-watching the bed, waiting for the least quiver of lids. But he did rub his thumb against the doctor's wrist, in order that Edward might know he was listening. Edward's fingers tightened in understanding.

"We'll prove he's lying," Skye orated. "About everything."

How? Hugh wondered bleakly. So far, without Othy's lies, they hadn't been able to prove Hugh's innocence. He wondered more bleakly what Othy had said, whether he'd accused Hugh of both the murder and the abortion. The police wanted to believe Fred O., he was one of their own, not a dark alien stranger.

All at once Hugh was again ebbing and flowing. He mustn't go now, it was important he hear this. Frantically, he tried to remain on shore, but helplessly, he was wafted away.

When he woke there were no voices. He was in the same bed in the same room. He saw his hands on the whiteness of the sheet. They were clean hands. Swollen, stained with methiolate, bandaged across the right knuckles, but unbloody, ungrimed, clean. He noticed the sleeves above his hands. Someone had undressed him, washed him, put him into white pajamas. Not his own pajamas, his were blue.

He didn't know if his voice would carry. His mouth hurt. "What time is it?" It was twilight.

"He's coming out of it."

He smelled Ellen's perfume. He managed to lift his eyelids. Just to see her face. She was a blur bending over him. He croaked, trying to grin, "Hello. I must look awful."

"You do." She turned away. He couldn't lift his hand to deter her.

But his eyes were focusing and he saw at the foot of the bed Skye Houston and Dr. Edward. He said, "Hello," to them too.

Their faces suddenly seemed to fill out. Edward came around to the side of the bed and took the pulse again. "He'll come out of it in a few minutes." The police must be gone.

"I am out of it." They didn't seem to hear him. If he could turn his head, he could find Ellen. He tried to say her name but it wouldn't come forth. He tried whispering, "What time is it?" He said aloud, "What time is it?" He didn't know why he kept asking.

Skye looked at his wrist. "Almost six o'clock."

"I thought it might be tomorrow," he whispered. It didn't hurt as much to whisper.

All he wanted now was to sleep, but Edward kept saying, "Come on, Hugh. Open your eyes. Come on, you can open your eyes." The new medical theory, only enough drug to accomplish what must be done for patients, then bring them out of it as quickly as possible.

"I'm not asleep," Hugh said, and, "Ellen?"

"Yes, darling."

He didn't know if that was what she said but she was beside him, holding his hand.

He closed his eyes. "You know I didn't do what he said."

"I know."

"It was he who ran me off the road."

"We know," Skye said. "You've told us often enough."

He couldn't remember. He tried to joke. "I've been talking in my sleep?"

"Constantly."

"Othy hit me. And she kept laughing, laughing . . ." He opened his eyes and peered for Edward. The doctor was on the other side of the bed. "Hysteric, you know." Politely, he redirected his attention to Skye. Skye was his lawyer, the one who was going to get him out of this trouble. "The police officer has the report. And Venner. White-trash Venner."

"I've seen it," Skye stated.

Then they must have known Othy attacked him. Unless damn Venner altered the report. He'd been asleep all day, he shouldn't be so tired. But of course, it was the medication, to kill pain, maybe an extra dose to keep him quiet when the marshal came. He had to know why the marshal came. His voice sounded slow, too faint, and he shook his head in annoyance. That was a mistake. A million pains jumped within his skull. But they woke him up. He saw the patio beyond French doors. He was at Skye's.

"Why was the marshal here? And Ringle?"

"You were conscious?" It was Ellen who asked.

"Briefly." He didn't look at her but his fingers tightened on hers. "Why?" he asked.

Houston's expression was troubled.

"I have to know," Hugh said. "I'm strong enough."

Without embellishment, Skye recited, "Othy turned himself in early this morning. Admitted he'd lied before, out of fear. Admitted Bonnie Lee came to him in her trouble. He still denies he fathered the baby, insists it was one of her Indio friends."

That much could be true. She would have fastened onto the one who could do the most for her. Unlike the high school boys, Fred O. had a job, lived in a big city.

"She had fifty dollars."

"No! She had seventeen cents and the little I gave her."

"Fifty dollars hidden under the lining of her handbag." She'd kept it clutched to her. "Some of it she earned; some she took from her father's wallet. Othy drove her to your motel. When she came out, it was done. The police lab has moved into that unit; Ellen is staying here."

"They won't find anything."

Skye said, "Let them probe. It will give us more time. I've spent the day asking questions of anyone and everyone who admits knowing Fred O."

Hugh demanded, "He says I killed her?"

"He's read the autopsy report too; he knows how badly she was cut up. He says he didn't know where to take her, what to do with her. She couldn't travel back home in that shape. Neither of them had motel money. He'd parked the car while he tried to figure out what to do, it just happened to be on Indian School Road. Suddenly she started gasping, and keeled over, dead."

If true, it made the abortionist and the murderer one man.

"He admits he panicked. He put her in the canal. He says the head blow was caused by some debris in the canal. He brought in a jacket and travel bag he says were hers."

"The police believe his story?"

"They don't reject it."

Because part of it was true. Because he had driven her from the abortionist's, had stopped on the Indian School Road. But she wouldn't have died of the operation, not that soon. Not unless her heart gave out.

"They came here to arrest me."

"To take you in for questioning," Skye amended.

"Has Othy been arrested?"

"He's out on bail. His part was minor; he could get merely a suspended sentence."

"He killed her!" Hugh cried hoarsely. "Don't you see, that's why he's made this confession. He's running scared."

Skye said, "Don't despair. The police are checking and double-checking and looking for witnesses—"

"When are they coming back for me?"

"Not until the doctor lets you out of bed. I hope that won't be for several days. I need the time."

It was essential he talk to Edward alone. He closed his eyes. "I'm awfully tired." The reaction was what he wanted.

Ellen released his hand. "We'd better go, let him rest." She was, of course, speaking to Skye.

"Yes, it's almost dinnertime anyway. Would you join us, Dr. Willis?"

Hugh narrowed his eyes. Edward was moving to the doorway where the others were standing. "I wish I could but I haven't seen my family since yesterday. They're sort of expecting me at home."

Hugh waited, timing it for Skye and Ellen to step out of the room, the doctor on the threshold. It hurt to raise his voice, "Edward, before you go . . ."

But it worked. Edward excused himself and returned. The others went on down the corridor.

Hugh whispered, "Close the door." Edward gave him a dubious glance. "Close it. As if you're going to do another examination or are getting me the bedpan."

Silently Edward walked back, closed the door. He returned to the bedside.

"How bad is the damage?"

"Not bad."

"Level with me. I'm in the business myself."

"I'm leveling, Hugh. You have a couple of cracked ribs. I've bound them. You're badly bruised but no bones broken."

"Kidney damage?"

"Nothing that shows up. I took a couple of stitches in your lower lip."

Hugh scowled. "He kicked me. Bastard." No wonder he couldn't talk right. He was afraid to ask the main question but he did, watching Edward with care. "What about skull damage?"

"None." Edward sighed soft relief. "None at all."

Was he leveling? Hugh pressed it. "My eyes. They blur."

Edward grinned. "With the dope I've pumped into you, it's a wonder you can see your hand in front of your face."

Hugh lifted his swollen hand. He could see it plain. "Steady too."

Edward said, "Fortunately, when you keeled over on them, they didn't try first aid. They got you to me at the hospital without delay."

"Skye was there."

"That was a bit of luck. Ellen couldn't have managed alone."

And why was Skye there at that hour? He didn't ask Edward. "Does the family know?"

"You're bunking with an old friend for a day or so. Reunion celebration."

"They believe it?"

"Why not? I'm quite good at dissembling." Edward touched his shoulder. "Don't worry about that part of it. I'll cover. You're in good shape considering everything, Hugh. Another day in bed—"

Hugh interrupted bluntly. "I need some medicine."

The suggestion confused Edward.

"I want you to shoot me full of B-12. And I want some biphetamine. Strong."

Edward wasn't slow to understand. "You can't—"

"I have to. I haven't seen Doc Jopher yet."

"Someone else can go."

He remembered not to shake his head but he made it emphatic. "I have to do it myself."

"Tomorrow."

"Tomorrow may be too late."

Edward knew this was true, but refusal was on his face. "I can't let you do this—"

Hugh interrupted factually. "I'm going to do it. With or without help."

Edward capitulated. "When do you want these things?"

"As soon as you can make it back here."

On reluctant feet, Edward started to the door. "I can probably get the supplies in Scottsdale."

"I'm trusting you to say nothing."

"You can trust me." Edward closed the door after him.

The medication was wearing off and his strength was returning. He ached in every bone and muscle but he was no longer in danger of fading out. He had a terrific thirst. He managed slowly to turn himself and raise onto his left elbow. It was a bit more difficult to reach across with his right hand and lift the water glass on the bed table, but he did it. He drank a little water, slowly. When he'd finished and put down the glass, he didn't sink back onto the pillow as he wanted to do. Modern medicine taught you to try your strength, to get on your feet as soon as possible; to get on them even when you couldn't believe it was possible. There was no head injury. Medically, it wouldn't hurt him to try to get up.

He waited until he had become accustomed to the half-reclining position and then, using the palms of his swollen hands for leverage, he pushed up until his shoulders rested against the headboard. The effort set his head to spinning like a phonograph record.

When he had rested a little, he would try to swing his legs out of the bed. If he could stand upright, he could stagger into the adjoining bathroom. There was a soft rap on the door. It had been too much to hope that he would be left alone.

It was Ellen who looked in. When she saw his position she rushed across the room. "You shouldn't be sitting up."

"I was just changing position." He tried to smile. "To see if I could."

"Why didn't you ring?" She indicated the small china bell on the bed table.

"I didn't need help," he assured her.

She was settling him with her lovely, strong hands. Scolding as his mother would have. He let her arrange the pillows, tuck him in. "I just came to see if you needed anything. Are you hungry?"

"I couldn't eat. And I don't need a thing." He thanked her.

"If you want anything, please ring," she urged. "You know I'm staying here tonight." There were circles under her eyes. She probably hadn't slept at all.

"Edward's coming back to give me another shot. After that I'll get settled for the night," he told her. She started back across the room. "If you sit up waiting for that bell to ring, you'll be the one in the hospital. Promise me you'll go to bed soon."

"I'll sleep if you will," she smiled.

"Skye too."

"He has to go back to town. He's interviewing more of the bus drivers."

Hugh asked point-blank, "Have either of you slept today?"

She said, "I rested a bit when the police were here." Her hand turned the doorknob. "If you want anything—"

"Good night," he said firmly.

Once they got to bed, they wouldn't wake easily. They'd be too worn out to be checking on him all evening. After her footsteps could no longer be heard in the corridor, Hugh managed to push out of bed and get to his feet. Once the dizziness had cleared, he was able to make it to the bathroom. He hurt all over, he was weak; however, it wasn't too much of an ordeal. He didn't stay up long. He was only too glad to return to the bed. But next time it would be easier.

He was too impatient to rest for long. Edward wouldn't let him down, not Edward, but he should have returned by now. Again Hugh forced himself up and out of the bed. By slow stages he walked the length of the room, to the door. He rested briefly against it before starting his tedious return. Halfway, he stopped before the mirror and forced himself to look into it. The gargoyle who gazed back at him was uglier than he had imagined. Well, Ellen had Skye for company.

He heard the doorknob turn, and moved too quickly. The room tilted, the Navajo rug at his feet quivered like sand. Quickly he clutched the bureau, held tight. It was Edward who opened the door.

Hugh groaned. "I was afraid Ellen had caught me out again." He let go too soon and swayed like a metronome.

"Here, let me help you."

"No." Hugh grimaced. "I've got to learn." Slowly but with increasing confidence, he covered the space to the bed, sank down on it.

Edward prepared the shot. "Double dose?"

"Yes, please." The needle connected. It hurt.

"It won't help too much tonight. But you'll be in better shape tomorrow."

"It'll help some. The bennies?"

The doctor handed him a glassine container of capsules. "Go easy on them."

"I only want one. To keep me on my feet."

Edward put away his materials. "I can't dissuade you?"

Hugh sat up again. "I don't want to do this. I have to." He touched Edward's arm. "One more favor. Give orders outside that I'm not to be disturbed for several hours. I need that much time."

"I'll tell Ellen. Skye has gone out."

"Thanks for everything. And say a prayer this is it."

"I've been on my knees all week," Edward said.

When Edward was gone, Hugh got up again and walked to the closet. They had taken his clothes away. For the ragbag, or perhaps Skye kept them as evidence.

He couldn't go to Jopher's in pajamas. He'd have to borrow from Skye. If Ellen should catch him at this, it would be necessary to tell her of his plan. He didn't want to add that trouble, but if it happened, he could handle it. The capsule had already begun to work; he felt capable of handling any problem.

Soundlessly he opened the door to the corridor. The light had been left on. From the living room he could hear music; Ellen was there. Using the wall for support he padded in the opposite direction, until halfway along he found what must be Skye's room. He entered, put on a light, and closed the door behind him. In the dressing room, there was a king-size walk-in closet. He leafed through the clothes with growing concern at their immaculate tailored condition. But he found what he wanted on a hook, a pair of worn Levis, bleached to a mottled blue. With them over his arm he stepped over to the shoe cabinet and easily found a pair of old tennis shoes, stained beyond repair, fraying at the seams. Skye was human, he didn't discard his old shoes. Against all his upbringing, Hugh forced himself to open drawers. He collected a faded-blue sports shirt, its freshness would be gone by the time he struggled into it, a pair of shorts, and a pair of heavy white tennis socks. The latter would take up some of the extra space in the tennis shoes. Skye was bigger than he. He remembered a belt as he started away. He didn't select the oldest one of well-rubbed leather, it could be a cherished relic. There was a fairly old black one which could be replaced. He'd have to punch some extra holes in it.

He was weaker now, not alone from the exertion but from the tension of haste, the fear of discovery. He retraced his faltering way to his own room, closed the door and locked it. He didn't stop to rest but crossed to the patio doors, drawing the curtains across them, after they too were locked. Dressing wasn't easy. Each move awakened a fresh vise of pain. That Skye was several inches taller didn't matter with Levis, he could roll the legs above his ankles. The belt took care of the waistline inches. That the shoes were oversize helped give him the appearance he needed, that of a poor lout wearing hand-me-downs.

It was essential that he find the keys to the Cadillac. He would have to drive it, notorious as it was; he couldn't borrow. His personal belongings should be here in the bedroom. At the hospital the nurses always stashed them in the top bureau drawer, the natural place. He found them there, the wallet, the keys, as well as all the peddler's pack from his pockets, loose silver, the half roll of mints and the open pack of gum, his cigarettes and lighter. He transferred them to his pockets. He could go.

Quietly he unlocked the corridor door. On his way back across the room, he noted the glassine bottle and put that into his pocket. He left by way of the patio. The car was parked where he expected, in the rear, shielded by the whitewashed walls from the road.

Hugh edged himself under the wheel, careful not to wrench his battered bones. He drove without lights out of the grounds. The gate was ajar; he left it open after he'd nosed through. He put on the lights as he started over the meandering lane back to Tatum, and found the jog which would carry him to Camelback Road. He slowed here to a standstill. There were no other cars to harry him. From his wallet he took the precious scrap of paper and in the dash lights read again the directions to Doc Jopher's house.

Camelback was long and dark and sparsely traveled at this hour. Hugh held a steady pace, not too fast, not too slow, to Scottsdale Road. At the intersection of lights, he turned north. Within moments, he had left all town traffic behind. One pickup truck rattled past him, otherwise he saw no cars as he proceeded.

He continued on, as slowly now as he felt he might without attracting stray attention, until the speedometer showed he had covered the designated miles. With the moon low on the horizon, it was difficult to recognize the turn-off lanes until you were upon them. Not that there were many. He turned on mileage alone, and wasn't sure he had the right lane until he reached the venerable cottonwood growing undisturbed in the middle of it.

As all travelers must over this road, he circled the tree and crept on along the bumpy, narrowing way. Over a rise, down a decline, on into rural darkness until he saw far ahead a prick of light. It could have been a distant firefly. But as he came closer, it became a miniature green-glow square of a shaded window. Soon the house took shape, a kindergarten scrawl against the night sky. It was away from the road, on a rise, across a neglected field.

Before he reached its gate his wheels clattered across the warped boards of a bridge spanning a dry stream. Within that house, the sound would give warning of an approaching car. A few yards and he had reached the gate, never mended, the paint peeling from the white palings.

There was no need to dismount to open the gate. It swung loosely, nudged by how many cars over the years? Hugh's headlights picked out no driveway, only the choice of crisscrossing tire tracks on the stubble. Hugh made his own as had those who had come before him, in slow approach over the beaten field toward the knoll. His pulses were beating too fast, not in fear but in desperate hope.

Close up the house was frame, once white, built country style, a box with a pointed roof set atop it. The small porch and the front door faced to the west, overlooking the lane he had traveled after leaving the highway. Someone could have watched his lights from the time he first turned into it. Yet the place was so motionless, it was impossible to believe that there was anyone within.

He drove past the porch and parked at the far side, where his car would not be seen. As he silenced the motor, the drone of crickets seemed to increase sharply. Hugh climbed the three sagging steps to the porch. The moment he set foot there, the barking of a dog sounded in fury from inside the house.

Hugh did not stop moving. He crossed to the screen door. It sagged on its hinges and in several places the screen had broken from the frame. But when he took hold of it, it was hooked fast. He felt around for a doorbell and found where it had been. The push button had been wrenched out of its socket.

He gave a tentative knock on the frame of the screen, rattling the entire door. The sound of barking increased and Hugh pushed the door tight with the flat of his hand while he waited. From the appearance of the screen, the dog might be in the habit of charging at strangers.

He waited. He was considering another knock when a dim porch light came on over his head. It startled him and he stumbled back, releasing his hold on the screen door. Someone was fumbling with a bolt. In another moment, the front door was opened to give a partial view of a big man standing inside. There was no sign of the dog. When the door opened, it had ceased barking.

Hugh put a touch of the South in his voice. "Are you Doc Jopher?"

The man peered out. "Yes, I'm the doctor." He pushed into the aperture and peered more intently. "What you want with me? Speak up, boy, what you want?" The sour smell of old wine came from his breath, fouling the clean night air.

"I got a little trouble," Hugh began softly.

"What kind of trouble? Speak up."

"Well, it's like this—" He tried to say what the doctor might expect of a boy in his position. "I'm in trouble. My girl friend —you see, she—"

"You get your own kind of doctor," the old man returned almost angrily. "I don't do no work for the colored."

He started to push the door shut and Hugh spoke up fast. "I got money." There was little evidence of a decent living in this broken-down house and the broken-down segment of man visible in the doorway. It didn't appear that Doc Jopher was in the business. If so, he drank up his fees. "I got plenty of money," Hugh emphasized. At least he was holding Jopher's interest, the door remained ajar. "I can get hold of most a hundred dollars." If he had operated on Bonnie Lee for fifty, the double amount should be tempting.

He had awakened cupidity. Even in the poor light, he could see the flicker of it over the shadowed face. Doc Jopher wet his lips and asked suspiciously, "How'd you know to come here?"

"I heard some fellows talking where I work."

"They didn't tell you I do colored folks. They didn't say that."

"I guess they didn't say." Hugh drooped his head. "I didn't think about that. I got most a hundred dollars to spend—" He couldn't believe that Jopher would care about the color of skin if the money was there.

"It ain't that I'm bigoted," Doc Jopher said as if arguing with himself. "It's just they ought to go to their own doctors."

He peered, but not at Hugh now, over his head. He might have spotted the pinpoint lights of a car. If so, the motor was not yet audible. His eyes moved back to Hugh's face and unwillingly he opened the door wider. "Well, come in," he said crossly. "I can't talk business with you out there on the porch." He unhooked the decrepit screen and pushed it open with his other hand.

Hugh caught the screen and followed the old man across the threshold. He forgot about the dog until he heard the throaty growl. Across the room he discovered it, an old molting collie, shapeless in a shapeless soft chair.

"Come in," the doctor repeated. "He won't bite you."

Hugh closed the front door. "I'm not afraid. I got a dog of my own."

"Get out of that chair, Duke." Doc Jopher waggled his puffy hand in the direction of the dog. "Let the company sit down." The animal didn't move.

"This is all right," Hugh said, taking quick hold of a straight chair, unpadded, once part of a dining-room set. He didn't sit down, for Jopher was still standing, but he would quickly if the man insisted on ousting the animal. The sagging cretonne on Duke's chair was gray with old dirt.

"I can't teach him, seems like. Minute I turn my back, he's up there like he owned it." Obviously Duke did. "Sit down, boy," he told Hugh. He himself went to the table in the center of the room under a green-shaded hanging lamp. He took up a wine bottle and poured sparingly into the sticky tumbler beside it.

He was a shapeless mass of man, shapeless as the dog and the chair, yet he had retained height. He was almost as tall as Hugh. His head was large, his jowls sagged, his large nose was pocked as a drunkard's. His rheumy blue eyes peered from overhanging eyebrows. He needed glasses, possibly he wore them for work. His hair was white and thick and the only clean-looking thing about him. His baggy gray trousers were stained with wine, his western shirt with sweat.

Although the back windows were open, the heat of the day was motionless, unbearable, under the low ceiling of the small square room. The room wasn't dirty, it just wasn't clean. There was a threadbare old carpet on the floor, several chairs like the one Hugh had taken, the center table, an old sideboard at the rear, and against the wall by a closed door an old-fashioned sofa with a raised headrest. Its black leather covering was cracked into brown lines like a crazy map. Was this the operating table? It wasn't the heat and the smell which sickened Hugh's stomach. A half-opened door at the rear, just beyond the dog's chair, gave a glimpse of a kitchen sink and drainboard. There were no dirty dishes visible, no clutter at all. Under the sink was the dog's plate, a small scatter of food remaining on it; beside it a bowl of water set on a newspaper. The closed door near the couch undoubtedly led to bedroom and bath.

There was a picture in a gold frame hung on the mottled gray of the wallpaper. It was of a country cottage, smothered with roses, banked in green, shaded by leafy trees with a brook at their feet. In spite of what this man was, in spite of what he had done, the pathos of that picture smote Hugh. That it was there, a home, an old home far from this desert wasteland. That this misshapen old relic was once a country child, was once a boy with dreams, once a student with aspirations, once a Doctor of Medicine. The poignant cry rose silently in him: What can happen to a man? Why?

As if in answer to the unspoken question, the old man sampled the wine, licked his lips, and took another small suck at the glass. He then sat down in an old-fashioned rocker, pushed aside the evening paper, pushed aside a small wooden-cased radio, so that there was no obstruction between his eyes and Hugh across the room. He said, "I wasn't expecting company."

He never stopped drinking while Hugh was there, although he never replenished the glass with more than an inch of the yellowish wine. And he never did more than sip of it. He wasn't drunk, perhaps it was too early for that. But he was probably never sober.

He asked again, squinting in the direction of Hugh, "Who was it you said sent you here?"

"I didn't say no one sent me," Hugh replied. "I heard the fellows talking. One of them said you took care of his girl."

"And he said I did it for a hundred dollars?"

"He said he didn't have no more'n a hundred dollars and you took care of her." He wouldn't name a name. The doctor listened to the radio and read the papers. The police had cleared him, but if he had done the operation, he must know that eventually the truth would out. Fred O.'s name might not yet have been made public, and it was doubtful if Jopher would know him by his right name, yet Hugh wouldn't chance naming him. Not yet.

"Where'd you get that much money?" The dim eyes could see Hugh's battered appearance and they were suspicious.

"I worked for it. And some I borrowed from a loan company."

The answer must have been satisfactory. The doctor rocked in his chair. "Why don't you marry your girl?"

"I can't." Hugh wasn't expecting this kind of questioning, he hadn't prepared for it. He made it up as he went along. "She's already married. She's got her a husband in the army. Over in Europe. He's been gone most a year."

The sudden cackle was startling. "You're in a pretty bad spot, aren't you, boy?"

"Yessir, I am. I sure am, Boss." He mustn't pile it on too thick. Wino though the doctor was, he had the remnant of a shrewd brain.

The doctor measured out another drink. There wasn't much left in the bottle. "Well, I just might take care of you." He sipped and rocked. "If you got the money on hand, cash on the barrel. That's the only way I do business, cash on the barrel."

"I got it," Hugh affirmed.

"All right." The eyes sharpened. "You bring her out here tonight."

"Bring her tonight?" Hugh couldn't control his shock at the words. He hadn't planned on producing the imaginary girl, only the money for the trap. "You mean tonight?"

"That's what I said. Tonight. If you want me to do it." A slack smile came to the big mouth. "I'm thinking of taking a little trip down to Nogales tomorrow."

Did he need the hundred dollars to skip town while the heat was on? Possibly the police hadn't canceled out the possibility of Jopher's guilt; it could be Ringle was still nosing around. Innocent or guilty, Doc Jopher, unless his need was great, surely wouldn't be doing business until this canal case had been resolved. But the need could be for drink alone; it could be to replenish his wine cupboard that the doctor was going to Nogales. A hundred dollars would buy more spirits across the border than here. And the doc doubtless had half a dozen secret ways to carry it back over into Arizona. Exchange of favors.

Hugh was reluctant. "What time would you want me to come back?"

"Soon's you can make it. I'm not going nowhere tonight."

"I'll have to go tell her," Hugh said. He didn't know what he was going to do. But the boy he was acting would have been no less uncertain about it. It was difficult to get up from the chair; movement activated his pain.

"Don't forget to bring the money. It won't do you no good coming back here unless you can put cash on the barrel." The voice was good-natured.

"I'll bring it." Hugh started to the door, clumsy-footed, but the doctor wouldn't figure it was from pain. He'd expect "boy" to walk that way. The dog raised a lazy head and growled.

Doc Jopher's voice chuckled. "Where'd you get that fat lip, boy?"

Hugh half turned. There was no evil knowledge on the sodden face. Simply amusement.

Hugh touched his hand to his swollen mouth. "I got in a little trouble," he mumbled.

He went on out, closing the door on the doctor's wheezing laughter.

Hugh returned to the house by way of the kitchen door. He hadn't the strength to walk further. He went through to the living room. Ellen was alone in front of the fire, a book in her hands but she wasn't reading. There was coffee on the table. When she saw him, it was as if she were seeing a specter. The book dropped; she was on her feet. "What are you doing here? Where did you get those clothes?"

He just made it to the couch. "I borrowed them from Skye. I didn't have time to ask his permission." He tried to light a cigarette; his hand fumbled.

She held her lighter. She asked, "Where have you been?"

The smoke made his head whir, but he needed it. "I've been to see Doc Jopher."

She disbelieved, and then she accepted the truth. "He is the one?"

"I don't know yet. I'm to return. With my girl. And a hundred dollars."

"He accepted you?" She indicated his appearance.

"To him I'm a poor colored boy who's got a girl in trouble. He doesn't do colored, but for a hundred dollars he'll forget his principles." He said hopelessly, "Where can I get a hundred dollars at this time of night?" He'd expected Skye to be home; Skye could arrange it.

"I cashed a check yesterday. I could almost make it."

"I have about twenty." He hoped again.

"Won't he be suspicious of your producing that much tonight?"

"I've explained that. Work and a loan company." He put out his hand. "Will you—"

"You can't go now." She was appalled. "Not until you've rested."

"I must get back. Before he's too drunk to answer questions."

Her hand on his arm restrained him. "Wait until Skye returns. He can go with you to help."

Hugh's mouth flicked a smile. "There are plenty of white Negroes but I'm afraid Doc Jopher doesn't know it."

"Skye is as dark as I am," she returned. "Sun glasses would take care of his eyes—if Doc Jopher doesn't know about blue-eyed Negroes. And he could darken his hair."

"Skye is too well known. I can't take any chances now of Jopher getting suspicious." He rejected the idea entirely. "I must do this myself, Ellen." He tried to make her see it. "All I need is his admission that Iris was there, and the police can take over. They'll find the evidence. Not only of her presence but with luck of Fred O.'s as well." If nowhere else, on the old screen door.

"Then why can't they do it without you?"

"Because they don't believe he's guilty."

"But you think they'll believe you if you say he is?" There was a touch of scorn.

He didn't think they would, with no witnesses, only his word. But they wouldn't dare not check it out. He said, "It's the only hope left."

Without further word, she left the room. He poured himself a cup of coffee and with it swallowed another capsule. He needed as much artificial energy as he could tolerate for this night's work.

He was drinking a second cup of coffee when she returned. Her handbag was held close to her; she didn't open it. She asked, "What about your girl?"

He had this planned. "I won't have to produce the girl. I'll tell him she's out in the car. I'm sure he'll answer questions when he sees the money. He needs that money."

She said decisively, "I'm your girl."

"No!" The tortured word sprang from him. To think of her in that foul room was inconceivable. "I don't want you there."

"You need me," she said.

"I don't. I won't take you there. You don't know—"

"I'm not milk and sugar," she said. "I'm not afraid. I can play a part as well as you."

He looked long at her and made the final decision. "No."

"Then you aren't going, Hugh." Her hands tightened on the closed purse. "Because I won't let you go alone. Not in your condition."

He could wait for Houston. Wait for how long? For Doc Jopher to open another bottle of wine, to be too fuddled to speak? Ellen would not change her decision. He knew her strength too well to hope for that. He was defeated.

She saw it without his admission. "It won't take me five minutes to get ready." She handed the purse to him. "You'll wait for me?"

He took it. "I'll wait." It was his word.

He put the money together, crumpling the bills, some into one pocket, some into another. He kept out three twenties for her to carry. He might need to play for time.

She returned in little more than the five minutes. She hadn't disguised herself; she wore the same dress but had changed her pumps for beach sandals. With her lipstick rubbed away and her hair pulled back from her face into a rubber band, she didn't look the same girl. "I'm ready," she said. She put on a dark plaid coat. It was too big for her. "I found it in the hall closet."

He gave her the twenties and explained why. She divided them, two in the pocket of the coat, another in her handbag.

"The car is out back," he said. It took a little time to get to his feet but he was all right, no feeling of blackout, only the constant aching pains.

Half across the room she said, "Let me make sure I have the house key. Skye lent me one." She opened the purse, resting it on the back of the couch.

"The kitchen door was unlocked." He was impatient to get on with it.

"Marcia must have forgotten it when she left. We mustn't leave the house open."

While she searched, the portable bar caught his attention and with it a half-formed idea. He went to it and found among the bottles one of bourbon, half filled. Winos drank wine because wine was cheap. The promise of a real drink might make Jopher more talkative than the money.

"I found it," Ellen said.

Hugh shoved the bottle into his jacket pocket. It was very visible.

When they reached the car, she asked, "Shall I drive?"

"I can manage it." Physically it would have helped but he didn't want the effort of giving directions. He knew the way.

As they covered the now seemingly brief miles, neither of them tried to make conversation. The roads were lonely, only occasionally did the lights of a car flash in the rear-view mirror and disappear. He wished Ellen a million and one miles away, yet he knew his chances of success were better with her along. After they had turned into the country lane, he asked, "Can you talk southern?"

She shrugged. "I've been told not too well, northern comes through. If I have to speak I'll stay with 'Yes, suh' and 'No, suh'—" She saw the lonely house ahead. "That's it?"

"Yes. Don't be afraid, he won't touch you." But he was the one who was afraid.

As before, he put the car where it would be partially hidden at the far side of the house. He didn't dare add a drink to his medication but he opened the bottle and rinsed his mouth with the bourbon. Then he spilled a little on his hand and rubbed it on his shirt. He wanted Jopher to thirst. When he and Ellen approached the house, the dog set up his noisy barking. Under his breath, Hugh said, "He barks but he doesn't leave his easy chair."

They climbed the broken steps to the porch. Again Hugh rattled the screen. This time the porch light did not go on. The door opened its cautious slit, revealing the blurred eyes and big nose.

"So you're back," Doc Jopher said. He unhooked the screen. "Come in, come in, don't stand there."

Hugh pushed Ellen ahead, keeping himself between her and the doctor. While Jopher locked the door, Hugh pointed her toward the side windows where she could breathe a little fresh air. The dog muttered sleepily from his easy chair.

"You got the money?" Jopher demanded.

"Sure, I got it," Hugh answered, somewhat truculently.

The doctor poked his eyes at Ellen. "You sit down and keep quiet, girl." His voice was thick. "We'll take care of you after we get our business out of the way."

He saw Hugh's bottle as he passed. "You been celebrating, boy?" he asked slyly. "I might join you for a little drink when I'm through working." He shambled to the table and drained the last traces of wine from his glass. For some reason the dog lifted his head and growled. "You be quiet, Duke." The doctor nodded at Ellen. "He won't hurt you. He's a good old dog. I don't know what I'd do without old Duke." As if the sip had revived him, he turned to Hugh with sharp eyes. "Now, boy, you give me that hundred dollars and we'll get this over with."

Hugh didn't move. He let his voice be laden with doubt. "You're sure you'll do a good job on my girl? I wouldn't want nothing to happen to her."

Doc Jopher didn't take offense. "I'll do a good job." He held out his shaking hand for the money.

"I wouldn't want nothing to happen to her," Hugh repeated with hesitation. "Like what happened to that little white girl who got drowned in the canal."

"It wasn't my fault what happened to that girl," Doc Jopher said amiably. "She was all right when she left here."

Hugh began shaking as if with a chill. Fearful that the import of what he'd said would trickle through the doctor's sodden brain. And then he realized the doctor didn't care; this poor colored couple couldn't give him away without involving themselves. That business was over and done, and he couldn't wait too long between drinks.

"If you want me to take care of your girl, you just put up your money." The doc was losing patience. "Stop worrying about what don't concern you."

Hugh reached into his pocket. He began bringing out the crumpled bills, one at a time. "Fred O. says it's your fault," he whined. "He says you killed Bonnie Lee."

Ellen gave a little moan in the background. He didn't know if it was she or the assumed character giving way.

"Then he's lying to you, boy. He knows that girl walked out of here on her own two feet." Doc Jopher's palsied hand stretched out greedily.

Hugh fed it with a few bills. "That's what you say." He made his distrust evident by withdrawing, holding fast to the money in his fist. "But I don't see no operating table here. How you going to operate on somebody without no place to do it?"

The doctor's arm swept toward the battered couch. "Right there's where I'm going to do it. Like I always do. If it's a hospital you want, what'd you come here for?"

He mustn't let the doctor reject him, not this near to success. Hugh was quickly obsequious, the way he should be. "Oh, nossuh, nossuh." He made the accent strong. "I don't want no hospital, nossuh!"

"Then let's get this over with." The outstretched hand quivered across the table.

Hugh began to smooth a bill, and again he hesitated. "Don't you have no"—not instruments—"no tools?"

Doc Jopher's face twisted into a mammoth scowl. "Of course I got instruments," he thundered. "I'm a doctor, not a damn hatpin quack!" He lifted his glass to drink but it was empty. He slammed it on the table; it didn't break. The money was there in plain view, the money he evidently needed so desperately. For he made the great effort, erasing the wrath, putting on the kindly-old-man demeanor he wore for all the world to see. "Come here, you."

Unsure, Hugh followed him across to the couch.

"Stoop down, boy, you're younger'n I am. Stoop down and hand me that bag you find underneath there."

Hugh went to one knee. From the lint and dust he brought out the doctor's bag. Like his own but so old, so very old.

"Hand it here," Jopher said.

Hugh passed it up. He started to rise but the doctor halted him.

"Reach under again. There's a washbasin there. Feel it? Bring it out. That's right."

Hugh stood up, holding the chipped basin. Folded into it was a rubber sheet.

The doctor's forefinger indicated it. "Shake it out, spread it over the couch." There were old stains on the fabric but it wasn't dirty. It had been scrubbed. "That's right. Set that washbasin down, at the foot. There. Now, come over here."

Doc Jopher returned to the table, plumped his instrument bag in the center, under the pool of light. Hugh edged himself to a place across from him.

"Now, you look here." Jopher opened the bag. It wasn't locked. "You see this 'tool'?" He mocked the word. He was humoring a dumb, ignorant colored boy. Because he must have that money. Now. Tonight. Not when another case turned up. "And this?" He laid the clean, worn instruments in a row on the wine-mucked table. His hands were tender, fondling them. "Doctor's tools," he said, but this was to himself. "The finest you can buy." He straightened up tall; his watery eyes prodded Hugh. "You satisfied, boy?" He took silence for assent. "Then pay up and we'll get this job done. You can stay right here and watch I don't make no mistakes."

Hugh had more than he needed to go to the police. He passed across the rest of the money.

Doc Jopher counted in a monotone. The dog growled. "Keep quiet, Duke." He finished counting, not quite believing his tally. "There ain't but forty dollars here."

"She's got the rest of it," Hugh said quickly. He went over to where Ellen was. She looked up at him for direction. He gave an imperceptible nod and she got up from the chair. On some excuse, they must get out of here now. Unexpectedly, the dog's growl menaced.

The doctor said sharply, "Do you have that money or don't you?"

Ellen opened her purse and found the one twenty. The others she took from the coat pocket. As he took them, Hugh muttered, "Get ready to run if I can't. Send police . . ."

Holding the bills, he started back to the table. And saw the kitchen door opening. In the opening Ringle towered, a monstrous shadow. He moved without sound into the room. Behind him crept the cat smile of Venner.

Ringle spoke. "I'll take that money, Doc."

Slowly Doc Jopher turned and saw them. For a moment he stood there, peering through his bleared eyes, not understanding. Then as Ringle advanced into the pool of lamplight, all hope sagged out of his old body, leaving it an empty sack. He fumbled for the wine bottle; its emptiness was the final betrayal. Still holding the bottle, he sank into the rocking chair. After a moment he put it to his mouth. His tongue licked the stain from the rim.

Ringle took a ponderous step toward Hugh. With satisfaction he recited, "I'm arresting you and Doc Jopher on conspiracy to commit an illegal operation. And for contributing to the death of a minor."

Hugh cried out, "Don't you understand?" but he saw that it was useless. He shouted, "Run, Ellen," as he himself advanced toward the two detectives. The club of Ringle's hand knocked him to the floor. She didn't make it. Venner, triumph staining his eyes, caught her at the door.

Hugh didn't lose consciousness. He knew every anguished moment of being hauled up and away, half flung into the back of the police car with Ellen and the old doctor. He knew the writhing pain of every yard of the drive back to Scottsdale. Ellen held him against her shoulder. His mouth was bleeding again.

Half along the way he became aware of Jopher's whisper. "The bottle. You didn't break the bottle when you fell?" He hadn't. The two detectives in the front seat weren't paying any heed. Venner was riding the wheel, Ringle growling into the radio. Hugh worried the bourbon from his pocket and thrust it into the avid hands. The doctor opened it, wiped the rim with his open palm and took a long, shuddering swallow. He recapped and fumbled it back toward Hugh.

"Keep it," Hugh slurred. "You need it."

Doc Jopher sighed. "You're a gentleman." He tipped it again briefly before putting it into his own pocket.

The expression on the faces of the deputies on duty at the Scottsdale station was to be expected, an almost weary and matter-of-fact acceptance that two shabby young Negroes were guilty until proven innocent. There was confirmation, seeing Ringle and Venner in charge. When they recognized Jopher, their mouths took on cynical knowledge.

"Sit down over there." Ringle pointed to the straight chairs against the wall. "We're waiting till the marshal gets here."

Hugh came out of despair. Marshal Hackaberry had been summoned, either by Ringle or as a result of Ringle's radio communication. Ellen helped him to a chair, eased him into it. She sat beside him. The shine of anger never left her eyes. Hugh spoke under his breath. "When the marshal comes, he'll let us telephone Skye," and he said, "Take that crazy rubber band off your hair."

She said, "Skye isn't home." She let her hair fall about her face. Without apology she told him, "I left a note where we'd be. On the couch when I was opening my purse."

At the time he might have been annoyed. Now he was grateful.

She said, "I'll try, but if he was home, he'd have traced us by now."

And if he didn't get here in time, Hugh wouldn't be believed. He'd be formally charged. But Skye should have returned by this hour—and then he saw by the wall clock that it wasn't yet midnight. It had seemed near to dawn.

Doc Jopher was incongruously at ease in this room with its too-bright lighting. He knew all the officers by name. And it would seem they had a special niche for him, as for one of the pet regulars, no matter the crime. He didn't move toward the chairs but away from them.

Ringle ordered again, "You too, Doc. Over there."

"I just want a cup of water." He drew his mouth into a pout. "Can't I have a cup of water?"

"Get your water and sit down." Ringle went to the desk just outside the marshal's door. He had a report to write.

Doc Jopher walked to the water fountain and filled a cup.

The deputy at communications said, "Sorry we got no ice, Doc."

"How do you like that?" Venner had spied the bottle. "Now Scottsdale's furnishing setups." He brayed laughter. "How do you like that?" He went over to make sure Ringle had caught the joke.

Jopher drank the water with dignity and filled the cup again. He ambled over to the chair next to Hugh and sat down, not spilling a drop. He proceeded to mix bourbon in the cup. If he was drunk, he was brilliantly so. The laughter at his antics was his applause. No one made a move to take his bottle.

He tasted and smacked his lips. But mixing a highball at the police station wasn't just a stunt to amuse an audience. Hugh recognized again the shrewd brain, the doctor who knew his tolerance to alcohol and who measured his dosage. There had been no room in the cup for more than a flavoring. In spite of the drinks on the way, the drive in must have brought to him a measure of sobriety. Which he had no intent of destroying. He knew the ropes. He knew the buffoon got a better deal from the cops than a straight man would.

He sipped and smacked until the laughter died. Then he began to talk. "Look, Mr. Ringle, you know I wasn't going to do nothing to this girl. I was just leading the niggers on to see how far they'd go." His appeal was jovial. "Then I was going to kick them out, you bet I was, right on their butts. First thing in the morning I was going to get me to a telephone and tell you all about it."

Ringle didn't look up. "Save it for the judge, Doc."

"You got no right to arrest me," Jopher complained. "You're a Phoenix cop. I live in the county."

This time Ringle looked at him. "Come off it, Doc. If you want to get technical, Marshal Hackaberry's got the right. He's county and city both."

"Well, I don't call that fair," Jopher said.

"You'll have to take that up with Hackaberry."

Jopher sulked audibly while he emptied his cup. "Is there any rule about getting a drink of water?" he began.

But the sound of boots on the outside stairs hushed him. He pushed the paper cup quickly under the chair.

The marshal came in. A swift glance covered the room and filed essential information. His boots were noisy as he stalked across to Ringle at the desk.

Ringle was standing. "We caught them both red-handed," he said with satisfaction. "Densmore was setting up another girl with the doc."

The marshal's side glance at the three was brief.

"You have your report?"

"I'm working on it."

"We'll go inside," Hackaberry announced.

He waited for Ringle and Venner to precede him. One of the deputies came over to the three. He gestured with his thumb.

"Me too?" Jopher asked in disdain.

"You too."

With Ellen's assistance, Hugh fumbled to his feet. The deputy asked, "Need any help?"

"I can make it."

The marshal was waiting. He didn't say anything about Hugh's condition, he merely observed it. When they came abreast, Hugh asked him, "May I call my lawyer?"

"He's not home. Go on, call him. I did, but he's not home."

Ellen went to the booth. The marshal motioned Hugh into the office. The deputy went with him. There were chairs for everyone tonight. This wasn't the informal gathering. The deputy helped Hugh to sit down. He didn't know how long he could last. His pain was frantic, but he mustn't black out until he could defend himself.

Ellen joined him, shaking her head. A deputy stood guard at the door. Ringle ignored everyone, pushing his pencil stub across the paper. Venner scuffed about the small room, whistling tunelessly between his teeth, too excited for silence. And Doc Jopher protested his innocence in a dozen maudlin ways. Still the marshal didn't join them. Not even when Skye came rushing in.

He scraped a chair over to where Hugh and Ellen were. "My God, what have you got yourself into?" he asked under his breath, and of Ellen, "Why did you let him go out?"

"I couldn't stop him." With fury, she said, "Ringle knocked him down."

"He just pushed too hard." Hugh smiled wryly and felt the encrusted blood flow again. He covered it with his stained handkerchief.

"When I read Ellen's note I checked here before tearing out to Doc's. I was afraid your idea might backfire."

"I've got Jopher," Hugh mumbled. "He admitted Bonnie Lee was there."

"Can you make it stand up?"

"The police can. We tried to call you."

"I've spent the evening at the bus depot," Skye said. "I found some men who can quote Fred Othy on Bonnie Lee. Before he got cautious." Before she was with child. "Just what happened at Doc's?"

It was too hard to talk; Hugh let Ellen whisper it. She hadn't finished before Fred O. was brought in by an officer. And the marshal followed.

When Othy saw Hugh and the doctor, he began a shrill protest. "Whose idea is it dragging me down here in the middle of the night? I've told you what happened."

The officer said, "Sit down and shut up." There was a small scuffle before the officer put him into a chair.

"I'm not going to be framed," Othy yelled. "I want a lawyer."

"Look, you're not arrested," the officer said. "What you want with a lawyer, when you're not even arrested?" Temporarily, Fred O. subsided.

Skye intercepted Hackaberry. What they said was private. When Skye took a place by Hugh's side, he didn't speak. The marshal went to his desk. "Okay, Ringle."

Ringle's report made it clear that he and Venner hadn't just happened to turn up at Jopher's. A Scottsdale cruiser had spotted Hugh's car heading north. The deputies didn't have to move in; they knew the road. Knew that particular lane, where Hugh turned off, led only to Doc Jopher's and tilled fields beyond. The information was relayed to the Phoenix detectives.

Ringle abandoned the report for discourse. It was easier for him. "We didn't drive up to the house. That dog of Doc's would raise the dead the way he barks when he hears anybody coming. But his ears aren't as good as they once were if you come quiet. I noticed that the last time we were out at Doc's. I had on my crepe soles and he never heard me till I was on the porch. So tonight when we got the call, I changed to them."

Venner said, "I had a pair of sneakers," but he didn't try to take the stage from Ringle.

The big detective continued placidly, "We knew we'd have to catch Densmore red-handed or not get nowhere. We left the car down the lane and the dog never heard us approach. We saw the whole thing through the window." His chuckle was only in the shape of his lips. "With that old dog snoring in his chair right on the other side." The moment of fun was so brief it might have been imagined. "Densmore passed some money to the doc, then the two of them went over to the couch and Densmore took out the doc's bag from underneath and handed it to him."

Oh, God, they hadn't been able to hear, only to see what went on!

"Next thing Densmore took a basin and a rubber sheet from under the couch. He spread the sheet on top and put the basin on it. They came back to the table then and the doc took some instruments out of his bag. After he and Densmore looked them over, Densmore gave the doc the rest of the money he was holding. Then Densmore went over to get the girl, and that's when we moved. We weren't going to let them go through with it."

"You don't understand!" Hugh repeated his cry.

"Keep quiet," the marshal barked. "You'll get your chance to talk."

Ringle went on smoothly, "We entered by the kitchen door." He didn't mention how they had made entry through Jopher's locked doors. "Took them red-handed. I had it figured by then why we couldn't get nothing on Densmore. He didn't use the motel room or his own stuff. He was working in partners with Doc."

Venner said, "Yeah." With satisfaction.

"That's it?" the marshal asked Ringle.

"That's about it." He put his big hands on his knees. "The details will be in the report."

The silence seemed long before the marshal addressed Hugh. "What have you to say?"

Hugh didn't try to rise. It was difficult enough just to speak.

He said, "I never saw Doc Jopher until tonight. I was never in that house until tonight. Doc Jopher was the one who aborted Bonnie Lee."

"He's lying," Othy snorted. "It was him."

"You keep quiet," the marshal ordered. "Wait your turn." He gestured Hugh, "Go on. So why did you go to Doc's tonight?"

Hugh told him. Forcing down the pain which enveloped him; forbidding it to take over until he was done. He told how he knew what he must do, and what he did; from the hapless search for Mahm Gitty to the conclusion at Jopher's.

The marshal must know it was the truth. It was the truth. Yet he said noncommittally, "That's your story." One story against another story and another story.

Hugh insisted, "Send your lab men out there. They'll find her fingerprints. Othy's too. Doc Jopher admitted he did it." He had a witness. He indicated Ellen. "Before both of us."

Othy hooted. "You going to listen to two niggers and a drunk old hoss doctor?" But fear was on him.

It could have been the professional insult. It could have been the bottle Hugh had given him. It could have been Doc Jopher knew when to sing. "Othy brought the girl to me. He waited while I took care of her."

Othy was on his feet. "Shut your mouth, you fat slob!"

Doc Jopher's eyes became venomous stones. "She walked out of there with him. She was just as live as him or me when she walked out with him."

Marshal Hackaberry said dispassionately to Othy, "The lab's found some dog hairs in your mother's car. You folks don't have a dog. Doc does. Might be they'll match up."

Othy shouted, "I didn't kill her. It was the doc!" The officer restrained him.

The marshal raised a decisive voice. "She was killed by a blow on the head. It was inflicted while she was alive. There was no debris in the canal. The Zanjaros checked after the locks were closed for the night. The locks were still closed when the girl's body was found. Nothing could have gone through them."

Doc Jopher's words quavered. "You know I didn't kill that poor little girl, Marshal. I wouldn't do a thing like that. Maybe I tried to help her in a way I oughtn't. Like I've tried to help other poor little girls that come crying to me. It's not my fault

I got a soft heart. I can't stand to hear them crying when I'm a doctor and know I can help them. But I wouldn't kill anybody."

It could have been a performance, the tragedian now. But at least a part of it was real. And it was real later when the deputy started to take him away.

"If you lock me up, who's going to take care of poor old Duke?" He began to cry. Real tears.

The marshal said brusquely, "Don't worry about that, Doc. We'll see to Duke until you get back."

For he would come back. Even if it came to complicity in murder, he wouldn't serve too long. He knew the ropes, the ingratiating deeds, the good behavior, the sentiment he could engender. He'd come back to carry on with his butcher's business.

Before that, a cursing Fred Othy had been led out. Last of all, Ringle and Venner went away. Ringle, stolidly; so he'd made one miscalculation, but on the whole he wasn't dissatisfied. He'd helped run Othy and Jopher to ground, not by risk and chance but by unspectacular routine. Venner departed with the hate still ugly in his eyes, with more hate for an innocent Hugh than for a guilty. The Venners would not be changed in their generation.

Hugh witnessed it all. And the aftermath hubbub of Ellen and Skye and the marshal filling in details. He didn't want to spoil their celebration but he knew he couldn't hold on much longer. If he could get outside to the car, he could lie down and wait.

He heard the marshal's slow western twang. It wasn't triumphant. "With any luck, we'll send Doc Jopher up for a longer spell than usual. But there'll be another Jopher. And another telephone number. And another old woman. Another and another and another. There'll always be abortionists just as there'll always be prostitutes and pimps and pushers. When man wants an evil, he'll always find someone evil to supply him."

Carefully, Hugh lifted himself from the chair. He took one step, and the floor rose up and crashed into his face.

8

SUCH A short time ago, he had traveled this road from Westwood to Phoenix. Now, such a long time later, he was traveling it from Phoenix back to Westwood. He had been light-hearted then; he wondered if he would ever again know that same careless happiness. He wondered if he would ever be cleansed of his innocent guilt.

By mid-afternoon he would be in Blythe; before sundown, in Indio. He would not stop in either place. After being treated as an invalid for almost a week, he was in pretty good shape. Even if his face did still bear considerable resemblance to that of a broken-down prizefighter's. By evening he would be making the rounds at Med Center. Just as if nothing had happened. Just as if he'd never been away.

His name had been in the papers. Not in the headlines, not as a suspected criminal, not as a Negro. Embedded in the story of the arrest of Fred Othy and Dr. Oren Jopher was a paragraph:

"Marshal H. C. Hackaberry stated that the discovery of Dr. Jopher's part in the case was made through the co-operation of Dr. Hugh Densmore of Los Angeles, a visitor in Phoenix. Dr. Densmore first became suspicious of Dr. Jopher's activities after learning from a friend, Skye Houston, attorney, of the conflicting stories given the police by the suspect, Fred Othy."

No more than that. It all might have to come out at the trial. He would return as a witness. Along with little Lora and bewildered Mr. Crumb and a handful of bus drivers and Doc Jopher turning state's witness. But he wouldn't be afraid to speak up then. He was no longer the expendable one.

Fred O. continued to deny killing Bonnie Lee. And why had he? She must have threatened to expose him, as they sat there in the car on Indian School Road after it was over. She hadn't come to Phoenix for this ugly thing; she had come with her secret hoard to buy a beautiful wedding dress, to begin a grand new life. Had she demanded that he free himself and marry her? Or did she make what would be the first of interminable demands for money? Whatever it was, he had panicked and killed her.

There was so much to remember. Not just the sad and the bitter moments, but the good ones as well. You'd think he was a bloody hero the way the family carried on. And Skye. And a friendly marshal. Everyone but Ellen. She didn't care to talk about it.

The road was winding through Wickenberg. Hugh spoke to her. "Hungry?"

Her smile was wide. "After your grandmother's breakfast?"

He wondered if she had been remembering too. The big farewell dinner his grandmother served last night. With Skye the honor guest. And Skye and Ellen silhouetted in the doorway as they said good-bye to each other.

Hugh had walked away, leaving them together. That was when Edward, just emerging from the dining room, put an envelope in his hand. "Houston asked me to give you this." The bill. Hugh didn't open it until he was alone. Not that he was afraid to see it. Whatever the amount, he could pay. He had a future ahead. When he did look at it, he couldn't believe. Carefully itemized, the total read: $10,000. Across it was stamped: *Paid in Full.* And scrawled, by Skye's own hand, was the notation. "I told you I was expensive. I didn't tell you my war chest was already full. I don't need your money. I'll take it out in trade when I get my ulcer."

Remembering so many things he would never forget. They were in open country again. Sand and horizon and the far-off hills. Hugh said, it had to be said, "If things had been different, it might have been you and Skye, mightn't it?"

She didn't hesitate. "They would have had to be very different."

"If he hadn't been married—"

Her words were simple. "If he hadn't been white."

Somehow it surprised him. "That would matter to you?"

"Yes," she said. "It's too soon. I'm not that strong."

"You have more strength than any woman I know."

"Not enough for that."

She was silent for a little while. Then she said, "I love Skye. I'll always love him. There are different ways of loving. Even if he weren't white, even if he weren't married, I wouldn't marry him unless I couldn't have the man I want."

Hugh couldn't look at her. There was a truck ahead, he had

to keep his eyes on the road. He waited until the truck driver gave him the signal to come around, and until he had negotiated the passing. Then he spoke, quite casually, he hoped.

"How long will you be in Los Angeles?"

"It depends upon how interesting I find your campus."

"I won't have much time," he despaired. "I've two weeks' vacation to make up."

"I'm in no hurry," she said.

For an instant, he took his eyes off the road. She was smiling. Not at him, but at the certainty of the coming-true of the plans they both were making.

THE SCORE

Richard Stark

ONE

I

WHEN THE bellboy left, Parker went over to the house phone and made his call. He gave the operator downstairs the number he wanted, and waited while the phone clicked and ticked and snicked in his ear. He was feeling impatient, and he was about to go downstairs and put in the call from a pay phone when all the clicking finally quit and a ringing sound started instead.

Parker counted the rings, just as Paulus was doing at the other end, and while he waited and counted he looked around at the room. It was just a hotel room, the same as any. Because it was in Jersey City, it might be a little grimier than most, that's all.

On the eighth ring, the nosy operator came on, saying, "Your party doesn't seem to be answering, sir."

"He moves slow," Parker told her. "Let it ring."

"Yes, sir."

He tensed and relaxed his shoulder muscles, hunching and relaxing, hunching and relaxing. He'd flown up, and being in a plane always made his shoulders stiff. Thirteen, fourteen, fifteen. Sixteen. Where the hell was he?

The ringing stopped, just before seventeen, and a voice said, "Hello?" The voice sounded wary. Paulus had always been a damn fool.

"Hello," said Parker. "I'm here."

"Oh. You made good time."

There was nothing to say to that. Parker waited.

Paulus cleared his throat, and said, "Come on over."

"Now?"

"Sure. We're all here. You got the address?"

If he said no, Paulus would sure as hell give it to him over the phone. Wary one second, bigmouthed the next. He said, "I've got it."

"Fine."

"I'll want to change first. I just got in."

"Any time."

Parker hung up, shook his head, and lit a cigarette. Paulus would die in jail; it had to happen. He was a good organizer, a good tactician, but he moved through the world like a movie spy, screaming for some cop to look at him twice.

Parker unpacked his suitcase, stripped, took a shower, put on fresh clothes, and left the hotel. Downstairs, he bought a city map at the tobacco counter and sat in one of the leatherette chairs to find his route. Cabdrivers keep a log, so he didn't want to take a cab.

He found Fourth Street, found the block the address should be on, and traced it out from where he was. It was maybe twelve blocks at the most, so he could walk it. If it had been farther away, he would have walked a couple of blocks and then taken a cab to within a few blocks of the address. This way was even better.

He tucked the map in his inside jacket pocket, left the lobby, and started walking. He walked four blocks. Halfway down the fifth block he realized he'd made a wrong turn. He turned around and started back. A guy who'd just come around the corner looked startled, hesitated, made his face blank, and came on. They passed each other, the guy looking straight ahead. Parker had seen that face before, in the hotel lobby.

Fine. Well, it was nice to know before getting into the operation too deep. Paulus had been overdue for years, and this was the time.

Except the guy hadn't looked like law. He was undersized. Most police departments have a height requirement, to boost their self-confidence. And he'd been dressed like a bum, in work pants and brown leather jacket, and wore on his face the gray, pinched look of the loser. He didn't look like law at all.

Parker hesitated at the corner, not looking back. The simplest thing would be to go to the hotel, pack, check out, go to Newark Airport, call Paulus from a pay phone there to warn him, and take the next plane to Miami. If the guy had looked even a little bit like law, that's what Parker would have done. But this way, it was a problem. Before he could know what to do, he'd have to find out what the guy was.

He turned right and started walking again. He'd heard the sound of a train whistle a while ago, one of those diesel blasts, from over in this direction.

He hadn't been law, but Parker already knew that. What he'd been, he still didn't know. He put the wallet in his own pocket; maybe Paulus would know. Then he left and walked down to the next intersection and looked at the street signs. There was a streetlight there; under it Parker opened his city map and found out where he was and how to get where he was going.

It was six blocks before he saw anybody at all.

2

PAULUS OPENED the door, looking wary, and then smiled a greeting when he saw it was Parker. "Come on in," he said, holding the door wide. "We been waiting for you." He was short, slender, balding, forty. He was wearing a thin brown suit and a thin brown tie, and he looked like a timid accountant.

Parker stepped into the apartment, took the door away from Paulus and shut it. "The deal's queered," he said.

They were standing in a little empty foyer with a spaceship light fixture up above and an oriental rug below. Paulus blinked rapidly and said, "What? What? What do you mean?"

"Somebody was following me."

Paulus switched to relief again, the way he'd done when he'd seen it was Parker at the door. "Oh," he said, throwing it away. "That doesn't mean anything."

"It doesn't mean anything?"

"I know all about it, Parker." Paulus patted at his arm, trying to get him moving. "Come on in, we're all here, Edgars will explain it to you."

Parker didn't move. "*You* explain, Paulus," he said.

Paulus looked troubled, unhappy. "I think it would be better if Edgars told you the situ—"

"I think it would be better if *you* did," Parker told him. "He's dead."

Paulus now was just blank. "What? Who?"

"Edward Owen. The guy who was tailing me."

"You *killed* him? For Christ's sake, why?" Paulus' tone was intense, but his volume had dropped, as though he didn't want any chance of somebody else in the apartment hearing him.

Parker answered him at normal volume. "He was tailing me. I stopped him to find out why, and he pulled a knife."

Paulus shook his head. "I don't know, Parker," he said. "That's a hell of a thing. I don't know what to tell you."

"Tell me how come you knew I was going to be tailed. Tell me why I was being tailed. And tell me whose idea it was to tail me."

"It was Edgars'," Paulus said, still very soft-voiced. "Owen was his man."

Parker glanced at the entranceway that led deeper into the apartment. "Who the hell is Edgars anyway? I don't remember the name."

"You don't know him, he's never worked an operation like this before."

"Then what's he doing here?"

"He set this one up."

"Oh, Christ." Parker shook his head. "The deal's no good," he said. "I can see that already. See you around, Paulus." He reached for the doorknob.

"Wait a second, wait a second." Paulus was getting agitated, but his voice wasn't rising. "Let me explain, will you?"

"You don't have to. This moron Edgars is an amateur, but he's the one setting this job up. He doesn't know me, so he doesn't trust me, so he puts a tail on me to see if I come straight here or do I go see somebody else first because maybe I'm planning a cross."

"You can't blame him, Parker, he—"

"I don't blame him. I don't work with him, either."

A heavy type in a brown suit with a beer can in his hand came through the entranceway, scowling. "What's the holdup here?" He looked at Paulus, and then at Parker. He had heavy black brows, and they were down in a V now to show he was irritated.

Paulus was now really fidgeting. "Edgars," he said, "this is Parker. There's been a—something's come up—there was a misunderstanding."

"What kind of a misunderstanding?" He was trying to act dangerous, but instead he was acting like a ward politician.

Parker waited to see how Paulus would handle it, but Paulus couldn't handle it at all. All he could do was fidget and look around and clear his throat. So Parker said, "You put a man to tail me."

Edgars shrugged. "So what? I want to know who I do business with, that's all."

"He pulled a knife when I called him."

Edgars scowled. "He did? That was stupid; I don't condone that. I'll have a talk with him."

"Not right away you won't."

"What's that supposed to mean?"

"Tell him, Paulus."

Edgars turned his head and scowled at Paulus, waiting. Paulus fidgeted and cleared his throat, and finally he said, "He's dead, that's what he means."

"Dead! You killed him?"

Parker shrugged, and it was Paulus who answered: "He didn't have any choice, Edgars. Your man pulled a knife on him. He didn't know the situation."

"I don't like that," said Edgars. "I don't like that at all."

Parker took the dead man's wallet out and held it out to Edgars. "I took this off him."

Edgars took the wallet and frowned at it. "I don't understand this," he said.

Parker nodded. "I know. See you, Paulus." He reached for the doorknob again.

Edgars said, "Hold on there. Where the hell are you going?"

"I'm out," Parker told him. He pulled the door open.

"Wait." Edgars waved his hands a little. "Will you wait a goddam minute?"

"For what?"

Edgars grimaced, looked again at the wallet he was holding and then at Paulus. Paulus just looked uncomfortable. Edgars said, "Paulus, tell the others we'll be in in a minute."

"Sure thing." Paulus went, happy to be off the hook.

Parker was still standing in the doorway, half in and half out. Edgars said to him, "Wait one minute while we talk, all right?"

Parker shrugged. He'd come this far, he could stick around a little longer. He came back in and shut the door.

Edgars looked around the empty foyer and said, "I wish there was some place we could sit down."

"It doesn't matter."

"All right, I guess not." Edgars looked at the wallet again with distaste and stuck it into a side pocket of his suitcoat. Then he gnawed his lower lip and glanced at the entranceway leading into the apartment. Looking off that way, he said, "Maybe Paulus told you, this is the first time I've been involved in something like this."

"He told me. He didn't have to, but he did."

Edgars managed a sour grin and looked out at Parker from under his eyebrows. "Sticks out all over, huh?"

"Yes."

"You and Paulus and the others," Edgars said, "you all know each other, know what to expect from each other. I don't know any of you at all. When I'm around you, my back itches."

Parker nodded. "Sure."

"You boys aren't exactly saints."

"So why get involved?"

"A quarter of a million dollars, for one thing. And personal reasons."

"Paulus is in with you," Parker told him. "And the others. You don't need me."

"They tell me you're the best. They tell me you can keep an operation together better than anybody, and you can get the best men to work with you."

"So why should I work with you?"

Edgars nodded. "That's a fair question," he said. He reached inside his coat and took out a cigar in an aluminum tube. While he opened it, he said, "I've made mistakes already, I can see that. Putting Owen on you. Maybe getting Paulus. I don't know what else." He motioned with his head, saying, "There's three men in there knew I was putting Owen on you, knew I'd put Owen on each of them when they showed up. They didn't act happy about it, but they didn't stop me. I need somebody to stop me making mistakes."

Parker shook his head. "That's not my kind of work."

"Wait a minute, now, don't get me wrong. I don't want to *run* this deal, for Christ's sake."

"You give a good imitation."

"I've been setting it up, that's all. I've been trying to get a group of professionals together to work *with* me on this, without getting a fast shuffle for me out of it."

"Sure," said Parker. "You had a problem, I see that."

"So what else could I do?"

"Stay all the way out, or come all the way in. Half and half doesn't do it."

"How can I come all the way in until I know what I'm getting myself into?"

"Then stay out."

Edgars shook his head stubbornly. "There's too much at stake."

"Not my problem."

Edgars gnawed his lip. He had the cigar unwrapped now but hadn't lit it. He rolled it back and forth between his fingers. After a minute, he shrugged heavy shoulders and said, "All right. All the way in. I'll give you the setup and then I'll do whatever you say."

Parker considered. "Paulus is in there," he said, "and Wycza. Who's the third?"

"Grofield."

"All right. They're all all right. This is a five-man operation?"

"Oh, no. These are just the department heads."

Parker stared at him. "The what?"

"It'll take probably twenty-five or thirty men," Edgars told him.

Parker looked at him as though he were crazy. "You don't have anything at all," he told him. "Twenty-five or thirty men? If a job takes more than four or five men, it's no job. You can put that down as a rule."

"This is a special case."

"Sure it is. Goodbye, Edgars."

"Will you God damn it stop leaving?"

Parker didn't like to do a lot of superfluous talking, but he took the time now to tick off the points for Edgars: "You got an operation needs an army, and the more men in a job the more chance it'll go sour. You got an operation set up by an amateur, for personal reasons. Amateurs get their ideas from the movies, which means flashy and impractical, and personal reasons are no good in a job because they get in the way of clear thinking. Forget it, Edgars."

"God damn it, Parker, you're the man I've been waiting for." Edgars was smiling happily now. He said, "I *know* this is a good solid deal, but I want a professional to *tell* me so, and you're it. All you have to do is hear me out. When I'm done if you don't think it's workable, then I'll give up the whole idea and I'll pay your fare back where you came from. Fair enough?"

Parker studied him. "Aren't you afraid I'll tell you it's no good, and then go do it on my own?"

"No, I'm not."

"Why not? I'm no saint."

"No, but you're a good businessman."

"What gives you that idea? You don't know anything about me at all."

"I've got a hunch, that's all. Will you listen to the deal?"

Parker thought about it. He didn't see any way an operation requiring twenty-five or thirty men could be workable, and he didn't see any way an operation Edgars was connected with could be workable, but he was here already so he might as well listen. He nodded. "All right."

"Fine. Come on in. You want a beer?"

"All right."

"I'll get it." They crossed the living room, a square sparsely furnished room lit by pole lamps, and Edgars pointed at a door just off the hallway. "They're in there. I'll be right in."

They separated at the hallway, Edgars going for the beer, Parker going into the room with the others. It was a long narrow room with another spaceship ceiling light. The walls were tan, with lighter squares where paintings had once hung, and there was a wall-to-wall green carpet on the floor. Paulus and Grofield and Wycza were sitting around a dining-room table. There was a slide projector on the table and a screen set up at the far end of the room.

Paulus gave him a nervous smile. Wycza, a huge bald man who did professional wrestling when times were bad, waved a beer can in greeting. Grofield, an intense, lean, handsome man who sometimes acted in summer stock theaters, said, "Hail, Parker. Long time no see."

"How are you, Grofield?"

Paulus said, "Are you in, Parker?"

"I don't know yet."

Grofield said, "Herr Edgars is a mysterious type. Did he tell *you* what the job is?"

"Not yet."

Edgars came in, then, with a double handful of beer cans, and Grofield said, "All fools in a circle."

Edgars laughed. "I hope not, Grofield," he said, and passed the beer around. Then he checked his slide projector, turned it on, and said, "Paulus, would you get the light, please?" He was full of confidence again.

Paulus got up and switched off the light. The projector was beaming a harsh white light at the screen, and it reflected back to give the five men pale faces and vague outlines.

There was a clicking, and the blank face of the screen was replaced by a black and white map. Edgars' voice said, "There it is. Copper Canyon, North Dakota."

Parker looked at the map, trying to make sense out of it, but it was just geometric confusion. He lit a cigarette, and waited.

Edgars moved around the table to the front of the room. He had a pointer with him now, like a geography teacher. "This wavy line," he said, and the pointer ran along a U-shaped irregular line that edged the town on three sides, "is the cliffs. The city is built inside a box canyon, with vertical cliffs on three sides, too steep and too tall to be passable. The only way in or out of town is here"—the pointer tapped—"at the open side of the canyon. State road 22A comes in here, and this here is a spur line of the Dakota and Western Railway. The one road and the railway line are the only means of entry to the town."

Parker silently shook his head. Everything Edgars said made the deal sound worse. You don't go into a box with only one exit, never.

Edgars kept moving the pointer, tapping here and there. "It's a one-industry town," he said. "Copper. The mine entrances are at the rear of the canyon, here, and the refinery is spread along here. Twelve buildings, storm fencing along here, two gates here and here, both with armed guards day and night, though the plant is working only during the day. There are two banks, here and here, in about the middle of town, opposite each other on Raymond Avenue, the continuation of 22A. There are three jewelry stores, here and here and here, all on Raymond Avenue. The police station is here, on Caulkins Street, near the east gate to the plant."

Parker waited for him to get to the point. He kept telling them about things, banks and jewelry stores and factory gates, but he hadn't gotten around yet to telling them what he thought they were going to hit. The fan in the slide projector made a humming sound, and Edgars kept on pointing at things.

"The telephone company building," he was saying, "is over here on Blake Street, a block from Raymond. There's a local radio station, with studios here on Whittier Street, but it shuts down operation between midnight and six-thirty in the morning, and there's no one on duty there during the night. The Nationwide Finance and Loan Corporation has offices on the second floor of the Merchants' Bank building. Most stores and other commercial operations are centered along this four-block stretch of Raymond Avenue, with the banks and jewelry stores." The pointer was removed, and Edgars' pale face turned to them. "That's it," he said.

Wycza said, "That's what?"

But Parker already had it. "You're crazy," he said.

"Am I?" Edgars was grinning, pleased with himself. "There are three men on duty in the police station at night, two out in the patrol car and the third in the station to take calls. The plant security force at night is also three, one man on each gate and one man in the front office of the main building to take calls. The banks and jewelry stores and so on have no night security of their own at all. The telephone company has three woman employees on duty at night, and the door to their building isn't even kept locked. After midnight, the radio station isn't broadcasting. There is one road and one railway line to watch, to keep townsmen in and reinforcements out. Due to vandalism of juvenile delinquents, there's been a midnight curfew in town for the last four years."

Wycza was beginning to get it. He said, "Hey, wait a minute, wait a minute."

Grofield laughed out loud.

Paulus whispered, "Sweet Jesus."

"We go in at midnight," Edgars told them. "We pop every safe in town, and we're out by six A.M. Two miles south of where this map leaves off there's the main east-west highway, and from there the whole state network of roads is open to us."

Parker said, "State police."

The pointer slapped the map, down near the bottom. "Substation here on 22A, two miles south of the town limits. State and city are differing political faiths, there's friction. State troopers never patrol north of the city line."

Parker said, "All night diner."

Edgars shook his head. "None. Curfew, remember? There's a Howard Johnson out on the highway; that's where the troopers go."

Parker shook his head. “Five minutes after we leave, they’ll be burning up the phone wires behind us. There’ll be a roadblock at the highway before we get to it.”

“We can arrange things to give ourselves more time. Break radio and telephone equipment, wreck a truck or two across the road, tie and gag policemen and telephone operators and the rest. We’ll have to figure out where we hide out afterwards, of course. We wouldn’t want to be on the road too long.”

Paulus, over on his side of the table, was shaking his head in wonder. “It could be done,” he whispered. “It honest to Christ could be done.”

But Parker wasn’t satisfied. The operation broke too many rules. Set up by an amateur. Requiring too many men. Involving going into a box with only one way out. And it was just too big and fantastic an idea to begin with, it was science fiction.

Edgars said, “It’s time to talk about money. Payday at the refinery is Friday. Thursday night there’s approximately sixty thousand in the refinery safe. The two banks should have between fifty and seventy-five thousand in cash each. Give them the low figure, that’s a hundred thousand from the two banks. Three jewelry stores, cash and gems, among them they ought to be good for another fifty thousand at the very least. The loan company and department store and other stores and commercial operations, maybe fifty thousand more all told. There’s a minimum of a quarter million dollars in that town, maybe more. With twenty-five men on equal shares, that’s a minimum of ten thousand a man.”

“Ten thousand? That’s not much, for the risk.”

“That’s a *minimum*. There may be more.”

Paulus said, “Maybe it could be done with less men, Parker.”

“You’d know more about that than I would,” Edgars told him.

Grofield said, musingly, “If it could be done at all, it would be fascinating.”

Wycza said, “I don’t like that state police barracks. And I don’t like not having any getaway figured out.”

“One thing at a time,” said Paulus. “Why don’t we think about manpower first?”

Edgars’ face, even in the semidarkness, showed an excitement that didn’t go with his ward politician features. “The way

I thought of it," he said, "would be almost like a commando raid. Each of the five of us would captain a group of five men, including himself. Each of our groups would have specific objectives. My group would take out the police station and radio station and plant security men and telephone company building. Parker's group would go for the refinery safe, with the payroll. Paulus' group would take the Merchants' Bank and Nationwide Finance. Grofield's group would take City Trust and Raymond Jewelers, right next door to it. Wycza's group the other two jewelry stores and the other commercial buildings along Raymond Avenue."

Parker shook his head. They were now talking about his business, his specialty. Whether he took the job seriously or not, he couldn't avoid thinking about it, and about the best way to handle it.

He said, "You don't want to do it that way. You waste manpower. You have four men stand around with nothing to do but watch a fifth man work on a bank vault. You don't need all those men."

Edgars watched him. "How, then? How should it be set up?"

Parker got to his feet and walked to the end of the room. He studied the map projected on the screen, and said, "To begin with, you need four men on stationary plant for as long as we're in there. One at the police station, one at the telephone company, one at the factory front office. Those three to handle any phone calls or anything like that. And the fourth man in a parked car down by the town line, so he can warn the rest of us if anybody's coming in. We'd need walkie-talkies for that. They're cheap, in any Army-Navy store."

"That's four," said Edgars.

Parker pointed at the map. "Five men hit the police station. One stays. That leaves four to hit the telephone company. One stays. Three to hit the west gate of the plant, take care of the guard, get into the main building without being seen by the guard at the east gate."

"No trouble," said Edgars. "The gates are six long blocks apart, and the main building is right near the west gate."

Parker glanced at him. "Any business at night? Truck deliveries or anything?"

"Not usually."

"So there's another man on plant. With a guard uniform on, at the east gate. Sign at the west gate, 'Closed, use other entrance.' That leaves two. One of them has to stay in the office of the main building, and the other one tackles the safe."

"Fine!" said Edgars. "That's fine! Just five men!"

"So far. Everything else you want is on Raymond Avenue, right?"

"Right. So's the west gate to the plant, down at the end of Raymond Avenue."

"I see that. All right, you need four more men, two on each side of the street. One opens the safes, the other one transfers the loot to the cars. We need four cars. One at the town line, for the lookout. One at the plant. Two along Raymond Avenue. Four cars, four walkie-talkies, a lot of guns, ten men."

Edgars moved closer, and for a few seconds his bulky shoulder cast a black shadow on the screen. He moved back out of the way and stood gazing at the map. "Ten men," he said. "I wouldn't have believed it."

"You need three box men. Paulus is good at that, so you need two more. You seem to know the town, Edgars, so you ought to be the lookout."

"You're in, Parker?"

Parker looked at the map. "Not yet," he said. "I want to see a getaway route that makes sense. I don't like the idea of driving four cars out of town past that state police barracks at six o'clock payday morning."

Wycza said, "I don't like that state police barracks at all."

Parker went on, "I want to see a hideout we can get to but the law can't. I want to be sure there's no other way to get information out of that town but what we've already covered, and I want to be sure there's nobody else we have to worry about in that town but what we've already covered."

"We can straighten those points out, Parker," Edgars assured him.

"Then let's do it." Parker looked down at the slide projector. "What's the rest of the slides in that box?"

"His trip to Ausable Chasm," said Grofield.

"Shut up, Grofield." Parker said it quietly, not bothering to look at him.

Edgars said, "Pictures of the banks, the plant gates, the police station and everything else."

"They'll come in handy some other time. What about getaway route? What about hideout? You got a map of the whole state there?"

"No, I don't."

"You've got to get one. You're from out around there, aren't you?"

"I was." His voice was bitter.

The personal reasons again. Parker didn't give a damn about them. He said, "You get a state map, a couple of them. A roadmap and a topographical map. You look at them till you find a spot we can hole up. If we leave there at six, we've got maybe an hour before the alarm's out. You find us a place fifty miles away or less, that we can get to without being noticed and without leaving tracks, and that the law wouldn't come in after us."

Edgars nodded. "All right, I'll do it."

Wycza said, "What about that goddam trooper barracks? Edgars, ain't there any side road, dirt road, anything at all to take us *around* that barracks?"

"Nothing," Edgars told him. "Flat dead countryside, that's all."

Wycza got to his feet and stretched. His knuckles scraped against the ceiling. He said, "I just don't like that barracks there, that's all."

"Neither do I," Parker told him. "Edgars, switch off that projector, we don't need that map right now. Paulus, give us some light."

When they had light, Parker said, "I don't like four cars going *into* town past that state police barracks, and I don't like them coming out again past the barracks."

Grofield said, "What about holing up inside the town? The old double feint. I've seen you use that a dozen times, Parker."

"It's no good here," Parker told him.

Edgars said, "What is it?"

"It works in some jobs, not this one. You do the job, then make like you're going to run for it. You run maybe two blocks, and hole up. They throw out roadblocks all over the state and wait for you to show up. You don't, so they figure you must of holed up in town. They take the roadblocks down and start looking for you in town, and that's when you leave town."

Edgars laughed. "You're in when they're looking for you out, and out when they're looking for you in."

"Right."

Grofield said, "What's wrong with doing it here?"

"Too small a town, number one. Only one road out, number two. They could put up one dinky roadblock and leave it there for thirty years, till we showed our faces."

Grofield shrugged. "So we have to go past the troopers, that's all."

Paulus said, "Going in's no problem. We can slip in over a couple days."

"So half the townspeople can make you in the rogue's gallery. No good, Paulus. We go in the night it happens and go back out the same night."

"These are details we can work out," Edgars told them.

"We work them out soon," Parker said, "or there's no job."

Edgars said, "Tomorrow morning I'll get the maps. We can meet back here again tomorrow night. Nine o'clock?"

Nine o'clock was all right with everybody. Edgars said, "This thing will work, I know it will. The town's wide open for it, and you people have the knowledge to do it."

"We'll see," Parker told him.

They left one at a time. Wycza went first, and Parker second. Parker walked back to the hotel and went up to his room. He lay down on the bed in darkness and stared at the ceiling, thinking about the job.

It was a crazy one. It broke practically every rule there was. But if the remaining loose ends could be tied up, it just might be workable.

A lot depended on the men. Wycza was all right, steady and fast. Grofield acted sometimes like he didn't take anything seriously, but he knew when to cut that out and get down to work. Paulus was a fidgety type, but first rate on safes and bank vaults.

But what about Edgars? He had some sort of grudge against somebody in that town, and that wasn't good. Also, he was an amateur at this kind of thing. But in some ways he wasn't an amateur at all. The way he'd reacted to the news about Owen, for instance. Sore at first, but after a while catching on, and then not bringing the subject up again. He was a tough man to figure. First he tried to bluff his way, and then he put all his cards on the table, but there was always the impression there were still a few cards left up his sleeve.

It might be a good idea to find out what Edgars' normal line was. It just might be that his personal reasons were something that would queer the operation from the start.

There were still too many doubts; Parker wasn't sure yet whether he wanted to be in this one or not. He didn't really need the dough yet, not for living expenses, but his cash reserve was low. The main reason he'd decided to come on up here and look this over was that he'd been getting bored. . . .

3

HE'D BEEN swimming when the call came. Boredom had driven him from the room, and then boredom drove him from the beach. He put his beach robe back on over his trunks, stuck cigarettes and matches in the pocket, and walked through the sand and bodies toward the hotel which was squatting there like a big white birthday cake.

He was a big man, broad and flat, with the look of a brutal athlete. He had long arms, ending in big flat hands gnarled with veins. His face—it was his second, done by a plastic surgeon—looked strong and self-contained. Women asprawl on the sand in two-piece bathing suits raised their heads to look at him as he went by; he was aware of the looks but didn't respond. It didn't interest him right now.

He knew what the problem was, had known for a couple of weeks now. It had been six months since he'd worked. Inactivity always got to him like this after a while.

He walked on through the sand to the hotel and entered the beach elevator. Two women got on right after him. They were in bathing suits, with towels draped across their shoulders. They were young and good-looking, with the impatient eyes of northern secretaries on vacation. They looked at him and he looked at the elevator boy and said, "Eight." Then he faced front.

Riding up, he didn't think about the women at all, but about the last job. He and Handy McKay had gotten the statuette for Bett Harrow's father, and a few thousand extra for themselves.* Now Handy was retired again, running a diner in Presque Isle, Maine. Parker wasn't retired, didn't want to be retired. But he didn't have anything lined up either. After that last job, he'd spent a while in Galveston, and then he'd gone to New Orleans for a few weeks, and now here he was in Miami. He'd had one woman in Galveston, a couple in New Orleans, but none here. He didn't have the interest.

* *The Mourner.*

"Him and Wycza and some others, they're opening a branch office in Jersey City. Maybe they could use another field man."

"The main operation going to be in Jersey City?"

"No, I don't know where the head office is. That's just a branch, to get organized."

"I might send them a résumé. What's the address?"

"Three nine nine Crescent, four A."

"Are they open for business yet?"

"You probably ought to call first and check. The number's 837-2598."

Parker was writing it all down. "I wouldn't call long distance," he said. "I'd just send them a résumé. What do they pay, do you know?"

"That I don't, Chuck, sorry. Ought to be good wages, though, the way Paulus was talking."

"Is he the sales manager?"

"No, I don't think so. There's some sort of regional manager setting things up, the way I get it."

"I might look into it. Thanks for thinking of me."

"Any time, Chuck. Send me a bathing beauty."

Parker left the booth, had a beer to get rid of some change and to cool off a little, and then walked back to the hotel. He phoned down to have his bill made up, made a reservation on a jet flight to Newark, and packed. He left the hotel room, and five hours later he walked into the hotel room in Jersey City. Then he met Edgars and heard the proposition.

Knock over a city. A whole goddam city.

It was so stupid it might even work. But it would have to be planned right. This one would have to be planned right on down to the shoe leather.

If Edgars wouldn't louse it up some way.

If they had every communications outlet in town figured.

If they could work out a sensible getaway route to a reliable hideout.

If they could get the right men.

If they could think of every possibility.

Right now, it was still just an idea, not a job yet. Maybe it never would be a job. He'd sleep on it.

4

"FIRE DEPARTMENT," said Parker. "They got to be in touch with other fire departments around the state."

Edgars frowned around his cigar. "God damn it," he said. "I forgot about that."

They were sitting around the dining-room table again, the five of them. Paulus was taking notes. The screen was up, at the far end of the room. The projector stood slightly up-angled on the table like a naval gun, but they weren't using it right now, so the spaceship ceiling light was on.

Wycza said, "That's another man. To sit by the phone in the fire house. And now we got firemen to keep on ice. Firemen, policemen, gate guards, telephone girls, the whole goddam town."

Parker nodded. "There's too many angles."

Paulus looked up from his note-taking. "Why not just take the payroll? In and out fast. We five right here could do it, keep it simple and neat."

Edgars shook his head. "No good at all," he said. "Don't you remember that map?" He put his hands down on the tabletop. "Here's your payroll, with a cliff in back, a cliff on the right, a cliff on the left, and the whole city spread out in front. You couldn't get through the city in the first place, and if you did there's still only one road out."

"Past that goddam state police barracks," said Wycza.

Edgars said, "That's right. Nobody's ever even tried to steal that payroll, because it just can't be done."

Parker said, "It's no good trying for any one thing in that town, the payroll or a bank. You've got to hit the whole town, or nothing."

"What about the fire department?" asked Paulus. "That's an eleventh man."

Grofield said, "Not necessarily. Give them a diversion."

Wycza looked at him. "A what?"

"A fire."

They all looked at him. Grofield grinned and shrugged, then turned to Paulus, sitting next to him on the right. Still grinning, he drove his left fist at Paulus' face. Paulus cried out and threw his hands up. Grofield's left stopped in midair, and his right hand dug painfully into Paulus' ribs. "Feint," he said. "Feint and attack. Give the boys of the fire brigade a real rip-snorter to think about, in a quiet corner of town where they'll see no evil, hear no evil, get wise to no evil."

Paulus said, "You keep your hands to yourself, buddy." He'd dropped the pencil he was taking notes with, and stooped over to get it.

Grofield grinned at his back. "Just a graphic illustration of the point, dear heart," he said. "Essence of theater."

"That's not a bad idea," said Edgars.

Parker shook his head. "A six-hour fire? They'll be done before we are."

Wycza said, "We need an eleventh man, that's all."

"We need one, anyway," Parker told him. "We need one man loose, to trouble shoot any place something unexpected comes up. If we need another one for the fire department, that's twelve." He turned to Edgars. "Where's the firehouse?"

"Across the street from the police station."

Paulus said, "So we've *got* to cover them. Twelve men. We're going right back up to twenty-five again."

Edgars took the cigar out of his mouth and looked insulted. "Why? Twelve men, what's so bad about that? Twelve men to take a whole city."

"Maybe we're not done yet," Paulus told him.

"Night people," said Grofield, "that's what we've got to think about. Who are the night people? Cops, firemen, telephone girls, we've got them. What about milkmen?"

Edgars shook his head. "They're union, they deliver in the daytime."

"Post office," said Grofield. "They've got to have somebody around for special-delivery letters. Western Union office. Railroad station. Cabdrivers."

"You don't have to worry about cabdrivers," Edgars told him. "I told you there was a curfew. There's no taxi customers after midnight."

"What about emergencies?" Grofield asked him. "Ladies having babies, children swallowing pins, men with appendicitis. Ambulances racing back and forth amid the booming safes."

Parker said, "That's right. Hospital. You got a hospital in this town?"

"No. The fire department has an ambulance, to take any emergency cases to the hospital in Madison, fourteen miles away on the highway."

Paulus said, "So the fire department man covers the ambulance, too."

Parker asked Edgars, "You know the train schedules? Anything going in or out between midnight and six in the morning?"

"No. It's just a spur line in. There's one passenger train a day, and two freight trains. The railroad station is closed between eight at night and eight in the morning."

"Good," said Paulus. "That takes care of the railroad station."

"Western Union," said Grofield. "Post office."

"The post office closes," said Edgars. "I'm sure it does. I don't know what they do about special delivery letters. Maybe they drive them in from Madison."

"But Western Union?"

"They've got an office on Raymond Avenue. I don't know if it closes nights or not. I should, but I don't."

"We have to know," Parker told him. "You got a contact in that town?"

"No."

"If everything else closes down," said Paulus, "the Western Union office probably does, too. They wouldn't have much business at night."

"No business at all," said Edgars. "Most likely any telegrams that come at night are driven in from the Madison office, the same as special-delivery letters. I can't remember if I've ever seen the Western Union office open at night, but I don't see why it would be."

"We have to know," Parker repeated. "If it's open, it's got to be covered, and that means another man."

"The only way to find out," Edgars told him, "is to go to Copper Canyon and look for yourself."

"I know."

"I'll write it down," said Paulus.

"More night people," said Grofield. "Who can think of more night people? You say there's no all-night diner?"

Edgars shook his head. "No. No business stays open at all, because of the curfew."

"That's a very small-town thing, a curfew," said Grofield. "Big cities talk about it, but small towns do it."

Wycza said, "What about a newspaper?"

"A weekly," Edgars told him. "It comes out on Thursday, for the convenience of the shoppers."

"No reporters on at night?"

"No. Most of the paper is written by the secretaries of women's organizations."

They were all silent, then, all trying to think of other people who might be out and around late at night. After a minute, Paulus said, "That's it, then. We need another man, to cover the fire department. And we have to find out about the Western Union office."

Wycza said, "What about the getaway?"

"I got the two maps like Parker suggested," Edgars answered. "There's no other way to get out of town except the road, but I think I've found the hideout."

"I don't like that barracks," Wycza said.

Grofield said, "An idle thought. What about the mine?"

They looked at him. Edgars said, "What about it?"

"Are there no entrances other than at the back of the canyon? No shafts leading out anywhere else? No emergency exits?"

Edgars shook his head. "I don't think so. All the shafts go straight down in from the canyon. There's no reason for any other way in."

"Just a thought." Grofield smiled. "I visualized us trundling away on ore carts with the loot, like the seven dwarfs."

"We have to go past the barracks," Parker said. "There's no other choice. We space it so we don't have a convoy go by all at once, and we'll be all right." He turned to Edgars. "What about the hideout?"

"Let me get the maps." He stood up. "More beer?"

They all wanted more beer. He went away and came back with a double handful of beer cans. He set them down on the table, and took two maps out of his hip pocket. He spread them out on the table, covering most of the table's surface. One was a state roadmap, the other a topographical map.

They were all standing now, leaning over the maps. Edgars

pointed to the topographical map, saying, "See, there's Copper Canyon. That's a mesa back of it, it gradually levels down again. Out in front, it's lowland for over a hundred miles. Down in here is one of the coal beds, lignite coal. This is just about the edge of the Badlands here. This whole section here is full of lignite coal. Some of it's right out on the surface, burning, been burning for years."

Parker didn't give a damn about lignite coal, burning or not. He said, "The hideout."

"I'm getting to it. Like I said, this section here is just about the edge of the Badlands, so it's away from the tourist areas and it's away from the mining operations. There was a strip mine working there a few years ago, but they're gone now; they cleaned out what they could get and left. There's an eighty-foot-deep ravine there now, where they scraped the topsoil off and took the coal out. There's nobody there now at all. There's some kind of sulphur by-product oozes out of the ground, pollutes the water, and stinks the place up, so nobody goes near it. But the mining company built a road into it, and their old sheds should still be there, on the lip of the ravine."

"What kind of road?" Parker asked him.

"Dirt. But passable. They brought trucks in and out."

"How do we get to it?"

Edgars switched over to the other map. "See, here's 22A here, coming out of Copper Canyon. We pick up the highway here, and turn left. Then there's this smaller road here, goes off to the right. We'd be on the highway maybe three miles. This small road we stay on for five or six miles, and then the mining company road goes off that to the left."

"This land is all flat here?"

"It's plains land. Rolling land."

"When we turn off the small road onto the mining company road, can we be seen from the highway?"

"No, not a chance. That's wild country in there, and there's some trees."

"How many miles in on the mining company road?"

"Maybe seven."

"And how many miles from Copper Canyon to the highway?"

"Eight."

Parker ran his finger along the map. "Eight miles to the

highway, then three miles to the secondary road, six miles to the mining company road, seven miles in from there. Twenty-four miles."

"Looks good," said Paulus.

Grofield said, "How much traffic on that highway early in the morning?"

"Six in the morning?" Edgars shook his head. "None."

"Good," said Paulus. "We won't be seen."

"No good," Parker told him. "If anybody does see us, we'll stick out like a sore thumb. Four cars in a row on an empty highway, all turn off together. All it needs is one trooper to see us."

Wycza said, "What about a truck? A big-ass tractor trailer. We stash it outside of town and switch to it when the job's done."

"Too much loot to be transferred."

Grofield said, "We bring the tractor trailer into town with us. Instead of loading two cars along the main drag, we load the tractor trailer. Then we have a car at the plant, the way we figured, and another car parked near the town line for a look-out. We leave that one, and just take the tractor trailer and the other car. They space five minutes apart, and it doesn't look so bad. You see tractor trailers all hours."

Wycza said, "All right, that's even better."

"It would work," said Edgars. "It would sure work all right."

Parker stood looking at the two maps and thinking it over. Twelve men. In at midnight, out by six in the morning. Everything covered, if they'd thought of everything, and if Edgars had his facts straight.

It was a job. It would work. The thing looked like idiocy at first, but it would work.

He nodded. "All right," he said. "Who's financing?"

Edgars looked blank. "Financing?"

"This is going to cost," Parker told him. "Walkie-talkies, the truck, the cars. Transportation out there. Food and water stashed at the hideout ahead of time. Guns. It'll cost dough to get this thing set up."

Edgars still looked blank, and now a little worried besides. Paulus explained it to him. "Every job has to be financed," he said. "Whoever puts up the dough gets it back doubled if the job works out."

"You mean, one of us?"

Parker shook his head. "No. It's better to get your financing done by somebody outside the operation. Otherwise the man who put the money in tries to run things."

"This is all new to me," Edgars told them.

"I'll go over to New York tomorrow," Grofield said. "I've got a couple contacts over there. How much you figure?"

Parker frowned, thinking it out. "Four thousand," he said.

Edgars said, "Four *thousand*!"

"I told you, it's going to cost. The truck, the cars, the—"

"Why not just steal the truck?"

"You want to leave Copper Canyon in a hot truck on every state trooper's list for a thousand miles around?"

"You mean, you just go to a used-truck dealer and buy a truck?"

"No, not that either. Then you got problems with registration. There's outlets where you can pick up a mace pretty cheap."

Edgars couldn't seem to get the bewildered look off his face. "A mace? What's a mace?"

"A car with papers that look good and license plates that look good."

"But they aren't really?"

"They aren't really."

Edgars sat down, shook his head, and drank some beer. "I didn't know there was this much to it," he said. "How many people have to know about this deal?"

"Just the ones in on it. Twelve men."

"But Grofield's going to go talk to somebody about financing, and you're going to buy a stolen truck. . . ."

"The man that finances doesn't know what the job is. Just that there's a job, and it needs so much to get set up, and it should be done by such and such a date."

"How you going to get a man to put money into a deal without knowing what it is?"

"He relies on the men in the deal. If he knows them, knows they do good work, he takes a chance on them."

"What about where you buy the truck? You don't tell him anything either?"

"Why should we?"

Edgars shrugged and spread his hands. "All right," he said. "You people know what you're doing."

"We rather hope so," said Grofield. He turned to Parker. "Come along with me tomorrow, okay? I know one guy in particular, he knows you. If he sees you're in he'll cover us with no trouble."

"All right."

"Now," said Paulus. "About personnel."

They all sat down at the table again, and Edgars cleared away the maps. Parker said, "We need three jug men. You're one, Paulus. You work one side of Raymond Avenue, and Wycza can carry for you. Grofield, you'd be a good man for the phone company, keep the ladies from getting too scared."

Grofield smiled thinly. "You know my boyish charm," he said. "I'll be happy to keep the ladies company."

"Edgars, you ought to be lookout at the town line. You know the town, know the circumstances there. You can figure anything that moves quicker than anybody else."

Edgars said, "I thought I'd be better off taking care of the police station. I know a little something about police procedure there, I could probably fake it better than anybody else if a phone call came in or anything like that."

Parker shrugged. "Wherever you think you'd do the most good."

"Police station."

"All right." Parker turned to Paulus. "You got a list of the jobs? Wait a minute, the other two juggers first. I'll see if I can get Handy McKay. He could get in at the payroll as fast as anybody I know." He looked around the table. "We need another jugger. A vault man. Any ideas?"

Paulus said, "What about Rohatch? He's a geech, but he's good at vaults."

Grofield shook his head and said, "I heard he died. The liver got him."

Wycza said, "I worked once or twice with a fella named Kemp. Any of you know him?"

"He's unreliable," said Paulus primly. "He's on the needle. He may even be in jail by now for all I know."

Wycza said, "All right, forget him. How about Wiss? Little guy, but fast."

"I've worked with him," said Parker. "While I was having that trouble with the Outfit. He's a good man."

"I'll see can I get in touch with him," said Wycza.

Edgars said, "What about you, Parker? What's your job going to be?"

It was Wycza who answered. "He ought to be the loose one, the trouble shooter."

Edgars nodded. "Fine by me."

"I'm writing all this down," said Paulus.

Parker said to him, "What other jobs?"

"You want Wiss to work the other side of Raymond Avenue, right? So you need someone to work with him, like Wycza's working with me."

"We'll let him pick his own sideman. Lookout's next. We want somebody fast, and cool."

"Salsa," said Grofield. "That bastard could hunker down in Times Square and disappear. You'd never see him, and he wouldn't move for a hundred years if he had to. But when it was time to move, zoom."

"I know Salsa," said Parker. "He's a good man."

"I'll get word to him."

Parker turned to Paulus. "What's left?"

"Just three. Fire department, gate guard, and plant office. Three men in place."

"I know the guy for the gate guard," said Wycza. "Pop Phillips. He wears some kind of uniform just about every job he takes."

"Good old Phillips," said Grofield. "Pop Phillips, the sweet old rummy."

"He don't drink when he's on a job," Wycza told him.

"You're right, he doesn't. But he's got bad breath."

Parker said, "Shut up, Grofield. Okay, Wycza, get Phillips. Now we need two more."

"The Chambers brothers," said Paulus.

Grofield shook his head. "Ernie's in jail."

"What the hell for?"

"Statutory. You know how those hillbillies like young meat."

"What about his brother?"

Grofield shrugged. "He's as good as the next man."

"I'll get in touch with him," said Paulus, and wrote it down.

Parker said, “If Littlefield’s still working, he’d be a good man for the plant office.”

“I worked with him last year,” said Wycza. “He was still going strong then.”

“Get in touch with him, will you?”

“Right.”

Paulus looked up from his notes. “That’s all,” he said. “Except Wiss’s sideman. He can get him himself.”

“Day after tomorrow,” said Parker. “Here again. Nine o’clock.”

Edgars got to his feet and rubbed his hands together. “This is going to work out,” he said. “It’s going to work out.”

They left the apartment one at a time. This time Parker waited, to be the last out. When he was alone with Edgars he said, “Something I wanted to ask you.”

“What?”

“What about Owen?”

“Owen? What about him?”

“He’s dead.”

“I know that.” Edgars was frowning at him, but then his face lit up with understanding. “Oh. You mean, what’s my attitude?”

“That’s right.”

“I couldn’t care less, Parker. He was just a bum I picked up here in town. He was more stupid than I thought, and exceeded his orders. That’s over with.”

Parker nodded. “All right,” he said. “See you day after tomorrow.”

“Right.”

TWO

I

PARKER PUMPED change into the phone box and listened to it booming. Then he waited.

He was in a phone booth next to a gas station. June sunlight poured down everywhere. Grofield was in his car, a three-year-old black Rambler sedan, parked just down the block; they were on their way over to New York to see about financing, and Parker wanted to make the call now, early, to give Handy time to get here.

The booming was replaced by a ringing sound, and then by a male voice. Parker said, "Arnie LaPointe, please." You couldn't get in touch with Handy direct. Like Parker with Joe Sheer, Handy had a middleman.

The voice said, "Speaking."

"This is Parker. If you see Handy McKay around, ask him to give me a call."

"I'm not sure I'll see him."

"This is a pay phone, I can't hang around too long."

"I just don't know when I'll see him."

"When you do, tell him I saw the monk and he's still mourning." That was a reference to the last job they'd worked together, so Handy would know it was him.

"If I see him, I'll tell him. What's your number there?"

"This is Jersey City. The number's OL 3-4599."

"I don't promise anything."

"Sure."

Parker hung up and waited. He pushed open the booth door to get some air, and lit a cigarette. He could see Grofield sitting in the car, relaxed and easy. Grofield was too playful sometimes, but he knew when to cut that out. The operation was shaping up to have good men in it, and with good men in a deal it was tough for the deal to go sour. Not impossible, but tough.

A gas station attendant in blue overalls came over, wiping his hands on an orange rag. He said, "Anything wrong?"

"They're calling me back."

"Okay." He went away again.

Parker finished his cigarette, flicked it out into the street. He leaned against the side of the booth, folded his arms, and waited some more.

He waited fifteen minutes and then the phone rang. He picked it up and said, "Charles Willis here."

It was Handy McKay's voice: "What's the story?"

"Thought you might like to come visit. I got a new place."

"Social call?"

"We might work a little."

"Not for me, remember? I retired."

"You might like the weather here. And there's thousands of things to see. Maybe twenty thousand."

"Don't tempt me. This time I'm retired for good. I got the diner going, and I'm settling down, and everything's fine."

"I was looking for company. Open a can or two with me, you know?"

"Yeah?" There was a pause, and he said, "What about Wiss? He's good company."

"He's already coming."

"Oh, yeah? What do you want, a crowd?"

"Yes."

"Jesus, now you got my curiosity up. But it's still no soap. Wait a second, how about Kerwin?"

"That's an idea. You just don't want to travel, huh?"

"Not any more. I'm settled down."

"All right. I'll drop in sometime."

"Do that. I'll fry you an egg."

"Sure."

He hung up and left the phone booth and walked down to Grofield's car. He slid in and said, "McKay's out. He's retired."

"Again?"

"This time he says it's for good. He suggested Kerwin."

"I don't know him."

"He's a good man."

Grofield shrugged. "I'll take your word for it. Call him."

"He lives in Brooklyn. I'll call him from the city, after we see your man. Who is he, by the way?"

"Ormont. Chester Ormont."

"Four thousand might be steep for him."

"We'll see."

Grofield started the engine, and they drove away from there. They went through the Holland Tunnel into the city, and took the West Side Highway up to 72nd Street, and then crosstown through the park to the East Side. Grofield parked illegally on East 67th Street, between Fifth and Madison, and they walked down the block to the address. It was a fashionable brownstone, with a doctor's shingle in the window. They went up the stoop and inside, into the dimness, and there was a nurse in a white uniform at a desk. She smiled impersonally and said, "Name, please?"

"Grofield. About my back."

"You've been to see the doctor before?"

"Yes."

"Have a seat, please, the doctor will be with you in just a minute."

They went into the waiting room, a large airy room done in Danish modern. Two stuffed matrons sat in opposite corners of the room, like welterweights between rounds. One was reading *Fortune*, and the other was reading *Business Week*. Grofield picked up a copy of *Time* from the central table, and he and Parker sat down to wait.

After about five minutes, the nurse appeared and took one of the women away with her. A little while later a white-haired old man came in on a cane and took the absent woman's seat and *Fortune*. Some time after that the other woman was escorted away by the nurse.

They waited about forty minutes, and then the nurse came to the door and said, "Mister Grofield?"

Grofield said, "Come on." He and Parker followed the nurse out of the waiting room, down a cream-colored hall, and into an office. There was no one in the office. The nurse said, "Doctor Ormont will see you in just a minute." She went away.

They sat in brown leather chairs and waited. They could hear a murmuring from somewhere else on the first floor. Five minutes went by, and then the door opened and a heavy impatient-looking man with pink scrubbed hands came in. He smiled sourly at them, said, "How are you, Grofield?" and went around behind his desk.

"Just terrible, Doctor," said Grofield. "I've got this terrible pain in my back."

"Never mind that," said the doctor. "This office isn't bugged."

Grofield burst out laughing. "Doctor, you're priceless!"

The doctor didn't get it, and didn't want it. He looked at Parker and said, "You remind me of somebody."

Grofield said, "This is Parker, with a face job. Not just the nose, the whole face. What do you think of that?"

"Parker, eh? Who did the job?"

"A doctor out west," Parker told him. "You wouldn't know him."

"He did a good job." The doctor switched his attention to Grofield. "You've got something on, eh?"

"So we have. We need financing."

"Obviously. This isn't a social call."

"Of course not. It's this pain in my back, it's killing me."

Parker said, "Cut it out, Grofield."

"Right you are." Grofield sobered, and said, "We need four G's."

"Thousand? Four thousand?"

"Right the first time."

"That's a hell of a bite." The doctor frowned, and stared at papers on his desk as though one of them had written on it the answer to a question that had been bothering him for months. "How long?" he asked.

"Couple of weeks. Maybe a month."

"Anyone else I know in on it?"

"I don't think so. Just me and Parker."

"But there's others in."

"Oh, sure."

The doctor considered again, then looked at Parker. "You're in it?"

Parker nodded. He knew Ormont wasn't very bright; the only thing to do was wait till he got everything straightened out inside his head.

Ormont said, "When do you need it by?"

Grofield shrugged. "Now. As soon as possible."

"Tomorrow afternoon, the earliest. The absolute earliest."

"All right, fine. I'll come in and get it."

Ormont nodded heavily. "Tomorrow afternoon. Two o'clock. I won't be having office hours then, just ring the bell."

"Will do."

They all got to their feet. Ormont said, "Good to see you again, Parker. The face is a very good job."

Parker nodded again. There wasn't anything to say; he'd never been any good at small talk.

Ormont said, "Sorry to keep you waiting the way I did. But we've got to keep up appearances. My nurse isn't in on it."

"That's all right."

They went out. When they were back in the car, Grofield started laughing again. "This office isn't bugged! Parker, if you had a sense of humor you'd bust a gut right now. This office isn't bugged! I wouldn't take a million dollars for that man."

Parker lit a cigarette and waited for Grofield to get over it.

2

TWELVE MEN made the dining room uncomfortably full. Edgars had set up folding chairs for the extras and had distributed beer. Then he and Parker and Paulus had taken turns filling the new men in on the operation. Edgars had run his slides, showing them the map, and also the photos of Raymond Avenue and the banks and the two gates to the plant and the police station and everything else. The room had filled with smoke, even with both windows open.

Handy McKay was the only one selected who hadn't chosen to come in at least to listen. The rest were all there. Wiss and Kerwin, the other two safe and vault experts, both small, narrow men with an intense and concentrated look. Wiss had brought, to work with him, a rangy fortyish man named Elkins, with whom Parker had worked in the past. Chambers was there, a big awkward-looking hillbilly with a brother in jail for statutory rape. And Pop Phillips, an old guy who looked like Hollywood's idea of a night watchman. And Littlefield, a stocky man in his fifties who looked as though he made his living selling gold-mine stock. And Salsa, in his late thirties, tall and slender, who looked like a gigolo and used to be one.

When the talk and the slide show was finished, and when Edgars had distributed more beer, Paulus asked if there were any questions. Wiss said, "One. What's the split?"

"Even," Paulus told him. "Every man a twelfth."

"That's not the regular way."

Parker said, "This isn't the regular job. It's more men than usual, and more things to do."

Wiss shrugged. "It don't matter to me. What's a twelfth of two hundred fifty grand?"

"That's minimum," said Edgars, "just a minimum."

Paulus said, "A little over twenty thousand."

Wiss said, "Twenty thousand's all right."

Littlefield, looking like a man at a board meeting, said, "You got financing yet?"

"Picked it up yesterday," Grofield told him.

"How much?"

"Four G's."

"That's eight thousand off the top. You couldn't cut it any closer than that?"

Parker said, "You heard the setup. You got any way to shave it?"

Littlefield shook his head. "I guess not. But eight thousand's a big bite."

"Less than seven hundred a man," Paulus told him.

Elkins, the man Wiss had brought with him, said, "How long you figure to stay out at this mine?"

Wycza laughed. "Till it cools," he said.

"Maybe three, four days," Parker told him. "We can stash cars there ahead of time, make our split there."

Chambers, the hillbilly, stretched his long legs out and said, "What's the chance of aerial surveillance? What if the state boys throw helio-copters out?"

"Helicopters," said Paulus.

Edgars said, "There's sheds there, and trees back a ways from the ravine edge. We can all get under cover."

Chambers nodded and scratched his chin. "The truck, too?"

"I'm pretty sure."

Chambers looked at him sideways. "Pretty sure? Pretty sure don't cut it."

"If we can't hide it up top," Edgars told him, "we can always take it down into the ravine. There's an overhang on the south side, we can stick it in under there."

"Just don't like helio-copters."

There was silence then. Parker looked around. Kerwin and Pop Phillips and Salsa hadn't asked anything, but all three of them looked as though they were thinking hard. Parker said, "Everybody in?"

Pop Phillips shook his head. "I'm not quite sure, Parker," he said. "It strikes me as being a pretty ostentatious sort of proposition."

Kerwin said, "How many safes?"

Edgars answered him. "The two bank vaults, the loan company, the three jewelry stores, maybe ten or twelve other stores that'd be worth it."

"How you want to do it, noisy or slow?"

Parker looked at Edgars. "Any people live along Raymond Avenue?"

"No, it's all commercial. There's no homes less than a block away."

"So you want juice," said Kerwin. "That's a hell of a lot of juice to carry around."

Paulus said, "Why not drill? Blow the vaults, but drill the others."

Wiss, the other safe man, said, "Drilling's just as loud, and slower."

"You got a hell of a lot of safes there," Kerwin said.

"But three men doing it," Parker told him. "You hit the payroll, while Paulus and Wiss start on the banks. Then the three of you take the rest of the town."

Kerwin nodded. "Maybe so. You got to blow the vaults, no choice there. But I don't like blowing everything, that's too much juice to carry around."

Paulus said, "Drilling doesn't take long. It might even be, a couple of those safes, all you'll need is a sledge on the combination."

Wiss said, "I don't mind drilling. But you want speed on this job."

Professionals bickering about their specialty; it was taking them away from where they ought to be. Parker said, "You three work it out later. Any way you want to do it is okay."

Elkins, Wiss's partner, said, "What about alarms?"

"What about them?" Edgars asked him. "We'll have the police station sewed up."

"I meant bells. You don't want the main street sounding like New Year's Eve."

"Oh. There aren't any bells."

"None at all?"

"Every business along Raymond Avenue is hooked up to a burglar alarm system at police headquarters. Trip the alarm in one of the banks or a store, and a bell rings in the police station, and a light comes on to show the man on duty where the break is."

Elkins nodded, and said, "That's all right, then."

Salsa spoke up for the first time. He had a trace of accent in his voice. "How soon do you plan to do this?"

"Couple of weeks," Parker told him. "Depends how long it takes to get set."

"What do we do in the meanwhile?"

"We'll get to that. First, is everybody in? Anybody want to drop out? Phillips?"

Pop Phillips shook his head thoughtfully. "I don't know," he said. "This looks all right to the rest of you, eh? I can't help but feel we're biting off more than we can chew, but if you're all convinced it's feasible, then I imagine that'll have to be good enough for me."

"Only if you're sure," Parker told him.

"That's just his way, Parker," Wycza told him. Phillips had been suggested by Wycza. "If he says he's in, he's in. Right, Pop?"

"I rely on your judgment," Phillips told him. He looked like a rummy night watchman, baggy pants and all, but sounded like a retired schoolteacher. He'd taken two falls in his lifetime and had done a lot of reading in prison.

"I guess we're all in," said Paulus.

"All fools in a circle."

"Shut up, Grofield."

"You men give me confidence. This is going to be easier than I thought."

"I only wish Ernie could be here to see this. He *hates* little towns."

"It'll be pleasant, I must admit, to be in uniform once again. I sometimes think I missed my calling."

"More beer?"

They all wanted more beer. When Edgars brought it back and distributed it, Parker got to his feet and said, "We've got some setting up to do. Paulus, you and Wiss ought to take a run out to Copper Canyon and look it over. See if there's any problems we haven't covered."

Wiss said, "I don't like showing my face."

"We'll sell insurance," Paulus told him. "Don't you worry, I've done this before. I've got identity cards and brochures and everything. All you do is do a bad job selling insurance, and in between you look around."

Parker said, "If Wiss don't want to, he don't have to. Kerwin?"

Kerwin shrugged. "All right by me."

"Wycza, you and Salsa go out there and take a look at this mining place. But don't stay in Copper Canyon." He turned to Edgars. "What's some other town nearby, bigger than Copper Canyon?"

"Madison."

"All right. Stay at Madison. Chambers, you pick us up a truck, right?"

"I surely will."

"The biggest they make."

"That's the one I'll get, all right."

"Wiss, get together with Paulus and Kerwin before they leave, work up a list of the supplies you need. Then you and Elkins go get the stuff."

Elkins nodded. Wiss said, "Who's handling the cash?"

"Grofield."

"Treasurer and disburser, at your service."

"Littlefield, pick yourself up a car. You and Phillips drive on out there to Madison and start moving groceries out to the mine. Enough for twelve men for a week, just in case. We'll need water, too. Edgars tells me the water there's polluted."

Littlefield said, "Is this the car we'll use in the job?"

"Right. So stay away from Copper Canyon. Arrange with the boys for when any of them wants to bring a car out to stash at the mine, so you can drive them back. The back money pays for your car and the truck and that's it."

Salsa said, "What about the lookout's car? I'm lookout, town line."

"Get yourself a car in town, when we start the operation."

Salsa nodded. "That's good."

Parker told him, "What you want to do right away is pick us up walkie-talkies. Four of them, for you, me, Wycza and Grofield. Grofield'll be at the telephone company, and he can get in touch with anybody else by phone. Wycza and Elkins will be coming together at the truck all the time, so they only need one walkie-talkie between them."

"Four walkie-talkies," said Salsa. "Very good."

"Buy them here in the East."

Salsa nodded.

Edgars said, "What about me? What do you want me to do?"

Parker shook his head. "Just stay loose. You'll have things to do later."

"Well, what about you? What are you going to do?"

"Guns."

Phillips leaned across the table and said, "Let me have some of that notepaper, will you, Paulus? And does anyone have a pencil? Then we'll make arrangements for rendezvous at the mine, for those of you with cars to leave there."

Wiss said, "Kerwin, Paulus, let's go out in the kitchen and talk."

Littlefield turned to Grofield. "We'll have to work out expenses," he said. "The car, and food, and living expenses."

"No living expenses," Grofield told him. "We shaved that much out already."

Littlefield pursed his lips. "If you think it works better that way."

Grofield grinned at him. "You want me to go get some more? And you pay it back double, so that way you pay your living expenses twice."

"That's the way my income tax will read," Littlefield told him.

"Income tax?" Grofield stared at him. "You pay income tax?"

"On every penny."

"I bet *your* return shakes them up."

"I account for every penny of income," Littlefield told him, "but I am forced, of course, to invent my sources."

"Why bother?"

Littlefield leaned closer to him. "You're a young man, you can still learn. Pay attention to this. You can steal in this country, you can rape and murder, you can bribe public officials, you can pollute the morals of the young, you can burn your place of business down for the insurance money, you can do almost anything you want, and if you act with just a little caution and common sense you'll never even be indicted. But if you don't pay your income tax, Grofield, you will go to jail."

"Oh, sure," said Grofield. "Sure thing."

"Parker knows I'm right. You pay tax, don't you, Parker?"

Parker nodded. Under the Charles Willis name he owned pieces of a few losing businesses here and there, and they gave him the background to cover his income on his tax return.

Grofield shook his head. "I don't get it. You're putting me on."

"Income tax is Federal," Parker told him.

"So's a bank, for Christ's sake."

"I don't mean Federal offense, I mean Federal, whose money it is. A bank is stockholders, but income tax is government money."

Pop Phillips said, "Those are words of wisdom, Grofield. I only fell twice, and once it was income tax. I got three years, and I'm still paying the back taxes. Why do you think I'm not retired?"

"I'll put you on to my accountant," Littlefield said. "He'll get you straightened out."

Grofield got to his feet, looking agitated. "That's a lot of crap. Don't talk to me about that. Income tax!"

Littlefield shrugged. "You'll go to jail," he said.

Parker saw Grofield getting mad, and said, "Back to business. We got a lot to set up tonight."

3

"MACHINE GUNS," said the blind man. "They're expensive, machine guns."

"I know," said Parker.

"And hard to come by."

"I know."

"The government tries to keep tabs on them. It's tough to find one without a history."

"I need three. And three rifles. And eight handguns."

"Rifles, handguns," said the blind man. "No problem. Machine guns, that's a problem."

Parker shook his head in irritation, though the blind man couldn't see it. He'd come to the blind man because he was the one to talk to if you wanted machine guns. Parker would have preferred to go to Amos Klee, in Syracuse, but Klee was only good on handguns. It was the blind man, called Scofe, who should be able to supply the machine guns.

Parker said, "You don't have them? You can't get them?"

"Sit," said the blind man. "Sit, sit. Let me think."

Parker sat, and let him think.

They were in the filthy back room of a cluttered hobby shop on Second Avenue in Albany, New York. Scofe owned the hobby shop, and it was run by a sloppy woman with red hair who didn't trust anybody. The filth and the clutter and Scofe's blindness and the woman's surliness combined to keep customers at a minimum. Scofe didn't need much to support himself anyway and he got most of his income from guns. He was good with his hands, could disassemble and reassemble a rifle faster than most men with eyes, and was even a good shot. He fired at sound targets, a small bell hung up in a breeze or—his favorite kind of target—a child's toy of the click-click type.

Scofe scratched his chin. He hadn't shaved for a few days, and his fingernails made a harsh dry sound against his beard stubble. He said, "Shotgun no good? I got good shotguns, sawed-off or what you want."

"Machine guns. Three."

"You know what the Germans call a machine gun? *Kugelspritz.* Bullet squirter. All noise, no accuracy."

"Three."

Scofe shrugged, and made a motion as though washing his hands. "Not my affair. I got a Schmeisser, a burp gun. Old, but in good condition."

"That's one."

Scofe chuckled, his shoulders rising and falling. "Parker," he said. "Parker, Parker. I hear you got a new face, but your voice don't change, or your style. You don't like me, do you, Parker?"

"I don't give a damn about you."

"You don't like the dirty old blind man. He smells bad. Yah, Parker?"

"Maybe I'll go to Amos Klee."

"For machine guns? No, Parker. For machine guns, you come to Scofe. You want the burp gun?"

"Let me see it."

Scofe pointed. "Over there you see a shelf. Long boxes on it, battleship models. Bottom box, second from the left. Bring it here."

Parker got the box. The ones he had to move were light, but the one he wanted was heavy. He started to open it and Scofe said, "I'll open it, Parker. Bring it here."

Parker brought it over to him. Scofe was sitting in a squeaky kitchen chair next to a table, an old scarred worktable with nothing on it. Parker handed him the box and Scofe put it on the table, half-turned to be closer to the table, and took the top off the box. It was full of parts. Scofe's hands touched the parts, his long fingers moving like worms in a garden. Parker watched him as he put the parts together, feeling in the bottom of the box for screws, using a small metal screwdriver he took from his hip pocket. He put the parts together, and when he was done there was a burp gun on the table. "There," he said. "You like it?"

Parker picked it up. There was rust on it, a little, not much. It was an old gun, but it looked to be in good shape. The places where it was rusted were where identification marks had been filed away, leaving the metal rough.

"Well?"

"How much."

"I don't haggle, Parker, you know I never haggle."

"How much?"

"One twenty-five."

Parker put the gun back down on the table. "What else you got?"

Scofe chuckled again. His hands reached out and found the gun and he disassembled it again, putting everything back in the model battleship box. When he was finished, he put the top on the box again and said, "You want to put it back? You're not interested?"

"Leave it out a while. What else you got?"

"You take the burp, I can let you have two Tommys, a hundred apiece."

"Where are they?"

"You know me, Parker, they aren't bad guns. I don't touch bad guns."

Parker knew that, but he wanted to see them before making up his mind. He said, "You know me. I always look first."

"I never look first, Parker. The smelly old blind man never looks at all." He swiveled around and pointed to a corner. "Road-racer sets there," he said. "Big square boxes. Fourth and fifth down. They're all assembled."

Parker went over. The fourth and fifth boxes were heavier than the first three. Parker felt the sixth box, and it was heavy, too. He carried the fourth and fifth over to the table, opened them, and looked at two Thompson .45 submachine guns, each equipped with a twenty-shot clip. They both looked all right. He put the tops back on the boxes and said, "These are good. I'll take three of these."

"Those two are all I got."

"Then I want a road-racer set. The sixth from the top."

"You're a bastard, Parker. You're a rotten bastard. You're a filthy rotten son of a bitch. You take advantage of a poor old blind man, you'd spit on your own mother. You're a cesspool, a walking cesspool, you're vomit, you're a cheap two-bit rotten punk."

"Shut up, Scofe."

Scofe shut up. He stuck his right hand up to his face and gnawed on a knuckle. He looked like an old squirrel.

Parker said, "One hundred each for three Tommys."

"Two Tommys. And one twenty-five for the burp."

"I don't want the burp."

"Then one fifty each for the Tommys."

"Goodbye, Scofe."

"I don't haggle, Parker, you know me."

Parker turned away and started for the front of the store. He opened the door and went through, leaving the door open behind him, and walked down between the display cases. The sullen woman watched him suspiciously.

Parker got halfway to the street door and then Scofe called, "Parker! Hey! Come back here!"

Parker turned around and went back. The woman kept watching him. He went into the back room again and said, "What?"

"Put these boxes away. You can't leave these boxes out."

"I'm going to see Amos Klee."

"You're a liar."

"He can get me guns. I wait a few days, that's all. He'll scout around for me."

Scofe twisted his head back and forth. "If I could *see* you!"

"It's all in my voice, Scofe."

"I hate you like poison. Like poison."

"I don't like to deal with you, Scofe. You smell bad. What's your price, the three Tommys?"

"Three-fifty. That's it, that's the lowest."

"Deal."

"Tell my woman to come in here."

Parker went to the door and motioned to the woman. "Come in here."

She came in, and Scofe said, "Every transaction cash. This transaction, you pay the cash, then we see what else you want."

The woman said, "How much?"

"Three-fifty. For three road racers."

Parker took an envelope out of his jacket pocket, and counted three hundred and fifty dollars onto the table, while the woman watched. When he was done, she said, "Okay."

"You're all right, Parker." Scofe raised his head and smiled. He was filthy, and his eyes were covered by a white film, and his teeth were brown. When he smiled, he looked like a parody of something unspeakable. "You're all right," he said again. "You don't mean all those things you say to me."

Parker went over and got the sixth heavy road-racer box. He

put it with the first two, and picked up all three. He said to the woman, "Come out with me and open the car door."

Scofe said, "What about the other stuff you wanted?"

"Never mind."

"You're going to Klee?"

Parker ignored him. He said to the woman, "Come on," and started for the front of the store.

"You scum! You vomit! You stinking cesspool!"

Parker walked through the store to the street, the woman coming behind him. She opened the rear door of the car, and Parker put the three boxes on the seat. He closed the door and nodded to the woman. She said, "He's getting worse."

Parker hadn't expected her to talk. He stopped and looked at her and said, "He's stupid. There's others in the same business."

"He don't get half the business he used to. You, too, you're going somewhere else now."

"Tell him, not me."

"It's because he's blind."

"He ought to be used to it by now."

Parker went around and got behind the wheel. It was a one-year-old Mercury, painted blue and white, a mace he'd picked up yesterday in Harrisburg, Pennsylvania. He'd drive it out to North Dakota, stash it at the mine, and drive away in it after the job. Then he'd get rid of it. The Pennsylvania plates and registration paper looked good enough if he stayed out of Pennsylvania. From the little mileage on it, he thought it had probably been taken right from a dealer. Even with planned obsolescence, it would last as long as he'd need it.

He made a U-turn on Second Avenue and went up the hill and over to the Thruway entrance. The way he'd originally figured, he'd go back to Jersey City and stay over tonight, then pick up Edgars in the morning and head west. But now, having to stop off in Syracuse to see Klee, he'd have to make better time than that, get Edgars to leave tonight. If everything worked out, they could maybe pull it next Thursday night.

He picked up the ticket at the Thruway entrance and headed south. He was impatient, but he stayed just under the speed limit. He didn't want a trooper looking into the road-racer boxes on the back seat.

4

"THIS IS Jean," said Edgars. He seemed uncomfortable.

Jean wasn't uncomfortable at all. She was a hard-looking blonde of about thirty, short, with hard, conical breasts. She was sitting on the sofa in the living room of Edgars' apartment, her legs crossed and skirt hiked up to show her tan.

Parker looked at Jean and then at Edgars. He said, "So what?"

Edgars swallowed. "She's coming along," he said.

"Since when?"

"Since always. She's always been with me."

"Always?" Parker looked at her. She wouldn't be with anybody always, and especially not Edgars.

"She doesn't have anything to do with the business arrangement," Edgars said. "I always had her go out to a movie or something when we had a meeting. And she can wait for us in Madison or somewhere until we're done."

Jean smiled lazily, looking at Parker like a nightclub booker at an audition, waiting for the new act to do something interesting. She said, "I'll get along."

Parker looked at Edgars and shook his head. "No dice. She can wait for you here."

"Why? She'll keep out of the way, I guarantee it."

"She'll keep out of the way better in Jersey City."

"Parker, I give you my word—"

"I don't want your word."

Jean said, "Who's the boss around here, anyway, honey?"

"Nobody," Parker told her. "And that's just the kind of trouble you bring with you." He turned to Edgars. "She stays here."

Edgars was embarrassed and uneasy. He felt like a fool, in front of the woman. He said, "Nobody else will even *see* her. I guarantee it. We'll take her part way and leave her in Madison or somewhere. I'll never say a word to any of the others; they won't even know she exists."

Jean laughed and said, "Just a quiet little mouse, that's me. Quiet little mouse."

Parker said, "She'll show up in the middle of it. At the town, or the hideout."

Edgars shook his head. "No, she won't, Parker. I'm not a professional at this kind of thing, like you, but I know better than that. She doesn't know where the job *is*, except North Dakota, and she doesn't know where the hideout is either."

"Except North Dakota," said Jean, and laughed again. She looked at Parker, a challenge in her eyes, and said, "You don't have to worry about me, Parker. I know my business, too."

"We leave her farther away than Madison," Parker said. He didn't like giving in on this thing, but looking at Edgars he saw he would have to. The trouble the woman could cause if they took her along was less than the trouble Edgars could cause, lousing up the operation out of pique and embarrassment, if they didn't take her along. "We leave her in some town this side of the North Dakota line."

"*I* pick the town," she said.

Edgars nodded, grateful for the compromise. "All right," he said. "I understand what you mean, Parker. That's why I kept her out of sight all the time."

"Sometimes I feel like a sheep or something," she said. "Couldn't you bastards at least lower your voices? You talk about me like I'm not even here, and I'm getting irritated."

They both ignored her. Parker said to Edgars, "I got to make a stop in Syracuse, so we'll have to leave tonight."

"Tonight? I'm not packed or anything."

"So pack."

Jean said, "What about me? Half my stuff's still over to the old place."

Edgars wanted to hold onto her, but he knew she was a liability. He sounded irritated when he said, "So go over to the old place and *get* your stuff."

"Jesus," she said. "It's like the army. Alert! Alert! Alert! Pack your bag in the middle of the night and run your ass off."

"I told you before about that language."

"Up yours," she said.

Parker said, "Argue later. Right now, pack."

She turned to Parker, saying, "Drive me over to the old place."

"Take a cab."

"*You're* the one in the hurry, ugly."

"You better take her," Edgars said. "Otherwise, she'll be gone for hours. I'd take her, but I got to pack. And I don't have a car." He said the last with surprise.

Parker was about ready to tell them both to go to hell, but then he thought of Edgars and his private reasons. The bitch might know something about them. He said, "All right, let's go."

"Be right back, honey." She twisted the last word like a knife.

They left the building and got into the Mercury, and Parker said, "Where to?"

"Just straight ahead awhile. I'll show you where to turn. Don't worry, ugly, you won't get lost with me."

"I know."

They rode four blocks in silence, and then she told him to turn right. It was after eleven at night, the middle of the week, and not much traffic on the streets. Parker drove along steadily, trying to think of a way to lead in to the questions he wanted to ask. Being no good at small talk was sometimes a disadvantage.

Ahead of him, a traffic light switched to red. He stopped and waited, and no cars came along from right or left to take advantage of the green light.

She said, "What do you know about him?"

Was she going to volunteer it all herself? He said, "Edgars, you mean?"

"Who else? What kind of a bird is he?"

So that took care of that. She knew less about Edgars than Parker did. On the off-chance, he said, "I thought you knew him from always."

She laughed. "That's his story. On my side, 'always' looks like three weeks."

"Since he came to town."

"I guess."

"You didn't sound like North Dakota."

"Compliments yet."

"That wasn't a compliment."

The light changed again, and he drove on. Two blocks farther on she told him to make a left. Her voice was cold as ice. He got stopped by another traffic light, went two more blocks and she said, "Just ahead on the right."

There was a fireplug handy. He parked next to it. She said, "You want a ticket?"

"What do you care?"

"Not a thing, ugly. Wait here, I'll be as quick as I can."

"I'll come along."

"Why?"

"So you'll be quicker."

"Mister Edgars has such sweet friends."

It was a brick apartment building, the entrance flanked by coachlamps bearing twenty-five-watt bulbs. There was a small green elevator, which took them slowly to the third floor. As they walked down the hall, she rummaged in her purse for a key and said, "If my roomie's in, try not to be any uglier than you have to."

She unlocked a door and pushed it open. The apartment was dark. She felt along the wall and found the light switch. It was a ceiling light that came on, showing a large room full of clutter. Newspapers, magazines, paperback books, scattered all over the place. A studio couch was covered by wrinkled sheets and blankets; a pillow was on the floor next to it. There were wicker chairs and end tables and two lamps. A gray carpet was on the floor.

"My roomie's a mess. Come in, if you're coming. Shut the door. You want a drink?"

"No. Just pack."

"I'm going to love traveling with you, ugly. You mind if I take a shower?"

"Yes."

"Tough. That's just plain tough."

"If you want to know how far you can push me," he told her, "you can find out right now."

She hesitated, and then she shrugged. "I don't care. You didn't want me to come along, you talked about me like I wasn't there, so I got sore. What do you expect?"

"I didn't expect you at all."

"Well, I'm here. I'll keep out of the way like a good girl, and I won't make trouble with Edgars or anybody else. All right?"

Parker shrugged. "That's all I ask."

"So I'll take a very quick shower. Quickest ever, I promise. Okay?"

Parker looked at his watch. "We want to be out of here in twenty minutes."

"Fifteen. Okay?"

She was making an effort, so he ought to make an effort, too. He made an effort, relaxed his face a little, and said, "Okay."

"There's booze in the kitchen, if you want a drink. And I won't call you ugly any more. Okay?"

Now she was overdoing it. "Just get moving," he said.

"You're hard to get along with, you know that?"

He didn't say anything at all to that, so after a minute she went on into the other room. Parker found the kitchen, found a bottle of Philadelphia and a glass and a tray of ice cubes, and made himself a drink. He could hear the shower running.

She was available. Some other time, he'd probably do something about it, but not now. He ran to a pattern that way; right after a job he was raring, he couldn't get enough. Then it would slacken off, gradually, over months, until he didn't give a damn at all. When he was working, he was an ascetic, not out of choice but just because that's the way he was built.

He stood in the kitchen doorway, looking at the messy living room and pulling at his drink. He heard the shower stop, and then she called, "You get a drink?"

"Yes."

"Make me one?"

He went back to the kitchen and made her one, just whiskey over ice in a glass. He carried the two glasses across the living room and into a small airless bedroom with a closed Venetian blind over the one window. She was wearing a white terrycloth robe, and a suitcase was open on the double bed. Her hair was wet, plastered to her head, and her face was scrubbed clean of make-up. That way she looked younger and less hard. Without the shrill good looks that cosmetics gave her, she had a plain and somewhat thin face.

"Just put it on the dresser," she said. "You want to dry my back?"

"You do it." He turned away.

"Wait a second."

"Why?"

She was studying him with confusion. "You a good friend of Edgars, or what?"

"What," he said.

"You always in such a goddam hurry like this?"

"I am this time."

"I try to be friendly, and you put me down. What's the matter with you?"

They were going to be traveling halfway across the country together, and she could always louse up Edgars' effectiveness in the operation some way if she wanted to, so he made the effort again and said, "Maybe it'll be different afterwards."

"Afterwards what? You mean after this big secret mission you and charming Billy got on?"

"That's right."

She shrugged. "Okay, I'll dry my own back. It wouldn't stay wet till then, anyway."

Parker went back to the living room, tipped a wicker chair forward to dump newspapers and magazines out of it onto the floor, and sat down. He looked at his watch; six minutes had gone by.

When she came out, dressed in black skirt and white blouse and tan summer coat, carrying a suitcase in each hand, he looked at his watch again. Exactly fifteen minutes. She said, "Well? Do I get the gold star?"

"Yeah."

"Sure. Gold-star mother. I had a boy in the service, but he died. Here, you're the gentleman, carry these things. I'll be right back." She put the suitcases down and went into the kitchen. She came back carrying the bottle.

5

"THERE'S THE turnoff," Edgars said. He pointed.

Parker turned the Mercury off the highway and onto the secondary road. The highway had been concrete, three lanes wide, straight as a bowling alley. The secondary road was blacktop, two lanes wide, and curved a lot. But the road surface was good, they could still make good time.

In the trunk of the car, along with the three road-racer sets from Scofe, were three rifles and eight pistols from Amos Klee. The rifles were a Higgins Model 45, chambered for .30-30, a Ruger .44 carbine, and a Winchester Standard 70, chambered for .30-06. The pistols were mostly S&W, .32 or .38 revolvers. Two boxes on the floor behind the front seat contained ammunition.

Yesterday they'd left the blonde, Jean, in a motel outside Thief River Falls, Minnesota. The name of the city struck Edgars as funny, which is why they picked it. Edgars wrote down the motel phone number, so he could call her from time to time and let her know everything was all right.

One way or another, she'd apparently made up her mind about Parker the first night, back in Jersey City. On the trip out she kept to herself, saying little, sitting on the back seat with her feet on the ammunition boxes, working her way through bottle after bottle. Every time they stopped, Edgars had to go buy her another bottle. "Gold-star mother," she said to Parker once, and started to cry. But she cried silently and didn't bother him. She was only about thirty, so the gold-star mother stuff was crap. Probably meant a boy friend killed in the army. Every tramp has an excuse.

But yesterday they'd unloaded her at Thief River Falls. Edgars gave her a bottle and some money, and promised to call every other day. Then he and Parker drove the last stretch to North Dakota. At Madison they picked up the highway that connected with 22A, the road into Copper Canyon. Three miles this side of it they came to the secondary road that headed toward the abandoned strip mine.

Parker glanced at the speedometer. "You said six miles to the dirt road?"

"About that."

They rode in silence, till Edgars said, "There it is."

Parker looked again at the speedometer. Six point two. He nodded, and made the turn.

The dirt road was in worse condition than the blacktop road; it hadn't been kept up since the mining company had moved on. Parker kept it at thirty, and the car jounced badly, but never badly enough to force him to slow down. He checked the rear-view mirror from time to time, but the land here was clay or something and there was practically no dust raised in their wake. That was good.

They ran through a small woods that was choked with underbrush and then they emerged suddenly on a brown flat plain. Just ahead were squat small buildings, some of corrugated metal, some of wood siding. There was a station wagon parked up close to one of the wooden buildings. As Parker drove the Mercury closer a man came into view, walking leisurely toward them. It was Littlefield.

Parker braked to a halt, and Littlefield came around to his side and said, "You made good time. How you like it here?"

"Where do I put the car?"

Littlefield pointed. "That one over there. We ripped some of the wall down on the other side, so we could get cars in."

Parker nodded, and drove forward again. Seen up close, the buildings were just sheds, each with a single door and one or two windows in each wall. Parker made a circle past the shed Littlefield had pointed out, and swung around to face it. It was one of the corrugated ones, and a couple of pieces of the wall were lying on the ground to one side. Parker drove through the open space and stopped.

There was just a dirt floor inside, and darkness, and dry heat. Parker felt sweat breaking out on his face before he was out of the car. There was a Plymouth already in there; with Parker's Mercury added the shed was full.

"Christ," said Edgars. "Hot."

They went back out to the sunlight and walked around the shed and over to Littlefield, who was standing next to the station wagon, watching them. Littlefield was wearing gray work pants and a flannel shirt and a cowboy hat. He didn't look like a member of the board of directors any more; out here he looked like a hanging judge.

Littlefield said, "We set this one up for living quarters. You go on in, I'll stay out here and watch for them."

"Better get the wagon out of sight."

"One car don't make any difference."

"Get it out of sight anyway."

Littlefield pursed his lips and went away to get the car out of sight.

Parker and Edgars went into the wooden shed. Inside, it was one large room, and it seemed a little cooler than outside. Folded army cots were stacked in a corner near some cardboard cartons. A folding table and some folding chairs were set up in the middle of the room.

Five men were in the room. Kerwin and Wycza and Salsa and Pop Phillips were sitting around the table, playing poker. Paulus was in the corner, inventorying the contents of the cartons.

Phillips waved a greeting. "Welcome to our happy home," he said.

Edgars said, "It looks okay, doesn't it?"

"It's okay," Parker told him. But he felt exposed, these little sheds on the flat brown plain.

Phillips said, "It was a deal of work for two old men, I'll tell you that. Me and Littlefield, we took down some walls to make garages, we transported food, we buried jugs of water under one of the sheds, we swept up, hung some curtains, planted azaleas outside the windows, and hired a butler."

"It looks good," Parker said. He looked at Kerwin. "How's the town?"

"Easy."

"Can we do it this week?"

"Sure."

"No problems?"

"None."

"Of course," Pop Phillips said, "Wycza and Salsa, here, they did help a bit. But for two old codgers, Littlefield and me, we did our share."

"Sure you did," Wycza told him. Wycza always seemed proud of Phillips, as though he'd invented him.

Paulus, from the corner, said, "I'm not sure we've got enough food."

"We've got enough," Phillips told him. "We've got plenty, don't you worry."

Littlefield stuck his head in the doorway. "Somebody coming." He went away again.

Parker went over to a window and watched a green Ford coming closer. It stopped. Littlefield went over to talk to the driver and then pointed. The car moved again. When it went by, Parker saw it was Wiss and Elkins.

Salsa came over. "I got the walkie-talkies. Shall I explain them to you?"

"Sure."

They went over to where the walkie-talkies were, nesting in four boxes like outsize shoeboxes. Salsa explained they were a matched set, he'd had them fixed for him. Talk into any one and the voice came out of all the other three. You couldn't talk to just one of the other walkie-talkies, but you couldn't talk to any walkie-talkies except these three, either. "I told the man we were a group of hunters," he said. He smiled, and his teeth were white and even. The Latin lover, with a tan. "I told the truth," he said. "We are a group of hunters."

"They look good," Parker told him. "Good work."

Wiss and Elkins came in then, and Wiss said to Phillips, "I need a cool place to keep the juice. Littlefield says to talk to you."

"One second." Phillips looked at his cards, said, "Fold," and got to his feet. "I'll show you. Sit in for me, Elkins."

Elkins sat down at the table, and Wiss and Phillips left. Salsa, still standing beside Parker, said, "This Thursday?"

"Right."

"Three days. Good. Three days before, four days after. One week is about all I will be able to take of this place."

Parker nodded. Their original plan had been to stay in towns around the general area until the night of the raid, but they'd decided instead to gather here today, and stay until after the job was finished. This way there wouldn't be any strangers in nearby towns for the locals to remember later.

Edgars came over and said, "We're set, huh? This is like I told you, isn't it?"

"It's fine. When Phillips comes back, have him show you some place to stow the ammunition. That shed's too hot."

"Will do."

Littlefield stuck his head in again. "Chambers' coming."

Parker followed him outside and watched. Chambers was wrestling the truck across the uneven ground, and the trailer, empty, was jogging back and forth. The cab was a Mack, painted red, and the trailer a metal-color Fruehauf, just about the biggest standard size made. Neither cab nor trailer had any sort of company name or markings visible on them.

Parker stuck his head back in the door and called, "Edgars! Where's the road down into the ravine?"

Edgars came outside and pointed. "Down past those sheds. You see the dropoff?"

"All right."

Chambers had pulled the truck to a stop near the shed. Parker went over and climbed up into the cab and shut the door. Chambers was grinning, his face dirty, streaked with sweat. "This is a big old bastard," he said.

"How was the road, coming in?"

"Not too bad. Couldn't top thirty-five, but I got no load. When we come back with the ass full of men and gold, she'll sit just fine on that road. You got a cigarette?"

Parker gave him a cigarette and lit one for himself. Chambers said, "I got it offen Chemy. He says to tell you hello, and his brother run that woman off. That make sense to you?"

"Yeah. Edgars says the road down to the bottom's over that way. Let's see if this truck'll do it."

"If it don't, we can sing hymns while we fall."

Chambers started the truck forward again, slowly, and after a minute Parker could see the edge. The brown earth just stopped, and there was midair. Across the way, a good distance off, the earth started again; over there he could see the sheer brown wall going downward.

"Son of a bitch," said Chambers. "I bet that's it there." He pointed out the cab window.

Chambers stopped the truck, and they both got down and

walked over to look at the road. Down below, eighty feet down, there was a flat brown expanse with nothing growing on it. Two streams of red water angled and wandered through it. It looked like a sunny part of Hell.

"Look at that," said Chambers. "Red water. What do you think, maybe it's wine."

"There's the road."

They both looked at it. It ran down the side of the wall, one lane wide, a dirt road with two broad ruts running down it. It went down at a steep slope, but it was straight all the way, reaching bottom at the far end of the ravine, where the ravine sloped up somewhat. The ruts circled there and came back along the ravine floor.

"I don't know," said Chambers. "I don't like the looks of it."

"Ore trucks did it."

"They're built low to the ground. Low center of gravity. I got me an empty trailer on there."

"It's straight. Just take it slow, that's all."

"Come on along, Parker. It's your idea."

They went back and got into the cab again. Chambers released the brake and eased the truck forward to the edge and slowly down the incline. They could hear the trailer couplings banging.

"She wants to run," said Chambers. "She wants to fly down this goddam road."

"You'll make it," Parker told him. "No problem."

"Sure."

The truck inched down the wall to the bottom, and Chambers swung the wheel to bring it around facing the other way. He stopped it, shifted into neutral, and said, "Give me another cigarette."

They smoked a minute in silence, Chambers wiping sweat off his face onto his sleeve, and then Parker said, "Looks like they cut into the wall over there. Let's go over and look."

"I shoulda got me a biddy panel truck."

Chambers wrestled the truck forward, and they came to a part where the side of the ravine angled inward sharply from top to bottom, leaving a narrow strip of the bottom in shadow. Chambers backed and filled till he got the truck in close to the side, in the shadow, and then they both got out and looked at it. Parker said, "We want to get some black paint. That metal shines too much."

"Brown paint. Make it blend right in. Camio-flage."

"All right, brown."

"Now we walk up, right?"

"Right."

"Christ. I'd be better off working."

"Come on."

Chambers took a step, stopped, and said, "Rotten eggs. Smell it?"

"That's your wine rivers. Sulphur."

"Real homey place."

They walked back up the road to the top and went into the shed where the others were. Grofield was there now, making everybody present. Parker looked at him and waited for him to say, "All fools in a circle."

But what he said was, "Come, Watson, come! The game is afoot!"

"This isn't summer stock."

"Good old Parker. This Thursday, huh?"

"This Thursday." He turned to Littlefield. "All the cars stashed?"

"Right. Six of them. Two each in three sheds."

"We better put the sides back on, in case anybody comes out here. What about the wagon?"

"I put it down in the woods, off the road."

"Good."

Parker and Wycza and Salsa and Grofield went out and put the torn-down sections of wall back into place, hiding the cars inside. Two men would be leaving in each car, after the job, each car going off to a different destination. Wiss and Elkins would leave together, and Wycza and Phillips, Paulus and Littlefield, Chambers and Salsa, Grofield and Kerwin. Parker would take Edgars with him, pick up the blonde at Thief River Falls, and drive them as far as Chicago. After that, they were on their own; Chicago was where Parker would dump the Mercury.

After they got the walls back up, and returned to the living-in shed, Parker found Littlefield and said, "One last trip to town for you. We need brown paint, to cover the truck."

"Right. What if I go in after dark?"

"If you can find a store open."

"There's a hardware store I seen open nights in Madison."

"Good."

Parker dragged a couple of food cartons over to the table and sat down on them. "Deal me in," he said. Behind him, Grofield was reciting, playing Falstaff and Hal both, *Henry IV, Part I*, Act 1, Scene 2.

6

CHAMBERS BROUGHT the truck up at eleven-thirty, using the parking lights only. The rest were waiting for him in the darkness at the top. In the last three days, they hadn't seen a single stranger, afoot or in a car or even in a plane. They might as well have been the last people on earth.

Parker and Salsa and Edgars carried machine guns—Parker had discovered, to his surprise, that Edgars already knew how to operate a Tommy—and Grofield, Chambers and Littlefield carried rifles. Salsa and Parker both also wore pistols, as did Kerwin and Phillips and Paulus and Wycza and Wiss and Elkins. Parker and Salsa and Wycza and Grofield had walkie-talkies strapped to their backs.

Chambers was to drive the truck, Littlefield the station wagon. Phillips and Edgars and Grofield were to ride in the wagon, the rest in the truck.

Chambers cut the parking lights as soon as he stopped the truck. There was no moon, but the sky was clear and full of stars. There was enough vague light to see by, sufficient for everyone to board.

Six men climbed into the back of the truck and sat along the sides, bracing themselves for the bumpy ride to come. Paulus and Wycza and Kerwin on one side, Wiss and Elkins and Salsa on the other. The safe men's equipment was to ride in the station wagon, where it would get a less bumpy trip.

Parker went over to the station wagon and said to Littlefield, "Remember, give us five minutes. We'll run slower than you, you can catch up when we get to town."

"Right."

"Don't catch up before we pass the trooper barracks."

"I remember, Parker."

"See you later."

Parker went back to the truck, took off his walkie-talkie, and climbed up into the cab with Chambers. He put the walkie-talkie on the floor between his legs and said, "All set."

Chambers put on his parking lights again, and the truck jolted forward.

It was seven miles to the secondary road, and they did it at a crawl, not because of the bumps but because of the bad visibility. Chambers leaned far over the wheel, peering out through the windshield at the dimly seen dirt road. Beside him, Parker lit a cigarette and sat quiet. The last few minutes before a job, he was always quiet, almost in suspended animation. He had no imagination for the few hours ahead, nor worry, nor anticipation, nor anything else. His consciousness worked at the level of recording the jouncing of the truck cab and the feel of the cigarette smoke and the darkness beyond the windshield.

They got to the secondary road and made their turn, and Chambers sighed. He sat back more comfortably, switched on his headlights, and the truck picked up speed. After a minute, Chambers said, "You ever get scared, times like this, Parker?"

Parker roused himself, and said, "No."

"You're lucky. I could use me a jolt of store-bought blended right about now." He laughed, a little shakily. "If them streams would of been wine," he said, "they'd be dry right now. You know, I can smell sulphur in this cab? This here's a good road, there'll be no problem coming back. Be light then, too."

Chambers talked on, working off nervous energy, and Parker sat silent beside him. They made the six miles to the highway and turned left. Up to now they hadn't seen any other traffic, but a mile along the highway they saw headlights in front of them. They came on, moving fast, and a foreign sports car raced by, looking to them in the cab of the truck so low and small it could have gone under the truck instead of next to it.

"Maybe I'll buy me one of them," said Chambers.

Parker leaned forward a little bit and looked at the rear-view mirror outside the right window. A way back, he could see headlights. "If that's Littlefield," he said, "I'll crack his skull."

"Don't worry 'bout Littlefield. He knows what he's doing."

By the time they made the turnoff onto 22A, the headlights had dropped farther back. They rolled along, right on the speed limit, and after they passed the trooper barracks—a squat brick building with yellow lights behind the windows, off to their left, surrounded by flat emptiness—Parker said, "Slow down a little now. Give Littlefield a chance to catch up." The headlights of the station wagon were much farther back now, almost invisible.

Ahead of them, on the right, was a sign. They came closer, and the truck lights illuminated it:

WELCOME

to

COPPER CANYON

"Son of a gun," said Chambers. "Son of a gun."

THREE

I

OFFICERS FELDER and Mason were on night-duty in Copper Canyon's only prowl car. They rode along in companionable silence, looking for but not expecting to see violators of the city curfew. It was just a few minutes after midnight, and here and there lights were still on behind windows, but the sidewalks were empty. The radio hissed like coffee brewing; at the other end, Officer Nieman had nothing to say.

The prowl car was a Ford, two years old, painted light green and white, with *Police* written in large letters on the doors and hood and trunk. The dashboard lights were green, and there was a small red dot of light, like a ruby, on the radio. Officer Mason wanted a cigarette but couldn't have one, because Officer Felder, who was driving, was allergic to cigarette smoke. Officer Mason said, "What say we take a break? I could use a smoke."

"Let me swing down around by the west gate. George is on there tonight."

"Fine by me."

They were on Blake Street, east of Raymond Avenue. Officer Felder drove over to Raymond Avenue and turned right, and the west gate to the refinery was six blocks dead ahead.

A few cars were parked along Raymond Avenue, as usual. Between Loomis and Orange Streets, against the right-hand curb, there was a huge tractor trailer parked. It was brown, all over brown. Officer Mason looked at it and thought to himself, *Funny color for a truck.*

He reached into his pocket and pulled out a pack of cigarettes. He got one out, then got his lighter out. He was ready.

They were almost to the gate when the hissing radio suddenly spoke. "Officer Felder, Officer Mason. Officer Felder, Officer Mason."

Officer Mason looked at it in surprise. What the hell kind of way to talk was that? They were on first-name basis, always. What the hell was this all about?

He grinned and said to Officer Felder, "Old Fred's gettin' highfalutin."

"He's just kidding around."

Officer Mason picked up the microphone and said, "Yes, *sir*, Officer Nieman, what can I do for you, sir?"

"Come on in to the station. Something's come up."

"What's come up?"

"Just get in here. Make it fast."

There was something funny in Officer Nieman's voice, some sort of agitation. Officer Mason said, "Okay, Fred, here we come." He hung up the microphone again and said to Officer Felder, "*Some*thing's sure got him upset. You hear his voice?"

"I heard it." Officer Felder had already made the turn into Caulkins Street, and was driving toward police headquarters.

"That's a funny thing," said Officer Mason.

"What is?"

"Kidding around one minute, then all upset the next."

"Maybe he wasn't kidding around. Maybe he got all formal and everything because he was upset already. Got rattled or something."

"Well, let's see what it is."

The police station was a modern building. It, and the fire department building across the street, had both been built five years ago, both with the same architect. They were built of tan brick, broad low buildings one story high, very similar in appearance except for the wide garage-type doors across half of the fire department building façade. Flanking the police station entrance were large modernistic faceted green lights, and across the street the fire department entrance was flanked by similar lights in red.

Officer Felder pulled to the curb in front of the building, in the No Parking zone, one of the few in town. They both got out of the car and went up the cement walk past the well-tended lawn into the building. They entered upon a hallway, and the Command Room—as the architect had called it—where Fred Nieman would be, was to the left. It was a large room, with desks along one wall, and a counter in front of the area where the radio and booking desk were located.

They went into the Command Room, and Fred Nieman looked at them from over by the radio. He didn't stand up or say anything or do anything. He offered them a weak and sheepish smile, and just sat there.

A voice behind them said, quietly, "There's seven guns on you. Either of you make a single solitary move, you're dead seven times."

The two officers froze. Both of them thought immediately that it was some sort of gag, and both looked at Officer Nieman to find a clue in his face. But Nieman's face was pale and frightened and sheepish, slit by a nervous, ashamed smile.

Footsteps sounded on the black composition flooring, coming from behind them, going to right and to left. Two men came around in front of them, both in dark work clothing, both wearing black hoods, slit three times for eyes and mouth. One of the two was carrying a Thompson submachine gun and had what looked like a walkie-talkie strapped to his back. The other one had a walkie-talkie, too, and carried a rifle.

Mason thought, *A war attack. Commies!* But even while he was thinking it, he knew that wasn't it. This was something else. It might even be something worse.

Another black-hooded man, this one with a rifle but no walkie-talkie, stood up from where he'd been crouched beside the radio, out of sight from the door, and said, "Okay, Fred boy, git on over there by your pals."

Officer Nieman got shakily to his feet and went around the end of the counter and came across the floor toward Mason and Felder. His face was pale, and shone with sweat under the fluorescent lights. A look of apology and shame was all over his face. Mason, watching him, thought Fred might even faint.

A hand came from behind Mason and took the revolver out of his holster. Another hand unarmed Felder.

The one with the machine gun said, "Listen close. For the next few hours, you got nothing to do but sit. You just sit, and don't get cute ideas, and you'll be all right. You." He pointed the machine gun at Mason. "What's your name?"

"Officer Mason."

"First name."

"Jim. James."

"All right, Jim. You, what's your name? First name."

"Albert."

"They call you Al, or Bert?"

"Al."

"Okay, Jim, Al, turn around, and do it slow."

They turned around. There were four more of them back there, hooded, in work clothes, one with another Thompson submachine gun, one with another rifle, and two with revolvers. They were just standing there, pointing all that death at Mason and Felder.

The spokesman said, "All right, Jim, Al, you've seen enough. Turn around again."

They turned around. Mason was trying to think, trying to figure out their game. What the hell was all this?

The spokesman was saying, "Who's got the prowl car key?"

Felder said, "Me. I have." Mason was gratified to hear a quaver in Felder's voice; he didn't want either of his brother officers to be less frightened than he was, and he was terrified.

"Bring it over here, Al. Hand it to me."

Felder did as he was told.

"Now go back where you were, Al. The two of you, Al, Jim, get your handcuffs out. Reach them behind you. Don't turn around, Jim, just reach back. Now put your hands together behind you."

Mason put his hands behind his back, and felt the cold metal of the cuffs close around his wrists. He looked at Nieman's face and suddenly realized why Nieman had been so formal when he'd called in; he was trying to warn them.

Mason said, softly, "I'm sorry, Fred, I didn't get it."

"Didn't get what?" It was the one who'd been hidden behind the radio, stepping forward.

Mason closed his mouth. Now he'd done it!

The one with the rifle and the walkie-talkie said, "All the world's a stage, and all the men and women merely players. Fred's seen too many movies. He tried to signal these two by calling them by their last names."

"Son of a bitch!" The one who'd been hidden behind the radio came closer and raised the rifle and slashed at Fred Nieman's head with the butt. Nieman ducked away, raising his arms, and the rifle butt thudded into his shoulder, knocking him down.

The spokesman said sharply, "Cut that out! We need him."

"You hear what he tried to pull?"

"It didn't work. It never does. Fred, how's your shoulder?"

Nieman sat on the floor, holding his shoulder, and didn't speak.

The one who'd hit him said, "You better answer, boy, double quick."

"It's all right."

"Good," said the spokesman. "All right, Al, Jim, come on over this way. Al, lie down between these two desks here. Face down, that'll be more comfortable, with your hands behind you that way. Jim, you over here between these two desks."

It was tough to get down without his hands to help him. He dropped to his knees and was stuck, until hands came along to lower him more or less gently the rest of the way. He felt his ankles being tied, and then a new voice said, "Open your mouth, Jim."

He opened his mouth. A piece of sponge was stuck into it and then a cloth tied around his head, covering his mouth, to keep the sponge in.

He couldn't see anyone now. All he could see was desk legs and chair legs and the wall. But his ear was pressed against the floor, and he could loudly hear them walking around.

A new voice said, "All right, Fred, get back to the radio. You just sit there, and if a call comes in from anywhere, you handle it like it was a normal night. And don't try anything else cute. I'll know if you do."

It was a familiar voice to Mason, the first familiar voice to come out from one of those black hoods. It was an arrogant voice, and an angry voice, and a familiar voice. Who? Who the hell was it?

All at once he knew, and his terror doubled. He heard the footsteps receding and then the familiar voice saying, "Now we're alone, boys. Just you three and me. And this Tommy gun."

Edgars! It was Edgars!

2

CHAMBERS FELT all right now, all the nervousness gone, all the jumpiness out of his system. All he'd needed was to get *started*, get *into* this thing. From the second he'd clubbed that smart-ass cop, every bit of jitters just washed right on out of him.

They'd left Edgars in there with the cops, and the other six went outside to stand on the lawn. Parker came over and said, "You got that out of your system now?"

"I guess I do. I feel a lot better."

"Don't do it any more."

"Not if I don't have to."

"You don't have to club anybody. Watch them if they behave, kill them if they cause trouble. Nothing in between."

"All right by me."

"Good. Everybody set?"

Everybody said they were set. Chambers felt a small irritation, at being chewed out by Parker right there where everybody could hear, but he shrugged it off. Minor irritations couldn't bother him now. He felt good.

Parker had propped the Tommy against the outer wall of the police station, and had unlimbered the walkie-talkie. Chambers looked across the street at the fire department building, waiting, and behind him Parker said, "Salsa. You set up?" His voice had an echo, tinny and small, coming out of the walkie-talkie on Grofield's back.

Then it was Salsa's voice, coming over both of them: "Set. I'm in a car on Raymond Avenue, facing out, right side as you are going out of town, one block in from that welcome sign."

"Anybody come in since us?"

"Not in or out."

"All right. Wycza?"

"Here."

"We got police headquarters. Going after the firehouse now. If you see the prowl car, don't worry. I'll be driving it."

Wycza laughed, and said, "Want us to start now?"

"Wait till we've got the firehouse and the telephone company. I'll let you know."

"Right."

Chambers had been fidgeting back and forth, standing in the darkness on the police station lawn. Now he said, "Come on, Parker, let's roll it. We don't got all night."

"Don't be so nervous."

"Then let's just roll, what do you say?"

"All right."

The six of them walked over the lawn and the sidewalk and crossed the street, Chambers in the lead, the rifle held at a loose approximation of port arms. His face was sweating, making the hood stick to his flesh, but he didn't really mind that. Just so they were *moving*.

Too bad Ernie wasn't here.

Four big garage doors, painted red, across the front of the building in a row. To the right of them was the regular entrance, flanked by red lights. Like a cat house; Chambers grinned under the hood, feeling his skin stretch.

Chambers and Parker were in the lead when they went in. A hall went ahead and then turned right. After the turn, it ran straight and long, but only the nearest fluorescent light was lit, leaving the rest of the hall in darkness. The first door at the right was open, spilling more light into the hall.

Two men in dark blue uniforms had been sitting on opposite sides of a desk, playing cards. They stared, dropped their cards, and jumped clumsily to their feet. One of them kicked his chair over, getting up.

It was a room very similar to the Command Room in police headquarters, but a little smaller, with fewer desks, fewer pieces of electronic equipment, and less open floor space. Lined around the walls were framed photographs of groups of men standing in front of fire engines, some horse-drawn.

Chambers moved to the left of the door and sensed Parker moving to the right. This was the part he liked, moving fast and moving sure, moving like the pieces of a clock. Let somebody else make the plans; all Chambers wanted was to know his own part in it.

Parker was saying, "You don't have to raise your hands, you aren't armed. You, what's your name?"

"Dee—Deegan."

"First name."

"George."

"And you?"

"Johanson, William Johanson."

"They call you Bill or Will?"

"Uh, Bill."

"All right, Bill, George, just pay attention."

While Parker gave them the spiel, using their first names a lot, telling them how nothing would happen to them if they didn't try nothing stupid, Chambers moved around and pulled a chair out from a desk with his foot and sat down. He kept the rifle level, hoping one of these bastards would make a run for it or something; he'd do just like Parker said, he'd gun him down in a second. But he knew neither of them would try anything; both paunchy geeks in their fifties, scared so bad they had to change their drawers.

Chambers wasn't so sure about Parker. He was supposed to be sharp and cool and efficient and all that, but Chambers wasn't so sure. What was all this crap about the first names? Who cared what kind of first names these stupes had? It was a waste of time.

When Parker was done, Grofield and Phillips came up and hogtied the one named Johanson William Johanson, tieing wrists and ankles and gagging him. Then Parker said to the other one, "How many men on tonight?"

"Fuh—four."

"Including you two?"

"Oh, no. I'm sorry. S-s-six."

"All right, George, just relax. Nobody's going to hurt you. Where are the other four?"

"Down the hall. They're asleep, mister."

"We'll wake them easy. Which room?"

"Last two on the left."

"Thanks, George." Parker turned his head and spoke to Chambers. "We'll let you know when it's clear."

"Sure thing."

Parker and the others went out to tie and gag the other

four sleeping beauties, and Chambers said, sarcastically, "Okay, now, George, just sit right down there. Right there where you were."

George sat down.

"What kind of card game was that, George?"

"Gin."

"Gin. Is that right? You got any of that other kind of gin here, George? You know the kind I mean?"

"No, we don't. I'm sorry, we don't have anything like that."

"That's a real pity, George." Chambers grabbed the bottom of his hood, just under his chin, and flapped it, to get some air inside. "This is a real nice firehouse you got here, George," he said.

"What are you people going to do?"

"Oh, now, don't go asking questions. Remember what happened to that curious cat."

Chambers stretched, and then set the rifle down on the desktop beside him, where it was handy. He said, "You know what you're supposed to do, you get any kind of call, right?"

"Yes. I know."

"Good boy, George. I sure do wish you had some of that other kind of gin."

"I'm sorry. How—how long is this going to be? I mean, before you let us go."

"Curiosity, George."

"But what if there's a fire?"

"Why, we'll just toast marshmallows, George." Chambers laughed, and stuck a hand up under his hood to wipe the sweat from his face.

Parker stuck his head in and said, "Clear. We're moving on now."

"Have a good time, y'all."

"We'll keep you posted. By phone."

Parker went out again.

This was the dull part. From now on, just sitting and waiting, this was going to be the dull part. If Ernie was here, they could Indian wrestle or something. He should of asked to be put on the truck detail, instead of Wycza. Let Wycza sit here all night.

He looked at George, speculatively, trying to find a sign in

George's face to indicate he might maybe try something pretty soon, make life interesting somehow. But there was no sense even hoping; George just wasn't the heroic type, that's all there was to it.

He stretched again. He wished he could take the hood off, but he couldn't. He'd taken one fall, and his picture was on file. A dumb fall. Him and Ernie, seventeen years of age for him and nineteen for Ernie, they were just razzing this clown with the tape recorder, down having old rumpots sing folk songs into it, and someway or other it all got out of hand, and when they were done they hadn't just beat the tape recorder in with lumber chunks like they'd intended, they'd beat the clown in, too. Then they had no more sense but to go right straight on home, and get picked up by the sheriff the next morning. Nobody much believed their story about stopping the clown from trying to rape some little girl that run away and likely too mortified to come forward and testify, but they stuck to the story anyway and got smaller sentences than they might of otherwise. Eight years apiece, for manslaughter. Out in less than three years.

There was a time, once, when three years in a state pen couldn't hurt anybody, but that time's long gone. Go look for a job, and the paperwork starts. When was you in the army? Why not? Where were you instead? What were you in the pen for? We'll call you if there's an opening.

Not all jobs were like that. Nobody cares what you did a while back if all they want you for is to operate a shovel or work in a harvest gang. Heavy work for low wages, all you can use.

There's more than one way to make a living. And if you want more of a living than you can get with a shovel, and if nobody'll give you a sniff at any sort of a job better than that, there's *still* ways to make a living.

Chambers stretched and scratched himself, and watched old George. That damn fool Ernie. Why take off after a sixteen-year-old chippy *anyway*? Who cares how willing she was?

Chambers sighed, and shifted position, and felt the sweat dribbling down. Too bad Ernie wasn't here.

3

GROFIELD HEARD background music. Always, everywhere he went. Sometimes lush and full, with a lot of strings. Sometimes rapidfire, with xylophones and brass, that busy-Manhattan-street-with-yellow-taxicabs music. Sometimes strident, harsh, dramatic. But always music, in the air around his head like a halo.

Right now, next to Parker in the front seat of the prowl car, the music he was hearing was low, slow, like a heavy pulse beat; a bass drum, and a bass fiddle, and maybe a few other instruments, all low-pitched, pounding out a slow relentless beat, gradually building up.

Parker was driving, and wearing a hat he'd taken off one of the cops. The walkie-talkie was on the seat between them, and the Tommy between their knees, barrel down against the floor, stock jutting up onto the seat. Grofield's rifle was in his arms, butt in his lap and barrel pointing up past his right ear. His walkie-talkie was on the floor between his legs.

Behind them, in the other car, were Phillips and Littlefield and Kerwin. The two cars drove over Caulkins Street to Raymond Avenue, and turned left. A block and a half up they saw the truck, but nobody in or near it. Grofield heard the music build up in tempo as they went by, rolling slow and silent, Parker's face all jutting angles in the green dashlights. Grofield turned his head to look at the truck, anonymous-looking truck, imagining the angle of the follow shot, the camera, having trailed up to now, now speeding, going past on the other side, keeping the truck always centered beyond the prowl car, and intercutting to the faces inside, Parker and himself.

He felt he ought to say something, but nothing came to mind. Nothing that wasn't banal, too damn typical of this scene. None of the really great playwrights had ever written this scene; the fifth-raters who had written it would all, to a man, put in his mouth at this point the line, "Well, this is it, boss."

He remained silent.

Three more blocks and they turned left on Blake Street. The telephone company building was one block over, on the corner. Parker stopped the car, and the background music stopped, too, leaving a dramatic silence. Parker got out of the car, carrying the Tommy but leaving the walkie-talkie, and Grofield got out on his side, strapped his walkie-talkie on, and picked up his rifle. The station wagon had stopped behind them, and the other three had gotten out. They'd all had their hoods off while riding, and now they put them back on.

The telephone company building was three stories high, made of the yellow brick that seemed to be standard around here for nonresidential buildings. The walk up to the door was flanked by flowers. There was a dim light beyond the entrance door, and lights behind four of the windows on the second floor left.

They went in without talking. The walkie-talkie on Grofield's back made a tiny jangling sound as he moved, barely loud enough for even him to hear it. That would be amplified on the soundtrack, serve instead of background music. He tried to walk so as to give the jangling a proper slow rhythm.

Inside, a globe hanging from the ceiling was lit, showing a hall, and a wide flight of metal stairs leading up. They went up, sliding their feet onto each step with small shushing sounds, to avoid any clatter, and at the top they saw a door with light behind the frosted glass.

They pushed open the door and went in, Parker first, Grofield after him, and the others behind. Parker said, "Stop, ladies. If anybody screams, I shoot."

Three women. One at a desk, writing with a ballpoint pen. The other two on chairs before a long switchboard filling the right-hand wall, looking like a flat black computer. All three stared. Two opened their mouths, but none of them screamed.

Parker said, "All stand up. Move to the center of the room."

The woman at the desk found part of her voice and said, "What are you men doing here?"

"Do as the gentleman tells you, dear," said Grofield. "Don't interfere with the schedule."

He watched the three women move uncertainly to the center of the room. The two operators looked terrified, period. The woman who'd been at the desk looked both terrified and indignant. But there wouldn't be any screaming, and there wouldn't be any running or anything like that. They'd behave.

Parker lowered the Tommy and pointed at the woman from the desk. "What's your name?"

"Mrs. Sawyer."

"What's your first name, Mrs. Sawyer?"

"Edith."

"Introduce me to the other ladies, Edith."

"I don't know what you have in—"

"Just tell me their names, Edith."

One of the operators blurted, "I'm Linda Peters."

"Thank you, Linda. What's your friend's name?"

The friend spoke for herself. "Mary Deegan."

"Mary Deegan. Tell me, Mary, you related to George Deegan, over at the firehouse?"

"He's my uncle."

"Well, he's in good hands, Mary. Just like you."

Grofield liked to watch Parker work. See him before a job, or after, you'd think he was just a silent heavy, quick-tempered and mean, about as subtle as a gorilla. But on a job, dealing with any people that might be in the way, he was all psychology.

Terrify them first. Terrify them in such a way that they'll freeze. Not so they'll make noise, or run, or jump you, or anything like that, just so they'll freeze. Then talk to them, calm and gentle. Get their first names, and use the first names. When a man uses your first name, calmly and without sarcasm, he's accepting your individuality, your worthiness to live. The use of your first name implies that this man really doesn't want to harm you.

The fright to freeze them, and then the reassurance to keep them frozen. And it worked almost every time.

Parker was explaining it to them now, telling them all they had to know. He was telling them he was sorry two of them would have to be tied and gagged, but it wouldn't be for long. They were watching him, the three of them, hanging on his words.

That was another part of the psychology. Bunch them together right away, in a little group. It reassures them, to be in a group, and it cuts down the possibility of individual initiative.

Each member of the group waits for some other member of the group to lead the way.

Parker even arranged the tieing and gagging differently. Phillips and Littlefield brought over two of the chairs, took the casters off them so they wouldn't roll, and had Mrs. Edith Sawyer and Linda Peters sit down in them. Their ankles were tied to the center chair leg, their wrists were tied behind their backs, and the sponge-and-cloth gags were applied. Then Parker and the others left, and Grofield was on his own.

The operator still loose was Mary Deegan. Grofield said to her, "Mary, do you suppose there's a telephone book around here anywhere?"

"Well, yes. Of course." Her fright was fading, and she was now becoming bewildered.

"Good. Mary, I want you to get that book, and sit down at Edith's desk there, and copy down some phone numbers for me. Will you do that like a good girl?"

"The book's in the desk drawer."

"Well, then, get it."

She went over and sat behind the desk, and looked at him doubtfully. "It's all right for me to open the drawer?"

"Mary, you don't have a gun in that drawer. And if you do, you have more sense than to show it to me. Go ahead and open the drawer."

She opened the drawer, and put the phone book on the desk.

"Good girl. Now, give me the phone number for police headquarters. Got it? Now the firehouse."

She looked up. "Do you really have my uncle prisoner, too?"

"Tut, tut! Prisoner me no prisoner, nor uncle me no uncle." Though she couldn't see it under the hood, he smiled, then said, "A paraphrase of Shakespeare. Your uncle is in good hands. Write down the number, and maybe later you can talk to him."

She wrote down the number.

"Let's see. One more. The night phone at the refinery."

She wrote that one, too.

"Good girl. Just leave the paper there, and rise and go to yon computer, if you would. Resume your seat there." He sat down at the desk, put the rifle down on its top, and pointed to the phone in front of him. "Can I work this? Or do you have to do something there?"

"You can work it."

"Fine." He picked up the receiver, and dialed police headquarters.

It was answered after one ring: "Police headquarters, Officer Nieman." The officer's voice sounded a little thin and strained.

"Hello, Fred, let me talk to E. The man with the machine gun." He felt the women's eyes on his face as he said the last words, and even though he wore a hood he forced himself not to smile.

Edgars came on the line, sounding wary. "Yeah?"

"G here at the phone company. Everything's fine. You can reach me at 7-3060. Got that?"

"Got it. Everything's under control here, too. You're the first call."

"May I be the only."

"Right."

Grofield broke the connection and called the firehouse. The shaky voice this time said only, "Hello?"

"Hello, George. I want to talk to C."

"Who?"

"The man with the rifle."

"Oh. Oh!"

Chambers came on, saying, "How's it going, man?"

"Fine. Everything under control. Let me give you the number here, in case you have to reach me."

"Hold on. George, give me a pencil. And a sheet of paper. Okay, go ahead."

Grofield gave him the number, and then hung up and got to his feet. He took the walkie-talkie off, set it on the desk next to the rifle, and hunched his shoulders to get the stiffness out of them. He looked over at Mary Deegan and said, "Mary, you got direct distance dialing here?"

"Not yet."

"If anybody wants to call out of town, they've got to go through you, right?"

"Yes."

"Good." He picked up the rifle and walked across the room to her. "If anybody calls you, I want to listen in. How do we work that?"

"You could sit there, I guess. Put that headset on, and plug that jack in there."

"Fine. Now we're set, aren't we?"

"I suppose so."

Grofield leaned back in the chair, feeling the unfamiliar closeness of the headset against his ears. The music had a high richness to it now, and he was bringing it back from over Germany, the co-pilot dead in the seat beside him. They'd said daylight low-level precision bombing was impossible, but he'd helped to prove them wrong. Radio silence, radio silence. The earphones were silent on his head.

Six years, eleven jobs. Every one of them had had the moments of high drama, complete with music and camera angles and dramatic lighting effects but they'd all had stretches like this, too, of waiting, silence, and boredom.

Twenty thousand. Maybe more. Too late to get into summer stock now, but there was always winter stock in Florida or Texas or somewhere. This time, why not spend the money the smart way? Produce. Get into the money end of the damn racket for once.

But you couldn't produce stock and act in it both. He'd already tried it, in Maine, three summers ago. But he liked to act and he hated paperwork, and the summer had been a disaster. So he'd do the same as always, act for peanuts in winter stock, throw away the dough on a convertible and a good apartment and good times, and by the end of the season he'd be broke again, looking around for another job. Number twelve.

All except number one had been fine. Competent professional jobs, because he was working with the right people. The first one had been a mess. Begun as a gag, actually gone through with only because nobody wanted to be the first to quit, and successful by pure luck.

In Pennsylvania it was. A repertory company, twelve of them on a shares basis, and the company not even earning enough to maintain itself. Four of the guys had started talking about stealing, as a gag: "If business keeps up this lousy, we'll have to knock over a gas station or two." Then the gag got specific; a supermarket in a suburban area forty miles away.

When it stopped being a gag and started being reality Grofield couldn't say for sure. But it became reality, as they worked out plan after plan for weeks, and then they went ahead and did it, wearing masks, carrying prop guns loaded with blanks, in an old beat-up Chevrolet with mud smeared on the license plates. They got forty-three hundred dollars, and they never were caught.

That was number one, and afterward Grofield swore it would never happen again; you couldn't bank on dumb luck forever. But he was still in general contact with a guy he'd known in the army, and one time he mentioned the supermarket score to him—the only one he'd told about it, up till then—and the guy laughed and offered him a spot driving in a jewelry store heist. It was just driving the car, and he was broke again, summer stock being over and nothing having turned up in the city. So he did it.

And he was still doing it. He was probably the only actor in the United States who could really afford to work at Equity minimum.

Over on the desk, the walkie-talkie spoke, in a tin imitation of Parker's voice, saying, "Radio station taken care of. Nobody was there."

Wycza's voice said, "Shall we start?"

"Wait till we get the west gate."

"It's almost twelve-thirty."

"I know."

Mary Deegan said, suddenly, "You're going to steal the payroll, aren't you?"

"Ask me no questions, I'll tell you no lies. I tell you what, let's play Twenty Questions. You know how to play Twenty Questions?"

"Wha—what?"

"Twenty Questions. Do you know how to play it?"

She nodded, doubtfully.

"Good." He looked around, saw the walkie-talkie. "I'm thinking of something mineral."

All at once she started to cry. She ducked her head and whispered, "I'm, I'm sorry. It's my nerves."

"That's all right, Mary. It's just stage fright, don't worry about it."

4

KERWIN DIDN'T take any part in wrecking the radio station equipment. For himself, he didn't even think it was necessary, but Parker and the others did, so let them do it.

He stood in the doorway, watching the street. The prowl car was parked there, at the curb, with the station wagon behind it. There was absolute silence from the street, but from inside there were the crashes of metallic breakage.

Kerwin liked metal. He liked machinery, liked to watch it work, liked to fiddle with it and learn about it and understand it. At home, he was a ham radio operator, and a do-it-yourselfer. He owned two prewar cars, and they both ran like watches. In one corner of his basement there was a model train layout, full of drawbridges and complex signal systems; he ran the model railroad with his neighbor, and two pipes under the driveway between their houses carried track which linked their systems.

He liked machinery and he hated to see it destroyed. When it came to safes, he liked to use drill and screwdriver and wrench and his own hands; men who relied on nitro were just bums and amateurs, not professional safemen at all. And when it came to the kind of wreckage Parker and Littlefield and Phillips were doing in the radio station now, Kerwin wanted no part of it. He didn't approve.

The sounds stopped. A few seconds later, they came out, all wearing their hoods, and Parker said, "Clear?"

Kerwin nodded. "Clear."

They went out and got into the two cars, Parker and Phillips in the prowl car, Kerwin and Littlefield in the wagon. They drove back up Whittier to Raymond, turned left, and drove down to the end, to the west gate of the plant.

This part had no effect on Kerwin at all. People were just fuses; they had to be deactivated before you could get to work. He and Littlefield waited while the prowl car nosed forward to the gate, and the guard came out of his booth, waving in a friendly way. Then the guard stopped, and raised his hands, and Kerwin saw Phillips get out of the car, walk around it, disarm the guard, and walk him back into his shack.

Littlefield cleared his throat, and said, "Think they need us?"

"If they do, they'll motion to us."

"I guess so."

Parker had gotten out of the car now, too, and had gone into the shack. After a couple of minutes, Phillips came out wearing the guard's uniform. He attached a metal sign to the already-closed gate, and got into the car just as Parker also came out of the shack.

Littlefield cleared his throat again. "It's certainly running smooth," he said.

Kerwin glanced at him and saw how tightly he was holding to the steering wheel. "Nothing to be nervous about," he said.

"That's right." Littlefield coughed, and cleared his throat.

The prowl car had backed away from the gate, and swung to the right. Littlefield put the wagon in gear, and followed the prowl car down Copper Street toward the other gate. Closed luncheonettes and bars and barber shops and tailors were on their right, and the fence on their left. Beyond the fence were the dark bulks of the plant buildings, and beyond them, in total darkness, the sheer wall of the canyon.

Again, the station wagon hung back while the prowl car drove up to the gate. The same actions were repeated, and then Parker waved to them to come forward. Phillips had opened the gate, and was standing there looking natural and easy in the guard uniform. He gave them a mock salute as the wagon passed him, following Parker along the blacktop company street between the buildings.

By the time Littlefield stopped in front of the main building, Kerwin had his bag of tools ready in his lap. They got out of the car, joined Parker, and the three of them went into the building.

As far as Kerwin was concerned, defusing people was Parker's job. Kerwin's job was simply to stand there and add numerical strength. He entered the office with Parker and Littlefield, and belatedly drew the revolver from his shoulder holster. Guns were about the only machines he wasn't interested in; he held this one absent-mindedly, waiting without listening while

Parker talked to the frightened man a while, and then Parker and Littlefield tied and gagged him. Once they were done, he put the revolver away again—the safety hadn't been off yet tonight—and said, "Where is it?"

"Through here."

Littlefield was sitting at the desk now, clearing his throat and watching the telephone. Kerwin followed Parker through a doorway, across an office, down a hall, and through another office. He waited while Parker forced a locked door, then went into the room and looked at the safe.

It was dark green, with yellow designs. Approximate exterior dimensions, four feet high, two and a half feet wide, three feet deep. Simple combination lock. Parker had turned on the office lights, because the windows here faced the rear of the building. Kerwin walked over and set his bag on a desk and patted the top of the safe.

Parker said, "You all set?"

"Mmm? Yes, of course."

5

PAULUS SAT on the floor in the back of the truck, and fidgeted. It was pitch black in the truck, nothing to see, nothing to do. Paulus liked to be able to observe what was going on, to see symmetry in the motion around him, and to see whether or not things were going right. Sitting here in the truck, in darkness, while actions important to him were going on outside, was torture.

From time to time, Wycza's walkie-talkie spoke out in Parker's voice, saying where they were, what they'd done. That they'd ruined the equipment in the radio station. A little later, that they'd captured the guard on the west gate. Just the bare facts, unadorned.

It wasn't enough. Paulus wanted to be able to *see*. He wanted to look at the radio station equipment and *know* it was no longer workable. He wanted to see the guard, find out his name, watch his reactions, gauge the possible danger he might be during the course of the night. He wanted to know precisely the situation at the telephone company, the firehouse, the police station. He wanted to see exactly where Salsa was stationed near the town line. He wanted to have a clipboard, and a list, and a pencil with which to check off completed items satisfactorily handled. He wanted to see symmetry and balance and precision.

A match flared; Wycza lighting a stub of cigar. In the small light, Paulus again saw the plank floor and metal sides of the truck, saw Wycza and Wiss and Elkins sitting, like himself, on the floor, saw his own sturdy suitcase full of tools and the weatherbeaten black bag—like a doctor's bag—in which Wiss kept his equipment. He looked at his watch, but he wasn't fast enough; Wycza blew out the match.

He shook his head in annoyance. It was important to know the time, know whether or not they were keeping to the schedule. He reached for his own matches.

But a clinging self-consciousness wouldn't let him light a match just to see his watch; he didn't want the others to know he felt that strongly about knowing the time. So he got out his cigarettes, too, though he didn't particularly want a cigarette. He struck the match, lit the cigarette, and kept the match aflame till he'd read his watch.

Twelve thirty-five.

Not too bad. He'd be in at the bank vault well before one. He shook the match out, and sat holding the cigarette, not smoking it.

The walkie-talkie spoke again: "Got the east gate. Going into the main office now. You can get started, W."

They had to use the initials because of Grofield. He was at the telephone company, with one of the walkie-talkies, and the women there could hear everything it said. It was Paulus who'd suggested the initials.

Wycza was saying, "Okay. You gonna prowl now?"

"After we get the main office."

"Check."

Paulus clambered to his feet, felt around in the dark, and picked up his suitcase. He moved toward the rear of the truck, and before he got there Elkins pushed the door open and jumped down to the street. Elkins reached up and took the black bag from Wiss, and Wiss clambered down more carefully. Paulus waited for Wycza, and as Wycza passed said, "You go first, I'll hand you my suitcase."

"Sure."

Being the last out, Paulus was careful to close the truck doors again. He took the suitcase back from Wycza and stepped up on the sidewalk. Wiss and Elkins had already started across the street.

Directly ahead of Paulus was the Merchants' Bank building, with the offices of Nationwide Finance & Loan Corporation on the second floor. The building was modernistic, made mostly of glass and chrome. Even the doors were mainly glass.

Paulus set his suitcase down near the doors and waited for Wycza to let him in. Wycza got his revolver from its shoulder holster, and used the butt to break the door glass. There were quieter, more scientific ways to do it, but they weren't worried about noise here, and the scientific ways were all slower. Wycza reached through, unlocked the doors from the inside, and pushed them open.

Paulus followed him inside. Wycza had put his revolver away now and taken out a flashlight. The narrow beam showed wood-paneled counters with marble tops, and cream composition flooring, and a free form copper bas relief sprawled out on one wall. The vault door was in plain sight on the rear wall, huge and round and complex, looking like an escape hatch on a spaceship or the entrance to a torpedo tube in a submarine.

After the front door, there were no more obstacles to the vault, no doors to unlock or gates to jimmy. They lifted a flap at the end of the counter, walked through the loan department, took a left around a railing, and there was the vault door in front of them. Desks and railings and countertops hid them almost completely from the street.

While Wycza held the flashlight, Paulus studied the vault door. He nodded in recognition of the type, walked back and forth to consider it from various angles, and rubbed the knuckles of his hands together as he thought it out. Drill four holes, load, blast. He pursed his lips, and nodded. Now he was absorbed, completely absorbed.

Wycza said, "Any problems?"

"I don't think so. Shine the light here a minute."

He knelt and opened the suitcase, got the drill, selected a bit, changed his mind and selected another. He looked around and said, "Find me an outlet."

"Over here."

"Am I going to need the extension?"

"No." Wycza laughed. "Handy, huh? The architect had you in mind."

"Good of him." Paulus carried the drill over to the vault, went down on one knee. "Hold the light steady, now."

The drill began to whine.

6

HE'D MISSED THE CURFEW.

His name was Eddie Wheeler, he was nineteen years old, he worked at Brooks' Pharmacy, and he was now in the Campbell house, having been engaged in premarital intercourse with Betty Campbell, whose parents were visiting relatives all this week in Bismarck.

He'd fallen asleep, entwined in Betty's arms.

"It's one o'clock," he whispered. There wasn't any need to whisper—he and Betty were the only ones in the house—but he whispered anyway. For the same lack of reason, they hadn't turned on any lights, but depended on the illumination coming faintly through the window from a streetlight outside.

"What are you going to do?" Betty was half-sitting, half-lying on the bed, holding a sheet up to her throat.

Eddie felt around on the floor for his other shoe. "What can I do? I've got to get home."

"Stay here tonight."

"And what do I tell my folks? Where do I say I spent all night?"

"But what if the police catch you?"

"What can they do to me?" He found the other shoe, put it on, tied the laces. "They'll just give me a warning, that's all."

"It's my fault, Eddie, I shouldn't have gone to sleep."

"We *both* went to sleep." He got to his feet. "I'll call you tomorrow."

"Wait, I'll walk you downstairs."

"No, stay there, go back to sleep."

"I've got to lock the door anyway."

He was concentrating so hard on getting away, slipping across town to his own house without being caught by the police, that he barely paid attention to her when she got out of bed, slim and pale and naked as a nymph, and quickly shrugged into a bathrobe. Almost six months they'd been sleeping together now, and she still got into a robe any time she got out of bed, still covered herself with a sheet before and after, still made him turn his back while she undressed and got into bed. It was silly, but there it was. And it was a small price to pay.

Six months, and this was the first time anything had distracted him from staring at any rare glimpse of her she offered. The goddam curfew.

They went down the carpeted stair together, she barefoot, and over to the front door. His heart was pounding, he felt like a desperado. He opened the door a little and peeked out, and saw no cars moving, no people at all. "I'll call you tomorrow," he whispered.

"Kiss me good night, Eddie."

"Oh. I forgot."

She was soft and warm from bed, and he forgot his nervousness for a few seconds, caught up in the sense of her. But the breeze from the slightly open door was cool on the back of his neck, reminding him, and he was the first to break the kiss. He told her again he'd call her tomorrow. Her robe had parted, and her breasts were pale and full and soft, but he turned away and sidled out onto the porch. They whispered good night to each other, and she closed the door. He heard the snick of the lock.

Nothing moving. Orange Street was dark and silent. A block and a half away, Raymond Avenue was a bit brighter, but just as silent. It was after one o'clock in the morning.

Which would they patrol most, Raymond Avenue or the side streets? Raymond Avenue was so brightly lit, a curfew-breaker might tend to keep away from it; wouldn't the police think of that? They'd patrol the side streets most, wouldn't they? And just cross Raymond Avenue from time to time, going from one side of town to the other?

All right. So he'd go straight to Raymond Avenue, and down Raymond to Blake Street, and then over Blake Street the two blocks to his house. On Orange and Blake, he could duck into a driveway if he saw headlights. On Raymond, he could hide in a store doorway.

Reluctantly, he left the protection of the porch, went down to the sidewalk, and turned right. He walked along quickly, his shoulders hunched, his hands in his pants pockets. He kept looking back over his shoulder, but he didn't see any headlights.

Raymond Avenue. He turned left. He went half a block, and out of the corner of his eye he saw something wrong.

Broken glass.

The bank door was broken.

He stopped in his tracks, forgetting everything else, and stared at the broken glass of the bank door. Parked here was a big brown tractor trailer, but nobody in or near it. But in the bank . . .

He went over to the glass front and peered in. There was a light back there, he could just barely make it out. And a man standing there.

Bank robbers!

He took three quick steps, beyond the bank's glass front. Had they seen him? He didn't think so. No, they would have come after him. Bank robbers, and that must be their truck.

What in hell was he going to do? He stared around wildly, and two blocks farther down, at the corner of Whittier Street, he could see the telephone booth. There was a phone booth right on the corner there, he'd used it himself a few times. He could go there and phone police headquarters.

Where was the police car? A minute ago he'd been grateful for its absence, but now he felt indignant that it wasn't here. That was the police for you, never around when you wanted them. If there weren't any bank robbers, the police car would be right here this second, the cops giving him a bad time for being out after curfew.

Did he dare phone in? He was still breaking the law himself.

Don't be silly. Giving the warning about a bank robbery would make up for being out late. They wouldn't even mention it.

He started off again, this time going at a trot, hurrying down the two blocks to Whittier Street, looking down the cross-streets in hopes of seeing the headlights of the police car, but seeing nothing. At the phone booth, he paused to catch his breath and to find a dime, and then he stepped into the booth and closed the door. It was a glass-and-metal booth, mostly windows, and when he closed the door the light came on. Startled, he snapped the door open again, and the light went off.

That was all he needed, the light on, so the robbers could see him making the call.

He did it the simplest way. Dropped the dime in, dialed operator, and when the girl came on said, "Police headquarters, please. This is an emergency."

"Yes, sir."

It seemed like a pretty long pause, but finally he heard a ringing sound, and then a male voice said, "Police headquarters, Officer Nieman."

"I—" He didn't know how to phrase it. He cleared his throat, and blurted it out: "There's a bank robbery going on! The Merchants' Bank."

"What? Who are you?"

"Eddie Wheeler. They broke the door, and they're back by the vault."

"What are you doing out at this time of night?"

"For Pete's sake, will you listen to me? There's a—"

It was like a crack of thunder, the sudden sound, not too far away. Eddie looked up, startled, knowing they'd blown open the vault door. "They just blew up the vault!"

A different voice answered him. "Where are you?"

"I'm in the phone booth at Raymond and Whittier."

"Stay there, the prowl car will be right there."

"All right."

The connection was broken.

Even with the light off, Eddie felt exposed, in the glass phone booth. He stepped out, and went over to lean against the side of the nearest building, Komray's Department Store. He stared down toward the bank, waiting and watching, wondering what was keeping the police.

The prowl car, when it arrived, came without siren or flashing red light. It seemed to roll along leisurely, and then it stopped at the curb by the phone booth. Eddie stepped toward it, away from the wall, and saw the driver getting out. "They're down at the Merch—"

The driver was wearing a hood.

Eddie just stared at him. The driver came around the front of the car, and he was holding a pistol aimed right at Eddie's stomach. He said, "You ought to know better than to be out after curfew, Eddie."

"You're one of them!"

"Walk down Whittier, Eddie. Ahead of me. Do like you're told and you won't get hurt."

Eddie turned, and started walking. He didn't believe it, didn't believe that he wouldn't get hurt. He was going to be murdered, he knew it.

He thought of Betty's breasts, gleaming behind the robe. He thought of her asking him to stay the night. He thought of sex with her, thought of the glimpses of her body.

Why didn't I stay?

"Turn right, Eddie."

It was the loading dock behind the department store. God, it was dark back there! Eddie hesitated, and the hooded man said, "I don't want to kill you, Eddie. I got nothing against you. I'm going to tie you and gag you, and early in the morning somebody'll find you here, safe and sound. But if you try anything cute, I'll have to cut you down."

Eddie swallowed, painfully.

"Why you out after curfew anyway, Eddie?"

"I wish I knew."

He walked into the darkness.

7

ONE A.M.

Most of Copper Canyon was asleep. Three policemen, six firemen, three telephone company employees, three plant employees, and a boy named Eddie Wheeler were all awake. Most of these were tied and gagged; none of them was sure he'd live till morning. Aside from these sixteen, there were about twenty other citizens awake in Copper Canyon; insomniacs reading, couples making love, two young mothers warming baby bottles.

The Merchants' Bank and City Trust had both been blown open. Wycza was carrying trays of money from Merchants' to the truck, Elkins was carrying trays of money from City to the truck. Paulus was working on the Nationwide Finance & Loan Corporation safe, and Wiss was working on the Raymond Jewelers safe. At the plant, Kerwin hadn't yet opened the safe containing the payroll; he worked slowly, because he enjoyed his work.

Parker was in the prowl car, driving aimlessly this way and that, the walkie-talkie on the seat beside him. At the firehouse, Chambers had commandeered the playing cards and was dealing out hand after hand of solitaire, waiting for George to make a run for the door. At the telephone company, Grofield was playing charades with George's niece Mary; she was laughing. At police headquarters, in the Command Room, Edgars sat inside his hood and brooded on his own plans.

Pop Phillips was half-asleep, sitting on a tilted-back chair in the guard shack by the east gate. In the main plant building, Littlefield sat in a coil of tension, waiting for the phone to ring and wondering what he would do if it did. At the other end of town, Salsa sat with stolid patience in a brand new Oldsmobile, watching the empty street. There was a car a little ways ahead, parked at the curb, and a streetlight shone on its license plate, a dull tan with the number in dark brown. Below the number was the legend PEACE GARDEN STATE; Salsa wondered idly what that meant.

*

Two A.M.

Eddie Wheeler was asleep, his face against cold asphalt. In the morning he would have the beginnings of a bad headcold, but he'd be alive. Officer Mason, three firemen, and Mrs. Sawyer at the phone company were all also asleep, leaving ten of the prisoners still awake.

Kerwin had finished the plant safe, finally, and loaded the payroll into the station wagon. He had driven down Raymond Avenue to the truck, transferred the payroll—in white canvas bank bags—to the truck, and carried his bag of tools to Credit Jewelers, where he was now once again opening a safe. Paulus was walking through Komray's Department Store with a flashlight, looking for the office. Wiss had just left the five-and-dime and was entering the shoe store next door. Wycza and Elkins were loading the truck.

Pop Phillips was asleep. Littlefield was chain-smoking. Salsa was standing beside the Oldsmobile, stretching his legs. Chambers was cheating at solitaire. Parker was driving around in the prowl car. Edgars was moodily studying the submachine gun, waiting for the time to be right. Grofield knew Mary Deegan wanted him to kiss her, but he couldn't figure out how to do it without removing the hood.

Three A.M.

Five prisoners remained awake; Officer Nieman, George Deegan and his niece, one other fireman, and the guard from the west gate. All other citizens were asleep, except one insomniac who had two chapters to go in the mystery he was reading.

Wiss and Paulus and Kerwin were opening safes; Wycza and Elkins were emptying them. Salsa was back in the Oldsmobile, thinking of women. Edgars was growing impatient. Grofield's hood was off; so were Mary Deegan's panties.

Three forty-five A.M.

Wycza opened the cab door of the truck, stepped up, sat down to rest a minute, and switched on his walkie-talkie. "This is W," he said. "You there, P?" He felt stupid, using initials; you might know Paulus would dream up something like that.

Parker answered: "What's up?"

"Everything's open. We'll be done quicker than we thought. All five of us are loading now."

"How much longer?"

"Half an hour, maybe less."

"S, you hear that?"

Salsa picked up the walkie-talkie. "I hear it. That's very good." He put the walkie-talkie down on the seat again and lit a new cigarette.

Parker said, "G, you there?"

Grofield had been trying to explain to Mary Deegan why he couldn't take her along, and she'd begun to get mad, had just pointed out that she could identify him now. He was grateful for the interruption. He went over and picked up the walkie-talkie and said, "Right here."

"Spread the word. We'll be ready to clear out in half an hour."

"Right."

Grofield went over to the desk and picked up the phone. Mary followed him, saying, "I don't see why you can't take me."

"In a minute, all right? Just one minute." He dialed police headquarters, went through Officer Nieman, got Edgars, told him, "We'll be moving out in half an hour."

"So soon? Thanks." Edgars hung up, picked up the machine gun, and sprayed bullets into Officers Nieman and Mason and Felder. He went down the well-remembered hall to the armory, shot the lock off, went in and opened the metal box in the corner. World War II souvenirs, impounded by the police, including three live hand grenades. He took them, left the building, and went across the street to the firehouse.

Grofield's second call was to Littlefield, who jumped when the phone rang as though he'd been hit by a live wire. He fumbled the receiver, dropped it, picked it up again, and tried to clear his throat while he was saying hello. Grofield told him about the speed-up, and Littlefield nearly fainted from relief. But after that, he wasn't tense any more; if the phone rang again, no matter who it was calling, he wouldn't be nervous or frightened at all.

Grofield called the firehouse, got Chambers, and said, "It's running faster than we thought. We'll be going in about half an hour."

"Boy, you'll never know how— Hey!"

"What?"

It sounded like a machine gun, roaring away there at the other end. Then the line went dead.

Forgetting himself, Grofield shouted, "Chambers! Chambers!" But the line was dead.

Mary was staring at him wide-eyed. "What is it? What's the matter?" The other two women were stirring, disturbed out of sleep.

Grofield had the walkie-talkie now, was saying, "P. Listen, something's gone wrong."

"What?"

"The firehouse. I don't know what it is. Sounded like machine-gun fire, and then we were cut off."

Parker cursed, and said, "W, you hear that?"

"I hear it."

"Take the wagon. I'll meet you at the firehouse."

The first explosion woke Pop Phillips. He jumped up, startled, looking around, not knowing what had knocked him out of sleep.

Parker heard the explosion, cursed again, and gunned the prowl car forward.

Citizens heard the explosion, and some of them started phoning police headquarters to find out what it was, but nobody answered at police headquarters. Some of them dialed operator, but no operator answered either; Mary Deegan was trying to get Grofield's attention, and failing.

The firehouse was on fire; half the front wall had been blown away, and, inside, flames leaped around the fire engines as the gasoline in their tanks burned. Parker got out of the prowl car, looking around, and didn't see Chambers or anyone else. The station wagon raced up, squealed to a stop, and Wycza jumped out, saying, "What the hell happened?"

"I don't know. Come on."

They went across the street to the police station. Edgars was nearest; he ought to know what had happened.

Edgars wasn't in the Command Room. Phones were ringing, but Officer Nieman lay bleeding in the middle of the floor, nearly shot in two.

"Edgars," said Wycza.

Parker grimaced. “I knew there was something wrong with that bastard, I knew it.”

Wycza said, “One of them groaned.” He went over, knelt, said, “This one’s alive.”

It was Officer Mason. He whispered, “Edgars. Edgars.”

“Yeah,” said Wycza. “We know.”

Parker came over. “Did he say Edgars? Does he know Edgars?”

Officer Mason whispered again, and Wycza leaned close to hear him. Parker watched impatiently, and said, “What did he say?”

Wycza looked up. “Chief of police. Edgars used to be chief of police here.”

The second explosion was a lot bigger than the first.

8

HE HADN'T wanted to kill Chambers, but Chambers had tried to get in his way. He didn't know what the others would think of that; they might be sore at him, but it didn't matter. He wasn't interfering with them, and they shouldn't interfere with him.

He came up to the east gate, and Pop Phillips came out of the shack, saying, "What the hell was that explosion?"

"A vault, I guess. There's something I've got to do in here."

"A vault?" Phillips frowned. "They don't need *that* much nitro," he said.

Edgars went on by him, and walked along the company road. He knew which building contained the furnaces and fuel; he went straight to it, and there he used the second of his grenades. He threw it, then flattened himself behind a wall, but the explosion knocked him off his feet anyway.

He picked himself up, found the machine gun, and started running. He ran back to the gate, and Phillips shouted, "What's going on?"

"Just stay there! Stick to your position!"

Edgars ran down Copper Street toward Raymond Avenue. Off to his right, part of the plant had started to burn; orange flames were shooting up, dirtying the night sky.

"Goodbye, Copper Canyon. I'll burn you to the ground."

He turned at Hector Avenue. Hector was four blocks east of, and parallel with, Raymond Avenue. The railroad station was on Hector Avenue, two blocks away.

They'd never proved anything on him, the bastards. People had sat there in front of that grand jury and spouted all their stories about him, but they'd never been able to prove a thing. Brutality? A kickback from Regal Ford on the purchase of the new prowl car? Kickbacks from the suppliers of radio equipment, weapons and ammunition, uniforms, all the rest of it? You needed witnesses, you needed *proof.* Well they couldn't get proof. He wasn't dumb enough to be caught by these hicks, not in a million years.

They couldn't return a single indictment, not a one. On over fifty charges of one kind and another, they hadn't been able to dredge up enough proof to hit him with even one little indictment. He laughed at them. He sat there as safe as houses, and laughed at them.

So they threw him out. The call to the mayor's office, and the whole crowd there; Thorndike, the mayor, and Ableman, the general manager of the plant, and all the rest of them. Notoriety, they said. Bad press. The lost confidence of the voters. They wanted his resignation.

"But the grand jury cleared me!"

Ableman was the one who answered him: "No, they didn't. They couldn't pin anything on you, but they didn't clear you."

"You don't get any resignation from me."

Thorndike: "It'll look worse for you if I have to dismiss you."

"You do, and you'll regret it."

But he did. And he was going to regret it.

Just ahead was the railroad station. And just beyond it was Ekonomee Gas.

Ekonomee Gas was a filling station, an independent not connected with any of the major gasoline companies. Ekonomee, like many similar independents, had no underground storage tanks. The station was built next to the railroad line, and a short spur track ran across the rear of the station property. Ekonomee bought gasoline in tank car lots, and piped the gas straight from the tank car into the pumps. There were always three or four tank cars full of gasoline on the spur behind Ekonomee Gas.

That was the place for the last grenade. That one ought to start a lovely fire. Two fires then, one at the plant and one at Ekonomee. Maybe three, if the firehouse had caught. In any case, they'd have plenty of time to spread. There was no longer any fire-fighting equipment in town. The radio station was disabled, the transmitting equipment at police headquarters had been riddled with machine-gun bullets, and once he'd blown up Ekonomee he'd go over to the telephone company and put *that* out of commission.

No fire-fighting equipment in town, and no way to call to Madison or anywhere else to get some help. It would be hours before they could get organized to fight the fire, hours. With luck, the whole goddam town would burn down.

And Parker and the others would have to help. All this racket would attract the attention of the state police, at the barracks down 22A. Parker and the others would have to put that barracks out of commission; they'd have no choice.

"I *told* you you'd regret it, Thorndike!"

He ran past the railroad station, over the blacktop driveway of Ekonomee and around the corner of the building. Three tank cars there. The spreading fire back at the plant glinted in smudged reflection on their sides.

Edgars paused at the corner of the building. He had the last grenade in his hands, and heard someone shout his name. He turned and saw two of the others running toward him, the prowl car standing behind them. "Keep away!" he shouted. "Keep away!"

"Stop!"

He pulled the pin. He whirled, and threw the grenade at the tank cars.

9

THE BLAST knocked Wycza off his feet. He went sprawling, his revolver flying out of his hand. He rolled and started to his feet, and a second blast knocked him down again. He was a wrestler sometimes and his body reacted instinctively to a lack of balance, adjusting itself, shifting, rolling, avoiding falls that could hurt.

He made it to his feet this time, and saw Parker braced against one of the pumps. The gas station building had fallen forward, and leaping flames behind it lit the whole area. He looked around but couldn't see Edgars.

He shouted the name, and Parker shook his head, pointing at the rubble. "Under there."

"We've got to get out of here, Parker."

"I know."

They ran back to the car, and Parker got his walkie-talkie. "G! Get hold of Littlefield, fast. Tell him to get down to the east gate, we'll pick him up there. Then you get over to Raymond, on the double."

Wycza, getting into the prowl car on the passenger side, heard Grofield's voice saying, "What the hell's going on?"

"Later. Get moving. S, watch that road, the troopers may come in. If they do, don't stop them, just warn us."

Salsa's voice said, "Will do."

"I never did like that trooper barracks," said Wycza. "I never did."

Parker had started the prowl car. He spun out away from the station, headed toward Raymond Avenue.

People were coming out on the sidewalks. Some of them, recognizing the prowl car, waved their arms, wanting the police to stop and answer questions. Wycza looked at them and muttered, "It's sour, Parker. It's gone sour."

"I know. You drive the truck, I'll take the wagon. Get your people in it and get going. Pick up Salsa and Grofield. I'll get Littlefield and Phillips."

"Right."

Raymond Avenue. Parker turned the wheel hard right, and braked next to the truck. “Don’t wait for me,” he said.

Wycza grinned under the hood. “Don’t worry.” He clambered out of the prowl car and ran around the truck cab.

They were all clustered there, Paulus and Kerwin and Wiss and Elkins. Wycza told them, “Get in. All in back, I got others to pick up.”

Everybody moved but Paulus, who wasted time asking, “What’s going on? What’s happening?”

“Get in or I leave you.”

Wycza got up in the cab, kicked the engine on, and pulled away from the curb. They’d taken the truck around the block when they’d first come in, so it would be facing the right way; he was grateful for that now.

He went four blocks and there was Grofield waiting for him, on a corner, without his hood. And not alone.

Wycza braked to a stop, and Grofield pulled open the door. Wycza said, “Get her the hell out of here!”

“She’s coming along.”

Wycza wouldn’t agree to that for a second, but there wasn’t time to argue. They were both in the cab, so he hit the accelerator again. “Parker’ll kill you,” he said.

“Let me worry about it.”

The girl said, “Don’t worry about me. You don’t have to worry about me. What’s going on?”

Grofield said, “We’ll find out later, honey. Just be quiet now.”

Wycza said, “Throw her out when we pick up Salsa. I’m telling you.”

“She’s coming along, so shut up, huh?”

“There’s no room for Salsa.”

“She’ll sit on my lap.”

Wycza ground his teeth in frustration. Of all the stupidities tonight, Edgars’ had suddenly taken second place behind Grofield’s. “I’m liable to kill you myself,” he said, and stopped the truck again to pick up Salsa.

Salsa squeezed into the cab and reported, “No troopers yet.”

They were all crammed in together, Grofield in the middle, the girl on his lap, the girl holding Wycza’s walkie-talkie and Grofield’s rifle. Salsa had a machine gun on the floor between his feet, and a walkie-talkie in his lap.

Wycza said, "Tell Parker it's still clear."

"Sure," said Salsa. He picked up the walkie-talkie.

"No sense telling him about the broad." Wycza turned his head and gave Grofield a cold eye, then looked front again. "He'll find out soon enough."

"Sure," said Salsa. The presence of the girl didn't seem to ruffle him a bit. He spoke into the walkie-talkie, saying, "Everything's clear so far. We're out of town, and no troopers have come in yet."

Parker's voice came out of both walkie-talkies in the cab: "I've got Littlefield and Phillips, I'm coming out now."

Wycza looked in the rear-view mirror. Behind him was the town. He saw flames shooting upward, deep within it, and way back on Raymond Avenue he saw a pair of headlights. "He'd better move," he muttered.

Ahead, on the right, was the trooper barracks, still lit up. As they passed it, they saw two men in uniform running from the front door toward one of the cars. Wycza said, "Salsa, keep an eye on them. See which way they go."

"Right."

Wycza's foot was heavy on the accelerator. The truck was doing seventy now, and the speedometer was still creeping upward. He kept telling himself he should get down to the speed limit, but he couldn't lift his foot off the accelerator; it was as though his foot were nailed there.

He'd never taken a fall. He'd never spent even one night in jail. He kept thinking about that now, never a single night in jail. And he didn't want to go to jail, because he knew what would happen to him if he went to jail. He would die. A year, maybe two years, and he'd be dead.

There were things he needed, in order to stay alive. Food and shelter and water, of course, but other things, too, that for him were just as important. Exercise, for instance. He had to be able to run, to run for miles, and to do it every single day. He had to be able to go into a gym and work out whenever he wanted. He had to keep using his body, or it would dry up and die.

And women. He needed women almost as much as he needed exercise. Not in the goddam truck on the get, but other times, other places. And sunshine, plenty of sunshine.

And certain kinds of food; steak, and milk, and green vegetables. And food supplements, vitamin pills and mineral pills and protein pills.

Not in jail. In jail, he wouldn't be able to exercise his body as much as was necessary. And there'd be no women. And little sunshine. And none of the foods or pills he needed. In jail, he would shrivel up like a leaf in September. He'd shrink and get pasty, his teeth would rot, his muscles would sag, his body would shrink in on itself and start to decay.

"They're going toward the town."

Wycza nodded. "Good. Tell Parker."

He wasn't going to jail. If it came down to it, if it ever came right down to it, he knew he wouldn't go to jail. There are two ways to die, fast and slow, and he'd prefer the fast way. He wouldn't go to jail because in order to put him in jail they'd have to lay hands on him, and before they'd be able to lay hands on him they'd have to kill him.

Salsa was talking to Parker on the walkie-talkie: "State police, coming in."

"Yeah, I see the red light. I'm going to park and let them go by."

Then the cab was silent. Everybody was listening, waiting for the walkie-talkies to speak again. Wycza glanced at the speedometer; five miles to go to the highway. Doing seventy-five now.

"They went by. They're headed for the fire. I'm coming out now."

Salsa said, "Fine. I can't see the barracks any more, but I didn't see any other cars leave there."

"There's nothing coming this way. I just passed the town line."

Wycza realized he'd been hunching his shoulders over the wheel. He sat back now, and let them relax; they'd started to ache. He lifted his foot from the accelerator, and let the truck slow down to the speed limit.

"We made it anyway," he said.

The girl said, "You don't have to worry about me, you really don't."

"I'm not going to," Wycza told her. "Grofield is." Ahead was the highway turnoff.

10

FOUR A.M.

Most of Copper Canyon was awake. The sidewalks were full of people, and other people were standing on their porches, and other people had gotten into their cars and were jamming up the streets around the fires.

There were three fires. Behind the plant fence, four buildings were aflame. On Caulkins Street, the firehouse was still burning, but was nearly out; the exterior walls, made of brick, were unharmed except for the chunk blown out by the hand grenade, but the interior of the building had been gutted. The square block bounded by Orange Street and Hector Avenue and Loomis Street and George Avenue was one mass of flame. The railroad station was in that block, and Ekonomee Gas, and a few other buildings, stores mostly, plus the garage and storage building of Elmore Trucking. Just at four o'clock, the fire leaped Loomis Street; two residences on the south side of the street caught fire as embers fell on their roofs.

The two state troopers had discovered the destruction of Copper Canyon's fire-fighting apparatus, had radioed to the barracks to have fire engines rushed in from Madison and Polk, and had entered police headquarters, baffled by the absence of all local police officials. Just at four A.M. they entered the Command Room and found the three bodies; all three were now dead.

In all the confusion, with the gigantic distraction of the triple fire, no one had yet noticed the broken windows and gaping doorways along Raymond Avenue.

Eight miles south, a brown tractor trailer was making the turn from 22A to the highway, eastbound. Two miles behind it a station wagon was speeding along at eighty miles an hour.

Three other cars were leaving the state trooper barracks two miles south of town, but all three of them were heading north, toward Copper Canyon.

Five A.M.

The three fires were one. The plant fire had moved south,

and the Ekonomee fire had moved north, and they'd met at Caulkins Street, one block west of the firehouse. The suction of the fires was forcing winds into Copper Canyon from the south, fresh cold air rushing in to supply more oxygen for the flames, hot dry air blasting upward along the rear canyon wall. The direction of the wind confined the fire, for the most part, to the area north of Loomis Street, but nearly everything in an area three blocks wide and five blocks long was or had been aflame.

Fire engines from Madison and Polk had arrived half an hour ago. The firemen were primarily trying to contain the blaze, trying to keep it from stretching east and west of the area it had already consumed. The morning and evening shifts of the town police department had come out in uniform to help the state police maintain some sort of order, keeping the curious back out of harm's and the firemen's way.

Somebody had found Eddie Wheeler, and he'd been brought to one of the troopers, so now the law knew about the robberies, or at least some of them. The two women at the telephone company had been found and released, so now the law also knew that the robbers had taken a hostage with them. Eddie Wheeler had described the truck he'd seen, and state police cars were combing the highway and route 22A and other secondary routes in this part of the state, but they hadn't as yet found any brown truck. Two police helicopters were being readied at Bismarck, the state capital, and would be in the air shortly. Reporters and wire service stringers were driving pell-mell toward Copper Canyon from all over the state.

It would be late afternoon before the fire would be completely extinguished, and tomorrow morning before the rubble would have cooled enough to permit inspection. Bodies would be found in the ruins, and tentatively identified, but the body of Edgars would never be discovered, it had been too close to the hottest core of the fire. All the next day, merchants and accountants would be toting up figures, learning just exactly how much had been stolen in all. Police technicians would be dusting virtually the whole town for fingerprints, and would find none left by the robbers, but would be surprised that there were still on various surfaces in police headquarters fingerprints left by former Chief of Police Edgars, who'd left town nearly a year ago and was not likely to show his face here ever again.

The roadblocks would be left up for another day, to be on the safe side. The two helicopters would continue their search. The police expected to apprehend the responsible parties very soon.

Eddie Wheeler spent the rest of the week in his own bed, with a headcold. By the time he was well enough to get up and move around, Betty's parents were back in town.

Three days after the holocaust, two architects and a lawyer and a minister formed the Citizens for Copper Canyon, CCC. Their goal was to convince their fellow citizens to rebuild the gutted section of town according to this plan they'd whipped up. Copper Canyon Plaza. Official buildings here at this end, new railroad station at the other end, the fountain here, the gardens here, and so on. The architects would be happy to prepare plans for the new integrated area, and the lawyer would be happy to handle the legal work involved. The minister was selfless.

FOUR

I

PARKER WATCHED Wycza drive the truck over to the edge and start it down the road to the bottom of the ravine. The loot was still in it; it would be light in an hour, so the best thing was to get the truck out of sight right away. Tomorrow night would be soon enough to make the split.

After the taillights had dropped down out of sight, he turned and went back toward the shed, thinking about the job. It had been beautiful. It could have been the cleanest and sweetest job he'd ever been in on. The closest thing to a foul-up was that night-owl kid that stumbled over Paulus working the bank. And that had turned out to be no problem; they'd handled it smooth and quiet and sweet. The whole thing was smooth and quiet and sweet, no killings, no messiness, no problems.

Except Edgars.

He'd known, God damn it, he'd known all along there was something wrong with Edgars. Edgars and his personal reasons. Those personal reasons had to blow the whole job sky high, they *had* to.

It had still worked out. They'd had to leave a little of the take behind, dribs and drabs from a couple of store safes, nothing important. They'd had to do the get a hell of a lot faster than they'd planned. But still and all it had worked out. Chambers was dead, and Edgars was dead, and there was no telling how many locals were dead, but at least they'd managed to get themselves out from under with the loot.

The dead locals were what bothered him. He didn't give a damn one way or the other, not personally, couldn't care less if they lived or died, but it was never good to cut down a citizen in a robbery. There's trouble enough from the law if they're just after you for a payroll, but if they're after you for Murder One you're in big trouble.

He pushed open the door of the shed and looked in. They were all there, Paulus and Wiss and Elkins and Kerwin and Littlefield and Salsa and Grofield and Phillips.

And Grofield's girl, sitting with Grofield on one of the army cots.

Parker looked at her, and then looked at Grofield. Grofield had the look on his face that a man gets when he's done something too stupid to be possible and he knows it but still wants to justify it.

Parker motioned to him to come outside. Grofield murmured something at the girl and got to his feet. She made as though to come along, but he shook his head and murmured some more, and this time she nodded and sat down again on the army cot. Her hands were in her lap, her knees were together, and her face looked pinched and frightened. She looked like the heroine of a silent movie.

Parker stepped aside and let Grofield out, then followed him and shut the door. He led the way out toward the edge, walking forward through the dim starlight, the sheds bulking around him. He stopped near the edge and said, "You can bury her down there some place."

"Forget it, Parker. You don't kill that girl."

"That's right, I don't. She's your responsibility."

"You don't have to worry about her, Parker." Grofield's voice had the shaky belligerence of a man who's pretty sure he's in the wrong but will be damned if he'll admit it.

"I'm not worrying about her, Grofield. *You* worry about her. In a day or two, she'll want to go home."

"No, she won't."

"When she tells you she's changed her mind, she wants to go home, but she'll never tell anybody where we are or what we look like or what our names are, that's when you take care of her."

"It won't happen. She won't say that."

"And you take her down there and bury her. Deep, Grofield. I don't want her found."

"What if it doesn't happen? What if she doesn't change her mind?"

"We'll be here three or four days. Then what?"

"New York. We'll get a place in the Village for the summer. In the fall we'll go south and do winter stock together. She's always wanted to be an actress."

"I always thought you were a pro."

"I am. I know what I'm doing."

Parker shook his head. "I didn't know I'd have to spell it all out for you. All right, listen."

"None of this is necessary, Parker, honest to Christ."

"Shut up and listen. You know how to keep the law off your tail. She doesn't. They'll pick her up for jay-walking in New York City, and before the cop gets the ticket wrote out she'll be so rattled she'll spill the whole works."

"No, she won't. She can learn."

"Shut up. That's just one thing. She'll louse up somehow, and get the law down on you. Number two, she'll change her mind. Maybe tomorrow, maybe six months from now. She thought it'd be exciting to run off with an honest-to-god bank robber, and how long you think she'll think it's exciting?"

"I can keep her interested, Parker. That girl's never been anywhere or done anything. I'll show her New York this summer, Miami this winter, a season of winter stock, maybe New England next summer, maybe after a while go out and try Hollywood. She won't get bored, believe me."

"No, she'll get homesick."

"Parker, listen. She told me about herself. Her folks are dead; she was living with her uncle. Just the two of them."

"That's another thing. She'll not only get homesick for the uncle, the uncle'll keep the law looking for her."

"No, he won't. She doesn't know it yet, but the uncle's dead. He was that fireman, that George."

Parker looked at him in the small light; too small to see his face. "You think that's good?"

"She's got no home to get sick for, no place to go back to."

"She'll want to be at the funeral, number one. Number two, you were part of the gang that killed him."

"That was Edgars, that wasn't us. I can tell her about that so she'll believe me. And so what about the funeral? I can keep her from even thinking about it."

"The other two women at the phone company know she went with you. The law know she's with us."

"She'll dye her hair. She wanted to anyway, but her uncle wouldn't let her. For Christ's sake, Parker, she's twenty-two years old, she's nobody's ward."

"I don't want her going back. I don't want her saying it was a guy named Parker and a guy named Grofield and a guy named this and that, and that's Grofield's picture there, and that's Phillips' picture there, and all that crap."

"She won't go back, Parker."

"I know that. I want to be sure *you* know it."

"Parker, I wouldn't have brought her along if I wasn't sure."

"Yeah. Go get her. Send her out here."

"Parker, I don't want you to lay a hand on her."

"That's not my job. That's your job. I want to talk to her."

Grofield shuffled his feet, and the silence lengthened between them until he finally said, "You going to tell her about her uncle?"

"Maybe."

"Then tell her about Edgars."

"Go get her, Grofield."

"Don't try to *push* her away, Parker."

"I won't. Go get her."

"All right."

Grofield took a few steps away, and then Parker called his name and said, "I want to see her alone first."

"I know. I figured that out already."

Parker looked up at the sky. Four-thirty in the morning, it was still fully night, but the stars seemed to be getting a bit fainter, the sky a bit less totally black. Except for the stars, there was no light anywhere; black cloth covered the windows of the shed they were living in.

There was a crunching sound from the left, opposite the shed. Parker listened to it, frowning, and then realized who it was. "Wycza," he said.

Wycza loomed up out of the darkness. "That's a long walk," he said.

"What do you think about Grofield's girl?"

"I think he's stupid."

"That's *him*. What about *her*?"

"I dunno. She doesn't yack a lot. He didn't have to twist her arm to bring her. I dunno about her."

"This could have been a sweet job."

"Tell me about that Edgars sometime."

"I wish I knew myself."

The girl was suddenly there, saying softly, "You wanted to talk to me?"

Parker turned and said, "Yeah. Wait there a second." He turned back to Wycza. "What happens if it rains out here?"

"You mean with the sheds?"

"Yeah."

"I guess they leak. But I don't think it rains here this time of year."

"Is that right?" Parker turned to the girl. "Does it rain here this time of year?"

"Not very often." Her voice was very low and soft, but not shy in particular, just self-contained. The frightenedness that had been in her face before was completely missing from her voice.

Parker didn't give a damn about rain or leaking sheds; he wanted to rattle her by talking at her instead of to her for a while, to see how she'd react. He said to Wycza, "What'll we do if it does rain? You got any ideas?"

"Not me."

He turned to the girl. "What about you? You got any ideas?"

"You robbed the banks, didn't you?"

He was alert now. "That's right," he said, and waited.

But what she said was, "They keep their money in those canvas sacks, don't they? You could cut them open and spread the sacks out on the roof on the parts where it leaks."

Wycza laughed, and said, "I'll be seeing you, Parker." He trudged away toward the shed.

Parker said, "They'll have helicopters out. We can't have bank sacks on the roof."

"Oh, I'm sorry. I didn't think of that."

"Did you ever hear of a guy named Edgars?"

"The man who used to be police chief?"

"That's the one."

"He was with you tonight, wasn't he?"

"What did he have against your town?"

"There was a big scandal. A grand jury asked him questions and tried to get evidence against him about something; I don't know exactly what. I don't think they ever tried him for anything, but he was dismissed anyway."

"That figures. He tried to blow up your whole damn city tonight."

"I saw the fires."

"Blew up part of the plant, and a gas station by the railroad depot, and the firehouse."

"The firehouse?"

"Killed the man I had in there guarding your uncle."

"Oh." She was silent, but he didn't have anything to say to her, he could outwait her. After a minute she said, "My uncle?"

"He got it, too. Everybody in the firehouse. The man I had in there was named Chambers. Hillbilly from Kentucky or somewhere like that. Has a brother named Ernie, in jail now. He's the one was supposed to drive the truck."

"What are you trying to do to me?"

He took a last drag on his cigarette, and flicked the butt out over the edge. "See if you'll crack."

"Why?"

"You know my name. You know my face. I don't want you going back and talking to the law."

"I see."

They waited again. Parker got out his cigarettes, lit one, then said, "You want one?"

"Yes, please."

He lit it for her. She looked up and studied his face in the matchlight, and when it was dark again she said, "The simplest thing would just be to throw me off the cliff here, wouldn't it?"

"It would."

"Why don't you? You're not afraid of Grofield."

"I don't kill as the easy way out of something. If I kill, it's because I don't have any choice."

"You mean self-defense."

"Wrong. I mean it's the only way to get what I want."

"Do you want me to promise I'll stay with Grofield forever? Maybe I will, maybe I won't. I know I won't go back to Copper Canyon, and there's no reason for me to go to the police."

"Why'd you come along with Grofield?"

"He's my chance. He's smart and exciting and fun, and he knows a lot of things. He can show me the whole world, and make it all fun. I had to scream and holler before he'd take me along, so don't blame him too much."

"Grofield'll be in jail within five years."

"Why do you say that?"

"Because he's impulsive. He's smart, but he doesn't always act smart. Also, he doesn't pay his income tax. Also, he spends too loose and works too often."

"So maybe I can help him, then."

Parker debated. He walked up and down along the cliff edge, thinking it out. The girl was a lot better than he'd expected. The only false note was that she'd run off in the first place, that she'd decided to come along with Grofield. She was too cool and sure of herself to be the run-off type. But maybe the running off was cool and methodical, too, maybe she was just running a calculated risk. Looked at that way, it made better sense.

And made her a better risk for him, too.

He said, "Go tell Grofield to show you where his car is. That's where you two will stay nights; we can't have you in the shed with the rest of us."

"All right. Thank you."

She went away, and Parker stayed outside a while longer. Far to the east, a narrow band of faint lightness was beginning to mark the horizon. Parker walked back and forth, back and forth, unwinding, getting the tension out of his body and mind.

He'd never been involved with such a contradictory job in his life. A job where he deliberately put himself in a box with only one exit, but in this particular case it didn't matter. A job where everything went smooth and sweet and precise, right up to the end, and then all hell broke loose, with one madman going around trying to blow up the city and another madman bringing a girl along for the ride. But the first madman's explosions and fires helped to cover the getaway in spite of themselves, and the second madman's girl turned out to be a safe risk.

Thinking of the girl, he felt a quickening in his loins, the sudden return of desire that always followed a job. He walked back and forth, back and forth, smoking his cigarette, thinking of women, thinking about the next opportunity he'd have to get next to a woman.

Not Grofield's girl. Messing with another man's woman was always dangerous, and never more dangerous than while hiding out. Besides, she acted too cool and composed for his taste. He wanted something with more abandon to her.

He knew who, knew exactly who. Three or four days, and he'd go see her.

Somebody had to tell her Edgars wouldn't be showing up.

2

THE HELICOPTER passed over again with a great flapping sound, like a huge bird of prey, and everyone in the shed crouched instinctively lower and stared upward at the roof.

It was late afternoon, and stifling hot in the shed. They were all there, all eleven of them. Parker and Wycza and Phillips and Salsa and Elkins were sitting around the card table, a hand of seven-card stud half dealt in front of them, halted temporarily while they all listened to the helicopter. Grofield and his girl were sitting on an army cot in the corner, with Littlefield standing next to them; the three of them had been playing charades and Littlefield had stopped in the middle of the third word. Wiss and Paulus and Kerwin, the three safe men, had been shop-talking in a corner, but they too were now quiet.

Pop Phillips said, "It's enough to make a man think of reforming."

"Tire tracks," said Parker. He looked over at Littlefield. "What about them?"

"Brushed away," Littlefield told him. "All brushed away."

Wycza said, "What about on the road going down, where I took the truck?"

"That's all hard-packed," Littlefield told him. "No tracks show."

Paulus said, "I don't like this place. Edgars set this place up, what do we know about it? We ought to get the hell out of here."

Parker shook his head. "And go where? None of us knows this territory. The roadblocks'll still be up."

"I just don't like this place. I want out of here tonight."

Parker shrugged and looked at his hole cards. Five and seven of spades. Six of spades and queen of hearts up, so far. Three cards to go.

Two days to go. This was always the worst part, afterward. The best jobs were the ones you could walk away from and keep on going. But the jobs where you had to hole up for a while, they were bad for the nerves. Particularly with a crowd this size. Eleven people stuck in a big empty shed with no interior walls, no proper furniture, no way to get away from each other. A lot of jobs that had run sweet all the way through suddenly went sour at this point, after the tough part was supposedly all over. One or two people decided not to wait it out any more, took off, got themselves picked up and backtracked, and there was the law all of a sudden at the hideout door.

Paulus said, "We make the split tonight, and then I go. Littlefield? You're supposed to ride with me, you want to come along?"

Littlefield seemed to consider it, and then said, "I don't think so, Paulus. I think I'll stay here and keep out of jail, if I can get a ride with somebody else."

Salsa said, "Chambers was supposed to ride with me. You can take his place."

"Thank you."

Paulus said, "Well, *I'm* going. Tonight, right after the split."

Parker, looking at his cards, said, "We don't split tonight. We make the split day after tomorrow."

Paulus said, "I'm taking *my* share tonight."

Wycza said, "Shut your face, Paulus, you ain't going nowhere."

"I don't *like* this place, I tell you!"

Grofield said, "Shut up a second. Listen. Is he coming back?"

The sound of the helicopter had faded to a murmur, but that murmur had remained unchanged as the copter circled the general area over the mining cut. Now the murmur was getting louder again.

Phillips said, "What does he think he *sees* out there?"

Nobody answered him. The murmur increased and then faded again, without having come close. It faded almost out of hearing, and then came back a little, and then faded again.

Salsa said, "He's doing a grid-check, that's all. A methodical search pattern. These sheds were a landmark for him, a hub, but now he's got some other hub."

"I hope you're right," said Phillips.

They listened some more. The helicopter was a distant hum, and then silence. Very briefly, a humming again, like a far-off bee, and then silence. Still silence. Silence.

Parker said, "Deal. He's gone."

Elkins picked up the cards and dealt another round. Parker got the jack of spades. He called Phillips' bet without raising, and got the four of spades on the sixth card. He bumped small, fed Phillips' large return raise, bet more heavily after the last card, and took the pot.

Paulus said, "I'm going tonight, and I'm going with my piece of the score."

Parker and Wycza looked at each other. It was Wycza who said it: "You're staying here, Paulus, and we're making the split the day after tomorrow. Now shut your trap about it."

Paulus shut his trap, but he looked mutinous.

Grofield guessed Littlefield's charade: "All the world's a stage, and all the men and women merely players."

Phillips took the next pot. Raking it in, he said, "All things come to him who waits."

"That's the tough part," Parker told him.

3

PARKER CAME awake all at once to find Wycza's hand on his shoulder. Wycza whispered, "Paulus."

Parker nodded and got to his feet. The shed was full of the hushes of sleeping breath. Cots were placed every which way around the room, and men were sleeping on all of them.

Wycza whispered, "Salsa, too?"

Parker nodded.

They moved forward, and Wycza touched Salsa's shoulder. Salsa too came straight awake and sat up. Wycza whispered Paulus' name, and then the three of them went outside and shut the shed door behind them.

It was cool at night here, and tonight there was a dampness in the air that hadn't been present before. The stars were obscured, the sky heavy and black.

Parker whispered, "Where?"

"I heard him when he started the car. He took it down below."

"Gone to get his share."

"Yeah."

Salsa said, "He may start up before we can get down. He'll be tough to get hold of, in his car."

Parker said, "Is there any other way out of there?"

Wycza shook his head. "Just this one road. Chambers and I looked that over when we first come out."

"We can block it at the top with one car."

"Okay, good."

They went to the shed where they'd stashed the wagon, and pulled the corrugated sections of wall away, moving as silently as they could. The darkness was almost complete. Parker backed the wagon out, turning the parking lights on, and with that small illumination drove over to the dropoff and the beginning of the road down to the bottom. He left the wagon parked across the road at the very top, pointing out into space. He switched the lights off and climbed out, and rejoined Wycza and Salsa, a little way off, standing at the edge over the road. They stood there and waited.

"Here he comes," said Salsa.

Wycza said, "The damn fool's using his parking lights."

Salsa said, "I wouldn't try to come up that without light."

They waited. The car crept slowly upward and was almost to the wagon before it stopped. The parking lights went out immediately. Paulus didn't make a sound.

Whispering, Wycza asked, "What do we do with him?"

"I don't want to have to bury him," said Parker.

"We tie him and leave him on one of the cots," said Salsa. "Grofield's girl can feed him."

"I don't work with him again," said Wycza. "That much I know."

Paulus' voice came up to them suddenly, with startling loudness: "Get that car out of the way!"

"Forget it, Paulus."

"I'll ram it!"

Salsa squatted down on his heels and called softly down to Paulus: "Don't make things so difficult for yourself. Come back to the shed and we'll tie you up a few days."

"There'll be law here by tomorrow! Edgars set us up to be collared, don't you damn fools *see* that?"

Salsa said, "You're all excited, Paulus. Don't they know we have rifles, machine guns? Don't they know how many of us there are? If they thought we were in here, would that helicopter pilot come back two three times all by himself, and down so low?"

"Why'd he come back, then?"

"Paulus, you don't know anything about search patterns, do you?"

"This place is naked, we stick out like boils. I want to be away from here, a thousand miles away from here."

Parker was tired, and a little chilly. He wanted to be back asleep. He said, "Quit screwing around, Paulus, you aren't going anywhere."

"God damn you, Parker!"

The headlights of Paulus' car came on all at once, on high beam, flooding the station wagon with light, light reflecting away on all sides to show Parker and Wycza standing big and heavy by the edge, Salsa hunkered down like a bandit beside them, the three looking down over the edge at the car just below them. Paulus' car was so close, they could have stepped down onto the roof.

The car began to back, Paulus gunning the engine. Salsa called something to him, but the roaring of the engine drowned it out. The car backed downward, and then they could see Paulus at the steering wheel, facing backward, twisted around and straining to see. There was only darkness behind the car, tinged with red by the taillights.

Paulus was excited, so maybe he forgot to reverse the turning direction on the steering wheel when going backward. Or maybe he just couldn't see well enough back there. His left rear wheel went off the edge.

Salsa hollered, "Jump!"

Parker dropped down to the road surface, landing on his hands and feet, going down to his knees and getting up again.

But Paulus was on the wrong side of the car to jump. And the engine was still roaring, so his foot was still heavily on the accelerator. The car seemed to tremble a minute, while Parker ran down toward its headlights, and then it swung sharp left, the front of the car with its blinding headlights snapping out into space to stare out over the ravine, and then it dropped.

Parker was running back up the other way long before they heard the crashing sound down below. He ran up to the wagon, and Wycza and Salsa were there. He said, "Wycza, get Phillips. Have him show you the shovels. Get Elkins and come down, bring a car. Salsa, let's go."

They got into the wagon, and Parker backed it away from the edge, then turned the wheel hard and they started down. Parker had the parking lights on again and went as fast as he could.

Salsa, sitting on the outside near the cliff, said, "It's burning."

"We got to put it out."

"That Paulus was a real chancy type."

"He always tensed up, always."

"I guess none of us works with him again, huh?" Salsa grinned. "You sure get the interesting jobs, Parker."

"Crap."

At the bottom they made the U-turn. Paulus' wreck was ahead of them, outlined by flames; it looked like a mound of black spare parts.

It wasn't much of a fire; by the time Parker and Salsa got there the only things left burning were the upholstery and the roof padding and the body hanging halfway out the front seat.

"He's taking it with him," said Salsa. "His split, you know?"

Parker was down on one knee, feeling the ground, trying to find loose sand. "We got to get that fire *out.*"

"Wait, Parker. Here they come with the shovels."

The other car was coming. Wycza and Elkins climbed out and passed out shovels. The four of them started digging, throwing dirt generally on the wreck and especially on the parts that were still burning. When the fire was put out, they brought the two cars closer in and switched on their parking lights to see by. Then they kept shoveling.

They moved around, not taking too much dirt from any one place, spreading it out so the ground wouldn't look more than usually uneven. When they were done, the mound of earth over the wreck was nearly waist-high, but it would look all right from the air.

"One thing," said Elkins, "now it's a nine-way split."

"He took his with him," said Salsa. He seemed pleased by the remark.

4

THE STINK of sulphur was everywhere. In the dimness of twilight, the red waters of the stream looked a dark maroon, and velvety. Parker threw a machine gun into the stream and watched the bubbles rise, then turned back to the station wagon.

Grofield was coming over with the two rifles, wrinkling his nose. "I counted two-and-seventy stenches, all well defined, and several stinks."

Parker shrugged. He wasn't talking; when he opened his mouth he smelled the stink more.

The rear of the wagon was still full of revolvers. Parker picked up four of them by the trigger guards and carried them over to the stream and threw them in. Nobody'd stumble over them here, not too readily.

The guns could have been kept, but it would have been a false economy, and maybe dangerous. Until the next job, none of them would be needing a gun, and certainly not a rifle or chopper. In the meantime, they were difficult to transport, difficult to hide, and a cheap little rap if the law happened to stumble across them. So guns were just part of the overhead, bought before each job and gotten rid of afterward. Sometimes, if the job was done somewhere close to someone like Scofe, the blind man, or Amos Klee, the guns were sold back again at half-price, but only if that was the easiest way to get rid of them.

After they'd all been dumped into the sulphurous stream, Parker and Grofield drove the station wagon over to the truck. Wycza and Salsa and Elkins were there, dragging the bags and trays of the score down to the end of the truck by the open doors. Parker swung the wagon around and backed it up to the rear of the truck, and then he and Grofield got out and started transferring the stuff from truck to wagon. There was another car there, too; when they finished filling the wagon they loaded the rest into the trunk of the other car.

This was the third day. Tonight, if everything was clear, they'd leave this place. The sky was overcast and heavy, had been all day, building up from a lighter cloudiness yesterday. It hadn't rained yet; with luck, it wouldn't for a day or two.

Parker and Grofield and Wycza rode up in the station wagon, and the other two in the car. When they passed the mound of dirt covering Paulus' wreck, Grofield said, "If it rains, the dirt'll get washed away."

"You got any ideas?"

"No. I was just saying."

Parker grunted. What was the sense of talking about a problem if you didn't have a way to solve it?

They drove up to the top and unloaded the two cars, carrying everything into the shed. Phillips and Littlefield and Wiss and Kerwin came out to help, making it like a bucket brigade, passing the sacks and bags and trays from hand to hand, piling it all up in a corner of the shed. Grofield's girl sat on an army cot and watched it mount up. In the last few days, sleeping in Grofield's car, with no fresh clothes to change to, she'd gotten a little bedraggled-looking, but it didn't really hurt her appearance. She'd gotten, if anything, sexier looking now. Parker had seen Salsa and a couple of the others looking at her. If they couldn't all leave here tonight, there might be trouble yet.

When the cars were unloaded, Parker and Wycza put them back in their sheds and put the sides up, then went back to the living shed, where the others had started the count.

They'd taken nothing but money. They'd left the jewelry store stock alone because the only way to make a profit on jewelry was to sell it back to the insurance company covering the store's loss, and in an operation like this, with so much other stuff taken, it would be too risky to try to get in touch with the insurance companies. As for the money, they'd taken only bills, leaving all sacks of change. Change was too heavy to carry, too bulky for the value, and too awkward to spend.

It took a long time to make the count; and outside, evening became night. The black curtains were put up in front of the windows and the electric lanterns were lit, and they went on counting. Their final total was $294,660.

Next, Grofield made his accounting of the $4,000 front money. He had a list of who had gotten how much and for what, and he had $730 left. He added $7,270 to it from the score to make the $8,000 that was to be paid to the doctor in New York. The $8,000 was put in an unmarked canvas sack and given to Grofield to deliver.

That left $287,390. Phillips got out pencil and paper and did the long division, and it came out $31,932.22. “Plus a fraction,” Phillips told them. “Two two two, it keeps going on.”

They worked it out. If each man took $31,900 there’d be $290 left over. Salsa said, “Give it to Grofield for a wedding present.” He bowed and smiled at Grofield’s girl.

That was the way they did it. Salsa presented the girl with the $290, making a little ceremony out of it. Parker watched Grofield watching Salsa, but Salsa didn’t push it, and the tense minute passed.

When the split was finished, Phillips got ready to leave. His cut was still sitting on the card table, not yet claimed. He put on an old black-and-red check hunting jacket and a gray cap, and then he looked exactly like a dairy farmer getting ready to go out and milk the cows. He stuck a pipe in his mouth to complete the picture and went out to get the station wagon, which was dirty enough by now to add to the general picture. He drove off in the wagon, and the rest settled down to wait. Phillips was the best man to try this because he looked the least like a desperado. He was to drive around the general area —but not too close to Copper Canyon—and see if things had quieted down yet or not. When he came back, he’d tell them if it was safe to leave here. If he didn’t come back, that would be an answer, too.

While he was gone, Parker and Wycza took shovels over to one of the sheds with a dirt floor and dug a deep hole and buried the money sacks and trays in it. The others were gathering up the gear in the living shed, getting ready to move it out if Phillips said everything was okay.

He was gone three hours. It was a little after eleven when he came back, his headlights gleaming ahead of him. He left the wagon in front, came into the shed, and said, “As clear as water. No roadblocks or anything. I heard on the radio where they think we escaped into Canada already.”

“That’s the one direction none of us goes,” said Parker. “They’ll still be watching the border.”

Phillips got his little cardboard suitcase and shoveled his share of the score into it. They all had suitcases or bags of one kind or another for their part of the loot.

They all worked together, moving all the equipment out of the shed and loading it into the station wagon. Army cots, the card table and folding chairs, cartons of rubbish, unused food, everything went into the station wagon, filling it from front to back with just enough room for Phillips to get behind the wheel. He drove it down to put it with the truck, and Wycza took his own car and followed, to drive Phillips back up.

They got their cars out of the sheds and, using as little light as possible, arranged the sheds to look the same as when they'd come here. Sooner or later the truck and station wagon would be found, but they were at the bottom where, because of the fumes, people were less likely to go. Hunters or kids or whatnot might come around these sheds up at the top any time. It might be months before the truck and wagon were found, and even then there was nothing in either to connect them directly with the score. Unless the law had one or the other identified, maybe when they'd driven out.

They left at fifteen-minute intervals, Wycza and Phillips first. Kerwin and Grofield and Grofield's girl left in the second car, and Wiss and Elkin in the third, and Salsa and Littlefield in the fourth.

Parker was last. He took one more look around, then loaded his luggage into the trunk of the Mercury. It was one o'clock Monday morning. Parker drove out to the highway and turned east.

5

THE BLONDE looked past him and said, “Where’s Edgars?”

“He isn’t coming.” Parker pushed on by her and dropped his suitcase on the floor. The room was stuffy, smelling of woman and alcohol. The windows were closed, the Venetian blinds shut, the drapes pulled. The sun was shining outside, but she had the lights on in here.

She shut the door after him and said, “What happened to him?” She seemed sober, or close enough to it. She was wearing a blue robe, and she was barefoot; red nail polish was half chipped off her toenails.

Parker said, “He died. Open a window.”

“I like the windows shut. How come he died?”

“Because he was a damn fool.” Parker went over to a window, yanked the drapes aside, pulled the blinds up, and opened the window all the way. A cool breath of fresh air came in.

“You move right in, don’t you?”

“You been out of this room at all?”

“What do you care?”

Parker crossed the room and opened the other window. Now a breeze came through, clearing out the underground aura.

She said, “You killed him, huh?”

“No. He killed himself.”

“That big hooraw at Copper Canyon, that was you people, wasn’t it?”

“What big hooraw?”

She shrugged and went over to the dresser, where the bottle and glass were. She poured and said, “What do I care if he’s alive or dead?”

“He was sick in the head. He tried to blow up the whole town, and one of his grenades knocked a wall over on him.”

“What was the matter with him?”

“He had a peeve against the town. We had a nice quiet operation going, and all of a sudden he blew up. Killed one of the boys, and a lot of locals, started fires all over the place, and got himself killed by a wall.”

She shook her head, a sour grin on her face. "I pick 'em, don't I? Tell me, Parker, what's wrong with you?"

"There's nothing wrong with me."

"There's got to be something, Parker, or I wouldn't pick you."

"You didn't pick me. Get another glass."

"Oh, don't act so goddam tough. Where are you going from here?"

"Drive to Chicago, take a plane to Miami. You like Miami?"

"How the hell do I know? This is the farthest I've ever been from New York in my life."

Parker looked at her, and thought of Grofield's girl. Where do you find one like that? Forget it, there'd be something wrong with her, too. He stretched and said, "Get the glass, I'm thirsty."

"Will you treat me nice? Will you for Christ's sake treat me nice?"

He looked at her. "What happens if I treat you nice?"

"How do I know? Nobody ever did. Maybe I turn into a butterfly."

"Let's find out. Come here."

She put the glass down on the dresser and came over. There was a pensive expression on her face, and she seemed oddly shy. It was out of character.

He reached for her, and she said, "The windows are all open."

"Will you forget the goddam windows?"

"All right. Anything you say."

His hands removed her robe. "Butterfly. Sure."

BIOGRAPHICAL NOTES

NOTE ON THE TEXTS

NOTES

Biographical Notes

Fredric Brown (October 29, 1906–March 11, 1972) Born William Fredric Brown in Cincinnati, Ohio, only child of Karl Lewis Brown, who worked in the newspaper industry, and Emma (Graham) Brown. Graduated high school in 1922 and worked for two years as an office boy for the Conger & Eel machine tool supply company. Mother died in 1923. Read voraciously, his favorite authors included Edgar Rice Burroughs, Sax Rohmer, H. G. Wells, and Jules Verne; briefly attended Hanover College in Indiana and the University of Cincinnati. Father died in 1926. Married Helen Brown in 1929; they had two sons, James Ross (b. 1930) and Linn Lewis (b. 1932). Moved to Milwaukee, Wisconsin, in 1930. Worked as proofreader for printing company and, from 1937, for the *Milwaukee Journal*. Began writing proofreading column for *The American Printer* in 1936 and became prolific contributor to trade journals such as *Feedstuffs*, *Excavating Engineer*, and *Ford Dealer Service Bulletin*; published first crime story in 1938 in *Street & Smith Detective Story*, and thereafter many crime and science fiction stories in *Detective Fiction Weekly*, *Thrilling Detective*, *Planet Stories*, *Astounding Science Fiction*, *Unknown Worlds*, and other publications; "Madman's Holiday" (1943) was adapted into RKO film *Crack-Up* (1947). Moved family to Albuquerque, New Mexico, for a few years in the early 1940s before returning to Milwaukee. *The Fabulous Clipjoint*, published by E. P. Dutton in 1947, won the Edgar Allan Poe Award of the Mystery Writers of America for Best First Novel. Divorced Helen Brown in 1947 and moved to New York City, where he married Elizabeth Charlier in 1948. They lived in Taos, New Mexico, 1949–52, and southern California, 1952–54, before settling in Tucson, Arizona, partly because of Brown's asthma. Continued to write stories, some of which he later expanded into novels, that appeared frequently in publications including *Weird Tales*, *Manhunt*, *Alfred Hitchcock's Mystery Magazine*, and *Playboy*. A number of his stories were adapted for television, including "Arena" (1944), the credited source for a *Star Trek* episode in 1967. Published a total of twenty-three crime novels, including *The Screaming Mimi* (1949), filmed as *Screaming Mimi* in 1958, *Night of the Jabberwock* (1950), *The Far Cry* (1951), *The Deep End* (1952), *The Lenient Beast* (1956), *Knock Three-One-Two* (1959), *The Murderers* (1961), and *The Five-Day Nightmare* (1962), as well as five science fiction novels, including *Martians, Go Home* (1955) and *The Mind Thing* (1961). An autobiographical novel set in the early 1920s, *The Office*, appeared in 1958. Due to declining health exacerbated by heavy drinking, Brown published little after the early 1960s. Died in Tucson.

Dan J. Marlowe (July 10, 1914–August 22, 1986) Born Daniel James Marlowe, in Lowell, Massachusetts, first child of Daniel Marlowe, a mechanic for a printing press manufacturer, and Helen Gilogly Marlowe. Mother died of influenza in 1920. After her death Marlowe lived with his paternal grandmother and aunts in Woburn, Massachusetts, until 1926, when his father married Helene Pendergrast in New London, Connecticut. Graduated from high school in New London and received accounting certificate from Bentley School in Boston in 1934. Held position as assistant manager at two country clubs in Connecticut, 1934–41, while largely supporting himself as a professional gambler. Worked as a timekeeper for United Aircraft in Stratford, Connecticut, during World War II. Moved to Washington, D.C., where he became credit manager for a tobacco wholesaler. Married Evelyn Chmura in 1945. Following her sudden death from acute hemorrhagic pancreatitis in August 1956, Marlowe drank heavily and wandered around the United States working at various jobs. Lived in New York City, 1957–58, while working on his first novel. *Doorway to Death*, with hotel bell captain Johnny Killain as its detective-protagonist, was published in 1959 as a paperback original by Avon Books; it was followed by five other paperback originals, 1959–61, four of which featured Johnny Killain. Marlowe settled in Harbor Beach, Michigan, where he later served as city councilman, 1967–70. *The Name of the Game Is Death* (1962), published in paperback by Fawcett Gold Medal, sold well, and was praised by Anthony Boucher in *The New York Times Book Review* as "extraordinarily effective in its presentation of a viewpoint quite outside of humanity's expected patterns." Al Nussbaum, who was wanted for a series of bank robberies, including one in which his partner killed a security guard, contacted Marlowe under a false name to express his admiration for *The Name of the Game Is Death*. After Nussbaum was arrested by the FBI in November 1962 Marlowe corresponded with him about writing and crime ("It's not every writer who is fortunate enough to get his technical information from the horse's mouth") and enlisted him as a researcher and collaborator, a relationship that continued after Nussbaum was paroled in 1974. Also collaborated extensively with William Odell, a retired Air Force colonel who had flown combat missions in Europe, North Africa, and the Pacific in World War II. Published novels *Strongarm* (1963), *Never Live Twice* (1964), *Death Deep Down* (1965), *The Vengeance Man* (1966), *The Raven is a Blood Red Bird*

(1967), with Odell credited as co-author, and *Route of the Red Gold* (1967). *One Endless Hour* (1969), sequel to *The Name of the Game Is Death* in which the unnamed protagonist is now called "Earl Drake," was followed by a ten-volume series, beginning with *Operation Firefall* (1969) and continuing through *Operation Counterpunch* (1976), that recast "Earl Drake" as a secret government agent. Published pornographic novels and stories under various pseudonyms. After possibly suffering a stroke, developed long-term amnesia in July 1977 that left him unable to remember his life past the age of twenty-five. Moved to California, where he shared an apartment with Nussbaum in the Tarzana neighborhood of Los Angeles, 1978–82. Resumed writing stories. Under the pseudonym Gar Wilson, Marlowe wrote *Guerilla Games* (1982), the second book in the Phoenix Force series, a spin-off of Don Pendleton's Executioner series. Moved into his own apartment in Tarzana, where he died alone of a heart attack.

Charles Williams (August 13, 1909–April 5, 1975) Born in San Angelo, Texas, oldest of six children of Orris Lloyd Williams and Maude Tennery Williams. Attended Brownsville High School; left school after the tenth grade. Enlisted in the Merchant Marine in 1929, where he served for ten years, traveling widely in the Caribbean, Central America, and South America; trained as radio operator. Married Lasca Foster in 1939. Worked as a radio inspector for RCA, 1939–42, at Puget Sound Navy Yard, 1942–46, and at Mackay Radio & Telegraph in San Francisco. The first of his twenty-two novels, *Hill Girl* (1951), was published as a paperback original by Fawcett Gold Medal after being rejected by numerous other publishers, and its success allowed him to quit his job and write full-time. His subsequent novels included *Big City Girl* (1951), *River Girl* (1951), *Hell Hath No Fury* (1953), *A Touch of Death* (1954), *The Big Bite* (1956), *Girl Out Back* (1958), *Talk of the Town* (1958), *All the Way* (1958), and *The Long Saturday Night* (1962), as well as several with nautical settings: *Scorpion Reef* (1955), *The Sailcloth Shroud* (1960), *Aground* (1960), *Dead Calm* (1963), and *And the Deep Blue Sea* (1971). Lived with Lasca in Lima, Peru, for a year, and in Tucson, Arizona, 1952–55. Daughter Alison born in 1953. The family later lived in Key West, Florida, 1955–57, and Palo Alto, California, 1957–60. His books sold well in Europe, and in 1960 Williams moved with his family to Lausanne, Switzerland. Received screenwriting credit for René Clément's *Les Félins* (1964) and Claude Sautet's *L'Arme à gauche* (1965), based on *Aground*. Family returned to California in 1965. Published novel *The Wrong Venus* (1966) and wrote screenplay for film adaptation *Don't Just Stand There!* (1968), directed by Ron Winston, as well as screenplay for Delbert Mann's *The Pink Jungle* (1968), an adaptation of Alan

Williams's novel *Snake Water*. Orson Welles acquired the rights to *Dead Calm* and began filming an adaptation, titled *The Deep*, in 1967 that was never completed. (The novel was later successfully filmed under its original title by Phillip Noyce in 1989.) In contrast to his European popularity, sales of Williams's books in the United States suffered a decline in the 1970s. Lasca Williams died of cancer in 1972. After her death Williams divided his time between Los Angeles and a residence in northern California near the Klamath River. Published his last novel, *Man on a Leash*, in 1973. Collaborated with Nona Tyson on screen adaptation of *Hell Hath No Fury* (screenplay was filmed in 1990 by Dennis Hopper as *The Hot Spot*). Worried about his finances and depressed since the death of his wife, Williams fatally shot himself in his apartment in Van Nuys, California.

Dorothy B. Hughes (August 10, 1904–May 6, 1993) Born Dorothy Belle Flanagan in Kansas City, Missouri, the oldest child of Frank S. Flanagan and Calla Belle Haley Flanagan. Later recalled that she wanted to be a writer at the age of six, when she first learned how to read. Graduated from the University of Missouri–Columbia in 1924 with a degree in journalism. Worked as a journalist in Missouri, New York, and New Mexico, and did graduate work at Columbia University and the University of New Mexico. Published book of poems, *Dark Certainty* (1931), in the Yale Series of Younger Poets. Married Levi Allen Hughes Jr. in Santa Fe, New Mexico, in 1932. They had three children, Helen (Holly), b. 1932, Antony, b. 1935, and Susan, b. 1940. Published *Pueblo on the Mesa* (1939), a history of the first fifty years of the University of New Mexico. Her first suspense novel, *The So Blue Marble* (1940), was followed by *The Cross-Eyed Bear* (1940), *The Bamboo Blonde* (1941), *The Fallen Sparrow* (1942), *The Blackbirder* (1943), *The Delicate Ape* (1944), *Dread Journey* (1945), *Ride the Pink Horse* (1946), *The Scarlet Imperial* (1946), and *In a Lonely Place* (1947), as well as *Johnnie* (1944), a comic novel. Reviewed crime fiction for the *Albuquerque Tribune*, 1941–55, and the *Los Angeles Daily News*, 1947–54. Several of Hughes's novels were adapted as Hollywood films: *The Fallen Sparrow* (1943), directed by Richard Wallace and starring John Garfield; *Ride the Pink Horse* (1947), directed by and starring Robert Montgomery; and *In a Lonely Place* (1950), directed by Nicholas Ray and starring Humphrey Bogart and Gloria Grahame. Family moved to Los Angeles in 1944. Published comic novel *The Big Barbecue* (1949), suspense novels *The Candy Kid* (1950) and *The Davidian Report* (1952), and short stories "The Homecoming" (1946), "You Killed Miranda" (1958), and "The Black & White Blues" (1959). Returned to Santa Fe, New Mexico, after the death of her mother in 1961. Reviewed crime fiction for the *Los*

Angeles Times, 1962–78. Published her final novel, *The Expendable Man* (1963), later explaining she had stopped writing novels in order to care for her mother as well as to support her children and grandchildren. Published short stories "Danger at Deerfawn" (1964) and "Everybody Needs a Mink" (1965). Husband died in 1975. Named Grand Master of the Mystery Writers of America in 1978. Published *Erle Stanley Gardner: The Case of the Real Perry Mason* (1978), which won her an Edgar Award for Best Critical/Biographical Work in 1979. Died from the complications of a stroke.

Richard Stark Pseudonym of Donald E. Westlake (July 12, 1933–December 31, 2008). Born Donald Edwin Westlake in Brooklyn, New York, son of Albert Joseph Westlake and Lillian Bounds Westlake; he was raised in Yonkers and Albany. Wrote fiction from an early age. Served in the U.S. Air Force, 1954–56. Attended Champlain College in Plattsburgh, New York, and Harpur College (later SUNY Binghamton) in Binghamton, New York, without graduating. Married Nedra Henderson in 1957; they had two sons, Sean and Steven. Moved to New York City in 1959, where he worked briefly for a literary agency. Wrote twenty-one pseudonymous paperback softcore sex novels published from 1959 to 1965. The first of fifty-four novels published under his own name, *The Mercenaries* (1960), was nominated for an Edgar Award, and was followed by *Killing Time* (1961). Adopted the pseudonym Richard Stark for his first novel featuring the professional thief Parker, *The Hunter* (1962), and thereafter alternated chiefly between the Westlake and Stark bylines. He also published five novels under the name Tucker Coe, beginning with *Kinds of Love, Kinds of Death* (1966), and four novels as Samuel Holt, beginning with *One of Us Is Wrong* (1986). The novels published as Westlake included *The Busy Body* (1966); *God Save the Mark* (1967), winner of the Edgar for Best Novel; *The Hot Rock* (1970); *Adios Scheherazade* (1970); *Bank Shot* (1972); *Jimmy the Kid* (1974); *Dancing Aztecs* (1976); *Kahawa* (1981); and *The Ax* (1997). Sixteen Parker novels were published from 1962 to 1974, including *The Outfit* (1963), *The Score* (1964), *The Seventh* (1966), *The Rare Coin Score* (1967), *Slayground* (1971), and *Butcher's Moon* (1974); several were adapted into films, notably John Boorman's *Point Blank* (1967), based on *The Hunter*, and John Flynn's *The Outfit* (1973). There were also four Stark titles featuring Parker's sometime associate Grofield, beginning with *The Damsel* (1967). Westlake later wrote that after the publication of *Butcher's Moon*, "Richard Stark just up and disappeared. He did a fade. . . . when I say he was gone, I mean his voice was gone, erased clean out of my head." The Parker character returned in *Comeback* (1997), which was followed by seven more titles; the last Parker novel, *Dirty Money*, appeared in 2008. Westlake also wrote several screenplays, including *The Stepfather* (1987) and *The Grifters* (1990), based on the novel by Jim Thompson. Named a Grand Master by the Mystery Writers of America in 1993. After his first marriage ended in divorce, Westlake married Sandra Korb Foley in 1967; they had a son, Paul, before their divorce. In 1979 Westlake married Abigail Adams, with whom he lived in Ancram, New York. Died of a heart attack while on vacation in Mexico.

Note on the Texts

This volume collects five American crime novels of the 1960s: *The Murderers* by Fredric Brown (1961); *The Name of the Game Is Death* by Dan J. Marlowe (1962); *Dead Calm* by Charles Williams (1963); *The Expendable Man* by Dorothy B. Hughes (1963); and *The Score* by Richard Stark (1964). A companion volume in the Library of America series, *Crime Novels: Four Classic Thrillers 1964–1969*, collects four later works: *The Fiend* by Margaret Millar (1964); *Doll* by Ed McBain (1965); *Run Man Run* by Chester Himes (1966); and *The Tremor of Forgery* by Patricia Highsmith (1969).

Fredric Brown was working as a television writer in Los Angeles when he wrote *The Murderers*, his twenty-seventh novel. *The Murderers* was published in hardcover in New York by E. P. Dutton on August 21, 1961. A hardcover English printing was published in London in 1962 by T. V. Boardman & Co. as part of its "Bloodhound" series of mysteries. Brown did not revise the book after its initial publication. This volume prints the text of the E. P. Dutton edition.

From 1959 to 1961 Dan J. Marlowe published his first six novels as paperback originals, five with Avon and one with Berkley. When Marlowe began working on *The Name of the Game Is Death* he wrote an 8,000-word biography of its protagonist, later recalling that "I knew him to the extent that made it difficult for him to do something in the course of the story that wasn't in character." He submitted an outline of the novel to Thomas Dardis, the editor-in-chief of Berkley Books, but Dardis rejected it, as did another editor at a different publisher. Marlowe continued to work on the novel during a stay in Hollywood, Florida. When it was "a little more than half written" he submitted a partial manuscript to Fawcett Gold Medal, a leading publisher of paperback originals, where it was accepted for publication. (Knox Burger, the editor of Gold Medal, later told Marlowe: "In that one you did something I don't see enough of: You struck a note and held it.") Marlowe finished the novel while staying in Woburn, Massachusetts, and sent the manuscript to Fawcett Gold Medal in August 1961. *The Name of the Game Is Death* was published in paperback in Greenwich, Connecticut, by Fawcett Gold Medal on January 29, 1962. An English paperback printing was published in London in 1963 by Frederick Muller Ltd.

At the suggestion of his friend Al Nussbaum, an imprisoned bank robber, Marlowe wrote *One Endless Hour* (1969), a sequel to *The*

Name of the Game Is Death in which the unnamed narrator, who had previously used the aliases "Roy Martin" and "Chet Arnold," adopted "Earl Drake" as a new alias. Fawcett Gold Medal then suggested making "Earl Drake" the hero of a new series of novels in which the former criminal became an undercover government agent. Marlowe agreed, and eventually published ten novels in the series, beginning with *Operation Fireball* (1969). When Fawcett issued a new edition of *The Name of the Game Is Death* in 1973, Marlowe made significant revisions in the text. Most of these changes were stylistic, but in some instances he altered the characterization of the protagonist to conform with the new Earl Drake series. The revised text was published in England in 1973 by Gold Lion in hardcover and (under the title *Operation Overkill*) by Coronet in paperback. This volume prints the text of the 1962 Fawcett Gold Medal edition because the novel here stands on its own and is not presented as part of the Earl Drake series.

Charles Williams was living in Lausanne, Switzerland, when he wrote *Dead Calm*, his nineteenth novel and one of several, including *Scorpion Reef* (1955), *The Sailcloth Shroud* (1960), and *Aground* (1960), to have a nautical setting. (Williams had served as a radio operator in the Merchant Marine before World War II.) *Dead Calm* was published in hardcover in New York by the Viking Press on October 10, 1963. The book sold more than 6,500 copies by March 1964, when it was reprinted by Viking. An English hardcover printing was published in London by Cassell in 1964. Williams did not make any changes to the novel after its publication. This volume prints the text of the 1963 Viking edition.

Dorothy B. Hughes published fourteen novels from 1940 to 1952. For the next decade she devoted most of her time to her family while continuing to review crime fiction in several newspapers. As she later told an interviewer: "My mother was very ill and lived with me. The children were in that state of getting started in marriage, with grandchildren for me to help care for. And I simply hadn't the tranquility required to write. I wasn't frustrated because I was reviewing mysteries, and reviewing has always been very important to me." After the death of her mother in 1961 Hughes wrote what would become her last novel. *The Expendable Man* was published in hardcover in New York by Random House on February 5, 1963. It was praised by Anthony Boucher in *The New York Times Book Review* as "Mrs. Hughes's finest work to date, of unusual stature both as a suspense story and as a straight novel." An English printing was published in London by Andre Deutsch in 1964. Hughes did not revise the novel after its publication. This volume prints the text of the 1963 Random House edition.

Donald E. Westlake began publishing novels under his own name in 1960. Westlake had long admired the "compulsive strength" of the crime novels published in the Fawcett Gold Medal series of paperback originals, and in 1962 he wrote "a Gold Medal book" about a professional thief named Parker. As he recalled in an introduction written in 1981 for a new edition of *The Hunter*, he put "a Gold Medal pen-name" on the typescript: "*Richard*, from Richard Widmark in *Kiss of Death* (1947), and *Stark*, because I wanted a name/word that meant stripped-down, without decoration." Gold Medal rejected the novel, but Bucklin Moon, a senior editor at Pocket Books, expressed interest and asked Westlake if he "could rewrite the book so that Parker gets away, and then give us two or three books a year about him?" Westlake eventually agreed to write a series about Parker and changed the ending of the novel so that the character survived. *The Hunter* was published under the name Richard Stark by Pocket Books in December 1962 and was followed by three more titles—*The Man with the Getaway Face*, *The Outfit*, and *The Mourner*—in 1963.

The fifth novel in the series, *The Score*, was published in paperback in New York by Pocket Books on August 15, 1964. An English paperback printing was published in London by Coronet Books in 1971 under the title *Killtown*. (This new title was also used when Berkley Medallion reissued the first fourteen books in the series in 1973 under the rubric "The Violent World of Parker.") Westlake/Stark made no changes to the novel after its publication. The text printed here is taken from the 1964 Pocket Books edition.

This volume presents the texts of the original printings chosen for inclusion here, but it does not attempt to reproduce nontextual features of their typographic design. The texts are presented without change, except for the correction of typographical errors. Spelling, punctuation, and capitalization are often expressive features and are not altered, even when inconsistent or irregular. The following is a list of typographical errors corrected, cited by page and line number: 28.38, compatable; 29.31, by own; 38.14, Willie; 39.10, Willie; 49.3, M.G.A.; 55.19, Seaton's; 79.9, forgiveable; 89.34–35, role and; 96.9, little "I'm; 104.4, Tiajuana; 104.29, celebate; 119.26, told the Jocelyn; 124.14, said, "To; 130.32, "Would; 142.14, swallowed.; 149.7, taped; 155.2, attented; 160.36, scowling "What's; 166.11, ask my; 182.34, Chatahoochee,; 191.27, Pike's Peak.; 212.3, bumper-to bumper; 215.9, Same'.; 257.20, country; 484.12, desk; 484.18, stationary; 493.21, went his; 543.38, marshall,; 593.16, sister's; 605.14, down the; 640.33, previous; 661.10, Damnvenner; 678.14, truclulantly.; 710.30, could done; 710.39, Edgar's; 721.11, heart.", 721.11, said "Essence; 723.17, suggested."; 735.23, whitehaired; 821.22, up the;.

Notes

In the notes below, the reference numbers denote page and line of this volume (the line count includes headings). No note is made for material included in standard desk-reference books. Quotations from Shakespeare are keyed to *The Riverside Shakespeare*, ed. G. Blakemore Evans (Boston: Houghton Mifflin, 1974). For references to other studies and further biographical background than is contained in the Biographical Notes, see Jack Seabrook, *Martians and Misplaced Clues: The Life and Work of Fredric Brown* (Bowling Green, OH: Bowling Green State University Popular Press, 1993); Newton Baird, *A Key to Fredric Brown's Wonderland: A Study and an Annotated Bibliographical Checklist* (Georgetown, CA: Talisman Literary Research, 1981); Charles Kelly, *Gunshots in Another Room: The Forgotten Life of Dan J. Marlowe* (Asclepian Imprints Ltd., 2012); Donald E. Westlake, *The Getaway Car: A Donald Westlake Nonfiction Miscellany* (Chicago: University of Chicago Press, 2014); David Bordwell, "Donald Westlake and the Richard Stark Machine," in *Perplexing Plots: Popular Storytelling and the Poetics of Murder* (New York: Columbia University Press, 2022); Sarah Weinman, "On the World's Finest Female Noir Writer, Dorothy B. Hughes," *Los Angeles Review of Books*, August 12, 2012; Hernán Migoya, *Charles Williams: La tormenta y la calma* (Semana Negra de Gijón [Spain]; 1999); Walt Sheldon, "My Friend Fredric Brown," and Ed Gorman, "Fifteen Impressions of Charles Williams," in Lee Server, Ed Gorman, and Martin H. Greenberg, eds., *The Big Book of Noir* (New York: Carroll & Graf, 1998); Brian Ritt, *Paperback Confidential: Crime Writers of the Paperback Era* (Eureka, CA: Stark House Press, 2013); Lee Server, *Encyclopedia of Pulp Fiction Writers* (New York: Facts on File, 2002); Jeffrey Marks, *Atomic Renaissance: American Women Mystery Writers of the 1940s and 1950s* (Lee's Summit, MO: Delphi Books, 2010).

THE MURDERERS

3.17 Wilshire Derby] Brown Derby, famously hat-shaped restaurant located at 3377 Wilshire Boulevard in Los Angeles (1937–80); part of a chain that also included the Hollywood Brown Derby at 1628 North Vine Street.

3.26–29 born of farmer parents . . . not yet dead or buried.] A parody of the Apostle's Creed, with "Pasadena Playhouse" in the role of Pontius Pilate. The Pasadena Playhouse was a community theater built in 1925; its associated school of theater arts, whose graduates included many prominent film performers, operated as an accredited college from 1937 to 1969.

6.34 musky] Muscatel.

16.36 Charlie Parker and Pres] Saxophonists Charles "Yardbird" Parker Jr. (1920–1955) and Lester "Pres" Young (1909–1959).

18.27 "The Untouchables"] Hour-long television crime series (1959–1963) starring Robert Stack (1919–2003) as Chicago-based Prohibition agent Eliot Ness.

20.2 vipers] Marijuana users.

20.35 "Sam Hall"] Folk song of British origin, sung by a criminal condemned to death.

22.3 *Lady Loverly's Chatter*] A book with this title, punning on D. H. Lawrence's *Lady Chatterley's Lover* (1928), was in fact published in 1945 by Arthur Yeoman Press; authorship was attributed to Mart Reb.

22.8 what cyanide smells like] In 1937 the California legislature made execution by cyanide gas the method of capital punishment to be used in all future death sentences imposed in the state. A total of 190 men and four women were executed in the gas chamber at San Quentin State Prison from 1938 to 1967.

23.34 Doris's MG] A British sports car.

30.35–36 Partita in D Minor . . . Segovia] Andrés Segovia (1893–1987) first performed his guitar transcription of Johann Sebastian Bach's Violin Partita in D Minor in 1935, and recorded it a number of times thereafter.

31.24–25 one Capistrano type swallow] Allusion to "When the Swallows Come Back to Capistrano" (1940), popular song by Leon René (1902–1982) first recorded by The Ink Spots.

31.35 Van Cliburn] Cliburn (1934–2013) became an international celebrity as a young American pianist winning the International Tchaikovsky Competition in Moscow in 1958.

31.38 Villa-Lobos] Brazilian composer Heitor Villa-Lobos (1887–1959).

32.24–26 Cosmo Alley . . . Unicorn] Cosmo Alley, at 1608 Cosmo Street, and the Unicorn, at 8907 Sunset Boulevard, were Hollywood nightclubs.

40.28 Desilu] Desilu Productions, television production company (1950–67) founded by Desi Arnaz (1917–1986) and Lucille Ball (1911–1989); its early successes included *I Love Lucy* and *The Untouchables.*

40.31–32 Gunsmoke, Have Gun, and Wagon Train] Successful television Westerns: *Gunsmoke* (1955–75), starring James Arness (1923–2011) as Matt Dillon; *Have Gun—Will Travel* (1957–63), starring Richard Boone (1917–1981) as Paladin; *Wagon Train* (1957–65), starring Ward Bond (1903–1960) as Seth Adams, replaced by John McIntire (1907–1991) as Christopher Hall after Bond's death in 1960.

44.21–22 Ginsberg . . . *Evergreen Review*] Poet Allen Ginsberg (1926–1997); *Evergreen Review*, literary magazine founded in 1957 by Barney Rosset (1922–2012), publisher of Grove Press.

46.34 High noon . . . Gary Cooper] Gary Cooper (1901–1961) starred as Marshal Will Kane in the Western *High Noon* (1952), directed by Fred Zinnemann (1907–1997).

49.3 M.C.A.] M.C.A., Music Corporation of America. Founded in Chicago in 1924 as a music booking agency, M.C.A. opened a Los Angeles office in 1937 and soon became one of the leading talent agencies in Hollywood. M.C.A. later expanded into television and film production, and dissolved its talent agency in 1962 in response to a federal antitrust suit.

58.8–9 .32 revolver . . . break action] A revolver with a hinged frame; when unlocked, the barrel is pushed down, opening the cylinder and allowing the weapon to be loaded.

69.11 Sullivan] *The Ed Sullivan Show*, long-running television variety show (1948–1971); from 1948 to 1955 its official title was *Toast of the Town*.

70.2–3 *Don Juan in Hell* . . . Rathbone] Spoken arts recordings: George Bernard Shaw's *Don Juan in Hell* (Columbia Masterworks, 1952), featuring Charles Laughton, Charles Boyer, Agnes Moorehead, and Cedric Hardwicke; Stephen Vincent Benét's *John Brown's Body* (Columbia Masterworks, 1953), produced by Charles Laughton and featuring Tyrone Power, Judith Anderson, and Raymond Massey; Christopher Fry's *The Lady's Not for Burning* (Decca, 1951), featuring John Gielgud and Pamela Brown. Various recordings of Laurence Olivier reading from *Henry V*, *Hamlet*, and *Richard III* were issued from 1947 to 1955. Caedmon Records released numerous albums of Dylan Thomas (1914–1953) reading his poetry, stories, and his play *Under Milk Wood*. Basil Rathbone's many recordings included notably his 1959 Caedmon Records album *Basil Rathbone Reads Edgar Allan Poe*.

72.12–13 Raskolnikov . . . *Crime and Punishment*?"] Rodion Raskolnikov, protagonist of *Crime and Punishment* (1866), novel by Fyodor Dostoevsky (1821–1881).

78.36 ridin' th' Katy . . . reefer] The Missouri-Kansas-Texas Railway; a refrigerated boxcar.

79.32 pearl diving] Dishwashing.

80.6 B. and O.] Baltimore and Ohio Railroad.

82.31–33 poem of Kenneth Patchen's . . . on a record] *Kenneth Patchen Reads His Poetry with the Chamber Jazz Sextet* (Cadence Records, 1957). Patchen (1911–1972) first published the poem in 1943.

92.12 Lon Chaney] Chaney (1883–1930) was noted for his extraordinary use of makeup and disguise in such films as *The Hunchback of Notre Dame* (1923), *The Phantom of the Opera* (1925), and *The Unholy Three* (1925).

92.22–29 Cyrano de Bergerac . . . Mack the Knife] The oversized nose attributed to the sixteenth-century writer Cyrano de Bergerac in the eponymous play (1897) by French poet Edmond Rostand (1868–1918) was familiar to American audiences through stage (1947) and screen (1950) portrayals by the Puerto Rican actor José Ferrer (1912–1992); American musician and actor Bobby Darin (1936–1973) had an international hit in 1959, with his recording of "Mack the Knife," adapted by Marc Blitzstein (1905–1964) from "Moritat vom Mackie Messer" from *The Threepenny Opera* (1928) by German playwright Bertolt Brecht (1898–1956) and composer Kurt Weill (1900–1950).

107.3 Kerouac] Jack Kerouac (1922–1969) became a best-selling writer with the publication of *On the Road* (1957), *The Subterraneans* (1958), and *The Dharma Bums* (1959).

108.34–37 Saroyan's *The Time of Your Life* . . . Nick] *The Time of Your Life* (1939), play by William Saroyan (1908–1981), set in Nick's Pacific Street Saloon, Restaurant, and Entertainment Palace in San Francisco. The streetwalker Kitty Duval is the principal female role.

THE NAME OF THE GAME IS DEATH

150.13 B.P.O.E. Does] Female auxiliary of the Benevolent Protective Order of Elks.

181.16 give you the office] Signal surreptitiously.

181.23 Joliet] The Illinois state penitentiary at Joliet.

197.21 John L. Sullivan's] Sullivan (1858–1918), American boxer considered heavyweight champion in both bare-knuckle and gloved bouts; he was defeated by James "Jim" Corbett (1866–1933) in 1892.

199.10–11 Northern Star . . . Delaware Park] Northern Star, American thoroughbred horse, foaled in 1948, that raced from 1950 to 1953.

199.19–20 Pimlico Futurity . . . the Bradley camp] Platter defeated By Jimminy by a neck in the 1943 running of the Pimlico Futurity, a race for two-year-old thoroughbreds; Edward R. Bradley (1859–1946) was a leading breeder of racehorses.

207.13–19 Ak-Sar-Ben to Woodbine . . . Tenacious] Ak-Sar-Ben, racetrack in Omaha, Nebraska (1919–95); Woodbine, racetrack in Toronto, Ontario, opened 1956; Arlington Classic Stakes, annual horse race held at Arlington Heights, Illinois; Santa Anita Derby, annual horse race in Arcadia, California; Garden State Stakes, annual race formerly held at Cherry Hill, New Jersey; Tenacious won multiple races in New Orleans from 1957 to 1961.

207.37–38 Citation . . . Noor] Citation won multiple races from 1947 to 1951, including the Triple Crown in 1948; Noor won multiple races from 1947 to 1950, winning over Citation on four occasions.

208.1–2 Count Fleet . . . the Walden] Count Fleet won the Walden Stakes (at Pimlico Race Course in Baltimore, Maryland) in 1942 and the Triple Crown in 1943.

215.8–9 'But They Get There Just the Same.'] Refrain from the traditional song "All Around the Mountain."

230.1–5 Cobb . . . Heilmann] Ty Cobb (1886–1961) and Tris Speaker (1888–1958) briefly played outfield together for the Philadelphia Athletics in 1928. Bob Fothergill (1897–1938) and Harry Heilmann (1894–1951) were both playing for the Detroit Tigers in 1928.

DEAD CALM

275.3–5 Ingram . . . Rae] John Ingram and Rae (Osborne) Ingram appeared previously in Williams's novel *Aground*, published in 1960. There are scattered allusions to episodes from that book throughout *Dead Calm*, including a virtual plot summary in chapter 10 (see pages 370.20–374.4).

278.24 Moonbeam McSwine] Unwashed rural beauty who was a running character in Al Capp's comic strip *Li'l Abner* (1934–1977).

290.25 the doghouse] A small cabin or compartment on a yacht that is partially raised above the deck.

319.33–34 Salmon P. Chase] Chase (1808–1873) served as secretary of the treasury under Abraham Lincoln (1861–64) and as chief justice of the United States (1864–73).

327.23 "Charmaine"] Popular song that was a major hit for Guy Lombardo (1902–1977) and His Orchestra in 1927.

365.24 Cape Stiff] Nickname for Cape Horn.

368.34 "*Je vous en prie, madame.*"] French: "You're welcome, madame."

369.29 John Birch Society] Extreme right-wing political organization founded in 1958 by candy manufacturer Robert W. Welch Jr. (1899–1985).

369.36–37 what the leopard . . . Kilimanjaro] See the opening passage of the short story "The Snows of Kilimanjaro" (1936) by Ernest Hemingway (1899–1961): "Kilimanjaro is a snow-covered mountain 19,710 feet high, and is said to be the highest mountain in Africa. Its western summit is called by the Masai 'Ngaje Ngai,' the House of God. Close to the western summit there is the dried and frozen carcass of a leopard. No one has explained what the leopard was seeking at that altitude."

370.15 Kinsey questionnaire] Survey questionnaire used by Alfred Kinsey (1894–1956) as research for his books *Sexual Behavior in the Human Male* (1948) and *Sexual Behavior in the Human Female* (1953).

390.22 Burl Ives] Musician and actor (1909–1995) who became widely known for his renditions of folk songs such as "The Blue-Tail Fly" and "The Big Rock Candy Mountain."

412.22 Hotspur] Henry Percy, son of the Earl of Northumberland in Shakespeare's *Richard II* and *Henry IV, Part I.*

THE EXPENDABLE MAN

463.6 'The Children's Hour'?"] Poem (1860) by Henry Wadsworth Longfellow (1807–1882) that includes the lines: "From my study I see in the lamplight, / Descending the broad hall stair, / Grave Alice, and laughing Allegra, / And Edith with golden hair."

464.13 Johnny Mathis] Mathis (b. 1935) enjoyed a string of hit singles including "Wonderful! Wonderful!" (1956), "It's Not for Me to Say" (1957), "Chances Are" (1957), and "Misty" (1959).

482.21 Territory of Arizona] Arizona Territory was formally established in 1863; Arizona was admitted to the Union as a state in 1912.

485.39–40 Gordo and Charlie Brown and Dick Tracy] *Gordo* (1941–85), comic strip by Gus Arriola (1917–2008); Charlie Brown, leading character in comic strip *Peanuts* (1950–2000) by Charles M. Schulz (1922–2000); *Dick Tracy*, comic strip created by Chester Gould (1900–1985) in 1931 and continued by other artists after 1977.

496.8 Zanjaros] Zanjeros, Spanish for "ditch riders," workers who distribute water from irrigation ditches and canals.

502.14 "Good-bye, Girls, I'm Through,"] Popular song by John L. Golden (1874–1955) and Ivan Caryll (1861–1921), from the musical *Chin Chin* (1914).

519.32–33 in another country, and the wench was dead.] See Christopher Marlowe (1564–1593), *The Jew of Malta*, Act 4, Scene 1: "But that was in another country; / And besides, the wench is dead."

560.31 "*¿Inglés, también?*"] Spanish: "English, too?"

579.31 cabbages and kings] See Lewis Carroll (1832–1898), "The Walrus and the Carpenter," from *Through the Looking-Glass, and What Alice Found There* (1872): "'The time has come,' the Walrus said, / 'To talk of many things: / Of shoes—and ships—and sealing wax— / Of cabbages—and kings—'"

599.24 Don Loper] Loper (1906–1972) was a costume and necktie designer who worked in many capacities for the American film studio Metro-Goldwyn-Mayer (MGM).

601.29 what Ellison so well describes as invisible.] See Ralph Ellison (1914–1994), *Invisible Man* (1952): "I am a man of substance, of flesh and bone, fiber and liquids—and I might even be said to possess a mind. I am invisible, understand, simply because people refuse to see me."

632.32 "They also serve who only stand and wait."] The last line of the sonnet "On His Blindness" (1652) by John Milton (1608–1674).

649.17 *Sartoris*] Novel (1929) by William Faulkner (1897–1962), an abridged version of the work later published as *Flags in the Dust* (1973).

THE SCORE

712.37 Ausable Chasm] A sandstone gorge through which the Ausable River runs in the Adirondacks, near Keeseville, New York; it first opened as a tourist attraction in 1870.

760.27–28 Chemy . . . his brother run that woman off.] The allusion is to an episode in the earlier Richard Stark novel *The Outfit* (1963).

762.18–19 "Come, Watson, come! The game is afoot!"] See "The Adventure of the Abbey Grange," in *The Return of Sherlock Holmes* (1904) by Arthur Conan Doyle (1859–1930).

772.28–29 "All the world's a stage . . . merely players."] See Shakespeare's *As You Like It*, II.vii.139–140.

785.14 Equity] Actors' Equity Association, theatrical labor union formed in 1913.

This book is set in 10 point ITC Galliard, a face designed for digital composition by Matthew Carter and based on the sixteenth-century face Granjon. The paper is acid-free lightweight opaque that will not turn yellow or brittle with age. The binding is sewn, which allows the book to open easily and lie flat. The binding board is covered in Brillianta, a woven rayon cloth made by Van Heek–Scholco Textielfabrieken, Holland.

Composition by Dianna Logan, Clearmont, MO.

Printing by Sheridan Grand Rapids, Grand Rapids, MI.

Binding by Dekker Bookbinding, Wyoming, MI.

Designed by Bruce Campbell.